CRESCENT CITY

HOUSE
of
SKY
and
BREATH

SARAH J. MAAS

BLOOMSBURY PUBLISHING

NEW YORK · LONDON · OXFORD · NEW DELHI · SYDNEY

BLOOMSBURY PUBLISHING
Bloomsbury Publishing Inc.
1385 Broadway, New York, NY 10018, USA
29 Earlsfort Terrace, Dublin 2, Ireland

BLOOMSBURY, BLOOMSBURY PUBLISHING, and the Diana logo are trademarks of
Bloomsbury Publishing Plc

First published in the United States in 2022
Paperback edition first published in the United States in 2023

ISBN: HB: 978-1-63557-407-4; PB: 978-1-63973-175-6; eBook: 978-1-63557-408-1
Special edition: 978-1-63973-287-6

4 6 8 10 9 7 5

Typeset by Westchester Publishing Services
Printed and bound in the U.S.A.

To find out more about our authors and books visit www.bloomsbury.com and sign up for our
newsletters, including news about Sarah J. Maas.

Bloomsbury books may be purchased for business or promotional use. For information
on bulk purchases please contact Macmillan Corporate and Premium Sales Department at
specialmarkets@macmillan.com

For Robin Rue,
fearless agent and true friend

LUNATHION

CRESCENT CITY

THE ANGELS' GATE

CENTRAL BUSINESS DISTRICT

THE MEAT MARKET

THE MERCHANTS' GATE

WESTERN ROAD

ISTROS RIVER

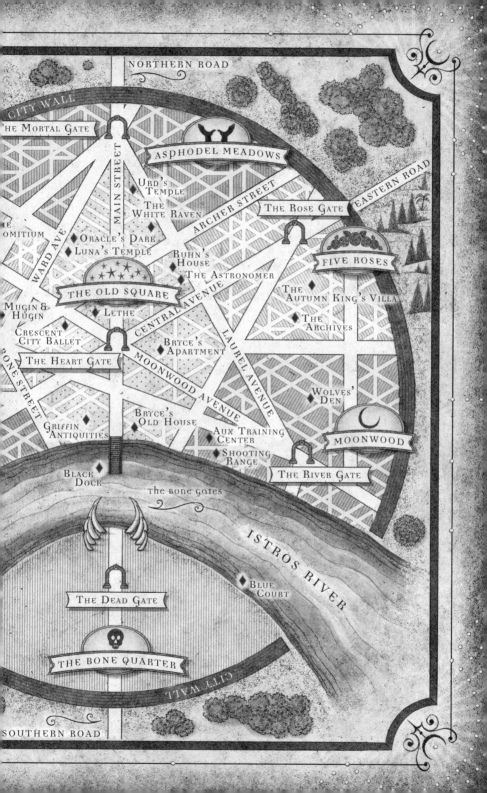

THE FOUR HOUSES OF MIDGARD

*As decreed in 33 V.E. by the Imperial Senate
in the Eternal City*

HOUSE OF EARTH AND BLOOD

Shifters, humans, witches, ordinary animals, and many others
to whom Cthona calls, as well as some chosen by Luna

HOUSE OF SKY AND BREATH

Malakim (angels), Fae, elementals, sprites,* and those who
are blessed by Solas, along with some favored by Luna

HOUSE OF MANY WATERS

River-spirits, mer, water beasts, nymphs, kelpies, nøkks,
and others watched over by Ogenas

HOUSE OF FLAME AND SHADOW

Daemonaki, Reapers, wraiths, vampyrs, draki, dragons,
necromancers, and many wicked and unnamed things
that even Urd herself cannot see

*Sprites were kicked out of their House as a result of their participation in the
Fall, and are now considered Lowers, though many of them refuse to accept this.*

PROLOGUE

Sofie had survived in the Kavalla death camp for two weeks.

Two weeks, and still the guards—dreadwolves, all of them—had not sniffed her out. Everything had gone according to plan. The reek of the days crammed into the cattle car had covered the telltale scent in her blood. It had also veiled her when they'd marched her and the others between the brick buildings of the camp, this new Hel that was only a small model of what the Asteri planned to do if the war continued.

Two weeks here, and that reek had become etched into her very skin, blinding even the wolves' keen noses. She'd stood mere feet from a guard in the breakfast line this morning and he hadn't so much as sniffed in her direction.

A small victory. One she'd gladly take these days.

Half of the Ophion rebel bases had fallen. More would soon. But only two places existed for her now: here, and the port of Servast, her destination tonight. Alone, even on foot, she could have easily made it. A rare benefit of being able to switch between human and Vanir identities—and of being a rare human who'd made the Drop.

It technically made her Vanir. Granted her a long life span and all the benefits that came from it that her human family did not and would never have. She might not have bothered to make the Drop had her parents not encouraged it—with the healing abilities she would gain, it provided extra armor in a world designed to kill her kind. So she'd done it under the radar, in a back-alley, highly illegal Drop center, where a leering satyr had been her Anchor, and handing over her firstlight had been the cost of the ritual. She'd spent the years since then learning to wear her humanity like a cloak, inside and out. She might have all the traits of the Vanir, but she'd never *be* Vanir. Not in her heart, her soul.

Yet tonight . . . tonight, Sofie did not mind letting a little of the monster loose.

It would not be an easy journey, thanks to the dozen small forms crouched behind her in the mud before the barbed-wire fence.

Five boys and six girls gathered by her thirteen-year-old brother, who now stood watch over them like a shepherd with his flock. Emile had gotten all of them out of the bunks, aided by a gentle human sun-priest, who was currently serving as lookout at the shed ten yards away.

The children were gray-skinned, gaunt. Eyes too big, too hopeless.

Sofie didn't need to know their stories. They were likely the same as hers: rebel human parents who'd either been caught or sold out. Hers had been the latter.

Pure dumb luck had kept Sofie out of the dreadwolves' clutches, too—at least until now. Three years ago, she'd been studying late at the university library with her friends. Arriving home after midnight, she'd spied the broken windows and shattered front door, the spray paint on the siding of their ordinary suburban house—*REBEL SHITS*—and begun running. She could only credit Urd for the fact that the dreadwolf guard posted at the front door hadn't seen her.

Later, she'd managed to confirm that her parents were dead. Tortured until the brutal end by the Hind or her elite squadron of dreadwolf interrogators. The report Sofie spent months working her way up through Ophion to attain had also revealed that her grandparents had been herded off upon reaching the Bracchus camp in the north, and shot in a lineup of other elders, their bodies left to crumple into a mass grave.

And her brother . . . Sofie hadn't been able to find anything on

Emile until now. For years, she'd been working with the Ophion rebels in exchange for any snippet of information about him, about her family. She didn't let herself think about what she'd done in return for that information. The spying, the people she'd killed to collect whatever intel Ophion wanted—these things weighed on her soul like a leaden cloak.

But she'd finally done enough for Ophion that they'd informed her Emile had been sent here, and survived against all odds. At last, she had a location for him. Convincing Command to let her come here . . . that had been another labyrinth to navigate.

In the end, it had required Pippa's support. Command listened to Pippa, their faithful and fervent soldier, leader of the elite Light-fall unit. Especially now that Ophion's numbers had taken such steep hits. Sort-of-human Sofie, on the other hand . . . She knew she was an asset, but with the Vanir blood in her veins, they'd never fully trust her. So she occasionally needed Pippa. Just as much as Pippa's Lightfall missions had needed Sofie's powers.

Pippa's help hadn't been due to friendship. Sofie was fairly certain that friends didn't exist within the Ophion rebel network. But Pippa was an opportunist—and she knew what she stood to gain should this op go smoothly, the doors that would further open to her within Command if Sofie returned triumphant.

A week after Command had approved the plan, over three years after her family had been snatched from their home, Sofie walked into Kavalla.

She'd waited until a local dreadwolf patrol was marching by and stumbled into their path, a mere mile from here. They immediately found the fake rebel documents she'd planted in her coat. They had no idea that Sofie also carried with her, hidden in her head, information that could very well be the final piece of this war against the Asteri.

The blow that could end it.

Ophion had found out too late that before she'd gone into Kavalla, she'd finally accomplished the mission she'd spent years preparing for. She'd made sure before she was picked up that Pippa and Ophion knew she'd acquired that intel. Now they wouldn't back out of their promises to retrieve her and Emile. She knew there would be Hel to pay for it—that she'd gone in secret to gather the information, and was now using it as collateral.

But that would come later.

The dreadwolf patrol interrogated her for two days. Two days, and then they'd thrown her into the cattle car with the others, convinced she was a foolish human girl who'd been given the documents by a lover who'd used her.

She'd never thought her minor in theater would come in handy. That she'd hear her favorite professor's voice critiquing her performance while someone was ripping out her fingernails. That she'd feign a confession with all the sincerity she'd once brought to the stage.

She wondered if Command knew she'd used those acting abilities on them, too.

That wasn't her concern, either. At least, not until tomorrow. Tonight, all that mattered was the desperate plan that would now come to fruition. If she had not been betrayed, if Command had not realized the truth, then a boat waited twenty miles away to ferry them out of Pangera. She looked down at the children around her and prayed the boat had room for more than the three passengers she'd claimed would be arriving.

She'd spent her first week and a half in Kavalla waiting for a glimpse of her brother—a hint of where he might be in the sprawling camp. And then, a few days ago, she'd spotted him in the food line. She'd faked a stumble to cover her shock and joy and sorrow.

He'd gotten so tall. As tall as their father. He was all gangly limbs and bones, a far cry from the healthy thirteen-year-old he should have been, but his face . . . it was the face she'd grown up with. But beginning to show the first hints of manhood on the horizon.

Tonight, she'd seized her chance to sneak into his bunk. And despite the three years and the countless miseries they'd endured, he knew her in an instant, too. Sofie would have spirited him away that moment had he not begged her to bring the others.

Now twelve children crouched behind her.

The alarms would be blaring soon. They had different sirens

for everything here, she'd learned. To signal their wake-ups, their meals, random inspections.

A mournful bird's call fluttered through the low-hanging mist. *All clear.*

With a silent prayer of thanks to the sun-priest and the god he served, Sofie lifted her mangled hand to the electrified fence. She did not glance at her missing fingernails, or the welts, or even feel how numb and stiff her hands were, not as the fence's power crackled through her.

Through her, into her, *becoming* her. Becoming hers to use as she wished.

A thought, and the fence's power turned outward again, her fingertips sparking where they curled against the metal. The metal turned orange, then red beneath her hand.

She sliced her palm down, skin so blisteringly hot it cleaved metal and wire. Emile whispered to the others to keep them from crying out, but she heard one of the boys murmur, "*Witch.*"

A typical human's fear of those with Vanir gifts—of the females who held such tremendous power. She did not turn to tell him that it was not a witch's power that flowed through her. It was something far more rare.

The cold earth met her hand as she rent the last of the fence and peeled the two flaps apart, barely wide enough for her to fit through. The children edged forward, but she signaled for them to halt, scanning the open dirt beyond. The road separating the camp from the ferns and towering pines lay empty.

But the threat would come from behind. She pivoted toward the watchtowers at the corners of the camp, which housed guards with sniper rifles forever trained on the road.

Sofie took a breath, and the power she'd sucked from the fence again shuddered through her. Across the camp, the spotlights ruptured in a shower of sparks that had the guards whirling toward it, shouting.

Sofie peeled the fence apart wider, arms straining, metal biting into her palms, grunting at the children to *run, run, run*—

Little shadows, their light gray uniforms tattered and stained and too bright in the near-full moon, hurried through the fence and across the muddy road to the dense ferns and steep gully beyond. Emile went last, his taller, bony body still a shock to her system, as brutal as any power she could wield.

Sofie did not let herself think of it. She raced after him, weak from the lack of food, the grueling labor, the soul-draining misery of this place. Mud and rocks cut into her bare feet, but the pain was distant as she took in the dozen pale faces peering from the ferns. "*Hurry, hurry, hurry,*" she whispered.

The van would wait only so long.

One of the girls swayed as she got to her feet, aiming for the slope beyond, but Sofie gripped her beneath a bony shoulder, keeping her upright as they staggered along, ferns brushing their legs, roots tangling their feet. Faster. They had to be *faster*—

A siren wailed.

This one, Sofie had not heard before. But she knew its blaring screech for what it was: *Escape.*

Flashlight beams shot through the trees as Sofie and the children crested the lip of a hill, half falling into the fern-laden gully. The dreadwolves were in their humanoid forms, then. Good—their eyes weren't as sharp in the dark this way. Bad, because it meant they carried guns.

Sofie's breathing hitched, but she focused, and sent her power slicing behind her. The flashlights went dark. Even firstlight could not stand against her power. Shouting rose—male, vicious.

Sofie hurried to the front of the group and Emile fell to the back to make sure none were forgotten. Pride swelled in her chest, even as it mingled with terror.

She knew they'd never make it back to the camp alive if they were caught.

Thighs burning, Sofie sprinted up the steep side of the gully. She didn't want to think what the children were enduring, not when their knobbly-kneed legs looked barely able to hold them up. They reached the top of the hill just as the dreadwolves howled, an inhuman sound breaking from humanoid throats. A summons to the hunt.

She pushed the children faster. Mist and ferns and trees and stones—

When one of the boys collapsed, Sofie carried him, focusing on the too-delicate hands gripping the front of her shift.

Hurry, hurry, hurry—

And then there was the road, and the van. Agent Silverbow had waited.

She didn't know his real name. Had refused to let him tell her, though she had a good idea of what—who—he was. But he'd always be Silver to her. And he had waited.

He'd said he wouldn't. Had said Ophion would kill him for abandoning his current mission. *Pippa* would kill him. Or order one of her Lightfall soldiers to do it.

But he'd come with Sofie, had hidden out these two weeks, until Sofie had sent forth the ripple of firstlight last night—the one signal she'd dared make with the Vanir prowling the death camp—to tell him to be here in twenty-four hours.

She'd told him not to use his powers. Even if it would've made this far safer and easier, it would have drained him too much for the escape. And she needed him at full strength now.

In the moonlight, Silver's face was pale above the imperial uniform he'd stolen, his hair slicked back like any preening officer. He grimaced at Emile, then at the eleven other kids—clearly calculating how many could fit into the nondescript white van.

"All," Sofie said as she hurtled for the vehicle, her voice raw. "All, Silver."

He understood. He'd always understood her.

He leapt out of the car with preternatural grace and opened the rear doors. A minute later, squeezed against Silver in the front of the van, his warmth heating her through her threadbare clothes, Sofie could hardly draw breath fast enough as he floored the gas pedal. His thumb brushed over her shoulder, again and again, as if reassuring himself that she was there, that she'd made it.

None of the children spoke. None of them cried.

As the van barreled into the night, Sofie found herself wondering if they still could.

It took them thirty minutes to reach the port city of Servast.

Sofie leaned on Silver, who saw to it, even while racing down the bumpy, winding country road, that the children found the food in the bags he'd stashed in the back. Only enough for three, but the children knew how to stretch a scant spread. He made sure Sofie ate, too. Two weeks in that camp had nearly wrecked her. She didn't understand how these children had survived months. Years. Her brother had survived *three years*.

Silver said quietly as they rounded a sharp curve, "The Hind is close by. I received a report this morning that she was in Alcene." A small city not two hours away—one of the vital depots along the Spine, the north-south network of train tracks that provided ammo and supplies to the imperial troops. "Our spies indicated she was headed this way."

Sofie's stomach tightened, but she focused on donning the clothes and shoes Silver had brought for her to change into. "Then let's hope we make it to the coast before she does."

His throat bobbed. She dared ask, "Pippa?"

A muscle ticked in his jaw. He and Pippa had been jockeying for a promotion into Command's inner ranks for years now. *A crazed fanatic*, Silver had called Pippa on more than one occasion, usually after her Lightfall squadron had led a brutal attack that left no survivors. But Sofie understood Pippa's devotion—she herself had grown up passing as fully human, after all. Had learned exactly how they were treated—how Pippa had likely been treated by the Vanir her entire life. Some things, some experiences, Silver could never understand.

Silver said, "No word yet. She'd better be where she promised to be." Disapproval and distrust laced every word.

Sofie said nothing else as they drove. She wouldn't tell him the details of the intelligence she'd gathered, for all that he had done and meant to her, despite the silent hours spent together, bodies and souls merging. She wouldn't tell anyone—not until Command came through on their promises.

The Asteri had probably realized what she'd discovered. They'd no doubt sent the Hind after her to stop her from telling anyone else.

But the more immediate threat came from the dreadwolves closing in with every mile they hurried toward Servast, hounds on a scent. Silver's frequent glances in the rearview mirror told her that he knew it, too.

The two of them could take on perhaps a handful of wolf shifters—they'd done so before. But there would be more than a handful for an escape from Kavalla. Far more than they could face and live.

She'd prepared for that eventuality. Had already handed over her comm-crystal to Command before entering Kavalla. That precious, sole line of communication to their most valued spy. She knew they'd keep the small chunk of quartz safe. Just as Silver would keep Emile safe. He'd given her his word.

When they emerged from the van, mist wreathed the narrow docks of Servast, writhing over the chill, night-dark waters of the Haldren Sea. It wended around the ancient stone houses of the port town, the firstlight in the few lampposts above the cobblestone streets flickering. No lights shone behind the shuttered windows; not one car or pedestrian moved in the deep shadows and fog.

It was as if the streets of Servast had been emptied in advance of their arrival. As if its citizens—mostly poor fisher-folk, both human and Vanir allied with the House of Many Waters—had hunkered down, some instinct bleating that the fog was not to be braved. Not this night.

Not with dreadwolves on the prowl.

Silver led the way, hair peeking from beneath the cap he'd donned, his attention darting this way and that, his gun within easy reach at his side. She'd seen him kill efficiently with his power, but sometimes a gun was easier.

Emile kept close to Sofie as they crept down the age-worn

streets, through the empty markets. She could feel eyes on her from behind the closed shutters. But no one opened a door to offer help.

Sofie didn't care. As long as that boat waited where she'd been told it would be, the world could go to Hel.

Mercifully, the *Bodegraven* was idling at the end of a long wooden dock three blocks ahead, silver letters bright against her black hull. A few firstlights glowed in the small steamer's portholes, but the decks remained quiet. Emile gasped, as if it were a vision from Luna.

Sofie prayed the other Ophion boats would be waiting beyond the harbor to provide backup, exactly as Command had promised in return for the valuable asset she'd gone into the camp to retrieve. They hadn't cared that the valuable asset was her brother. Only what she told them he could do.

She scanned the streets, the docks, the skies.

The power in her veins thrummed in time to her heart. A counter-beat. A bone-drum, a death knell. A warning.

They had to go *now*.

She started, but Silver's broad hand clamped on her shoulder.

"They're here," he said in his northern accent. With his sharp senses, he could detect the wolves better than she could.

Sofie surveyed the sloping rooftops, the cobblestones, the fog. "How close?"

Dread filled Silver's handsome face. "Everywhere. They're fucking everywhere."

Only three blocks separated them from salvation. Shouts echoed off the stones a block away. "*There! There!*"

One heartbeat to decide. One heartbeat—Emile halted, fear bright in his dark eyes.

No more fear. No more pain.

Sofie hissed at Silver, "*Run*." Silver reached for his gun, but she shoved his hand down, getting in his face. "Get the kids to the boat and go. I'll hold the wolves off and meet you there."

Some of the children were already bolting for the dock. Emile waited. "Run!" she told Silver again. He touched her cheek—the softest of caresses—and sprinted after the children, roaring for the captain to rev the engines. None of them would survive if they didn't depart now.

She whirled to Emile. "Get on that boat."

His eyes—their mother's eyes—widened. "But how will you—"

"I promise I will find you again, Emile. Remember all I told you. *Go.*"

When she embraced his lanky, bony body, she let herself inhale one breath of his scent, the one that lay beneath the acrid layers of dirt and waste from the camp. Then Emile staggered away, half tripping over himself as he marked the lingering power building at her fingertips.

But her brother said softly, "*Make them pay.*"

She closed her eyes, readying herself. Gathering her power. Lights went out on the block around her. When she opened her eyes to the newfound darkness, Emile had reached the dock. Silver waited at the ramp, beckoning beneath the one streetlight that remained lit. Her stare met Silver's.

She nodded once—hoping it conveyed all that was within her heart—and aimed for the dreadwolves' howls.

Sofie sprinted right into the golden beams of the headlights of four cars emblazoned with the Asteri's symbol: *SPQM* and its wreath of seven stars. All crammed full of dreadwolves in imperial uniforms, guns out.

Sofie instantly spied the golden-haired female lounging in the front of the military convertible. A silver torque glimmered against her neck.

The Hind.

The deer shifter had two snipers poised beside her in the open-air car, rifles trained on Sofie. Even in the darkness, Lidia Cervos's hair shimmered, her beautiful face passive and cold. Amber eyes fixed on Sofie, lit with smug amusement. Triumph.

Sofie whipped around a corner before their shots cracked like thunder. The snarl of the Hind's dreadwolves rumbled in the mist behind her as she charged into Servast proper, away from the harbor. From that ship and the children. From Emile.

Silver couldn't use his power to get her. He had no idea where she was.

Sofie's breath sawed out of her chest as she sprinted down the empty, murky streets. A blast from the boat's horn blared through the misty night, as if pleading with her to hurry.

In answer, half a dozen unearthly howls rose up behind her. All closing in.

Some had taken their wolf form, then.

Claws thundered against the pavement nearby, and Sofie gritted her teeth, cutting down another alley, heading for the one place all the maps she'd studied suggested she might stand a chance. The ship's horn blasted again, a final warning that it would leave.

If she could only make it a bit deeper into the city—a bit deeper—

Fangs gnashed behind her.

Keep moving. Not only away from the Vanir on her tail, but from the snipers on the ground, waiting for the open shot. From the Hind, who must know what information Sofie bore. Sofie supposed she should be flattered the Hind herself had come to oversee this.

The small market square appeared ahead, and Sofie barreled for the fountain in its center, punching a line of her power straight for it, shearing through rock and metal until water sprayed, a geyser coating the market square. Wolves splashed into the water as they surged from the surrounding streets, shifting as they cornered her.

In the center of the flooded square, Sofie paused.

The wolves in human forms wore imperial uniforms. Tiny silver darts glimmered along their collars. A dart for every rebel spy broken. Her stomach flipped. Only one type of dreadwolf had those silver darts. The Hind's private guard. The most elite of the shifters.

A throaty whistle sounded through the port. A warning and a farewell.

So Sofie leapt onto the lip of the fountain and smiled at the wolves closing in. They wouldn't kill her. Not when the Hind was waiting to interrogate her. Too bad they didn't know what Sofie truly was. Not a human, nor a witch.

She let the power she'd gathered by the docks unspool.

Crackling energy curled at her fingertips and amid the strands of her short brown hair. One of the dreadwolves understood then—matched what he was seeing with the myths Vanir whispered to their children.

"*She's a fucking thunderbird!*" the wolf roared—just as Sofie unleashed the power she'd gathered on the water flooding the square. On the dreadwolves standing ankle-deep in it.

They didn't stand a chance.

Sofie pivoted toward the docks as the electricity finished slithering over the stones, hardly sparing a glance for the smoking, half-submerged carcasses. The silver darts along their collars glowed molten-hot.

Another whistle. She could still make it.

Sofie splashed through the flooded square, breath ragged in her throat.

The dreadwolf had been only half-right. She was part thunderbird—her great-grandmother had mated with a human long ago, before being executed. The gift, more legend than truth these days, had resurfaced in Sofie.

It was why the rebels had wanted her so badly, why they'd sent her out on such dangerous missions. Why Pippa had come to value her. Sofie smelled like and could pass for a human, but in her veins lurked an ability that could kill in an instant. The Asteri had long ago hunted most thunderbirds to extinction. She'd never learned how her great-grandmother had survived, but the descendants had kept the bloodline secret. *She* had kept it secret.

Until that day three years ago when her family had been killed and taken. When she'd found the nearest Ophion base and showed them exactly what she could do. When she told them what she wanted them to do for her in exchange.

She hated them. Almost as much as she hated the Asteri and the world they'd built. For three years, Ophion had dangled Emile's whereabouts above her, promising to find him, to help her free him, if she could do *one more mission*. Pippa and Silver might believe in the cause, though they differed in their methods of how to fight for it, but Emile had always been Sofie's cause. A free world would be wonderful. But what did it matter if she had no family to share it with?

So many times, for those rebels, she had drawn up power from the grid, from lights and machines, and killed and killed, until her soul lay in tatters. She'd often debated going rogue and finding her brother herself, but she was no spy. She had no network. So she'd stayed, and covertly built up her own bait to dangle before Ophion. Made sure they knew the importance of what she'd gleaned before she entered Kavalla.

Faster, faster she pushed herself toward the dock. If she didn't make it, maybe there would be a smaller boat that she could take to the steamer. Maybe she'd just swim until she was close enough for Silver to spot her, and easily reach her with his power.

Half-crumbling houses and uneven streets passed; fog drifted in veils.

The stretch of wooden dock between Sofie and the steamer pulling away lay clear. She raced for it.

She could make out Silver on the *Bodegraven*'s deck, monitoring her approach. But why didn't he use his power to reach her? Another few feet closer, and she spied the hand pressed to his bleeding shoulder.

Cthona have mercy on him. Silver didn't appear badly hurt, but she had a feeling she knew what kind of bullet he'd been hit with. A bullet with a core of gorsian stone—one that would stifle magic.

His power was useless. But if a sniper had hit Silver on the ship . . . Sofie drew up short.

The convertible sat in the shadows of the building across from the docks. The Hind still lounged like a queen, a sniper beside her with his rifle trained on Sofie. Where the second had gone, she didn't know. Only this one mattered. This one, and his rifle.

It was likely chock-full of gorsian bullets. They'd bring her down in seconds.

The Hind's golden eyes glowed like coals in the dimness. Sofie gauged the distance to the end of the dock, the rope Silver had thrown down, trailing with every inch the *Bodegraven* chugged toward the open water.

The Hind inclined her head in challenge. A deceptively calm voice slid from between her red lips. "Are you faster than a bullet, thunderbird?"

Sofie didn't wait to banter. As swift as a wind through the fjords of her native land, she hurtled down the dock. She knew the sniper's rifle tracked her.

The end of the dock, the dark harbor beyond, loomed.

The rifle cracked.

Silver's roar cleaved the night before Sofie hit the wood planks, splinters cutting into her face, the impact ricocheting through one eye. Pain burst through her right thigh, leaving a wake of shredded flesh and shattered bone, so violent it robbed even the scream from her lungs.

Silver's bellow stopped abruptly—and then he yelled to the captain, "*Go, go, go, go!*"

Facedown on the dock, Sofie knew it was bad. She lifted her head, swallowing her shriek of pain, blood leaking from her nose. The droning hum of an Omega-boat's energy rocked through her even before she spied the approaching lights beneath the harbor's surface.

Four imperial submersible warships converged like sharks on the *Bodegraven*.

Pippa Spetsos stood aboard the rebel ship *Orrae*, the Haldren Sea a dark expanse around her. In the distance, the firstlights of the towns along Pangera's northern coast twinkled like gold stars.

But her attention remained fixed on the gleam of Servast. On the little light sailing toward them.

The *Bodegraven* was on time.

Pippa pressed a hand against the cold, hard armor covering her breast, right above the sinking sun insignia of the Lightfall unit. She would not loose that final breath of relief—not until she saw Sofie. Until she'd secured the assets Sofie carried with her: the boy and the intel.

Then she'd demonstrate to Sofie precisely how Command felt about being manipulated.

Agent Silverbow, the arrogant bastard, had followed the woman he loved. She knew the asset Sofie brought with her meant little to him. The fool. But the possibility of the intel that Sofie claimed to have spent years covertly gathering for Ophion . . . even Silverbow would want that.

Captain Richmond stepped up beside her. "Report," she ordered.

He'd learned the hard way not to disobey her. Learned exactly who in Command supported her, and would rain down Hel on her behalf. Monitoring the approaching vessel, Richmond said, "We've made radio contact. Your operative is not on that ship."

Pippa went still. "The brother?"

"The boy is there. And eleven other children from Kavalla. Sofie Renast stayed behind to buy them time. I'm sorry."

Sorry. Pippa had lost track of how many times she'd heard that fucking word.

But right now . . . Emile had made it to the ship. Was gaining him worth losing Sofie?

It was the gamble they'd taken in even allowing Sofie to go into Kavalla: possibly losing one valuable asset in the quest to seize another. But that was before Sofie had left—and then informed them, right before entering the camp, that she'd attained vital intel on their enemies. To lose Sofie now, with that crucial intel on the line . . .

She hissed at the captain, "I want—"

A human sailor barreled out the glass-enclosed bridge door, skin eerily pale in the moonlight. He faced the captain, then Pippa, uncertain whom to report to. "The *Bodegraven*'s got four Omegas on her tail, closing in fast. Agent Silverbow is down—gorsian bullet to the shoulder."

Pippa's blood chilled. Silverbow wouldn't be any help with a gorsian bullet in him. "They're going to sink that ship, rather than let those children go."

She had not yet become so numb to the horrors of this world that it didn't roil her stomach. Captain Richmond swore softly.

Pippa ordered, "Prepare the gunners." Even if the odds were slim that *they* would survive an assault by the Omegas, they could provide a distraction. The captain grunted his agreement. But the sailor who'd come rushing out of the bridge gasped and pointed.

On the horizon, each and every light in Servast was winking out. The wave of darkness swept inland.

"What in Hel—"

"Not Hel," Pippa murmured as the blackout spread.

Sofie. Or . . . Her eyes narrowed on the *Bodegraven*.

Pippa ran for the bridge's better view. She arrived, panting, Richmond beside her, in time to see the *Bodegraven* racing for them—the submerged lights of the four Omega-boats flickering behind, closing in.

But as they did, a mighty white light soared beneath the surface. It wrapped its long arms around the nearest Omega.

The white light leapt away a moment later, flying for the next boat. No submersible lights glowed in its wake. On the radar before her, the Omega-boat vanished.

"Holy gods," Richmond said.

Something like that, Pippa wanted to say. It was Sofie's strange gift: not only electricity, but firstlight power, too. Energy of any type was hers to command, to suck into herself. Her kind had been hunted to extinction by the Asteri centuries ago because of that mighty, unconquerable gift—or so it had seemed.

But now there were two of them.

Sofie said her brother's powers dwarfed her own. Powers Pippa now witnessed as the light leapt from the second boat—another blackout—and raced for the third.

She could make out no sign of Emile on the *Bodegraven*'s deck, but he had to be there.

"What can bring down an Omega with no torpedoes?" murmured one of the sailors. Closer now, the light swept beneath the surface for the third boat, and even with the distance, Pippa could see the core of long, bright white tendrils streaming from it—like wings.

"An angel?" someone whispered. Pippa scoffed privately. There were no angels among the few Vanir in Ophion. If Pippa had her way, there'd be no Vanir among them at all . . . save for ones like this. Vanir powers, but a human soul and body.

Emile was a great prize for the rebellion—Command would be pleased indeed.

The third Omega submersible went black, vanishing into the inky deep. Pippa's blood sang at the terrible glory of it. Only one Omega left.

"Come on," Pippa breathed. "Come on . . ." Too much rested on that boat. The balance of this war might hang on it.

"Two brimstone torpedoes fired from the remaining Omega," a sailor shouted.

But the white light slammed into the Omega, miles' worth of first-light sending the final ship spiraling into a watery abyss.

And then a leap outward, a whip of light illuminating the waves above it to turquoise. A stretching hand.

A sailor reported hoarsely, awe and anticipation in every word, "Brimstone torpedoes are gone from the radar. Vanished."

Only the lights of the *Bodegraven* remained, like dim stars in a sea of darkness.

"Commander Spetsos?" Richmond asked.

But Pippa ignored Richmond, and stalked into the warmth of the bridge's interior, yanking a pair of long-range binoculars from a hook just inside the door. Within seconds, she was out on the wind-whipped deck again, binoculars focused on the *Bodegraven*.

Emile stood there, aged but definitely the same child from Sofie's photos, no more than a lean figure alone at the prow. Staring toward the watery graveyard as they passed over it. Then to the land beyond. He slowly sank to his knees.

Smiling to herself, Pippa shifted the view on the binoculars and gazed toward the thorough blackness of Pangera.

Lying on her side, the lap of waves against the quay and the drip of her blood on the surface beneath the wooden slats the only sounds she could hear, Sofie waited to die.

Her arm dangled off the end of the dock as the *Bodegraven* sailed toward those savior lights on the sea. Toward Pippa. Pippa had brought battleships to guide the *Bodegraven* to safety. Likely to ensure Sofie was on it, along with Emile, but . . . Pippa had still come. Ophion had come.

Tears slid along her cheeks, onto the wood slats. Everything hurt.

She'd known this would happen, if she pushed too far, demanded too much power, as she had tonight. The firstlight always hurt so much worse than electricity. Charred her insides even as it left her craving more of its potent power. It was why she avoided it as much as possible. Why the idea of Emile had been so enticing to Command, to Pippa and her Lightfall squadron.

There was nothing left inside her now. Not one spark of power. And no one was coming to save her.

Footsteps thudded on the dock, rattling her body. Sofie bit her lip against the flashing pain.

Polished black boots stopped inches from her nose. Sofie shifted her good eye upward. The Hind's pale face peered down.

"Naughty girl," the Hind said in that fair voice. "Electrocuting my dreadwolves." She ran an amber eye over Sofie. "What a remarkable power you have. And what a remarkable power your brother has, downing my Omega-boats. It seems all the legends about your kind are true."

Sofie said nothing.

The spy-breaker smiled slightly. "Tell me who you passed the intel to, and I will walk off this dock and let you live. I'll let you see your darling little brother."

Sofie said through stiff lips, "No one."

The Hind merely said, "Let's go for a ride, Sofie Renast."

The dreadwolves bundled Sofie into a nondescript boat. No one spoke as it sailed out to sea. As an hour passed, and the sky lightened. Only when they were so far from the shore that it was no longer a darker shadow against the night sky did the Hind lift a hand. The engines cut off, and the boat bobbed in the waves.

Again, those polished, knee-high boots approached Sofie. She'd been bound, gorsian shackles around her wrists to stifle her power. Her leg had gone numb with agony.

With a nod to a wolf, the Hind ordered that Sofie should be hauled to her feet. Sofie bit down her cry of pain. Behind her, another wolf opened the transom gate, exposing the small platform off the boat's back. Sofie's throat closed up.

"Since your brother has bestowed such a death upon a multitude of imperial soldiers, this will be an apt punishment for you," the Hind said, stepping onto the platform, not seeming to care about the water splashing over her boots. She pulled a small white stone from her pocket, lifting it for Sofie to see, and then chucked it into the water. Observed it with her Vanir-sharp eyes as it dropped down, down, down into the inky blackness.

"At that depth, you'll likely drown before you hit the seafloor," the Hind observed, her golden hair shifting across her imperious face. She slid her hands into her pockets as the wolves knelt at Sofie's feet and bound them together with chains weighted with lead blocks.

"I'll ask you again," the Hind said, angling her head, silver torque glinting at her neck. "With whom did you share the intelligence you collected before you went into Kavalla?"

Sofie felt the ache of her missing fingernails. Saw the faces in that camp. The people she'd left behind. Her cause had been Emile—yet Ophion was right in so many ways. And some small part of her had been glad to kill for Ophion, to fight for those people. Would keep fighting for them, for Emile, now. She gritted out, "I told you: no one."

"Very well, then." The Hind pointed to the water. "You know how this ends."

Sofie kept her face blank to conceal her shock at her good luck, one last gift from Solas. Apparently, even the Hind was not as clever as she believed herself to be. She offered a swift, horrible death—but it was nothing compared to the endless torture Sofie had expected.

"Put her on the platform."

A dreadwolf—a hulking, dark-haired male—objected, sneering, "We'll get it out of her." Mordoc, the Hind's second in command. Almost as feared as his commander. Especially with his particular gifts.

The Hind didn't so much as look at him. "I'm not wasting my time on this. She says she didn't tell anyone, and I'm inclined to believe her." A slow smile. "So the intel will die with her."

It was all the Hind needed to say. The wolves hauled Sofie onto the platform. She swallowed a cry at the wave of agony that rippled through her thigh. Icy water sprayed, soaking through her clothes, burning and numbing.

Sofie couldn't stop her shaking. Tried to remember the kiss of the air, the scent of the sea, the gray of the sky before dawn. She would not see the sunrise, only minutes away. She'd never see another one again.

She had taken the beauty and simplicity of living for granted. How she wished she'd savored it more. Every single moment.

The deer shifter prowled closer. "Any last words?"

Emile had gotten away. It was all that mattered. He'd be kept safe now.

Sofie smiled crookedly at the Hind. "*Go to Hel.*"

Mordoc's clawed hands shoved her off the platform.

The frigid water hit Sofie like a bomb blast, and then the lead at her feet grabbed all that she was and might have been, and pulled her under.

The Hind stood, a phantom in the chilled mist of the Haldren Sea, and watched until Sofie Renast had been wrapped in Ogenas's embrace.

PART I
THE CHASM

1

For a Tuesday night at the Crescent City Ballet, the theater was unusually packed. The sight of the swarming masses in the lobby, drinking and chatting and mingling, filled Bryce Quinlan with a quiet sort of joy and pride.

There was only one reason why the theater was so packed tonight. With her Fae hearing, she could have sworn she heard the hundreds of voices all around her whispering, *Juniper Andromeda*. The star of tonight's performance.

Yet even with the crowd, an air of quiet reverence and serenity filled the space. As if it were a temple.

Bryce had the creeping sensation that the various ancient statues of the gods flanking the long lobby watched her. Or maybe that was the well-dressed older shifter couple standing by a reclining statue of Cthona, the earth goddess, naked and awaiting the embrace of her lover, Solas. The shifters—some sort of big cats, from their scents, and rich ones, judging by their watches and jewelry—blatantly ogled her.

Bryce offered them a bland, close-lipped smile.

Some variation of this had happened nearly every single day since the attack this past spring. The first few times had been overwhelming, unnerving—people coming up to her and sobbing with gratitude. Now they just stared.

Bryce didn't blame the people who wanted to speak to her, who *needed* to speak to her. The city had been healed—by her—but its people . . .

Scores had been dead by the time her firstlight erupted through Lunathion. Hunt had been lucky, had been taking his last breaths, when the firstlight saved him. Five thousand other people had not been so lucky.

Their families had not been so lucky.

So many dark boats had drifted across the Istros to the mists of the Bone Quarter that they had looked like a bevy of black swans. Hunt had carried her into the skies to see it. The quays along the river had teemed with people, their mourning cries rising to the low clouds where she and Hunt had glided.

Hunt had only held her tighter and flown them home.

"Take a picture," Ember Quinlan called now to the shifters from where she stood next to a marble torso of Ogenas rising from the waves, the ocean goddess's full breasts peaked and arms upraised. "Only ten gold marks. Fifteen, if you want to be in it."

"For fuck's sake, Mom," Bryce muttered. Ember stood with her hands on her hips, gorgeous in a silky gray gown and pashmina. "Please don't."

Ember opened her mouth, as if she'd say something else to the chastised shifters now hurrying toward the east staircase, but her husband interrupted her. "I second Bryce's request," Randall said, dashing in his navy suit.

Ember turned outraged dark eyes on Bryce's stepfather—her only father, as far as Bryce was concerned—but Randall pointed casually to a broad frieze behind them. "That one reminds me of Athalar."

Bryce arched a brow, grateful for the change of subject, and twisted toward where he'd pointed. On it, a powerful Fae male stood poised above an anvil, hammer raised skyward in one fist, lightning cracking from the skies, filling the hammer, and flowing down toward the object of the hammer's intended blow: a sword.

Its label read simply: *Unknown sculptor. Palmira, circa 125 V.E.*

Bryce lifted her mobile and snapped a photo, pulling up her messaging thread with *Hunt Athalar Is Better at Sunball Than I Am.*

She couldn't deny that. They'd gone to the local sunball field one sunny afternoon last week to play, and Hunt had promptly wiped the floor with her. He'd changed his name in her phone on the way home.

With a few sweeps of her thumbs, the picture zoomed off into the ether, along with her note: *Long-lost relative of yours?*

She slid her phone into her clutch to find her mother watching. "What?" Bryce muttered.

But Ember only motioned toward the frieze. "Who does it depict?"

Bryce checked the sliver of writing in the lower right corner. "It just says *The Making of the Sword.*"

Her mother peered at the half-faded etching. "In what language?"

Bryce tried to keep her posture relaxed. "The Old Language of the Fae."

"Ah." Ember pursed her lips, and Randall wisely drifted off through the crowd to study a towering statue of Luna aiming her bow toward the heavens, two hunting dogs at her feet and a stag nuzzling her hip. "You stayed fluent in it?"

"Yep," Bryce said. Then added, "It's come in handy."

"I'd imagine so." Ember tucked back a strand of her black hair.

Bryce moved to the next frieze dangling from the distant ceiling on near-invisible wires. "This one's of the First Wars." She scanned the relief carved into the ten-foot expanse of marble. "It's about . . ." She schooled her expression into neutrality.

"What?" Ember stepped closer to the depiction of an army of winged demons swooping down from the skies upon a terrestrial army gathered on the plain below.

"This one's about Hel's armies arriving to conquer Midgard during the First Wars," Bryce finished, trying to keep her voice bland. To block out the flash of talons and fangs and leathery wings—the boom of her rifle resounding through her bones, the rivers of blood in the streets, the screaming and screaming and—

"You'd think this one would be a popular piece these days," Randall observed, returning to their sides to study the frieze.

Bryce didn't reply. She didn't particularly enjoy discussing the events of the past spring with her parents. Especially not in the middle of a packed theater lobby.

Randall jerked his chin to the inscription. "What's this one say?"

Keenly aware of her mother marking her every blink, Bryce kept her stance unaffected as she skimmed the text in the Old Language of the Fae.

It wasn't that she was trying to hide what she'd endured. She *had* talked to her mom and dad about it a few times. But it always resulted in Ember crying, or ranting about the Vanir who'd locked out so many innocents, and the weight of all her mother's emotions on top of all of *hers* . . .

It was easier, Bryce had realized, to not bring it up. To let herself talk it out with Hunt, or sweat it out in Madame Kyrah's dance classes twice a week. Baby steps toward being ready for actual talk therapy, as Juniper kept suggesting, but both had helped immensely.

Bryce silently translated the text. "This is a piece from a larger collection—likely one that would have wrapped around the entire exterior of a building, each slab telling a different part of the story. This one says: *Thus the seven Princes of Hel looked in envy upon Midgard and unleashed their unholy hordes upon our united armies.*"

"Apparently nothing's changed in fifteen thousand years," Ember said, shadows darkening her eyes.

Bryce kept her mouth shut. She'd never told her mom about Prince Aidas—how he'd helped her twice now, and had seemed unaware of his brothers' dark plans. If her mom knew she'd consorted with the fifth Prince of Hel, they'd have to redefine the concept of *going berserk*.

But then Ember said, "Couldn't you get a job *here*?" She gestured with a tan hand to the CCB's grand entrance, its ever-changing art exhibits in the lobby and on a few of the other levels. "You're qualified. This would have been perfect."

"There were no openings." True. And she didn't want to use her princess status to get one. She wanted to work at a place like the CCB's art department on her own merit.

Her job at the Fae Archives . . . Well, she definitely got that because they saw her as a Fae Princess. But it wasn't the same, somehow. Because she hadn't wanted to work there as badly.

"Did you even *try?*"

"Mom," Bryce said, voice sharpening.

"Bryce."

"Ladies," Randall said, a teasing remark designed to fracture the growing tension.

Bryce smiled gratefully at him but found her mother frowning. She sighed up at the starburst chandeliers above the glittering throng. "All right, Mom. Out with it."

"Out with what?" Ember asked innocently.

"Your opinion about my job." Bryce gritted her teeth. "For years, you ragged on me for being an assistant, but now that I'm doing something better, it's not good enough?"

This was so not the place, not with tons of people milling about within earshot, but she'd had it.

Ember didn't seem to care as she said, "It's not that it's not good enough. It's about where that job is."

"The Fae Archives operate independently of *him.*"

"Oh? Because I remember him bragging that it was pretty much his personal library."

Bryce said tightly, "Mom. The gallery is gone. I need a job. Forgive me if the usual corporate nine-to-five isn't available to me right now. Or if CCB's art department isn't hiring."

"I just don't get why you couldn't work something out with Jesiba. She's still got that warehouse—surely she needs help with whatever she does there."

Bryce refrained from rolling her eyes. Within a day of the attack on the city this spring, Jesiba had cleared out the gallery—and the precious volumes that made up all that remained of the ancient Great Library of Parthos. Most of Jesiba's other pieces were now in a warehouse, many in crates, but Bryce had no idea where the sorceress had spirited off the Parthos books—one of the few remnants of the human world before the Asteri's arrival. Bryce hadn't dared question Jesiba about their current whereabouts. It was a miracle that the Asteri hadn't been tipped off about the contraband books' existence. "There are only so many times I can ask for a job without looking like I'm begging."

"And we can't have a princess do that."

She'd lost count of how often she'd told her mom she wasn't a princess. Didn't want to be, and the Autumn King sure as shit didn't want her to be, either. She hadn't spoken to the asshole since that last time he'd come to see her at the gallery, right before her confrontation with Micah. When she'd revealed what power coursed through her veins.

It was an effort not to glance down at her chest, to where the front of her gauzy, pale blue dress plunged to just below her breasts, displaying the star-shaped mark between them. Thankfully, the back was high enough to hide the Horn tattooed there. Like an old scar, the white mark stood out starkly against her freckled, golden-tan skin. It hadn't faded in the three months since the city had been attacked.

She'd already lost count of how many times she'd caught her mom staring at her star since arriving last night.

A cluster of gorgeous females—woodland nymphs, from their cedar-and-moss scents—meandered past, champagne in hand, and Bryce lowered her voice. "What do you want me to say? That I'll move back home to Nidaros and pretend to be normal?"

"What's so bad about normal?" Her mother's beautiful face blazed with an inner fire that never banked—never, ever died out. "I think Hunt would like living there."

"Hunt still works for the 33rd, Mom," Bryce said. "He's second in command, for fuck's sake. And while he might appease you by saying he'd *love* to live in Nidaros, don't think for one minute he means it."

"Way to throw him under the bus," Randall said while keeping his attention on a nearby information placard.

Before Bryce could answer, Ember said, "Don't think I haven't noticed things between you two are weird."

Trust her mom to bring up two topics she didn't want to talk about in the space of five minutes. "In what way?"

"You're together but not *together*," Ember said bluntly. "What's that about?"

"It's none of your business." It really wasn't. But as if he'd heard her, the phone in her clutch buzzed. She yanked it out and peered at the screen.

Hunt had written, *I can only hope to have abs like those one day.*

Bryce couldn't help her half smile as she peered back at the muscular Fae male on the frieze before answering. *I think you might have a few on him, actually . . .*

"Don't ignore me, Bryce Adelaide Quinlan."

Her phone buzzed again, but she didn't read Hunt's reply as she said to her mother, "Can you please drop it? And don't bring it up when Hunt gets here."

Ember's mouth popped open, but Randall said, "Agreed. No job or romance interrogations when Hunt arrives."

Her mother frowned doubtfully, but Bryce said, "Mom, just . . . stop, okay? I don't mind my job, and the thing between me and Hunt is what he and I agreed on. I'm doing fine. Let's leave it at that."

It was a lie. Sort of.

She actually *liked* her job—a lot. The private wing of the Fae Archives housed a trove of ancient artifacts that had been sorely neglected for centuries—now in need of researching and cataloging so they could be sent on a traveling exhibit next spring.

She set her own hours, answering only to the head of research, an owl shifter—one of the rare non-Fae staff—who only worked from dusk to dawn, so they barely overlapped. The worst part of her day was entering the sprawling complex through the main buildings, where the sentries all gawked at her. Some even bowed. And then she had to walk through the atrium, where the librarians and patrons tended to stare, too.

Everyone these days stared—she really fucking hated it. But Bryce didn't want to tell her mom any of that.

Ember said, "Fine. You know I just worry."

Something in Bryce's chest softened. "I know, Mom. And I know . . ." She struggled for the words. "It really helps to know that I can move back home if I want to. But not right now."

"Fair enough," Randall chimed in, giving Ember a pointed glance before looping his arm around her waist and steering her toward another frieze across the theater lobby.

Bryce used their distraction to take out her phone, and found that Hunt had written two messages:

Want to count my abs when we get home from the ballet?

Her stomach tightened, and she'd never been more grateful that her parents possessed a human sense of smell as her toes curled in her heels.

Hunt had added, *I'll be there in five, by the way. Isaiah held me up with a new case.*

She sent a thumbs-up, then replied: *Pleaaaaaase get here ASAP. I just got a major grilling about my job. And you.*

Hunt wrote back immediately, and Bryce read as she slowly trailed her parents to where they observed the frieze: *What about me?*

"Bryce," her mom called, pointing to the frieze before her. "Check out this one. It's JJ."

Bryce looked up from her phone and grinned. "Badass warrior Jelly Jubilee." There, hanging on the wall, was a rendering of a pegasus—though not a unicorn-pegasus, like Bryce's childhood toy—charging into battle. An armored figure, helmet obscuring any telltale features, rode atop the beast, sword upraised. Bryce snapped a photo and sent it to Hunt.

First Wars JJ, reporting for duty!

She was about to reply to Hunt's *What about me?* question when her mom said, "Tell Hunt to stop flirting and hurry up already."

Bryce scowled at her mom and put her phone away.

So many things had changed since revealing her heritage as the Autumn King's daughter and a Starborn heir: people gawking, the hat and sunglasses she now wore on the street to attain some level of anonymity, the job at the Fae Archives. But at least her mother remained the same.

Bryce couldn't decide whether that was a comfort or not.

Entering the private box in the angels' section of the theater—the stage-left boxes a level above the floor—Bryce grinned toward the heavy golden curtain blocking the stage from sight. Only ten minutes remained until the show began. Until the world could see how insanely talented Juniper was.

Ember gracefully sank into one of the red velvet chairs at the front of the box, Randall claiming the seat beside her. Bryce's mother didn't smile. Considering that the royal Fae boxes occupied the wing across from them, Bryce didn't blame her. And considering that many of the bejeweled and shining nobility were staring at Bryce, it was a miracle Ember hadn't flipped them off yet.

Randall whistled at the prime seats as he peered over the golden rail. "Nice view."

The air behind Bryce went electric, buzzing and alive. The hair on her arms prickled. A male voice sounded from the vestibule, "A benefit to having wings: no one wants to sit behind you."

Bryce had developed a keen awareness of Hunt's presence, like scenting lightning on the wind. He had only to enter a room and she'd know if he was there by that surge of power in her body. Like her magic, her very blood answered to his.

Now she found Hunt standing in the doorway, already tugging at the black tie around his neck.

Just . . . gods-damn.

He'd worn a black suit and white shirt, both cut to his powerful, muscled body, and the effect was devastating. Add in the gray wings framing it all and she was a goner.

Hunt smirked knowingly, but nodded to Randall. "You clean up good, man. Sorry I'm late." Bryce could barely hear her dad's reply as she surveyed the veritable malakim feast before her.

Hunt had cut his hair shorter last month. Not too short, since she'd staged an intervention with the stylist before the draki male could chop off all those beautiful locks, but gone was the shoulder-length hair. The shorter style suited him, but it was still a shock weeks later to find his hair neatly trimmed to his nape, with only a few pieces in the front still unruly enough to peek through the hole in his sunball hat. Tonight, however, he'd brushed it into submission, revealing the clear expanse of his forehead.

That was still a shock, too: no tattoo. No sign of the years of torment the angel had endured beyond the *C* stamped over the slave's tattoo on his right wrist, marking him a free male. Not a full citizen, but closer to it than the peregrini.

The mark was hidden by the cuff of his suit jacket and the shirt beneath, and Bryce lifted her gaze to Hunt's face. Her mouth went dry at the bald hunger filling his dark, angular eyes. "You look okay, too," he said, winking.

Randall coughed, but leafed through the playbill. Ember did the same beside him.

Bryce ran a hand down the front of her blue dress. "This old thing?"

Hunt chuckled, and tugged on his tie again.

Bryce sighed. "Please tell me you're not one of those big, tough males who makes a big fuss about how he hates getting dressed up."

It was Ember's turn to cough, but Hunt's eyes danced as he said to Bryce, "Good thing I don't have to do it that often, huh?"

A knock on the box door shut off her reply, and a satyr server appeared, carrying a tray of complimentary champagne. "From Miss Andromeda," the cloven-hoofed male announced.

Bryce grinned. "Wow." She made a mental note to double the size of the bouquet she'd planned to send to June tomorrow. She took the glass the satyr extended to her, but before she could raise it to her lips, Hunt halted her with a gentle hand on her wrist. She'd officially ended her No Drinking rule after this spring, but she suspected the touch had nothing to do with reminding her to go slow.

Arching a brow, she waited until the server had left before asking, "You want to make a toast?"

Hunt reached into an inner pocket of his suit and pulled out a small container of mints. Or what seemed like mints. She barely had time to react before he plopped a white pill into her glass.

"What the *Hel*—"

"Just testing." Hunt studied her glass. "If it's drugged or poisoned, it'll turn green."

Ember chimed in with her approval. "The satyr said the drinks are from Juniper, but how do you know, Bryce? Anything could be in it." Her mom nodded at Hunt. "Good thinking."

Bryce wanted to object, but . . . Hunt had a point. "And what am I supposed to do with it now? It's ruined."

"The pill is tasteless," Hunt said, clinking his flute against hers when the liquid remained pale gold. "Bottoms up."

"Classy," she said, but drank. It still tasted like champagne—no hint of the dissolved pill lingered.

The golden sconces and dangling starburst chandeliers dimmed twice in a five-minute warning, and Bryce and Hunt took their seats behind her parents. From this angle, she could barely make out Fury in the front row.

Hunt seemed to track the direction of her attention. "She didn't want to sit with us?"

"Nope." Bryce took in her friend's shining dark hair, her black suit. "She wants to see every drop of Juniper's sweat."

"I'd think she saw that every night," Hunt said wryly, and Bryce waggled her eyebrows.

But Ember twisted in her seat, a genuine smile lighting her face. "How are Fury and Juniper doing? Did they move in together yet?"

"Two weeks ago." Bryce craned her neck to study Fury, who seemed to be reading the playbill. "And they're really good. I think Fury's here to stay this time."

Her mom asked carefully, "And you and Fury? I know things were weird for a while."

Hunt did her a favor and made himself busy on his phone. Bryce idly flipped the pages of her playbill. "Working things out with Fury took some time. But we're good."

Randall asked, "Is Axtar still doing what she does best?"

"Yep." Bryce was content to leave her friend's mercenary business at that. "She's happy, though. And more important, June and Fury are happy together."

"Good," Ember said, smiling softly. "They make such a beautiful couple." And because her mom was . . . well, her mom, Ember sized up Bryce and Hunt and said with no shame whatsoever, "You two would as well, if you got your shit together."

Bryce slouched down in her seat, lifting her playbill to block her red-hot face. Why weren't the lights dimming yet? But Hunt took it in stride and said, "All good things come to those who wait, Ember."

Bryce scowled at the arrogance and amusement in his tone, throwing her playbill into her lap as she declared, "Tonight's a big deal for June. Try not to ruin it with nonsensical banter."

Ember patted Bryce's knee before twisting back to face the stage.

Hunt drained his champagne, and Bryce's mouth dried out again at the sight of the broad, strong column of his throat working as he swallowed, then said, "Here I was, thinking you loved the banter."

Bryce had the option of either drooling or turning away, so rather than ruin her dress, she observed the crowd filtering into their seats. More than one person peered toward her box.

Especially from the Fae boxes across the way. No sign of her father or Ruhn, but she recognized a few cold faces. Tristan Flynn's parents—Lord and Lady Hawthorne—were among them, their professional snob of a daughter Sathia sitting between them. None of the glittering nobility seemed pleased at Bryce's presence. Good.

"Tonight's a big deal for June, remember," Hunt murmured, lips quirking upward.

She glowered. "What?"

Hunt inclined his head toward the Fae nobility sneering across the space. "I can see you thinking about some way to piss them off."

"I was not."

He leaned in to whisper, his breath brushing her neck, "You were, and I know it because I was thinking the same thing." A few cameras flashed from above and below, and she knew people weren't snapping photos of the stage curtain.

Bryce peeled back to survey Hunt, the face she knew as well as her own. For a moment, for a too-brief eternity, they stared at each other. Bryce swallowed, but couldn't bring herself to move. To break the contact.

Hunt's throat bobbed. But he said nothing more, either.

Three fucking *months* of this torture. Stupid agreement. Friends, but more. More, but without any of the physical benefits.

Hunt said at last, voice thick, "It's really nice of you to be here for Juniper."

She tossed her hair over a shoulder. "You're making it sound like it's some big sacrifice."

He jerked his chin toward the still-sneering Fae nobility. "You can't wear a hat and sunglasses here, so . . . yeah."

She admitted, "I wish she'd gotten us seats in the nosebleed section."

Instead, Juniper—to accommodate Hunt's wings—had gotten them this box. Right where everyone could see the Starborn Princess and the Fallen Angel.

The orchestra began tuning up, and the sounds of slowly awakening violins and flutes drew Bryce's attention to the pit. Her muscles tensed of their own volition, as if priming to move. To dance.

Hunt leaned in again, voice a low purr, "You look beautiful, you know."

"Oh, I know," she said, even as she bit her lower lip to keep from grinning. The lights began dimming, so Bryce decided to Hel with it. "When do I get to count those abs, Athalar?"

The angel cleared his throat—once, twice—and shifted in his seat, feathers rustling. Bryce smiled smugly.

He murmured, "Four more months, Quinlan."

"And three days," she shot back.

His eyes shone in the growing darkness.

"What are you two talking about back there?" Ember asked, and Bryce replied without tearing her gaze from Hunt's, "Nothing."

But it wasn't nothing. It was the stupid bargain she'd made with Hunt: that rather than diving right into bed, they'd wait until Winter Solstice to act on their desires. Spend the summer and autumn getting to know each other without the burdens of a psychotic Archangel and demons on the prowl.

So they had. Torturing each other with flirting was allowed, but sometimes, tonight especially . . . she really wished she'd never suggested it. Wished she could drag him into the coat closet of the vestibule behind them and show him precisely how much she liked that suit.

Four months, three days, and . . . She peeked at the delicate watch on her wrist. Four hours. And at the stroke of midnight on Winter Solstice, *she* would be stroking—

"Burning fucking Solas, Quinlan," Hunt grunted, again shifting in his seat.

"Sorry," she muttered, thankful for the second time in an hour that her parents didn't have the sense of smell that Hunt possessed.

But Hunt laughed, sliding an arm along the back of her chair, fingers tangling in her unbound hair. He seemed contented. Assured of his place there.

She glanced at her parents, sitting with similar closeness, and couldn't help but smile. Her mom had taken a while to act on her desires with Randall, too. Well, there'd been some initial . . . stuff. That was as much as Bryce let herself think about them. But she knew it had been nearly a year before they'd made things official. And they'd turned out pretty damn well.

So these months with Hunt, she cherished them. As much as she cherished her dance classes with Madame Kyrah. No one except Hunt really understood what she'd gone through—only Hunt had been at the Gate.

She scanned his striking features, her lips curving again. How many nights had they stayed up, talking about everything and nothing? Ordering in dinner, watching movies or reality shows or sunball, playing video games, or sitting on the roof of the apartment building, observing malakim and witches and draki dart across the sky like shooting stars.

He'd shared so many things about his past, sad and horrible and joyous. She wanted to know all of it. And the more she learned, the more she found herself sharing, and the more she . . .

Light flared from the star on her chest.

Bryce clapped a hand over it. "I shouldn't have worn this stupid dress."

Her fingers could barely cover the star that was blaring white light through the dim theater, illuminating every face now turned her way as the orchestra quieted in anticipation of the conductor's approach.

She didn't dare look toward the Fae across the space. To see the disgust and disdain.

Ember and Randall twisted in their seats, her dad's face scrunched with concern, Ember's eyes wide with fear. Her mom knew those Fae were sneering, too. She'd hidden Bryce from them her whole life because of how they'd react to the power that now radiated from her.

Some jackass shouted from the audience below, "*Hey! Turn off the light!*" Bryce's face burned as a few people chuckled, then quickly went silent.

She could only assume Fury had been nearby.

Bryce cupped both hands over the star, which had taken to glowing at the *worst* fucking times—this was merely the most mortifying. "I don't know how to turn it off," she muttered, making to rise from her seat and flee into the vestibule behind the curtain.

But Hunt slid a warm, dry hand over her scar, fingers grazing her breasts. His palm was broad enough that it covered the mark, capturing the light within. It glowed through his fingers, casting his light brown skin into rosy gold, but he managed to contain the light.

"Admit it: you just wanted me to feel you up," Hunt whispered, and Bryce couldn't help her stupid, giddy laugh. She buried her face in Hunt's shoulder, the smooth material of his suit cool against her cheeks and brow. "Need a minute?" he asked, though she knew he was glaring daggers at all the assholes still gawking. The Fae nobility hissing about the *disgrace*.

"Should we go?" Ember asked, voice sharp with worry.

"No," Bryce said thickly, putting a hand over Hunt's. "I'm good."

"You can't sit there like that," Ember countered.

"I'm good, Mom."

Hunt didn't move his hand. "We're used to the staring. Right, Quinlan?" He flashed Ember a grin. "They won't fuck with us." An edge laced his smile, a reminder to anyone watching that he wasn't only Hunt Athalar, he was also the Umbra Mortis. The Shadow of Death.

He'd earned that name.

Ember nodded again approvingly as Randall offered Hunt a grateful dip of the chin. Mercifully, the conductor emerged then, and a smattering of applause filled the theater.

Bryce inhaled deeply, then slowly exhaled. She had zero control over when the star flared, or when it stopped. She sipped from her champagne, then said casually to Hunt, "The headline on the gossip sites tomorrow is going to be: *Horndog Umbra Mortis Gropes Starborn Princess at Ballet.*"

"Good," Hunt murmured. "It'll improve my standing in the 33rd."

She smiled, despite herself. It was one of his many gifts—making her laugh, even when the world seemed inclined to humiliate and shun her.

His fingers went dark at her chest, and Bryce heaved a sigh. "Thanks," she said as the conductor raised his baton.

Hunt slowly, so slowly, removed his hand from her chest. "Don't mention it, Quinlan."

She glanced sidelong at him again, wondering at the shift in his tone. But the orchestra began its lilting opening, and the curtain drew back, and Bryce leaned forward breathlessly to await her friend's grand entrance.

2

Bryce tried not to shiver with delight when Hunt knocked her with a wing while they walked up the sagging stairs to Ruhn's house.

A small get-together, Ruhn had said when he'd called to invite them to swing by after the ballet. Since the thought of her mother grilling her again about her job, sex life, and princess status was sure to drive her to drink anyway, Bryce and Hunt had dumped her parents back at their hotel, changed at the apartment—Hunt had insisted on that part with a grumbled *I need to get the fuck out of this suit*—and flown over here.

The entire Old Square had apparently turned up as well: Fae and shifters and people of all Houses drank and danced and talked. On the pathetic excuse for a front lawn, a cluster of green-haired river nymphs and fauns both male and female played cornhole. A cluster of Fae males behind them—Aux members, from their muscles and stick-up-the-ass posture—were engaged in what looked like an absolutely *riveting* game of bocce.

The arid day had yielded to a whisper-sweet night, warm enough that every bar and café and club in the Old Square—especially around Archer Street—teemed with revelers. Even with the booming music erupting from Ruhn's house, she could make out the thump of the bass from the other houses along the street, the bar at the corner, the cars driving by.

Everyone was celebrating being alive.

As they should be.

"Fury and June are already here," Bryce called to Hunt over the noise as they strode up the rickety, beer-splattered steps into Ruhn's house. "June said they're in the living room."

Hunt nodded, though his focus remained fixed on the partying crowd. Even here, people noted from all directions as the Starborn Princess and the Umbra Mortis arrived. The crowd parted for them, some even backing away. Bryce stiffened, but Hunt didn't halt his easy pace. He was accustomed to this shit—had been for a while now. And though he was no longer officially the Shadow of Death, people hadn't forgotten what he had once done. Who he'd once served.

Hunt aimed for the living room to the left of the foyer, the ridiculous muscles along his shoulders shifting with the movement. They were put on near-obscene display by the black tank top he wore. Bryce might have survived the sight of it, had it not been for the white sunball hat, twisted backward the way Hunt usually wore it.

She preferred that hat to the fancy suit, actually.

To her shock, Hunt didn't protest when a reveling air sprite floated past, crowning him and then Bryce with glow-stick necklaces made from firstlight. Bryce removed the plastic tube of light and looped it into a bracelet snaking up her arm. Hunt left his hanging over his chest, the light casting the deep muscles of his pectorals and shoulders in stark relief. Gods spare her.

Hunt had only taken one step into the living room when Tristan Flynn's voice boomed from the foyer behind them: "The *fuck*, Ruhn!"

Bryce snorted, and through the crowd she spied the Fae lord at one end of the beer pong table on which he'd painted an image of an enormous Fae head devouring an angel whole.

Ruhn stood at the other end of the table, both middle fingers raised to his opponents, his lip ring glinting in the dim lights of the foyer. "Pay up, assholes," her brother said, the rolled cigarette between his lips bobbing with his words.

Bryce reached a hand for Hunt, fingers grazing his downy soft wings. He went rigid, twisting to look at her. Angels' wings were highly sensitive. She might as well have grabbed him by the balls.

Face flushing, she jabbed a thumb toward her brother. "Tell June and Fury I'll be there in a sec," she called over the noise. "I want to say hi to Ruhn." She didn't wait for Hunt to reply before wending her way over.

Flynn let out a cheer as she appeared, obviously well on his way to being smashed. Typical Tuesday night for him. She considered sending a photo of his wasted ass to his parents and sister. They might not sneer so much at her, then.

Declan Emmet appeared slightly more sober as he said from Flynn's side, "Hey, B."

Bryce waved, not wanting to shout over the crowd gathered in what had once been a dining room. It had recently been transformed into a billiards and darts room. Absolutely fitting for the Crown Prince of the Valbaran Fae, Bryce thought with a half smile as she sidled up to the male beside her brother. "Hi, Marc."

The towering leopard shifter, all sleek muscle beneath his dark brown skin, peered down at her. His striking topaz eyes sparkled. Declan had been seeing Marc Rosarin for a month now, having met the tech entrepreneur during some fancy party at one of the big engineering companies in the Central Business District. "Hey, Princess."

Flynn demanded, "Since when do you let Marc get away with calling you Princess?"

"Since I like him better than you," Bryce shot back, earning a clap on the shoulder from Marc and a grin from Ruhn. She said to her brother, *A small get-together, huh?*

Ruhn shrugged, the tattoos along his arms shifting. "I blame Flynn."

Flynn lifted his last beer up in acknowledgment and chugged.

"Where's Athalar?" Declan asked.

"With June and Fury in the living room," Bryce said.

Ruhn waved his greeting to a passing partier before he asked, "How was the ballet?"

"Awesome. June killed her solos. Brought the house to its feet."

She'd had chills along her entire body while her friend had danced—and tears in her eyes when Juniper had received a standing ovation after finishing. Bryce had never heard the CCB so full of cheering, and from Juniper's flushed, joyous face as she'd bowed, Bryce knew her friend realized it, too. A promotion to principal was sure to come any day now.

"Hottest ticket in town," Marc said, whistling. "Half my office would have sold their souls to be there tonight."

"You should have told me," Bryce said. "We had a few extra seats in our box. We could have fit them."

Marc smiled appreciatively. "Next time."

Flynn began reracking the beer pong cups, and called to her, "How are Mommy and Daddy?"

"Good. They fed me a bottle of milk and read me a bedtime story before I left."

This earned a chuckle from Ruhn, who had once again become close with Ember. Her brother asked, "How many interrogations since they got here last night?"

"Six." Bryce pointed to the foyer and living room beyond. "Which is why I'm going to go have a drink with my friends."

"Open bar," Declan said, gesturing magnanimously behind him.

Bryce waved again, and she was off. Without Hunt's imposing form, far fewer people turned her way. But when they did . . . pockets of silence appeared. She tried to ignore them, and nearly sighed with relief when she spied a familiar pair of horns atop a head of gracefully curling hair tucked into Juniper's usual bun. She was seated on the stained living room sectional, thigh to thigh with Fury, their hands interlaced.

Hunt stood before them, wings held at a casual angle as he talked with her friends. He looked up as Bryce entered the living room, and she could have sworn his black eyes lit.

She reined in her joy at the sight as she plopped onto the cushions beside Juniper, cuddling close. She nuzzled June's shoulder. "Hi, my talented and brilliant and beautiful friend."

Juniper laughed, squeezing Bryce. "Right back at you."

Bryce said, "I was talking to Fury."

Juniper smacked Bryce's knee, and Fury laughed, observing, "Already acting like a prima donna."

Bryce sighed dramatically. "I can't wait to see June throw temper tantrums about the state of her dressing room."

"Oh, you're both horrible," Juniper said, but laughed along with them. "One, I won't even *have* a dressing room to myself for years. *Two*—"

"Here we go," Fury said, and when June made a noise of objection, she only chuckled and brushed her mouth over the faun's temple.

The casual, loving bit of intimacy had Bryce daring a glance toward Hunt, who was smiling faintly. Bryce avoided the urge to fidget, to think about how that could so easily be them, cuddling on the couch and kissing. Hunt just said, voice gravelly, "What can I get you, Quinlan?" He inclined his head toward the bar in the rear of the room, barely visible with the crowds mobbing the two bartenders.

"Whiskey, ginger beer, and lime."

"You got it." With a mockery of a salute, Hunt stalked off through the crowd.

"How's the whole no-sex thing going for you, Bryce?" Fury asked wryly, leaning forward to peer at her face.

Bryce slumped against the cushions. "Asshole."

June's laugh fizzled through her, and her friend patted her thigh. "Remind me why you two aren't hooking up?"

Bryce peered over the back of the couch to make sure Hunt still stood at the bar before she said, "Because I am a fucking idiot, and you two jerks know that."

Juniper and Fury snickered, the latter taking a sip of her vodka soda. "Tell him you've changed your mind," the merc said, resting the glass on her black leather-clad knee. How Fury could wear leather in this heat was beyond Bryce. Shorts, T-shirt, and sandals were all she could endure with the sizzling temperatures, even at night.

"And break our bargain before Winter Solstice?" Bryce hissed. "He'd never let me live it down."

"Athalar already knows you want to break it," Fury drawled.

"Oh, he totally knows," Juniper agreed.

Bryce crossed her arms. "Can we not talk about this?"

"Where would the fun be in that?" Fury asked.

Bryce kicked Fury's leather boot, wincing as her gold-sandaled foot collided with unforgiving metal. "Steel toes? Really?"

"This is a veritable frat party," Fury said, smirking. "There might be some asses to kick if someone makes a move on my girlfriend."

Juniper glowed at the term. *Girlfriend.*

Bryce didn't know what the Hel she was to Hunt. *Girlfriend* seemed ridiculous when talking about Hunt fucking Athalar. As if Hunt would ever do anything as normal and casual as dating.

Juniper poked Bryce in the arm. "I mean it. Remind me why you guys still need to wait for solstice to do the deed."

Bryce slouched, sinking down a few inches, her feet sending the empty beer cans under the coffee table clattering. "I just . . ."

That familiar buzz of power and maleness that was Hunt filled the air behind her, and Bryce shut her mouth a moment before a plastic cup of amber liquid garnished with a wedge of lime appeared before her. "Princess," Hunt crooned, and Bryce's toes curled—yet again. They seemed to have a habit of doing that around him.

"Do we get to use that term now?" June perked up with delight. "I've been *dying*—"

"Absolutely not." Bryce swigged from her drink. She gagged. "How much whiskey did you have the bartender *put* in here, Athalar?" She coughed, as if it'd do anything to ease the burn.

Hunt shrugged. "I thought you liked whiskey."

Fury snorted, but Bryce got to her feet. Lifted the cup toward Hunt in a silent toast, then lifted it to June. "To the next principal dancer of the CCB."

Then she knocked back the whole thing and let it burn right down to her soul.

Hunt let himself—just for one fucking second—look at Bryce. Admire the steady, unfaltering tap of her sandaled foot on the worn wood floor to the beat of the music; the long, muscled legs that gleamed in the neon firstlights, her white shorts offsetting her summer tan. No scars remained from the shit that had occurred this spring, aside from that mark on her chest, though the thick scar from years ago still curved along her thigh.

His fierce, strong, beautiful Bryce. He'd done his best not to gape at the shape of her ass in those shorts as they'd walked over here, the sway of her long hair against her lower back, the ample hips that swished with each step.

He was a stupid fucking animal. But he'd always been a stupid fucking animal around her.

He'd barely been able to focus on the ballet earlier—on June's dancing—because Bryce had looked so . . . delicious in that blue dress. Only her parents sitting a few feet in front of him had kept him from thinking too much about sliding his hand up her thigh and underneath that gauzy material.

But that wasn't part of the plan. Earlier this spring, he'd been fine with it. Aching for her, but fine with the concept of getting to know each other better before sex entered the equation. Yet that ache had only gotten worse these past months. Living together in their apartment was a slow kind of torture for both of them.

Bryce's whiskey-colored eyes shifted toward him. She opened her mouth, then shut it at whatever she beheld in his expression.

The memory of those days following Micah's and Sandriel's demises cooled his rising lust.

Let's take things slow, she'd requested. *I feel like we tumbled into all of this, and now that things are getting back to normal, I want to do this right with you. Get to know you in real time, not while we're running around the city trying to solve murders.*

He'd agreed, because what else could he do? Never mind that he'd come home from the Comitium that night planning to seduce Quinlan within an inch of her life. He hadn't even gotten to the kissing part when she'd announced she wanted to hit the brakes.

He knew more lay behind it. Knew it likely had something to do with the guilt she harbored for the thousands of people who hadn't been saved that day. Allowing herself to be with him, to be happy . . . She needed time to sort it out. And Hunt would give it to her. Anything Bryce wanted, anything she needed, he'd gladly give it to her. He had the freedom to do so now, thanks to the branded-out tattoo on his wrist.

But on nights like these, with her in those shorts . . . it was really gods-damned hard.

Bryce hopped up from the couch and padded over to him, leaving Juniper and Fury to chat, Fury busy reloading the arts page of the *Crescent City Times* for the review of Juniper's performance. "What's up?" Hunt said to Bryce as she took up a place beside him.

"Do you actually like coming to these parties?" Bryce asked, gesturing to the throng, firstlight glow stick around her wrist gleaming bright. "This doesn't disgust you?"

He tucked in his wings. "Why would it disgust me?"

"Because you've seen all the shit that's happening in the world, and been treated like dirt, and these people . . ." She tossed her sheet of hair over a shoulder. "A lot of them have no idea about it. Or just don't care."

Hunt studied her tight face. "Why do we come to these parties if it bothers you?"

"Well, tonight we're here to avoid my mom." Hunt chuckled, but she went on, "And because I want to celebrate June being a genius." She smiled at her friend on the couch. "And we're here because Ruhn asked me to come. But . . . I don't know. I want to feel normal, but then I feel guilty about that, and then I get mad at all these people who don't care enough to feel guilty, and I think the poison-testing pill you no doubt put in my whiskey had some sort of sad-sack potion in it because I don't know why I'm thinking about this right now."

Hunt huffed a laugh. "Sad-sack potion?"

"You know what I mean!" She glared. "This really doesn't bug you?"

"No." He assessed the party raging around them. "I prefer to see people enjoying their lives. And you can't assume that because they're here, it means they don't care. For all you know, a lot of them lost family and friends this spring. Sometimes people need stuff like this to feel alive again. To find a kind of release."

Wrong word. He sure as fuck hadn't found release recently, other than by his own hand. He tried not to think about whether Bryce had opened the drawer in her left nightstand, where she kept her toys, as often as he'd jacked off in the shower.

Four months left until Winter Solstice. Only four.

Bryce nodded, her mind clearly still on the conversation at hand. "I guess I just . . . Sometimes I catch myself enjoying a moment, and worry I'm enjoying it *too* much, you know? Like something could come along and ruin all of this if I let myself have too much fun or get too accustomed to feeling happy."

"I know the feeling." He couldn't stop himself from letting his fingers curl in the ends of her hair. "It's going to take time to adjust."

He was still adjusting, too. He couldn't get used to walking around without a pit in his stomach as he wondered what horrors the day would bring. Being in charge of himself, his future . . . The Asteri could take it all away again, if they wished. Had only let him live because he and Bryce were too public to kill—the Asteri wanted them to lie low forever. And if they didn't . . . Well, Rigelus had been very clear on his call to Bryce months ago: the Bright Hand of the Asteri would kill everyone Bryce and Hunt cared about if they stepped out of line. So lying low it would be.

Hunt was happy to do precisely that. To go to the ballet and these parties and pretend that he'd never known anything different. That Bryce didn't have the Horn tattooed into her back.

But each morning, when he donned his usual black armor for the 33rd, he remembered. Isaiah had asked him for backup right after Micah's death, and Hunt had gladly given it. He'd stayed on as Isaiah's unofficial commander—unofficial only because Hunt didn't want the paperwork that came with the real title.

The city had been quiet, though. Focused on healing. Hunt wasn't going to complain.

His phone buzzed in the back pocket of his black jeans, and he fished it out to find an email from Isaiah waiting for him. Hunt read it and went still. His heart dropped to his feet and back up again.

"What's wrong?" Bryce peered over his shoulder.

Hunt passed her the phone with a surprisingly steady hand. "New Archangels have been chosen for Micah's and Sandriel's territories."

Her eyes widened. "Who? How bad are they?"

He motioned for her to read Isaiah's email, and Bryce, that first-light glow stick still coiled around her wrist, obeyed.

Roll out the welcome mat, Isaiah had written as his only comment on the forwarded email from the Asteri's imperial secretary announcing the new positions.

"They're not bad," Hunt said, staring blankly at the revelers now gathering around a Fae male doing a keg stand in the corner. "That's the problem."

Bryce's brows bunched as she scanned the email. "Ephraim—he currently shares Rodinia with Jakob. Yeah, he seems decent enough. But he's going to northern Pangera. Who . . . Oh. Who the Hel is Celestina?"

Hunt frowned. "She's stayed out of the spotlight. She oversees Nena—population, like, fifty. She has one legion under her command. *One.* She doesn't even have a triarii. The legion is literally controlled by the Asteri—all watchdogs for the Northern Rift. She's a figurehead."

"Big promotion, then."

Hunt grunted. "Everything I've heard about her sounds unusually nice."

"No chance it's true?"

"Where Archangels are concerned? No." He crossed his arms.

Fury said from the couch, "For what it's worth, Athalar, I haven't heard anything bad, either."

Juniper asked, "So this is promising, right?"

Hunt shook his head. This wasn't a conversation to have in public, but he said, "I can't figure out why the Asteri would appoint her *here*, when she's only handled a small territory until now. She must be their puppet."

Bryce tilted her head to the side, looking at him in that stark, all-seeing way that made his balls tighten. Gods, she was beautiful. "Maybe it's just a good thing, Hunt. So many shitty things have happened to us that we might not trust when something actually *is* good. But maybe we got lucky with Celestina's appointment."

"I'm inclined to think Urd's dealing us a decent hand," Juniper agreed.

Fury Axtar said nothing, her eyes shining as she thought. The merc would likely be the only one to fully grasp the workings of the Asteri. Not that she'd ever reveal the details of her dealings with them.

"Celestina wants to meet what remains of Micah's triarii when she arrives. Apparently, there's going to be some sort of restructuring," Hunt said as Bryce handed back his phone. "Whatever that means. The press release won't go live until tomorrow morning. So keep it quiet." The three females nodded, though he had a feeling Fury wouldn't keep her word. Whoever she answered to, whatever valuable clients she served, would likely hear before dawn.

Bryce hooked her red hair behind her pointed ears. "When's Celestina coming?"

"Tomorrow evening." His throat constricted.

Juniper and Fury fell into quiet conversation, as if to grant them privacy. Bryce, catching their drift, lowered her voice. "You're a free male, Hunt. She can't order you to do anything you don't want to do." Her warm fingers wrapped around his wrist, thumb brushing over the branded-out *SPQM*. "You *chose* to reenlist in the 33rd. You have the rights of a free citizen. If you don't like her, if you don't want to serve her, then you don't need to give her a reason in order to leave. You don't need her permission."

Hunt grunted his agreement, though he still had a fucking knot in his chest. "Celestina could make life very difficult for us."

Bryce held up a hand. Starlight radiated, turning her skin iridescent. A drunk asshole nearby let out an *ooooooh*. Bryce ignored him and said, "I'd like to see her try. I'm the Super Powerful and Special Magic Starborn Princess, remember?" He knew she was joking, but her mouth thinned. "I'll protect you."

"How could I forget, oh Magically Powerful and Super Special . . . whatever you said."

Bryce grinned, lowering her hand. She'd been meeting with Ruhn once a week to explore her magic—to learn more about what lay within her veins, fueled by the power of so many. Her magic only manifested as starlight—a purely Fae gift. No shadows, like Ruhn possessed, or fire, like her father. But the sheer force of her power came from all those who'd given a droplet of their magic to the Gates over the years. All combined to make some kind of fuel to increase the potency of her starlight. Or something like that. Bryce had tried to explain it—why the magic manifested as a Fae talent—but Hunt didn't care where it came from, so long as it kept her safe.

The magic was protection in a world designed to kill her. From a father who might very well want to eliminate the threat of a daughter who surpassed him in power, if only by a fraction.

Hunt still had trouble fathoming that the female standing beside him had become more powerful than the Autumn King. Hunt's power technically still outranked hers, and her father's, but with the Horn etched in her back, who really knew the depths of Bryce's power? Considering Rigelus's order to lie low, it wasn't like Bryce could explore how the Horn affected her magic, but given what it had done this spring . . . He doubted Bryce would ever be tempted to experiment with it anyway.

He caught Axtar watching Bryce, but the merc said nothing.

So Hunt continued, only loud enough to indicate that he wanted Fury and Juniper to also hear, "I don't know what this Celestina thing is about, but the Asteri do nothing out of the kindness of their hearts."

"They'd need hearts to do that," Juniper whispered with uncharacteristic venom.

Fury's voice lowered. "The war is getting worse in Pangera. Valbara is a key territory full of vital resources. Appointing someone who all reports claim is *nice* seems idiotic."

Juniper raised her brows. Not at the claim about the Asteri, Hunt guessed, but that Fury had willingly mentioned the war overseas. The merc rarely, if ever, talked about it. What she'd done over there. What she'd seen. Hunt, having fought in many of those battles, had a good idea of both.

"Maybe they really do want a puppet," Juniper said. "Someone who's a figurehead, so they can order all of Valbara's troops over-seas with no resistance."

Fury tucked a strand of her hair behind an ear. From all appear-ances, Axtar seemed human. But she was definitely Vanir—of what breed, what House, Hunt had no idea. Flame and Shadow seemed likeliest, but more than that, he couldn't guess. The merc said, "Even Micah might have resisted that order."

Bryce's face paled at the bastard's name. Hunt repressed the urge to fold a wing around her. He hadn't told her of his own nightmares—of being forced to watch, over and over, as Micah bru-talized her. And the nightmares of how she'd raced through the streets, demons from Hel's darkest pits swarming her. Of brim-stone missiles shooting for her in the Old Square.

"We can guess all night," Bryce said, mastering herself. "But until you have that meeting tomorrow, Hunt, we won't know. Just go in there with an open mind."

"You mean, don't start a fight." His mouth twitched to the side. Fury snickered.

Bryce put a hand on her hip. "I mean, don't go in there playing Scary Asshole. Maybe try for an Approachable Asshole vibe."

Juniper laughed at that, and Hunt chuckled as well. Unable to stop himself from knocking Bryce with a wing for the second time that night, he promised, "Approachable Asshole it is, Quinlan."

3

Ruhn Danaan knew three things with absolute certainty:

1. He had smoked so much mirthroot that he couldn't feel his face. Which was a damn shame because there was a female currently sitting on it.
2. He had downed an obscene amount of whiskey, because he had no idea what the female's name was, or how they'd gotten to his bedroom, or how he'd wound up with his tongue between her legs.
3. He really fucking loved his life. At least . . . right now.

Ruhn dug his fingers into the soft, spotted flanks of the delectable creature moaning above him, dragging his lip ring across that spot he knew would—

Yeah. There it was. That groan of pure pleasure that shot right to his cock, currently aching behind the fly of his black jeans. He hadn't even undressed before going to town on the sweet faun who'd shyly approached him at the beer pong table. He'd gotten one look at her large green eyes, the long legs that ended in those pretty little hooves, and the creamy skin of her neck, above those high, perky breasts, and known precisely where he wanted this night to end.

Good thing she'd had the same idea. Had told him precisely what she wanted in that whisper-soft voice.

Ruhn flicked his tongue across the taut bud of her clit, savoring the meadow-soft taste of her in his mouth. She arched, thighs straining—and came with a series of breathy moans that nearly had him spilling in his pants.

Ruhn gripped her bare ass, letting her ride his face through each wave of pleasure, moaning himself as he slipped his tongue inside her to let her delicate inner muscles clench around him.

Fuck, this was hot. *She* was hot. Even through the haze of drugs and booze, he was ready to go. All he needed was the okay from those full lips and he'd be buried in her within seconds.

For a heartbeat, like an arrow of light fired through the blissed-out darkness of his mind, he remembered that he was, technically, betrothed. And not to some simpering Fae girl whose parents might be pissed at his behavior, but to the Queen of the Valbaran Witches. Granted, they'd sworn no vows of faithfulness—for fuck's sake, they'd barely spoken to each other during the Summit and in the months afterward—but . . . did it cross some line, to fuck around like this?

He knew the answer. The weight of it had lain heavy on him for months. And perhaps that was why he was here right now: it did cross a line, but a line he had no say in. And yes, he respected and admired Hypaxia Enador—she was alarmingly beautiful, brave, and intelligent—but until the High Priestess bound their hands at Luna's Temple, until that titanium ring went on his finger . . . he'd savor these last months of freedom.

He hoped it would be months, anyway. Hypaxia had not given his father any indication of a timeline.

The faun stilled, chest heaving, and Ruhn let his thoughts of his betrothed fade away as he swallowed the taste of the faun deep into his throat.

"Merciful Cthona," the faun breathed, rising on her knees to pull herself off his face. Ruhn released the firm cheeks of her ass, meeting her bright gaze as she peered at him, a flush across her high cheekbones.

Ruhn winked up at her, running a tongue over the corner of his mouth to get one final taste of her. Gods, she was delectable. Her throat bobbed, her pulse fluttering like a beckoning drum.

Ruhn ran his hands up her bare thighs, fingers grazing over her narrow hips and waist. "Do you want to—"

The door to his bedroom burst open, and Ruhn, pinned beneath the female, could do nothing but twist his head toward the male standing there.

Apparently, the sight of the Crown Prince of the Valbaran Fae with a female straddling his face was common enough that Tristan Flynn didn't so much as blink. Didn't even smirk, though the faun leapt off Ruhn with a squeak, hiding herself behind the bed.

"Get downstairs," Flynn said, his usually golden-brown skin pale. Gone was any hint of drunken revelry. Even his brown eyes were sharp.

"Why?" Ruhn asked, wishing he had time to talk to the female quickly gathering her clothes on the other side of the bed before he headed for the door.

But Flynn pointed to the far corner—the pile of dirty laundry, and the Starsword propped against the stained wall beside it. "Bring that."

Ruhn's raging hard-on had vanished, thankfully, by the time he made it to the top of the stairs above the foyer. Music still shook the floors of the house, people still drank and hooked up and smoked and did whatever bullshit they usually enjoyed during these parties.

No sign of danger, no sign of anything except—

There. A prickle at the back of his neck. Like a chill wind had skittered over the top of his spine.

"Dec's new security system picked up some kind of anomaly," Flynn said, scanning the party below. He'd gone into pure Aux mode. "It's making all the sensors go off. Some kind of aura—Dec said it felt like a storm was circling the house."

"Great," Ruhn said, the hilt of the Starsword cool against his back. "And it's not some drunk asshole dicking around with magic?"

Flynn assessed the crowds. "Dec didn't think so. He said from the way it circled the house, it seemed like it was surveilling the area."

Their friend and roommate had spent months designing a system to be placed around their house and the surrounding streets—one that could pick up things like the kristallos demon, formerly too fast for their technology to detect.

"Then let's see how it likes being watched, too," Ruhn said, wishing he was slightly less high and drunk as his shadows wobbled around him. Flynn sniggered.

The mirthroot took hold for a moment, and even Ruhn laughed as he moved for the staircase. But his amusement faded as he checked the rooms on either side of the foyer. Where the fuck was Bryce? He'd last seen her with Fury, Juniper, and Athalar in the living room, but from this angle atop the stairs, he couldn't see her—

Ruhn had made it three steps down the front staircase, dodging discarded beer cans and plastic cups and someone's zebra-print bra, when the open front doors darkened.

Or rather, the space within them darkened. Exactly as it had when those demons had stormed through the Gates.

Ruhn gaped for a moment at the portal to Hel that had just replaced his front doors.

Then he reached for the sword half-buckled at his back, working past his brain fog to gather shadows in his other hand. Laughter and singing and talking stopped, and the firstlights guttered. The music shut off as if someone had yanked the power cord from the wall.

Then Bryce and Athalar were at the archway into the living room, his sister now wearing Athalar's hat, and the angel armed with a gun discreetly tucked against his thigh. Athalar was the only person Ruhn would allow to bring a gun into one of his parties. And Axtar—who was now nowhere to be seen.

Ruhn drew his sword as he leapt down the rest of the stairs, managing to land gracefully on the other side of his sister. Flynn and Dec fell into place beside him. His shadows swirled up his left arm like twining snakes.

A faint light glowed from Bryce— No, that was the glow stick on her arm.

A figure stalked from the darkness in the doorway. Straight out of Hel. And in that moment, Ruhn knew three more things.

1. He wasn't looking at a portal to Hel after all. Shadows swirled there instead. Familiar, whispering shadows.
2. It wasn't just the glow stick coiled around Bryce's arm that was shining. The star-shaped scar beneath her T-shirt blazed with iridescent light.
3. As a familiar golden-haired Fae male strode from those shadows and into the foyer, Ruhn knew his night was about to take a turn for the worse.

4

Oh, *come on*," Bryce hissed at the glowing scar between her breasts. Or what she could glimpse of it with the neckline of her T-shirt and her bra in the way. It lit up the fabric of both, and if she hadn't been facing the towering Fae male who'd appeared out of a cloud of shadows, she *might* have used the moment to ponder why and how it glowed.

Partygoers had stopped dead in their revelry. Waiting for whatever shit was about to go down.

And what asshole had turned off the music? Dramahounds.

"What the fuck are you doing here?" Ruhn prowled closer to the stranger.

The male's tan face might have been ruggedly good-looking were it not for the complete lack of feeling there. His light brown eyes were dead. Humorless. His thin white sweater over black jeans and combat boots told Bryce he'd come from somewhere colder.

The crowd seemed to sense danger, too, and backed away until only Hunt, Bryce, Ruhn, and his friends remained facing the stranger. She had no idea where Fury and Juniper were. The former was likely strategically positioned in the room to make sure she could intercept any danger before it reached her girlfriend. Good.

The stranger stalked forward, and Bryce braced herself, even as Hunt casually angled himself between her and the male. Bryce held in her grin at the gesture. And found that grin vanishing instantly when the blond spoke, his accent rolling and rich.

"I was invited."

The stranger turned to her and smirked, lifeless as a dead fish. "I don't believe we've met." A nod toward her—her chest. "Though I know who you are, of course." His eyes flicked over her. "You look better than expected. Not that I was expecting much."

"What the *fuck* are you doing here, Cormac?" Ruhn ground out, stepping closer. But he sheathed the Starsword down his back once more.

The blond—Cormac—faced her brother. He sniffed once, then chuckled. "You smell like cunt."

Bryce nearly gagged at the thought. Cormac went on as Ruhn bristled, "And I told you: I was invited."

"Not to this fucking house," Flynn said, moving to Ruhn's side, Declan flanking his other. A lethal unit.

Cormac assessed his surroundings. "You call this a house? I hadn't realized your standards had dropped so low, Lord Hawthorne."

Declan snarled. "Fuck off, Cormac." Marc came up behind him, teeth bared with silent menace.

Any other opponent, Bryce knew the group would likely obliterate, but this male was Avallen Fae: powerful, trained in combat from a young age, and merciless.

The male said, as if seeing her try to puzzle him out, "I'm your cousin, Bryce."

Hunt—the fucking bastard—snorted.

"I don't have any Fae cousins." Bryce snapped. If only the stupid scar would halt its glowing. If only people would go back to partying.

"That light says otherwise," Cormac said with blatant confidence. "I might be Ruhn's cousin directly through his mother's kin, but your father, King Einar, is Fae, and his line once crossed with ours long ago." He held up his hand, and flame wreathed his fingers before winking out.

Bryce blinked. Her mother had never once spoken the Autumn King's name, and Bryce had only learned it through the news when she was old enough to use a computer.

"Why are you here?" Ruhn bit out.

From the corner of her vision lightning sizzled at Hunt's fingertips. One strike, and Hunt could fry this fucker.

Yet Cormac smiled. His dead eyes gleamed with nothing but contempt as he bowed mockingly to Bryce. "I'm here to meet my bride."

The words shot through Hunt's mind fast enough that they doused his lightning, but Bryce tipped her head back and laughed.

No one else joined her.

And when Bryce had finished, she smirked at Cormac. "You're hilarious."

"It is no joke," Cormac said, face darkening. "It's been decreed."

"By who?" Hunt snapped.

The Avallen male sized up Hunt with palpable disdain. Not someone used to being questioned, then. Spoiled little prick. "By her sire, the Autumn King, and mine, the High King of the Avallen Fae." Making this shithead a Crown Prince.

Bryce said coolly, "Last I checked, I wasn't on the market."

Hunt crossed his arms, becoming a wall of muscle beside her. Let Cormac see precisely who he'd be tangling with if he took another step closer to Bryce. Hunt willed tendrils of his lightning to crackle along his shoulders, his wings.

"You're an unwed Fae female," Cormac said, unmoved. "That means you belong to your male kin until they decide to pass you to another. The decision has been made."

From the living room archway, a delicate, dark figure emerged. Axtar. She palmed a gun, but kept it at her thigh. No sign of Juniper—presumably, the faun was staying wherever Fury had instructed her to hide.

Cormac glanced toward the merc, and even his sneer faltered.

Every power broker on Midgard knew of Fury Axtar. What she was capable of, if provoked.

Ruhn pointed to the door and snarled at Cormac, "Get the fuck out of my house. I don't care if you use your shadows or your own feet, but get out."

Yet Cormac glowered at the Starsword peeking over Ruhn's broad shoulder. "Rumor has it that the sword sings for my bride, too."

A muscle feathered in Ruhn's jaw. Hunt didn't know what to make of that.

But Bryce stepped forward, star still blazing. "I'm not your bride, asshole. And I'm not going to be, so scuttle back to whatever hole you crawled out of and tell your kings to find someone else. And tell them—"

"You've got a mouth on you," Cormac murmured.

Hunt didn't particularly like the male's appreciative tone. But he kept his power reined in. Even a zap of lightning against Cormac could be seen as a declaration of war.

Fae were highly sensitive babies. Their tantrums could last centuries.

Bryce smiled sweetly at Cormac. "I get that you want to play Broody Prince, but don't ever fucking interrupt me again."

Cormac started. Hunt hid his smirk, even as his blood heated at Bryce's irreverence.

Bryce went on, "My brother told you to leave his house." Her skin began to glow. "You don't want *me* to have to ask you."

The hair on Hunt's neck rose. She'd blinded people with that power—and that had been before the Drop. With all that magic backing her starlight . . . He hadn't yet seen how it would manifest. Half hoped he'd find out now, with this asshole as a test subject.

Hunt eyed Flynn, Declan, and Marc—all of whom were tense and primed to leap into the fray. And Ruhn . . .

Hunt didn't know why Ruhn's apparent satisfaction surprised him. He'd expected wounded male pride, perhaps, at Bryce showing him up in his own home. Yet pride did shine from Ruhn's face—for Bryce. Like the prince had been waiting for his sister to step into her power for a while now and he was honored to have her at his side.

Hunt's attention shot back to Cormac as the Avallen Prince held up his hands and slowly smiled at Bryce. The expression was as dead as his eyes. "I've seen all I needed to."

"What the fuck are you talking about?" Ruhn demanded. Shadows rippled from his shoulders, a dark contrast to the light emanating from Bryce.

But shadows also swirled behind Cormac—darker, wilder than Ruhn's, like a stampede of stallions waiting to gallop over all of them. "I wanted to confirm that she has the gift. Thank you for demonstrating." He set one foot into those untamed shadows. Bowed his head to Bryce. "I'll see you at the altar."

Bryce's star winked out the moment he vanished, leaving only drifting embers behind.

Bryce was dimly aware of the party ending: people filtering out through the front door, the countless eyes on her as she stood in the foyer, typing into her phone.

"There's a train at seven tomorrow morning," Bryce announced to Hunt, who lingered at her side. As if afraid the Avallen male would reappear to snatch her away.

Not just any Avallen male: Prince Cormac. Her . . . fiancé.

"There's no way your mom will go," Hunt said. "If by some miracle she isn't suspicious that you're bumping them onto a train five hours earlier, then Randall will be."

Juniper scrolled on her phone at Bryce's other side. "Social channels are empty right now, but . . ."

"All it takes is one person," Fury finished from where she monitored the front of the house with the same vigilance as Hunt. "I think I made my point clear about the consequences of that, though."

Gods bless her, Fury really had. *If any of you post, talk, or so much as think about what went down here tonight,* she'd declared with quiet authority to the awed partygoers, *I'll hunt you down and make you regret it.*

No one had said anything, but Bryce had noticed more than a few people deleting pictures from their phones as they hurried out.

Hunt said, "Getting your parents out of the city without them being suspicious *or* finding out will be tricky, to say the least." He angled his head. "You sure it's not easier to tell them?"

"And risk my mom going ballistic? Doing something reckless?" And that was to say nothing about what Randall might do if he thought the Autumn King was threatening Bryce's happiness and control over her own life. Whatever her mom left of the Autumn King, Randall would be sure to put a bullet in it. "I'm not risking them like that."

"They're adults," Fury said. "You can trust them to make rational choices."

"Have you met my mom?" Bryce burst out. "Does *rational* ever spring to mind when you think about her? She makes sculptures of babies in beds of lettuce, for fuck's sake."

"I just think," June jumped in, "that they're going to find out anyway, so maybe it's better if it comes from you. Before they hear it from someone else."

Bryce shook her head. "Nope. I want to be far, far away when they find out. And get a few hundred miles between them and the Autumn King, too."

Hunt grunted his agreement, and she threw him a grateful nod.

The sound of Declan shutting the front door pulled her attention from the angel as the Fae male leaned back against it. "Well, my buzz is officially ruined."

Flynn slumped onto the lowest steps of the staircase, a bottle of whiskey in his hand. "Then we better start getting it back." He swigged deeply before passing it up to Ruhn, who leaned against the banister with crossed arms, his blue eyes blazing into a near-violet. He'd been quiet these last few minutes.

Bryce had no idea where to start with him. About Cormac, about the power she'd shown in Ruhn's own house, about the star glowing for the Avallen Prince . . . any of it. So she said, "I take it that's the cousin from your Ordeal."

Ruhn, Dec, and Flynn nodded gravely. Her brother drank from the bottle of whiskey.

"How close did Cormac get to killing you during your Ordeal?"

Hunt asked. Ruhn must have told him about it at some point this summer.

"Close," Flynn said, earning a glare from Ruhn.

But Ruhn admitted, "It was bad." Bryce could have sworn he didn't look at her as he added, "Cormac spent his whole life thinking he'd get the Starsword one day. That he'd go into the Cave of Princes and be proven worthy. He studied all the lore, learned all the lineage, pored over every account detailing the variations in the power. It, ah . . . didn't go down well when I got it instead."

"And now his fiancée has a claim to it, also," Flynn said, and it was Bryce's turn to glare at the lord. She could have lived without anyone bringing that up again.

Ruhn seemed to force himself to look at Bryce as he said, "It's true." So he'd seen her glare, then. "The sword's as much yours as it is mine."

Bryce waved a hand. "I'll take it on weekends and holidays, don't worry."

Hunt tossed in, "And it'll get *two* Winter Solstices, so . . . double the presents."

Ruhn and the others gawked at them like they had ten heads, but Bryce grinned at Hunt. He returned it with one of his own.

He got her—her humor, her fears, her hedging. Whatever it was, Athalar *got* her.

"Is it true?" Juniper looped her elbow through Bryce's and pressed close. "About the legality of an engagement against Bryce's will?"

That wiped the smile from Hunt's face. And Bryce's. Her mind raced, each thought as swift and dizzying as a shooting star.

"Tell me there's a way out of this, Ruhn." She walked to her brother and snatched the whiskey bottle from him. A faint light flared at his back—the Starsword. It hummed, a whining sound like a finger tracing the rim of a glass.

Ruhn's stare met hers, questioning and wary, but Bryce stepped back. The sword stopped singing.

It's not going to bite, you know.

Bryce nearly flinched as her brother's voice filled her mind. He used the mind-speaking rarely enough that she often entirely forgot he had the gift.

It's your sword. Not mine. You're as much a Starborn Prince as I am a princess.

He shot back, eyes glinting with stars, *I'm not the kind of male whose sense of pride is so brittle that I need to cling to a shiny weapon. If you want to use it, it's yours.*

She shook her head. *You retrieved the blade—and apparently had to deal with Cormac while doing it. That fact alone entitles you to keep it.*

Ruhn's laughter filled her mind, full of amusement and relief. But his face remained serious as he said to the group, now staring at them, "I didn't pay attention in class when we covered Fae law. Sorry."

"Well, I did," Marc said. "And I've already put some of my firm's associates on researching it. Any legal case or precedent that's been uploaded into a database, short of whatever's hidden in the Asteri Archives, we'll be able to comb through."

Declan added, "I'll go hunting, too." But even Dec, with his hacking skills, couldn't pierce the security around the private, ancient files of the Asteri.

"Thank you," Bryce said, but she didn't allow that shred of hope to balloon in her chest. "Update me when you have anything."

Ruhn started talking, but Bryce tuned him out, handing off the bottle of whiskey to Juniper before slipping out onto the sagging front porch, dodging discarded cups and cans. Hunt was a storm wind at her back as she strode onto the small slice of grassy front lawn and breathed in the bustle of the Old Square before her.

"Why are you being so calm about this?" Hunt asked, his arms crossed. The dry, warm night breeze ruffled his hair, his gray wings.

"Because this is some move in a game the Autumn King is playing," Bryce said. "He's anticipating that I'm going to run to his house and fight him. I'm trying to figure out why that would help him. What his endgame is."

And what her own might be.

"Connecting the two most powerful Fae royal bloodlines is a

pretty clear endgame," Hunt growled. "And you're Starborn on top of it—you told me you've got the gifts of one of the first of the Starborn. *And* you've got the Horn. That makes you a massive bargaining chip for more power."

"That's too simple for the Autumn King. His games play out over years—centuries. This engagement is the first step. Or maybe we're already several steps along." She just needed to find some way to get a few steps ahead of *that* without revealing her hand. The engagement would have to stand. For now.

"It's bullshit."

Bryce steeled her spine. "I was really enjoying this summer, you know. Today seems Hel-bent on ruining it for both of us."

Hunt ducked his head. "You'd almost think this was planned by the gods. They probably have a special task force: How to Fuck Over Bryce and Hunt in One Day."

Bryce chuckled. "Celestina might wind up being a blessing. But . . ." She asked Hunt, "You think the Autumn King might have timed this to coincide with you getting the news about Celestina?"

"To what end?"

"To rattle us. To make us act, I don't know." She dared say, "Maybe he thought you'd go after him, and it'd make you look bad in front of the new Archangel."

Hunt stilled, and Bryce became keenly aware of the distance between their bodies. "Again," he said, voice husky, "to what end?"

"If you did something illegal," Bryce mused, heart beginning to thunder as he stepped closer, "like . . ."

"Kill a Crown Prince of the Fae?"

Bryce chewed on her lip. "Celestina needs to set an example of how she plans to rule. And punishing a powerful angel, a *notorious* angel acting out of line . . . that'd be the perfect way to demonstrate her power. And thus get you out of the picture for the Autumn King. He knows we're a team."

"A team," Hunt said slowly. As if, out of everything she'd laid out, *that* was what he chose to dwell on.

"You know what I mean," Bryce said.

"I'm not sure I do." Had his voice dropped lower?

"We're roomies," she said, her own voice getting breathy. "Roomies."

"Occasional Beer Pong Champions?"

Hunt snatched the hat off her head and plunked it back on his own, backward as usual. "Yes, the Autumn King truly fears our unholy beer pong alliance."

Bryce smiled, letting it chase away the darkness lurking in her soul. But Hunt added, "We can't forget that Avallen has their own angle. Why'd they agree to the union?"

"You know what?" Bryce said. "Who cares about any of them? My father, the Avallen Fae—screw them." Only with Hunt could she be dismissive about this. He'd have her back, no matter what. "At least until we get my parents onto that train."

"You still haven't given me a convincing plan for how *that* will happen. For all we know, they're learning about this on the news."

"Oh, my phone would already be exploding if my mother had heard." She ran a hand through her hair. "Maybe I should ask Fury to sneak into their hotel and disable their phones."

"Is it bad if I think she should go one step further and tie them up, throw them in the trunk of a car, and drive them home so they get there before the news breaks? Because that's what Fury will likely do if you send her to that hotel."

Bryce laughed, and the sound sang through her like silver bells. "Okay, no Fury." She looped her arm through Hunt's, savoring the muscled mass of him as she steered them toward the low gate and sidewalk beyond. "Let's watch old episodes of *Beach House Hookup* and come up with ways to trick my parents."

One of his wings brushed along her back in the softest of caresses. Every inch it touched lit up like firstlight. "Sounds like a normal Tuesday night."

They meandered home, and despite Bryce's flippant words, she found herself slipping into a state of roiling darkness and thoughts like shooting stars. She'd been a fool to think she could lie low forever. She'd been willing to follow the Asteri's order to lead a boring, normal life, but the rest of the world had different plans for her. And Hunt.

She was bringing her phone to her ear to call her parents with the news that *Oh, so sad, but Jesiba needs me to head over to her ware-house tomorrow and I think this might lead to a second chance at a job with her, so do you mind getting on the earlier train?* when she and Hunt walked off the elevator and found the door to their apartment ajar.

If her mom and Randall had come over unexpectedly . . .

Syrinx was barking inside, and Bryce lunged for the door, the memory of another night washing red over her senses. Now, as then, the scent of blood was a coppery tang in the air, in the hallway, on the threshold of her door—

Not again. Not her parents—

Hunt shoved her back as he angled himself at the doorway, gun out and lightning wreathing his other hand, violence written in every taut line of his body, his raised wings.

Surprise flared in his dark eyes, and then he lowered the gun. Bryce beheld what was in the center of the great room and swayed into Hunt with relief and shock.

Yes, the gods had clearly formed a How to Fuck Over Hunt and Bryce task force.

Inside lay Ithan Holstrom, bleeding all over her pale wood floors.

5

Tharion Ketos had royally fucked up.

Literally. The River Queen had been *pissed*.

Which was why he was now struggling to keep his feet on a small fishing vessel in a sea so stormy it made even his iron stomach churn. Up and down, down and up, the boat bobbed in the rain and swells, wind threatening to flay his skin to the bone, despite his thick black sweater and the tactical vest atop it.

He should be lounging on a rock in the Istros right now, preferably in plain sight of whatever females walked along the quay. He certainly enjoyed finding not-so-covert photos of him on social media, with captions like: *So hot it's a miracle he doesn't turn the Istros to steam!*

That had been a particular favorite. Too bad it had also landed him here. Punished by the River Queen because her daughter had cried over it.

He was accustomed to cold, had explored as deep as his mer's gifts would allow without his skull cracking like an egg, but this northern stretch of the Haldren Sea was different. It sucked the life from one's bones, its grayness creeping into the soul.

Though swimming would be a Hel of a lot less nauseating.

Tharion ducked his head against the lashing rain, his dark red hair plastered to his scalp, dripping icy water down his neck. Gods, he wanted to go home. Back to the dry, blistering heat of a Lunathion summer.

"Submersible's within range," the captain called. The female dolphin shifter was tucked in the safety of the command vestibule. Lucky asshole. "We're starting to get a live feed."

Barely able to maintain his grip on the rain-slick rail of the boat, Tharion aimed for the vestibule. It could only fit two people, so he had to wait until the first mate—a shark shifter—squeezed out before entering. The warmth was like a kiss from Solas himself, and Tharion sighed as he slid the door shut and observed the small screen beside the wheel.

The images from the trench were murky: flurries of floating bits in a whole lot of darkness. If they'd been on a battleship—Hel, even a yacht—they'd have had giant screens with crystal clarity. But this fishing boat, capable of slipping past the Pangeran navy's radar, had been the best bet.

The captain stood before the screen, pointing with a brown finger to a rising number in its upper right corner. "We're nearing the requested depth."

Tharion sank into the swivel chair anchored into the floor. Technically, it was the captain's chair, but he didn't care. He was paying for this expedition. Granted, it was with his Blue Court–issued credit card, but he could damn well sit where he wanted to.

The captain raised a dark brow. "You know what you're looking for?" She'd come highly recommended by a few spies in his employ—a discreet and bold female who wouldn't flee at the first hint of imperial battleships.

Tharion surveyed the screen. "A body."

The captain whistled. "You know the odds of that are—"

"She was tied to lead blocks and dropped into the water around here." By the Hind.

"If she's not in the House of Many Waters, she's long dead."

No shit. "I just need to find her." What remained of her, after two weeks at the bottom of the sea. Frankly, her bones and body had likely exploded from the pressure.

His queen had learned of the poor girl's fate through whatever the rivers and seas whispered to her. He'd known it was how the River Queen kept tabs on her sisters, who ruled the other bodies of water around Midgard, but he hadn't realized how precise the information could be—she'd been able to tell him to hunt for lead blocks, and where to look. And what manner of Vanir, exactly, Sofie was: a thunderbird. Ogenas have mercy on them all.

It was on the slim chance that Sofie's Vanir body had survived the plunge—and hadn't been picked apart yet by scavengers—that he'd come. His queen seemed to be under the impression that Sofie was an asset, even dead.

His queen had refused to tell him more than that. She'd only said that he was to retrieve the body and bring it back to the Blue Court. Presumably to search it for intel or weapons. He prayed he wouldn't be the one to do it.

"We're at depth," the captain announced, and the camera feed halted. More white bits swirled past as the camera pivoted to reveal the silty, alien seafloor. "Any idea where to start, Captain?"

Captain. Tharion still found the title ridiculous, and more than a little painful. The case that had earned him the recent promotion had been his sister's murder. He'd have traded in the title in a heartbeat if it meant he could have Lesia back. Hear his younger sister's boisterous laugh one more time. Catching and killing her murderer hadn't eased that feeling.

"Based on the current, she should have landed around here," Tharion said, letting his water magic drift to the bottom, cringing at the ocean's viciousness. Not at all like the clear calm of the Istros. Granted, plenty of monsters dwelled within the Blue River, but the turquoise water sang to him, laughed with him, cried with him. This sea only bellowed and raged.

Tharion monitored the camera feed. "Rotate the camera to the west—and move the submersible ahead about ten yards."

Through the glare of the firstlight beams atop the remote submersible, more fleshy white bits floated by. This was what the wraith Viktoria had been damned by Micah to endure. The former Archangel had shoved her essence into a magically sealed box while the wraith remained fully conscious despite having no corporeal form, and dropped her to the floor of the Melinoë Trench.

That the trench's bottom was another fifteen miles deeper than the seafloor before them sent a shiver along Tharion's tiger-striped forearms. The wraith's shoebox-sized Helhole had been bespelled against the pressure. And Viktoria, not needing food or water, would live forever. Trapped. Alone. No light, nothing but silence, not even the comfort of her own voice.

A fate worse than death. With Micah now sitting in a trash bag in some city dump, would anyone dare retrieve the wraith? Athalar had shown no signs of rebellion, and Bryce Quinlan, the last Tharion had heard, was content to return to a normal life.

Hel, after this spring, hadn't everyone wanted to return to normal?

The River Queen didn't seem to want to. She'd sent him hunting for a rebel spy's remains. To retrieve her Very Fucking Important corpse.

Even if the mere fact that the River Queen was searching for the body of a rebel spy could damn her. Damn all of them.

And he'd be first in the line of fire. But he never dared to challenge her about the contradictions of it: she punished him for making her daughter cry, yet what would happen should he be killed or harmed during one of her punishments? Wouldn't her daughter cry then?

Her daughter, as capricious as her mother—and as jealous. If she was a bit of a possessive monster, it was because her mother had taught her well.

He'd been a fool not to see it before he'd taken her maidenhead and sworn himself to her a decade ago. Before he'd ever made himself her betrothed. Beloved of the River Queen's daughter. A prince-in-training.

A fucking nightmare.

Judging by the fact that he had kept his job these ten years, and even been promoted, her mother apparently still had no idea what to do with him. Unless her daughter had intervened on his behalf, to keep him safe. The thought of that alone—that he had to stay on her good side—had made him keep his hands to himself and his cock in his pants. Fins. Whatever.

And he'd accepted the punishments, however unfair and undeserved and dangerous, that were thrown his way.

"I'm not seeing anything." The captain adjusted the control toggle on the dash.

"Keep moving. Do a complete scan within a one-mile perimeter." He wouldn't return to his queen empty-handed if he could help it.

"We'll be here for hours," the captain countered, frowning.

Tharion just settled into the chair, glancing to the first mate sheltering against the side of the vestibule.

They knew what they were getting into by coming here. Knew what kind of storms stalked these seas at this point in the year. If the shifter got tired of the wind and rain, he could jump beneath the waves.

Even if a shark in these waters was the least of the terrors.

Three and a half hours later, Tharion lifted a hand. "Go back to the right. No—yeah. There. Can you get closer?"

The remote submersible had floated past boiling-hot sea vents, past muck and rock and all manner of strange creatures. But there, tucked among a cluster of red-and-white tuber worms . . . a square rock.

Only Vanir or human hands could have made it.

"I'll be damned," the captain murmured, leaning toward the screen, the light illuminating her angular face. "Those are lead blocks."

He suppressed a shiver. The River Queen had been right. Down to the last detail. "Circle them."

But . . . Chains draped from the block onto the seafloor. They were empty.

The captain observed, "Whoever those chains held is long gone. They either got eaten or they exploded from the pressure."

Tharion marked the chains, nodding. But his gaze snagged on something.

He glanced at the captain to see if she'd noticed the anomaly, but her face revealed no sign of surprise. So Tharion kept silent, letting her bring the small submersible back up to the surface, where the first mate hauled it onto the deck.

Two hours later, back on land—soggy and muddy from the rain—Tharion calmed his chattering teeth long enough to call his queen.

The River Queen answered after the first ring. "Talk."

Used to the curt, yet ethereal voice, Tharion said, "I found the lead blocks. The chains were still attached."

"So?"

"There was no body." A sigh of disappointment. He shivered yet again—not entirely from the cold. "But the shackles had been unlocked."

The sigh paused. He'd learn to read her pauses, as varied as the life in her river. "You're sure of this?"

He refrained from asking why the currents hadn't told her about this particularly vital detail. Maybe they were as capricious as she. Tharion said mildly, "No signs of damage. At least as far as I could tell on the crappy screen."

"You think Sofie Renast freed herself?"

"I don't know." Tharion climbed into the black SUV that he'd drive to the private heliport in the north of Pangera, and turned the heat to full blast. It'd probably take the entire hour's drive inland to warm his frozen body. "But I sure as Hel don't think she ever made it to the seafloor."

Tharion drove down the rough road, mud spraying, windshield wipers swishing faintly.

His queen said, "Then either someone got there before us . . . or Sofie is alive. Interesting, that the water did not whisper of that. As if it were silenced." Tharion had a feeling he knew where this was going. "Find her," she ordered. "I'd bet my court that she's look-ing for her brother. She went to great lengths to free him from Kavalla. The sea whispered that he is as gifted as she. Find him, and we find her. And vice versa. But even if we only find the boy . . . he will be valuable indeed."

Tharion didn't dare ask why she wanted either of them. He could invent reasons for wanting the rebel, but the boy . . . Emile Renast had his sister's gift, and that was it. A powerful one, but he was a kid. Hadn't even made the Drop. And as far as Tharion knew, his queen wasn't in the habit of using child soldiers. But Tharion couldn't say anything other than: "I'll begin the search immediately."

6

Bryce tore through the cabinet beneath her sink. Bottles of hair products, old makeup palettes, dead blow-dryers flew out and scattered behind her. Where the *fuck* had she put it—

There. Bryce yanked out the white first aid kit, Syrinx doing a little dance next to her. As if the golden-furred chimera had found it himself. Cheeky pup.

Leaping to her feet as she opened the lid, she rifled through the antiseptic ointment, bandages, and vial of pain-relieving potion. She frowned down at Syrinx. "This stuff never goes bad, right?"

Syrinx scrunched his snout, huffing as if to say, *Beats me!*

Bryce scratched under his chin and returned to the great room to find Hunt crouching beside Ithan, whom they'd laid out on the coffee table. Ithan's face . . . Burning Solas.

Well, he was awake. And talking. She hoped he hadn't heard her and Hunt bickering over where to put his barely conscious form a moment ago. Hunt had wanted to set Ithan on the couch, and Bryce hadn't been able to stop herself from shrieking about ruining the white cushions. So the coffee table it was.

Hunt and Ithan were murmuring too low for Bryce to understand, and they halted as she approached. Though she could detect no outward sign of it, Hunt's lightning seemed to crackle in the air around him. Or maybe that was Hunt's presence, once again doing funny things to her senses. Bryce lifted the first aid kit. "Found it."

Ithan grunted. "It's . . . it's not as bad as it looks."

"Your mouth literally started bleeding again saying that," Bryce said, dropping the kit on the table next to Ithan before fishing inside for sterile wipes. She hadn't seen him since the attack last spring. Hadn't spoken to him.

Bryce waved a hand over the bruised and swollen face that held no resemblance to the handsome, charming features she'd once known so well. "I don't even know where to start with this . . . mess." She didn't just mean his face.

"You and me both," Ithan mumbled, and hissed as Bryce dabbed at a slice across his brow. He pulled his head from her reach. "It'll heal. That one's already smaller."

"I'd guess claws made that," Hunt said, arms crossed. Syrinx hopped onto the sectional, turned in a circle three times, then curled up in a ball.

Ithan said nothing. Bryce reached for the wound again, but he pulled his head farther back, wincing in pain.

"Why the fuck are you here, Ithan?" Hunt's voice was like gravel.

Ithan's brown eyes, one half-swollen, met Bryce's. Ire glowed in them. "I didn't tell them to bring me here. Perry . . . my pack's Omega . . . She arranged it."

A fuzzy memory of a brown-haired female emerged. Perry . . . Ravenscroft. Amelie's younger sister. "*She* did this to you?"

Ithan huffed a raw laugh, then winced. His ribs must be—

Bryce lifted Ithan's bloody gray T-shirt, revealing disgustingly carved abs and—"Holy shit, Ithan."

He yanked the shirt back over the extensive bruising. "It's fine."

"Those look like broken ribs," Hunt said wryly.

"Definitely broken ribs, Athalar," Bryce replied, sitting back on her heels. "And a broken arm, from the way he's cradling it."

"Skull fracture's healed," Hunt observed with equal distance, as if they were on one of his favorite Vanir crime procedurals. Ithan's eyes flashed again.

"I'm sensing hostility and a good dose of male pride," Bryce said.

"Throw in some stubbornness and I'd say we've got ourselves a classic case of stupidity," Hunt answered.

"What *the fuck* is wrong with you two?" Ithan demanded.

Bryce smiled at Hunt, all thoughts of the betrothal and her father and the Asteri vanishing at the amusement glittering in the angel's eyes. But she stopped smiling as she faced Ithan again.

"I promise to clean you up as quickly as possible, and you'll be on your way," she said.

"Take your time. It's not like I have anywhere to go."

Hunt stilled. "Amelie kicked you out?"

"Sabine kicked me out," Ithan growled. "She, Amelie, and the others did . . . this."

"Why?" Bryce managed to say.

Ithan met her stare. "Why do you think?" Bryce shook her head, disgust creeping through her. Ithan said, "You know how Sabine operates. Some reporter cornered me at a bar a few weeks ago about the attack last spring, and I talked about . . . what happened. How I helped you. The article came out this morning. Sabine apparently wasn't a fan."

"Oh?" Hunt lifted a brow.

Ithan's bruised throat bobbed. "I might have also defended you," he said to Bryce. "Against a nasty quote from Sabine."

Bryce resisted the urge to pull out her phone to search for the article. Nothing in there would make her feel better about this. So she said, "Sabine's a City Head. This is really what she wants to waste her time on?"

"Wolves don't talk shit about other wolves."

"But you did," Hunt countered.

"So did Sabine." He said sadly, wearily to Bryce, "The Prime called you a wolf. That's good enough for me. I, ah . . . It didn't sit well, what Sabine said. But I guess the article didn't sit well with her, either. So I'm out."

Bryce exhaled a long, long breath.

"Why bring you here?" Hunt asked.

Ithan grimaced with pain. "Perry remembered that we were friends, once upon a time." He tried and failed to rise. "But give me a few minutes, then I'll be gone."

"You're staying here," Bryce said. Honestly, after the night she'd had, it was the last thing she wanted. Especially when she still had to call her mom and convince her to get out of town. Gods, if Ember found out Ithan was here, she'd never leave. She'd loved him like a son. Bryce shook off the thought. "You're lucky Sabine didn't kill you."

"Trust me, she wanted to," Ithan said bitterly. "But I wasn't worth the legal headache that would cause."

Bryce swallowed. Connor's little brother had once been her best friend, after Danika. Fury and June had come after that. Gods, how many messages had she and Ithan swapped over the years? How many juvenile jokes had they shared? How many times had she bounced in the stands at one of his sunball games, screaming her lungs out for him?

The male before her was a stranger.

"I should go," Ithan said thickly. Like he remembered their history, too. Read it on her face.

"Sit the fuck down," Hunt said. "You can't even walk."

"Fine," Ithan conceded. "One night."

He had to be desperate, then.

Fighting the tightness in her chest, Bryce pulled out her phone. "Good." She noted the time. Almost midnight. Her parents were likely about to go to bed. "I have to make a call."

Hunt fixed a cup of decaf just to give himself something to do as Ithan lay bleeding on the coffee table behind him. Bryce's voice as she spoke to her parents filtered down the hall in bits and pieces.

We'll plan a long weekend next time. Maybe Hunt and I can come up to you guys. I think he'd love to finally see Nidaros.

Hunt's lips quirked upward. Bringing him home to her parents, huh? No matter that she was lying through her teeth.

The coffee machine finished a heartbeat before Bryce said, "All right. I'll meet you at your hotel at six. Yep. Bright and early. Okay. Love you. Bye."

Hunt blew on the steaming-hot coffee as Bryce padded back down the hall. "Everything good?" he asked her.

"Aside from the fact that I have to be up in a few hours, sure." Bryce slid her phone onto the kitchen counter. "Tickets are switched." She peered at Ithan, whose eyes were closed. But Hunt had no doubt the wolf was listening.

"Right," Bryce said. "Beds."

"I'm good on the couch," Ithan croaked.

Hunt was inclined to agree, but Bryce said, "Oh no. You're in my room. I won't have you bleeding all over my white couch."

Hunt said roughly, "I'll sleep on the couch. Holstrom, you can have my room."

"Nope," Bryce countered. "It's fine. My bed is big."

Hunt shot back, "Then *you* sleep on the couch and give Holstrom the bed."

"With my back problems?" Before Hunt could ask what the Hel she was talking about, she said, "I'm tired, and I don't want to argue. Conversation over."

Ithan cracked open an eye. Hunt reined in his growl of frustration.

Fifteen minutes later, Hunt lay in his own bed, teeth gritted as he stared at the ceiling, with only a snoring Syrinx for company.

It was fine. Totally fucking fine that Ithan Holstrom was sharing Bryce's bed.

Totally. Fucking. Fine.

His bed, his blood roared. Even if he hadn't been near it in months. His bed, *his* Bryce, who'd emerged from the bathroom in her sleep shorts and a faded, threadbare T-shirt that did nothing to hide the shadow of her nipples behind the purple fabric. Thankfully, Holstrom's eyes were too swollen for Hunt to notice if the male looked. Not that it really mattered. He trusted Bryce. Knew precisely what—and who—she wanted.

But . . . it didn't matter that Holstrom had come to Bryce's defense during the attack, or in some stupid article. He'd been a nasty fuck to her in the two years before that. And had let Amelie run rampant, tormenting Bryce over the death of his brother.

And fine—trust aside, maybe he was slightly on edge. Holstrom was good-looking, when he wasn't beaten to Hel and back. He'd been a star sunball player at CCU. Hunt remembered watching a few of the games in the 33rd's lounge in the Comitium, marveling at Holstrom's speed and agility. The male hadn't played the sport for two years now, but he was still built.

Stupid, jealous idiot. For fuck's sake, having Holstrom here bothered him more than that asshole Cormac claiming he'd marry Quinlan.

He hated himself just a little bit as he pulled his phone from the nightstand and typed in *Ithan Holstrom Sabine Fendyr Bryce Quinlan.*

The article popped up immediately.

Hunt skimmed it. Read what Sabine had said and focused on his breathing. On not leaping into the skies and shredding the Prime Apparent into pieces.

"Bryce Quinlan is nothing but a spoiled party girl who was conveniently in the right place during the attack. My wolves saved innocents. She's a pathetic fame-chaser."

Hunt ground his teeth so hard his jaw hurt. Toward the bottom, he found Holstrom's sound bite.

"The wolves only went to Asphodel Meadows because of Bryce. She got the call for help out, and held the line until we could provide backup. She saved this city. She's a hero, as far as I'm concerned. Don't let anyone convince you otherwise. Especially people who weren't even in this city during the attack."

Well, Hunt didn't blame Sabine for being pissed. The truth hurt.

Hunt sighed and was about to set his phone back onto the night-stand when it buzzed with a message from Isaiah. *Thoughts???*

He knew Isaiah was asking about Celestina's appointment. *Too early to tell*, he wrote back. *Too early for hope, too.*

Isaiah answered immediately. *She'll be here tomorrow evening at five. Try to play nice, Hunt. She's not Micah.*

Hunt sent back a thumbs-up. But sleep was a long time coming.

Bryce gazed at her bedroom ceiling, listening to the wet, labored breathing of the male beside her.

Her mom and dad had bought her lies—hook, line, and sinker. Of course, it meant she'd be getting up in four hours, but it was a price worth paying. No news about her engagement had been leaked yet. She could only pray it wouldn't until their train was out of the city.

Ithan shifted slightly, the sound of the blankets loud in the silence. It was strange to have him here, his scent filling her nose. So similar to Connor's scent—

"I could have slept on the couch," Ithan said into the darkness.

"I don't trust Athalar not to smother you with a pillow."

Ithan huffed a laugh. "He holds a grudge, huh?"

"You have no idea."

Silence fell again, thick and heavy. She'd wanted Ithan right where she could see him. It was as simple as that. Wards on this place or not, she wasn't about to leave him unguarded when Sabine and Amelie might change their minds about the paperwork being too much trouble. She'd lost one Holstrom already.

"Danika had me keyed to the locks," Ithan said. "Right before . . . everything. She showed me this place—wanted me in on the sur-prise. That's how I got in."

Bryce's throat clogged. "Oh."

"Is it true that Danika helped you make the Drop?"

Since her voice had been broadcast through the Gates into every part of the city, it was common knowledge that Danika Fendyr had something to do with Bryce's Drop, but rumors about exactly what ranged widely.

"Yeah," Bryce said. "She, ah . . . She was my Anchor."

"I didn't know that was possible."

"Me neither."

His breathing thinned. Bryce said, "I . . . Ithan, when I saw Danika during the Search, she told me that the others—Connor and Nathalie and the whole Pack of Devils—held off the Reapers to buy her time to be there with me. They saved me, too. Connor saved me."

Ithan said nothing for a long moment. When was the last time they'd spoken like this? Calm, quiet. Without hate spewing like acid, burning everything it touched? Then Ithan said, "He loved you more than anyone."

Her heart strained. "He loved *you* more than anyone."

"He thought you were his mate."

Bryce shut her eyes against the punch that slammed into her gut. "In the wolf sense of the word?"

"What other sense is there? Yeah, the wolf sense."

There were several definitions of the term *mate*—though Bryce supposed that to Ithan, to a shifter, only one mattered: one's true lover, predestined by Urd.

The Fae had a similar concept—a mate was a bond deeper than marriage, and beyond an individual's control. The angels, she knew, used the term far more lightly: for the malakim, it was akin to a marriage, and matings could be arranged. Like breeding animals in a zoo.

But for Connor, if he'd thought Bryce was his mate . . . Her stomach twisted again.

"Did you love him?" Ithan whispered.

"You know I did," Bryce said, voice thick.

"We waste so much time. Maybe it's our curse as immortals. To see time as a luxury, a never-ending ocean." He loosed a long breath. "I wasted a lot of it."

Bryce couldn't tell what he was referring to. "Real poetic of you."

Ithan let out a soft laugh. In the air-conditioned dark, Bryce asked, "Why did you quit sunball?"

She felt Ithan tense, the mattress shifting. "Because it's a stupid game," he said, voice empty, and turned onto his side with a groan.

Bryce had no idea how to respond. So she closed her eyes, rubbing idly at the scar on her chest, and prayed for Luna to send her into a dreamless, heavy sleep.

7

This is bullshit." Ruhn paced the ornate rugs of his father's study as the grandfather clock in the corner chimed two in the morning. "You *know* it's total fucking bullshit."

Lounging in a crimson leather armchair by the darkened fireplace, the Autumn King said nothing. The experiments and nonsense he worked on day and night boiled and bubbled away, the sound a steady hum in the background.

"What's the matter, cousin? Feeling possessive of your sister?" Cormac smirked from where he leaned against the black marble mantel, white sweater stretched tight over his muscled chest. Not one golden hair on his head out of place.

Fucker.

Ruhn ignored Cormac's taunt and said to his father, "We live in a modern city. In modern times. There are lawyers by the dozen who have endless resources to challenge this—and courts that might be amenable to setting a new precedent that protects the rights of Fae females."

"Bryce will arrive willingly at the marriage altar," his father said. "As will you."

Cormac's mouth curled upward. "I hear you're engaged to Hypaxia Enador. Congratulations." Ruhn scowled at him. Cormac went on, sizing up Ruhn, "Of course, the marriage is unorthodox, considering your bride's family and bloodline."

Ruhn stiffened. "You've got some shit to spew about Hypaxia, then let's hear it."

But Cormac said to the Autumn King, "He doesn't know?"

His father, damn him, seemed bored as he said, "It didn't seem necessary. My order is law."

Ruhn glanced between them. "What is this?"

His father, features tightening with distaste—as if disappointed that Ruhn hadn't learned it himself—said, "The late Queen Hecuba had two daughters, from different sires. Hypaxia's sire, Hecuba's coven learned afterward, was a powerful necromancer from the House of Flame and Shadow. Hypaxia seems to have inherited his gifts alongside her mother's."

Ruhn blinked. Slowly. Hypaxia could raise and speak to the dead. All right. He could live with that. "Cool."

Flames danced along his father's hair, dancing over his shoulders. "Her older sister, however, was sired by a shape-shifting male. A stag."

"So?"

Cormac snorted. "Hypaxia's half sister is better known as the Hind." Ruhn gaped at him. How had he not known this? "She didn't inherit any witch gifts," Cormac continued, "and was handed over to her father's kin. The crown naturally went to Hypaxia. But it seems that since your bride has been crowned queen, the question of her necromancy has become . . . an issue for the witches."

"It's of no bearing on this conversation," his father said. "Ruhn shall marry her, necromancy or not, odious sister or not."

"My father found Hypaxia's background to be problematic," Cormac said.

"Then it is a good thing your father is not marrying her," the Autumn King countered.

Cormac shut his mouth, and Ruhn held in his grin of delight.

But his father went on, "Ruhn shall marry Hypaxia, and Bryce Quinlan shall marry you, Prince Cormac. There will be no more debate."

"You do remember that Bryce and Athalar are together?" Ruhn said. "Try to get between them, and you'll get a refresher course on why he was called the Umbra Mortis."

"Last my spies reported, she still does not bear his scent. So I can only assume they have not consummated their relationship."

Just talking about this with his father was gross.

Cormac cut in, "One day, she'll be Queen of Avallen. She'd be a fool to throw it away on a bastard angel."

Ruhn spat, "You need Bryce more than she needs either of you. She's Starborn."

The Autumn King's teeth flashed. "If Bryce wished to remain free of our household, then she should not have been so brazen about showing off her power."

"Is that what this is about?" Fire seared through Ruhn's veins. "That she *showed you up*? That she has more power than you? What—you needed to put her back in her place?"

"You're delusional," Cormac's grin promised violence. "I am stooping to marry your sister. Many of my people will consider the union a disgrace."

"Careful," the Autumn King warned, true anger sparking in his whiskey-colored eyes. "Regardless of her human lineage, Bryce is an heir to the Starborn line. More so than my son." He threw a frown dripping with disdain at Ruhn. "We have not seen starlight with such force for thousands of years. I do not take handing her over to Avallen lightly."

"What the fuck are you getting from it?" Nausea clawed its way up Ruhn's throat.

His father answered, "Your sister has one value to me: her breeding potential. Both of our royal houses will benefit from the union."

Cormac added, "And the continued commitment to the alliance between our peoples."

"Against what?" Had everyone lost their minds?

"A weakening of magic in the royal bloodline," Cormac said. "As recent generations have demonstrated." He waved with a flame-crusted hand toward Ruhn and his shadows.

"Fuck you," Ruhn hissed. "Is this about the war in Pangera? The rebellion?" He'd heard rumors recently that Ophion had taken out four Omega submersibles in the north. *Four.* Some insane shit had to be going on over there. His father had even hinted at it in the late spring, when he'd announced Ruhn's betrothal. That war was coming, and they needed to shore up allies.

"It is about ensuring that the Fae retain our power and birth-right," his father said. His icy voice had always belied the merciless flame in his blood. "Your sister can imbue that into her offspring with Cormac."

Cormac grunted his agreement, flames winking out.

Ruhn tried again. "For fuck's sake, leave Bryce out of this. Don't we have other royals we can pair off to punch out some babies?"

"I didn't remember you whining so much, Ruhn," Cormac said.

"Before or after you tried to kill me? Or when you buried a sword in Dec's gut?"

Cormac's eyes gleamed like hot coals. "Just wanted to feel you boys out." He pushed off the mantel and strode for the shut doors. "You know," Cormac drawled over his shoulder, "the Starborn used to intermarry. Brother wed sister, aunt married nephew, and so on. All to keep the bloodline pure. Since you seem so heavily invested in who shares Bryce's bed, perhaps the old traditions could be revived for you two."

"Get the Hel out," Ruhn snarled. His shadows writhed at his fingertips, whips ready to snap for the Avallen Prince's neck.

"You might rebel all you like, Ruhn Danaan, but you are a Crown Prince, as I am. Our fates are the same. But I know which one of us will rise to meet it."

Then he was gone.

Our fates are the same. Cormac meant that they would both be kings, but Ruhn knew his fate was more complicated than that.

The royal bloodline shall end with you, Prince. The Oracle's voice floated through his mind, twisting up his insides. He might very well not live long enough to see himself crowned. His blood chilled. Was it because Cormac would lead some sort of coup?

He shook it off, turning to his father. "Why are you doing this?"

"That you have to ask shows me you're no true son of mine."

The words seared through him. Nothing could ever hurt worse than what had already been done to him by this male, the scars he bore on his arms from it, mostly covered by the sleeves of his tattoos. But the words . . . yeah, they stung.

Ruhn refused to let the old bastard see it, though. Would never let him see it. "And I suppose you think Cormac will become that true son by marrying Bryce."

His father's lips curled upward, eyes as lifeless as the Pit. "Cormac has always been the son I should have had. Rather than the one I was burdened with."

8

"Today's the big day, huh?"

Hunt turned from where he'd been staring at the coffee machine, willing the grinding of the beans to drown out the thoughts roaring in his head. Bryce leaned against the white marble counter behind him, clad in leggings and an old T-shirt.

Hunt tucked in his gray wings and saluted. "Approachable Asshole, reporting for duty." Her lips curved upward, but he asked, "How'd it go with your parents?" She'd left well before he was up.

"Perfectly." She feigned brushing dirt off her shoulders. "Not a whisper about the engagement. I think Randall suspected *something*, but he was game to play along."

"Five gold marks says your mom calls before noon to start yelling."

Her grin was brighter than the morning sun streaming outside the windows. "You're on." She angled her head, surveying his daily uniform: his usual black battle-suit for the 33rd. "You should see the decorations that went up overnight—apparently, the city's rolling out the welcome mat, and sparing no expense. Banners, flowers, sparkly-clean streets, even in the Old Square. Not one drop of drunken-idiot vomit to be seen or smelled."

"The appointment of a new Governor is a pretty big deal," he said, wondering where she was going with this.

"Yep." Then Bryce asked casually, "Want me to come with you today?"

There it was. Something in his chest kindled at the offer. "No hand-holding needed, Quinlan. But thanks."

Bryce's eyes glowed—pure Fae predator lurking there. "Remember what we did to the last two Archangels, Hunt," she said quietly. That was new—the raw power that thundered beneath her words. "If Celestina does something fucked up, we'll react accordingly."

"Bloodthirsty, Quinlan?"

She didn't smile. "You might be heading in there without me today, but I'm a phone call away."

His chest ached. She'd do it—back him up against a fucking Archangel, Solas burn him. "Noted," he said thickly. He nodded toward the hallway. "How's our guest?"

"He looks a lot better this morning, though the broken ribs have some mending left to do. He was still sleeping when I left."

"What's the plan?" Hunt kept his voice neutral. He'd slept terribly last night, every sound sending him lurching from sleep. Bryce, of course, appeared as beautiful as ever.

"Ithan can stay as long as he wants," Bryce said simply. "I'm not turning him over to Sabine."

"Glad to hear it," Ithan said from behind her, and even Hunt started.

The male had crept up with preternatural silence. He *did* look better. Blood still crusted Holstrom's short golden-brown hair, but the swelling around his eyes had vanished, leaving only a few purple streaks. Most of the cuts were healed, except the thick slash across his brow. That'd take another day or two. Ithan pointed past Hunt. "Is that coffee?"

Hunt busied himself with pouring three cups, passing one to Quinlan first. "A drop of coffee in a cup of milk, just as you like it."

"Asshole." She swiped the mug. "I don't know how you drink it straight."

"Because I'm a grown-up." Hunt passed the second mug to Ithan, whose large hands engulfed the white ceramic cup that said *I*

Survived Class of 15032 Senior Week and All I Got Was This Stupid Mug!

Ithan peered at it, his mouth twitching. "I remember this mug."

Hunt fell silent as Bryce let out a breathy laugh. "I'm surprised you do, given how drunk you were. Even though you were a sweet baby frosh."

Ithan chuckled, a hint of the handsome, cocky male Hunt had heard about. "You and Danika had me doing keg stands at ten in the morning. How was I supposed to stay sober?" The wolf sipped from his coffee. "My last memory from that day is of you and Danika passed out drunk on a couch you'd moved right into the middle of the quad."

"And why was that your last memory?" Bryce asked sweetly.

"Because I passed out next to you," Ithan said, grinning now.

Bryce smiled, and damn if it didn't do something to Hunt's heart. A smile of pain and joy and loss and longing—and hope. But she cleared her throat, peering at the clock. "I need to get into the shower. I'll be late for work." With a swish of her hips, she padded down the hallway.

Syrinx scratched at Hunt's calf, and Hunt hissed, "Absolutely not. You had one breakfast already." Probably two, if Bryce had fed him before going to meet her parents. Syrinx flopped down beside his steel bowl and let out a whine. Hunt tried to ignore him.

He found Ithan watching him carefully. "What?" Hunt said, not bothering to sound pleasant.

Ithan only sipped from his mug again. "Nothing."

Hunt gulped a mouthful of coffee. Glanced down the hall to make sure Bryce was indeed in her room. His voice dropped to a low growl. "Allow me to repeat what I said to you last night. You bring trouble in here, to Bryce, and I will fucking gut you."

Ithan's mouth twitched upward. "I'm shaking, Athalar."

Hunt didn't smile back. "Are you suddenly cool with her because she's a princess? Because of the Horn and the Starborn shit?"

Ithan's nose crinkled with the beginnings of a snarl. "I don't care about any of that."

"Then why the fuck did you bother to defend her in that article? You had to know there'd be consequences with Sabine. You practically called Sabine out."

"Danika showed up for her. My brother and the rest of the Pack of Devils showed up for her this spring. If they're not holding a grudge, then how can I?"

"So you needed permission from your dead brother to be nice to her?"

Ithan's snarl rattled the cabinets. "Bryce was my best friend, you know. She had Danika, yeah, but I only had *her*. You've known Bryce for what—a few months? We were friends for five *years*. So don't fucking talk about me, my brother, or her as if you know anything about us. You don't know shit, *Umbra Mortis*."

"I know you were a dick to her for two years. I watched you stand by while Amelie Ravenscroft tormented her. Grow the fuck up."

Ithan bared his teeth. Hunt bared his own right back.

Syrinx hopped to his feet and whined, demanding more food.

Hunt couldn't help his exasperated laugh. "Fine, fine," he said to the chimera, reaching for his container of kibble.

Ithan's eyes burned him like a brand. Hunt had seen that same take-no-shit face during televised sunball games. "Connor was in love with her for those five years, you know." The wolf headed over to the couch and plopped onto the cushions. "Five years, and by the end of it, he'd only managed to get her to *agree* to go on a date with him."

Hunt kept his face unreadable as Syrinx devoured his second—potentially third—breakfast. "So?"

Ithan turned on the morning news before propping his feet on the coffee table and interlacing his hands behind his head. "You're at month five, bro. Good luck to you."

The Fae Archives hummed with activity—loud enough that Bryce had grown accustomed to keeping in her earbuds all day, even with the door to her tiny office on Sublevel Alpha shut.

It wasn't that it was *loud*, exactly—the archives had the usual hush of any library. But so many people visited or studied or worked in the cavernous atrium and surrounding stacks that there was a constant, underlying roar. The scuff of footsteps, the waterfall fountain pouring from the atrium's ceiling, the clack of keyboards blending with the crinkle of turning pages, the whispers of patrons and tourists mingling with the occasional giggle or snap of a camera.

It grated on her.

Gone were the solitary days in the gallery. The days of blasting her music through the sound system.

Lehabah was gone, too.

No incessant chatter about the latest episode of *Fangs and Bangs*. No whining about wanting to go outside. No dramatic monologues about Bryce's cruelty.

Bryce stared at the dark computer screen on her glass desk. She reached out a foot to stroke Syrinx's coat, but her toes only met air. Right—she'd left the chimera home to watch over Ithan.

She wondered if Syrinx even remembered Lehabah.

Bryce had visited the Black Dock during the days after the attack, searching for a tiny onyx boat among the mass of Sailings. None had appeared.

Lehabah had no remains anyway. The fire sprite had been snuffed out like a candle the moment a hundred thousand gallons of water had come crashing down upon her.

Bryce had gone over it, again and again. Usually during her dance classes with Madame Kyrah, amid her panting and sweating. She always arrived at the same conclusion: there was nothing she might have done to stop Lehabah's death.

Bryce understood it, could rationally talk about it, and yet . . . The thoughts still circled, as if dancing right along with her: *You might have found a way. Revealed yourself as Starborn earlier. Told Lehabah to run while you faced Micah.*

She'd talked about it with Hunt, too. And he'd pointed out that all of those options would have resulted in Bryce's own death, but . . . Bryce couldn't get past the question: Why was Lele's life any less valuable than Bryce's? Her Starborn Princess status meant nothing. If it came down to it, Lele had been the better person, who had suffered for decades in bondage. The fire sprite should be free. Alive, and free, and enjoying herself.

Bryce picked up the desktop phone, dialing. Jesiba answered on the third ring. "Another question, Quinlan? That's the third one this week."

Bryce drummed her fingers on her glass desk. "I've got a nine-thousand-year-old Rhodinian bust of Thurr here." Basically a broody male who was supposed to pass for the nearly forgotten minor storm deity. All that remained of him in their culture was the behemoth of a planet named after him. And Thursdays, apparently. Bryce had already sent a photo of it to Hunt, with the comment, *Bryce Quinlan Presents: The Original Alphahole Smolder.* "A museum is interested, but they're worried the former owner fudged some documents about its history. They want to make sure it's legit before showing it to the public. Any idea who to call in Rhodinia to verify?"

"If I'm doing your job for you, then why am I not being paid for it?"

Bryce ground her teeth. "Because we're friends?"

"Are we?"

"You tell me."

Jesiba huffed a soft laugh. The enchantress who'd defected from her witch-clan and sworn allegiance to the House of Flame and Shadow still lurked around Lunathion, but Bryce hadn't seen her in months. Not since the day Jesiba had found Bryce poking around the watery ruins of the gallery library and told her not to come back.

Not in a mean way. Just in a *This gallery is now permanently closed, and those books you're looking for are hidden away where no one will ever find them* sort of manner.

Jesiba said, "I suppose I should consider it an honor, to be called a friend by the Starborn Princess daughter of the Autumn King." A slight pause, and Bryce knew what was coming next. "And the future Queen of Avallen."

Bryce swiftly opened a news website as she hissed, "Who told you?"

"Some of the people I've turned into animals have remained in my employ, you know. They tell me what they overhear on the streets. Especially the sewer rats who hope to regain their true forms one day."

Bryce truly wasn't sure if Jesiba was serious. She sighed again. "I don't suppose you have any insights as to *why* the Autumn King suddenly decided to ruin my life."

Jesiba tsked. "Males will always try to control the females who scare them. Marriage and breeding are their go-to methods."

"Satisfying as it is to think of my father being afraid of me, that can't be it."

"Why not? It's been months. You've done nothing with your new power, your titles. Or the Horn in your back. He grew tired of waiting. I wouldn't be surprised if he did this just to learn how you'd react."

"Maybe." Bryce doodled on a piece of scrap paper beside her computer. A little heart that said *BQ + HA*.

"What *are* you going to do about it?" Jesiba asked, as if she couldn't help it.

"Pretend it's not happening until I can't any longer?"

Jesiba chuckled again. "I worried, you know, when I learned you were Starborn. I've watched many succumb to the allure of being the Chosen One. Perhaps you and your brother have more in common than I realized."

"I think that's a compliment?"

"It is. Ruhn Danaan is one of the few who's ever been strong enough to shun what he is." Bryce grunted. "You don't plan on doing anything with it, then," Jesiba asked, more quietly than Bryce had ever heard. "Your talent. Or the Horn."

"*Definitely* not the Horn. And it seems most of the Starborn power's value lies in what I can breed into the Fae bloodline." Bryce straightened, twirling her pencil between her fingers. "And what good does blinding people do? I mean, it *does* have its uses, but surely there are deadlier weapons to wield?" Like Hunt's lightning.

"You killed an Archangel without access to that power. I imagine that you can now do a great many things, Quinlan."

Bryce stiffened at the words, spoken so casually over an open line. She had no idea what Jesiba had done with the Godslayer Rifle. Honestly, she never wanted to see it again.

Bryce lowered her voice, even though she knew no one was near her little subterranean office. "I was given an order by the Asteri to lie low. Forever."

"How terribly boring of you to obey them."

Bryce opened her mouth, but the intercom on her desk buzzed. "Miss Quinlan, you're needed in the northern wing. Doctor Patrus wants your opinion on that sculpture from Delsus?"

Bryce pushed the button. "Be there in five." She said to Jesiba, "I'm going to send you some photos of this piece. I'd appreciate it if you'd deign to give me your opinion. And let me know if you have any contacts in Rhodinia who can help verify its authenticity."

"I'm busy."

"So am I."

"Perhaps I'll turn you into a toad."

"At least toads don't wear stupid heels to work," Bryce said, sliding her feet back into the white stilettos she'd chucked beneath her desk.

Jesiba let out another soft, wicked laugh. "A word of advice, Quinlan: think through the advantages of a marriage to Cormac Donnall before you decide to be a cliché and refuse."

Bryce stood, cradling the phone between her ear and shoulder. "Who says I'm not?"

There was a lengthy pause before the sorceress said, "Good girl," and hung up.

9

Anything?"

"Nothing at all—though you were right about the all-out decorations. I nearly flew into about six different banners and wreaths on my way over this morning. But no reports or sightings of the Governor. Pretty normal day so far, to be honest." Hunt's low voice ran invisible hands along Bryce's arms as she picked at the remnants of her lunch: a gyro grabbed from the archives' staff cafeteria. He added, "Though not if you count me receiving a photo of some marble abs while I was showing crime scene pictures to Naomi."

"Thought you'd enjoy that."

His laugh rumbled over the line. It shot through her like starlight. If he was able to laugh today, good. She'd do whatever she could to keep a smile on Hunt's face. He cleared his throat. "Thurr was pretty jacked, huh?"

"I'm petitioning for the exhibit to sell replicas in the gift shop. I think the old ladies will go wild over it." That earned her another beautiful laugh. She bit her lip against her broad smile. "So Celestina's now due to arrive at six, then?" Apparently, she'd been delayed by an hour.

"Yep." Any hint of amusement faded.

Bryce stirred her computer to life. So far, the news sites reported nothing beyond the headline that Lunathion—that all of Valbara—would have a new leader.

Bryce was willing to admit she'd spent a good hour skimming through various images of the beautiful Archangel, pondering what sort of boss she'd be for Hunt. She found no hint about any romantic entanglements, though Micah hadn't often broadcast who he'd been fucking. It wasn't that Bryce was *worried*, though she'd certainly felt a scrap of *something* when she'd seen precisely how stunning Celestina was, but . . . she needed a mental picture of who Hunt would be seeing day in and day out.

Bryce chucked her lunch into the trash beside her desk. "I could come over after work. Be with you for the grand arrival."

"It's all right. I'll fill you in afterward. It might take a while, though, so feel free to eat without me."

"But it's pizza night."

Hunt laughed. "Glad you've got your priorities straight." His wings rustled in the background. "Any word about Prince Dickhead?"

"Nothing on the news, nothing from my mom."

"Small blessing."

"You owe me five gold marks."

"Add it to my tab, Quinlan."

"Don't forget that my mom will probably be pissed at *you* for not telling her."

"I already have my bug-out bag packed and ready to flee to another territory."

She chuckled. "I think you'd have to go to Nena to escape her." Hunt laughed with her. "Don't you think she—"

A glow flared at her chest. From the scar.

"Bryce?" Hunt's voice sharpened.

"I, uh . . ." Bryce frowned down at the glowing star between her breasts, visible in her low-cut dress. Not again. Its glowing had been rare until now, but after last night—

She looked up.

"My boss is here. I'll call you back," she lied, and hung up before Hunt could reply.

Bryce lifted her chin and said to Cormac Donnall, lurking in the doorway, "If you're looking for *How Not to Be an Asshole*, it's shelved between *Bye, Loser* and *Get the Fuck Out*."

The Crown Prince of Avallen had changed into a climate-appropriate gray T-shirt that did little to hide the considerable muscles of his arms. A tattoo of strange symbols encircled his left biceps, the black ink gleaming in the bright lights.

He examined her closet-sized office with typical Fae arrogance—and disapproval. "Your star glows in my presence because our union is predestined. In case you were wondering."

Bryce barked out a laugh. "Says who?"

"The Oracle."

"Which one?" There were twelve sphinxes around the world, each one bitchier than the last. The meanest of them, apparently, dwelled in the Ocean Queen's court Beneath.

"Does it matter?" Cormac turned, noting the shell-white dress Bryce wore, the gold bracelets, and, yes, her ample cleavage. Or was he gazing at the star? She supposed it made no difference.

"I just want to know whose ass to kick."

Cormac's mouth quirked upward. "I don't know why I expected a half-breed to be as docile as a pure-blooded female."

"You're not doing yourself any favors."

"I did not say I preferred a tamer female."

"Gross. What did the Oracle say to you, exactly?"

"What did she say to *you* before she began clawing at her blinded eyes?"

She didn't want to know how he'd found out. Maybe her father had told him—warned him about his bride. "Old news. I asked first."

Cormac glowered. "The Oracle of Avallen said I was destined to unite with a princess who possessed a star in her heart. That our mingling would bring great prosperity to our people."

Bryce drummed her fingers on her glass desk. "A lot of room for interpretation there." Trust an Oracle to call sex *mingling*.

"I disagree."

Bryce sighed. "Tell me why you're here, then leave, please. I have work to do."

Cormac studied the small torso of Thurr on her desk. "I wanted to see where my betrothed works. To gain some insight into your . . . life."

"You say that as if it's a foreign thing for females to have jobs."

"In Avallen, it is." He leaned against the doorjamb. "My people have let the old traditions remain untouched. You will need to adjust."

"Thanks, but no. I like my TV and phone. And I like being considered a person, not livestock for breeding."

"Like I said last night, you don't have a choice." His voice was flat, his eyes hollow.

Bryce crossed her arms, realized it put her cleavage and the star on better display, and lowered them to her sides once more. "Can I . . . pay you to drop this whole engagement thing?"

Cormac laughed. "I have more gold than I know what to do with. Money holds little power over me." He crossed his arms as well. "You have a chance to help your people and this world. Once you bear me a few heirs, you can take whatever lovers you wish. I will do the same. This marriage doesn't need to burden either of us."

"Except for the part where I have to sleep with you. And live in your backwater land."

His lips curled upward. "I think you'll find the first part to be rather enjoyable."

"Spoken with true male arrogance."

He shrugged, clearly confident that she *would* enjoy him. "I haven't had any complaints yet. And if our union helps our people, and strengthens the royal bloodlines, then I'll do it."

"The Fae are no people of mine." They never had been, and certainly not now, after they'd locked out innocent citizens in this city and refused to come to anyone's aid during the attack last spring. She pointed to the open door. "Bye."

He simmered with disgust. "Your father let you run wild for too long."

"My father's name is Randall Silago. The Autumn King is just a male who gave me genetic material. He will never have a place in my life. Neither will you."

Cormac took a step back from the doorway, shadows swirling. His golden hair glowed like molten metal. "You're immortal now, as well as Starborn. Time to act like it."

Bryce slammed the door in his face.

Hunt considered the beautiful Archangel seated at Micah's old desk. Glowing skin as dark as onyx brought out the light brown of her eyes, and her delicate mouth seemed permanently set in a patient smile. It was that smile—that gentle, kind smile—that threw him. "Take a seat, please," Celestina said to him, Naomi, and Isaiah.

Hunt nearly choked at the word. *Please.* Micah would never have said anything of the sort. Isaiah appeared equally baffled as they settled into the three chairs before the simple oak desk. Naomi kept her face wholly blank, her black wings rustling.

Behind the Governor's gleaming white wings, the wall of windows revealed an unusual number of angels soaring by. All hoping to catch a glimpse of the female who had entered the Comitium in a grand procession thirty minutes ago.

The lobby ceremony had been the start of Hunt's utter confusion. Rather than strutting magnanimously past the gathered crowd, the voluptuous, lush-bodied Archangel had taken her time, pausing to greet the malakim who stepped forward, asking for their names, saying things like *I'm so very happy to meet you* and *I look forward to working with you.* Cthona spare him, but Hunt honestly thought she might be serious.

He didn't let his guard down, though. Not when she'd reached him, Naomi, and Isaiah, standing before the elevator doors to escort her to her new residence and office; not when she'd taken his hand with genuine warmth; and certainly not now that they sat here for this private meeting.

Celestina surveyed them with unnerving clarity. "You three are all that remains of Micah's triarii."

None of them replied. Hunt didn't dare mention Vik—or beg the Archangel to pull her out of Melinoë's inky depths. To spare her from a living Hel. It had been months. Odds were that Vik had gone insane. Was likely begging for death with each moment in that box.

The Governor angled her head, her tightly curling black hair shifting with the movement. She wore pale pink-and-lilac robes, gauzy and ethereal, and the silver jewelry along her wrists and neck glowed as if lit by the moon. Where Micah had radiated dominance and might, she shimmered with feminine strength and beauty. She barely came up to Hunt's chest, yet . . . she had a presence that had Hunt eyeing her carefully.

"Not ones for talking, are you?" Her voice held a musical quality, as if it had been crafted from silver bells. "I suppose my predecessor had rules quite different from mine." She drummed her fingers on the desk, nails tinted a soft pink. "Allow me to make this clear: I do not wish for subservience. I want my triarii to be my partners. I want you to work alongside me to protect this city and territory, and help it meet its great potential."

A pretty little speech. Hunt said nothing. Did she know what he'd done to Sandriel? What Bryce had done to Micah? What Micah had done in his quest to supposedly protect this territory?

Celestina wrapped a curl around a finger, her immaculate wings shifting. "I see that I shall have to do a great deal of work to earn your trust."

Hunt kept his face bland, even as he wished that she'd be equally as forthright as Micah. He'd always hated his owners who'd disguised their dead souls in pretty speeches. This could easily be part of a game: to get them to trust her, come limping into her soft arms, and then spring the trap. Make them suffer.

Naomi's sharp chin lifted. "We don't wish to offend you, Your Grace—"

"Call me Celestina," the Archangel interrupted. "I abhor formalities." Micah had said the same thing once. Hunt had been a fool to buy it then.

Isaiah's wings shifted—like his friend was thinking the same.

His friend, who still bore the halo tattoo across his brow. Isaiah was the better male, the better leader—and still a slave. Rumors had swirled in the months before Micah's demise that the Archangel would free him soon. That possibility was now as dead as Micah himself.

Naomi nodded, and Hunt's heart tightened at the tentative hope in his friend's jet-black eyes. "We don't wish to offend you . . . Celestina. We and the 33rd are here to serve you."

Hunt suppressed his bristle. *Serve.*

"The only way you could offend me, Naomi Boreas, would be to withhold your feelings and thoughts. If something troubles you, I want to know about it. Even if the matter is due to my own behavior." She smiled again. "We're partners. I've found that such a partnership worked wonders on my legions in Nena. As opposed to the . . . systems my fellow Archangels prefer."

Torture and punishment and death. Hunt blocked out the sear of white-hot iron rods pounding his back, roasting his skin, splitting it down to the bone as Sandriel watched from her divan, popping grapes into her mouth—

Isaiah said, "We're honored to work with you, then."

Hunt pushed aside the bloody, screaming horrors of the past as another lovely smile bloomed on the Governor. "I've heard so many wonderful things about you, Isaiah Tiberian. I'd like you to stay on as leader of the 33rd, if that is what you wish."

Isaiah bowed his head in thanks, a tentative, answering smile gracing his face. Hunt tried not to gape. Was he the only asshole who didn't believe any of this?

Celestina turned her gaze upon him. "You have not yet spoken, Hunt Athalar. Or do you wish to go by Orion?"

"Hunt is fine." Only his mother had been allowed to call him Orion. He'd keep it that way.

She surveyed him again, elegant as a swan. "I understand that you and Micah did not necessarily see eye to eye." Hunt reined in his urge to growl in agreement. Celestina seemed to read his inclination. "On another day, I'd like to learn about your relationship with Micah and what went wrong. So we might avoid such a situation ourselves."

"What went wrong is that he tried to kill my—Bryce Quinlan." Hunt couldn't stop the words, or his stumble.

Naomi's brows nearly touched her hairline at his outburst, but Celestina sighed. "I heard about that. I'm sorry for any pain you and Miss Quinlan suffered as a result of Micah's actions."

The words hit him like stones. *I'm sorry.* He'd never, not in all the centuries he'd lived, heard an Archangel utter those words.

Celestina went on, "From what I've gathered, you have chosen to live with Miss Quinlan, rather than in the barracks tower."

Hunt kept his body loose. Refused to yield to the tension rising in him. "Yeah."

"I am perfectly fine with that arrangement," Celestina said, and Hunt nearly toppled out of his chair. Isaiah looked inclined to do the same. Especially as the Archangel said to Isaiah and Naomi, "If you should wish to dwell in your own residences, you are free to do so. The barracks are good for building bonds, but I believe the ones between you are quite unshakable. You are free to enjoy your own lives." She glanced at Isaiah, to the halo still tattooed on his brow. "I am not one to keep slaves," she said, disapproval tightening her face. "And though the Asteri might brand you as such, Isaiah, you are a free male in my eyes. I will endeavor to continue Micah's work in convincing them to free you."

Isaiah's throat worked, and Hunt studied the window—the shining city beyond—to give him privacy. Across the room, Naomi followed his lead.

Celestina couldn't be serious. This had to be an act.

"I'd like to hit the ground running," the Governor went on.

"Each morning, let's gather here so you can update me on any news, as well as your plans for the day. Should I have tasks for you or the 33rd, I shall convey them then." She folded her hands in her lap. "I am aware that you are skilled at hunting demons, and have been employed to do so in the past. If any break into this city, gods forbid, I'd like you to head up the containment and extermination unit against them."

Hunt jerked his chin in confirmation. Easy enough. Though this spring, dealing with the kristallos had been anything but easy.

Celestina finished, "And should an issue arise before our meeting tomorrow morning, my phone is always on."

Naomi nodded again. "What time tomorrow?"

"Let's say nine," Celestina said. "No need to drag ourselves out of bed simply to look busy." Hunt blinked at her. "And I'd like the others to get some rest after their journey."

"Others?" Isaiah asked.

The Archangel frowned slightly. "The rest of the triarii. They were delayed by a few hours due to some bad weather up north."

All three of them stilled. "What do you mean?" Hunt asked quietly.

"It was in the formal letter you received," she said to Isaiah, who shook his head.

Celestina's frown deepened. "The Asteri's Communications Minister is not usually one to make mistakes. I apologize on their behalf. The Asteri found themselves with a predicament after losing two Archangels, you see. You are all that remains of Micah's triarii, but Sandriel had a full stable in that regard. I had no triarii of my own in Nena, as the legion there technically answers to the Asteri, but Ephraim wanted to bring his own triarii with him. So rather than have his group get too large, it was split—since ours is so depleted."

Roaring erupted in Hunt's head. Sandriel's triarii. The actual scum of the universe.

They were coming here. To be part of *this* group. In *this* city.

A knock sounded on the door, and Hunt twisted as Celestina said, "Come in."

Lightning crackled at Hunt's fingertips. The door opened, and in swaggered Pollux Antonius and Baxian Argos.

The Hammer and the Helhound.

10

Absolute quiet settled over the Governor's office as Hunt and his friends took in the two newcomers.

One was dark-haired and brown-skinned, tall and finely muscled—the Helhound. His jet-black wings shimmered faintly, like a crow's feathers. But it was the wicked scar snaking down his neck, forking across the column of his throat, that snared the eye.

Hunt knew that scar—he'd given it to the Helhound thirty years ago. Some powers, it seemed, even immortality couldn't guard against.

Baxian's obsidian eyes simmered as they met Hunt's stare.

But Pollux's cobalt eyes lit with feral delight as he sized up Naomi, then Isaiah, and finally Hunt. Hunt allowed his lightning to flare as he stared down the golden-haired, golden-skinned leader of Sandriel's triarii. The most brutal, sadistic asshole to have ever walked Midgard's soil. Motherfucker Number One.

Pollux smirked, slow and satisfied. Celestina was saying something, but Hunt couldn't hear it.

Couldn't hear anything except Pollux drawling, "Hello, friends," before Hunt leapt from his chair and tackled him to the floor.

* * *

Ithan Holstrom dabbed a damp washcloth at the last of the cuts healing on his face, wincing. Bryce's bathroom was exactly as he'd expected it to be: full of at least three kinds of shampoos and conditioners, an array of hair treatments, brushes, curling rods of two different sizes, a blow-dryer left plugged into the wall, half-burned candles, and makeup scattered up and down the marble counter like some glittery bomb had gone off.

It was almost exactly the same as her bathroom at the old apartment. Just being here made his chest tighten. Just smelling this place, smelling *her* made his chest tighten.

He'd had little to distract himself today, sitting alone with her chimera—Syrinx, Athalar had called him—on the couch, nearly dying of boredom watching daytime TV. He didn't feel like trawling the news for hours, awaiting a glimpse of the new Archangel. None of the sports channels had interesting coverage on, and he had no desire to listen to those assholes talk anyway.

Ithan angled his face before the mirror to better see the cut lacing across his brow. This particular beauty had been from Sabine, a swipe of a claw-armed fist.

He had a feeling the blow had been intended for his eyes. Sure, they'd have healed after a few days or weeks, sooner if he'd gone to a medwitch, but being blinded wasn't at the top of his to-do list.

Not that he really had anything *else* on his to-do list today.

His phone buzzed on the counter, and Ithan peered down to see three different news alerts and photo essays about the arrival of Celestina. Had shit not gone down with Sabine, he'd probably be gearing up to meet the beautiful malakh as part of the wolves' formal welcome. And fealty-swearing bullshit.

But now he was a free agent. A wolf without a pack.

It wasn't common, but it did happen. Lone wolves existed, though most roamed the wilds and were left to their own devices. He'd just never thought he'd be one.

Ithan set down his phone, hanging up the washcloth on the already-crowded towel bar.

He willed the shift, inhaling sharply and bidding his bones to melt, his skin to ripple.

It occurred to him a moment after he took his wolf form that the bathroom wasn't quite large enough.

Indeed, a swish of his tail knocked over various bottles, sending them scattering across the marble floor. His claws clicked on the tiles, but he lifted his muzzle toward the mirror and met his reflection once more.

The horse-sized wolf that stared back was hollow-eyed, though his fur covered most of his bruising and the cuts, save for the slash along his brow.

He inhaled—and the breath stuck in his ribs. In some empty, strange pocket.

Wolf with no pack. Amelie and Sabine had not merely bloodied him, they'd exorcised him from their lives, from the Den. He backed into the towel rack, tossing his head this way and that.

Worse than an Omega. Friendless, kinless, unwanted—

Ithan shuddered back into his humanoid form. Panting, he braced his hands on the bathroom counter and waited until the nausea subsided. His phone buzzed again. Every muscle in his body tensed.

Perry Ravenscroft.

He might have ignored it had he not read the first part of the message as it appeared.

Please tell me you're alive.

Ithan sighed. Amelie's younger sister—the Omega of the Black Rose Pack—was technically the reason he'd made it here. Had said nothing about her sister and Sabine ripping him to shreds, but she'd carried him into the apartment. She was the only one of his former pack to bother to check in.

She added, *Just write back y/n.*

Ithan stared at the message for a long moment.

Wolves were social creatures. A wolf without a pack . . . it was a soul-wound. One that would cripple most wolves. But he'd been struck a soul-wound two years ago and had survived.

Even though he knew he couldn't endure taking his wolf form again anytime soon.

Ithan took in the bathroom, the various crap Bryce had left

lying around. She'd been a wolf without a pack for those two years, too. Yeah, she had Fury and Juniper, but it wasn't the same as Danika and Connor and the Pack of Devils. Nothing would ever be the same as that.

Ithan typed back *Yes*, then slid his phone into his pocket. Bryce would be home soon. And she'd mentioned something about pizza.

Ithan padded out into the airy apartment, Syrinx lifting his head from the couch to inspect him. The chimera lay back down with a puff of approval, lion's tail waggling.

The silence of the apartment pressed on Ithan. He'd never lived on his own. He'd always had the constant chaos and closeness of the Den, the insanity of his college dorm, or the hotels he'd stayed at with the CCU sunball team. This place might as well have been another planet.

He rubbed at his chest, as if it'd erase the tightness.

He'd known precisely why he'd disobeyed Sabine's order this spring when Bryce had screamed for help. The sound of her pleading had been unbearable. And when she'd mentioned children at risk, something had exploded in his brain. He had no regrets about what he'd done.

But could he endure its consequences? Not the beating—he could weather that shit any day. But being here, alone, adrift . . . He hadn't felt like this since Connor and the others had died. Since he'd walked away from his sunball team and stopped answering their calls.

He had no idea what the Hel he'd do now. Perhaps the answer wasn't some big, life-altering thing. Maybe it could be as simple as putting one foot in front of the other.

That's how you wound up following someone like Amelie, a voice that sounded an awful lot like Connor's growled. *Make better choices this time, pup. Assess. Decide what you want.*

But for now . . . one foot in front of the other. He could do that. If just for today.

Ithan walked to the door and pulled the leash off the hook on the wall beside it. "Want a walk?" he asked Syrinx. The beast rolled onto his side, as if saying, *Belly rub, please.*

Ithan slung the leash back onto its hook. "You got it, bud."

"Approachable Asshole, huh?"

Bryce leaned against the bars of the immaculate cell beneath the Comitium, frowning at where Hunt sat on a steel-framed cot, head hanging. He straightened at her words, gray wings tucking in. His face— Bryce stiffened. "What the *fuck*, Hunt?"

Black eye, swollen lip, cuts along his temple, his hairline . . . "I'm fine," he grumbled, even though he looked as bad as Ithan. "Who called you?"

"Your new boss—she filled me in. She sounds nice, by the way." Bryce pressed her face through the bars. "Definitely nice, since she hasn't kicked your ass to the curb yet."

"She did put me in this cell."

"Isaiah put you in the cell."

"Whatever."

"Don't *whatever* me." Gods, she sounded like her mother.

His voice sharpened. "I'll see you at home. You shouldn't be here."

"And you shouldn't have gotten into a stupid fight, but here you are."

Lightning forked down his wings. "Go home."

Was he—was he really pissed she was here? She snorted. "Were you intentionally trying to sabotage yourself today?"

Hunt shot to his feet, then winced at whatever pain it summoned in his battered body. "Why the fuck would I do that?"

A deep male voice answered, "Because you're a stupid bastard."

Bryce grimaced. She'd forgotten about Pollux.

Hunt snarled, "I don't want to hear your fucking voice."

"Get used to it," said another male voice from the elevator bay at the end of the white hall.

Bryce found a tall, lean angel approaching with a natural

elegance. Not beautiful, not in the way that Hunt and Pollux and Isaiah were, but . . . striking. Intense and focused.

Baxian Argos, the Helhound. An angel with the rare ability to shift into the form that had given him his nickname.

Hunt had told her about him, too. Baxian hadn't ever tortured Hunt or others, as far as she knew—but he'd done plenty of awful things in Sandriel's name. He'd been her chief spy-master and tracker.

Baxian bared his teeth in a fierce smile. Hunt bristled.

Like Hel would these males make her back down.

Pollux crooned from his cell, his pretty-boy face as battered as Hunt's, "Why don't you come a little closer, Bryce Quinlan?"

Hunt growled. "Don't talk to her."

Bryce snapped, "Spare me the protective alphahole act." Before Hunt could reply, she'd stalked over to Pollux's cell.

Pollux made a show of looking her over from head to stilettos. "I thought your kind usually worked the night shift."

Bryce snickered. "Any other outdated jabs to throw my way?" At Pollux's silence, Bryce said, "Sex work is a respectable profession in Crescent City. It's not my fault Pangera hasn't caught up with modern times."

Pollux brimmed with malice. "Micah should have killed you and been done with it."

She let her eyes glow—let him see that she knew all he'd done to Hunt, how much she detested him. "That's the best you can come up with? I thought the Hammer was supposed to be some kind of sadistic badass."

"And I thought half-breed whores were supposed to keep their mouths closed. Fortunately, I know the perfect thing to shove in that trap of yours to shut you up."

Bryce winked saucily. "Careful. I use teeth." Hunt coughed, and Bryce leaned forward—close enough that if Pollux extended an arm, his hand could wrap around her throat. Pollux's eyes flared, noting that fact. Bryce said sweetly, "I don't know who you pissed off to be sent to this city, but I'm going to make your life a living Hel if you touch him again."

Pollux lunged, fingers aiming for her neck.

She let her power surge, bright enough that Pollux reared back, an arm flung over his eyes. Bryce's lips quirked to the side. "I thought so."

She backed away a few steps, pivoting toward Hunt once more. He cocked an eyebrow, eyes shining beneath the bruises. "Fancy, Quinlan."

"I aim to impress."

A low laugh whispered behind her, and Bryce found the Helhound now leaning against the wall opposite the cells, beside a large TV.

"I take it I'll be seeing more of you than I'd like," Bryce said.

Baxian sketched a bow. He wore lightweight black armor made of overlapping plates. It reminded her of a reptilian version of Hunt's suit. "Maybe you'll give me a tour."

"Keep dreaming," Hunt muttered.

The Helhound's dark eyes gleamed. He turned on his heel and said before entering the elevator, "Glad someone finally put a bullet through Micah's head."

Bryce stared after him in stunned silence. Had he come down here for any reason other than to say that? Hunt whooshed out a breath. Pollux remained pointedly silent in his cell.

Bryce gripped the bars of Hunt's cell. "No more fights."

"If I say yes, can we go home now?" He gave her a mournful pout almost identical to Syrinx's begging.

Bryce suppressed her smile. "Not my call."

A fair female voice floated from an intercom in the ceiling. "I've seen enough. He's free to go, Miss Quinlan." The bars hissed, the door unlocking with a clank.

Bryce said to the ceiling, "Thank you."

Pollux growled from his cell, "And what of me? I didn't start this fight." The shithead had balls. Bryce would give him that.

Celestina answered coolly, "You also didn't do anything to defuse it."

"Forgive me for fighting back while being pummeled by a brute."

From the corner of her eye, Bryce could have sworn Hunt was grinning wickedly.

The Governor said, voice taking on a no-bullshit sharpness, "We shall discuss this later." Pollux was wise enough not to snap a reply. The Archangel went on, "Keep Athalar in line, Miss Quinlan."

Bryce waved at the camera mounted beside the TV. When Celestina didn't answer, Bryce stepped back to allow Hunt out of the cell. He limped toward her, badly enough that she looped her arm around his waist as they aimed for the elevator.

Pollux sneered from his cell, "You two mongrels deserve each other."

Bryce blew him a kiss.

11

Tharion needed a new job.

Honestly, even years into the position, he had no idea how he'd wound up in charge of the River Queen's intelligence. His schoolmates probably laughed every time his name came up: a thoroughly average, if not lazy, student, he'd gotten his passing grades mostly through charming his teachers. He had little interest in history or politics or foreign languages, and his favorite subject in school had been lunch.

Maybe that had primed him. People were far more inclined to talk over food. Though anytime he'd tortured an enemy, he'd puked his guts up afterward. Fortunately, he'd learned that a cold beer, some mirthroot, and a few rounds of poker usually got him what he needed.

And this: research.

Normally, he'd tap one of his analysts to pore over his current project, but the River Queen wanted this kept secret. As he sat before the computer in his office, all it took was a few keystrokes to access what he wanted: Sofie Renast's email account.

Declan Emmet had set up the system for him: capable of hacking into any non-imperial email within moments. Emmet had charged him an arm and a fin for it, but it had proved more than useful. The first time Tharion had used it had been to help track down his sister's murderer.

The sick fuck had emailed himself photos of his victims. Even what Tharion had done to him afterward hadn't erased the image seared into his brain of his sister's brutalized body.

Tharion swallowed, looking toward the wall of glass that opened into clear cobalt waters. An otter shot past, yellow vest blazingly bright in the river water, a sealed tube clenched between his little fangs.

A creature of both worlds. Some of the messenger otters dwelled here, in the Blue Court deep beneath the Istros, a small metropolis both exposed and sealed off from the water around them. Other otters lived Above, in the bustle and chaos of Crescent City proper.

Tharion couldn't ever move Above, he reminded himself. His duties required him here, at the River Queen's beck and call. Tharion peered at his bare feet, digging them into the cream shag carpet beneath his desk. He'd been in human form for nearly a day now. He'd have to enter the water soon or risk losing his fins.

His parents found it odd that he'd chosen to live in one of the dry glass-and-metal buildings anchored into a sprawling platform at the bottom of the river, and not near them in the network of underwater caves that doubled as apartments for the mer. But Tharion liked TV. Liked eating food that wasn't soggy at best, cold and wet at worst. He liked sleeping in a warm bed, sprawled over the covers and pillows, and not tucked into a seaweed hammock swinging in the currents. And since living on land wasn't an option, this underwater building had become his best bet.

The computer pinged, and Tharion pivoted back to the screen. His office was in one of the glass-domed bubbles that made up the Blue Court Investigative Unit's headquarters—the River Queen had only allowed their construction because computers had to stay dry.

Tharion himself had been forced to explain that simple fact.

His queen was almighty, beautiful, and wise—and, like so many of the older Vanir, had no idea how modern technology worked. Her daughter, at least, had adapted better. Tharion had been instructed to show her how to use a computer. Which was how he'd wound up here.

Well, not here in this office. But in this place. In his current life.

Tharion skimmed through Sofie Renast's email archive. Evidence of a normal existence: emails with friends about sports or TV or an upcoming party; emails from parents asking that she pick up groceries on her way home from school; emails from her little brother. Emile.

Those were the ones that he combed through the most carefully. Maybe he'd get lucky and there'd be some hint in here about where Sofie was headed.

On and on, Tharion read, keeping an eye on the clock. He had to get in the water soon, but . . . He kept reading. Hunting for any clue or hint of where Sofie and her brother might have gone. He came up empty.

Tharion finished Sofie's inbox, checked the junk folder, and then finally the trash. It was mostly empty. He clicked open her sent folder, and groaned at the tally. But he began reading again. Click after click after click.

His phone chimed with an alert: thirty minutes until he needed to get into the water. He could reach the air lock in five minutes, if he walked fast. He could get through another few emails before then. *Click, click, click.* Tharion's phone chimed again. Ten minutes.

But he'd halted on an email dated three years ago. It was so simple, so nonsensical that it stood out.

Subject: Re: Dusk's Truth

The subject line was weird. But the body of her email was even weirder.

Working on gaining access. Will take time.

That was it.

Tharion scanned downward, toward the original message that Sofie had replied to. It had been sent two weeks before her reply.

From: BansheeFan56

Subject: Dusk's Truth

Have you gotten inside yet? I want to know the full story.

Tharion scratched his head, opened another window, and searched for *Dusk's Truth.*

Nothing. No record of a movie or book or TV show. He did a search on the email system for the sender's name: *BansheeFan56*.

Another half-deleted chain. This one originating from BansheeFan56.

Subject: Project Thurr
Could be useful to you. Read it.

Sofie had replied: *Just did. I think it's a long shot. And the Six will kill me for it.*

He had a good feeling he knew who "the Six" referred to: the Asteri. But when Tharion searched online for *Project Thurr*, he found nothing. Only news reports on archaeological digs or art gallery exhibits featuring the ancient demigod. Interesting.

There was one other email—in the drafts folder.

BansheeFan56 had written: *When you find him, lie low in the place I told you about—where the weary souls find relief from their suffering in Lunathion. It's secure.*

A rendezvous spot? Tharion scanned what Sofie had started to reply, but never sent.

Thank you. I'll try to pass along the info to my

She'd never finished it. There were any number of ways that sentence could have ended. But Sofie must have needed a place where no one would think to look for her and her brother. If Sofie Renast had indeed survived the Hind, she might well have come here, to this very city, with the promise of a safe place to hide.

But this stuff about Project Thurr and Dusk's Truth . . . He tucked those tidbits away for later.

Tharion opened a search field within Declan's program and typed in the sender's address. He started as the result came in.

Danika Fendyr.

Tharion burst from his office, sprinting through the glass corridors that revealed all manner of river life: mer and otters and fish, diving birds and water sprites and the occasional winding sea serpent. He only had three minutes before he had to be in the water.

Thankfully, the hatch into the pressurization chamber was open when he arrived, and Tharion leapt in, slamming the round door behind him before punching the button beside it.

He'd barely sealed the door when water flooded his feet, rushing into the chamber with a sigh. Tharion sighed with it, slumping into the rising water and shucking off his pants, his body tingling as fins replaced skin and bone, his legs fusing, rippling with tiger-striped scales.

He pulled off his shirt, shuddering into the scales that rippled along his arms and halfway up his torso. Talons curled off his fingers as Tharion thrust them into his hair, slicking back the red strands.

Fucking inconvenient.

Tharion glanced at the digital clock above the air lock door. He was free to return to human form now, but he liked to wait a good five minutes. Just to make sure the transformation had been marked by the strange magic that guided the mer. It didn't matter that he could summon water from thin air—the shift only counted if he submerged completely in the currents of wild magic.

Danika Fendyr had known Sofie Renast. Had swapped emails during a six-month window leading up to Danika's death, all relating to something about Dusk's Truth and this Project Thurr, except that one detailing a secure spot.

But had Danika Fendyr known Emile as well? Had Emile been the person Sofie had meant to pass along the safe location info to? It was a stretch, but from what the River Queen had told him, everything Sofie had done before her death had been for her brother. Why wouldn't he be the person she was eager to hide, should she ever get him free from Kavalla? The trouble now was finding them somewhere in this city. *Where the weary souls find relief from their suffering*, apparently. Whatever that meant.

Tharion waited until five minutes had passed, then reached up with a muscled arm to hit the release button beside the air lock door. Water drained out, clearing the chamber, and Tharion remained seated, staring at his fins, waving idly in the air.

He willed the change, and light shimmered along his legs, pain lancing down them as his fin split in two, revealing his naked body.

His pants were soaked, but Tharion didn't particularly care as he shoved his legs back into them. At least he hadn't been wearing shoes. He'd lost countless pairs thanks to close calls like this over the years.

With a groan, he eased to his feet and opened the door once more. He donned one of the navy windbreakers hanging from the wall for warmth, BCIU written in yellow print on the back. Blue Court Investigative Unit. It was technically part of Lunathion's Auxiliary, but the River Queen liked to think of her realm as a separate entity.

He checked his phone as he stalked down the hall toward his office, skimming the field reports that had come in. He went still at one of them. Maybe Ogenas was looking out for him.

A kingfisher shifter had called in a report three hours ago—out in the Nelthian Marshes. A small, abandoned boat. Nothing unusual, but its registration had snagged his eye. It had made berth in Pangera. The rest of the report had Tharion hurrying to his office.

An adolescent-sized life vest with *Bodegraven* written on its back had been found in the boat. No one remained on board, but a scent lingered. Human, male, young.

What were the odds that a life jacket from the same ship Sofie Renast's brother had been on had appeared on a wholly different boat, near the very city the emails between her and Danika had indicated was safe to hide in?

Emile Renast had to have been on that boat. The question was: Did he have reason to suspect that his sister had survived the Hind? Were they currently en route to be reunited? Tharion had a few guesses for where Danika's cryptic instructions might imply—none of them good. He might have no idea what his queen wanted with either Sofie or Emile, enough that she'd wanted the former alive or dead, but he had little choice in following this lead.

He supposed he'd forfeited the right to choices long ago.

Tharion took a wave skimmer up the Istros, aiming for the marshland an hour north of the city. The river cut along the coast here, wending between the swaying, hissing reeds. Along one seemingly random curve, the small skiff had been driven up onto the grasses, and now tilted precariously to one side.

Birds swooped and soared overhead, and eyes monitored him unblinkingly from the grasses as he slowed the wave skimmer to examine the boat.

He shuddered. The river beasts nested in these marshes. Even Tharion had been careful about what watery paths he took through the grasses. The sobeks might know better than to fuck with the mer, but a female beast would go down snapping for her young.

A thirteen-year-old boy, however gifted, would be a rich dessert.

Tharion used his water magic to guide him right up to the boat, then hopped aboard. Empty cans of food and bottles of water clanked against each other with the impact of his landing. A sweep of the sleeping area below revealed a human, male scent, along with blankets and more food.

Small, muddy footprints marked the deck near the steering wheel. A child had indeed been on this boat. Had that child sailed from Pangera all the way here alone? Pity and dread stirred in Tharion's gut at all the abandoned trash.

He turned on the engine and discovered plenty of fuel— indicating that the boat hadn't run out of firstlight and been ditched here. So this must have been an intentional landing. Which suggested that Sofie must have passed that information about the meeting spot along to Emile after all. But if he'd discarded the boat here, in the heart of sobek territory . . . Tharion rubbed his jaw.

He made a slow circle of the reeds around the boat. Listening, scenting. And—fuck. Human blood. He braced himself for the worst as he approached a red-splattered section of reeds.

His relief was short-lived. The smell was adult, but . . . that was an arm. Ripped away from the body, which must have been dragged off. Trauma to the biceps in line with a sobek bite.

Fighting his roiling stomach, Tharion crept closer. Scented it again.

It was fresher than the boy's scent on the boat by a day or so. And maybe it was a coincidence that there was a human arm here, but Tharion knew the dark gray of the torn sleeve that remained on the arm. The patch of the golden sun bracketed by a gun and a blade still half-visible near the bite.

The Ophion insignia. And the additional red sinking sun above it . . . Their elite Lightfall squadron, led by Pippa Spetsos.

Carefully, as silently as he could, Tharion moved through the reeds, praying he didn't stumble into any sobek nests. The human scents were more numerous here. Several males and a female, all adult. All coming from inland—not the water. Ogenas, had Pippa Spetsos herself led the unit here to get the boy? They must have tried to creep up on the boat from the reeds. And apparently one of them had paid the ultimate price.

Ophion had sent their best unit here, despite their numerous recent losses. They needed Lightfall in Pangera—and yet they were expending resources on this hunt. So they likely weren't seeking the boy out of the goodness of their hearts. Had Emile abandoned the boat here not because Sofie had told him to, but because he'd sensed someone on his tail? Had he fled to this city not only to find his sister at the arranged spot, but also to get free of the rebels?

Tharion retraced his steps back to the boat, scanning it again. He slung himself belowdecks, pulling aside blankets and garbage, skimming, scanning—

There. A marked-up map of the Valbaran coast. With these marshes circled. These marshes . . . and one other marking. Tharion winced. If Emile Renast had fled on foot from here to Crescent City . . .

He pulled out his phone and dialed one of his officers. Ordered them to get to the marshes. To start at the boat and work their way by land toward the city. And bring guns—not just for the beasts in the reeds, but for the rebels who might be following the kid.

And if they found Emile . . . He ordered the officer to track him for a while. See who he met up with. Who the boy might lead them to.

If the boy had even walked out of these marshes alive.

12

Hunt stretched out his legs, adjusting his wings so he didn't crush them between his back and the wooden bench. Bryce sat beside him, pistachio ice cream melting down the sides of her cone, and Hunt tried not to stare as she licked away each dribbling green droplet.

Was this punishment for his fight with Pollux? To sit here and watch this?

Hunt focused instead on the scooter she'd apparently ridden at breakneck speed to the Comitium. She'd walked with him when they left, though, pushing it beside her all the way to the park. He cleared his throat and asked, "Something up with your bike?"

Bryce frowned. "It was making a weird noise earlier. Didn't seem wise to get back on it." She arched a brow. "Want to be a gentleman and carry it home for me?"

"I'd rather carry *you*, but sure." The scooter would be heavy, but nothing he couldn't deal with. He remembered his own ice cream—coffee—in time to lick away the melted bits. He tried not to note the way her eyes tracked each movement of his tongue. "What kind of noise was it making?"

"A kind of rasping sputter whenever I idled." She twisted to where her beloved bike leaned against a banner-adorned lamp-post. "It's gonna have to go into the shop, poor thing."

Hunt chuckled. "I can bring it up to the roof and check it out."

"So romantic. When do the wedding invites go out for you two?"

He laughed again. "I'm shocked Randall didn't make you learn how to fix your own bike."

"Oh, he tried. But I was a legal adult by that point and didn't have to listen." She glanced at him sidelong. "Seriously, though—you know how to fix a bike?"

Hunt's amusement slipped a notch. "Yeah. I, ah . . . know how to fix a lot of machines."

"Does your lightning give you an affinity for knowing how they work, or something?"

"Yeah." Hunt trained his gaze upon the Istros. The relentless sun was finally setting, casting the river in reds and golds and oranges. Far below the surface, little lights glowed, all that showed of the mighty, sprawling court beneath the water. He said quietly, "Sandriel took advantage of that—she often had me take apart Ophion's mech-suits after battles, so I could learn how they worked and then sabotage them before discreetly sending the machines back to the front for the rebels to use unwittingly." He couldn't look at her, especially when she remained silent as he added, almost confessing, "I learned a lot about how machines work. How to make them *not* work. Especially at key moments. A lot of people likely died because of that. Because of me."

He'd tried convincing himself that what he did was justified, that the suits themselves were monstrous: fifteen feet high and crafted of titanium, they were essentially exoskeletal armor that the human standing within could pilot as easily as moving their own body. Armed with seven-foot-long swords—some of them charged with firstlight—and massive guns, they could go head-to-maw with a wolf shifter and walk away intact. They were the human army's most valuable asset—and only way of withstanding a Vanir attack.

Sandriel ordering him to take apart and mess with the suits had nothing to do with that, though. It had been about pure cruelty and sick amusement—stealing the suits, sabotaging them, and returning them with the humans none the wiser. It was about watching with glee as the pilots squared off against Vanir forces, only to find that their mech-suits failed them.

Bryce laid a hand on his knee. "I'm sorry she made you do that, Hunt."

"So am I," Hunt said, exhaling deeply, as if it could somehow cleanse his soul.

Bryce seemed to sense his need to shift the subject, because she suddenly asked, "What the Hel are we going to do about Pollux and Baxian?" She threw him a wry look, drawing him out of the past. "Aside from pummeling them into tenderized meat."

Hunt snorted, silently thanking Urd for bringing Bryce into his life. "We can only hope Celestina keeps them in line."

"You don't sound so certain."

"I spoke to her for five minutes before Pollux came in. It wasn't enough to make a judgment."

"Isaiah and Naomi seem to like her."

"You talked to them?"

"On the way in. They're . . . concerned about you."

Hunt growled. "They should be concerned about those two psychopaths living here."

"Hunt."

The sun lit her eyes to a gold so brilliant it knocked the breath from him. She said, "I know your history with Pollux. I understand why you reacted this way. But it can't happen again."

"I know." He licked his ice cream again. "The Asteri sent him here for a reason. Probably to rile me like this."

"They told us to lie low. Why goad you out of doing so?"

"Maybe they changed their minds and want a public reason to arrest us."

"We killed two Archangels. They don't need any further charges to sign our death sentences."

"Maybe they do. Maybe they worry we *could* get away with it if it went to trial. And a public trial would mean admitting our roles in Micah's and Sandriel's deaths."

"I think the world could easily believe you killed an Archangel. But a widdle nobody half-human like me? *That's* the thing they don't want leaking out."

"I guess. But . . . I just have a hard time believing any of this.

That Pollux and Baxian being here isn't a sign of shit about to go down. That Celestina might actually be a decent person. I've got more than two hundred years of history telling me to be wary. I can't deprogram myself." Hunt shut his eyes.

A moment later, soft fingers tangled in his hair, idly brushing the strands. He nearly purred, but kept perfectly still as Bryce said, "We'll keep our guards up. But I think . . . I think we might need to start believing in our good luck."

"Ithan Holstrom's arrival is the exact opposite of that."

Bryce nudged him with a shoulder. "He's not so bad."

He cracked open an eye. "You've come around quickly on him."

"I don't have time to hold grudges."

"You're immortal now. I'd say you do."

She opened her mouth, but a bland male voice echoed through the park: *The Gates will be closing in ten minutes. Anyone not in line will not be granted access.*

She scowled. "I could have lived without them using the Gates to broadcast announcements all day."

"You're the one to blame for it, you know," he said, mouth kicking up at one corner.

Bryce sighed, but didn't argue.

It was true. Since she'd used the crystal Gates to contact Danika, it had awoken public interest in them, and revived awareness that they could be used to speak throughout the city. They were now mostly used to make announcements, ranging from the opening and closing times at the tourist sites to the occasional recording of an imperial announcement from Rigelus himself. Hunt hated those the most. *This is Rigelus, Bright Hand of the Asteri. We honor the fallen dead in beautiful Lunathion, and thank those who fought for their service.*

And we watch all of them like hawks, Hunt always thought when he heard the droning voice that disguised the ancient being within the teenage Fae body.

The Gate announcer fell quiet again, the gentle lapping of the Istros and whispering palm trees overhead filling the air once more.

Bryce's gaze drifted across the river, to the mists swirling on its opposite shore. She smiled sadly. "Do you think Lehabah is over there?"

"I hope so." He'd never stop being grateful for what the fire sprite had done.

"I miss her," she said quietly.

Hunt slid an arm around her, tucking her into his side. Savoring her warmth and offering his own. "Me too."

Bryce leaned her head against his shoulder. "I know Pollux is a monster; and you have every reason in the world to want to kill him. But please don't do anything to make the Governor punish you. I couldn't . . ." Her voice caught, and Hunt's chest strained with it. "Watching Micah cut off your wings . . . I can't see that again, Hunt. Or any other horror she might invent for you."

He ran a hand over her silken hair. "I shouldn't have lost control like that. I'm sorry."

"You don't need to apologize. Not for this. Just . . . be cautious."

"I will."

She ate more of her ice cream, but didn't move. So Hunt did the same, careful not to drip into her hair.

When they'd eaten it all, when the sun was near-vanished and the first stars had appeared, Bryce straightened. "We should go home. Ithan and Syrinx need dinner."

"I'd suggest not telling Holstrom that you group him with your pet."

Bryce chuckled, pulling away, and it was all Hunt could do to not reach for her.

He'd decided to Hel with it all when Bryce stiffened, her attention fixed on something beyond his wings. Hunt whirled, hand going to the knife at his thigh.

He swore. This was not an opponent he could fight against. No one could.

"Let's go," Hunt murmured, folding a wing around her as the black boat neared the quay. A Reaper stood atop it. Clothed and veiled in billowing black that hid all indication of whether the Reaper was male or female, old or young. Such things did not matter to Reapers.

Hunt's blood chilled to ice as the oarless, rudderless boat drifted right to the quay, utterly at odds with the elegant banners and flowers adorning every part of this city. The boat halted as if invisible hands tied it to the concrete walkway.

The Reaper stepped out, moving so fluidly it was as if it walked on air. Bryce trembled beside him. The city around them had gone quiet. Even the insects had ceased their humming. No wind stirred the palms lining the quay. The banners hanging from the lamp-posts had ceased their flapping. The ornate flower wreaths seemed to wither and brown.

But a phantom breeze fluttered the Reaper's robes and trailing veil as it aimed for the small park beyond the quay and the streets past that. It did not look their way, did not halt.

Reapers did not need to halt for anything, not even death. The Vanir might call themselves immortal, but they could die from trauma or sickness. Even the Asteri were killable. The Reapers, however . . .

You could not kill what was already dead. The Reaper drifted by, silence rippling in its wake, and vanished into the city.

Bryce braced her hands on her knees. "Ugh, ugh, *ughhh*."

"My sentiments exactly," Hunt murmured. Reapers dwelled on every eternal isle in the world: the Bone Quarter here, the Cata-combs in the Eternal City, the Summerlands in Avallen . . . Each of the sacred, sleeping domains guarded by a fierce monarch. Hunt had never met the Under-King of Lunathion—and hoped he never would.

He had as little as possible to do with the Under-King's Reap-ers, too. Half-lifes, people called them. Humans and Vanir who had once been alive, who had faced death and offered their souls to the Under-King as his private guards and servants instead. The cost: to live forever, unaging and unkillable, but never again to be able to sleep, eat, fuck. Vanir did not mess with them.

"Let's go," Bryce said, shaking off her shiver. "I need more ice cream."

Hunt chuckled. "Fair enough." He was about to turn them from the river when the roar of a wave skimmer's engine sounded. He turned toward it on training and instinct, and halted when he marked the red-haired male atop it. The muscled arm that waved toward them. Not a friendly wave, but a frantic one.

"Tharion?" Bryce asked, seeing the direction of Hunt's focus as the mer male gunned for them, leaving roiling waves in his wake.

It was the work of a moment to reach them, and Tharion cut the engine and drifted for the quay, keeping well away from the black boat tied nearby.

"Where the fuck have *you* been this summer?" Hunt asked, crossing his arms.

But Tharion said breathlessly to Bryce, "We need to talk."

"How did you even find us?" Bryce asked as they rode the elevator in her apartment building minutes later.

"Spy-master, remember?" Tharion grinned. "I've got eyes everywhere." He followed Bryce and Hunt into the apartment.

Bryce's attention immediately shot to Ithan—who was exactly where she'd left him that morning: on the couch, Syrinx sprawled across his lap. His face had healed even more, the raw scar nearly vanished.

Ithan straightened as Tharion entered. "Relax," she said, and didn't spare the wolf another glance as Hunt and Tharion aimed for the couch.

Bryce let out a warning hiss at the mer's still-wet clothes.

Hunt rolled his eyes and sat at the dining table instead. "This is why people shouldn't get white couches," the angel grumbled, and Bryce scowled.

"Then *you* can clean off the river water and dirt," she shot back.

"That's what insta-clean spells are for," Hunt replied smoothly. Bryce scowled.

"Domestic bliss, I see," Tharion said.

Bryce snickered, but Ithan asked from the couch, "Who are you?"

Tharion flashed him a smile. "None of your business."

But Ithan sniffed. "Mer. Oh—yeah, I know you. Captain Whatever."

"Ketos," Tharion muttered.

Hunt tipped his head to Ithan. "You've landed a grave blow to Captain Whatever's ego, Holstrom."

"The gravest blow comes from my dearest friends failing to extol my many qualities when I'm challenged," Tharion said, pouting.

"Dearest friends?" Hunt asked, raising a brow.

"Prettiest friends," Tharion said, blowing a kiss to Bryce.

Bryce laughed and twisted away, putting her phone on silent before sending off a message to Ruhn. *Get over here ASAP.*

He replied instantly. *What's wrong?*

NOW.

Whatever it was that Tharion wanted with such urgency, Ruhn should know about it, too. She wanted him to know about it. Which was . . . weird. Yet nice.

Bryce slid her phone into her back pocket as Tharion gestured toward the neon-pink lace bra dangling off the folding door to the laundry machines. "Hot," the mer said.

"Don't get her started," Hunt muttered.

Bryce glared at him, but said to Tharion, "It's been a while." The mer was as attractive as she remembered. Perhaps more so, now that he was slightly disheveled and muddy.

"We talking about your sex life, or the time since I've seen you?" Tharion asked, glancing between her and Hunt. Hunt glowered, but Bryce smiled fiendishly. Tharion went on, heedless of Hunt's ire, "It's been a busy summer." He jumped onto a stool at the kitchen counter and patted the one beside him. "Sit, Legs. Let's have a chat."

Bryce plopped next to him, hooking her feet on the bar below.

Tharion asked, suddenly serious, "Did Danika ever talk about someone named Sofie?" Ithan grunted in surprise.

Bryce's mouth scrunched to the side. "Sofie who?"

Before she could ask more, Hunt demanded, "What the fuck is this about?"

Tharion said smoothly, "Just updating some old files."

Bryce drummed her fingers on the marble counter. "On Danika?"

Tharion shrugged. "Glamorous as my life might seem, Legs, there's a lot of grunt work behind the scenes." He winked. "Though not the sort of grunting I'd like to do with you, of course."

"Don't try to distract me with flirting," Bryce said. "Why are you asking about Danika? And who the Hel is Sofie?"

Tharion sighed at the ceiling. "There's a cold case I'm working on, and Danika—"

"Don't lie to her, Tharion," Hunt growled. Lightning danced along his wings.

A thrill shot through Bryce at it—not only the power, but knowing he had her back. She said to Tharion, "I'm not telling you shit until you give me more information." She jabbed a thumb toward Ithan. "And neither is he, so don't even ask."

Ithan only smiled slowly at the mer, as if daring him to.

Tharion sized them all up. To his credit, he didn't back down. A muscle ticked in his cheek, though. As if he waged some inner debate. Then the mer captain said, "I, ah . . . I was assigned to look into a human woman, Sofie Renast. She was a rebel who was captured by the Hind two weeks ago. But Sofie was no ordinary human, and neither was her younger brother—Emile. Both he and Sofie pass as human, yet they possess full thunderbird powers."

Bryce blew out a breath. Well, she hadn't been expecting *that*.

Hunt said, "I thought thunderbirds had been hunted to extinction by the Asteri." *Too dangerous and volatile to be allowed to live* was the history they'd been spoon-fed at school. *A grave threat to the empire.* "They're little more than myths now."

All true. Bryce remembered a Starlight Fancy horse called Thunderbird: a blue-and-white unicorn-pegasus who could wield all types of energy. She'd never gotten her hands on one, though she'd yearned to.

But Tharion went on, "Well, somehow, somewhere, one survived. And bred. Emile was captured three years ago and sent to the Kavalla death camp. His captors were unaware of what they'd grabbed, and he wisely kept his gifts hidden. Sofie went into Kavalla and freed him. But from what I was told, Sofie was caught by the Hind before she reached safety. Emile got away—only to run from Ophion as well. It seems like he came this way, but various parties are still *very* interested in the powers he possesses. And Sofie, too, if she survived."

"No one survives the Hind," Hunt said darkly.

"Yeah, I know. But the chains attached to the lead blocks at the bottom of the ocean were empty. Unlocked. Seems like Sofie made it. Or someone snatched her corpse."

Bryce frowned. "And the River Queen wants both the kid and Sofie? Why? And what does this have to do with Danika?"

"I don't know what my queen's ultimate goal is. All I know is that she's very keen on finding Sofie, alive or dead, and equally keen on attaining Emile. But despite what that suggests, she's not affiliated with Ophion in any way." Tharion rubbed at his jaw. "In the process of trying to figure out this clusterfuck, I found some emails between Sofie and Danika talking about a safe place in this city for Sofie to lie low should she ever need it."

"That's not possible," Ithan said.

Hunt rose from the table and stalked to Bryce's side. His power shimmered up her body, electrifying her very blood at his nearness. "Is the River Queen insane? Are *you* insane? Searching for rebels and not turning them in is a one-way ticket to crucifixion."

Tharion held his stare. "I don't really have a choice here. Orders are orders." He nodded to them. "Clearly you guys know nothing about this. Do me a favor and don't mention it to anyone, okay?" The mer stood and turned toward the door.

Bryce hopped off her stool and stepped into his path. "Oh, I don't think so." She let a fraction of her starlight shine around her. "You don't get to tell me that Danika was in contact with a known rebel and then waltz out of here."

Tharion chuckled, cold frosting his eyes. "Yeah, I do, Legs." He took a blatantly challenging step toward her.

Bryce held her ground. Was surprised and delighted that Hunt let her fight this battle without interfering. "Do you even care that this oh-so-powerful thunderbird is a kid? Who survived a fucking *death camp*? And is now scared and alone?"

Tharion blinked, and she could have strangled him.

"I know this is a dick thing to say," Ithan added, "but if the kid's got that power, why didn't he use it to get out of Kavalla himself?"

"Maybe he doesn't know how to use it yet," Tharion mused. "Maybe he was too weak or tired. I don't know. But I'll see you guys later." He made to step past Bryce.

She blocked him again. "Emile aside, Danika wasn't a rebel, and she didn't know anyone named Sofie Renast."

Ithan said, "I agree."

Tharion said firmly, "The email was linked to her. And the email address was *BansheeFan56*—Danika was clearly a Banshees fan. Skim through any of her old social media profiles and there are ten thousand references to her love of that band."

Solas, how many Banshees shirts and posters had Danika amassed over the years? Bryce had lost count.

Bryce tapped her foot, her blood at a steady simmer. Hadn't Philip Briggs said something similar when she and Hunt had interrogated the former leader of the Keres rebel sect in his prison cell? That Danika was a rebel sympathizer? "What did the emails say?"

Tharion kept his mouth shut.

Bryce bristled. *"What did the emails say?"*

Tharion snapped, a rare show of temper apparently getting the better of him, "Does Dusk's Truth mean anything to you? What about Project Thurr?" At her blank look, and Ithan's, the mer said, "I thought so."

Bryce clenched her jaw hard enough to hurt. After this spring, she'd realized she hadn't known as much about Danika as she'd believed, but to add even more to that list . . . She tried not to let it sting.

Tharion took another challenging step toward the door. But Bryce said, "You can't drop all that information and expect me not to do anything. Not to go looking for this kid."

Tharion arched a brow. "So softhearted. But stay out of it, Legs."

"No way," Bryce countered.

Hunt cut in, "Bryce. We were given an order by the Asteri—by Rigelus himself—to lie low."

"Then obey them," Tharion said.

Bryce glared at the mer, then at Hunt. But Hunt said, storms in his eyes, "The Asteri will slaughter us, along with your entire family, if word reaches them that you're involved with rebel activity in any way. Even if it's just helping to find a lost kid."

Bryce opened her mouth, but Hunt pushed, "We won't get a trial, Bryce. Only an execution."

Tharion crossed his arms. "Exactly. So, again: stay out of it, and I'll be on my way."

Before Bryce could snap her reply, the front door banged open, and Ruhn filled the doorway. "What the— Oh. Hey, Tharion."

"You invited him?" Tharion accused Bryce.

Bryce stayed silent, holding her ground.

"What's going on?" Ruhn asked, glancing to Hunt and Ithan. Ruhn startled at the sight of the wolf. "And what's *he* doing here?"

"Ithan's a free agent right now, so he's staying with us," Bryce said, and at Ruhn's puzzled look, added, "I'll fill you in later."

Ruhn asked, "Why's your heart racing?"

Bryce peered at her chest, half expecting her scar to be glowing. Mercifully, it lay dormant. "Well, apparently Tharion thinks Danika was involved with the rebels."

Ruhn gaped.

"Thanks, Bryce," Tharion muttered.

Bryce threw him a saccharine smile and explained Tharion's investigation to Ruhn.

"Well?" Ruhn asked when she'd finished, his face drained of color. "*Was* Danika a rebel?"

"No!" Bryce splayed her arms. "Solas, she was more interested in what junk food we had in our apartment."

"That's not all she was interested in," Ruhn corrected. "She stole the Horn and hid it from you. Hid it *on* you. And all that shit with Briggs and the synth . . ."

"Okay, fine. But the rebel stuff . . . She never even *talked* about the war."

"She would have known it'd endanger you," Tharion suggested.

Hunt said to Tharion, "And you're cool with being press-ganged into working on this shit?" His face remained paler than usual. Tharion just crossed his long, muscular arms. Hunt went on, voice lowering, "It won't end well, Tharion. Trust me on that. You're tangling in some dangerous shit."

Bryce avoided looking at the branded-out tattoo on Hunt's wrist.

Tharion's throat bobbed. "I'm sorry to have even come here. I know how you feel about this stuff, Athalar."

"You really think there's a chance Sofie is alive?" Ruhn asked.

"Yes," Tharion said.

"If she survived the Hind," Hunt said, "and the Hind hears about it, she'll come running."

"The Hind might already be headed this way," Tharion said thickly. "Regardless of Sofie, Emile and his powers remain a prize. Or something to be wiped out once and for all." He dragged his long fingers through his dark red hair. "I know I'm dropping a bomb on you guys." He winced at his unfortunate word choice, no doubt remembering what had happened last spring. "But I want to find this kid before anyone else."

"And do what with him?" Bryce asked. "Hand him over to your queen?"

"He'd be safe Beneath, Legs. It'd take a damn long while even for the Asteri to find him—and kill him."

"So he'd be used by your queen like some kind of weaponized battery instead? Like Hel am I going to let you do that."

"Again, I don't know what she wants with Emile. But she wouldn't harm him. And you'd be wise to keep out of her path."

Ithan cut in before Bryce could start spitting venom, "You really think the kid is coming here? That the Hind will follow?"

Hunt rubbed his jaw. "The 33rd hasn't heard anything about the Hind coming over. Or Ophion being in the area."

"Neither has the Aux," Ruhn confirmed.

"Well, unless one of the marsh sobeks swam all the way across the Haldren to take a bite out of an Ophion soldier, I can't think of any other reason why I found dismembered body parts of one here," Tharion said.

"I don't even know where to begin with that," Hunt said.

"Just trust me," Tharion said, "Ophion is on its way, if not already here. So I need to know as much as possible, and as quickly as possible. Find Emile, and we potentially find Sofie."

"And gain a nice child soldier, right?" Bryce said tightly.

Tharion turned pleading eyes on her. "Either the River Queen puts me in charge of hunting for them, or she assigns someone else, possibly someone less . . . independently minded. I'd rather it be me who finds Emile."

Ithan burst out, "Can we discuss that you guys are talking about *rebels* in this city? About *Danika* potentially being a rebel?" He snarled. "That's a serious fucking claim."

"Sofie and Danika exchanged a number of intentionally vague emails," Tharion said. "Ones that included an allusion to a safe hiding place here in Lunathion. A place *where the weary souls find relief from their suffering.* I'm guessing the Bone Quarter, though I'm not sure even Danika would be so reckless as to send them there. But anyway, it's not a claim. It's a fact."

Ithan shook his head, but it was Hunt who said, "This is a lethal game, Tharion. One I'd rather not play again." Bryce could have sworn his hands shook slightly. This had to be dragging up the worst of his memories and fears—he'd *been* a rebel, once. It had won him two hundred years of servitude.

And today had been long and weird and she hadn't even told Hunt about Cormac's visit at lunch.

But to let this boy be hunted by so many people . . . She couldn't sit by. Not for an instant. So Bryce said, "I can ask Fury tomorrow if she knows anything about Danika and Sofie. Maybe she can give some insight into where Danika might have suggested hiding."

"Ask her right now," Tharion said with unusual seriousness.

"It's Wednesday night. She and Juniper always have date night."

It was half a lie, and Hunt must have known it was for his sake, because his wing gently brushed over her shoulder.

But Tharion ordered, "Then interrupt it."

"Don't you know *anything* about Fury Axtar?" Bryce waved a hand. "I'll call her tomorrow morning. She's always in a better mood after she and June get it on."

Tharion glanced between her and Hunt, then to Ruhn and Ithan, both silently watching. The mer reached into his jacket and pulled out a folded stack of papers with a resigned sigh. "Here's a sampling of the emails," he said, handing them to Bryce, and aimed for the door again. He paused near Syrinx, then knelt down and petted his head, his thick neck. He straightened Syrinx's collar and earned a lick of thanks. Tharion's mouth curled up at the corners as he stood. "Cool pet." He opened the front door. "Don't put anything in writing. I'll be back around lunch tomorrow."

As soon as the mer shut the door, Hunt said to Bryce, "Getting involved with this is a bad idea."

Ruhn said, "I agree."

Bryce only clutched the papers tighter and turned to Ithan. "This is the part where you say you agree, too."

Ithan frowned deeply. "I can ignore the shit about Danika and Ophion, but there's a kid out there on the run. Who probably has nothing to do with Ophion and needs help."

"*Thank you,*" Bryce said, whirling on Hunt. "See?"

"It's Tharion's business. Leave it alone, Bryce," Hunt warned. "I don't even know why you had to ask about any of this."

"I don't know why you *wouldn't* ask," Bryce challenged.

Hunt pushed, "Is this really about finding the kid, or is it about learning something new about Danika?"

"Can't it be both?"

Hunt slowly shook his head.

Ruhn said, "Let's think this through, Bryce, before deciding to act. And maybe burn those emails."

"I've already decided," she announced. "I'm going to find Emile."

"And do what with him?" Hunt asked. "If the Asteri want him, you'd be harboring a rebel."

Bryce couldn't stop the light from shimmering around her. "He's thirteen years old. He's not a rebel. The rebels just *want* him to be."

Hunt said quietly, "I saw kids his age walk onto battlefields, Bryce."

Ruhn nodded solemnly. "Ophion doesn't turn away fighters based on their age."

Ithan said, "That's despicable."

"I'm not saying it isn't," Hunt countered. "But the Asteri won't care if he's thirteen or thirty, if he's a true rebel or not. You stand in their way, and they'll punish you."

Bryce opened her mouth, but—a muscle flickered in his cheek, making the bruise there all the more noticeable. Guilt punched through her, warring with her ire. "I'll think about it," she conceded, and stalked for her bedroom.

She needed a breather before she said or did more than she meant to. A moment to process the information she'd gotten out of Tharion. She hadn't put any stock in Briggs's claim about Danika and the rebels when he'd taunted her with it—he'd been trying to get at her in any way possible. But it seemed she'd been wrong.

She scoured her memory for any detail as she washed away her makeup, then brushed her hair. Male voices rumbled from the other side of the door, but Bryce ignored them, changing into her pajamas. Her stomach gurgled.

Was Emile hungry? He was a kid—alone in the world, having suffered in one of those gods-forsaken camps, no family left. He had to be terrified. Traumatized.

She hoped Sofie was alive. Not for any intel or amazing powers, but so Emile had someone left. Family who loved him for *him* and not for being some all-powerful chosen one whose people had long ago been hunted to extinction.

Bryce frowned in the mirror. Then at the stack of papers Tharion had handed her. The emails between Sofie and Danika—and a few between Sofie and Emile.

The former were exactly as Tharion had claimed. Vague mentions of things.

But Sofie and Emile's emails . . .

I had to leave your sunball game before the end, Sofie had written in one exchange more than three years ago, *but Mom told me you guys won! Congrats—you were amazing out there!*

Emile had replied, *I was ok. Missed 2 shots.*

Sofie had written back, at three in the morning—as if she'd been up late studying or partying—*I once had a game when I missed* ten *shots! So you're doing way better than me. :)*

The next morning, Emile had said, *Thanks, sis. Miss u.*

Bryce swallowed hard. Such an ordinary exchange—proof of a normal, decent life.

What had happened to them? How had he wound up in Kavalla? Part of her didn't want to know, and yet . . . She read the emails again. The loving, casual exchange between siblings.

Did any of the many people searching for Emile want to actually help him? Not use him, but just . . . protect him? Maybe he and Sofie would find each other at that rendezvous spot Danika had mentioned. Maybe they'd get lucky, and no one would ever find them.

Danika had always helped those who needed it. Bryce included.

And during the spring attack, when Bryce had run to Asphodel Meadows . . . it was the same feeling creeping over her now. The boy needed help. She wouldn't walk away from it. *Couldn't* walk away from it.

But how did Danika factor in to all of this? She needed to know.

Her stomach protested again. Right—dinner. With a silent prayer to Cthona to keep Emile safe, Bryce emerged from the bedroom and said, "I'm ordering pizza."

Ruhn said, "I'm in," as if he'd been invited, but Bryce glanced at the shut door to Hunt's bedroom.

If *she* needed a moment, he'd sure as Hel need a lot longer.

Hunt turned on the shower with a shaking hand. The blast and splatter of the water provided much-needed white noise, a quieting barrier against the world beyond his bathroom. He'd muttered something about needing a shower and walked in here, not caring what Danaan and Holstrom thought.

Hunt peeled out of his battle-suit, dimly aware of the bruises along his ribs and his face, the brawl with Pollux almost forgotten.

He couldn't stop shaking, couldn't stop the surge of acid through his veins that made every breath torturous.

Fucking Tharion. That stupid, arrogant asshole. Dragging them—dragging *Bryce*—into this. The River Queen might have no association with Ophion, but Emile was a rebel's brother. Danika had possibly been a rebel herself. It brought them far too close to Ophion's orbit.

Of course Bryce wouldn't have been able to drop it once she'd heard. He knew it was irrational to be pissed at her about it, because part of why he adored her was that she was the kind of person who *would* want to help, but . . . fucking Hel.

Hunt sucked in a breath, stepping into the now-warm stream, and clenched his jaw against the rising thunder in his blood and the memories that came with it.

Those strategy meetings in Shahar's war tent; the bloody, screaming chaos of battle; his roar as Shahar died, a piece of his heart dying with her; the bolt of unrelenting pain as his wings were sawed off tendon by tendon—

Hunt sucked in another breath, wings twitching, as if in an echo of that pain.

He couldn't let it happen again. If all of it had been for Bryce, to get here—then it had happened so that he'd know when to walk away, and keep her safe.

But he hadn't been able to find those words. Hunt focused on his breathing, on the sensation of his feet against the slick tiles, the dribble of water down his wings.

And couldn't help but think that warm water felt an awful lot like blood.

Thirty minutes later, they sat around the dining table, four boxes of pizza stacked before them.

"Carnivore's Delight," Bryce said with forced cheer to Hunt, sliding the meat-on-meat-on-meat pizza toward him. He offered a smile, but it didn't quite reach his eyes. She didn't ask about that haunted gleam, though. Not with Ruhn and Ithan here. Not when Hunt had already made it pretty clear what was going through his head.

They'd undoubtedly have it out the moment they were alone.

"Carnivore's Delight with extra sausage," she said to Ithan, winking as she handed over the box. She could have sworn Ithan blushed. "And pepperoni with grilled onions," she said to Ruhn.

"What'd you get?" her brother asked. An attempt at normalcy after Tharion's visit.

Hunt and Ithan said at the same time, "Sausage and onion with extra cheese."

Bryce laughed. "I don't know whether to be impressed or disturbed."

But Ithan and Hunt didn't smile. She caught Ruhn's glance from across the table, and her brother said into her mind, *Ignoring all the shit with Tharion and Emile, it's super fucking weird that Holstrom's here.*

She started on her pizza and sighed at the combination of meat and cheese and slightly sweet sauce. *I think it's super weird for him, too.*

Ruhn bit into his slice. *Honestly, don't flip the Hel out, but you're technically a Starborn Princess. And you're now harboring an exiled wolf. I hate this political crap, but . . . I wouldn't put it past Sabine to see this as an affront. The wolves are technically our allies.*

Bryce sipped from her beer. *It's not like he has any family left.* Her heart ached. *Believe me, he is fucking* miserable *that he has nowhere else to go.*

I can take him in. Her brother spoke with utter sincerity.

Isn't that the same political bullshit?

I can say that I'm hiring him to work for the Fae side of the Aux. Claim it's for a top secret investigation, which I suppose this stuff with Danika and Sofie and Emile is. Sabine can't get around that.

All right. But . . . give him a few days. I don't want him to think I'm kicking him out.

Why not? He was a dick to you.

There were five years before that when we were close.

So? He was a dick to you when you needed him most.

And I shut him out when he needed me *most.*

Bryce blinked, finding Hunt and Ithan watching her and Ruhn. The angel drawled, no hint of his previous haunted discomfort, "Some might consider it rude to have a silent conversation in front of other people."

Ithan raised his hand in agreement. How he'd figured out what was going on, she could only attribute to his keen wolf's abilities. Or his athlete's skill at reading opponents.

Bryce stuck out her tongue. "Sorry you're not magical, special Fae like us."

"Here we go," Hunt said, diving into his slice. "I was waiting for this day to come."

"What day?" Ithan swigged from his beer.

Hunt smirked. "When Bryce realizes how truly obnoxious being a princess allows her to be."

Bryce flipped him off. "If I have to suffer through the title, then you have to suffer through the effects."

Hunt opened his mouth, but Ithan said, "I heard you had your Ordeal that day this spring. Congrats?"

Bryce went still. "Yeah. Uh, thanks." She didn't want to think about it—the nøkk, Syrinx nearly drowning, the tank . . . Syrinx rubbed against her ankles, as if sensing her distress. And Hunt, also reading it, said to Ruhn, "You had your Ordeal in Avallen, right? And our new friend Cormac was there?"

Before Ruhn could answer, Flynn and Dec strode into the apartment with a key Bryce definitely hadn't authorized. She whipped her head to Ruhn. "You gave them fingerprint access and copies of my keys?"

Flynn slid into the chair beside hers and pulled her pizza toward himself. "We took Ruhn's fingerprints when he was passed out during the Summer Solstice, as a way into the system. Then Dec added ours alongside them."

Declan dropped into the chair beside Ruhn, taking one of her brother's slices and a beer from the bucket in the center of the table. "We made copies of the physical keys before he noticed they were gone."

"You're really making me look good, you two," Ruhn grumbled.

Bryce shoved out a hand. "I'm changing my fingerprint system to something more secure. Give me that key."

Flynn only slid it into his pocket. "Come get it, babycakes."

Hunt shot the Fae lord a glare, and Declan snickered. "Careful, Flynn," Dec warned.

Ithan snorted, and the two males eyed him up. Of course they'd already noticed him—they were trained warriors—but they hadn't yet deigned to acknowledge him.

Flynn flashed a charming smile full of teeth. "Hi, pup."

Ithan's fingers tightened into fists at the term. "Hey."

Declan gave a mirror grin to Flynn's. "Bryce needed a new pet?"

"Okay, okay," Bryce cut in. "Let's just say that we made a thousand dog jokes about Ithan, and he made a thousand Fae asshole jokes about you two idiots, and we now all thoroughly hate each other, but we can be adults and eat our food."

"I second that." Hunt dug into his third slice, using his other hand to clink beers with Bryce.

Flynn grinned again. "I thought I heard you ask Ruhn about his Ordeal. It was our Ordeal, too, you know."

"I know," Bryce said, flicking her hair over her shoulder. "But he won the prize sword, didn't he?"

"Ouch." Flynn clutched his chest.

"Cold, B," Declan said.

Ruhn chuckled and leaned back in his seat, finishing off his beer before he said, "I was twenty-seven. My—our father sent me to Avallen to . . . check out the ladies."

"There was a Fae female from a powerful family who the Autumn King wanted Ruhn to marry," Flynn explained. "Unfortunately, Cormac wanted to marry her, too. Neither married her in the end, of course."

Bryce groaned. "Please tell me all this tension between you two isn't over a girl."

"Only partially," Declan said. "It's also because Cormac and his twin cousins tried to kill us. Cormac literally put a sword through my gut." He patted his rock-hard abs.

"Aren't you Fae all . . . allies?" Ithan asked, brows raised.

Flynn nearly spat out his drink. "Valbaran Fae and Avallen Fae *hate* each other. The Avallen Fae are a bunch of backward assholes. Prince Cormac might be Ruhn's cousin, but he can drop dead for all we care."

"Strong family bonds, huh?" Hunt said.

Flynn shrugged. "They deserved what happened during the Ordeal."

"Which was what, exactly?" Bryce asked.

"Humiliation," Declan said with relish. "A few weeks into our visit, King Morven—Cormac's dad—ordered Ruhn to go see if he could retrieve the Starsword from the caves."

"Tell the whole story, Dec. *Why* did he order me to do that?" Ruhn growled.

Dec sheepishly grinned. "Because I bragged that you could."

Ruhn cracked open another beer. "And?"

"And I made fun of Cormac for not having gone to retrieve it yet."

"And?"

"And I said that one Valbaran Fae warrior was better than ten from Avallen."

Bryce laughed. "So Uncle Morven sent you off to teach you a lesson?"

"Yep," Flynn said. "All three of us. We didn't realize until we were in the mist—the caves are literally full of it—that he also sent Cormac and the asshole twins to hunt us in there."

"Starting blood feuds," Bryce said to Declan, raising her hand for a high five. "Nice work."

Declan clapped her hand, but Ithan asked, "So your Ordeals happened then?"

"Yeah," Ruhn said, face darkening. "We all got lost in the caves. There was some . . . scary shit in there. Ghouls and wraiths—they were old and wicked. The six of us went from trying to kill each other to trying to stay alive. Long story short, Flynn and Dec and I wound up in these catacombs deep beneath the cave—"

"Surrounded by bloodsucking spirits who were going to eat our bodies, then our souls," Flynn added. "Or was it our souls, then our bodies?"

Ruhn shook his head. "I got disarmed. So I looked in the sarcophagus in the center of the chamber where we were trapped, and . . . there it was. The Starsword. It was either die at the hands of those creatures or die trying to pull that sword from its sheath." He shrugged. "Thankfully, it worked."

Declan said, "Bastards ran screaming from the cave when Ruhn drew the sword. Right to where Cormac and the twins were hunting us." He grinned again. "The three of them had no choice but to flee back to their castle. King Morven was *not* happy. Especially when Ruhn returned with the Starsword and told him to go fuck himself."

Bryce lifted her brows at her brother. He smiled, lip ring glinting. "Not such a loser after all, huh?"

Bryce waved him off. "Whatever."

Flynn suddenly asked Ithan, gaze on his tattooed neck, "You gonna keep that ink?"

Ithan drained his beer. "What's it to you?"

Another charming grin. "Just want to know when I can tell you that Sabine and Amelie are two of the worst fucking people in this city."

Ithan grunted, but a ghost of a smile appeared on his lips.

Bryce glanced to Ruhn, who said into her mind, *Might not be such a bad idea for him to come stay with us.*

You really want to be roomies with a wolf?

Better than an angel.

Depends on what you're doing with that angel.

Gross, Bryce.

Bryce tuned back into the conversation as Declan asked with a wicked smile that told her he was about to start shit, "So, who's sleeping where in this apartment tonight?"

Bryce couldn't help glancing again at Hunt, who kept his face wholly neutral as he said, "I'm bunking with Bryce."

Bryce's mouth popped open, but Ithan said, "Good. She snores."

"Assholes," Bryce seethed. "You can both go sleep on the roof."

"Not enough distance from your snoring," Ithan said, smirking.

Bryce scowled, leaning down to pet Syrinx's velvety ears.

Hunt only winked. "I'll get earplugs."

13

Bryce barely slept. She was trying too hard to pretend that Hunt fucking Athalar was not sleeping beside her. The illusion was shattered every time she rolled over, got a face full of gray wings, and remembered that Hunt fucking Athalar was sleeping beside her.

They hadn't spoken about Tharion's visit. Or about her decision to find Emile. So any fight on that front was likely still on the horizon.

Naturally, Bryce woke up puffy-eyed, sweat-slicked, and with a pounding headache. Hunt was already up and making coffee, to guess by the sounds in the other room.

Bryce slithered out of bed, earning a disgruntled yip from Syrinx at being disturbed. Her ringing phone aggravated her headache, and it didn't get any better when she glanced at the caller ID.

She mustered her most chipper voice. "Hi, Mom."

"Hello, Bryce." Ember's voice was calm. Too calm.

Ithan smirked from the couch as she passed by, blindly walking toward the beckoning aroma of coffee. Gods, she needed some. Bryce asked her mom, "What's up? You guys get home okay?"

The wall of windows revealed a sunny day, witches and angels zooming by. And, Bryce realized in the morning light, the fact that she was still wearing her worn T-shirt that said *Nidaros Community Center Camp Summer 15023* and . . . little else. Oops. No wonder

Ithan was smirking. Her lilac lace demi-thong left little to the imagination. Bryce stifled the urge to tug her shirt's hem over her half-bare ass.

Hunt's eyes darkened, but he merely leaned against the counter and silently offered her a cup of coffee.

"Oh yes," Ember said. "We got home, had plenty of time to do some grocery shopping and run a few errands." Bryce put the phone on speaker and slid it onto the counter, backing away a few feet. Like it was a grenade of compressed firstlight about to explode.

"Great," Bryce said, and she could have sworn Hunt was trying not to laugh.

"We also had plenty of time," her mom went on, "to answer all the phone calls that we began to get, asking when the wedding is."

Hunt took a long sip of his coffee. Ithan just watched with a befuddled expression. Right. She hadn't told him.

Bryce gritted her teeth in an attempt at a smile. "You and Randall are renewing your vows?"

Her mom fell silent. A wave building, cresting, about to break. "Is this engagement some scheme to prompt Hunt to finally confess his love for you?"

Hunt choked on his coffee.

Oh gods. Bryce was half-tempted to pour the boiling coffee over her head and melt into nothing. "For fuck's sake," she hissed, snatching up her phone and taking it off speaker. Even if Hunt and Ithan, with their heightened hearing, could no doubt make out everything Ember said. "Look, it's not a *real* engagement—"

"It certainly sounds like it is, Bryce Adelaide Quinlan." Her mom's voice rose with each word. "And it sounds like you're engaged to the Crown Prince of Avallen! Do you *know* who his father is?"

"Mom, I'm not going to marry him."

"Then why do so many of my former school friends know about it? Why are there photos of you two having a private meeting at your office yesterday?"

Hunt's wings flared with alarm, and Bryce shook her head. *Later*, she tried to signal.

"Cormac ambushed me—"

"He did *what?*"

"In a nonphysical way. Nothing I couldn't handle. *And*," she said as her mom began objecting, "I have zero intention of marrying Prince Creepster, but you gotta trust me to deal with it." She gave Hunt a look as if to say, *You too.*

Hunt nodded, getting it. Drank some more coffee. Like he needed it.

Her mother, however, hissed, "Randall is in a *panic.*"

"Randall, or you? Because last I checked, Dad knows I can take care of myself." Bryce couldn't help the sharpness in her tone.

"You're playing games with Fae royals who will outsmart you at every turn, who have likely anticipated your reticence—"

Bryce's phone buzzed. She skimmed the incoming message. Thank Urd.

"I appreciate your confidence, Mom. I have to go. I've got an important meeting."

"Don't you try to—"

"*Mom.*" She couldn't stop herself, couldn't halt the roiling, rising power that made her body begin to shimmer, as if she were a pot boiling over with liquid starlight. "You don't get a say in what I do or don't do, and if you're smart, you'll stay the Hel out of this."

Stunned silence from her mother. From Hunt and Ithan, too.

The words kept flowing, though. "You have *no* fucking idea what I've been through, and faced, and what I'm now dealing with." Her mom and Randall would never know about what she'd done to Micah. She couldn't risk it. "But let me tell you that handling this bogus engagement is *nothing* compared to that. So *drop* it."

Another pause. Then her mother said, "I knew you bundled us off at the break of dawn for a reason. I want to *help* you, Bryce—"

"Thanks for the guilt trip," Bryce said. She could practically see her mother stiffening.

"Fine. We're still at your disposal should you need us, Your Highness."

Bryce started to answer, but her mother had hung up. She

slowly, slowly closed her eyes. Hunt said into the sudden, heavy quiet, "Cormac came by the archives?"

Bryce opened her eyes. "Only to swing his dick around." Hunt tensed, and Bryce added, "Not literally."

His expression turned wary. "Why didn't you tell me?"

"Because I got a phone call from Celestina that you were in a holding cell." She bared her teeth. "Spare me the territorial male act, okay?"

"Hide shit from your parents all you want, but don't keep stuff from me. We're a team."

"I just *forgot*. No big deal."

Hunt hesitated. "All right." He lifted his hands. "Okay. Sorry."

Silence fell, and she became keenly aware of Ithan's attention. "Hunt can fill you in on my joyous news," she said, glancing at the clock. "I do have a meeting, and I need to get dressed." Hunt arched a brow, but Bryce offered no explanation as she aimed for her bedroom.

She returned to the great room an hour later, showered and in work clothes. Hunt was already in his 33rd gear.

Bryce said to Ithan, who was doing push-ups in front of the TV with extraordinary ease, "I'll pop back in at lunch when Tharion swings by. Help yourself to whatever's in the fridge and call if you need anything."

"Thanks, Mom," Ithan said between reps, and Bryce stuck out her tongue.

Bryce unlocked the door, then buckled Syrinx's leash before slipping into the hall. She'd been lonely in the archives yesterday without his company. And maybe a little jealous about the fact that Syrinx had spent the day with Ithan.

And it would have been nice to watch him take a bite out of Prince Cormac's ass.

The elevator had just arrived when Hunt appeared behind her, and every muscle in her body turned electric. Had the elevator always been this small? Had his wings gotten larger overnight?

"Why are things so weird between us?" Hunt asked.

Going right for the throat, then. "Are things weird?"

"Don't play stupid. Come on—last night was weird. Right now is fucking weird."

Bryce leaned against the wall. "Sorry. Sorry." It was all she could think to say.

Hunt asked carefully, "When were you going to tell me about Cormac dropping by the archives? What the fuck did he say?"

"That you and I are losers and he thinks I'm an immature brat."

"Did he touch you?" Lightning skittered along Hunt's wings. The elevator lights guttered.

The elevator reached the ground floor before she could answer, and they fell silent as they passed Marrin, the doorman. The ursine shifter waved goodbye.

Only when they'd stepped onto the sizzling sidewalk did Bryce say, "No. Cormac's just a creep. Seems like this city is full of them these days." She gestured to the sky above, the angels soaring toward the sprawling complex of the Comitium in the CBD. The decorations in Celestina's honor seemed to have multiplied overnight. "No fights today, okay?"

"I'll try."

They reached the corner where Bryce would go right, Hunt to the left. "I mean it, Hunt. No more fights. We need to keep a low profile." Especially now. They were too close to Ophion for comfort.

"Fine. Only if you call me the moment Prince Asshole contacts you again."

"I will. Let me know if Tharion gets in touch. Or if you pick up anything about . . ." She glanced at the cameras mounted on the ornately decorated streetlamps and buildings. She couldn't say Emile's name here.

Hunt stiffened, wings tucking in. "We need to talk about that. I, ah . . ." Shadows darkened his eyes, and her heart strained, knowing what memories caused them. But here it was. The discussion she'd been waiting for. "I know you want to help, and I commend you for it, Bryce. But I think we really need to weigh everything before we jump in."

She couldn't resist the impulse to squeeze his hand. "Okay." His calluses brushed against her skin. "Good point."

"Tharion threw me off last night," he went on. "It dragged up a lot of old shit for me—and worries for you. But if you want to move forward with this . . . let's talk it through first."

"Okay," she said again. "But I'm still going to meet with Fury right now." She had too many questions *not* to meet with her.

"Sure," he said, though worry shone in his gaze. "Keep me updated." He slid his hand from hers. "And don't think we're done talking about this weirdness between us."

By the time Bryce had opened her mouth to answer, Hunt had already launched skyward.

Bryce slid onto a stool at the eight-seat counter that made up Tempest in a Teapot, her favorite tea bar in the city.

Nestled on Ink Street in the heart of the Old Square, most of the narrow, graffiti-painted alley was quiet, most of the shops shut. Only the tea bar and the tiny bakery operating out of a window between two tattoo parlors were open. Come lunch, the many eateries would roll up their doors and set out the little tables and benches that crowded either side of the street. Once the lunch crowd returned to their offices, the street would quiet again—until the after-work rush of people eager for a beer, a specialty cocktail, or more food. And sundown brought in a whole new crowd: drunk assholes.

"Morning, B," Juniper said, her curly hair pulled back into an elegant bun, brown skin glowing in the morning light. She stood alongside Fury, who'd perched herself on a barstool and was scrolling through her phone. "Just wanted to say hi before practice."

Bryce kissed her friend on her silken cheek. "Hi. You're gorgeous. I hate you."

Juniper laughed. "You should see me when I'm dripping with sweat in an hour."

"You'll still be gorgeous," Bryce said, and Fury nodded without taking her focus from her phone. "Did you guys order?"

"Yeah." Fury put away her phone. "So go ahead."

Juniper said, "Mine's to go, though." She tapped her navy dance bag, which was partially unzipped, the soft pink of her leotard peeking out. For a moment, Bryce allowed herself to look at her friend— really look at the beauty that was Juniper. Graceful and tall and thin, certainly not the *wrong body type*.

What would it have been like to be heading into morning practice? To have a dance bag full of gear and not a purse full of random crap on her shoulder? Heels braced on the rail beneath the bar, Bryce couldn't stop her feet from twitching, arching—as if testing the strength and pliancy of pointe shoes.

Bryce had known the high of performance well. Had craved it those years in Nidaros, dancing with her small team at the rec hall. She'd been the best dancer in town—in their entire mountainous region. Then she'd come to Lunathion and learned what a fragile bubble she'd been living inside. And, yeah, ultimately she didn't think she could have lasted as long as Juniper, but . . . seeing the faun standing there, some small part of her wondered. Yearned.

Bryce swallowed, then sighed, clearing away the cobwebs of her old dreams. Dancing in Madame Kyrah's class twice a week was pleasure enough. And though Kyrah had once graced the stage of CCB herself until she'd decided to open a studio, the dancer-turned-instructor understood.

So Bryce asked, "What are you guys rehearsing today?"

"*Marceline*," Juniper said, her eyes flickering. "But I don't have the lead."

Bryce's brows rose. "I thought you were rehearsing for it these last weeks."

Fury said tightly, "Apparently, Marceline's costume doesn't fit Juniper."

Bryce's mouth popped open.

"Roles are often determined that way," Juniper said quickly. "But I'm fine with soloist."

Bryce and Fury swapped a look. No, she wasn't. But after the disaster this spring, the CCB had put a hold on any "new" changes. Including June's promotion from soloist to principal.

Juniper had often wondered aloud over drinks or pastries whether that hold was because she'd been the only one in the bomb shelter to demand that they keep the doors open for humans to get in. Had gone hoof-to-toe with some of their wealthiest patrons, thinking nothing of the consequences for her career.

Of what it might mean for the first faun to ever grace the stage of that theater to curse out those patrons, to condemn them to their faces for their cowardice and selfishness.

Well, *this* was what it meant for her.

June slumped into the stool beside Bryce, stretching out her long legs. Another year of waiting in the wings for her chance to shine.

"So who got your shot at Marceline?" The group of principals and veteran soloists rotated through the main roles each night.

"Korinne," Juniper said, a shade too neutrally.

Bryce scoffed. "You're twenty times the dancer she is."

June laughed softly. "No way."

"Way," Fury added.

"Come on," Bryce said, elbowing Juniper. "No need to be humble."

June shrugged, then smiled at the barista as she handed over a green tea in a to-go cup. "Okay. Maybe *twice* the dancer she is."

Fury said, "There's my girl." She nodded her thanks to the barista as her own drink was deposited in a ceramic mug.

Juniper pulled off the lid of her to-go cup and blew on the steaming-hot brew inside.

Bryce asked, "Did you give any thought to that offer from the Heprin Company?"

"Yeah," June murmured. Fury suddenly became very interested in her drink.

"And?" Bryce pushed. "They're practically crawling to have you as principal." And so were about three other smaller dance companies in the city.

"They're great," June said quietly. "But they're still a step down."

Bryce nodded. She got it. She really did. For a dancer in Valbara, CCB was the pinnacle. The distant star to aspire to. And June had been *so close*. Close enough to touch that glimmer of principal dancer. Now she was in free fall.

"I want to hold out for another year," June said, putting the lid on her tea and standing. "Just to see if things change." Pain gleamed in her friend's large, beautiful eyes.

"They will," Bryce assured her, because hope was the only thing she could offer at the moment.

"Thanks," Juniper said. "I'm off. I'll see you at home later," she said to Fury, leaning in to kiss her swiftly. When she made to step away, however, Fury put a hand on her cheek, keeping her there. Deepened the kiss for a few heartbeats.

Then Fury pulled back, holding her girlfriend's stare, and said, "See you at home." Sensual promise laced every word.

Juniper was more than a bit breathless, her cheeks flushing, as she turned to Bryce and kissed her cheek. "Bye, B," she said, then was gone into the sun and dust.

Bryce glanced sidelong at Fury. "You've got it bad, huh?"

Fury snorted. "You have no idea."

"How was date night?" Bryce asked, waggling her eyebrows.

Fury Axtar sipped delicately from her tea. "Exquisite."

Pleasure and happiness quietly radiated from her friend, and Bryce smiled. "What are you drinking?"

"Chai with almond milk. It's good. Spicy."

"You've never been here?"

"Do I look like the kind of person who goes to tea bars?"

"Yes . . . ?"

Fury laughed, her dark hair swaying. She wore her usual head-to-toe black, despite the heat. "Fair enough. So, what's this urgent thing you need to talk to me about?"

Bryce waited until she'd ordered her matcha latte with oat milk before murmuring, "It's about Danika." She and Hunt might need to talk things over regarding Emile, but speaking about this with Fury wasn't a step toward anything, necessarily. She could learn the truth without being dragged into Ophion's orbit, right?

At this hour, only the barista and one other patron occupied the bar. The street was empty save for a few cats picking through piles of trash. Safe enough to talk without being overheard.

Fury kept her posture casual, uninterested. "Does it have to do with Ithan staying with you?"

"How did you even hear about that?" Fury smiled smugly, but Bryce shook her head. "Never mind. But no, that's separate."

"He's always had a thing for you, you know."

"Um, Ithan had a thing for Nathalie."

"Sure."

"Whatever." How to phrase any of this? "You knew about Danika and the synth stuff. I was wondering if there was anything else you might have been . . . keeping secret for her."

Fury sipped her chai. "Care to explain more?" Bryce made a face. "That wasn't really a request," Fury said, her voice lethally soft.

Bryce swallowed. And so quietly only Fury could hear, she told her about Sofie Renast and Tharion and the River Queen and the hunt to find Emile and all the power he possessed. About the abandoned boat in the marshes and Ophion hunting for the boy as well. About the potential meet-up location that Danika had hinted at three years ago and the vague mentions of Project Thurr and Dusk's Truth in those emails between Danika and Sofie.

When she'd finished, Fury drained her drink and said, "I'm going to need something a lot stronger than chai."

"I've been reeling since Tharion told me," Bryce admitted, voice still low. "But Danika and Sofie definitely knew each other. Well enough for Sofie to trust Danika to find her a potential place to hide, should she ever need one."

Fury drummed her fingers on the counter. "I believe you. But Danika never hinted at involvement with the rebels, and I never picked it up on my usual channels."

Bryce nearly sagged with relief. Maybe it hadn't gone too far, then. Maybe their acquaintance hadn't been related to Ophion at all. "Do you think the meeting location is the Bone Quarter?" She prayed it wasn't.

"Danika wouldn't have sent a kid there, even with thunderbird power in his veins. And she wouldn't be so stupid as to make it *that* obvious."

Bryce frowned. "Yeah. True."

"As for Dusk's Truth and Project Thurr . . ." Fury shrugged. "No idea. But Danika was always interested in weird, random shit. She could spend hours getting sucked into an interweb research hole."

Bryce smiled slightly. Also true. "But do you think Danika might have been keeping anything else a secret?"

Fury seemed to consider. Then said, "The only other secret I knew about Danika was that she was a bloodhound."

Bryce straightened. "A what?"

Fury signaled the barista for another chai. "A bloodhound—she could scent bloodlines, the secrets in them."

"I knew Danika had an intense sense of smell," Bryce acknowledged. "But I didn't realize it was *that* . . ." She trailed off, memory surfacing. "When she came home with me over winter break freshman year, she could pick out the family ties of everyone in Nidaros. I thought it was a wolf thing. It's special?"

"I only know about it because she confronted me when we first met. She scented me, and wanted to understand." Fury's eyes darkened. "We sorted our shit out, but Danika knew something dangerous about me, and I knew something dangerous about her."

It was as much as Fury had ever said about being . . . whatever she was.

"Why is it dangerous to be a bloodhound?"

"Because people will pay highly to use the gift and to kill anyone with it. Imagine being able to tell someone's true lineage—especially if that person is a politician or some royal whose parentage is in question. Apparently, the gift came from her sire's line."

Maybe that was another reason why Danika hadn't wanted to mention it. She'd never discussed the male who'd been ballsy enough to fuck Sabine.

Bryce asked, "You never thought to tell me this during the investigation?"

"It didn't seem relevant. It was only one of Danika's many powers."

Bryce lifted a hand to rub at her eyes, then halted, remembering her makeup. "What are the odds that Sofie knew that?"

"No idea," Fury said. "Slim, probably." Then she asked carefully, "You sure you want to start digging into this? Go after that kid?"

"It's not only for Emile's sake," Bryce confessed. "I want to know what Danika was up to. I feel like she was always two steps—more like *ten* steps—ahead. I want to know the full scope of it."

"She's dead, Bryce. Knowing or not knowing won't change that."

Bryce cringed at her friend's harsh words. "I know. But if Danika was tied up with Ophion, with Sofie . . . I want to find Sofie, if she's alive. Learn whatever it is that Sofie knew about Danika, and how they were even in contact. Whether Danika truly was aligned with Ophion."

"You're tangling in some dangerous shit."

"Hunt said the same thing. And . . . you're both right. Maybe that makes me stupid, for not walking away. But setting aside the fact that Emile is a kid being chased by some intense people, if I can locate him for Tharion—he'll lead me to Sofie, or the information about her. And her answers about Danika."

Fury saluted her thanks to the barista and sipped her second chai. "And what will you do once you learn the truth?"

Bryce chewed on her lip. "Pray to Cthona that I can accept it, I guess."

14

Hunt crossed his arms, trying to focus on the unit sparring in one of the Comitium's rooftop training areas and not the scorching heat threatening to singe his wings. Beside him, Isaiah also sweated away, dark eyes fixed on a pair of fighting soldiers. The female was faster and cleverer than the male she faced, but the male had a hundred pounds on her. Each of his blows must have felt like being hit by a semitruck.

"My money's on the male," Isaiah murmured.

"So's mine. She's too green to hold out much longer." Hunt wiped the sweat from his brow, grateful he'd cut his hair shorter before the heat had set in. Solas was slow-roasting them over a pit of coals. Thank fuck he'd changed in the barracks to shorts and a T-shirt.

"Won't really matter in the long run," Isaiah said as the male landed a blow to her jaw with the pommel of his sword. Blood sprayed from her mouth. "Not if we head into war."

The great equalizer.

Hunt said nothing. He'd barely slept last night. Hadn't been able to calm the thoughts that circled over and over. He'd wanted to talk to Bryce, but that acid in his veins had surged every time he'd gotten close, and dissolved all his words. Even this morning, all he'd been able to say was that they needed to talk.

But Bryce being Bryce, she'd seen all of that. Knew what haunted him. And held his hand as she said yes.

He checked his phone. Only an hour until Tharion would show up at the apartment to discuss things. Great.

"You think we'll wind up back there?" Isaiah went on, face distant. "On those battlefields?"

Hunt knew which ones he meant, though they'd fought on many. Sandriel had sent both him and Isaiah to slaughter human rebels decades ago, when Ophion had initially formed.

"I hope not," Hunt said, blocking out the images of those muddy massacres: the mech-suits smoldering with their pilots bleeding out inside them; heaps of broken wings piled high to the skies; some shifters going feral and feasting on the carrion alongside the crows.

He looked over at Isaiah. What would his friend say if he knew about Tharion? Isaiah's words from their last argument in Shahar's war tent still rang in his ears. *This is folly, Athalar! We fly into slaughter. We have no allies, no route of retreat—you two are going to* kill *us all!*

Hunt had ordered his friend out. Had curled up alongside Shahar, who'd listened to their argument from her bed behind the curtain of the tent. She'd promised him that Isaiah was wrong, that he was merely afraid, and Hunt had believed her. Because he was also afraid, he realized later. He'd believed her, and they'd fucked like animals, and a few hours after dawn, she was dead.

Hunt shook the memories of the past away and focused on the fight in front of him. The female ducked and slammed her fist into the male's gut. He went down like a sack of flour, and Hunt chuckled, memories and dread shaking loose. "A pleasant surprise," he said, turning his attention to the other soldiers paired off throughout the space. Sweat gleamed on bare skin, wings white and black and brown and gray rustled, and blood shone on more than a few faces.

Naomi was in the skies training a unit in dive-bombing maneuvers. It was an effort not to glance to the far ring, where Pollux and Baxian oversaw a unit practicing their shooting. The latter was currently in his large canine form, his coat a slick black.

It felt wrong to have those two pieces of shit here, instead of Vik and Justinian.

So wrong that he did look at them after all. Sized up the Helhound's animal form. He'd seen Baxian rip limbs from opponents with those jaws, and move as fast on land as he did in his malakh form. As if sensing his attention, Baxian turned his head. His dark eyes gleamed.

Hunt bristled at the blatant challenge in Baxian's gaze. It didn't lessen when Baxian shifted in a flash of light, a few angels nearby startling at the return of his humanoid form.

Isaiah murmured, "Relax," as Baxian said something to Pollux before stalking for them.

Baxian stood nearly as tall as Hunt, and despite the sweltering heat, he still wore head-to-toe black that matched his wings and his Helhound pelt. "I thought you were doing something far more interesting here in Valbara, Athalar. I'm surprised you haven't dropped dead from boredom."

Isaiah took that as a cue to check on the male who'd fallen, winking at Hunt as he left.

Traitor.

"Some of us crave a normal life, you know," Hunt said to Baxian.

Baxian snickered. "All those battles, all that glory you won for yourself, all that lightning in your veins . . . and you simply want a nine-to-five job?" He tapped the scar on his neck. "The male who gave me this would be horrified."

"The male who gave you that," Hunt said through his teeth, "always wanted peace."

"Didn't seem like it when your lightning flayed me."

"You handed over that rebel family to Sandriel without a second thought. I'd say you had it coming."

Baxian laughed, low and lifeless. The hot, dry breeze rustled his black wings. "You were always a literal sort of bastard. Couldn't read between the lines."

"What the fuck does that mean?" Hunt's power flared at his fingertips.

Baxian shrugged. "I might not have been a slave as you are— were." A nod toward his clear brow. "But I had as little choice in serving Sandriel as you did. Only I didn't make my displeasure known."

"Bullshit. You served her gladly. You don't get to rewrite your history now that you're here."

Baxian's wings rustled. "You never asked me why I was in her triarii, you know. Not once, in all those decades. You're like that with everyone, Athalar. Surface-level."

"Fuck off. Go back to your work."

"This is my work. The Governor just messaged me and told me to team up with you."

Hunt's stomach turned. Did Celestina somehow know about Tharion asking for help finding that thunderbird kid? What better way to monitor him than to shackle him to the Helhound? "Hel no," he said.

Baxian's mouth curled upward as he nodded toward Pollux. "I've been stuck with that prick for a hundred years. It's someone else's turn to deal with him." He pointed to Naomi.

Was it selfish to be glad he didn't have to deal with the Hammer? "Why not tell us during the meeting earlier?"

"I think she's been watching us this morning." Baxian inclined his head to the cameras. "Likely didn't want to alter our behavior before deciding who to pair up."

"To what end?"

As if in answer, Hunt's phone buzzed. He pulled it from his shorts to find a message from Celestina.

As Isaiah will be escorting me around the city to meet its various leaders, I am relying on you and Naomi to help our two new arrivals adjust. I'd like you to partner with Baxian. Show him the ropes. Not just the ins and outs of the 33rd, but also how this city operates. Ease him into life in Valbara.

Hunt considered, even as he inwardly groaned. He was acutely aware of those cameras—the Archangel might be observing his every expression. "She put Naomi in charge of helping Pollux adjust?"

Across the ring, Isaiah was now checking his phone, frowning deeply. He glanced to Hunt, face lit with alarm. Not at the honor of escorting the Governor, Hunt knew.

Hunt turned back to Baxian, who'd no doubt gleaned that Hunt had all the orders he needed. "There's no way Pollux will allow anyone to *show him the ropes.*"

Baxian shrugged. "Let Pollux dig his own grave here. He's too pissed about being separated from the Hind to understand his new reality."

"I didn't realize the Hammer was capable of caring for anyone like that."

"He isn't. He just likes to have control over his . . . belongings."

"The Hind belongs to no one." Hunt hadn't known Lidia Cervos well—their time had only briefly overlapped when he'd served Sandriel, and the Hind had spent most of it off on missions for the Asteri. Rented out like some sort of field-worker to do their spy-hunting and rebel-breaking. Whenever Lidia had been at Sandriel's castle, she'd either been in secret meetings with the Archangel, or fucking Pollux in whatever room they felt like using. Thank the gods the Hind hadn't come here. Or the Harpy.

But if Emile Renast was heading for this city . . . Hunt asked, "The Hind's really not coming to Lunathion?"

"No. Pollux got a call from her this morning. He's been moody ever since."

"Mordoc finally making his move?" The head of the Hind's dreadwolves was as formidable as his mistress.

Baxian snorted. "He's not Lidia's type. And doesn't have the balls to go head-to-head with Pollux."

"Did Mordoc go with her to Ephraim?" He had to step carefully.

"Yeah," Baxian said, attention on Pollux. "They're all in Forvos right now. Ephraim's been keeping them close for the last few weeks—it's pissed off the Hind. The Harpy's even madder."

So the Hind wasn't in pursuit of Emile. At least, not at present. Which left the Ophion agents as the main danger to the boy, he supposed. He made a mental note to tell Tharion when he saw him later and said, "I thought you and the Harpy were a pair—you don't seem too hung up on not seeing her."

Baxian let out another one of those low laughs that skittered over Hunt's bones. "She and Pollux would be a better pair than him and Lidia." *Lidia*. Hunt had never heard Baxian use the Hind's given name, but he'd used it twice now. "She'll make Ephraim miserable," Baxian went on, smiling to himself. "Too bad I can't see it."

Hunt almost pitied Ephraim for inheriting the Harpy. "And the Hawk?"

"Doing what he does best: trying to outdo Pollux in cruelty and brutality." The hawk shifter had long been Pollux's main rival for power. Hunt had steered clear of him for decades. So had Baxian, he realized. He'd never seen them interact.

"You're a free male," Hunt said carefully. "Sandriel's gone. Why keep serving at all?"

Baxian ran a hand over his closely buzzed hair. "I could ask the same question of you."

"I need the money."

"Is that so?" Baxian clicked his tongue. "Bryce Quinlan's an expensive girlfriend, I take it. Princesses like pretty things."

Hunt knew better than to deny that Bryce was his girlfriend. Not if it'd open a door for Baxian to taunt him. "Exactly."

Baxian continued, "I like her. She's got balls."

Isaiah shouted Hunt's name from across the space, and Hunt nearly sagged with relief to have an excuse to get out of this conversation. "Here's the first rule of getting adjusted: don't fucking talk to me unless I talk to you." As Isaiah's Second, he outranked Baxian.

Baxian's eyes flared, as if realizing it. "I'm taking this assignment seriously, you know."

Hunt gave him a savage grin. "Oh, I know." If he had to help Baxian adjust, he'd happily drag him into the current century. Hopefully kicking and screaming. "So am I."

Baxian had the good sense to look a little nervous.

Tharion wanted to own Bryce Quinlan's apartment. Badly.

But he sure as shit didn't make enough to afford it, and the sun would shine in Hel before the River Queen allowed him to live

Above. The thought had him scowling as he knocked on the apartment door.

The lock clicked, and Ithan Holstrom peered out from the doorway, brows high. "Bryce isn't back yet."

"She already told me." Tharion held up his phone, displaying the brief exchange with the Fae Princess from a few minutes ago.

I'm at your apartment and ready to go through your underwear drawer.

She'd written back immediately, *You're early. I'll be there in ten. Don't leave drool stains on the lace ones. Or worse.*

No promises, he'd answered, and she'd replied, *Just spare the pink bra, please.*

To Tharion's surprise, Ithan checked that the number under her contact info was indeed Bryce's. Smart kid. Ithan's jaw worked before he said, "I thought she was involved with Athalar."

"Oh, she is," Tharion said, pocketing his phone. "But Legs and I have an understanding when it comes to her underwear." He stepped forward, a blatant demand to be let in.

Ithan stiffened, teeth flashing. Pure wolf. But the male opened the door wider, stepping aside. Tharion kept a healthy distance away as he entered. How many sunball games had Tharion watched where this male had scored the winning shot? How many times had he yelled at his TV, ordering Ithan to *throw that fucking ball*? It was weird to see him face-to-face. To go toe-to-toe with him.

Tharion plopped onto the ridiculously comfortable white couch, sinking deep into the cushions. "It occurred to me after I left last night that you didn't say much about Danika."

Ithan leaned against the counter. "What do you mean?"

Tharion smirked. "You might be a jock, but you're not dumb. I mean about what I told Bryce last night."

"Why would Danika tell me anything about knowing a rebel?"

"You were pretty damn close with her."

"She was my Alpha."

"You weren't part of the Pack of Devils."

"No, but I would have been."

Tharion toed off his shoes and propped his bare feet on the

coffee table. Sports news blared on the TV. "Weren't you all set to go pro?"

Ithan's face tightened. "That's none of your business."

"Right. I'm just Captain Whatever." Tharion gave him a salute. "But if you knew about any involvement Danika had, if there was a place Danika might have told Sofie was safe for hiding here in the city that sounds like it might be *where the weary souls find relief*, or even if your brother—"

"Don't talk about my brother." Ithan's snarl rattled the glasses in the kitchen cabinets.

Tharion held up his hands. "Noted. So you don't know anything."

"We didn't talk about the rebellion, or the war, or anything of the sort." A muscle ticked in Ithan's jaw. "I don't appreciate being dragged into this. Or having Bryce dragged into it, either. You're endangering her simply by mentioning it. Hunting for a missing kid is one thing, but the shit with Ophion is deadly."

Tharion gave the male a winning smile. "I have my orders, and I'm bound to obey them."

"You're an idiot if you don't see the risk in spreading this intel about your queen searching for Emile."

"Maybe, but what she'll do to me if I disobey will be a Hel of a lot worse than what Sabine and Amelie did to you." Another grin. "And I won't have pretty Bryce to kiss my wounds after."

Ithan snarled again. Did the wolf have any idea what he revealed with that snarl alone? He'd been such a smart sunball player, never broadcasting his moves. Seemed like he'd lost the skill.

But Tharion went on, "Danika did a lot of shady shit before she died. Bryce knows that. You're not protecting her by refusing to talk." Tharion eased to his feet, then stalked for the fridge, keenly aware of the wolf's every breath.

He'd opened the door to rummage for snacks when Ithan said, "She was a history major."

Tharion arched a brow. "Yeah?"

Ithan shrugged. "She once told me she was doing research on something that would likely land her in a heap of trouble. But when

I asked her later what she'd gotten on the paper, she said she'd changed subjects. I always thought it was weird."

Tharion shut the fridge door and lounged against it. "Why?"

"Because Danika was relentless. If she was interested in something, she didn't stop. I didn't really believe that she'd have changed the subject of her paper without good reason."

"You think a college student found something top secret that led her to Ophion?"

"Danika wasn't ever only a college student."

"The same way you weren't ever just a college sunball player, huh?"

Ithan ignored the barb. "You asked me about Danika. Aside from everything that went down with the synth, that's the only thing I can think of. Sorry if it's not what you hoped for."

Tharion just looked at the male leaning against the counter. Alone.

Maybe he was a sappy bastard, but Tharion pointed toward the TV. "I missed the sunball game against Korinth last night and want to see the highlights. Mind if I watch with you while we wait for the others?"

Ithan frowned, but Tharion put a hand on his heart. "No secret spying stuff, I swear." He sighed. "I could use a few minutes of peace."

Ithan weighed the words, Tharion's expression, with a keen-eyed sharpness that the wolf had used on his opponents. Perhaps the sunball player wasn't dead after all.

But Ithan only said, "There's leftover pizza if you're hungry."

15

Ruhn met his sister outside the Fae Archives right as the lunch-time crowds spilled into the warren of streets in Five Roses.

Amid the throng, few of the milling Fae noticed them, too focused on getting food or scrolling through their phones. Still, Bryce slid on a sunball cap and a pair of sunglasses as she stepped onto the blisteringly hot street that even the trees and greenery of FiRo couldn't entirely cool.

"I'm not wearing that getup," Ruhn said. Certainly not in Fae territory. "People are going to figure out who you are pretty damn fast."

"I can't take any more of the gawking."

"Comes with the territory."

Bryce grumbled something Ruhn chose not to hear. "So Tharion's back at the house?" he asked as they headed toward her apartment.

"Yep. Already grilling Ithan." Which was why she'd asked him to come as backup. A fact that gave him no small amount of satisfaction.

They crossed a busy intersection teeming with Fae and shifters, the occasional draki making their way past. Ruhn said, "I take it you didn't invite me to walk you home for some muscle in the mean streets of Crescent City." He wryly nodded to the angels and witches soaring overhead, the little otter in his yellow vest scooting by, the family of some sort of equine shifters trotting between the cars.

She glared at him over her sunglasses. "I wanted to discuss something with you—and I don't trust the phone. Or messages."

Ruhn blew out a breath. "I know the shit with Cormac is absurd—"

"It's not about Cormac. It's about Danika."

"Danika?"

"I saw Fury this morning. She told me Danika was a bloodhound. Do you know what that is?"

"Yes," Ruhn said, surprise shooting through him. "You're simply . . . telling me this?"

His sister waved a dismissive hand. "Danika kept a lot of things from me. And I don't see the point in keeping secrets anymore."

"It's okay to be pissed at her, you know."

"Spare me the self-help lecture, okay?"

"Fair enough." He rubbed his jaw. "I guess this explains how Danika knew we were siblings before anyone else." He'd never forget running into Bryce and Danika at that frat party—his first time seeing his sister in years. And how Danika had stared at him. Then looked at Bryce, brows high. He'd known in that moment that Danika had guessed what no one else had, even as Bryce introduced him as her cousin. He'd chalked it up to her uncanny observation skills.

"I thought she was just *good* at scenting," Bryce said, fanning her face against the heat. "Not a genius or whatever. Do you think this could have anything to do with her connection to Sofie?"

"It seems like a stretch. Danika was a powerful, influential Vanir regardless of that gift. She could have been sought out by Sofie or Ophion for a host of other reasons."

"I know." They fell silent until Bryce halted outside the glass doors of her apartment building. "Maybe Sofie thought Danika could help free her brother from Kavalla or something. It sounded like she was working on that for years before she was able to get to him. Maybe she imagined Danika had the influence."

Ruhn nodded. He couldn't begin to imagine what it had been like—for Emile to endure, and for Sofie to spend every moment of every day praying and working for his survival. That she hadn't given up, that she'd accomplished it . . . Ruhn had no words. "*Did* Danika have that kind of sway, though?" he asked.

Bryce shook her head. "I mean, she might have been able to, but she never tried to do anything like that, as far as I know. And I don't see why Sofie would contact Danika, of all people, when Danika was here and Sofie was over in Pangera. It doesn't add up." Bryce flipped her ponytail over a shoulder and grunted her frustration. "I want to know what Sofie knew about Danika."

"I get that," Ruhn said carefully. "And I get why you want to find Emile, too. But I'll say this one more time, Bryce: if I were you, I'd stay out of whatever game Tharion and the River Queen are playing in looking for the kid. Especially if Ophion is on the hunt for Emile as well."

Bryce opened the door to her building, air-conditioning smothering them like a frosty blanket, and waved to Marrin. The ursine shifter waved back from the front desk, and Ruhn offered a half smile to the male before he stepped into the elevator after his sister.

Ruhn waited until the doors had shut before he said softly, "I know Athalar already said this to you last night, but the Asteri could kill you for even getting involved. Even if it's something as seemingly harmless as finding this kid."

Bryce idly wrapped the length of her ponytail around a wrist. "They could have killed me this spring, but they didn't. I'm guessing they won't now."

Ruhn toyed with his lip ring, tugging on the silver hoop as the elevator doors opened and they stepped out onto her floor. "If they want you alive, I'd start wondering why that is. You have the Horn in your back. That's no small thing." He couldn't help himself from glancing at his sister's back as he said it, eyeing the upper tendrils of the tattoo visible above her dress. "You're a power player now, Bryce, whether you like it or not. And trust me, I get it—it *sucks* to want to be normal but to have all this other shit that keeps you from being that way." His voice turned hoarse and she looked over a shoulder at him, face neutral. "But you're Starborn and you have the Horn. And you have a lot of power thanks to the Drop. The Bryce before this spring might have searched for Emile with few repercussions, but the Bryce who exists now? Any move you make will be politicized, analyzed— viewed as an act of aggression or rebellion or outright war. No matter what you say."

Bryce sighed loudly—but her eyes had softened. Either at what he'd said, or what he'd admitted to her about his own life. "I know," she said before unlocking the front door to her apartment.

They found Tharion on the couch with Ithan, the TV blasting the latest sports stats. Tharion munched on a piece of pizza, long legs sprawled out in front of him, bare feet on the coffee table.

Ruhn might have stepped inside to grab a piece of that pizza had Bryce not gone still.

A Fae sort of stillness, sizing up a threat. His every instinct went on high alert, bellowing at him to defend, to attack, to slaughter any threat to his family. Ruhn suppressed it, held back the shadows begging to be unleashed, to hide Bryce from sight.

Ithan called over to them, "Pizza's on the counter if you want some."

Bryce remained silent as fear washed over her scent. Ruhn's fingers grazed the cool metal of the gun strapped to his thigh.

"Your cat's a sweetheart, by the way," Ithan went on, not taking his focus from the TV as he stroked the white cat curled on his lap. Bryce slowly shut the door behind her. "He scared the shit out of me when he leapt onto the counter a few minutes ago, the bastard." The wolf ran his fingers through the luxurious coat, earning a deep purr in response.

The cat had stunning blue eyes. They seemed keenly aware as they fixed on Bryce.

Ruhn's shadows gathered at his shoulders, snakes ready to strike. He subtly drew his gun.

Behind her, a familiar ripple of ether-laced power kissed over her skin. A small reassurance as Bryce croaked, "That's not a cat."

Hunt arrived at the apartment just in time to hear Bryce's words through the shut front door. He was inside in a moment, his lightning gathered at his fingers.

"Oh, calm yourself," the Prince of the Chasm said, leaping onto the coffee table.

Swearing, Ithan lunged from the couch and jumped over it with preternatural grace. Tharion went for a knife at his thigh, a wicked blade with a curved tip. Designed to do its worst damage on the way out.

But Aidas said to Hunt, little fangs glinting, "I thought we were friends, Orion."

"It's Hunt," he gritted out, lightning skittering over his teeth, zapping his tongue.

One move and he'd fry the prince. Or try to. He didn't dare take his focus off Aidas to check on Bryce's positioning. Ruhn would make sure she stayed back.

"Regardless," Aidas said, padding across the coffee table and jumping onto the carpet. A glowing light filled the corner of Hunt's vision, and he found Ruhn standing on Bryce's other side, Starsword in hand.

But Bryce, damn her, walked forward. Hunt tried to block her, but she easily sidestepped him, her chin high as she said, "Good to see you again, Aidas."

Ruhn, Tharion, and Ithan all seemed to inhale at once.

Hunt hardly breathed as the cat trotted up to her and wended between her legs, brushing against her shins. "Hello, Princess."

Hunt's blood chilled. The demon prince purred the word with such intent. Such delight. Like he had some sort of claim on her. Hunt's lightning flared.

Aidas trotted for the counter and jumped onto it in one

graceful spring, then surveyed all of them. His blue gaze returned to Bryce at last. "Why don't you know how to use your powers yet?"

Bryce rolled her shoulders, cracking her neck, and held out a hand. A kernel of starlight flared in her palm. "I can use them."

A soft, hissing laugh. "Party tricks. I meant your real powers. Your heritage."

Hunt's fingers tightened on his gun. Bryce challenged, "What powers?"

Aidas's eyes glowed like blue stars. "I remember the last Starborn Queen, Theia, and her powers." He seemed to shudder. "Your light is her light. I'd recognize that luster anywhere. I'm assuming you have her other gifts as well."

"You *knew* the last Starborn Queen?" Ruhn asked. Starlight glinted among Ruhn's shadows, shimmering down the length of his sword.

Aidas's eyes now flared with a strange sort of rage as he looked upon the Fae Prince. "I did. And I knew the sniveling prince whose light *you* bear." A ripple of stunned silence went through the room.

Ruhn, to his credit, didn't back down an inch. But from the corner of Hunt's vision, he noted Ithan and Tharion creeping into mirroring positions behind the Prince of the Chasm.

Bryce said, more to herself than to the demon prince, "I hadn't realized they'd have individualized starlight. I always thought mine was only . . . brighter than yours." She frowned at Ruhn. "I guess it makes sense that there could be nuances to the light amongst the Fae that got interbred. Theia's elder daughter, Helena, had the gift—and married Prince Pelias. Your ancestor."

"He's your ancestor, too," Ruhn muttered.

"Pelias was no true prince," Aidas spat, fangs bared. "He was Theia's high general and appointed himself prince after he forcibly wed Helena."

"I'm sorry," Ithan said, scrubbing at his face, "but what the fuck is this about?" He glanced at the pizza on the table, as if wondering whether it had been spiked with something.

Welcome to our lives, Hunt wanted to say.

But Bryce's face had gone pale. "Queen Theia allowed this?"

"Theia was dead by that point," Aidas said flatly. "Pelias slew her." He nodded to the Starsword in Ruhn's hand. "And stole her blade when he'd finished." He snarled. "That sword belongs to Theia's *female* heir. Not the male offspring who corrupted her line."

Bryce swallowed audibly, and Ruhn gaped at his blade. "I've never heard any of this," the Fae Prince protested.

Aidas laughed coldly. "Your celebrated Prince Pelias, the so-called first Starborn Prince, was an impostor. Theia's other daughter got away—vanished into the night. I never learned of her fate. Pelias used the Starsword and the Horn to set himself up as a prince, and passed them on to his offspring, the children Helena bore him through rape."

That very Horn that was now tattooed into Bryce's back. A chill went down Hunt's spine, and his wings twitched.

"Pelias's craven blood runs through both of your veins," Aidas said to Ruhn.

"So does Helena's," Ruhn shot back, then recited, *"Night-haired Helena, from whose golden skin poured starlight and shadows."*

Bryce clicked her tongue, impressed. "You memorized that passage?"

Ruhn scowled, as if annoyed she'd focus on that when a demon prince was before them.

But Bryce asked Aidas, "Why are you telling us this now?"

Aidas shimmered with anger. "Because I was powerless to help then. I arrived too late, and was vastly outnumbered. After it was over—that's when I asked my eldest brother for a favor. To face Pelias on the battlefield and wipe him from this world." Aidas paced a few steps, tail swishing. "I tell you this now, Bryce Quinlan, so the past does not repeat itself. Are you doing anything to help in this endless war?"

"You mean the rebel cause?" Tharion asked, face taut with disbelief and dread.

Aidas didn't take his eyes off Bryce as he said, "It is the same war we fought fifteen thousand years ago, only renewed. The same war you fought, Hunt Athalar, in a different form. But the time is ripe again to make a push."

Ithan said slowly, "Hel is our enemy."

"Is it?" Aidas laughed, ears twitching. "Who wrote the history?"

"The Asteri," Tharion said darkly.

Aidas turned approving eyes on him. "You've heard the truth in some form, I take it."

"I know that the official history of this world is not necessarily to be believed."

Aidas leapt off the counter, trotting to the coffee table again. "The Asteri fed their lies to your ancestors. Made the scholars and philosophers write down their version of events under penalty of death. Erased Theia from the record. That library your former employer possesses," he said, turning to Bryce, "is what remains of the truth. Of the world before the Asteri, and the few brave souls who tried to voice that truth afterward. You knew that, Bryce Quinlan, and protected the books for years—yet you have done nothing with that knowledge."

"What the fuck?" Ithan asked Bryce.

Aidas only asked, "What was this world *before* the Asteri?"

Tharion said, "Ancient humans and their gods dwelled here. I've heard the ruins of their civilization are deep beneath the sea."

Aidas inclined his head. "And where did the Asteri come from? Where did the Fae, or the shifters, or the angels come from?"

Bryce cut in, "Enough with the questions. Why not just tell us? What does this have to do with my . . . gifts?" She seemed to choke on the word.

"The war approaches its crescendo. And your power isn't ready."

Bryce flicked the length of her ponytail over a shoulder. "How fucking cliché. Whatever my other powers are, I want nothing to do with them. Not if they somehow link me to you—the Asteri will consider that a serious threat. Rightly so."

"People died so you could have this power. People have been dying in this battle for fifteen thousand years so we could reach this point. Don't play the reluctant hero now. *That* is the cliché."

Bryce seemed at a loss for words, so Hunt stepped in. "What

about your eldest brother, with his armies? They seem perfectly content to slaughter innocent Midgardians."

"Those armies have always been to help you. Not to conquer."

"The attack on this city last spring suggests otherwise," Hunt argued.

"A mistake," Aidas said. "The beasts that swept in were . . . pets. Animals. Micah opened the doors to their pens. They ran amok as they saw fit. Fortunately, you took control of the situation before our intervention was required," he said, smiling at Bryce.

"A lot of people died," Ithan growled. "Children died."

"And more will soon die in this war," Aidas countered coolly. "Hel's armies shall strike at your command, Bryce Quinlan."

The words dropped like a bomb.

"Bullshit," Ruhn said, face crinkling as he snarled. "You're waiting for the right moment when we're all at war with each other, so you'll be able to find a way into this world at last."

"Not at all," Aidas said. "I already know the way into this world." He pointed with a paw to Bryce and inclined his head. "Through my lovely Bryce and the Horn on her back." Hunt suppressed a growl at the word *my* as all of them looked to her. Her eyes remained fixed on Aidas, her lips a thin line. The Prince of the Chasm said, "It's your choice in the end. It has always been your choice."

Bryce shook her head. "Allow me to get this straight: You're here to convince me to rebel against the Asteri in front of all these people? And what—sign up with Ophion? No, thank you."

Aidas only chuckled. "You should have looked more carefully at the cats picking through the trash in the alley of Ink Street this morning. Should have picked a more discreet location to discuss the rebellion with Fury Axtar." Bryce hissed, but said nothing as Aidas went on, "But yes—by all means, turn rebel. Help Ophion, if you need some authority to answer to. I can tell you before you undoubtedly ask, I have no information about the connection between Danika Fendyr and Sofie Renast."

Bryce growled, "I don't even *know* any Ophion rebels."

Aidas stretched out his front paws, back arching. "That's not true." Hunt stilled as the demon yawned. "There's one right behind you."

Bryce whirled, Hunt with her, lightning poised to strike.

Cormac Donnall stood in the doorway, shadows fading from his shoulders.

"Hello, Agent Silverbow," Aidas crooned, then vanished.

16

I'm sorry," Ruhn blurted, gaping at the Avallen Prince in the doorway, "you're *what*?" Bryce's gaze darted between her brother and their cousin. Ithan was sniffing delicately toward Cormac, clearly putting together who stood before them.

"Agent Silverbow?" Tharion demanded.

Ruhn went on, "Does your father know about this? Does *my* father?" Bryce swapped a glance with her brother. They could use this. Maybe she'd get out of the engagement—

Cormac's face darkened with menace. "No. Nor will they ever." Threat rumbled in every word.

Bryce might have joined in on the interrogation, had the star on her chest not flared through the fabric of her dress. She clapped a hand over it.

Trust Aidas to reveal Cormac's secret and then bail. Bryce had a strong feeling that the Prince of the Chasm had also let Cormac through the wards using his unholy power.

Fucking demon.

Cormac bristled as he glared around the room. "What the fuck do you know about Sofie Renast?"

Bryce pushed her hand harder against her chest, grinding against her sternum as she countered, "What the fuck do *you* know about Sofie Renast, *Agent Silverbow*?"

Cormac whirled on her, stalking closer. "Answer me."

Hunt casually stepped into his path. Lightning danced over his wings. Alphahole to the core, yet it warmed something in her.

Tharion slumped onto the couch, an arm slung lazily along the back cushions, and peered at his nails. He drawled to Cormac, "And you are?"

Shadows ran down Cormac's arms, trailing like smoke from his shoulders. Like Ruhn's shadows—only darker, more feral somehow. Some small part of her was impressed. The Avallen Prince growled, "Cormac Donnall. I'll ask one more time, mer. What do you know about Sofie?"

Tharion crossed an ankle over a knee. "How do you know I'm mer?" Solas, was Tharion riling him for the Hel of it?

"Because you reek of fish," Cormac spat, and Tharion, gods bless him, lifted an arm to sniff his armpit. Ithan chuckled. Most Vanir could detect when a mer was in their humanoid form by that scent of water and salt—not an unpleasant one, but definitely distinct.

Hunt and Ruhn weren't smiling. She had to admit her brother cut a rather imposing figure. Not that she'd ever tell him that.

Tharion smirked at Cormac. "I'm guessing Sofie is your . . . girlfriend?"

Bryce blinked. Cormac let out a snarl that echoed into her bones.

"Impressive," Hunt murmured to Bryce, but she didn't feel like smiling.

Cormac had turned on her once again. "You know Sofie."

"I don't—didn't," Bryce said, stepping to Hunt's side. "I never heard of her until yesterday, when *he* came to ask some questions." She shot a look at Tharion, who held up his long-fingered hands. "But I now have a Hel of a lot of my own questions to ask, so can we all just . . . sit down and talk? Instead of this weird standoff?" She shut the apartment door, and then claimed a seat at one of the stools by the kitchen counter, kicking off her heels beneath it. Ruhn slid onto the one at her left; Hunt perched on the one to the right. Leaving Cormac standing in the middle of the great room, eyeing all of them.

"Why do your shadows appear different from Ruhn's?" Bryce asked Cormac.

"*That's* the first thing you want to know?" Hunt muttered. She ignored him.

"How do you know Sofie?" was Cormac's only reply.

Bryce rolled her eyes. "I already told you—I don't know her. Tharion, can you put him out of his misery?"

Tharion crossed his arms and settled into the couch cushions. "I was asked to confirm her death." Bryce noted that Tharion's answer could be interpreted as ensuring a dangerous rebel was dead. Smart male.

"And did you?" Cormac's voice had gone low. His body shook, as if he was restraining himself from leaping upon Tharion. Embers sparked in his hair.

But Hunt leaned back against the counter, elbows on the stone. Lightning snaked along his wings; his face was deathly calm. The embodiment of the Umbra Mortis. A thrill shot through Bryce's veins as Hunt spoke. "You have to realize that you're not getting any other answers or leaving here alive without convincing us of some key things."

Gods-damn. He meant it. Bryce's heart thundered.

"So take a breath," Hunt said to the prince. "Calm yourself." The angel smiled, showing all his teeth. "And listen to the lady's advice and sit the fuck down."

Bryce pressed her lips together to keep from smiling. But Cormac—he did indeed take a breath. Another. Bryce glanced at Ithan, but his attention remained on Cormac as the prince breathed, studying his every movement like he was an opponent on the sunball field.

Ruhn, however, met her stare, surprise lighting his features. He said into her head, *I did not see this coming.*

Bryce might have replied, but the shadows on Cormac's arms faded. His broad shoulders relaxed. Then he stalked to the dining table and sat. His eyes were clear—calmer.

The star on her chest winked out as well. As if reassured that all was well.

"Good," Hunt said in that take-no-shit tone that did funny things to her insides. "First things first: How'd you get in? This place is warded to Hel and back."

"That cat—or not-cat. That somehow knew who—what I am." A glimmer of displeasure in his face hinted that the prince was only leaving that question aside for the moment. "It left a gaping hole in the wards."

Hunt nodded, like this wasn't a big fucking deal. "And why did you come here, at this exact moment?" He'd gone into full-on interrogation mode. How many times had he done this in the 33rd?

Cormac pointed to Tharion. "Because I believe we're hunting for the same person: Emile Renast. I want to know what you know."

Bryce couldn't stop her low sound of surprise. But Tharion's face remained stony. The expression of the River Queen's Captain of Intelligence. He asked, "Did Pippa Spetsos send you?"

Cormac barked a laugh. "No. Pippa is the reason Emile fled the *Bodegraven*."

"So who sent you to find Emile?" Hunt asked.

"No one," Cormac said, taking another long breath. "I was sent to this city for another reason, for many reasons, but this matter of finding Emile . . ." His jaw worked. "Sofie and I were close. I helped her free Emile from Kavalla. And before she . . ." He swallowed. "I made her a promise—not only as one agent to another, but as a . . . friend. To look after Emile. I failed her. In every way, I failed her."

Either he's an amazing actor, Ruhn said into her head, *or he was in love with Sofie.*

Agreed, Bryce said.

"Why did Emile run from Pippa?" Tharion asked.

Cormac ran his hands through his blond hair. "He was afraid of her. He's wise to be. Pippa is a fanatic on a fast track to promotion into Ophion Command. With so many of our bases recently destroyed, Ophion is nervous enough to start considering her ideas—and I worry they'll soon start following her as well. There are no lines she and her unit of Lightfall soldiers won't cross. Did your news over here get wind of that story about the leopard massacre a year ago?"

Bryce couldn't stop her shudder. Ithan said quietly, "Yeah."

Cormac said, "That was Pippa's idea, carried out by Lightfall. To use those Vanir kids and babies to lure their parents out of their hidden dens—and then kill them all. Simply for sport. For the Hel of it. Because they were Vanir and *deserved* to die. Even the children. She said it was part of cleansing this world. Working their way up to the top: the Asteri. Hence the Lightfall name."

Hunt looked to Tharion—who nodded gravely. Apparently, the Captain of Intelligence had heard that, too.

Cormac went on, "Pippa sees Emile as a weapon. The night of the escape, he took down those imperial Omegas, and she was practically beside herself with excitement. She spooked him with her eagerness to get him onto a battlefield, and he fled on an escape boat before I could convince him that I was there to help. The boy sailed to the nearest port, then stole another boat."

"Resourceful kid," Ithan muttered.

"I tracked him as far as these shores." Cormac jerked his chin at Tharion. "I saw you in the marshes at the abandoned boat. I figured you were on his trail as well. And I watched you find the remains of the Lightfall soldier's body—so you must have at least guessed that Pippa wants Emile for her Lightfall unit. If she catches him, she'll drag him back to Ophion's main base and turn him into a weapon. Into exactly what the Asteri feared when they hunted down the thunderbirds centuries ago."

His gaze shifted to Hunt. "You asked why I came here, at this exact moment? Because when the mer kept returning here, I figured you lot might be involved somehow—some of the very people I was sent here to meet. I hoped Emile might even be here." Again, his jaw tightened. "If you know where Emile is, tell me. He's not safe."

"I don't understand," Ruhn said. "You and Pippa are both in Ophion, yet you're trying to find Emile to . . . keep him out of Ophion's hands?"

"Yes."

"Won't Ophion be pissed?"

"Command will never know of my involvement," Cormac said. "I have other tasks here to complete."

Bryce didn't like the sound of that for one moment. She slid off the stool, taking a step toward the dining table. Her mouth began moving before she could think through her words. "You expect us to trust you about all of this when you were so fucking obsessed with a stupid piece of metal that you wanted to kill my brother?" She flung a hand in the general direction of Ruhn and the Starsword in his grip.

Ruhn grunted with surprise as Cormac retorted, "That was fifty years ago. People change. Priorities change."

But Bryce took one step closer to the dining table, not caring if Cormac deemed it a challenge. "Fae don't change. Not you old-school losers."

Cormac glanced between her and Ruhn with palpable disdain. "You Valbaran Fae are such babies. Did you not learn something of yourself, your destiny, *Prince* Ruhn, because of me nipping at your heels?"

"You put a sword through Dec's gut," Ruhn said mildly. "I'd hardly call that *nipping.*"

Tharion cut in, "Assuming we buy your story, why would a Fae Prince join Ophion?"

Cormac said, "I joined because I felt it was right. The details are unnecessary."

"Not if you might be working for the Asteri," Bryce said.

"You think I'd turn you over to the Asteri?" Cormac laughed, dead and cold. "I wouldn't wish that fate on anyone. The dungeons beneath their crystal palace are darker and deadlier than the Pit."

Hunt said icily, "I know. I was there."

Bryce hated the shadows in his eyes. Ones she'd do anything to help heal. Do anything to avoid renewing. Team Survive at All Costs—that was her team. She didn't care if that made her a coward.

Cormac went on, ignoring Hunt, "Sofie was an Ophion agent because the Asteri butchered her family. Her human family, and her thunderbird ancestors. All she wanted was to find her brother. Everything she did was for him."

Tharion opened his mouth, but Bryce lifted a hand, cutting him off as she said to Cormac, "Tharion came by yesterday to ask about a connection between someone I . . . knew and Sofie. He was being super shady"—a glare from Tharion at this—"so I managed to get some answers out of him, mainly that he's looking for Emile for the River Queen."

Cormac narrowed his stare on Tharion. "What does your queen want with the boy?"

Tharion shrugged.

Ruhn murmured, "Nothing good, I bet."

Tharion rumbled a warning growl at Ruhn, but Bryce continued, "I don't care about the politics. Emile's a kid, and lost—I want to find him." And get answers about Danika knowing Sofie, but . . . that could wait for a moment. She wanted to feel Cormac out first.

Indeed, the Avallen Prince's eyes softened a bit—with gratitude.

Could be faking that, Ruhn observed to her.

Could be, but my gut says he isn't, Bryce replied before she angled her head and asked Cormac, "The Hind's a pretty big deal. She went to all that trouble to kill Sofie just for freeing her brother? Or was it because Sofie's a thunderbird?"

Cormac's hands curled into fists at his side. "The Hind went to all that trouble because Sofie, as collateral to make sure the Ophion boat showed up for Emile, had gathered vital intel on the Asteri, and made sure Command knew it."

"What?" Hunt blurted, wings twitching.

"What kind of intel?" Tharion asked, face darkening.

Cormac shook his head. "Sofie was the only person who knew it. She just mentioned to me that it was something big—war-changing. That Ophion would kill to have it. And our enemies would kill to contain it."

Across the room, Ithan was wide-eyed. Had any of his training prepared him for this? Had any of hers?

Tharion said, "The Asteri probably sent the Hind to kill her before she could tell anyone else."

Cormac grimaced. "Yes. But I suspect the Hind knew Sofie could hold out against torture, and decided it was best the information die with her." He shuddered and said, "They ripped out her nails when she went into Kavalla, you know. She told me that they tore out the nails on one hand, and when they asked her for any information, she held out her other hand to them." He laughed to himself. "One of the guards fainted."

"Brave female," Ithan said softly, earning a thankful nod from Cormac that had Bryce wishing she'd said as much herself. Bryce studied her own manicured nails. Wondered if she'd be able to hold out if it ever came to that.

Cormac again turned to Tharion, his face bleak. "Tell me the Hind at least put a bullet in her head before she sent Sofie down to the deep."

"I don't know," Tharion said. "Her body wasn't there."

"What?" Shadows rippled from Cormac again.

Tharion went on, "The lead blocks, the chains were there. But Sofie's body was gone. And the shackles had all been unlocked."

Cormac shot to his feet. "Sofie is alive?"

Such raw hope filled his voice. Was it from genuine love? Or hope that the intel she carried lived on?

"I don't know," Tharion answered. Then he admitted, "But that's why I came to Bryce. She had a friend who knew Sofie years ago. I'm investigating any connections between them—I'm wondering if it might give us hints about Emile's whereabouts." Tharion shrugged. "I have good reason to believe that a safe meeting place was set up long ago for a scenario like this, and that Emile might be headed there—and Sofie, too, if she's alive."

Would Sofie have passed that vital intel to her brother? Bryce found Hunt giving her a *Don't even think about it* look.

Cormac said, pacing, "Sofie made the Drop—at an illegal center where it wouldn't be recorded. I thought that there was a chance she might have survived, but when she didn't contact me . . ." His eyes narrowed at the mer. "What else do you know?"

"I've told you everything," Tharion lied, crossing his legs.

Cormac gave a slashing, mocking grin. "And what of Danika Fendyr?"

Bryce stilled. "What about her?" Hunt gave her another look warning her to keep quiet.

Cormac said, "She and Sofie knew each other. She was the one who set up this safe place, wasn't she?"

"You don't know any of that for sure," Hunt said.

"I do," Cormac said, his gaze still on Bryce, on the star in her chest that had begun to glow dimly again. "It's why I agreed to marry Bryce."

Ruhn needed a moment to process everything. He watched his cousin warily.

But Bryce chuckled. "I thought you agreed to marry me because of my winning personality."

Cormac didn't smile. "I agreed to marry you because I needed access to you. And to you, cousin," he said to Ruhn.

Athalar demanded, "You couldn't just pay a friendly visit?"

"The Avallen Fae and the Valbaran Fae are not *friendly*. We are allies, but also rivals. I needed a reason to come here. I needed to come here to find Emile—it was a blessing from Urd that Ophion wanted me here for another mission, too."

Bryce glowered. "Forcing me into marriage seems extreme."

"It's the only currency I have. My breeding potential."

Ruhn snorted. He and his cousin had more in common than he'd realized. "Why do you need access to me?"

"Because you can mind-speak, can you not? It's how you and your friends survived in the Cave of Princes during your Ordeal. You fought as if you were of one mind. You never told my father, but he suspected. *I* suspected. It's a rare Starborn gift. A skill Ophion needs badly."

Ruhn said, "What about your cousins—the twins? They can mind-speak."

"They're not trustworthy. You know that."

Athalar cut in, "Don't let him rope you into whatever this is, Danaan. Searching for Emile independently is one thing. If you let him deliver his pitch, you're one step away from working with Ophion. The Asteri won't care whether you agree or reject his ass." He leveled a look at Cormac. "And let me remind you that Ophion is going up against legions that outrank them in power and size. If one of the Asteri walks onto a battlefield, you're all done."

The power of one Asteri, the holy star glowing within them, could level an entire army.

Hunt went on, "And if the Asteri catch wind that *Agent Silverbow* is trying to recruit Ruhn, we'll all be taken in for questioning. If we're lucky. If not, we'll be executed."

"You didn't seem to have such concerns when you rebelled, Fallen Angel," Cormac said.

"I learned the hard way," Hunt said through his teeth. Bryce stepped closer to him, fingers brushing his. "I'd prefer to protect my friends from learning that lesson."

It shouldn't have meant something to Ruhn, for Athalar to consider him a friend. But it did.

Hunt continued, "You're not only insane to tell us this—you're reckless. We could sell you out in a heartbeat."

Tharion added, "Or you're an Asteri mole seeking to entrap us."

Cormac drawled, "Trust me, I don't bandy about this information to just anyone." He sized up Athalar. "You might have made foolish mistakes in the past, Umbra Mortis, but I shall not."

"Fuck you." That one came from Bryce, her voice low and deadly.

Ruhn said to Cormac, hoping to take the temperature down a few degrees, "I'm not going to get involved with you or Ophion. I won't risk it. So don't even ask me to do whatever it is you want me to use my . . . mind-stuff for." He hated that his cousin knew. That Tharion was now watching him with a mixture of surprise, awe, and wariness.

Cormac laughed bitterly. "You can't risk your friends and family? What about the countless friends and family in Pangera who are tortured, enslaved, and murdered? I saw you entering this apartment earlier, and assumed you were assisting Captain Ketos in looking for Emile. I thought convincing you to help me might be that much easier. But it seems all of you wish to put your own lives before those of others."

"Fuck off," Hunt growled. "Did you see what happened here this spring?"

"Yes. It convinced me of your . . . compassion." He said to Bryce, "I saw that you raced to Asphodel Meadows. To the humans." He glanced at Ithan. "You too. I thought it meant you'd be sympathetic to their greater plight." He again addressed Bryce. "That's why I wanted to get near you. You and Danika saved this city. I realized you two were close. I wanted to see if you might have any insights—I've long suspected that Danika might have arranged a rendezvous spot for Sofie." He faced Tharion. "Where do you believe the meet-up point would be?"

"Nowhere good," Tharion muttered. Then he added, "You'll get the details when we're good and ready to tell you, princey."

Cormac bristled, flames sparking in his hair again, but Bryce cut in, "How did Danika and Sofie meet?" Apparently, Ruhn realized, this trumped everything else for his sister.

Cormac shook his head. "I'm not sure. But from what Sofie told me, Danika suspected something about the Asteri, and needed someone to go in to confirm those suspicions. Sofie was that person."

Bryce's eyes were bright—churning. It didn't bode well.

Bryce's brows knit, though. "Danika died two years ago. Sofie had this intel for that long?"

"No. From what I've gathered, three years ago, Danika needed Sofie to go in to get it, but it took Sofie that long to gain access. Danika died before Sofie could ever pass the information to her. When she finally got it, she decided to use it to manipulate Ophion into upholding their bargain to go help rescue Emile."

"So Danika worked for *Ophion*?" Ithan asked. The wolf's face was a portrait of shock.

"No," Cormac said. "She was connected to them, but didn't report to them. As far as I understood from Sofie, Danika had her own agenda."

Bryce watched Cormac, her head angled to the side. Ruhn knew that look.

Bryce was planning something. Had definitely already planned something.

Bryce stepped closer to Cormac. The padding of her bare feet was the only sound. Ruhn braced himself for whatever was about to come out of her mouth. "For what it's worth, I don't think Aidas is in the habit of allowing Asteri loyalists into my apartment."

"Aidas." Cormac started, face paling. "That cat was the Prince of the Chasm?"

"Yep," Bryce said. "And I think Aidas brought you here as a gift to me." Athalar blinked at her, but Bryce went on, "Talk all you like about tracking Tharion here, and wanting to recruit Ruhn, but don't for one minute think that Aidas wasn't involved in your being here at the exact moment he told me to learn about my powers." She crossed her arms. "What do you know about the Starborn gifts?"

Cormac said nothing. And Ruhn found himself saying, half in dread that Bryce was right, "I told you the other night that our cousin here was obsessed enough with the idea of getting the Starsword that he learned everything he could about Starborn powers. He's a veritable library of information."

Cormac cut him a glare. But he admitted, "I did spend . . . much of my youth reading about the various gifts."

Her lips curled upward. "Rebel prince and bookworm." Athalar looked at her like she'd lost her mind. "I'll make a deal with you."

Hunt growled his objection, but Ruhn's mind churned. This was the Bryce he knew—always angling for the advantage.

"No interest in helping out of the goodness of your heart, Princess?" Cormac taunted.

"I want out of this marriage," Bryce said smoothly, running a finger over the counter's edge. Ruhn pretended not to see Athalar's shudder. "But I know that if I end our engagement too soon, my . . . sire will send along someone who isn't as motivated to work with me." Truth. "So we'll team up with Tharion here to find Emile. And I'll even help you find out whatever intel it was that Danika wanted Sofie to learn. But I want this engagement ended when I say it's time. And I want you to teach me about my magic. If not, good luck to you. I'll be sure to point Pippa and her Lightfall unit right in your direction."

Hunt smirked. Ruhn avoided doing the same. Tharion just tucked his arms behind his head. Only Ithan seemed surprised. Like he'd never seen this side of Bryce.

"Fine," Cormac said. "But the engagement will only be broken once my work here for Ophion is done. I need the reason to be in Valbara."

Ruhn expected Bryce to object, but she seemed to think it over. "We do need the cover to be seen together," she mused. "Otherwise, anyone who knows what a piece of shit you are would wonder why the Hel I would stoop to hang with you. It'd be suspicious."

Hunt coughed into his shoulder.

Ruhn blurted, "Am I the only one here who thinks this is insane?"

Ithan said, "I think we're all dead meat for even talking about this."

But Hunt rubbed his jaw, solemn and weary. "We need to talk this over before deciding." Bryce's hand brushed over his once more.

Ruhn grunted his agreement and said to his cousin, "You've dropped a shit-ton of information on us. We need to process." He gestured toward the door in dismissal. "We'll contact you."

Cormac didn't move an inch. "I require your blood oath not to say a word of this."

Ruhn barked a laugh. "I'm not making a blood oath. You can trust us. Can we trust you?"

"If I can trust cowards who like painting their nails while the rest of the world suffers, then you can trust me."

Bryce said wryly, "Going in hard with the charm, Cormac."

"Swear a blood oath. And I'll leave."

"No," Bryce said with surprising calm. "I have a manicure in ten minutes."

Cormac glowered. "I'll require your answer tomorrow. In the meantime, I am entrusting my life to you." His eyes slid to Ruhn's. "Should you wish to hear my *pitch*, I'll be at the bar on Archer and Ward today. Your services would be . . . greatly valued."

Ruhn said nothing. The fucker could rot.

Cormac's eyes narrowed with cold amusement. "Your father remains unaware of your mind-speaking gifts, doesn't he?"

"Are you threatening me?" Ruhn snarled.

Cormac shrugged, walking toward the door. "Come meet me at the bar and find out."

"Asshole," Ithan murmured.

Cormac paused with his hand on the knob. He sucked in a breath, the powerful muscles of his back rippling. When he looked over his shoulder, the amusement and threats were gone. "Beyond Sofie, beyond Emile . . . This world could be so much more. This world could be *free*. I don't understand why you wouldn't want that."

"Hard to enjoy being free," Hunt countered darkly, "if you're dead."

Cormac opened the door, stepping into the swirling shadows. "I can think of no better reason to yield my life."

17

Does anyone else feel like they're about to wake up from a bad dream?" Ithan's question echoed into the fraught silence of the apartment.

Bryce checked the clock on her phone. Had it really been less than an hour since she'd walked down the teeming lunchtime streets with Ruhn? She rubbed idly at her star, still glowing faintly, and said to no one in particular, "I need to get back to the archives."

Ruhn exclaimed, "After all that, you're going back to *work*?"

But she strode across the room, throwing Hunt a glance that had him following. He always got her like that—they didn't need Ruhn's fancy mind-speaking to communicate.

She halted by the front door. None of Cormac's power lingered—not even a wisp of shadow. Not one ember. For a heartbeat, she wished she had the serenity of Lehabah to return to, the serenity of the gallery and its quiet library.

But those things were irrevocably gone.

Bryce said as calmly as she could to the males watching her, schooling her face into neutrality, "We just had a bomb dropped into our lives. A bomb that is now ticking away. I need to think. And I have a job that I'm contractually obligated to show up to."

Where she could close her office door and figure out if she wanted to run like Hel from that bomb or face its wrath.

Hunt put a hand on her shoulder, but said nothing. He'd leapt in front of a bomb for her months ago. Had shielded her body with his own against the brimstone missile. There was nothing he could do to shield her from this, though.

Bryce couldn't bear to see the worry and dread she knew would be etched on his face. He knew what they were walking into. The enemy and odds they faced.

She pivoted to Tharion instead. "What do you want to do, Tharion? Not because the River Queen is pulling your puppet strings—what do *you* want?"

"This apartment, for starters," Tharion said, leaning his head back against the cushions, muscled chest expanding as he heaved a breath. "I want to find answers. Regardless of my orders, I want the truth of what I am facing—the enemy at my front as well as my back. But I'm inclined to believe Cormac—he didn't display any signs of lying."

"Trust me," Ruhn growled, "he's more skilled than you know."

"I don't think he was lying, either," Hunt admitted.

Bryce rubbed at her neck—then straightened. "Any chance that Dusk's Truth is somehow related to the Lightfall squadron?"

Tharion arched a brow. "Why?"

Hunt picked up her thread immediately. "Lightfall. Also known as dusk."

"And Project Thurr . . . thunder god . . . Could it be related to the thunderbirds?" Bryce went on.

"You think it involved some kind of intel about Pippa's Lightfall squadron?" Ruhn asked.

"It seemed to be some sort of groundbreaking info," Tharion said. "And Thurr . . . It could have had something to do with the thunderbird stuff. Sofie sounded afraid of the Asteri's wrath in her reply to Danika . . . Maybe it was because she was afraid of them knowing she had the gift."

"These are all hypotheticals," Hunt said. "And big stretches. But they might lead somewhere. Sofie and Danika were certainly well aware of the threats posed by both Lightfall and the Asteri."

Ithan said, "Can we go back to how the Prince of the Chasm was *sitting on my lap*?"

"You've got a lot to catch up on," Hunt said, chuckling darkly. "Be glad you weren't here for the first summoning."

Bryce elbowed him. "I really do have to return to work."

Ruhn asked, "You don't think we should go to the Bone Quarter to look for Emile and Sofie?"

Bryce winced. "I'm not going to the Bone Quarter to look for *anyone* unless we're absolutely certain that they're there."

"Agreed," Tharion said. "It's too dangerous to go on a whim. We'll keep investigating. Maybe Danika meant something else by *weary souls*."

Bryce nodded. "None of us talks to anyone else. I think we all know we're going to be roasted on a spit if this leaks."

"One word from Cormac and we're dead," Ruhn said gravely.

"One word from us," Hunt countered, "and *he's* dead." He jerked his chin at Bryce. She finally met his stare, finding only razor-sharp calculation there. "Grab a gun."

Bryce scowled. "Absolutely not." She gestured to her tight dress. "Where would I hide it?"

"Then take the sword." He pointed to her bedroom hallway. "Use it as some sort of accessory. If anyone can pull it off, you can."

Bryce couldn't help her glance at Ithan. It gave away everything.

"You never gave Danika's sword back after the attack this spring?" the wolf asked a shade quietly.

"Sabine can fight me for it," Bryce said, and ignored Hunt's order to take the blade from its resting place in her closet. Bryce twisted the knob. "Let's take the day. Agree not to fuck each other over on this, pray Cormac isn't a lying sack of shit, and then reconvene tomorrow night."

"Done," Tharion said.

Bryce stepped into the hall, Hunt on her heels, and heard Ithan sigh behind her. "This was not how I expected my day to go," the wolf muttered to Tharion before ratcheting up the volume on the TV.

Same, Bryce thought, and shut the door.

Hunt's head spun as he and Bryce rode the elevator down to the apartment lobby. He'd been free for a few glorious months, only to wind up right back on the cusp of another rebellion.

The same war, Aidas had claimed. Just by a different name, with a different army. Hunt's hands slicked with sweat. He'd seen how this war turned out. Felt its cost for centuries.

He said to Bryce, unable to stop the trembling that now overtook him, the sense that the elevator walls were pushing in, "I don't know what to do."

She leaned against the rail. "Me neither."

They waited until they were out on the street, keeping their voices down, before Hunt continued, words falling out of his mouth, "This isn't something we can jump into for the Hel of it." He couldn't get a breath down. "I've seen wrecked mech-suits with their human pilots hanging out of the cockpit, organs dangling. I've seen wolves as strong as Ithan ripped in two. I've seen angels decimate battlefields without setting foot on the ground." He shuddered, picturing Bryce among all that. "I . . . Fuck."

She looped her arm through his, and he leaned into her warmth, finding himself frozen despite the hot day. "This sounds more like . . . spying than battle-fighting or whatever."

"I'd rather die on the battlefield than in one of the Hind's interrogation rooms." *I'd rather you die on a battlefield than in her hands.* Hunt swallowed. "Sofie was lucky that the Hind dumped her and was done with it." He halted at an alley, tugging Bryce into its shadows with him.

He let himself look at her face: pale enough that her freckles stood out, eyes wide. Scared. The scent hit him a moment later.

"We were never going to be allowed to live like normal people," Bryce breathed, and Hunt ran a hand through her hair, savoring the silken strands. "Trouble was always going to come find us."

He knew she was right. They weren't the sort of people who could live ordinary lives. Hunt fought past the shaking in his bones, the roaring in his mind.

She lifted a hand, and her warm palm cupped his cheek. He leaned into her touch, reining in a purr as her thumb brushed over his cheekbone. "You really don't think Cormac is luring us into a trap with this claim that Sofie knew some vital intel—the bait being that Danika was involved in some way?"

"It's possible," Hunt admitted. "But there was clearly a connection between Danika and Sofie—the emails prove it. And Cormac seemed pretty damned shocked to learn that Sofie was potentially alive. I think he believed the intel on the Asteri had died with Sofie. I wouldn't blame him for wondering if it could be in play once more."

"You think there's any chance Sofie told Emile before they were separated?"

Hunt shrugged. "They were in Kavalla together—she might have found an opportunity to tell him. And if he doesn't have the intel, and Sofie is alive, he might know where Sofie is headed right now. That makes Emile a pretty valuable asset. For everyone."

Bryce began counting on her fingers. "So we've got Ophion, Tharion, and Cormac all wanting to find him."

"If you want to find him, too, Bryce, then we need to navigate carefully. Consider if we really want to get involved at all."

Her mouth twisted to the side. "If there's a chance that we could discover what Sofie knew, what Danika guessed—separate from Cormac, from this shit with that Pippa woman and whatever the River Queen wants—I think that intel is worth the risk."

"But why? So we can keep the Asteri from fucking with us about Micah and Sandriel?"

"Yeah. When I met up with Fury this morning, she mentioned that Danika knew something dangerous about her, so Fury learned something big about Danika in return." Hunt didn't get the chance to ask what exactly that was before Bryce said, "Why not apply the same thinking to this? The Asteri know something dangerous about me. About you." That they'd killed two Archangels. "I want to even the playing field a bit." Hunt could have sworn her expression was one he'd glimpsed on the Autumn King's face as she went on, "So we'll learn something vital about *them*. We'll take steps to ensure that if they fuck with us, the information will leak to the broader world."

"This is a deadly game. I'm not convinced the Asteri will want to play."

"I know. But beyond that, Danika thought this intel might be important enough to send Sofie after it—to risk her life for it. If Sofie is dead, then someone else needs to secure that information."

"It's not your responsibility, Bryce."

"It is."

He wasn't going to touch that one. Not yet. "And what about the kid?"

"We find him, too. I don't give a shit if he's powerful—he's a kid and he's caught up in this giant mess." Her eyes softened, and his heart with them. Would Shahar have cared about the boy? Only in the way Ophion and the River Queen seemed to: as a weapon. Bryce asked, head tilting to the side, "And what about Cormac's talk of freeing the world from the Asteri? That doesn't hold any weight with you?"

"Of course it does." He slid a hand over her waist, tugging her closer. "A world without them, without the Archangels and the hierarchies . . . I'd like to see that world one day. But . . ." His throat dried up. "But I don't want to live in that world if the risk of creating it means . . ." *Get it out.* "If it means that *we* might not make it to that world."

Her eyes softened once more, and her thumb stroked over his cheek again. "Same, Athalar."

He huffed a laugh, bowing his head, but she lifted his chin with her other hand. His fingers tightened on her waist.

Bryce's whiskey-colored eyes glowed in the muted light of the alley. "Well, since we're dabbling in some seriously dangerous shit, now's probably as good a time as any to admit I don't want to wait until Winter Solstice."

"For what?" Fuck, his voice had dropped an octave.

"This," she murmured, and rose onto her toes to kiss him.

Hunt met her halfway, unable to contain his groan as he hauled her against him, lips finding hers at the same moment their bodies touched. He could have sworn the fucking world spun out from under him at the taste of her—

His head filled with fire and lightning and storms, and all he could think of was her mouth, her warm, luscious body, the aching of his cock pressing against his pants—pressing against *her* as her arms twined around his neck.

He was going to kick that wolf out of the apartment immediately.

Hunt twisted, pinning her against the wall, and her mouth opened wider on a gasp. He swept his tongue in, tasting the honeyed spice that was pure Bryce. She wrapped a leg around his waist, and Hunt took the invitation, hefting her thigh higher, pressing himself against her until they were both writhing.

Anyone might walk by the alley and see them. Lunchtime workers were streaming past. All it would take was one peek down the alley into the dusty shadows, *one* photograph, and this whole thing—

Hunt halted.

One photo, and her engagement to Cormac would be off. Along with the bargain Bryce had crafted with him.

Bryce asked, panting hard, "What's wrong?"

"We, ah . . ." Words had become foreign. All thought had gone between his legs. Between *her* legs.

He swallowed hard, then gently backed away, trying to master his jagged breathing. "You're engaged. Technically. You have to keep up that ruse with Cormac, at least in public."

She straightened her dress, and—shit. Was that a lilac lace bra peeking out from the neckline? Why the fuck hadn't he explored that just now? Bryce peered down the alley, lips swollen from his kisses, and some feral part of him howled in satisfaction to see that *he* had done that, *he* had brought that flush to her cheeks and wine-rich scent of arousal to her. She was *his*.

And he was hers. Utterly fucking hers.

"Are you suggesting we find a seedy motel instead?" Her lips curved, and Hunt's cock throbbed at the sight, as if begging for her mouth to slide over him.

He let out a strangled noise. "I'm suggesting . . ." Hel, what *was* he suggesting? "I don't know." He blew out a breath. "You're sure you want to do this now?" He gestured between them. "I know emotions are high after what we've learned. I . . ." He couldn't look at her. "Whatever you want, Quinlan. That's what I mean to say."

She was silent for a moment. Then her hand slid over his chest, landing upon his heart. "What do you want? Why is it only what I want?"

"Because you were the one who mentioned waiting until solstice."

"And?"

"And I want to make sure that you're fully on board with ending our . . . agreement."

"All right. But I also want to know what *you* want, Hunt."

He met her golden stare. "You know what I want." He couldn't stop his voice from lowering again. "I've never stopped wanting it—wanting you. I thought it was obvious."

Her heart was thundering. He could hear it. He glanced down at her ample chest and beheld a faint glimmering. "Your star . . ."

"Let's not even get started on this thing," she said, waving a hand at it. "Let's keep talking about how much you want me." She winked.

Hunt slung an arm around her shoulders, steering her back toward the bustling avenue. He whispered in her ear, "Why don't I just show you later?"

She laughed, the star's glow fading in the sunlight as they emerged onto the baking streets, and she slipped on her sunglasses and hat. "That's what I want, Hunt. That is *definitely* what I want."

18

Ithan rubbed at his face. This day had gotten . . . complicated.

"You look like you need a drink," Tharion said as he strode to the apartment door. Ruhn had left a moment ago. Ithan supposed he'd sit on his ass for a good few hours and contemplate the epic mess he'd somehow landed in the middle of. That Bryce seemed intent on involving herself in.

"How long have you guys been doing all this shit?"

"You know what happened during the Summit, right?"

"Demons wrecked the city, killed a lot of people. Two Archangels died. Everyone knows that."

Tharion's brows rose. "You ever learn how Micah and Sandriel died?"

Ithan blinked, bracing himself.

Tharion's expression was dead serious. "I am telling you this after I received a personal phone call from Rigelus three months ago, telling me to keep my mouth shut or I'd be killed, my parents with me. But as everything I'm doing these days seems to point toward that road anyway—you might as well know the truth, too. Since you'll likely wind up dead with us."

"Fantastic." Ithan wished Perry had dumped him anywhere but this apartment.

Tharion said, "Hunt ripped Sandriel's head from her shoulders after the Archangel threatened Bryce."

Ithan started. He'd known Athalar was intense as shit, but killing an Archangel—

"And Bryce slaughtered Micah after he bragged about killing Danika and the Pack of Devils."

Ithan's body went numb. "I . . ." He couldn't get a breath down. "Micah . . . what?"

By the time Tharion finished explaining, Ithan was shaking. "Why didn't she tell me?" That packless wolf inside him was howling with rage and pain.

Fuck, Sabine had no idea Micah had killed her daughter. Or . . . wait. Sabine *did* know. Sabine and Amelie had both been at the Summit, along with the Prime. They'd witnessed through the feeds what Tharion had just described.

And . . . and hadn't told him. The rest of the Den, fine, but Connor was his brother. The urge to shift, to bellow and roar, filled his blood, trembling along his bones. He suppressed it.

Tharion went on, unaware of the animal within trying to claw free. "The Asteri have made it clear to Bryce and Athalar: one word to anyone, and they're dead. The only reason they're not dead yet is because they've played nicely this summer."

Claws appeared at Ithan's fingertips. Tharion didn't fail to note them.

Through a mouth full of lengthening fangs, Ithan growled, "Micah killed my brother. And Bryce killed Micah because of it." He couldn't wrap his mind around it—that Bryce, *before* the Drop, had destroyed an Archangel.

It made no sense.

He'd had the audacity, the ignorance, to question her love for Danika and Connor. His claws and fangs retracted. That wolf inside ceased baying.

Ithan rubbed at his face again, shame an oily river through him that drowned that wolf inside his skin. "I need some time to process this." The wolf he used to be would have run to the sunball field to practice until he became nothing but breath and sweat and the thoughts sorted themselves out. But he hadn't set foot on one of those fields in two years. He wasn't going to start now.

Tharion headed for the door again. "I'm sure you do, but a word of advice: don't take too long. Urd works in strange ways, and I don't think it was a coincidence that you were brought here right as this shit started."

"So I'm supposed to go along with it on some hunch that fate is nudging me?"

"Maybe," the mer answered. He shrugged his powerful shoulders, honed from a lifetime of swimming. "But whenever you're tired of sitting on the couch feeling sorry for yourself, come find me. I could use a wolf's sense of smell."

"For what?"

Tharion's face turned grave. "I need to find Emile before Pippa Spetsos. Or Cormac."

The mer left him with that. For a long moment, Ithan sat in silence.

Had Connor known anything about Danika's involvement with Sofie Renast? Had Sabine? He doubted it, but . . . At least Bryce had been as much in the dark about this as he was.

Bryce, who had used Danika's sword during the attack on this city, and kept it ever since. Ithan glanced to the door.

He moved before he could second-guess the wisdom and morality of it, going right to the coat closet. Umbrellas, boxes of crap . . . nothing. The linen closet and the laundry closet didn't reveal anything, either.

Which left . . . He winced as he entered her bedroom.

He didn't know how he hadn't seen it the other night. Well, he'd been beaten to Hel and back, so that was excuse enough, but . . . the sword leaned against the chair beside her tall dresser, as if she'd left it there for decoration.

Ithan's mouth dried out, but he stalked for the ancient blade. Gifted to Danika by the Prime—an act that had infuriated Sabine, who'd long expected to inherit the family weapon.

He could still hear Sabine raging in the weeks after Danika's death, trying to find where Danika had left the sword. She'd practically torn that old apartment to pieces to find it. Ithan had thought it lost until he saw Bryce brandishing it this spring.

Breath tight in his chest, Ithan picked up the blade. It was light but perfectly balanced. He drew it from the sheath, the metal shining in the dim light.

Damn, it was gorgeous. Simple, yet impeccably made.

He blew out a long breath, chasing away the clinging cobwebs of memories—Danika carrying this sword everywhere, wielding it in practice, the blade somehow validation that even if Sabine sucked, with Danika, they had a bright future, with Danika, the wolves would become *more*—

He couldn't help it. He took up a defensive stance and swung the blade.

Yeah, it was perfect. A remarkable feat of craftsmanship.

Ithan pivoted, feinting and then striking at an invisible opponent. Sabine would lose her shit if she knew he was messing around with the blade. Whatever.

Ithan struck again at the shadows, shuddering at the beautiful song of the sword slicing through the air. And . . . what the Hel: he'd had a weird fucking morning. He needed to burn off some tension.

Lunging and parrying, leaping and rolling, Ithan sparred against an invisible enemy.

Maybe he'd gone crazy. Maybe this was what happened to wolves without a pack.

The sword was an extension of his arm, he thought. He slid over the glass dining table, taking on two, three, ten opponents—

Holstrom blocks; Holstrom presses—

Moving through the apartment, Ithan leapt up onto the coffee table in front of the sectional, wood shuddering beneath him, the narration loud and precise in his head. *Holstrom delivers the killing blow!*

He swiped the sword down in a triumphant arc.

The front door opened.

Bryce stared at him. Standing on the coffee table with Danika's sword.

"I forgot my work ID . . . ?" Bryce started, brows so high they seemed capable of touching her hairline. Ithan prayed Solas would melt him into the floor and boil his blood into steam.

It seemed the sun god was listening. The coffee table groaned. Then cracked.

And collapsed entirely beneath him.

Ithan might have continued to lie there, hoping some Reaper would come suck the soul from his body, had Bryce not rushed over. Not to him—not to help him up. But to investigate something just beyond his line of sight.

"What the Hel is this?" she asked, kneeling.

Ithan managed to move his ass off the debris, lifting his head to see her crouching over a stack of papers. "Was there a drawer in the table?"

"No. There must have been a secret compartment." Bryce flicked splinters of wood from the half-scattered pile. "This table was here when I moved in—all the furniture was Danika's." She lifted her gaze to him. "Why would she hide her old college papers in here?"

Ruhn held the Starsword to the grindstone. Black, iridescent sparks flew from the blade's edge. Behind him in the otherwise empty Aux armory, Flynn and Declan cleaned their array of guns at a worktable.

He'd planned to meet them here this afternoon. Had intended to hone the sword, clean and inspect his guns, and then cap the day off with a City Head meeting to discuss the new Archangel.

A normal day, in other words. Except for the colossal, life-threatening shit that had just gone down. Incredibly, the Prince of the Chasm was the least of his problems.

"Out with it," Flynn said without halting work on his handgun.

"What?" Ruhn asked, pulling the blade away.

Declan answered, "Whatever has kept you standing there in silence for ten minutes, not even complaining about Flynn's shitty playlist."

"Asshole," Flynn said to Dec, nodding toward where his phone blasted heavy metal. "This stuff is poetry."

"They've done studies where plants wither up and die when exposed to this music," Declan countered. "Which is precisely how I feel right now."

Flynn chuckled. "I'm guessing you're brooding about one of three things: horrible daddy, baby sister, or pretty fiancée."

"None of them, dickhead," Ruhn said, slumping into the chair across the table from them. He glanced to the doors, listening. When he was assured no one occupied the hall beyond, he said, "My lunch hour began with finding the Prince of the Chasm in feline form at Bryce's apartment, where he revealed that Cormac is an Ophion rebel, and it ended with learning that Cormac is on the hunt for a missing kid and the kid's spy sister. Who happens to be Cormac's girlfriend. And he's basically threatened to tell my father about my mind-speaking gifts if I don't meet him at some bar to hear his pitch for how I can be of use to Ophion."

His friends gaped. Declan said carefully, "Is everyone . . . alive?"

"Yes," Ruhn said, sighing. "I was sworn to secrecy, but . . ."

"So long as you didn't swear a blood oath, who cares?" Flynn said, gun forgotten on the table beside him.

"Trust me, Cormac tried. I refused."

"Good," Dec said. "Tell us everything."

They were the only two people in the world Ruhn would trust with this knowledge. Bryce—and Hunt—would kick his ass for saying anything, but too fucking bad. They had each other to vent to. So Ruhn opened his mouth and explained.

"And . . . that's where I'm at," Ruhn finished, toying with the ring through his lip.

Flynn rubbed his hands together. "This should be exciting." He was totally serious. Ruhn gawked at him.

But Declan was eyeing him thoughtfully. "I once hacked into an imperial military database and saw the uncensored footage from the battlefields and camps." Even Flynn's smile vanished. Declan went on, red hair gleaming in the firstlights, "It made me sick. I dreamed about it for weeks afterward."

"Why didn't you say anything?" Ruhn asked.

"Because there was nothing to be done about it. It seemed that way, at least." Declan nodded, as if to himself. "Whatever you need, I'm in."

"That easy, huh?" Ruhn said, brows lifting.

"That easy," Dec answered.

Ruhn had to take a moment. He had no idea what god he'd pleased enough to warrant being blessed with such friends. They were more than friends. They were his brothers. Ruhn finally said hoarsely, "We get caught, and we're dead. Our families with us." He added to Dec, "And Marc."

"Trust me, Marc would be the first one to say Hel yes to this. He hates the Asteri." Dec's smile turned subdued. "But . . . yeah, I think it's safer if he doesn't know." He frowned at Flynn. "Can you keep quiet?"

Flynn made an outraged sound.

"You talk when you're wasted," Ruhn chimed in. But he knew Flynn was a steel vault when he wanted to be.

Declan's voice deepened into a ridiculous mockery of Flynn as he said, "Oh, sexy nymph-writer, look at your boobs, they're so round, they remind me of these bombs the Aux is hiding in their armory in case of—"

"That was *not* what fucking happened!" Flynn hissed. "She was a reporter, first of all—"

"And it was twenty years ago," Ruhn cut him off before this could descend into further insanity. "I think you learned your lesson."

Flynn glowered. "So what now? You're going to go meet Cormac and hear him out?"

Ruhn blew out a breath and began cleaning the sword in earnest. Bryce was going to go ballistic. "I don't see how I have any other choice."

19

"What the fuck *is* this?" Bryce whispered as she knelt in the ruins of her coffee table and leafed through the stack of papers that had apparently been hidden inside.

"It's not only college papers," Ithan said, fanning out the pages beside her. "These are documents and images of newspaper clippings." He peered at them. "They all seem like they're regarding firstlight's uses—mostly how it was made into weapons."

Bryce's hands shook. She sifted through a few academic articles— all full of redactions—theorizing on the origin of worlds and what the Asteri even *were*.

"She never mentioned any of this," Bryce said.

"Think this is what Sofie Renast discovered?" he asked. "Like, maybe Danika sniffed something out about the Asteri with her . . ." He trailed off, then added, "Gifts?"

Bryce lifted her gaze to his carefully neutral face as he tried to recover from a stumble. "You knew about her bloodhound gift?"

Ithan shifted on his knees. "It wasn't ever talked about, but . . . yeah. Connor and I knew."

Bryce flipped another page, tucking that factoid away. "Well, why would it even matter if Danika had sniffed out something regarding the Asteri? They're holy stars." Beings that possessed the force of an entire star within them, unaging and undying.

But as Bryce skimmed article after article, Ithan doing the same beside her, she began to see that they challenged that fact. She made herself keep breathing steadily. Danika had been a history major at CCU. None of this stuff was out of the ordinary—except that it had been hidden. Here.

All we have as proof of their so-called sacred power is their word, Bryce read. *Who has ever seen such a star manifest itself? If they are stars from the heavens, then they are fallen stars.*

A chill ran down Bryce's spine, one hand drifting to her chest. She had a star within her. Well, starlight that manifested as a star-shaped thing, but . . . What was the Asteri's power, then? The sun was a star—did they possess the power of an actual sun?

If so, this rebellion was fucked. Maybe Danika had wondered about it, and wanted Sofie to verify it somehow. Maybe that was what the intel was about, what Danika had suspected and dreaded and needed to officially confirm: there was no way to win. Ever.

Bryce wished Hunt were here, but she didn't dare call him with this info. Though after what had happened between them in the alley during lunch, maybe it was good they weren't in close quarters. She didn't trust herself to keep her hands off him.

Because *gods-damn*. That kiss. She hadn't hesitated. Had seen Hunt, that usually unflappable exterior melting away, and . . . she'd needed to kiss him.

The problem was that now she needed more. It was unfortunate that Ithan was staying with her, and the kind of sex she planned to have with Hunt would rattle the walls.

But . . . Urd must have sent her back to the apartment just now. For this. She exhaled. Ran a hand over the pages. The final papers in the pile made Bryce's breath catch.

"What is it?" Ithan asked.

Bryce shook her head, angling slightly away from him to read the text again.

Dusk's Truth.

The same project that had been mentioned in the emails between Sofie and Danika. That Danika had said would be of interest to Sofie.

Danika had been digging into it since *college*? Bryce inhaled and turned to the next page.

It was completely blank. Like Danika had never gotten to writing down any notes about it.

"Dusk's Truth was one of the things that Danika mentioned to Sofie," Bryce said quietly. "Dusk's Truth and Project Thurr."

"What is it?"

She shook her head again. "I don't know. But there has to be a connection between all of it." She tossed the Dusk's Truth document back onto the pile.

Ithan asked, "So what now?"

She sighed. "I gotta get back to work."

He arched a brow in question.

"Job, remember?" She got to her feet. "Maybe, um . . . find someplace to hide this stuff? And don't play Warrior Hero anymore. I liked that coffee table."

Ithan flushed. "I wasn't playing Warrior Hero," he muttered.

Bryce snickered and grabbed her ID from where she'd left it hanging beside the door, but then she sobered. "You looked good wielding it, Ithan."

"I was just screwing around." His tone was tense enough that she didn't say anything more before leaving.

Ruhn found Cormac at the pool hall in FiRo, losing to a satyr, an old rock song crackling from the jukebox on the other side of the concrete-lined space.

Cormac said, focusing on his shot, "I'd never tell your father, by the way."

"And yet here I am," Ruhn said. The satyr noted the expression on Ruhn's face and made himself scarce. "Seems like your threat worked."

"Desperate times," Cormac muttered.

Ruhn grabbed the cue the satyr had discarded, eyeing the pool table. He spotted the satyr's next shot immediately and smirked. "He was probably going to kick your ass."

Cormac again assessed his shot. "I was letting him win. It was the princely thing to do."

Balls cracked, and Ruhn chuckled as they scattered. None found a pocket.

"Sure," Ruhn said, aligning the cue ball. Two balls found their homes with a satisfying *plink*.

Cormac swore softly. "I have a feeling this is more your element than mine."

"Guilty."

"You seem like a male who spends his time in places like this."

"As opposed to . . . ?"

"Doing things."

"I head up the Aux. It's not like I squat in dives all day." Ruhn looked pointedly around the bar.

"That party suggested otherwise."

"We like to enjoy ourselves here in sunny Lunathion."

Cormac snorted. "Apparently." He watched Ruhn pocket another ball, then blow his second shot by an inch. "You have more piercings since the last time I saw you. And more ink. Things must be dull around here if that's what you spend your time on."

"All right," Ruhn said, leaning against his cue. "You're a brooding hero and I'm a lazy asshole. Is that really how you want to start your pitch?"

Cormac made his move, one of the balls finally sinking into a pocket. But his second shot missed, leaving the angle Ruhn needed completely open. "Hear me out, cousin. That's all I ask."

"Fine." Ruhn took his shot. "Let's hear it." His voice was barely more than a whisper.

Cormac leaned against his cue and studied the empty bar before saying, "Sofie was in contact with our most vital spy in the rebellion—Agent Daybright."

Unease wended through Ruhn. He really, really didn't want to know this.

Cormac went on, "Daybright has direct access to the Asteri—Ophion has long wondered whether Daybright is one of the Asteri themselves. Daybright and Sofie used codes on crystal-fueled radios to pass along messages. But with Sofie's . . . disappearance, it's become too dangerous to keep using the old methods of communicating. The fact that the Hind was able to be on the scene so quickly that night indicates that someone might have intercepted those messages and broken our codes. We need someone who can mind-speak to be in direct contact with Agent Daybright."

"And why the fuck would I ever agree to work with you?" Beyond the threat of Cormac telling his father about his talents.

The mind-speaking was a rare gift of the Avallen Fae, inherited from his mother's bloodline, and had always come naturally to him. He'd been four the first time he'd done it—he'd asked his mother for a sandwich. She'd screamed when she'd heard him in her mind, and in that moment, he'd known that the gift was something to hide, to keep secret. When she'd rubbed her head, clearly wondering if she'd imagined things, he'd kept quiet. And made sure she had no reason to bring him to his father, who he knew, even then, would have questioned and examined him and never let him go. Ruhn hadn't made that mistake again.

He wouldn't let his father control this piece of him, too. And even if Cormac had sworn he wouldn't reveal it . . . he'd be stupid to believe his cousin.

"Because it's the right thing to do," Cormac said. "I've seen those death camps. Seen what's left of the people who survive. The children who survive. It can't be allowed to go on."

Ruhn said, "The prison camps are nothing new. Why act now?"

"Because Daybright came along and started feeding us vital information that has led to successful strikes on supply lines, missions, encampments. Now that we have someone in the upper echelons of the Asteri's rule, it changes everything. The information Daybright would pass to you can save thousands of lives."

"And take them," Ruhn said darkly. "Did you tell Command about me?"

"No," Cormac said earnestly. "I only mentioned that I had a contact in Lunathion who might be useful in reestablishing our connection with Daybright, and was sent here."

Ruhn couldn't fault him for trying. While he couldn't read

thoughts or invade people's unguarded minds as some of his cousins could, he'd learned that he could talk to people on a sort of psychic bridge, as if his mind had formed it brick by brick between souls. It was perfect for a spy network.

But Ruhn asked, "And it was coincidence that it happened to line up with Emile coming here, too?"

A slight smile. "Two birds, one stone. I needed a reason to be here, to cover for my hunt for him. Seeking out your gifts offered that to Ophion. As does my engagement to your sister."

Ruhn frowned. "So you're asking me to what—help out this one time? Or for the rest of my fucking life?"

"I'm asking you, Ruhn, to pick up where Sofie left off. How long you decide to work with us is up to you. But right now, Ophion is desperate for Daybright's information. People's lives depend on it. Daybright has alerted us three times now before an imperial attack on one of our bases. Those warnings saved thousands of lives. We need you for the next few months—or at least until we've attained the intel that Sofie knew."

"I don't see how I have any choice but to say yes."

"I told you—I won't tell your father. I just needed to get you here. To get you to listen. I wouldn't ask this of you unless it was necessary."

"How'd you even get caught up in all this rebel business?" Cormac's life had been pretty cushy, as far as Ruhn could tell. But he supposed that to an outsider, his own life looked the same.

Cormac weighed the cue in his hands. "It's a long story. I linked up with them about four years ago."

"And what's your title with Ophion, exactly?"

"Field agent. Technically, I'm a field commander of the northwestern Pangeran spy network." He exhaled slowly. "Sofie was one of my agents."

"But now you're trying to keep Emile away from Ophion? Having doubts about the cause?"

"Never about the cause," Cormac said quietly. "Only about the people in it. After the heavy hits to the bases this year, Ophion has about ten thousand members left, controlled by a team of twenty in

Command. Most of them are humans, but some are Vanir. Any Vanir affiliated with Ophion, Command or not, are sworn to secrecy, perhaps to stricter standards than the humans."

Ruhn angled his head and asked baldly, "How do you know you can trust me?"

"Because your sister put a bullet through the head of an Archangel and you've all kept quiet about it."

Ruhn nodded toward a pocket, but missed his final shot. Yet he said calmly, "I don't know what you're talking about."

Cormac laughed softly. "Really? My father's spies learned of it before the Asteri shut the information down."

"Then why treat her like some party girl?"

"Because she went back to partying after what happened last spring."

"So did I." But they were getting off topic. "What do you know about Agent Daybright?"

"As much as you do." Cormac's ball went wide by an embarrassing margin.

"How do I make contact? And what's the process after I receive information?"

"You pass it to me. I know where to send it in Command."

"And again, I'm supposed to simply . . . trust you."

"I've trusted you with information that could land me in the Asteri's cells."

Not just any prison. For this kind of thing, for someone of Cormac's rank—Ruhn's rank—it'd be the notorious dungeons beneath the Asteri's crystal palace. A place so awful, so brutal, that rumor claimed there were no cameras. No record, no proof of atrocities. Except for rare witnesses and survivors like Athalar.

Ruhn again lined up his final shot and called the pocket, but paused before making it. "So how do I do it? Cast my mind into oblivion and hope someone answers?"

Cormac chuckled, swearing again as Ruhn sank his last ball. Ruhn wordlessly grabbed the wooden triangle and began to rerack the balls.

Ruhn broke the balls with a thunderous crack, starting the next round. The three and seven balls landed in opposite pockets—solids, then.

Cormac pulled a small quartz crystal from his pocket and tossed it to Ruhn. "It's all hypothetical right now, given that we've never worked with someone like you. But first try to contact Daybright by holding this. Daybright has the sister to this comm-crystal. It possesses the same communicative properties as the Gates in this city."

The comm-crystal was warm against Ruhn's skin as he pocketed it. "How does it work?"

"That's how our radios reached Daybright. Seven crystals all hewn from one rock—six in radios in our possession, the seventh in Daybright's radio. They're beacons—on the same precise frequency. Always desiring to connect into one whole again. This crystal is the last one that remains of our six. The other five were destroyed for safety. I'm hoping that if someone with your powers holds it in your hand, it might link you with Daybright when you cast your mind out. The same way the Gates here can send audio between them."

Cormac's gaze had gone hazy—pained. And Ruhn found himself asking, "Is this crystal from Sofie's radio?"

"Yes." Cormac's voice thickened. "She gave it to Command before she went into Kavalla. They gave it to me when I mentioned I might know someone who could use it."

Ruhn weighed the grief, the pain in his cousin's face before he softened his tone. "Sofie sounds like a remarkable person."

"She was. Is." Cormac's throat bobbed. "I need to find her. And Emile."

"You love her?"

Cormac's eyes burned with flame. "I don't try to delude myself into thinking that my father would ever approve of a union with a part-human—especially one with no fortune or name. But yes. I was hoping to find a way to spend my life with her."

"You really think she's here, trying to meet up with Emile?"

"The mer didn't rule it out. Why should I?" Again those walls rose in Cormac's eyes. "If your sister knows anything about whether Danika found a hiding place for them, I need to know."

Ruhn noted the faint hint of desperation—of dread and panic—and decided to put his cousin out of his misery. "We suspect Danika might have told Sofie to lie low in the Bone Quarter," he said.

Alarm flared across Cormac's face, but he nodded his gratitude to Ruhn. "Then we will need to find a way to secure safe passage there—and find some way to search unseen and undisturbed."

Well, Ruhn needed a drink. Thank Urd they were already in a bar. "All right." He surveyed his cousin, the perfect blond hair and handsome face. "For what it's worth, if we can find Sofie, I think you should marry her, if she feels the same way about you. Don't let your father tie you into some betrothal you don't want."

Cormac didn't smile. He observed Ruhn with the same clear-eyed scrutiny and said, "The witch-queen Hypaxia is beautiful and wise. You could do far worse, you know."

"I know." That was as much as Ruhn would say about it.

She *was* beautiful. Stunningly, distractingly beautiful. But she had zero interest in him. She'd made that clear in the months after the Summit. He didn't entirely blame her. Even if he'd had a glimpse of what life might have been like with her. Like peering through a keyhole.

Cormac cleared his throat. "When you connect with Daybright, say this to confirm your identity."

As his cousin rattled off the code phrases, Ruhn made shot after shot, until only two balls remained and he blew an easy one and scratched the cue ball to give his cousin a chance. He didn't know why he bothered.

Cormac handed the cue ball back to him. "I don't want a pity win."

Ruhn rolled his eyes but took the ball back, making another shot. "Is there any intel I should be asking Daybright about?"

"For months now, we've been trying to coordinate a hit on the Spine. Daybright is our main source of information regarding when and where to strike."

The Spine—the north-south railway that cut Pangera in half. The main artery for supplies in this war.

"Why risk the hit?" Ruhn asked. "To disrupt the supply lines?"

"That, and Daybright's been getting whispers for months now about the Asteri working on some sort of new mech-suit prototype."

"Different from the mech-suits the humans use?"

"Yes. This is a mech-suit designed for Vanir to pilot. For the imperial armies."

"Fuck." He could only imagine how dangerous they'd be.

"Exactly," Cormac said. He checked his watch. "I need to head toward the Black Dock—I want to know if there's any hint that Emile or Sofie have been there. But contact Daybright as soon as you can. We need to intercept the Vanir suit prototype to study its technology before it can be used to slaughter us."

Ruhn nodded, resigned. "All right. I'll help you."

"Your friends will not be pleased. Athalar in particular."

"Leave Athalar to me." He didn't answer to the angel. Though his sister . . .

Cormac observed him once more. "When you want out, I'll get you out. I promise."

Ruhn sank his last ball into his chosen pocket and leaned the stick against the concrete wall. "I'll hold you to that."

20

The water dripping from Tharion's wave skimmer onto the plastic floor of the dry dock in the Blue Court was the only sound as he repaired the vehicle. His sweat dripped along with it, despite the chamber's cool temperature. He'd stripped off his shirt within minutes of arriving here, even its soft cotton too confining against his skin as he worked. Reeds had gotten stuck in the engine during his trip out to the marshes the other day, and though the engineering team could have easily fixed the issue, he'd wanted to do it himself.

Wanted to give his mind some time to sort everything out.

When he'd awoken that morning, talking to the Prince of the Chasm—pretending to be a cat, for Urd's sake—hadn't been remotely near the list of possibilities for his day. Nor had finding out that an Avallen prince was an Ophion rebel searching for Sofie Renast's younger brother. Or that Danika Fendyr had sent Sofie to gather some vital intel on the Asteri. No, he'd awoken with only one goal: learn what Ithan Holstrom knew.

A whole lot of nothing, apparently.

Some Captain of Intelligence. *Captain Whatever*, Holstrom had called him. Tharion was half-inclined to get it etched into a plaque for his desk.

But at least Holstrom had agreed to help out should Tharion

need his nose to find the kid. If Pippa Spetsos was hunting for Emile as Cormac had claimed, politics and Sofie and his queen aside . . . they needed to find the kid first. If only to spare him from being forced to use those thunderbird powers in horrible ways. Holstrom would be a valuable asset in that endeavor.

And besides—the wolf seemed like he needed something to do.

The door to the dry dock room whooshed open, ushering in a scent of bubbling streams and water lilies. Tharion kept his attention on the engine, the wrench clenched in his hand.

"I heard you were here," said a lilting female voice, and Tharion plastered a smile on his face as he looked over a shoulder at the River Queen's daughter.

She wore her usual diaphanous pale blue gown, offsetting the warm brown of her skin. River pearls and shards of abalone gleamed in her thick black curls, cascading well past her slim shoulders to the small of her back. She glided toward him on bare feet, the chill water coating the floor seemingly not bothering her at all. She always moved like that: as if she were floating underwater. She had no mer form—was only a fraction mer, actually. She was some kind of elemental humanoid, as at home in the open air as she was beneath the surface. Part woman, part river.

Tharion held up his wrench, a strip of river weed tangled around the tip. "Repairs."

"Why do you still insist on doing them yourself?"

"Gives me a tangible task." He leaned against the wave skimmer on the lift behind him, the water beading its sides cool against his hot skin.

"Is your work for my mother so unfulfilling that you need such things?"

Tharion offered a charming smile. "I like to pretend I know what I'm doing around machines," he deflected.

She gave him a light laugh in return, coming closer. Tharion kept himself perfectly still, refusing to shy from the hand she laid on his bare chest. "I haven't seen much of you lately."

"Your mother's been keeping me busy." *Take it up with her.*

A small, shy smile. "I'd hoped we could . . ." She blushed, and Tharion caught the meaning.

They hadn't done *that* in years. Why now? Water-spirits were capricious—he'd figured she'd gotten him, had him, lost interest, and moved on. Even if the vows between them still bound them together irreparably.

Tharion covered her small hand with his own, brushing his thumb over the velvety skin. "It's late, and I have an early start."

"And yet you're here, toiling on this . . . machine." She took after her mother when it came to technology. Had barely mastered the concept of a computer, despite lessons with Tharion. He wondered if she even knew the name for the machine behind him.

"I need it for tomorrow's work." A lie.

"More than you need me?"

Yes. Definitely yes.

But Tharion gave another one of those grins. "Another time, I promise."

"I heard you went into the city today."

"I'm always in the city."

She eyed him, and he noted the jealous, wary gleam.

"Who did you see?"

"Some friends."

"Which ones?"

How many interrogations had begun like this and ended in her crying to her mother? The last one had been only a few days ago. Afterward, he'd wound up on that boat in the Haldren Sea, hunting for Sofie Renast's remains.

He said carefully, "Bryce Quinlan, Ruhn Danaan, Ithan Holstrom, and Hunt Athalar." No need to mention Aidas or Prince Cormac. They weren't his friends.

"Bryce Quinlan—the girl from this spring? With the star?"

He wasn't surprised she only asked about the female. "Yeah." Another wary look that Tharion pretended not to notice as he said casually, "She and Athalar are dating now, you know. A nice ending after everything that went down."

The River Queen's daughter relaxed visibly, shoulders slumping. "How sweet."

"I'd like to introduce you sometime." A blatant lie.

"I shall ask Mother."

He said, "I'm going to see them again tomorrow. You could join me." It was reckless, but . . . he'd spent ten years now avoiding her, dodging the truth. Maybe they could change it up a bit.

"Oh, Mother will need more time than that to prepare."

He bowed his head, the picture of understanding. "Just let me know when. It'll be a double date."

"What's that?"

Television didn't exist down here. Or at least in the River Queen's royal chambers. So popular culture, anything modern . . . they weren't even on her radar.

Not that theirs could be considered a true betrothal. It was more like indentured servitude.

"Two couples going out to a meal together. You know, a date . . . times two."

"Ah." A pretty smile. "I'd like that."

So would Athalar. Tharion would never hear the end of it. He glanced at the clock. "I do have an early start, and this engine is a mess . . ."

It was as close to a dismissal as he'd ever dare make. He did have a few rights: she could seek him out for sex—as she'd done—but he could say no without repercussions; and his duties as Captain of Intelligence were more important than seeing to her needs. He prayed she'd consider fixing a wave skimmer one of those duties.

Ogenas be thanked, she did. "I'll leave you to it, then."

And then she was gone, the scent of water lilies with her. As the doors slid open to let her through, Tharion glimpsed her four mer guards waiting on the other side—the River Queen's daughter never went anywhere alone. The broad-chested males would have fought to the death for the chance to share her bed. He knew they detested him for having and rejecting that access.

He'd happily yield his position. If only the River Queen would let him.

Alone again, Tharion sighed, leaning his forehead against the wave skimmer.

He didn't know how much more of this he could take. It could be weeks or years until she and her mother would start pushing for the wedding. And then for children. And he'd be locked in a cage, here below the surface, until even his Vanir life expired. Old and dreamless and forgotten.

A fate worse than death.

But if this thing with Sofie and Emile Renast was indeed playing out in a big way . . . he'd use it as his temporary escape. He didn't give a shit about the rebellion, not really. But his queen had given him a task, so he'd milk this investigation for all it was worth. Perhaps see what the intel Sofie had gathered could gain *him*.

Until his own stupid choices finally called in a debt.

"And here's the common room," Hunt said through his teeth to Baxian as he shouldered open the door to the barracks hangout area. "As you already know."

"Always nice to hear from a local," Baxian said, black wings folded in tightly as he noted the dim space: the little kitchenette to the left of the door, the sagging chairs and couches before the large TV, the door to the bathrooms straight ahead. "This is only for triarii?"

"All yours tonight," Hunt said, checking his phone. After ten. He'd been on his way out at seven when Celestina had called, asking him to give Baxian a tour of the Comitium. Considering the sheer size of the place . . . it had taken this long. Especially because Baxian had oh-so-many *questions*.

The bastard knew he was keeping Hunt here. Away from Bryce and that sweet, sumptuous mouth. Which was precisely why Hunt had opted to grin and bear it: he wouldn't give the shithead the satisfaction of knowing how much he was pissing him off. Or turning his balls blue.

But enough was enough. Hunt asked, "You need me to tuck you into bed, too?"

Baxian snorted, going up to the fridge and yanking it open. The light bounced off his wings, silvering their arches. "You guys have crap beer."

"Government salary," Hunt said, leaning against the doorway. "Menus for takeout are in the top drawer to your right; or you can call down to the canteen and see if they're still serving. Good? Great. Bye."

"What's that?" Baxian asked, and there was enough curiosity in his tone that Hunt didn't bite his head off. He followed the direction of the Helhound's gaze.

"Um. That's a TV. We watch stuff on it."

Baxian threw him a withering glare. "I know what a TV is, Athalar. I meant those wires and boxes beneath."

Hunt arched a brow. "That's an OptiCube." Baxian stared at him blankly. Hunt tried again. "Gaming system?" The Helhound shook his head.

For a moment, Hunt was standing in Baxian's place, assessing the same room, the same strange, new tech, Isaiah and Justinian explaining what a fucking mobile phone was. Hunt said roughly, "You play games on it. Racing games, first-person games . . . giant time suck, but fun."

Baxian looked like the word—*fun*—was foreign to him, too. Solas.

Sandriel hated technology. Had refused to allow even televisions in her palace. Baxian might as well have been transported here from three centuries ago. Hunt himself had encountered tech in other parts of the world, but when most of his duties had kept him focused on Sandriel or her missions, he hadn't really had time to learn about everyday shit.

From the hallway behind him, low voices murmured. Naomi— and Pollux. Isaiah's soothing tones wove between them. Thank the gods.

Hunt found Baxian observing him warily. He threw a flat stare back, one he'd perfected as the Umbra Mortis. Baxian just aimed for the hallway. Hunt gave him a wide berth.

The Hammer filled the doorway of Vik's room, talking to Isaiah and Naomi in the hall. It was Pollux's room now. Hunt's magic rumbled, lightning on the horizon. Pollux sneered at Hunt as he stalked past. Bags and boxes were piled high behind him, a miniature city dedicated to the Hammer's vanity.

Hunt, keenly aware of all the cameras, of Bryce's plea to behave, continued on, nodding at Naomi and Isaiah as he passed.

"Well, here you go," Hunt said to Baxian, pausing before Justinian's old room. Baxian opened the door. The room was as bare and empty as Hunt's had been.

A duffel lay beside the narrow bed. All of Baxian's belongings fit in one fucking bag.

It didn't make a difference. The Helhound was an asshole who had done shit that even Hunt couldn't stomach. For him to be in Justinian's room, filling his place—

The crucifix in the lobby flashed in Hunt's mind, Justinian's agonized face as he hung on it. Hunt tried to banish the thought, but failed. He'd fucked up. Twice now, he'd fucked up. First with the Fallen rebellion, then this spring with the Viper Queen, and now . . . Was he really going to allow himself and Bryce to be dragged into something similar? How many people would be destroyed by the end?

Baxian said, stepping into his room, "Thanks for the tour, Athalar."

Hunt again glimpsed that sad, empty little room behind the Helhound. Perhaps something like pity stirred him, because he said, "I'll give you a lesson on video games tomorrow. I gotta get home."

He could have sworn a shadow dimmed in Baxian's eyes that appeared a Hel of a lot like longing. "Thanks."

Hunt grunted. "We'll link up after the morning check-in. You can shadow me for the day."

"Real generous of you," Baxian said, and shut the door without further reply.

Fortunately, Pollux shut his own door right then—slammed it in Naomi's face. Leaving Hunt with his two friends.

They headed for the common room without needing to say a word, waiting until they'd closed the door and ensured no one was in the bathroom before sinking onto the couch. Hunt really wanted to go home, but . . . "So this fucking sucks," he said quietly.

"Pollux should be drawn and quartered," Naomi spat.

"I'm amazed you're both still alive," Isaiah said to her, propping his feet on the coffee table and loosening the gray tie around his neck. Judging by the suit, he must have recently gotten in from escorting Celestina somewhere. "But as your commander, I'm grateful you didn't brawl." He gave Hunt a pointed look.

Hunt snorted. But Naomi said, "The two of them defile those rooms by staying in there."

"They're only rooms," Isaiah said, though pain tightened his face. "All that Vik and Justinian were . . . it's not in there."

"Yeah, it's in a box at the bottom of a trench," Naomi said, crossing her arms. "And Justinian's ashes are on the wind."

"So are Micah's," Hunt said softly, and they looked at him.

Hunt just shrugged.

"Were you really going to rebel this spring?" Naomi asked. They hadn't once spoken about it these past months. The shit that had gone down.

"Not by the end," Hunt said. "I meant everything I said on the boat. I changed my mind; I realized that wasn't the path for me." He met Isaiah's disapproving frown. "I still mean it."

He did. If Sofie and Emile and Ophion and Cormac and all that shit went away right now, he wouldn't fucking think twice about it. Would be *glad* for it.

But that wasn't how things were playing out. It wasn't how Bryce wanted it to play out. He could barely stand the sight of Isaiah's tattooed brow.

"I know," Isaiah said at last. "You've got a lot more on the line now," he added, and Hunt wondered if he'd intended the slight tone of warning in the words.

Wondered if Isaiah remembered how he and the other angels in the Summit conference room had bowed to him after he'd ripped off Sandriel's head. What would his friends do if he told them about his recent contact with an Ophion rebel? His head spun.

Hunt changed the subject, nodding to the hall behind the shut door. "You two going to stay here or find places of your own?"

"Oh, I'm out," Isaiah said, practically beaming. "Signed a lease this morning on a place a few blocks from here. CBD, but closer to the Old Square."

"Nice," Hunt said, and lifted a brow at Naomi, who shook her head.

"Free rent," she said, "despite the new hallmates." Pollux and Baxian would be staying here until Celestina deemed them well adjusted enough to live in the city proper. Hunt shuddered to think of them loose.

"Do you trust that they're going to behave?" he asked Isaiah. "Because I fucking don't."

"We don't have any choice but to trust that they will," Isaiah said, sighing. "And hope that the Governor will see them for what they are."

"Will it make any difference if she knows?" Naomi asked, tucking her hands behind her head.

"I guess we'll see," Hunt said, and glanced at his phone again. "All right. I'm out." He paused at the doorway, however. Looked at his two friends, wholly unaware of the shit that was coming their way. It'd be huge for either of them—potentially freeing for Isaiah—to bust Ophion. To capture Sofie Renast and her brother and haul in Cormac.

If he spoke up now, spilled his guts, could he spare Bryce from the worst of it? Could he avoid crucifixion—avoid having an empty room being all that was left of him one day, too? If he played it right, could he save them both—and maybe Ruhn and Ithan—and live to tell the tale? Tharion was likely dead fucking meat for not telling the authorities about his mission, queen or no, as was the Crown Prince of Avallen. But . . .

Isaiah asked, "Something on your mind?"

Hunt cleared his throat.

The words sizzled on his tongue. A parachute, and now would be the exact moment to pull it open. *We have a major problem with rebels converging on this city and I need your help to make sure they play right into our hands.*

Hunt cleared his throat again. Shook his head.

And left.

21

Dusk's Truth, huh?" Hunt's deep voice rumbled across the bed to Bryce as they lay in the darkness, Syrinx already snoring between them.

"Danika definitely thought she was onto something," Bryce replied. Hunt had missed dinner, leaving her to an unbearably awkward meal with Ithan. He'd been quiet and contemplative, wearing the game face she'd seen before big matches. She'd said as much to him, but he hadn't wanted to talk.

So Bryce had combed through Danika's papers and clippings again. Had found nothing new. She'd only filled Hunt in when he'd finally gotten home from the Comitium and they'd readied for bed. Any thoughts of continuing what had gone down in that alley had vanished by the time she'd finished.

Hunt hummed, shifting onto his side. "So you're really going to help Cormac, then."

"It's not about wanting to help him—it's more about wanting to help Emile. But I meant what I said to you in the alley: this is also about getting what I can out of the situation for our own advantage." An end to the betrothal, and some training. "And," she admitted, "learning about Danika."

"Does it matter? About Danika, I mean?"

"It shouldn't. But it does. For some reason, it does." She said carefully, "I know we discussed this earlier, but . . . I can't do this without you, Hunt."

He said softly, "I know. I'm just . . . Fuck, Quinlan. The thought of anything happening to you scares the shit out of me. I under-stand, though. That's what prompted me this spring . . . what I was doing with Vik and Justinian. It was for Shahar."

Her heart strained. "I know." And he'd been willing to give that up for her—for *them*. "So you're in?"

"Yeah. Whatever help I can give, I'll offer it. But we need an exit strategy."

"We do," she agreed. "Let's talk about it tomorrow, though. I'm exhausted."

"All right." His wing brushed her bare shoulder and she turned her head to find him with his head propped on a fist.

"Don't *do* that."

"What?" His eyes sparkled in the dimness.

She turned onto her own side and waved a hand toward him. "Look so . . . like that."

His lips curled upward. "Sexy? Attractive? Seductive?"

"All of the above."

He flopped onto his back. "I feel weird doing anything with Hol-strom a wall away."

She pointed to the aforementioned wall. "He's on the other side of the apartment."

"He's a wolf."

Bryce inhaled the musky, midnight scent of him. Arousal. "So let's be quiet, then."

Hunt's swallow was audible. "I . . . All right, I'll be straight with you, Quinlan."

She arched a brow.

He blew out a breath toward the ceiling. "It's been . . . a while. For me, I mean."

"Me too." The longest she'd ever gone without sex since her first time at seventeen. Well, ignoring what she and Hunt had done on the couch months ago—though that wasn't the kind of sex she wanted right now.

He said, "I guarantee that however long it's been for you, it's been longer for me."

"How long?"

Some part of her howled at the idea of anyone—any-fucking-one—putting their hands and mouth and other parts on him. Of *Hunt* touching anyone else. Wanting anyone else. Of him existing in a world where he hadn't known her, and some other female had been more important—

Some other female *had* been more important. Shahar. He'd loved her. Been willing to die for her.

He nearly died for you, too, a small voice whispered. But . . . this was different somehow.

Hunt grimaced. "Six months?"

Bryce laughed. "That's it?"

He growled. "It's a long time."

"I thought you were going to say *years*."

He gave her an affronted look. "I wasn't celibate, you know."

"So who was the lucky lady, then?" Or male, she supposed. She'd assumed he preferred females, but it was entirely possible he also—

"A nymph at a bar. She was from out of town and didn't recognize me."

Bryce's fingers curled, as if invisible claws appeared at their tips. "Nymph, huh."

Was that his type? Exactly like those dancers at the ballet? Delicate and svelte? Had Shahar been like that? Bryce had never searched for portraits of the dead Archangel—hadn't ever wanted to torture herself like that. But Sandriel had been beautiful as Hel, slim and tall, and Hunt had once mentioned that they were twins.

Bryce added, if only because she wanted him to feel a shred of the misery that now coursed through her, "Lion shifter. In a bathroom at the White Raven."

"The night of the bombing?" The words were sharp. As if her fucking someone while they'd known each other was unacceptable.

"Less than a week before," she said nonchalantly, quietly pleased at his sharpness.

"I thought you didn't like alphaholes."

"I like them for some things."

"Oh yeah?" He trailed a finger down her bare arm. "What, exactly?" His voice dropped to a purr. "You don't seem to enjoy males bossing you around."

She couldn't help her blush. "Every once in a while." It was all she could think to say as his fingers reached her wrist and he lifted her hand, bringing it to his mouth and pressing a kiss to her palm. "This one was especially good at being in charge."

"All right, Quinlan," he said against her skin. "I'm thoroughly jealous."

She chuckled. "So am I."

He kissed the inside of her wrist, lips grazing over sensitive flesh. "Before we went off on this stupid tangent, I was trying to warn you that it's been a while, so I might . . ."

"Be fast?"

He nipped at her wrist. "Be loud, asshole."

She laughed, running her fingers over his smooth, unmarked brow. "I could gag you."

Hunt barked out a laugh. "Please tell me you're not into that."

She let out a *hmmm*.

"For real?" He sat up slowly.

She lay back against the pillows, arms behind her head. "I'll try anything once."

A muscle throbbed in his neck. "All right. But let's start with the basics. If that gets boring, I promise to find ways to keep you interested."

"That doesn't get rid of the problem of Ithan's keen hearing."

He shifted against the bed, and Bryce found the blatant evidence of his interest pushing against his tight boxer briefs. Solas, he was huge.

She laughed softly, sitting up as well. "It really has been a while."

He trembled, though—with restraint. "Tell me yes, Bryce."

She went molten at the raw need in his words. "I want to touch you first."

"That's not a yes."

"I want *your* yes."

"Yes. Fuck yes. Now your turn."

She only smirked, pressing a surprisingly steady hand to his bare, muscled chest. He allowed her to push him back against the pillows. "I'll say yes when I've had my fill."

Hunt let out a low, rough noise.

"Not too late for a gag," Bryce murmured, pressing a kiss to his chest.

Hunt was going to burst out of his skin. He couldn't stand it: the sight of Bryce now straddling his thighs, wearing nothing but an old, soft T-shirt, the silken glide of her hair over his bare chest as she pressed a kiss between his pecs. Pressed another near his nipple.

There was another person in this apartment. One with exceptional hearing, and he—

Bryce's lips closed around his left nipple, wet heat sending Hunt's hips straining toward hers. She flicked her tongue across the taut bud, and Hunt hissed. "For fuck's sake."

She laughed around his nipple, then moved to the other. "Your chest is as big as mine," she muttered.

"That's the least sexy thing anyone has ever said to me," he managed to say.

She dug her long nails into his chest, the pain a light, singeing kiss. His cock throbbed in response. Gods spare him, he wouldn't last a minute.

Bryce kissed his right ribs. Ran her tongue along the muscles there. "How do you get these stupid muscles, anyway?"

"Exercise." Why was she talking? Why was *he* talking?

His hands shook, and he fisted them in the sheets. Syrinx had leapt off the bed, trotting to the bathroom and kicking the door shut with a hind leg. Smart chimera.

Her tongue teased over his left ribs, trailing downward as her fingers traced lines along his chest, his stomach. She kissed his belly button, and her head hovered mere inches from the edge of his boxer briefs, so close he was about to erupt at the sight of it—

"Aren't we supposed to do some kissing first?" His voice was guttural.

"Absolutely not," Bryce said, wholly focused on her task. Hunt couldn't get a breath down as her fingers curled on the waistband of his underwear and peeled it away. He could only let her do it, lifting his hips to accommodate her, baring all of him—

"Well, well, well," she crooned, sitting up. Hunt almost started whining at the distance she put between that mouth of hers and his cock. "This is a . . . big surprise."

"Stop playing, Quinlan." She had five seconds until he leapt on her and did everything he'd dreamed of for months now. Everything he'd planned to do during the longest night of the year.

She laid a finger on his lips. "Hush." She brushed her mouth over his. Slid her tongue along the seam of his lips. Hunt parted for her, and as her tongue slipped into his mouth, he caught it between his lips and sucked hard. Let her know precisely how he liked it.

Her whimper was a triumph. But Hunt kept still as she withdrew, straightening again, and lifted the shirt over her head.

Fuck, those breasts. Full and heavy and tipped in rosy nipples that had him seeing double—

He hadn't gotten enough of them that day they'd hooked up. Not even close. He needed to feast on these, needed their weight in his palms, those pretty nipples on his tongue—

She fisted her breasts, squeezing as she looked down at him. Hunt bucked his hips, driving his cock up before her in a silent request. Bryce only writhed, the plane of her stomach undulating as she squeezed her breasts again.

Hunt surged to grab her, to put his mouth where her hands were, but she held up a finger. "Not yet." Her eyes simmered like coals in the dimness. Her star began to glow faintly, as if it were under a black light. She traced her finger over the soft iridescence. "Please."

He panted through his teeth, chest heaving, but lay back on the pillows once more. "Well, when you put it so politely . . ."

She let out a sensuous laugh and leaned over him. Ran her nails along the shaft of his cock, then back down to its base. He shivered, pleasure singing along his spine as she said, "There's no way I can fit all of you in me."

He ground out, "Never know until we try."

Bryce smiled, and her head dipped as her fingers wrapped around his cock, barely able to grasp him fully. She squeezed his base right as her tongue lapped at his tip.

Hunt bucked, panting hard. Bryce laughed against his cock. "Quiet, remember?"

He was going to cut off Holstrom's ears. That would keep the wolf from hearing—

Bryce licked him again, tongue swirling, then slid his broad head into her mouth. Warm, wet heat enveloped him as she sucked tight and—

Hunt arched again, clapping a hand over his mouth as his eyes rolled back in his head. Yes. *Fuck* yes. Bryce withdrew, then slid her mouth further onto him. A few more strokes and he'd—

Hunt shifted, making to grab her, but she pinned his hips to the bed with a hand. Took him until he bumped against the back of her throat. He nearly flew out of his skin.

She sucked him hard, the pressure so perfect it was practically pain, withdrawing nearly to his tip before taking him all again. What didn't make it into her mouth was squeezed by her hand in flawless tandem.

Hunt took in the sight of his cock disappearing into her mouth, her hair whispering over his thighs, her breasts swaying—

"Quinlan," he groaned, a plea and a warning.

Bryce only slid him down her throat again, her free hand digging into the muscles of his thigh in silent permission. In her mouth—that was where she wanted him.

The thought alone unleashed him. Hunt couldn't stop himself as he raked his hands into her hair, fingers digging into her scalp, and rode her mouth. She met him thrust for thrust, moaning deep in her throat so that it echoed through him—

And then her hand slipped down to his balls, squeezing hard as her teeth grazed along his shaft—

Hunt shattered, biting down on his lip so hard the coppery tang of blood coated his tongue, bucking up into her, spilling down her throat.

Bryce swallowed as he came, the walls of her mouth fluttering against him, and he was going to fucking *die* from this, from her, from the pleasure she was wringing from him—

Hunt groaned, the last of himself shooting into her mouth. Then he was shaking and panting as she removed her mouth in one wet slide, then held his gaze.

She swallowed once more. Licked her lips.

Hunt tried and failed to get up. As if his body were stunned stupid.

Bryce smirked, a queen triumphant. Every fantasy he'd had of her these months—none of them came close to this. To what her mouth had been like, to what she looked like naked . . .

Hunt had managed to prop himself up on his elbows when Ithan yelled from the other side of the apartment, "*Please: have sex a little louder! I didn't hear everything that time!*"

Bryce burst out laughing, but Hunt could only stare at the little droplet that ran down her chin, gleaming in the dim light of her star. She noted the direction of his attention and wiped off her chin, rubbing her fingers together, then licking them clean.

Hunt growled, low and deep. "I'm going to fuck you senseless." Her nipples were hard as pebbles, and she squirmed against him. Nothing but those little lace panties separated her sweetness from his bare thighs.

But then Holstrom shouted, "*That sounds medically dangerous!*"

And Bryce laughed again, rolling off Hunt and reaching for his T-shirt. "Let's go to a sleazy motel tomorrow," she said, and promptly went to sleep.

Hunt, mind blasted apart, could only lie there naked, wondering if he'd imagined it all.

* * *

Hunt sat in a simple folding chair at the bottom of an abyss, nothing but blackness around him, the only light coming from the faint glow cast by his body. There was no beginning or end to the perpetual night.

He'd fallen asleep beside Quinlan, wondering if he should just slide his hand over her hip to reacquaint himself with that lovely spot between her legs. But Bryce wasn't there.

He didn't want Bryce in a place like this, so dark and empty and yet . . . awake. Wings rustled nearby—not the soft feathers of his wings, but something leathery. Dry.

Hunt stiffened, trying to shoot to his feet, but he couldn't. His ass stayed planted in the chair, though no ties bound him. His booted feet were glued to the black floor.

"Who's there?" The darkness absorbed his voice, muffling it. The leathery wings whispered again, and Hunt twisted his head toward the sound. Moving his head was about the only thing he could manage.

"A greater warrior would have freed himself from those bonds by now." The soft, deep voice slithered over his skin.

"Who the fuck are you?"

"Why do you not use the gifts in your blood to free yourself, Orion?"

Hunt gritted his teeth. "It's Hunt."

"I see. Because Orion was a hunter."

The voice came from everywhere. "What's *your* name?"

"Midgardians do not feel comfortable uttering my name on your side of the Rift."

Hunt stilled. There was only one being whose name was not uttered in Midgard.

The Prince of the Pit. Apollion.

His blood chilled. This was a fucked-up, weird-ass dream, no doubt caused by Quinlan literally blowing his mind into smithereens—

"It is no dream."

The seventh and most lethal of the demon princes of Hel was *in his mind*—

"I am not in your mind, though your thoughts ripple toward me like your world's radio waves. You and I are in a place between our worlds. A pocket-realm, as it were."

"What do you want?" Hunt's voice held steady, but—fuck. He needed to get out of here, to find some way back to Bryce. If the Prince of the Pit could get into Hunt's mind, then—

"If I went into her mind, my brother would be very angry with me. Again." Hunt could have sworn he heard a smile in the prince's voice. "You certainly worry a great deal about a female who is far safer than you at the moment."

"Why am I here?" Hunt forced out, willing his mind to clear of anything but the thought. It was difficult, though. This being before him, around him . . . This demon prince had killed the seventh Asteri. Had *devoured* the seventh Asteri.

The Star-Eater.

"I do like that name," Apollion said, chuckling softly. "But as for your question, you are here because I wished to meet you. To assess your progress."

"We got the pep talk from Aidas this afternoon, don't worry."

"My brother does not inform me of his movements. I do not know or care what he has or has not done."

Hunt lifted his chin with a bravado he didn't feel. "So let's hear it. Your proposal for how we should ally with you to overthrow the Asteri and set you up as our new masters."

"Is that what you think will happen?"

"Aidas already gave us a history lesson. Spare me."

The darkness rumbled with distant thunder. "You are foolish and arrogant."

"Takes one to know one, I suppose."

The darkness paused. "You are impertinent as well. Do you not know where I come from? My father was the Void, the Being That Existed Before. Chaos was his bride and my dam. It is to them that we shall all one day return, and their mighty powers that run in my blood."

"Fancy."

But Apollion said, "You're wasting the gifts that were given to you."

Hunt drawled, "Oh, I think I've put them to good use."

"You don't know a fraction of what you might do. You and the Starborn girl."

"Again, Quinlan got the whole 'master your powers' talk from Aidas today, and that was boring enough, so let's not repeat it."

"Both of you would benefit from training. Your powers are more similar than you realize. Conduits, both of you. You have no idea how valuable you and the others like you are."

Hunt arched a brow. "Oh yeah?"

The darkness rippled with displeasure. "If you are so dismissive of my assistance, perhaps I should send some . . . appetizers to test you and yours."

Hunt flared his wings slightly. "Why summon me? Just to give me this shove?"

Apollion's unholy essence whispered around him again. "The Northern Rift is groaning once more. I can smell war on the wind. I do not plan to lose this time."

"Well, I don't plan to have a demon prince for my ruler, so find a new five-year goal."

A soft laugh. "You do amuse, Orion."

Hunt snarled, and his lightning sizzled in answer. "I take it we're done here—"

The seething darkness and those leathery wings vanished.

Hunt jolted awake. He was already reaching for the knife on the nightstand when he halted.

Quinlan slept beside him, Syrinx on her other side, both of them snoring softly. In the darkness, her red hair looked like fresh blood across her pillow.

The Prince of the Pit had spoken to him. Knew who he was, who Bryce was—

The Prince of the Pit was a liar and a monster, and it was entirely likely that he was trying to lure Hunt and Bryce into some fool's quest with their powers. And yet . . . Fuck.

Hunt ran a shaking hand over his sweaty face, then settled back onto the pillows, brushing a knuckle down Bryce's soft cheek. She murmured, shifting closer, and Hunt obliged, sliding his arm over her waist and folding a wing around her. As if he could shield her from all that hunted them.

On both sides of the Northern Rift.

22

Ruhn finished off his beer, setting it on the coffee table before the massive TV in the living room. Declan, seated to his left, did the same. "All right," Dec said, "espionage time."

Flynn, smoking some mirthroot that Ruhn desperately needed a hit of, chuckled. "Our sweet son Ruhn is all grown up and spying for rebels."

"Shut up," Ruhn growled. "I knew I should have done this in private."

"Where would the fun be in that?" Dec asked. "Plus, shouldn't someone be here in case it's, I don't know, a trap or something?"

"Then why the fuck is he smoking?" Ruhn nodded to where Flynn blew smoke rings.

"Because I'm a self-destructive yet insanely charming idiot?" Flynn grinned.

"Emphasis on *insane*," Dec muttered.

But Ruhn wanted them with him tonight, when most of the city was asleep, as he attempted contact with Agent Daybright. He had the comm-crystal, though he wasn't exactly sure what to do with it—how to even begin connecting his abilities with its communication affinity. All hypotheticals, no guarantee of success. He couldn't decide whether or not it'd be a relief to fail. To be able to walk away from this.

"So, are we supposed to meditate with you or something?" Flynn set down the mirthroot.

"How the Hel would that help?" Ruhn asked.

"Solidarity?" Flynn suggested.

Ruhn snorted. "I'm good. Just . . . put a wooden spoon between my teeth if I go into some kind of fit."

Declan raised one. "Already thought of that."

Ruhn put his hand on his heart. "Thanks. I'm touched."

Flynn clapped Ruhn on the back. "We've got you. Do your thing."

There wasn't anything else to say, anything else Ruhn needed to hear, so he closed his eyes, leaning back against the cushions of the couch. He clenched the crystal in his fist, the stone eerily warm.

A mental bridge—that was how he always pictured the link he made between his mind and someone else's. So that was the image he summoned, funneling it through the crystal in his hand, as surely as Bryce had funneled her own powers through the crystal of the Gate this spring. Cormac had said the crystal had similar properties, so . . . why not?

Ruhn extended the bridge from himself, through the crystal, and then out into the vast unknown, sprawling into a darkness with no end. He clenched the crystal tighter, willing it to lead him where he needed to go, as if it were a prism filtering his powers out into the world.

Hello? His voice echoed down the bridge. Into nothing.

He visualized the crystal's milky core. Imagined a thread running from it, down along this mental bridge, out toward another end.

Hello? This is Agent . . .

Well, fuck. He should have come up with a code name. He sure as Hel couldn't risk his own name or identity, but he wanted something cool, damn it.

This is your new contact.

No answer from Daybright came. Ruhn kept extending the bridge, letting it span into nothingness. Pictured the crystal and its thread, letting himself follow its trail into the night.

I'm here to—

Yes?

Ruhn went still at the faint female voice. Light glowed down the bridge, and then there she was.

A female of pure flame. Or that was how she chose to appear. Not how Lehabah had been made of flame, with her body visible, but rather a female cloaked in it, only a flash of a bare wrist or an ankle or a shoulder through the veil. She was humanoid, but that was all he could glean. She looked like one of the radical sun-priests who'd gone rogue and immolated themselves to be close to their god.

Who are you? he asked.

Who are you? she challenged. Not one hint of her face.

I asked first.

Her flame flared, as if in annoyance. But she said, *The little black dog sleeps soundly on a wool blanket.*

Ruhn blew out a breath. There it was—the code phrase Cormac had given him to confirm her identity. He said, *And the gray tabby cleans her paws by the light of the moon.*

Utter nonsense.

But she said, *I'm Agent Daybright, in case that wasn't clear enough. Now . . . you are?*

Ruhn peered down at himself, swearing. He hadn't thought to hide his body—

But he found only a form of night and stars, galaxies and planets. As if his silhouette had been filled by them. He lifted a hand, finding not skin but the starry blanket of the sky covering his fingers. Had his mind instinctively shielded him? Or was this what he was, deep below the skin? Was this fire-being standing thirty feet down the mental bridge what *she* was, deep below her own skin? Or fur, he supposed.

She could be a faun or a satyr. Or a witch or a shifter. Or an Asteri, as Cormac had suggested. Maybe the fire was that of the holy star in her.

She merely stood there, burning. *Well?*

Her voice was beautiful. Like a golden song. It stirred his Fae soul, made it perk up. *I, ah . . . I hadn't gotten that far yet.*

She angled her head with what seemed like predatory intent. *They sent a novice?*

A chill skittered down his spine. She certainly spoke like one of the Asteri, regal and aloof. She looked over her shoulder. As if back toward the body connected to her mind.

Ruhn said, *Look, Agent Silverbow gave me this crystal, but had no idea if it could even work on a mind-to-mind level. So I wanted to attempt to make contact and let you know I'm here and this is the new mode of communication. So if it's an emergency, I don't need to waste time figuring out how to get in touch.*

That's fine.

He surveyed her again. *So, we trust each other that easily, then?* He couldn't stop his taunting question. *You're not at all worried the crystal fell into the wrong hands and the code phrases were compromised?*

Agents of the Asteri don't bumble about so much.

Damn. *I'll try harder to impress you the next time.*

Another soft laugh. *You already have, Agent Night.*

Did you just give me a code name? Night and Daybright. Night and Day—he liked that.

I figured I'd spare you the trouble of trying to invent something interesting. She turned back to her end of the bridge, flame flowing in her wake.

No messages for me to pass along? He didn't dare say Cormac's name. *Anything about the Spine?*

She kept walking. *No. But tell your commander that safe passage is granted under the cover of the waning moon.*

Ruhn bristled. Like Hel was Cormac his commander. *I don't know what that means.*

You're not supposed to. But Agent Silverbow will. And tell him I much *prefer this method of communicating.*

Then Daybright and her flame winked out, and Ruhn was alone.

"Why not tell me Agent Daybright was a female?" Ruhn asked Cormac the next morning, standing in his living room and gulping down his second cup of coffee, Flynn lounging beside him. He'd messaged his cousin to come here under the guise of wanting to discuss the terms of Bryce's engagement. Thankfully, his cousin hadn't needed much more than that before arriving.

Cormac shrugged, his gray T-shirt lightly coated in sweat, presumably from the scorching walk over here. "I thought you might share your father's outdated views that females should not be in the line of danger and balk at putting her at risk."

"Does anything I've ever done indicate I'd feel that way?"

"You're protective of your sister to a fault." Cormac frowned. "Did you *see* Daybright?"

"She appeared humanoid, cloaked in flame. I couldn't see anything, really."

"Good. I'm assuming you veiled yourself, too."

Only by pure dumb luck. "Yeah."

Cormac paced in front of the TV. "But she said nothing of Sofie?"

Ruhn hadn't even thought to ask. Guilt twisted in his gut. "No."

Cormac dragged his hands through his short blond hair. "And no updates on the Asteri's mech-suit prototype being sent along the Spine?"

"No. She only told me to tell you that safe passage is granted under the light of the waning moon."

Cormac sighed. Whatever that meant. But Declan asked as he emerged from the kitchen, cup of coffee in hand, "So what now? Ruhn waits for her to call with intel about this raid on the Spine?"

Cormac sneered at Declan. Avallen snob to the core. He said to Ruhn, "Remind me, cousin, why you felt the need to involve these two fools in our business?"

"Remind me," Ruhn countered, "why I'm working with someone who insults my brothers?"

Dec and Flynn smirked at Cormac, who seethed, but finally sighed. The Avallen Prince said, "To answer your question, Declan Emmet, yes: Ruhn will wait until Daybright contacts him with details on the Spine raid. Or until I have something for him to pass along, in which case he'll contact her again."

Flynn leaned back on the couch, propping his arms behind his head. "Sounds boring."

"Lives are at stake," Cormac gritted out. "This hit on the Spine, attaining that new mech-suit prototype before the Asteri can use it against us on the battlefields, will give us a fighting chance."

"Not to mention all the weapons you'll loot from the supply trains," Declan said darkly.

Cormac ignored his tone. "We don't do anything unless it's been approved by Command. So wait until you hear from me before you contact her again."

Fine. He could do that. Go about his life, pretending he wasn't a sort-of rebel. Only until he wanted out, Cormac had promised. And after that . . . he'd go back to what he'd been doing. To leading the Aux and hating his father yet dreading the day the male died. Until the next person who needed him for something came along.

Flynn grinned. "Bureaucracy at its finest."

Cormac scowled at the Fae lord, but stalked for the front door. "I need to head out."

"Hunting for Emile?" Ruhn asked. It was the middle of the morning—the kid would likely be lying low.

Cormac nodded. "Being a visiting prince allows me the cover of . . . sightseeing, as you call it here. And as a tourist, I've taken a keen interest in your Black Dock and its customs."

"Morbid," Declan said.

Ruhn blurted, "You can't think Emile's going to jump into one of the black boats in broad daylight."

"I'll look for him both by the light of the sun and the moon, until I find him. But I'd rather ask casual questions of the Reapers during the day."

"Are you insane?" Flynn said, laughing in disbelief.

Ruhn was inclined to agree. "Don't fuck with the Reapers, Cormac," he warned. "Even for Emile's sake."

Cormac patted a knife at his side. As if that would do anything to kill a creature that was already dead. "I know how to handle myself."

"I told you this would happen," Hunt snarled to Isaiah as their steps thundered along the hallway of Celestina's private residence atop the third tower of the Comitium. Celestina had called this meeting in her own home, rather than in the public office Micah had always used.

"We don't have the full scope yet," Isaiah shot back, adjusting his tie and the lapels of his gray suit.

Celestina had tried to ease the harsh modernism that Micah had favored: plush rugs now softened the white marble floors, angular statues had been replaced by lush-bodied effigies of Cthona, and vases of fluffy, vibrant flowers graced nearly every table and console they passed.

It was a nice contrast, Hunt might have thought. Had they not been called here for a reason.

He kept reminding himself of that reason, that this was a triarii meeting and not some one-on-one session. That he wasn't in Sandriel's castle of horrors, where a trip to her private chambers ended in blood and screaming.

He inhaled once, thinking of Bryce, of her scent, the warmth of her body against his. It settled the edge in him, even as something far more lethal opened an eye. What they were doing with Cormac, all this rebel shit they'd agreed to go through with last night . . .

Hunt glanced sidelong at Isaiah as the male knocked on the open double doors of Celestina's study. He could tell him. He needed someone like Isaiah, even-keeled and unflappable. Especially if Hel had a vested interest in the conflict. And Hunt himself.

He'd decided to ignore Apollion's commands. He had no interest in playing right into Hel's hands.

Celestina murmured her welcome, and Hunt braced himself as he followed Isaiah in.

Sunlight filled the glass-and-marble space, and all the hard-edged furniture had been replaced by lovely artisanal wood pieces, but Hunt only noted the two males sitting before the desk. Naomi leaned against the wall by the built-in bookcase to the right, face dark and lethal focus fixed upon the males.

Well, the one male. The reason they were here.

Pollux didn't turn as they entered, and Hunt aimed for the chair beside Baxian. Isaiah could sit next to Pollux. Isaiah threw him a *Thanks, asshole* look, but Hunt scanned Celestina's expression for clues.

Displeasure tightened the corners of her mouth, but her eyes were calm. Face full of contemplation. She wore pale purple robes, her curls spilling down her bare arms like a waterfall of night. She might have been a goddess, so still and lovely was she—might have been Cthona herself, voluptuous and full-bodied, were it not for the radiant wings that filled with the light of the sun shining through the windows behind her.

"I apologize for keeping my message brief," Celestina said to Hunt, Isaiah, and Naomi. "But I did not want the full account on the record."

Pollux and Baxian stared ahead at nothing. Or Hunt assumed that was the case, given that one of Baxian's eyes was swollen shut, and Pollux's face was one big magnificent bruise. That it remained this way after twelve hours suggested the initial damage had been impressive. He wished he could have seen it.

"We understand," Isaiah said in that take-no-shit commander's tone. "We share your disappointment."

Celestina sighed. "Perhaps I was naïve in believing that I could introduce two Pangerans to this city without a more thorough education in its ways. To hand over the responsibility"—she glanced at Naomi, then at Hunt—"was my mistake."

Hunt could have warned her about that. He kept his mouth shut.

"I would like to hear from you two, in your own words, about what happened," the Archangel ordered Pollux and Baxian. The tone was pleasant, yet her eyes glinted with hidden steel. "Pollux? Why don't you start?"

It was a thing of beauty, the way Pollux bristled in his seat, flowing golden hair still streaked with blood. The Hammer hated this. Absolutely fucking hated this, Hunt realized with no small amount of delight. Celestina's kindness, her fairness, her softness . . . Pollux was chafing even worse than Hunt. He'd served enthusiastically under Sandriel—had relished her cruelty and games. Perhaps sending him to Celestina had been a punishment that even the Asteri had not anticipated.

But Pollux growled, "I was having some fun at a tavern."

"Bar," Hunt drawled. "We call them bars here."

Pollux glared, but said, "The female was all over me. She *said* she wanted it."

"Wanted what?" Celestina's voice had taken on a decidedly icy tone.

"To fuck me." Pollux leaned back in his chair.

"She said no such thing," Baxian growled, wings shifting.

"And were you there every moment of the night?" Pollux demanded. "Though perhaps you were. You always pant after my scraps."

Hunt met Isaiah's wary stare. Some major tension had arisen between these two in the years since Hunt and Isaiah had left Sandriel's territory.

Baxian bared his teeth in a feral grin. "Here I was, thinking your *scraps* were panting after me. They always seem so . . . unsatisfied when they leave your room."

Pollux's power—standard malakim magic, but strong—rattled the pretty trinkets along the built-in bookcase.

Celestina cut in, "That is enough." Warm, summer-kissed power filled the room, smothering their own gifts. A feminine, unbreaking sort of magic—the kind that took no shit and would lay down the law if threatened. That was utterly unafraid of Pollux and the sort of male he was. She said to the Hammer, "Explain what happened."

"We went into the alley behind the *tavern*"—he threw that last word at Hunt—"and she was all over me, as I said. Then the bastard"—he threw that one at Baxian—"attacked me."

"And at what point did you not hear her say no?" Baxian challenged. "The first or the tenth time?"

Pollux snorted. "Some females say no when they want it. It's a game for them."

"You're fucking delusional," Naomi spat from across the room.

"Was I talking to you, hag?" Pollux snapped.

"*Enough.*" Celestina's power again filled the room, stifling any magic they might have summoned. She asked Baxian, "Why did you go into the alley after him?"

"Because I've spent decades with this asshole," Baxian seethed. "I knew what was about to happen. I wasn't going to let him go through with it."

"You did plenty of times under Sandriel," Isaiah said, voice low. "You and your whole triarii stood back."

"You don't know shit about what I did or didn't do," Baxian snapped at Isaiah, then said to Celestina, "Pollux deserved the beating I gave him."

The Hammer bared his teeth. Hunt could only watch in something like shock.

"That may be true," Celestina said, "but the fact remains that you two are in my triarii and your fight was filmed. And it's now online and being aired by every news station." Her gaze sharpened on Pollux. "I offered the female the chance to press charges—but she declined. I can only assume she is aware of what a circus it would be, and is frightened of the consequences for herself and her loved ones. I plan to fix that in this city. This territory. Even if it means making an example of one of my triarii."

Hunt's blood roiled, howling. Maybe this would be it. Maybe Pollux would finally get what was coming to him.

But Celestina's throat worked. "I received a call this morning, however, and have seen the wisdom in . . . granting you a second chance."

"*What?*" Hunt blurted.

Pollux bowed his head in a mockery of gratitude. "The Asteri are benevolent masters."

A muscle ticked in Celestina's smooth cheek. "They are indeed."

Naomi asked, "What about that one?" She gestured toward Baxian, who glared at her.

Celestina said, "I would like to grant you a second chance as well, Helhound."

"I *defended* that female," Baxian snapped.

"You did, and I commend you for that. But you did so in a public way that drew attention." Not only the city's attention. The Asteri's.

Again, Celestina's throat bobbed.

Isaiah asked a shade gently, "What can we do to help clean up this mess?"

She kept her stare on her wooden desk, thick lashes nearly grazing her high cheekbones. "It is already done. To give the media something else to focus on, the Asteri have blessed me with an opportunity. A gift."

Even Pollux dropped his simpering bullshit to angle his head. Hunt braced himself. This couldn't be good.

Celestina smiled, and Hunt saw it for the forced expression it was. "I am to mate Ephraim. With two Archangels now dead, there is a need to . . . replenish the ranks. On the Autumnal Equinox, we shall have our mating ceremony here in Lunathion."

A month away. The holiday known as Death's Day was a lively one, despite its name: it was a day of balance between the light and dark, when the veil between the living and dead was thinnest. Cthona began her preparations for her upcoming slumber then, but in Lunathion, raging costume parties were held along the Istros River at the various Sailing points. The biggest party of all surrounded the Black Dock, where lanterns were sent across the water to the Bone Quarter, along with offerings of food and drink. It had been a total shitshow every time Hunt had flown above the festivities. He could only imagine what Bryce would wear. Something as irreverent as possible, he imagined.

Celestina went on, "He shall stay here for a few weeks, then return to his territory. After that, he and I shall alternate visiting each other's territories." Until a baby was born, no doubt.

Naomi asked, "This is a good thing, right?"

Celestina again gave them that forced smile. "Ephraim has been my friend for many years and is a fair and wise male. I can think of no better partner."

Hunt sensed the lie. But such was the lot of Archangels: should the Asteri decide they were to breed, they obeyed.

"Congratulations?" Isaiah said, and Celestina laughed.

"Yes, I suppose those are in order," she said. But her amusement faded upon facing Pollux—the cause of this. He'd embarrassed this city, embarrassed her, and the Asteri had taken notice. And now she would pay. Not for what Pollux had tried to do to that female, but for getting caught by the public. The Asteri would take this opportunity to remind her exactly how much control they had over her. Her life. Her body.

Hunt didn't know why they bothered to care, why they'd gone so far out of their way to prove a point, but . . . nothing surprised him where they were concerned. Hunt's blood began to heat, his temper with it. Fucking monsters.

"With my mating announcement, we will have a media frenzy. The ceremony and party will be a high-profile event. Royals and dignitaries will attend, along with Ephraim's retinue."

Pollux straightened at that, delight in his bruised eyes. Celestina leveled that cold stare at him again. "I hope that with the Hind coming to visit, you will refrain from behaving as you did last night."

Baxian snorted. "Never stopped him before."

Pollux bared his teeth again, but Celestina went on, "Hunt, I'd like a word with you. The rest of you are dismissed." Hunt froze, but said nothing as the others filed out. Isaiah and Naomi gave him warning looks before shutting the doors behind them.

Alone with his Archangel, Hunt forced himself to breathe. To keep steady.

She was going to rip into him for not controlling Baxian last night. For not being there to stop him from brawling, even if he'd been given no order to watch over him at all hours of the day. The punishment was coming, he could sense it—

"The Autumn King informed me of Miss Quinlan's engagement to Crown Prince Cormac of Avallen," Celestina said.

Hunt blinked.

She continued, "I was hoping you could provide insight into the situation, considering that they will be expected to attend my mating celebration together."

He hadn't thought of that. That this would even be something to discuss. And after what they'd done last night . . . Could he stomach it, seeing her in the arms of another male, even if it was just pretend?

"It's an arranged marriage," Hunt said. "Their fathers insist."

"I'd assumed so." Celestina's mouth tightened. "I'm curious how *you* are feeling. You and Miss Quinlan are close."

"Yeah. We are." Hunt rubbed his neck. "We're dealing with it day by day," he admitted.

Celestina studied him, and Hunt made himself hold her gaze. Found nothing but . . . consideration and worry there. "You are exactly as I thought you'd be."

Hunt arched a brow.

Celestina's eyes fell to her hands, fingers twisting. "Shahar was my friend, you know. My dearest friend. We kept it quiet. The Asteri wouldn't have approved. Shahar was already defying them in small ways when she and I became close, and she thought they would see our friendship as an alliance and try to . . . stop it."

Hunt's heart stumbled. "She never said anything."

"Our correspondence over the years was covert. And when you rebelled . . . I had nothing to offer her. My legion in Nena is—was—an extension of the Asteri's forces."

"You could have offered your own power." Fuck, one more Archangel fighting with them that day—

"I have lived with the consequences of my choice since then," Celestina said.

"Why are you telling me this?"

"Because I heard the whispers that you did what I had longed to do since I learned about Shahar's death at Sandriel's hands. What I longed to do every time I had to sit in the Asteri's council room and listen to Sandriel spit on her sister's memory."

Holy shit.

"And I would like to apologize for my failure to extract you from the masters who held you in the years after Shahar fell."

"That's not your fault."

"I tried—but it wasn't enough."

Hunt's brows bunched. "What?"

She set her hands on the desk. Interlaced her fingers. "I amassed funds to . . . purchase you, but the Asteri denied me. I tried three times. I had to stop a century ago—it would have raised suspicions had I continued."

She had sympathized with the Fallen. With his cause. "All for Shahar?"

"I couldn't let someone she cared for rot away like that. I wish . . ." She blew out a breath. "I wish they'd let me buy you. So many things might be different now."

It could all be a lie. A lovely, clever lie to get him to trust her. If she'd sympathized with the Fallen, did she share the same sentiments about the Ophion rebels? If he told her all that was brewing in this city, would she damn them or help them?

"The doubt in your eyes shames me." For all the world, she sounded like she meant it.

"I just find it hard to believe that during all the shit I went through, someone was out there, trying to help me."

"I understand. But perhaps I might atone for my failures now. I'd like us to be . . . friends."

Hunt opened his mouth, then shut it. "Thank you." He meant it, he realized.

Celestina smiled, like she understood it, too. "I'm at your disposal should you need anything. Anything at all."

He weighed the kind expression on her face. Did she know about Ophion and Cormac and Sofie? She'd somehow learned about him killing Sandriel, so she clearly was able to attain secret information.

Hunt breathed deeply, calming himself as he said again, "Thank you." He rose from his chair. "Since we're being honest here . . . Sandriel's old triarii is poison. I don't know why Baxian is suddenly playing good guy, but I'm sorry I wasn't there to rein him in last night."

"I don't hold you accountable for that."

Something tight eased in Hunt's chest. He went on, "Okay, but the rest . . . They're dangerous people. Worse than the Princes of Hel."

She chuckled. "You compare them like you know from experience."

He did. But he hedged, "I hunted demons for years. I know a monster when I see one. So when the Harpy and the Hawk and the Hind come for the mating party . . . I'm begging you to be careful. To protect the people of this city. We might give Baxian shit about standing by while Pollux terrorized people, but . . . I had to stand by, too. I've seen what Pollux does, what he delights in. The Harpy is his female counterpart. The Hawk is secretive and dangerous. And the Hind . . ."

"I know very well what manner of threat Lidia Cervos poses."

Even Archangels feared the Hind. What she might learn. And Celestina, secret friend to Shahar, who still cared about her friend centuries later, who carried the guilt of not helping . . . "Whatever you need," Hunt said quietly, "anything you need to get through this mating ceremony, to deal with Sandriel's cabal, you let me know."

Perhaps the Asteri had redistributed Sandriel's triarii here not only to balance out the numbers, but to plant allies and spies. To report on Hunt—and Celestina.

She nodded solemnly. "Thank you, Hunt."

He strode for the door, tucking in his wings. He halted at the doorway. "You don't need to feel guilty, you know. About the shit that happened to me."

She angled her head. "Why?"

He gave her a half smile. "If I'd gone to you in Nena, I never would have come here. To Lunathion." His smile broadened as he walked out. "I never would have met Bryce."

And every horror, every nightmare . . . all of it had been worth it for her.

Hunt found Baxian waiting at the end of the hallway, the male's arms crossed, bruised face solemn. "How'd your special time go?" Baxian asked by way of greeting.

"What the fuck do you want?" Hunt strode toward the veranda

SARA J. MAAS

at the far end of the hall. He'd pay Bryce a lunchtime visit. Maybe they'd get naked. That sounded really fucking good.

"The old gang's getting back together in a few weeks. I assume you were warning Celestina about it."

"You're a bunch of sadistic psychos." Hunt stepped onto the empty veranda. The wind whipped at his hair, carrying the fresh scent of the Istros from across the city. Storm clouds gathered on the horizon, and lightning danced in his veins. "I'd hardly call you the *old gang.*"

Baxian's mouth twitched upward, bruises stretching.

Hunt said, "I'm not buying whatever bullshit you're selling by beating the Hel out of Pollux."

"New city, new rules," Baxian said, black feathers rustling. "New boss, who doesn't seem to like Pollux all that much."

"So?" Hunt spread his wings.

"So I don't have to pretend anymore," Baxian said. He lifted his face to the darkening sky. "Storm's coming. Be careful up there."

"Thanks for your concern." Hunt flapped once, feet lifting.

"I'm not trying to fuck you over."

"You're trying to be a pain in my ass, then?"

Baxian snorted. "Yeah, I guess."

Hunt settled back to the ground. "What was that shit with you and Pollux—about his seconds?"

Baxian slid his hands into his pockets. "He's a jealous fucker. You know that."

Hunt could think of only one person Pollux had ever shown any preference for beyond Sandriel. "You have a thing for the Hind?"

Baxian barked a laugh. "Fuck no. Pollux is the only person insane enough to go near her. I wouldn't touch Lidia with a ten-foot pole."

Hunt studied the male who had been his enemy for so long he'd lost track of the years. Something had changed. Something big, and primal, and . . . "What the fuck went on with Sandriel after I left?"

Baxian smirked. "Who says it had anything to do with Sandriel?"

"Why can't anyone give me a direct answer these days?"

Baxian cocked a brow. Thunder growled its warning in the distance. "You tell me your secrets, Athalar, and I'll tell you mine."

Hunt flipped him off. He didn't bother saying goodbye before launching into the darkening sky.

But he couldn't shake the sense that Baxian continued to watch him. As if he'd left something vital hanging in the balance. It seemed only a matter of time before it returned to bite him in the ass.

23

Ithan kept a step back from the small crowd of mer emergency workers gathered around Captain Ketos—and the body. He'd scented death before they'd even approached the pristine stretch of the Istros an hour north of Lunathion, a pretty green spot amid the oaks of the small forest. They'd taken wave skimmers up the Blue, as this section of the river was nearly inaccessible by foot. He supposed he might have made the run easily in his wolf form, but after getting one sniff of the corpse from a mile downriver, he was glad not to be in that body.

"Selkie female," Tharion was saying to the small group assembled, wiping the sweat from his brow. Even in the shadow of the mighty oaks, the sun baked the forest into kindling.

Ithan swigged from his canteen. He should have worn shorts and sandals instead of the black jeans and boots of the Aux. He had no business wearing these clothes anyway.

Tharion went on, surveying the little heap by the river's edge. It had been found this morning by a passing otter. "Killed execution-style."

Death was nothing new. Ithan just wished he hadn't become so well acquainted with it that at age twenty-two, it was already something he barely batted an eye at. But that was the life of a wolf. Of a Holstrom.

Tharion pointed. "Gorsian bullet to the right thigh to keep her from shifting into her seal form, then a slow bleed-out from a slice to her left femoral artery. Repeated lacerations indicate the murderer reopened the thigh incision continuously to keep her bleeding until she died."

Cthona spare him. "Or until whoever it was got their answers," Ithan said.

The group—three of Tharion's people—turned his way. He'd been brought for one reason—to use his nose. Apparently, that hadn't included speaking.

"Or that," Tharion said, crossing his arms with a pointedness that said:

Keep it quiet; I have the same instinct you do about this.

At least, that was what Ithan thought it conveyed. He'd gotten pretty good at assessing others' expressions and tells thanks to his years on the sunball field.

Tharion said to the group, "Right. Continue documenting the scene, then let's see if we can find a name for her." People peeled away to follow his orders, and Tharion stepped aside to sniff the air.

A male voice spoke from Ithan's left. "Hey, you used to play sunball, right?" Ithan found a ruddy-faced mer in a blue BCIU windbreaker standing a few feet away, a walkie-talkie in hand.

Ithan grunted. "Yeah."

"For CCU—you were that Holstrom kid."

Were. Everything in his life was *were* these days. *You were Connor's brother. You were part of a pack. You were in the Aux. You were a sunball player. You were Bryce's friend. You were normal. You were happy.*

"One and only."

"Why'd you quit? You could be, like, MVP in the pros right now."

Ithan didn't smile, tried his best to appear disinterested. "Had other plans."

"Than playing sunball professionally?" The male gaped. As if a selkie's ravaged body didn't lie mere feet away.

Everyone was watching now. Ithan had grown up with eyes on him like that—had triumphed and failed spectacularly in front of thousands of people, day after day, for years. It didn't make it easier.

"Holstrom." Tharion's voice cut through the air, mercifully drawing him from the conversation. Ithan gave the male a nod and aimed for where the captain stood beside the river. Tharion murmured, "Smell anything?"

Ithan inhaled. Blood and rot and water and iron and—

Another sniff, taking him deeper, pulling back layers. Salt and water and seal. That was the selkie. Then— "There's a human scent here. On her." He pointed to the selkie left amid the leaves and bone-dry brush. "Two of them."

Tharion said nothing, idly twirling a ribbon of water between his fingers. The mer were similar to the water sprites in that regard— able to summon water from thin air.

Ithan began to pace through the clearing, careful of the tracks— noting and scenting the slight disturbances in the dirt and leaves and sticks.

He sniffed again, brain downloading and sorting all those scents.

"Wouldn't your wolf form be easier?" Tharion asked, leaning against a tree.

"No," Ithan lied, and kept moving. He couldn't bear to take that form, to feel that empty-souled wolf.

He sniffed a few more times, then stalked up to Tharion and said quietly, "There's a human female scent all over this scene. But the second scent—it's a human male. A little strange, but human." Exactly as Ithan would have described a part-thunderbird human. "It's only on the selkie. A little whiff."

"So what does that tell you?" Tharion asked with equal quiet, monitoring the others documenting the crime scene.

"My guess?"

"Yeah, tell me your gut impressions."

Ithan noted the mer around him. Their hearing might not be as keen as his, but . . . "I think we should be somewhere more secure."

Tharion made a *hmm* of contemplation. Then he called to the group of investigators, "Any further insights, kids?"

No one answered.

Tharion sighed. "All right. Let's get her bagged up and brought back to the lab. I want tests done as soon as possible, along with an ID."

The others broke apart, heading to the aquatic vehicles lined up along the Blue River's edge, tethered in place with their water magic. Leaving Ithan and Tharion with the body.

The mer male arched a brow. "I need to head to the Blue Court, but I'd like to hear your findings while they're fresh. Do you have time?"

"I got nothing but time," Ithan answered.

He wondered when having all that time would stop feeling like such a chore.

"So, let's hear it," Tharion said as he slumped into his office chair and turned on his computer.

Ithan Holstrom stood at the wall of glass, gazing out at the deep blue of the Istros, observing the fish and otters dart past. The wolf had said little while Tharion had brought him Beneath, though from his wide eyes, it was clear he'd never been here before.

Ithan said without turning, "Let's assume the players involved are the ones we think they are. I think the selkie found the kid, helped him on his way toward Lunathion. Not soon afterward, given how his scent is still on her clothes, the selkie was found and tortured by a human woman for intel on Emile's location. From what we know about her, my guess is Pippa Spetsos."

Tharion's mouth twisted to the side. "My techs said the kill was about a day old. That line up with your info?"

"Yeah, though probably less than a day. But the kid's scent on her clothes was older than that. Only by six hours or so."

"Why?" Tharion propped his chin on his hands.

"Because she couldn't have gone in the water—or changed her clothes, if the scent was still on her. As far as I know, selkies rarely go a day before shifting and swimming. The water would have washed the kid's scent from her."

Tharion considered, turning over the information in his mind. "We didn't pick up any tracks from the kid in the clearing, though."

"No," Ithan agreed, turning back to him. "Emile was never in that clearing. The selkie must have come there afterward."

Tharion peered at the map of Crescent City and its surrounding lands behind his desk. "That spot is between the boat I investigated and the city. If he linked up with the selkie somewhere around there, he is indeed moving toward Lunathion. And if that kill is less than a day old, he might have just gotten here."

"And Pippa Spetsos, if that's whose scent was on the female, could be here as well."

"Or one of her soldiers, I guess," Tharion admitted. "Either way, Lightfall is near. We need to be careful."

"Pippa is a human woman."

"She's a dangerous rebel, capable of killing Vanir thanks to those gorsian bullets. And a psychopath who delights in killing even the most innocent. We're not going near her without prep and thought." Hopefully they would find Emile first and not need to deal with Pippa at all.

Ithan snorted. "We can take her. My brother took down Philip Briggs."

"Something tells me Pippa might be worse than Briggs."

"Come on," Ithan said, scoffing.

Tharion didn't bother to keep the gravity from his face. "I like being alive. I'm not going to risk death because you've got an outsize view of your wolf skills."

"Fuck you."

Tharion shrugged. "My river, my rules, pup."

Thunder from far above echoed in the quiet halls, rattling even the thick glass.

"I can go after her on my own."

Tharion smirked. "Not while you're stuck down here."

Ithan sized him up. "Really? You'd trap me?"

"For your own safety, yeah. You know what Bryce would do to me if you wound up dead? I'd never get to fondle her underwear again."

Ithan gaped at him. Then burst out laughing. It was a rich sound, a little hoarse—like he hadn't done it in a while. "I'm surprised Athalar lets you live."

"You know what Bryce would do to Hunt if *I* wound up dead?" Tharion grinned. "My sweet Legs has my back."

"Why do you call her that?" Ithan asked cautiously.

Tharion shrugged again. "You really want me to answer that?"

"No."

Tharion smirked. "Anyway, the real question is whether Emile is headed toward the place Danika hinted at in her email."

Holstrom had already filled him in on the papers and news clippings he and Bryce had uncovered yesterday, but none had any link to a potential rendezvous location.

The door to Tharion's office opened, and one of his officers, Kendra, strode in. The blond sentinel stopped short upon seeing Ithan, hair swaying around her. She looked to Tharion, who nodded. She was free to speak around the wolf.

"Boss wants you in her quarters. She's, ah . . . in a mood."

Fuck. "I thought I heard thunder." Tharion jerked his chin at the door as Kendra left. "There's a lounge down this hall on the left. Feel free to watch TV, help yourself to snacks, whatever. I'll be back . . . soon. Then we can start sniffing around for the kid." And hopefully avoid Pippa Spetsos.

He used the walk to his queen's quarters to steady his nerves against whatever storm was brewing. It had to be bad, if it was raining Above during the dry summer months.

Bryce fanned her face in the summer heat, thanking Ogenas, Bringer of Storms, for the rain that was moments away from falling. Or whatever Vanir might be throwing a temper tantrum. Judging by how swiftly the storm had swept in to ruin the otherwise flawless blue sky, odds were on the latter.

"It's not *that* hot," Ruhn observed as they walked down the sidewalk toward the Aux training facility on the edge of the Old Square and Moonwood. The empty, cavernous chamber was usually used for large meetings, but he'd reserved it once a week at this hour for their standing training.

They'd have a newcomer today. At least, if Prince Cormac deigned to show up to begin her training, as he'd promised.

"I don't know how you're wearing a leather jacket," Bryce said, her sweaty thighs sticking together with each step.

"Gotta hide the weapons," Ruhn said, patting the holsters beneath the leather jacket. "Can't have the tourists getting skittish."

"You literally carry a sword."

"That has a different impact on people than a gun."

True. Randall had taught her that a long time ago. Swords could mean hope, resistance, strength. Guns meant death. They were to be respected, but only as weapons of killing, even in defense.

Bryce's phone rang, and she checked the caller ID before shutting off the ringer and sliding it into her pocket.

"Who's that?" Ruhn asked, glancing at her sidelong as thunder grumbled. People began clearing the streets, darting into shops and buildings to avoid the downpour. With the arid climate, summer storms were usually violent and swift, prone to flooding the streets.

"My mom," Bryce said. "I'll call her later." She fished out a postcard from her purse and waved it at Ruhn. "She's probably calling about this."

"A postcard?" On the front, it said *Greetings from Nidaros!* in a cheery font.

Bryce slid it back into her purse. "Yeah. It's a thing from when I was a kid. We'd get into a huge fight, and my mom would send me postcards as a weird kind of apology. Like, we might not be talking in person, but we'd start communicating again through postcards."

"But you were living in the same house?"

Bryce laughed again. "Yeah. She'd put them under my door and I'd put them under hers. We'd write about everything *but* the fight. We kept doing it when I went to CCU, and afterward." Bryce riffled through her bag and pulled out a blank postcard of an otter waving that said, *Keep It Fuzzy, Lunathion!* "I'm going to send her one later. Seems easier than a phone call."

He asked, "Are you going to tell her about . . . everything?"

"Are you crazy?"

"What about the engagement being a ruse? Surely that'd get her off your back."

"Why do you think I'm avoiding her calls?" Bryce asked. "She'll say I'm playing with fire. Literally, considering Cormac's power. There's no winning with her."

Ruhn chuckled. "You know, I would have really liked to have her as my stepmom."

Bryce snickered. "Weird. You're, like, twenty years older than her."

"Doesn't mean I don't need a mom to kick my ass every now and then." He said it with a grin, but . . . Ruhn's relationship with his own mother was strained. She wasn't cruel, merely out to lunch. Ruhn took care of her these days. He knew his father certainly wouldn't.

Bryce spoke before she had the chance to consider it. "I'm thinking of going home to Nidaros for the Winter Solstice. Hunt's coming. You want to join?" Now that she and Hunt had adjusted their timeline, Bryce supposed she could be a decent human being and go home for the holiday.

That is, if her mom forgave her for the engagement. And not telling her about it.

Rain splattered the pavement, but Ruhn stopped. His eyes filled with such hope and happiness that Bryce's chest hurt. But he said, "Bringing Hunt home, huh?"

She couldn't help her blush. "Yep."

"Big step, bringing home the boyfriend."

She waved him off, but cringed at the rain that now became a deluge. They still had five blocks to the training center. "Let's wait it out," she said, ducking under an empty restaurant's awning. The Istros lay a block away, close enough that Bryce could see the veils of rain lashing its surface. Even the mer weren't out in this.

Rain streamed off the awning, thick as a waterfall, joining the veritable river already flowing down to the gaping sewer entrance at the corner of the block. Ruhn said over the din, "You really want me to come home with you?"

"I wouldn't have asked if I didn't." Assuming they were still alive by December. If this rebellion shit hadn't killed them all.

Ruhn's tattooed throat bobbed. "Thanks. I normally spend it with Dec and his family, but . . . I don't think they'll mind if I skip this year."

She nodded, awkward silence setting in. They usually had the training to occupy them during any tense silences, but now, trapped by the rain . . . she kept quiet, waiting to see what Ruhn might say.

"Why won't you touch the Starsword?"

She twisted, gesturing to the black hilt of the blade peeking over his shoulder. "It's yours."

"It's yours, too."

"I've got Danika's sword. And you found it first. Doesn't seem fair of me to claim it."

"You're more Starborn than I am. You should have it."

"That's bullshit." She backed up a step. "I don't want it." She could have sworn the rain, the wind, paused. Seemed to listen. Even the temperature seemed to drop.

"Aidas said you've got the light of the true Starborn Queen. I'm just the heir to some rapist asshole."

"Does it matter? I like that you're the Chosen One."

"Why?"

"Because . . ." She hooked her hair behind her ears, then fiddled with the hem of her T-shirt. "I already have this star on my chest." She touched the scar gently. The hair on her arms rose as if in answer. "I don't need a fancy sword to add to it."

"But I do?"

"Honestly? I think you don't know how special you are, Ruhn."

His blue eyes flickered. "Thanks."

"I mean it." She grabbed his hand, and light flared from her chest. "The sword came to you first for a reason. When was the last time two Starborn royals lived peacefully side by side? There's that dumb prophecy that the Fae have: *When knife and sword are reunited, so shall our people be.* You have the Starsword. What if . . . I don't know. What if there's a knife out there for me? But beyond that, what's Urd playing at? Or is it Luna? What's the end goal?"

"You think the gods have something to do with all this?"

Again, the hair on her arms rose; the star on her chest dimmed and went dark. She turned to the rain-lashed street. "After this spring, I can't help but wonder if there *is* something out there. Guiding all this. If there's some game afoot that's . . . I don't know. Bigger than anything we can grasp."

"What do you mean?"

"Hel is another world. Another *planet*. Aidas said so—months ago, I mean. The demons worship different gods than we do, but what happens when the worlds overlap? When demons come here, do their gods come with them? And all of us, the Vanir . . . we all came from elsewhere. We were immigrants into Midgard. But what became of our home worlds? Our home gods? Do they still pay attention to us? Remember us?"

Ruhn rubbed his jaw. "This is some seriously sacrilegious shit for a lunchtime conversation. The postcards with your mom, I can handle. This? I need some coffee."

She shook her head and closed her eyes, unable to suppress the chill down her spine. "I just have this feeling." Ruhn said nothing, and she opened her eyes again.

Ruhn was gone.

A rotted, veilless Reaper, black cloak and robes clinging to its bony body, rain sluicing down its sagging, grayish face, was dragging her unconscious brother across the drenched street. Its acid-green eyes glowed as if lit by Helfire.

The rain must have covered the creature's approach. The hair on her arms had been raised but she'd chalked it up to their dangerous conversation. No one was on the street—was it because everyone had somehow sensed the Reaper?

With a roar, Bryce darted into the driving rain, but she was too late. The Reaper shoved Ruhn into the gaping sewer drain with too-long fingers that ended in cracked, jagged nails, and slithered in after him.

24

Ruhn drifted.

One breath, he'd been talking to Bryce about gods and fate and all that shit. The next, something cold and rotting had breathed in his ear and he'd found himself here in this black void, no up or down.

What the fuck had happened? Something had jumped him and *fuck*, Bryce—

Night.

The female voice flitted in from everywhere and nowhere.

Night, open your eyes.

He twisted toward the voice. *Daybright?*

Open your eyes. Wake up.

What happened? How did you find my mind? I don't have the crystal.

I have no idea what happened to you. Or how I found your mind. I simply felt . . . I don't know what I felt, but the bridge was suddenly there. I think you're in grave danger, wherever you are.

Her voice echoed from above, from below, from within his bones.

I don't know how to wake up.

Open your eyes.

No shit.

She barked, *Wake up! Now!*

Something familiar echoed in her voice—he couldn't place it.

And then she was there, burning flame, as if the link between their minds had solidified. Bright as a bonfire, her hair floated around her head. Like they were both underwater.

Get up! she roared, flames crackling.

Why do I know your voice?

I can assure you, you don't. And you are about to be dead *if you don't wake up.*

Your scent—

You can't smell me.

I can. I know it.

I have never met you, and you have never met me—

How can you know that, if you don't know who I am?

OPEN YOUR EYES!

There was blackness, and the bellow of pouring water. That was Bryce's first, pathetic assessment of the sewer as she plunged into the subterranean river rushing beneath the city.

She didn't let herself think of what swam or floated in the water as she splashed for the stone path running along its side, hauling herself up as she scanned for the Reaper. For Ruhn.

Nothing but dimness, the faint trickle of light from the sewer grates overhead. She peered inward, to the star in her chest. Inhaled sharply. And when she exhaled, light bloomed.

It cast the sewer in stark relief, silvering the stones, the brown water, the arched ceiling—

Well, she'd found her brother.

And five Reapers.

The Reapers floated over the sewer's river, black robes drifting. Ruhn, unconscious, dangled between two of them. The Starsword was still strapped to him. Either they were too stupid to disarm him, or they didn't want to touch it.

"What the fuck do you want?" Bryce stepped closer. Water poured from the grates above, the river rising swiftly.

"We bear a message," the Reapers intoned together. Like they were of one mind.

"Easier ways to send it than this," she spat, advancing another step.

"No further," they warned, and Ruhn dropped an inch for emphasis. Like they'd dump his unconscious ass into the water and let him drown.

One of the Reapers drifted closer to Ruhn as they caught him. The hilt of the Starsword brushed against its robes. It hissed, recoiling.

Okay, they definitely didn't want to touch the sword.

Yet that became the least of her worries as five more Reapers drifted out of the darkness behind her. She reached for the phone in her back pocket, but the Reapers holding Ruhn dropped him another inch. "None of that," they said, the sound echoing from all around.

Wake up, she willed Ruhn. *Wake the fuck up and rip these shitheads apart.*

"What do you want?" she asked again.

"The Prince of the Pit sent us."

Her blood chilled. "You don't serve him. I doubt your king would be happy about it."

"We bear his message nonetheless."

"Put Prince Ruhn down and we can talk."

"And have you use the star on us? We think not."

She pivoted, trying to keep them all in her sights. Ruhn might survive being dumped in the river, but there were limits. How long could a Vanir who'd made the Drop go without oxygen? Or would it be a torturous process of drowning, healing, and drowning again, until even their immortal strength was spent and they finally died?

She didn't want to find out.

"What's your message?" she demanded.

"Apollion, Prince of the Pit, is ready to strike."

Her blood iced over to hear the name spoken aloud. "He's going to launch a war?" Aidas had said something like that yesterday, but he'd indicated that the armies would be for *her*. She'd thought he meant to help in whatever insanity Hel had planned.

"The Prince of the Pit wants a worthy opponent this time. One who will not break so easily, as Prince Pelias did so long ago. He insists on facing *you*, Starborn, at your full power."

Bryce barked a laugh. "Tell him I was literally on my way to training before you half-lives interrupted me." But her bones quaked to say it, to think about who they represented. "Tell him you just knocked out my tutor."

"Train harder. Train better. He is waiting."

"Thanks for the pep talk."

"Your disrespect is not appreciated."

"Yeah, well, your kidnapping my brother is definitely not appreciated."

They seethed with ire and Bryce cringed. "The Prince of the Pit already hunts through the Bone Quarter's mists to find the other one who might be his worthy opponent . . . or his greatest weapon."

Bryce opened her mouth, but shut it before she could blurt *Emile?* But *fuck*—Apollion was hunting for the kid, too? Was the Bone Quarter what Danika had meant after all? Her mind raced, plan after plan spreading out, then she said, "I'm surprised the Under-King lets Apollion wander around his territory unchecked."

"Even the caretakers of the dead bow to the Prince of the Pit."

Bryce's heart sank. Emile *was* in the Bone Quarter. Or at least Apollion thought so. What the fuck had Danika been thinking, telling Sofie it was safe there?

Before Bryce could ask more, the Reapers said as one, "You sold your soul away, Bryce Quinlan. When it is your time, we shall come to rip it to shreds."

"It's a date." She had to find some way to grab Ruhn, to be faster, smarter than them—

"Perhaps we shall have a taste of you now." They surged forward.

Bryce flared her light, falling against the curved wall of the tunnel. Water lapped over the edge of the walkway, spilling toward her neon-pink sneakers.

The Reapers exploded back, but despite their threats, kept Ruhn between them. So Bryce rallied that power inside her, let it crest in a blink, and then—

Another blast. Not from her, but somewhere else. A blast of pure night.

One moment a Reaper stood close to her. Then it was gone. Vanished into nothing. The others screeched, but—

Bryce shouted as Cormac appeared out of nothing, hovering over the river, arms around another Reaper—and vanished once more.

Again, he appeared. Again, he took another Reaper with him and vanished.

What was already dead could not be killed. But they could be . . . removed. Or whatever the fuck he was doing.

Cormac appeared again, blond hair shining, and yelled, *"USE THE FUCKING LIGHT!"*

She caught the direction of his stare: Ruhn. The Reapers who still held him aloft.

Bryce punched out her power, flaring bright as a supernova. The Reapers screamed and made good on their threat, hurling Ruhn toward the raging water—

Cormac caught Ruhn before he hit the frothing surface. Vanished again.

The Reapers whirled, screeching and hissing. Bryce flared her light anew, and they scattered into the darkest shadows.

Then Cormac returned, and tossed something to her—the Starsword. He must have taken it from Ruhn. Bryce didn't stop to think as she unsheathed it. Starlight erupted from the black blade. Like its metal had been kindled with iridescent fire.

A Reaper lunged, and Bryce swept the sword up, a blind, unwieldy block that she knew would have horrified Randall.

But blade met cloth and rotting flesh and ancient bone. And for the first time, perhaps the only time in that world, a Reaper bled.

It screamed, the sound as piercing as a hawk's cry. The others keened in horror and rage.

The Starsword sang with light, her power flowing into it. Activating it. And nothing had ever felt so right, so easy, as plunging the blade into the bony chest of the wounded Reaper. It arced, bellowing, black blood spurting from its withered lips.

The others screamed then. So loud she thought the sewer might come down, so loud she nearly dropped the blade to cover her ears.

The Reapers surged, but Cormac appeared before her in a plume of shadows. He grabbed her around the middle, nearly tackling her, and they were gone.

Wind roared and the world spun out from beneath her, but—

They landed inside the Aux training center. Ruhn was coughing on the floor beside her, the polished pine scrubbed clean except where the three of them dripped sewer water.

"You can fucking *teleport*?" Bryce gasped out, twisting to where Cormac stood.

But Cormac's gaze was on the Starsword, his face ashen. Bryce peered at the blade she clenched in a white-knuckled grip. As if her hand refused to let go.

With shaking fingers, she put it back into its sheath. Dimmed its light. But the Starsword still sang, and Bryce had no idea what to make of it.

Of the blade that had slain that which was unkillable.

PART II
THE ABYSS

25

Tharion warily watched the two sobeks lounging at his queen's feet, their scaly, powerful bodies draped over the dais steps. With their shut eyes, only the bubbles drifting from their long snouts revealed they lived—and were capable of snapping his arm off in one swift bite.

The River Queen's throne had been carved into a towering mountain of river corals rising from the rocky floor. Lunathion lay close enough to the coast that the water in this part of the Istros had plenty of salt to support the vibrant corals, as well as the bouquets of anemones, waving lace sea fans, and the occasional rainbow ribbons of iris eels all adorning the mount around and above her. He had a feeling her magic had also created a good chunk of it.

Tail pumping against the strong current that flowed past, Tharion bowed his head. "Your Majesty." At this point, the effort against the current was second nature, but he knew she'd selected this location for her throne so that any person appearing before her would be a bit off-kilter—and perhaps less guarded as a result. "You summoned me?"

"It has come to my attention," his queen said, her dark hair drifting above her, "that you asked my daughter on a date."

Tharion focused on keeping his tail moving, holding him in place. "Yes. I thought she'd enjoy it."

"You asked her on a date *Above*. Above!"

Tharion lifted his chin, hands clasped behind his back. A subservient, vulnerable position that he knew his queen preferred, exposing the entirety of his chest to her. His heart lay in range of the jagged sea-glass knife resting on the arm of her throne, or the beasts drowsing at her feet. She had the power to destroy him in an instant, but he knew she liked the feel of the kill.

He'd never understood it, until he'd found his sister's murderer and opted to tear the panther shifter apart with his bare hands.

"I only meant to please her," Tharion said.

But the River Queen's fingers dug into the carved arms of her throne. "You know how overwhelmed she becomes. She is too fragile for such things."

Tharion sucked in a deep breath through his gills. Exhaled it before saying, "She handled herself well at the Summit." A half-lie. She'd done absolutely nothing of value at the Summit, but at least she hadn't been cowering the whole time.

Anemones shrank into themselves, a swift warning of his queen's ire before she said, "That was in an organized, guarded place. Lunathion is a wild forest of distraction and pleasure. It will devour her whole." The iris eels sensed her tone and darted into the cracks and crevices around the throne.

"I apologize for any distress the suggestion caused you or her." He didn't dare so much as curl his fingers into a fist.

The queen studied him with the concentration of one of the sobeks at her feet, when the beasts were poised to strike. "What of your progress with the Renast boy?"

"I have good reason to believe he's just arrived in this city. I have my people looking for him." They hadn't found any new bodies today—for better or worse. He could only pray it didn't mean Pippa Spetsos had gotten her hands on the boy.

"I want that boy at the Blue Court the moment he's found."

Pippa or the River Queen. Above or Beneath. Emile Renast's options were limited.

Once the kid was down here, he wouldn't get back Above unless the River Queen wished it. Or the Asteri dispatched one of their elite aquatic units to drag him out. But that would mean they'd learned of the River Queen's betrayal.

But Tharion only nodded. As he had always done. As he would always do. "We'll apprehend Emile soon."

"Before Ophion."

"Yes." He didn't dare ask why she was bothering with any of it. From the moment she'd heard the rumors about the boy who could bring down those Omegas with his power-draining magic, she'd wanted Emile. She didn't share her reasons. She never did.

"And before any other of the River Courts."

Tharion lifted his head at that. "You think they know about Emile, too?"

"The currents whispered to me about it. I don't see why my sisters wouldn't hear similar murmurings from the water."

The queens of Valbara's four great rivers, the Istros, the Melanthos, the Niveus, and the Rubellus—the Blue, the Black, the White, and the Red, respectively—had long been rivals: all mighty and gifted with magic. All vain and ancient and bored.

While Tharion might not be privy to his queen's most intimate plans, he could only assume she wanted the boy for the same reason Pippa Spetsos did: to use him as a weapon. One that could be used to get the queens of the Black, White, and Red Courts to yield. With the boy in her thrall, she could potentially use him to siphon their powers, to turn all that elemental energy against them and expand her influence.

But if they knew of Emile as well, then did they already scheme, thinking to take the Blue Court? And if the Queen of the Red Court wished to overthrow his queen, to use Emile's gifts to drain her of power . . . would he fight it?

Years ago, he would have said Hel yes.

But now . . .

Tharion lifted his face toward the surface. That distant, beckoning ribbon of light.

He found her studying him again. As if she could hear every

thought in his mind. The sobek at her left cracked open an eye, revealing a slitted pupil amid green-marbled citrine.

His queen asked, "Are things so wonderful Above that you resent your time Beneath?"

Tharion kept his face neutral, kept swishing his fins with an idle grace. "Can't both realms be wonderful?"

The second sobek opened an eye as well. Would they be opening their jaws next?

They ate anything and everything. Fresh meat, trash, and, perhaps most important, the bodies of the shameful dead. Having one's black boat overturned on its way to the Bone Quarter was the deepest sort of humiliation and judgment: a soul deemed unworthy of entering the holy resting place, its corpse given over to the river beasts to devour.

But Tharion kept his hands clasped behind him, kept his chest exposed, ready to be shredded apart. Let her see his utter subservience to her power.

His queen only said, "Keep searching for the boy. Report as soon as you hear anything new."

He bowed his head. "Of course." He swished his fin, readying to swim off the moment she gave the dismissal.

But the River Queen said, "And Tharion?"

He couldn't stop his swallow at the smooth, casual tone. "Yes, my queen?"

Her full lips curved into a smile. So much like the beasts at her feet. "Before you invite my daughter on a date Above again, I think you should witness firsthand the disrespect those Above show the citizens of the Beneath."

The River Queen picked her punishments well. Tharion would give her that.

Swimming along the Old Square's section of the quay an hour later, he kept his head down as he speared trash.

He was her Captain of Intelligence. How many of his people had already noticed him here or heard about this? He stabbed a discarded, half-decayed pizza box. It fell into three pieces before he could tuck it into the giant bag drifting behind him on the current.

The River Queen wanted Emile badly, Pippa Spetsos was leaving a trail of bodies in her hunt for the kid, and yet *this* was his queen's priority for him?

Water splashed twenty feet above, and Tharion lifted his head to find an empty beer bottle filling—and then drifting down. Through the surface, he could just make out a blond female laughing at him.

She'd tried to fucking *hit* him with that bottle. Tharion rallied his magic, smiling to himself as a plume of water showered the female, earning a host of shrieks and growls from those around her.

Ten more bottles came flying down at him.

Tharion sighed, bubbles flowing from his lips. Captain Whatever, indeed.

The River Queen fancied herself a benevolent ruler who wanted the best for her people, yet she treated her subjects as harshly as any Asteri. Tharion wended between the mussel-crusted pillars of a dock, various crabs and bottom-scavengers watching him from the shadows.

Something had to change. In this world, in the hierarchies. Not only in the way Ophion wanted, but . . . this imbalance of power across all Houses.

Tharion pried a bike tire—for fuck's sake—from between two rocks, muscles groaning. A giant blue crab scuttled over, waving its claws in reprimand. *Mine!* it seemed to shout. Tharion backed off, gesturing to the trash. *Have at it,* he conveyed with a wave of his hand, and with a powerful thrust of his tail, swam farther along the quay.

The glowing firstlights cast ripples on the surface. It was like swimming through gold.

Something had to change. For him, at least.

Ruhn laid the Starsword on his father's desk as the Autumn King stalked through the study doors.

The top buttons of his father's black shirt were undone, his ordinarily smooth red hair a bit out of place. Like someone had been running their hands through it. Ruhn shuddered.

His father eyed the sword. "What is so important that you interrupted my afternoon meeting?"

"Is that what you're calling it these days?"

His father threw him an admonishing glance as he slid into his desk chair, surveying the bare Starsword. "You smell like trash."

"Thanks. It's a new cologne I'm trying out." Considering the insanity of the last hour, it was a miracle he could even joke right then.

Agent Daybright had been in his mind, screaming at him to wake up. That was all he'd known before he'd started puking water and the gods knew what else—*he* certainly didn't want to know—on the Aux training center floor.

Cormac had left by the time Ruhn mastered himself, apparently wanting to quickly search the area for any hint of Emile or Sofie. Bryce had still been in shock when Ruhn managed to ask what the fuck had happened.

But she'd told him enough—then kicked the Starsword toward him in the empty training hall and left. Which was when he'd rushed over here.

Flame sparked at his father's fingers—the first warning of his impatience. So Ruhn asked, "What's the lore behind this sword?"

His father arched a brow. "You've been its bearer for decades. Now you want to know its history?"

Ruhn shrugged. His head still pounded from the blow the Reapers had given him; his stomach churned like he'd been drinking all night. "Does it have any special powers? Weird gifts?"

The Autumn King swept a cold look over Ruhn, from his waterlogged boots to his half-shaved head, the longer hair scraggly thanks to the sewer trip. "Something has happened."

"Some Reapers tried to jump me, and the sword . . . reacted."

A light way of putting it. Had Bryce stayed away from the sword all these years because she somehow sensed that in her hand, it would unleash horrors?

He didn't want to know what his father would do with the truth.

A sword that could kill the unkillable. How many rulers in Midgard would scheme and murder to attain it? Starting with his father and ending with the Asteri.

Maybe they'd get lucky and the information would be contained to the Reapers. But the Under-King . . .

His father stilled. "How did the sword react?"

"Shouldn't a father ask if his son is all right? And why the Reapers attacked?"

"You appear unharmed. And I assume you did something to offend them."

"Thanks for your vote of confidence."

"Did you?"

"No."

"How did the sword react in the presence of the Reapers?"

"It glowed. They ran from it." It was only a half-lie. "Any idea why?"

"They are already dead. Blades hold no threat to them."

"Yeah, well . . . they freaked."

His father reached for the black blade but halted, remembering himself. It wasn't his blade to touch.

Ruhn reined in his smirk of satisfaction. But his father watched the various globes and solar system models across his office for a long moment.

Ruhn spied their own solar system in the center of it all. Seven planets around a massive star. Seven Asteri—technically six now—to rule Midgard. Seven Princes of Hel to challenge them.

Seven Gates in this city through which Hel had tried to invade this spring.

Seven and seven and seven and seven—always that holy number. Always—

"It's an ancient sword," the Autumn King said at last, drawing Ruhn from his wandering thoughts, "from another world. Made from the metal of a fallen star—a meteorite. This sword exists beyond our planet's laws. Perhaps the Reapers sensed that and shied away."

The Reapers had learned precisely how outside the planet's laws the sword was. It could fucking *kill* them.

Ruhn opened his mouth, but his father sniffed him again. Frowned. "And when were you going to tell me your sister was involved in this incident? She's even more reckless than you."

Ruhn stifled the spike of anger in his gut. "Only fit for breeding, right?"

"She should consider herself lucky I believe her valuable enough for that."

"You should consider yourself lucky that she didn't come in here to kick your ass for the betrothal to Cormac."

His father stalked to the elegant wood liquor cabinet behind his desk and pulled out a crystal decanter of what looked and smelled like whiskey. "Oh, I've been waiting for days now." He poured himself a glass, not bothering to offer Ruhn any, and knocked it back. "I suppose you convinced her not to."

"She decided all on her own that you weren't worth the effort."

His father's eyes simmered as he set the glass and decanter on the edge of his desk. "If that sword is acting up," the Autumn King said, ignoring his barb, "I'd suggest keeping it far from your sister."

Too late. "I offered it to her already. She didn't want it. I don't think she's interested in your politics."

But she had run into a sewer teeming with Reapers after him. Ruhn's heart squeezed tight.

His father poured himself another glass of whiskey. The only sign that something about this conversation rattled him. But the Autumn King's voice was bland as he said, "In ancient times, Starborn rivals would slit each other's throats. Even those of the children. She is now more powerful than you and I are, as you like to remind me."

Ruhn resisted the urge to ask whether that had played any part in his father's slaying of the last Starborn heir. "Are you telling me to kill Bryce?"

His father sipped from the whiskey this time before replying, "If you had any backbone, you would have done it the moment you learned she was Starborn. Now what are you?" Another sip before he said mildly, "A second-rate prince who only possesses the sword because she allows you to have it."

"Pitting us against each other won't work." But those words—*second-rate prince*—those gouged something deep in him. "Bryce and I are good."

The Autumn King drained the glass. "Power attracts power. It is her fate to be tied to a powerful male to match her own strength. I would rather not learn what comes of her union with the Umbra Mortis."

"So you betrothed her to Cormac to avoid that?"

"To consolidate that power for the Fae."

Ruhn slowly picked up the Starsword. Refused to meet his father's stare while he sheathed it down his back. "So this is what being king is all about? That old shit about keeping friends close and enemies closer?"

"It remains to be seen whether your sister is an enemy to the Fae."

"I think the burden of that's on you. Overstepping your authority doesn't help."

His father returned the crystal decanter to the cabinet. "I am a King of the Fae. My word is law. I cannot overstep my authority—it has no limits."

"Maybe it should." The words were out before Ruhn could think.

His father went still in a way that always promised pain. "And who will impose them?"

"The Governor."

"That doe-eyed angel?" A mirthless laugh. "The Asteri knew what they were doing in appointing a lamb to rule a city of predators."

"Maybe, but I bet the Asteri would agree that there are limits to your power."

"Why don't you ask them, then, Prince?" He smiled slowly, cruelly. "Maybe they'll make you king instead."

Ruhn knew his answer would mean his life or death. So he shrugged again, nonchalant as always, and aimed for the door. "Maybe they'll find a way to make you live forever. I sure as fuck have no interest in the job."

He didn't dare to look back before he left.

26

Bryce leaned against the alley side of a brick building bordering the Black Dock, arms crossed and face stony. Hunt, gods bless him, stood at her side, mirroring her position. He'd come right over the moment she'd called him, sensing that her eerily calm voice meant something big had gone down.

She'd only managed to say something vague about Reapers before they'd found Cormac here, prowling for any hint of Emile.

Cormac lounged against the wall across the alley, focus on the quay beyond. Not even the vendors selling touristy crap came here. "Well?" the Avallen Prince asked, not taking his attention from the Black Dock.

"You can teleport," Bryce said, voice low. *That* made Hunt's eyes widen. He kept himself contained, though, solid and still as a statue, wings tucked in—but brimming with power. One blink, and Hunt would unleash lightning on the prince.

"What of it?" Cormac asked with no small hint of haughtiness.

"What did you do to the Reapers you teleported out?"

"Put them about half a mile up in the sky." The Avallen Prince smiled darkly. "They weren't happy."

Hunt's brows rose. But Bryce asked, "You can go that far? It's that precise?"

"I need to know the spot. If it's a trickier location—indoors, or a specific room—I need exact coordinates," Cormac said. "My accuracy is within two feet."

Well, that explained how he'd shown up at Ruhn's house party. Dec's tech had picked up Cormac teleporting around the house's perimeter to calculate where he wanted to appear to make his grand entrance. Once he'd had them, he'd simply walked right out of a shadow in the doorway.

Hunt pointed to a dumpster halfway down the alley. "Teleport there."

Cormac bowed mockingly. "Left side or right side?"

Hunt leveled a cool stare at him. "Left," he challenged. Bryce suppressed a smile.

But Cormac bowed at the waist again—and vanished.

Within a blink, he reappeared where Hunt had indicated.

"Well, fuck," Hunt muttered, rubbing the back of his neck. Then, Cormac reappeared before them, right where he'd been standing.

Bryce pushed off the wall. "How the Hel do you do that?"

Cormac slicked back his blond hair. "You have to picture where you want to go. Then simply allow yourself to take that step. As if you're folding two points on a piece of paper so that the two points can meet."

"Like a wormhole," Hunt mused, wings rustling.

Cormac waved a dismissive hand. "Wormhole, teleportation, yes. Whatever you want to call it."

Bryce blew out an impressed breath. But it didn't explain— "How'd you know where to find me and Ruhn?"

"I was on my way to meet you, remember?" Cormac rolled his eyes, as if she should have figured it out by now. Asshole. "I saw you run into the sewer, and I did some mental calculations for the jump. Thankfully, they were right."

Hunt let out an approving grunt, but said nothing.

So Bryce said, "You're going to teach me how to do that. Teleport."

Hunt whipped his head to her. But Cormac simply nodded. "If it's within your wheelhouse, I will."

Hunt blurted, "I'm sorry, but Fae can just *do* this shit?"

"*I* can do this shit," Cormac countered. "If Bryce has as much Starborn ability as she seems to, she might also be able to do this shit."

"Why?"

"Because I'm the Super Powerful and Special Magic Starborn Princess," Bryce answered, waggling her eyebrows.

Cormac said, "You should treat your title and gifts with the reverence they are due."

"You sound like a Reaper," she said, and leaned against Hunt. He tucked her into his side. Her clothes were still soaked. And smelled atrocious.

But Hunt didn't so much as sniff as he asked Cormac, "Where did you inherit the ability from?"

Cormac squared his shoulders, every inch the proud prince as he said, "It was once a gift of the Starborn. It was the reason I became so . . . focused on attaining the Starsword. I thought my ability to teleport meant that the bloodline had resurfaced in me, as I've never met anyone else who can do it." His eyes guttered as he added, "As you know, I was wrong. Some Starborn blood, apparently, but not enough to be worthy of the blade."

Bryce wasn't going to touch that one. So she retied her wet hair into a tight bun atop her head. "What are the odds that I have the gift, too?"

Cormac gave her a slashing smile. "Only one way to find out."

Bryce's eyes glowed with the challenge. "It would be handy."

Hunt murmured, his voice awed, "It would make you unstoppable."

Bryce winked at Hunt. "Hel yeah, it would. Especially if those Reapers weren't full of shit about the Prince of the Pit sending them to challenge me to some epic battlefield duel. Worthy opponent, my ass."

"You don't believe the Prince of the Pit sent them?" Cormac asked.

"I don't know what I believe," Bryce admitted. "But we need to confirm where those Reapers came from—who sent them—before we make any moves."

"Fair enough," Hunt said.

Bryce went on, "Beyond that, this is twice now that we've gotten warnings about Hel's armies being ready. Apollion's a little heavy-handed for my tastes, but I guess he *really* wants to get the point across. And wants me leveled up by the time all Hel breaks loose. Literally, I guess."

Bryce knew there was no fucking way she'd ever stand against the Star-Eater and live, not if she didn't expand her understanding of her power. Apollion had killed a fucking Asteri, for gods' sakes. He'd obliterate her.

She said to Cormac, "Tomorrow night. You. Me. Training center. We'll try out this teleporting thing."

"Fine," the prince said.

Bryce picked lingering dirt from beneath her nails and sighed. "I could have lived without Hel getting mixed up in this. Without Apollion apparently wanting in on Sofie's and Emile's powers."

"Their powers," Cormac said, face thunderous, "are a gift and a curse. I'm not surprised at all that so many people want them."

Hunt frowned. "And you really think you're going to find Emile just hanging around here?"

The prince glowered at the angel. "I don't see you combing the docks for him."

"No need," Hunt drawled. "We're going to search for him without lifting a finger."

Cormac sneered, "Using your lightning to survey the city?"

Hunt didn't fall for the taunt. "No. Using Declan Emmet."

Leaving the males to their posturing, Bryce pulled out her phone and dialed. Jesiba answered on the second ring. "What?"

Bryce smiled. Hunt half turned toward her at the sound of the sorceress's voice. "Got any Death Marks lying around?"

Hunt hissed, "You can't be serious."

Bryce ignored him as Jesiba answered, "I might. Plan on taking a trip, Quinlan?"

"I hear the Bone Quarter's gorgeous this time of year."

Jesiba chuckled, a rolling, sultry sound. "You do amuse me every now and then." Pause. "You have to pay for this one, you know."

"Send the bill to my brother." Ruhn would have a conniption, but he could deal.

Another soft chuckle. "I only have two. And it'll take until tomorrow morning for them to reach you."

"Fine. Thanks."

The sorceress said a shade gently, "You won't find any traces of Danika left in the Bone Quarter, you know."

Bryce tensed. "What does that have to do with anything?"

"I thought you were finally going to start asking questions about her."

Bryce clenched the phone hard enough for the plastic to groan. "What sort of questions?" What the fuck did Jesiba know?

A low laugh. "Why don't you start by wondering why she was always poking around the gallery?"

"To see me," Bryce said through her teeth.

"Sure," Jesiba said, and hung up.

Bryce swallowed hard and pocketed her phone.

Hunt was slowly shaking his head. "We're not going to the Bone Quarter."

"I agree," Cormac grumbled.

"You're not going at all," she said sweetly to Cormac. "We'll only have two fares, and Athalar is my plus-one." The prince bristled, but Bryce turned to Hunt. "When the coins arrive tomorrow, I want to be ready—have as much information as possible about where those Reapers came from."

Hunt folded his wings behind him, feathers rustling. "Why?"

"So the Under-King and I can have an informed heart-to-heart."

"What was that shit Jesiba said about Danika?" Hunt asked warily.

Bryce's mouth hardened into a thin line. Jesiba did and said nothing without reason. And while she knew she'd never get answers out of her old boss, at least this nudge was something to go on. "Turns out we're going to have to ask Declan for an additional favor."

* * *

That night, still reeling from the events of the day, Ruhn flipped through the channels on the TV until he found the sunball game, then set down the remote and swigged from his beer.

On the other end of the sectional couch in Bryce's apartment, Ithan Holstrom sat hunched over a laptop, Declan beside him with a laptop of his own. Bryce and Hunt stood behind the two, staring over their shoulders, the latter's face stormy.

Ruhn had told none of them, especially Bryce, about the conversation with his father.

Ithan typed away, then said, "I'm super rusty at this."

Dec said without breaking his attention from the computer, "If you took Kirfner's Intro to Systems and Matrices, you'll be fine."

Ruhn often forgot that Dec was friendly with people other than him and Flynn. While none of them had attended college, Dec had struck up a years-long friendship with the ornery CCU computer science professor, often consulting the satyr on some of his hacking ventures.

"He gave me a B minus in that class," Ithan muttered.

"From what he tells me, that's practically an A plus," Declan said.

"Okay, okay," Bryce said, "any idea how long this is going to take?"

Declan threw her an exasperated look. "You're asking us to do two things at once, and neither is easy, so . . . a while?"

She scowled. "How many cameras are even at the Black Dock?"

"A lot," Declan said, going back to his computer. He glanced to Holstrom's laptop. "Click that." He pointed to a mark on the screen that Ruhn couldn't see. "Now type this code in to identify the footage featuring Reapers."

How Dec managed to direct Ithan to comb through the footage around the Black Dock from earlier today while *also* creating a program to search through years of video footage of Danika at the gallery was beyond Ruhn.

"It's insane that you made this," Ithan said with no small bit of admiration.

"All in a day's work," Dec replied, typing away. Pulling any footage from the gallery featuring Danika could take days, he'd said.

But at least the footage from the Black Dock would only take minutes.

Ruhn carefully asked Bryce, "You sure you trust Jesiba enough to follow this lead? Or at all?"

"Jesiba literally has a collection of books that could get her killed," Bryce said tartly. "I trust that she knows how to stay out of . . . dangerous entanglements. And wouldn't shove me into one, either."

"Why not tell you to look at the footage during the investigation this spring?" Hunt asked.

"I don't know. But Jesiba must have had a good reason."

"She scares me," Ithan said, gaze fixed on the computer.

"She'll be happy to hear that," Bryce said, but her face was tight.

What's up? Ruhn asked her mind-to-mind.

Bryce frowned. *You want the honest answer?*

Yeah.

She tucked a strand of hair behind an ear. *I don't know how much more of this "Surprise! Danika had a big secret!" stuff I can take. It feels like . . . I don't even know. It feels like I never really knew her.*

She loved you, Bryce. That's not in doubt.

Yeah, I know. But did Danika know about the Parthos books—or the other contraband tomes—in the gallery? Jesiba made it sound like she did. Like she took a special interest in them.

You guys never talked about it?

Never. But Jesiba was always monitoring those cameras, so . . . maybe she saw something. Danika was down there without me plenty of times. Though Lehabah was usually there, too.

Ruhn noted the pain that filled his sister's face at the fire sprite's name.

We'll figure it out, Ruhn offered, and Bryce gave him a thankful smile in return.

"Don't forget to keep an eye out for Emile around the docks," Bryce said to Ithan. Cormac had turned down the invitation to join them here—he'd said he wanted to continue hunting for Emile on the ground.

"I already added it to the program," Declan said. "It'll flag any Reaper or any person whose facial features and build match the kid's." Dec had managed to pull a still from the security footage in the town of Servast the night Emile and Sofie had separated.

Ruhn again considered his sister, who was peering over Declan's shoulder with an intensity he recognized. She wouldn't let go of any of this.

Would she be able to teleport? She'd told him that Cormac had agreed to try to teach her. And wouldn't that be something for the Autumn King to chew on—Bryce plus teleporting plus Starborn power plus Starsword with crazy killing abilities plus Bryce magically outranking their father equaled . . .

Ruhn kept his face neutral, tucking away thoughts of what a leveled-up Bryce might mean for the Fae.

Ithan finished typing in the code, and said without looking up, "Hilene is going to win this one."

Ruhn checked the sunball game just beginning its first period. "I thought Ionia was favored."

Ithan stretched out his long legs, propping his bare feet on a cushioned stool Bryce had dragged over from the windows to be a temporary replacement for the coffee table. "Jason Regez has been off the last two games. I played with him at CCU—I can tell when he starts to get in a funk. He'll fuck it up for Ionia."

Ruhn eyed Ithan. A few years off the sunball field hadn't gotten rid of the muscles on the male. He'd somehow gotten even bigger since then.

"I hate Ionia anyway," Dec said. "They're all swaggering assholes."

"Pretty much." Ithan typed in the next line of code that Declan fed him.

Bryce yawned audibly. "Can't we watch *Veiled Love*?"

"No," everyone answered.

Bryce elbowed Hunt. "I thought we were a team."

Hunt snorted. "Sunball always trumps reality shows."

"Traitor."

Ithan snickered. "I remember a time when you knew all the players on the CCU team and their stats, Bryce."

"If you think that was because I was remotely interested in the actual sunball playing, you're delusional."

Hunt laughed, some of the tightness on the angel's face lightening, and Ruhn smiled, despite the old ache in his heart. He'd missed out on those years with Bryce. They hadn't been speaking then. Those had been formative, pivotal years. He should have been there.

Ithan flipped Bryce off, but said to Declan, "Okay, I'm in."

Bryce scanned the screen. "Do you see any Reapers crossing in boats?"

"This is showing nothing landing at the Black Dock at all today. Or last night."

Athalar asked, "When's the last time any Reaper docked?"

Ithan kept typing, and they all waited, the only additional sound the swift clack of Declan's fingers on the keys of his computer. The wolf said, "Yesterday morning." He grimaced. "These two look familiar?"

Bryce and Ruhn scanned the image Ithan had pulled up. Ruhn had no idea why the fuck he bothered, since he'd been unconscious, but a shiver went down his spine at the sagging, graying faces, the crepe-like skin so at odds with the jagged, sharp teeth that gleamed as the Reapers stepped from the boat. Both had pulled back their veils during the trip across the Istros, but tugged them over their faces as they stepped onto the Black Dock and drifted into the city.

Bryce said hoarsely, "No. Gods, they're awful. But no—those weren't the ones who attacked."

"They might have been hiding out for a few days," Athalar said. "The Prince of the Pit only threatened us the other night, but he might have had them in place already."

Ruhn had no idea how the angel spoke so calmly. If the Star-Eater had come to *him* and wanted to have a one-on-one chat, he'd still be shitting his pants.

"I'm not seeing any kids lurking around the Black Dock, either,"

Ithan muttered, scanning the results. He twisted to Bryce. "No sign of Emile at all."

Ruhn asked, "Possible the kid took another way over? Maybe Danika found some sort of back door into the Bone Quarter."

"Not possible," Athalar said. "Only one way in, one way out."

Ruhn bristled. "That's what we've been taught, but has anyone ever tried to get in some other way?"

Athalar snorted. "Why would they want to?"

Ruhn glared at the angel but said, "Fair enough."

Ithan stopped on an image. "What about this one? He didn't take a boat over, just appeared from within the city—"

"That's the one," Bryce hissed, her face paling.

They all studied the still—the Reaper was half-turned to the camera as it entered the frame from a street near the Black Dock. He was taller than the others, but had the same grayish, soft face and those terrifying teeth.

Athalar whistled. "You sure know how to pick them, Quinlan."

She scowled at the angel, but asked Dec, "Where's it coming from? Can you add its face to the program and run a search on the city's footage?"

Declan's brows rose. "You know how long *that* will take? Every camera in Lunathion? It's why we're not even doing it for Emile. It'd take . . . I can't even calculate how long we'd need."

"Okay, okay," Bryce said. "But can we . . . track this one for a while?" She directed the last bit at Ithan, but the wolf shook his head.

"There must be a logical reason for this—like a gap in the camera coverage or something—but that Reaper just seems to . . . appear."

"Micah had the kristallos stay in known camera gaps," Hunt said darkly. "These Reapers could know about them, too."

Ithan pointed to the screen. "Right here is where they first appear. Before that, nothing."

Ruhn pulled up a map of the city in his Aux app. "There should be a sewer entrance right behind them. Possible they came out of there?"

Ithan moved the footage around. "The cameras don't cover that sewer entrance."

Bryce said, "So they probably knew it'd be a good entry point. And it'd make sense, given that they dragged us into the sewers." Where there were no cameras at all.

"Let me look around a little more," Ithan offered, and clicked away.

Athalar asked none of them in particular, "You think they were waiting for you, or for Emile?"

"Or both?" Ruhn asked. "Clearly, they wanted to stay hidden."

"But did the Prince of the Pit send them, or did the Under-King?" Athalar pushed.

"Good thing we've got a date with the being who can answer that," Bryce said.

Ruhn winced. He'd paid for the Death Marks that Jesiba had promised, but he wasn't happy about it. The thought of Bryce confronting the Under-King scared the Hel out of him.

"We need a plan for how we question him," Athalar warned her. "I doubt he'll appreciate being questioned at all."

"Hence the research," Bryce shot back, gesturing to the computer. "You think I'm stupid enough to go in and fling accusations around? If we can confirm whether or not those Reapers came directly from the Bone Quarter, we'll have steadier footing when we question him. And if we can get any hint of Emile actually going over to the Bone Quarter, then we'll have a good reason to ask him about that, too."

Ithan added, "Considering what Tharion thinks Pippa Spetsos has done while hunting for Emile, I'm half hoping the kid's already in the Bone Quarter." He dragged a hand through his short brown hair. "What she did to that selkie we found this morning was no joke."

The wolf had filled them all in on the work he'd done with Tharion earlier—the tortured body they suspected had been left behind by the rebel fanatic.

Bryce pivoted and began pacing. Syrinx trotted at her heels, whining for a second dinner. Ruhn refrained from remarking on how similar the motion was to one he'd seen their father do so many times in his study. Unable to stand it, he turned back to the sunball game.

Then Ithan said to Ruhn, picking up the thread of conversation from earlier, "See? Regez should have nailed that shot, but he balked. He's second-guessing himself. He's too deep in his head."

Ruhn glanced sidelong at the male. "You've never thought about playing again?"

A muscle ticked in Ithan's jaw. "No."

"You miss it?"

"No."

It was an obvious lie. Ruhn didn't fail to note that Bryce's eyes had softened.

But Ithan didn't so much as look in her direction. So Ruhn nodded to the wolf. "If you ever want to play a pickup game, me, Dec, and Flynn usually play with some of the Aux in Oleander Park over in Moonwood on Sundays."

"Where's my invite?" Bryce asked, scowling.

But Ithan said roughly, "Thanks. I'll think about it."

Hunt asked, "I'm assuming I don't get an invite, either, Danaan?"

Ruhn snorted at the angel. "You want an excuse for me to beat the shit out of you, Athalar, then I'm down."

Athalar smirked, but his gaze drifted to Bryce, who was now staring over Declan's shoulder at the lightning-fast footage zooming by on his laptop. Footage of Danika from years ago.

She straightened suddenly. Cleared her throat. "I'm going down to the gym. Call me if you find anything." She aimed for her bedroom, presumably to change. Ruhn watched Hunt glance between her disappearing form and the sunball game. Weighing which one to follow.

It took Athalar all of thirty seconds to decide. He ducked into his room, saying he was going to change for the gym.

When Ruhn was alone with Dec and Ithan, his beer half-finished, Ithan said, "Connor would have picked the game."

Ruhn raised an eyebrow. "I didn't realize it was a competition between them." Between a dead male and a living one.

Ithan just typed away, eyes darting over the screen.

And for some reason, Ruhn dared ask, "What would you have picked?"

Ithan didn't hesitate. "Bryce."

27

Bryce didn't go to the gym. Not yet, anyway. She waited in front of the elevator, and when Hunt appeared, she tapped her wrist and said, "You're late. Let's go."

He halted. "We're not working out?"

She rolled her eyes, stepping into the elevator and hitting the Lobby button. "Honestly, Athalar. We've got a kid to find."

"You really think Emile is *here*? What about the Bone Quarter?" Hunt asked as Bryce strode through the warren of stalls that made up one of the Meat Market's many warehouses. There was no missing her, not with her neon-pink sneakers and athletic gear, that high ponytail that swished back and forth, brushing tantalizingly close to the glorious curve of her ass. "The Reapers practically told you that he and Sofie are lying low over there. You're having Emmet and Holstrom comb through footage *because* you think Emile's over there."

She paused at an open seating area, surveying the crammed array of tables and the diners hunched over them. "Forgive me if I don't take those half-lifes at their word. Or want to wait around while Declan and Ithan stare at their screens. Jesiba said the coins will arrive tomorrow, so why not look at alternatives in the meantime?

What Danika said . . . *Where the weary souls find relief* . . . Couldn't that be here, too?"

"Why would Danika tell them to lie low in the Meat Market?"

"Why tell them to lie low in the *Bone Quarter*?" She sniffed and sighed with longing toward a bowl of noodle soup.

Hunt said, "Even if Danika or Sofie told Emile it was safe to hide out, if I were a kid, I wouldn't have come here."

"You were a kid, like, a thousand years ago. Forgive me if my childhood is a little more relevant."

"Two hundred years ago," he muttered.

"Still old as fuck."

He pinched her ass and she squeaked, batting him away, drawing more than a few eyes. Not exactly inconspicuous. How long until the Viper Queen heard they were here? Hunt tried not to bristle at the thought. He had zero interest in dealing with the shapeshifter tonight.

Hunt marked the faces that turned their way, the ones who moved off into the stalls and shadows. "And if this is where Sofie told him to hide, Sofie was a fool for listening to Danika. Though I really doubt Danika would have suggested it as a rendezvous point."

Bryce glared at him over a shoulder. "This kid stole *two* boats and made it all the way here. I think he can handle the Meat Market."

"Okay, buying that, you think he's simply going to be sitting at a table, twiddling his thumbs? You're no better than Cormac, stomping around the docks for any sign of this kid." Hunt shook his head. "If you do find Emile, don't forget you'll have Tharion and Cormac fighting you for him."

She patted his cheek. "Then it's a good thing I have the Umbra Mortis at my side, huh?"

"Bryce," he growled. "Be reasonable. I mean, look at where we are right now. This market's huge. Are we going to search through every warehouse ourselves?"

"Nope." Bryce put her hands on her hips. "That's why I brought backup."

Hunt's brows rose. She lifted her hand, waving at someone across the space. He followed her line of attention. Let out a low growl. "You didn't."

"You're not the only badass I know, Athalar," she trilled, approaching Fury and Juniper, the former in her usual all black, the latter in tight jeans and a flowing white blouse. "Hi, friends," Bryce said, smiling. She kissed June's cheek as if they were meeting for brunch, then gave Fury a once-over. "I said casual clothes."

"These are her casual clothes," Juniper said, laughter in her eyes.

Fury crossed her arms, ignoring them as she said to Hunt, "Gym clothes? Really?"

"I thought I *was* going to the gym," he grumbled.

Bryce waved him off. "All right. We divide and conquer. Try not to attract too much attention." The last bit she directed at Hunt and Fury, and the merc glowered with impressive menace. "Don't ask questions. Just watch—listen. June, you take the east stalls, Fury the west ones, Hunt the south, and me . . ." Her gaze drifted to the northern wall, where *Memento Mori* had been painted. The stalls beneath it—beneath the walkway above—lay within range of the door to the Viper Queen's quarters.

Fury eyed her, but Bryce winked. "I'm a big girl, Fury. I'll be fine."

Hunt grunted, but suppressed any hint of objection.

"That's not what I'm worried about," Fury said. Then asked quietly, "Who is this kid again?"

"His name is Emile," Bryce whispered. "He's from Pangera. Thirteen years old."

"And possibly very, very dangerous," Hunt warned, glancing at Juniper. "If you spot him, come find us."

"I can take care of myself, angel," Juniper said with impressive cool.

"She's a big girl, too." Bryce high-fived her friend. "Right. Meet back here in thirty?"

They parted, and Hunt watched Bryce weave through the tables of the dining area—watched the many patrons note her, but keep well away—before slipping between the stalls. Gazes slid back to him, questioning. Hunt bared his teeth in a silent snarl.

Moving off toward the area she'd ordered him to sweep, Hunt opened his senses, calmed his breathing.

Thirty minutes later, he'd returned to the dining area, Juniper appearing a moment later. "Anything?" he asked the faun, who shook her head.

"Not a whisper." The dancer frowned. "I really hope that kid isn't here." She scowled at the warehouse. "I hate this place."

"That makes two of us," Hunt said.

Juniper rubbed at her chest. "You should talk to Celestina about it—the things that happen here. Not only that fighting pit and the warriors the Viper Queen practically enslaves . . ." The faun shook her head. "The other things, too."

"Even Micah let the Viper Queen do what she wanted," Hunt said. "I don't think the new Governor is going to challenge her anytime soon."

"Someone should," she said quietly, eyes drifting to the *Memento Mori* on the wall. "Someday, someone should."

Her words were haunted and strained enough that Hunt opened his mouth to ask more, but Fury sauntered up, smooth as a shadow, and said, "No sign of the kid."

Hunt searched the space for Bryce, and found her at a stall far too close to the Fae-guarded door to the Viper Queen's private living area. The towering Fae sentries a mere fifty feet from her didn't so much as blink at her presence, though. She had a bag swinging from her wrist, and she was chatting away.

Bryce finished and walked toward them. Again, too many eyes watched her.

"She's got some pep in her step," Juniper observed, chuckling. "She must have gotten a good bargain."

The tang of blood and bone and meat stuffed itself up Hunt's nose as Bryce approached. "I got some lamb bones from the butcher for Syrinx. He goes crazy for the marrow." She added to Juniper, "Sorry."

Right. The faun was a vegetarian. But Juniper shrugged. "Anything for the little guy."

Bryce smiled, then surveyed them all. "Nothing?"

"Nothing," Hunt said.

"Me neither," Bryce said, sighing.

"What now?" Fury asked, monitoring the crowd.

"Even if Declan and Ithan can't find any footage of Emile around the Black Dock," Bryce said, "the fact that there's no hint of him here at the Meat Market leads us right back to the Bone Quarter again. So it gives us a bit more reason to even ask the Under-King about whether Emile is there."

Hunt's blood sparked. When she talked like that, so sure and unflinching . . . His balls tightened. He couldn't wait to show her just how insanely that turned him on.

But Juniper whispered, "A little boy in the Bone Quarter . . ."

"We'll find him," Bryce assured her friend, and threw an arm around Juniper's shoulders, turning them toward the exit. Hunt swapped a look with Fury, and they followed. Hunt let Bryce and Juniper drift ahead a few feet, and then, when he was sure they wouldn't be overheard, asked Axtar, "Why does your girlfriend hate this place so much?"

Fury kept her attention on the shadows between the stalls, the vendors and shoppers. "Her brother was a fighter here."

Hunt started. "Does Bryce know?"

Fury nodded shallowly. "He was talented—Julius. The Viper Queen recruited him from his training gym, promised him riches, females, everything he wanted if he signed himself into her employ. What he got was an addiction to her venom, putting him in her thrall, and a contract with no way out." A muscle ticked in Fury's jaw. "June's parents tried everything to get him freed. *Everything.* Lawyers, money, pleas to Micah for intervention—none of it worked. Julius died in a fight ten years ago. June and her parents only learned about it because the Viper Queen's goons dumped his body on their doorstep with a note that said *Memento Mori* on it."

The elegant dancer strode arm-in-arm with Bryce. "I had no idea."

"June doesn't talk about it. Even with us. But she hates this place more than you can imagine."

"So why'd she come?" Why had Bryce even invited her?

"For Bryce," Fury said simply. "Bryce told her she didn't have to join, but she wanted to come with us. If there's a kid running around lost in this place, June would do anything to help find him. Even come here herself."

"Ah," Hunt said, nodding.

Fury's eyes glittered with dark promise. "I'll burn this place to the ground for her one day."

Hunt didn't doubt it.

An hour later, Bryce's arms and stomach trembled as she held her plank on the floor of her apartment building's gym, sweat dripping off her brow and onto the soft black mat beneath. Bryce focused on the droplet as it splattered, on the music thumping in her earbuds, on breathing through her nose—*anything* other than the clock.

Time itself had slowed. Ten seconds lasted a minute. She pushed her heels back, steadying her body. Two minutes down. Three more to go.

Before the Drop, she'd usually managed a decent minute in this position. After it, in her immortal body, five minutes should be nothing.

Master her powers, indeed. She needed to master her body first. Though she supposed magic was ideal for lazy people: she didn't need to be able to hold a plank for ten minutes if she could just unleash her power. Hel, she could blind someone while sitting down if she felt like it.

She chuckled at the idea, horrible as it was: her lounging in an oversize armchair, taking down enemies as easily as if she were changing the channel with a remote. And she *did* have enemies now, didn't she? She'd killed a fucking Reaper today.

As soon as those Death Marks arrived from Jesiba tomorrow morning, she'd demand answers from the Under-King.

It was why she'd come down here—not only to validate her excuse for leaving the apartment. Well, that and seeing Danika on Declan's laptop as it scanned through footage. Her head had begun spinning and acid had been burning through her veins, and sweating it all out seemed like a good idea. It always worked in Madame Kyrah's classes.

She owed June a massive box of pastries for coming tonight.

Bryce checked the clock on her phone. Two minutes fifteen seconds. Fuck this. She plopped onto her front, elbows splaying, and laid her face directly on the mat.

A moment later, a foot prodded her ribs. Since there was only one other person in the gym, she didn't bother to be alarmed as she craned her neck to peer up at Hunt. His lips were moving, sweat beading his brow and dampening his tight gray T-shirt—gods-damn it. How could he look so good?

She tugged an earbud out. "What?" she asked.

"I asked if you were alive."

"Barely."

His mouth twitched, and he lifted the hem of his T-shirt up to clean his dripping face. She was rewarded with a glimpse of sweat-slicked abs. Then he said, "You dropped like a corpse."

She cradled her arms, rubbing the sore muscles. "I prefer running. This is torture."

"Your dance classes are equally grueling."

"This isn't as fun."

He offered her a hand, and Bryce took it, her sweaty skin sliding against his as he hauled her to her feet.

She wiped at her face with the back of her arm, but found it to be equally sweaty. Hunt returned to the array of metal machines that seemed more like torture devices, adjusting the seat on one to accommodate his gray wings. She stood in the center of the room like a total creep for a moment, watching his back muscles ripple as he went through a series of pull-down exercises.

Burning fucking Solas.

She'd blown this male. Had slid down that beautiful, strong body and taken his ridiculously large cock in her mouth and had nearly come herself as he'd spilled on her tongue.

And she knew it was ten kinds of fucked up, considering how much shit they were juggling and all that lay ahead, but . . . *look at him.*

She wiped at the sweat rolling down her chest, leaving a spectacularly unsexy stain beneath her sports bra.

Hunt finished his set but kept gripping the bar above his head, arms extended high above him, stretching out his back and wings. Even in a T-shirt and gym shorts, he was formidable. And . . . she was still staring. Bryce twisted back to her mat, grimacing as she put in her earbud and it blasted music. But her body refused to move.

Water. She needed some water. Anything to delay going back to that plank.

She trudged for the wet bar built into the far wall of the gym. The beverage fridge beneath the white marble counter was stocked with glass water bottles and chilled towels, and Bryce helped herself to both. A bowl of green apples sat on the counter, along with a basket full of granola bars, and she took the former, teeth sinking into the crisp flesh.

Fuck doing planks.

Savoring the apple's tart kiss, she glanced over toward Hunt, but—Where was he? Even that telltale ripple of his power had faded away.

She scanned the expansive gym, the rows of machines, the treadmills and ellipticals before the wall of windows overlooking the bustle of the Old Square. How had he—

Hands wrapped around her waist, and Bryce shrieked, nearly leaping out of her skin. Light erupted from her chest, but with the music thumping in her ears, she couldn't hear anything—

"Fucking *Hel*, Quinlan!" Hunt said, prying her earbuds away. "Listen to your music a little louder, will you?"

She scowled, pivoting to find him right behind her. "It wouldn't matter if you didn't *sneak up on me.*"

He flashed her a sweaty, wicked grin. "Just making sure my Shadow of Death skills don't get rusty before tomorrow's tea party with the Under-King. I thought I'd see if I could dim myself a bit."

Hence her inability to sense him creeping up. He rubbed at his eyes. "I didn't realize you'd be so . . . jumpy. Or *bright*."

"I thought you'd praise me for my quick reflexes."

"Good jump. You almost blinded me. Congrats."

She playfully slapped his chest, finding rock-hard muscles beneath the sweat-dampened shirt. "Solas, Hunt." She rapped her knuckles on his pecs. "You could bounce a gold mark off these things."

His wings rustled. "I'm taking that as a compliment."

She propped her elbows on the counter and bit into her apple again. Hunt extended a hand, and she wordlessly handed him one earbud. He fitted it to his ear, head angling as he listened to the song.

"No wonder you can't do a plank for more than two minutes, if you're listening to this sad-sack music."

"And your music is so much better?"

"I'm listening to a book."

She blinked. They'd often swapped music suggestions while working out, but this was new. "Which book?"

"Voran Tritus's memoir about growing up in the Eternal City and how he became, well . . . him." Tritus was one of the youngest late-night talk show hosts ever. And absurdly hot. Bryce knew the last fact had little to do with why Hunt tuned in religiously, but it certainly made her own viewing much more enjoyable.

"I'd say listening to a book while working out is even less motivational than this *sad-sack* music," she said.

"It's all muscle memory at this point. I only need to pass the time until I'm done."

"Asshole." She ate more of her apple, then changed the song. Something she'd first heard in the hallowed space of the White Raven dance club, a remix of a slower song that somehow managed to combine the song's original sensual appeal with a driving beat that demanded dancing.

The corner of Hunt's mouth kicked up. "You trying to seduce me with this music?"

She met his gaze as she chewed on another mouthful of apple. The gym was empty. But the cameras . . . "You're the one who snuck up to fondle me."

He laughed, the column of his throat working. A droplet of sweat ran down its powerful length, gleaming among all that golden-brown skin, and her breathing hitched. His nostrils flared, no doubt scenting everything that went hot and wet within the span of a breath.

He tucked in his wings, leaving the earbud in place as he took a step closer. Bryce leaned slightly against the counter, the marble digging into her overheated spine. But he only took the apple from her fingers. Held her gaze while he bit in, then slowly set the core on the counter.

Her toes curled in her sneakers. "This is even less private than my bedroom."

Hunt's hands slid onto her waist, and he hoisted her onto the counter in one easy movement. His lips found her neck, and she arched as his tongue slid up one side, as if licking away a bead of sweat. "Best be quiet, then, Quinlan," he said against her skin.

Lightning skittered around the room. She didn't need to look to know he'd severed the camera wires, and likely had a wall of power blocking the door. Didn't need to do anything other than enjoy the sensation of his tongue on her throat, teasing and tasting.

She couldn't stop the hands that slid into his hair, driving through the sweaty strands, all the way down his head until they landed on the nape of his neck. She drew him closer as she did so, and Hunt lifted his head from her neck to claim her mouth.

Her legs opened wider, and he settled between them, pressing hard as his tongue met hers.

Bryce groaned, tasting apple and that storm-kissed cedar scent that was pure Hunt, grinding herself against his demanding hardness. With his gym shorts and her skintight leggings, there was no hiding his erection, or the dampness that soaked through her pants.

His tongue tangled with hers, hands dropping from her waist

to cup her ass. She gasped as his fingers dug in, pulling her harder against him, and she hooked her legs around his middle. She couldn't taste him deep enough, fast enough.

His shirt came off, and then she was running her fingers over those absurd abs and side abs and pecs, down the shifting muscles of his back, frantic and desperate to touch all of him.

Her tank top peeled away, and then his teeth nipped at the swells of her breasts above the seafoam green of her sports bra, the fabric almost neon against her tan skin.

He bracketed her waist, calluses scraping her skin as he tilted her back, and Bryce let him lay her on the counter. She propped herself up on her elbows as he pulled away, graceful as an ebbing tide, hands running from her breasts to her sweaty stomach.

Hunt's fingers curled over the waistband of her black leggings, but paused. His gaze lifted to hers in silent request.

At the black fire she beheld there, the sheer beauty and size and perfection of him . . .

"Hel yes," she said, and Hunt grinned wickedly, rolling down her leggings. Exposing her midriff. Then her abdomen. Then the lacy top of her amethyst thong. Her pants and underwear were soaked with sweat—she didn't want to imagine what they smelled like—and she opened her mouth to tell him so, but he'd already knelt.

He pulled off her sneakers, then her socks, then the leggings. Then gently, so gently, he took her right ankle and kissed its inside. Licked at the bone. Then at her calf. The inside of her knee.

Oh gods. This was going to happen. Right here, in the middle of the building gym where anyone could fly past the wall of windows twenty feet away. He was going down on her right here, and she needed it more than she'd ever needed anything—

His tongue traced circles along the inside of her right thigh. Higher and higher, until she was shaking. But his hands slid up, looping through the waistband of her thong. He pressed a kiss to the front of her underwear, and she could have sworn he shuddered as he inhaled.

Bryce went liquid, unable to stop her writhe of demand, and Hunt huffed a warm laugh against her most sensitive place, kissing her again through the fabric of her underwear.

But then he kissed her left thigh, beginning a downward trajectory, pulling her underwear away as he went. And when the thong was completely gone, when she was bared to the world, Hunt's wings splayed above him, blocking her from the world's view.

Only his to see, his to devour.

Her breathing turned jagged as his mouth reached her left ankle, kissing again, and then he was sliding back up. He halted with his head between her thighs, though. Took her feet and propped them onto the counter.

Spread her legs wide.

Bryce moaned softly as Hunt surveyed her, the light glowing through his wings making him look like an avenging angel lit with inner fire.

"Look at you," he murmured, voice guttural with need.

She'd never felt so naked, yet so seen and cherished. Not as Hunt slid a finger through her wetness. "Fuck yeah," he growled, more to himself than to her, and she really, truly couldn't breathe as he knelt again, head poised where she needed him most.

Hunt softly, reverently, laid a hand on her, opening her for his own personal tasting. His tongue swept along her in an introductory *Hi, nice to fuck you* flit. She bit her lip, panting through her nose.

Yet Hunt bowed his head, brow resting just above her mound as his hands slid to her thighs once more. He inhaled and exhaled, shuddering, and she had no idea if he was savoring her scent or really needed a moment to calm the Hel down.

One or two more licks and she knew she'd lose her mind entirely.

Then Hunt pressed a kiss to the top of her sex. And another, as if he couldn't help it. His hands caressed her thighs. He kissed her a third time, raised wings twitching, and then his mouth drifted south, one hand with it.

Again, he parted her, and pressed his tongue flat against her as he dragged it up.

Stars sparked behind Bryce's eyes, her breasts aching so much she arched into the air, as if seeking invisible hands to touch them.

"That's it," Hunt said against her, and flicked his tongue over her clit with lethal precision.

She couldn't endure this. Couldn't handle one more second of this torture—

His tongue pushed into her, curling deep, and she bucked.

"You taste like gods-damn paradise," he growled, pulling back enough for her to note her wetness on his mouth, his chin. "I knew you'd taste like this."

Bryce clapped a hand over her mouth to keep from shouting as Hunt drove his tongue back into her, then dragged it all the way up to her clit. His teeth clamped down gently, and her eyes rolled back into her head. Burning Solas and merciful Cthona . . .

"Hunt," she managed to say, voice strangled.

He paused, ready to halt should she give the word. But that was the last thing she wanted.

Bryce met Hunt's blazing gaze, her chest heaving, head a dizzy, starry mess. She said the only thing in her head, her mind, her soul. "I love you."

She regretted the words the moment they left her mouth. She'd never said them to any male, hadn't even *thought* the words about Hunt, though she'd known for a while. Why they came out then, she had no idea, but—his eyes darkened again. His fingers tightened on her legs.

Oh gods. She'd fucked everything up. She was a stupid, horny idiot, and what the *fuck* had she been thinking, telling him that when they weren't even *dating*, for fuck's sake—

Hunt unleashed himself. Dipped his head back down between her thighs and feasted on her. Bryce could have sworn thunderstorms rumbled in the room. It was answer and acceptance of what she'd said. Like he was beyond words now.

Tongue and teeth and purring—all combined into a maelstrom of pleasure that had Bryce grinding against him. Hunt gripped her thighs hard enough to bruise and she loved it, needed it; she drove her hips into his face, pushing his tongue into her, and then something *zapped* right at her clit, as if Hunt had summoned a little spark of lightning, and her brain and body lit up like white fire, and oh gods, oh gods, oh gods—

Bryce was screaming the words, Hunt's wings still cocooning them as she came hard enough that she arced clean off the counter, fingers scrabbling in his hair, pulling hard. She was flaring with light inside and out, like a living beacon.

She could have sworn they fell through time and space, could have sworn they tumbled toward something, but she wanted to stay here, with him, in this body and this place—

Hunt licked her through every ripple, and when the climax eased, when the light she'd erupted with had faded, and that falling sensation had steadied, he lifted his head.

He met her stare from between her thighs, panting against her bare skin, lightning in his eyes. "I love you, too, Quinlan."

No one had said those words to Hunt in two centuries.

Shahar had never said them. Not once, though he'd stupidly offered the words to her. The last person had been his mother, a few weeks before her death. But hearing them from Quinlan . . .

Hunt lay beside her in bed thirty minutes later, the minty scent of their toothpaste and lavender of their shampoo mingling in the air. That had been weird enough: showering one after the other, then brushing their teeth side by side, those words echoing. Walking through the apartment, past Ruhn, Declan, and Ithan watching sunball analysts argue over tonight's game, wondering how so much and yet so little had changed in the span of a few minutes.

Going into the Bone Quarter tomorrow seemed like a far-off storm. A distant rumble of thunder. Any thought of their search at the Meat Market tonight dissolved like melting snow.

In the dimness, the TV still droning from the living room, Hunt stared at Bryce. She silently watched him back.

"One of us has got to say something," Hunt said, voice gravelly.

"What else is there to say?" she asked, propping her head on a fist, hair spilling over a shoulder in a red curtain.

"You said you love me."

"And?" She cocked an eyebrow.

Hunt's mouth twitched upward. "It was said under duress."

She bit her lip. He wanted to plant his teeth there. "Are you asking whether I meant it, or do you think you're that good with your mouth that I went out of my mind?"

He flicked her nose. "Smart-ass."

She flopped back onto the mattress. "They're both true."

Hunt's blood heated. "Yeah?"

"Oh, come on." She tucked her arms behind her head. "You have to know you're good at it. That *lightning* thing . . ."

Hunt held up a finger, a spark of lightning dancing at the tip. "Thought you'd enjoy that."

"If I'd known ahead of time, I might have been concerned about you deep-frying my favorite parts."

He laughed warmly. "I wouldn't dare. They're my favorite parts, too."

She lifted herself onto her elbows, unable to keep from fidgeting. "Does it weird you out? What I said?"

"Why should it? I reciprocated, didn't I?"

"Maybe you felt bad for me and wanted to make it less weird."

"I'm not the kind of person who lightly tosses those words around."

"Me neither." She reached over and Hunt leaned toward her hand, letting her brush her fingers through his hair. "I've never said it to anyone. I mean, like . . . romantically."

"Really?" His chest became unbearably full.

She blinked, her eyes like golden embers in the darkness. "Why the surprise?"

"I thought you and Connor . . ." He wasn't sure why he needed to know.

That fire banked slightly. "No. We might have one day, but it didn't get that far. I loved him as a friend, but . . . I still needed time." She smiled crookedly. "Who knows? Maybe I was just waiting for you."

He grabbed her hand, pressing a kiss to her knuckles. "I've been in love with you for a while. You know that, right?" His heart thundered, but he said, "I was . . . very attached to you during our investigation, but when Sandriel had me in that cell under the Comitium, she put on this fucked-up slideshow of all the photos on my phone. Of you and me. And I watched it and knew. I saw the photos of us toward the end, how I was looking at you and you were looking at me, and it was a done deal."

"Sealed with you jumping in front of a bomb for me."

"It's disturbing when you make jokes about that, Quinlan."

She chuckled, kissing his jaw. Hunt's body tensed, readying for another touch. Begging for another touch. She said, "I made the Drop for you. *And* offered to sell myself into slavery in your stead. I think I'm allowed to joke about this shit." He nipped at her nose. But she pulled back, gaze meeting his. Hunt let her see everything that lay there. "I knew the moment you went snooping for my dildos."

Hunt burst out laughing. "I can't tell if that's the truth."

"You handled Jelly Jubilee with such care. How could I not love you for it?"

He laughed again, ducking to brush a kiss to her warm throat. "I'll take that." He traced his fingers down her hip, the threadbare softness of her old T-shirt snagging against his callused skin. He kissed her collarbone, inhaling the scent of her, his cock stirring. "So what now?"

"Sex?"

He grinned. "No. I mean, fuck yes, but I don't want an audience." He gestured over his shoulder and wing to the wall behind him. "Shall we get a hotel room somewhere in the city?"

"Somewhere on another continent."

"Ah, Quinlan." He kissed her jaw, her cheek, her temple. He whispered into her ear, "I really want to fuck you right now."

She shuddered, arching against him. "Same."

His hand slid from her waist to cup her ass. "This is torture." He slipped his hand under her oversize shirt, finding her bare skin warm and soft. He traced his fingers along the seam of her lacy thong, down toward her thighs. Heat beckoned him, and she sucked in a breath as he halted millimeters short of where he wanted to be.

But she placed a hand on his chest. "What do I call you now?"

The words took a moment to register. "What?"

"I mean, what *are* we? Like, dating? Are you my boyfriend?"

He snorted. "You really want to say you're dating the Umbra Mortis?"

"I'm not keeping this private." She said it without an ounce of doubt. She brushed her fingers over his brow. Like she knew what it meant to him.

Hunt managed to ask, "What about Cormac and your ruse?"

"Well, after all that, I guess." If they survived. She whooshed out a breath. "*Boyfriend* sounds weird for you. It's so . . . young. But what else is there?"

If he had a star on his chest, Hunt knew it'd be glowing as he asked, "Partner?"

"Not sexy enough."

"Lover?"

"Does that come with a ruff and lute?"

He swept a wing over her bare thigh. "Anyone ever tell you that you're a pain in the ass?"

"Just ye olde lover."

Hunt hooked his finger under the strap of her thong and snapped it. She yowled, swatting away his hand.

But Hunt grabbed her fingers, laying them on his heart again. "What about *mate*?" Bryce stilled, and Hunt held his breath, wondering if he'd said the wrong thing. When she didn't reply, he went on, "Fae have mates, right? That's the term they use."

"Mates are . . . an intense thing for the Fae." She swallowed audibly. "It's a lifetime commitment. Something sworn between bodies and hearts and souls. It's a binding between beings. You say I'm your mate in front of any Fae, and it'll mean something big to them."

"And we don't mean something big like that?" he asked carefully, hardly daring to breathe. She held his heart in her hands. Had held it since day one.

"You mean *everything* to me," she breathed, and he exhaled

deeply. "But if we tell Ruhn that we're mates, we're as good as married. To the Fae, we're bound on a biological, molecular level. There's no undoing it."

"*Is* it a biological thing?"

"It can be. Some Fae claim they know their mates from the moment they meet them. That there's some kind of invisible link between them. A scent or soul-bond."

"Is it ever between species?"

"I don't know," she admitted, and ran her fingers over his chest in dizzying, taunting circles. "But if you're not my mate, Athalar, no one is."

"A winning declaration of love."

She scanned his face, earnest and open in a way she so rarely was with others. "I want you to understand what you're telling people, telling the Fae, if you say I'm your mate."

"Angels have mates. Not as . . . soul-magicky as the Fae, but we call life partners mates in lieu of husbands or wives." Shahar had never called him such a thing. They'd rarely even used the term *lover.*

"The Fae won't differentiate. They'll use their intense-ass definition."

He studied her contemplative face. "I feel like it fits. Like we're already bound on that biological level."

"Me too. And who knows? Maybe we're already mates."

It would explain a lot. How intense things had been between them from the start. And once they crossed that last physical barrier, he had a feeling the bond would be even further solidified.

So . . . maybe they *were* already mates, by that Fae definition. Maybe Urd had long ago bound their souls, and they'd needed all this time to realize it. But did it even matter? If it was fate or choice to be together?

Hunt asked, "Does it scare you? Calling me your mate?"

Her gaze dipped to the space between them, and she said quietly, "You're the one who's been defined by other people's terms for centuries." *Fallen. Slave. Umbra Mortis.* "I just want to make sure it's a title you're cool with having. Forever."

He kissed her temple, breathing in her scent. "Of everything I've ever been called, Quinlan, your mate will be the one I truly cherish."

Her lips curved. "Did you hear the *forever* part?"

"I thought that's what this thing between us is."

"We've known each other for, like, five months."

"So?"

"My mom will throw a fit. She'll say we should date for at least two years before calling ourselves mates."

"Who cares what other people think? None of their rules have ever applied to us anyway. And if we're some sort of predestined mates, then it doesn't make a difference at all."

She smiled again, and it lit up his entire chest. No, that was the star between her breasts. He laid a hand over the glowing scar, light shining through his fingers. "Why does it do that?"

"Maybe it likes you."

"It glowed for Cormac and Ruhn."

"I didn't say it was smart."

Hunt laughed and leaned to kiss the scar. "All right, my lovely mate. No sex tonight."

His mate. *His.*

And he was hers. It wouldn't have surprised him if her name were stamped on his heart. He wondered if his own were stamped on the glowing star in her chest.

"Tomorrow night. We'll get a hotel room."

He brushed another kiss against her scar. "Deal."

28

I'm glad to see you alive.

Ruhn stood on a familiar mental bridge, the lines of his body once more filled in with night and stars and planets. At the other end of the bridge waited that burning female figure. Long hair of pure flame floated around her as if underwater, and what he could make out of her mouth was curved upward in a half smile.

"So am I," he said. He must have passed out on the couch in Bryce's apartment. He'd still been there at two in the morning, watching old game highlights with Ithan. Dec had long since gone to spend the night at Marc's place. Neither had turned up any solid footage of Emile at the docks—or concrete proof of the Reapers being sent from the Under-King or Apollion. The search for Danika at the gallery would take days, Dec had said before leaving, and he did have other work to do. Ithan had instantly volunteered to keep combing through it.

The wolf pup wasn't bad. Ruhn could see them being friends, if their people weren't constantly at each other's throats. Literally.

Ruhn said to Agent Daybright, "Thanks for trying to wake me up."

"What happened?"

"Reapers."

Her flame guttered to a violet blue. "They attacked you?"

"Long story." He angled his head. "So I don't need the crystal to reach you? I can just be unconscious? Sleeping?"

"Perhaps the crystal was only needed to initiate contact between our minds—a beacon for your talents," she said. "Now that your mind—and mine—knows where to go, you don't require the crystal anymore, and can contact me even in . . . inopportune moments."

A pinprick of guilt poked at him. She was embedded in the higher ranks of the empire—had he endangered her when he'd been unconscious earlier, his mind blindly reaching for hers?

But Daybright said, "I have information for you to pass on."

"Yeah?"

She straightened. "Is that how Ophion agents speak these days? *Yeah?*"

She had to be old, then. One of the Vanir who'd lived for so long that modern lingo was like a foreign language. Or, gods, if she was an Asteri . . .

Ruhn wished he had a wall or a doorway or a counter to lean against as he crossed his arms. "So you're old-school Pangeran."

"Your position here isn't to learn about me. It's to pass along information. Who I am, who you are, is of no consequence." She gestured to her flames. "This should tell you enough."

"About what?"

Her flames pushed closer to her body, turning a vibrant orange—like the hottest embers. The kind that would burn to the bone. "About what shall happen if you ask too many prying questions."

He smiled slightly. "So what's the intel?"

"The hit on the Spine is a go."

Ruhn's smile faded. "When's the shipment?"

"Three days from now. It leaves from the Eternal City at six in the morning their time. No planned stops, no refueling. They'll travel swiftly northward, all the way to Forvos."

"The mech-suit prototype will be on the train?"

"Yes. And along with it, Imperial Transport is moving fifty crates of brimstone missiles to the northern front, along with a hundred and twelve crates of guns and about five hundred crates of ammunition."

Burning Solas. "You're going to stage a heist?"

"*I'm* not doing anything," Agent Daybright said. "Ophion will be responsible. I'd recommend destroying it all, though. Especially that new mech-suit. Don't waste time trying to unload anything from the trains or you'll be caught."

Ruhn refrained from mentioning that Cormac had suggested something different. He'd said Ophion wanted to attain the suit—to study it. And use those weapons in their war. "Where's the best place to intercept?"

He was really doing this, apparently. Pass this intel along, and he was officially aligning himself with the rebels.

"That's for Ophion Command to decide."

He asked carefully, "Will Pippa Spetsos be assigned to the hit?" Or was she in Lunathion looking for Emile, as Tharion suspected?

"Does it matter?"

Ruhn shrugged as nonchalantly as he could. "Just want to know whether we need to notify her."

"I'm not privy to who Command sends on their missions."

"Do you know where Pippa Spetsos is right now, though?"

Her flame guttered for a moment. "Why do you have such interest in her?"

He held up his hands. "No interest at all." He could sense her suspicion, though, so he asked, "Will there be armed guards with the shipment?"

"Yes. About a hundred wolves in and atop the cars, along with a dozen aerial angel scouts above. All armed with rifles, handguns, and knives."

Forested areas would be best for a strike, then, to avoid being seen by the malakim.

"Anything else?"

She angled her head. "None of this bothers you?"

"I've been in the Aux for a while. I'm used to coordinating shit." Nothing like this, though. Nothing that put him firmly in the Asteri's line of fire.

"That's a stupid thing to reveal. Ophion must have been desperate, if they sent someone as untrained as you to deal with me."

"Trust is a two-way street." He gestured to the space between them.

Another one of those soft laughs raked over his skin. "Do you have anything for me? What's this business with Pippa Spetsos?"

"Nothing at all. But—thanks for trying to save my ass earlier."

"I'd be a fool to let a valuable contact go to waste."

He bristled. "I'm touched."

She snorted. "You sound like a male used to being obeyed. Interesting."

"What the Hel is interesting about it?"

"The rebels must have something on you, to make you risk your position by doing this."

"I thought you didn't give a shit about my personal life."

"I don't. But knowledge is power. I'm curious about who you might be, if the Reapers tried to grab you. And why you allow the rebels to push you around."

"Maybe I wanted to join."

She laughed, the sound sharp as a blade. "I've found that the ruling class rarely do such things out of the kindness of their hearts."

"Cynical."

"Perhaps, but it's true."

"I could name a highly placed Vanir who's helping the rebels without being forced into it."

"Then they should put a bullet in your head."

Ruhn stiffened. "Excuse me?"

She waved a hand. "If you know their identity, if you're able to so blithely boast about it, if you are asking too many questions about Agent Spetsos, you're not an asset at all. You're a loose cannon. If the dreadwolves catch you, how long will it take for you to sing that person's name?"

"Fuck off."

"Have you ever been tortured? It's easy for people to claim they wouldn't break, but when your body is being pulled apart piece by piece, bone by bone, you'd be surprised what people offer to get the pain to stop, even for a second."

Ruhn's temper flared. "You don't know shit about me or what

I've been through." He was grateful the night and stars of his skin covered the marks his father's ministrations had left—the ones his ink couldn't hide.

Day's flame blazed brighter. "You should mind what you tell people, even among Ophion allies. They have ways of making people disappear."

"Like Sofie Renast?"

Her fire simmered. "Don't repeat her true name to anyone. Refer to her as Agent Cypress."

Ruhn gritted his teeth. "Do you know anything about Sofie?"

"I assumed she was dead, since you're now my contact."

"And if she isn't?"

"I don't understand."

"If she isn't dead, where would she go? Where would she hide?"

Daybright whirled back toward her end of the bridge. "This meeting is over." And before Ruhn could say another word, she vanished, leaving only drifting embers behind.

"Why the Hel would the Asteri create their own mech-suit for this war?" Hunt asked, rubbing his jaw as he leaned against the kitchen counter the next morning.

He tried not to look at the black box on the other end of the counter. But its presence seemed to . . . hum. Seemed to hollow out the air around it.

Considering the two Death Marks inside, it was no wonder.

Cormac sipped from his tea, face clouded. He'd arrived barely past dawn, apparently after Ruhn had called him to demand that he rush over, thus dragging Hunt from slumber—and Bryce's arms—with his knocking. "The suits are the one advantage we have. Well, that the humans have."

"I know that," Hunt countered tightly. "I've fought them. I know them inside and out."

And he'd taken them apart. And sabotaged them so their pilots didn't stand a chance.

He'd been content to let that knowledge serve him lately for stuff like fixing Bryce's bike—which he'd gone so far as to wash for her before handing it back over—but if the Asteri were making a mech-suit of their own for a Vanir soldier to use . . .

"I always forget," Ruhn murmured from where he sat on the couch beside Bryce, "that you fought in two wars." The one he'd waged and lost with the Fallen, and then the years spent fighting at Sandriel's command against the Ophion rebels.

"I don't," Hunt said, earning an apologetic wince from Ruhn. "We need to be careful. You're sure this information was real?"

"Yeah," Ruhn said.

Holstrom settled himself against the wall beside the counter, silently watching the exchange. His face revealed nothing. A laptop sat open on the couch, though, still combing through the years of gallery footage for any hint of Danika.

But this conversation with Cormac, this hit on the Spine . . . "You likely have double agents in Ophion," Hunt said to the Avallen Prince.

"Not Daybright," Cormac said with absolute certainty.

"Anyone can be bought," Hunt said.

Bryce said nothing, busy pretending that she was more interested in her pink toenails than this conversation. Hunt knew she was picking over every word.

He'd emerged from the bedroom intending to tell every single person who crossed his path that she was his mate, but Ruhn had been waiting with this news instead, apparently having slept on the couch.

"Regardless," Cormac said tightly, "I need to pass this information along."

"I'll go with you," Ruhn said. Bryce's mouth popped open in alarm.

"You could be walking right into a trap," Hunt warned.

"We don't have any choice," Cormac countered. "We can't risk losing this opportunity."

"And what do you risk losing if it's fake?" Lightning crackled at Hunt's fingers. Bryce's eyes flicked up to him at last, wary and full of caution.

She said before Cormac could answer, "This isn't our business, Hunt."

"Like Hel it isn't. We're tied into it, whether we want to be or not."

Golden fire filled her gaze. "Yes, but we have nothing to do with this hit; this intel. It's Ophion's problem to deal with." She straightened, giving Ruhn a scathing look that seemed to say, *You should stay out of it, too*, but faced Cormac. "So go report to Command and keep us out of it."

Cormac stared her down, his jaw working.

She gave him a slash of a smile that set Hunt's blood thrumming. "Not used to females giving you orders?"

"There are plenty of females in Command." Cormac's nostrils flared. "And I would advise you to behave as a Fae female ought to when we are seen together in public. It shall be hard enough to convince others of our betrothal thanks to that smell on you."

"What smell?" Bryce said, and Hunt braced his feet. She could take care of herself in a fight, but he'd still enjoy pummeling the bastard.

Cormac motioned between her and Hunt. "You think I can't scent what went down between you two?"

Bryce leaned back against the cushions. "You mean, that *he* went down on me?"

Hunt choked, and Ruhn let out a garbled string of curses. Ithan walked to the coffee machine and muttered something about it being too early.

Cormac, however, didn't so much as blush. He said gravely, "Your mingling scents will jeopardize this ruse."

"I'll take that into consideration," Bryce said, and then winked at Hunt.

Gods, she'd tasted like a dream. And the sweet, breathy sounds she made when she came . . . Hunt rolled out the tautness in his shoulders. They had a long day ahead of them. A dangerous day.

They were going to the Bone Quarter today, for fuck's sake. The street camera footage had pinpointed that the Reaper who'd attacked Bryce and Ruhn had been within a block of the Black Dock, but even with Declan's skills, they hadn't found any concrete proof of the Reaper sailing over. It was enough of a link that they'd question the Under-King about it, though. And if they got through that, then Hunt planned to have a long, long night. He'd already made a reservation at a fancy-ass hotel restaurant. And reserved a large suite. With rose petals and champagne.

Cormac drummed his fingers on the table and said to Bryce, "If you find Emile in the Bone Quarter, let me know immediately." Bryce, to Hunt's surprise, didn't object. Cormac pivoted to Ruhn, jerking his chin to the door. "We need to get going. If that supply train is leaving in three days, we can't waste a moment." He looked sharply at Hunt. "Even if it's bad intel."

"I'm ready." Ruhn got to his feet. He frowned at his sister. "Good hunting. Stay out of trouble today, please."

"Right back at you." Bryce grinned, though Hunt noted that her attention was on the Starsword—as if she were speaking to it, pleading with it to protect her brother. Then her gaze slid to Cormac, who already stood at the door. "Be careful," she said pointedly to Ruhn.

The warning was clear enough: *Don't trust Cormac entirely.*

Ruhn nodded slowly. The male might have claimed he'd changed since trying to kill the prince decades ago, but Hunt didn't trust him, either.

Ruhn turned toward Ithan as the wolf aimed for the discarded laptop on the couch. "Look, I hate to drag anyone else into our shit, but . . . you want to come?"

Holstrom jerked his chin toward the laptop. "What about the footage?"

"It can wait a few hours—you can look through any flagged sections when we get back. We could use your skills today."

"What skills?" Bryce demanded. Pure, protective alarm. "Being good at sunball doesn't count."

"Thanks, Bryce," Ithan grumbled, and before Ruhn could supply a reason for inviting the wolf, he said, "Sabine will have a fit if I'm caught helping you."

That was the least of what would happen if he was caught

aiding rebels. Hunt tried not to shift his wings, tried to halt the echo of agony through them.

"You don't answer to Sabine anymore," Ruhn countered.

Ithan considered. "I guess I'm already in this mess." Hunt could have sworn guilt and worry filled Bryce's face. She chewed her bottom lip, but didn't challenge Ithan further.

"Okay," Ithan continued, plugging in the laptop. "Let me get dressed."

Bryce turned warily toward the black box on the counter. The looming, thrumming Death Marks within. But she said, "Right, Athalar. Time to be on our way. Suit up."

Hunt followed Bryce back into her bedroom—their bedroom now, he supposed—to see her pick up a holster and prop her leg on the bed. Her short pink skirt slid back, revealing that lean, long expanse of golden leg. His mind went blank as she strapped the holster around her upper thigh.

Her fingers snagged on the buckle, and Hunt was instantly there to help, savoring the silken warmth of her bare skin. "You're really wearing this to the Bone Quarter?" He drifted a hand to toy with the soft pleats of the skirt. No matter that her gun would be useless against any Reapers that came their way.

"It's a thousand degrees today and humid. I'm not wearing pants."

"What if we get into trouble?" He might have taken far longer on the buckle than necessary. He knew she was letting him.

She smiled wickedly. "Then I suppose the Under-King will get a nice view of my ass."

He gave her a flat look.

Bryce rolled her eyes, but said, "Give me five minutes to change."

29

I think he knows we're coming," Bryce whispered to Hunt as they stood on the edge of the Black Dock and peered through the mist swarming the Istros. Thankfully, there had been no Sailings today. But a path through the mists spread ahead—an opening through which they'd sail to get to the Bone Quarter.

She knew, because she'd sailed through it herself once.

"Good," Hunt said, and Bryce caught his glance at the Starsword she'd sheathed down her back. Ruhn had left it for her with the note: *Bring it. Don't be stupid.*

For once in her life, she'd listened.

And Ruhn had listened when she'd encouraged him, in their swift mind-to-mind conversation, not to trust Cormac. His invitation to Ithan had been the result.

She could only pray they'd stay safe. And that Cormac was true to his word.

Bryce shifted, tucking the thoughts away, the half-rotted black wood beneath her shoes creaking. She'd wound up changing into black leggings and a gray T-shirt before leaving. Yet even with the mist, the heat somehow continued, turning her clothes into a sticky second skin. She should have stayed in the skirt. If only because it had allowed her to conceal the gun—which she'd left behind after Hunt had mortifyingly reminded her of its uselessness against anything they'd encounter in the Bone Quarter.

"Well, here goes," Bryce said, fishing out the onyx coin from the pocket in the back of her waistband. The stifling, earthen smell of mold stuffed itself up her nostrils, as if the coin itself were rotting.

Hunt pulled his coin from a compartment in his battle-suit and sniffed, frowning. "It smells worse the closer we get to the Bone Quarter."

"Then good riddance." Bryce flipped the Death Mark with her thumb into the fog-veiled water below. Hunt's followed. Both only made one ripple before they went rushing toward the Bone Quarter, hidden from view.

"I'm sure a few people have told you this," a male voice said behind them, "but that is a very bad idea."

Bryce whirled, but Hunt bristled. "What the fuck do you want, Baxian?"

The Helhound emerged like a wraith from the mist, wearing his own battle-suit. Shadows had settled beneath his dark eyes, like he hadn't slept in a while. "Why are you here?"

"I'd like to know the same," Hunt bit out.

Baxian shrugged. "Enjoying the sights," he said, and Bryce knew it for the lie it was. Had he followed them? "I thought we were supposed to be paired up, Athalar. You never showed. Does Celestina know about this?"

"It's my day off," Hunt said. Which was true. "So no. It's none of her business. Or yours. Go report to Isaiah. He'll give you something to do."

Baxian's attention shifted to Bryce, and she held his stare. His gaze dipped to the scar on her chest, only the upper spikes of the star visible above the neckline of her T-shirt. "Who are you going to see over there?" His voice had gone low, dangerous.

"The Under-King," Bryce said cheerfully. She could feel Hunt's wariness growing with each breath.

Baxian blinked slowly, as if reading the threat emanating from Athalar. "I can't tell if that's a joke, but if it isn't, you're the dumbest people I've ever met."

Something stirred behind them, and then a long, black boat appeared from the slender path in the mists, drifting toward the dock. Bryce reached out a hand for the prow. Her fingers curled over the screaming skeleton carved into its arch. "Guess you'll have to wait to find out," she said, and leapt in.

She didn't look back as Hunt climbed in after her, the boat rocking with his weight. It pulled away from the Black Dock along that narrow path, leaving Baxian behind to watch until the mists swallowed him.

"You think he'll say anything?" Bryce whispered into the gloom as the path ahead vanished, too.

Hunt's voice was strained, gravelly as it floated toward her. "I don't see why he would. You were attacked by Reapers yesterday. We're going to talk to the Under-King about it today. There's nothing wrong or suspicious about that."

"Right." This shit with Ophion had her overthinking every movement.

Neither of them spoke after that. Neither of them dared.

The boat sailed on, across the too-silent river, all the way to the dark and distant shore.

Hunt had never seen such a place. Knew in his bones he never wanted to see it again.

The boat advanced with no sail, no rudder, no rower or ferryman. As if it were pulled by invisible beasts toward the isle across the Istros. The temperature dropped with each foot, until Hunt could hear Bryce's teeth clacking through the mist, so thick her face was nearly obscured.

The memory of Baxian nagged at him. Snooping asshole.

But he had a feeling that the Helhound wouldn't go blabbing. Not yet. Baxian was more likely to gather intel, to shadow their every move and then strike when he had enough to damn them.

Hunt would turn him into smoldering cinders before he could do that, though. What a fucking mess.

The boat jolted, colliding with something with a *thunk*.

Hunt stiffened, lightning at his fingertips. But Bryce rose, graceful as a leopard, the Starsword's dark hilt muted and matte in the dimness.

The boat had stopped at the base of worn, crumbling steps. The mists above them parted to reveal an archway of carved, ancient bone, brown with age in spots. *Memento Mori*, it said across the top.

Hunt interpreted its meaning differently here than in the Meat Market: *Remember that you will die, and end here. Remember who your true masters are.*

The hair on Hunt's arms rose beneath his battle-suit. Bryce leapt from the boat with Fae elegance, twisting to offer a hand back to him. He took it, only because he wanted to touch her, feel her warmth in this lifeless place.

But her hands were icy, her skin drab and waxy. Even her shimmering hair had dulled. His own skin appeared paler, sickly. As if the Bone Quarter already sucked the life from them.

He interlaced their fingers as they strode up the seven steps to the archway and tucked all the worries and fears regarding Baxian, regarding this rebellion, deep within him. They'd only be a distraction.

His boots scuffed on the steps. Here, Bryce had once knelt. Right here, she'd traded her resting place for Danika's. He squeezed her hand tighter. Bryce squeezed back, leaning into him as they stepped under the archway.

Dry ground lay beyond. Mist, and grayness, and silence. Marble and granite obelisks rose like thick spears, many inscribed—but not with names. Just with strange symbols. Grave markers, or something else? Hunt scanned the gloom, ears straining for any hint of Reapers, of the ruler they sought.

And for any hint of Emile, or Sofie. But not one footprint marked the ground. Not one scent lingered in the mist.

The thought of the kid hiding out here . . . of any living being dwelling here . . . Fuck.

Bryce whispered, voice thick, "It's supposed to be green. I saw a land of green and sunlight." Hunt lifted a brow, but her eyes—now a flat yellow—searched the mists. "The Under-King showed me the Pack of Devils after the attack on the city." Her words shook. "Showed me that they rested here among shining meadows. Not . . . this."

"Maybe the living aren't allowed to see the truth unless the Under-King allows it." She nodded, but he read the doubt tightening her ashen face. He said, "No sign of Emile, unfortunately."

Bryce shook her head. "Nothing. Though I don't know why I thought it'd be easy. It's not like he'd be camped out here in a tent or something."

Hunt, despite himself, offered her a half smile. "So we head to the boss, then." He kept scanning the mists and earth for any hint of Emile or his sister as they continued on.

Bryce halted suddenly between two black obelisks, each engraved with a different array of those odd symbols. The obelisks—and dozens more beyond them—flanked what seemed to be a central walkway stretching into the mist.

She drew the Starsword, and Hunt didn't have time to stop her before she whacked it against the side of the closest obelisk. It clanked, its ringing echoing into the gloom. She did it again. Then a third time.

"Ringing the dinner bell?" Hunt asked.

"Worth a shot," Bryce muttered back. And smarter than running around shouting Emile's and Sofie's names. Though if they were as survival-savvy as they seemed, Hunt doubted either would come running to investigate.

As the noise faded, what remained of the light dimmed. What remained of the warmth turned to ice.

Someone—something—had answered.

The other being they sought here.

Their breath hung in the air, and Hunt angled himself in front of Bryce, monitoring the road ahead.

When the Under-King spoke, however, in a voice simultaneously ancient and youthful but cold and dry, the sound came from behind them. "This land is closed to you, Bryce Quinlan."

A tremor went through Bryce, and Hunt rallied his power, lightning crackling in his ears. But his mate said, "I don't get a VIP pass?"

The voice from the mist echoed around them. "Why have you come? And brought Orion Athalar with you?"

"Call him Hunt," Bryce drawled. "He gets huffy if you go all formal on him."

Hunt gave her an incredulous look. But the Under-King materialized from the mist, inch by inch.

He stood at least ten feet tall, robes of richest black velvet draping to the gravel. Darkness swirled on the ground before him, and his head . . . Something primal in him screamed to run, to bow, to fall on his knees and beg.

A desiccated corpse, half-rotted and crowned with gold and jewels, observed them. Hideous beyond belief, yet regal. Like a long-dead king of old left to rot in some barrow, who had emerged to make himself master of this land.

Bryce lifted her chin and said, bold as Luna herself, "We need to talk."

"Talk?" The lipless mouth pulled back, revealing teeth brown with age.

Hunt reminded himself firmly that the Under-King was feared, yes—but not evil.

Bryce replied, "About your goons grabbing my sweet brother and dragging him into the sewer. They claimed they were sent by Apollion." Hunt tensed as she spoke the Prince of the Pit's name. Bryce continued, utterly nonchalant, "But I don't see how they could have been sent by anyone but *you*."

The Under-King hissed. "Do not speak that name on this side of the Rift."

Hunt followed Bryce's irreverence. "Is this the part where you insist you knew nothing?"

"You have the nerve to cross the river, to take a black boat to my shores, and accuse me of this treachery?" The darkness behind the Under-King shivered. In fear or delight, Hunt couldn't tell.

"Some of your Reapers survived me," Bryce said. "Surely they've filled you in by now."

Silence fell, like the world in the aftermath of a boom of thunder.

The Under-King's milky, lidless eyes slid to the Starsword in Bryce's hand. "Some did *not* survive you?"

Bryce's swallow was audible. Hunt swore silently.

Bryce said, "Why did you feel the need to attack? To pretend the Reapers were messengers of—the Prince of the Pit." She clicked her tongue. "I thought we were friends."

"Death has no friends," the Under-King said, eerily calm. "I did not send any Reapers to attack you. But I do not tolerate those who falsely accuse me in my realm."

"And we're supposed to take you at your word that you're innocent?" Bryce pushed.

"Do you call me a liar, Bryce Quinlan?"

Bryce said, cool and calm as a queen, "You mean to tell me that there are Reapers who can simply defect and serve Hel?"

"From whence do you think the Reapers first came? Who first ruled them, ruled the vampyrs? The Reapers chose Midgard. But I am not surprised some have changed their minds."

Bryce demanded, "And you don't care if Hel steps into your territory?"

"Who said they were my Reapers to begin with? There are none unaccounted for here. There are many other necropolises they might hail from." And other half-life rulers they answered to.

"Reapers don't travel far beyond their realms," Hunt managed to say.

"A comforting lie for mortals." The Under-King smiled faintly.

"All right," Hunt said, fingers tightening around Bryce's. The Under-King seemed to be telling them the truth. Which meant . . . Well, fuck. Maybe Apollion *was* the one who'd sent the Reapers. And if that part was true, then what he'd said about Emile . . .

Bryce seemed to be following the same train of thought, because she said, "I'm looking for two people who might be hiding out here. Any insight?"

"I know all the dead who reside here."

"They're alive," Bryce said. "Humans—or part-humans."

The Under-King surveyed them once more. Right down to their souls. "No one enters this land without my knowledge."

"People can slip in," Hunt countered.

"No," the creature said, smiling again. "They cannot. Whoever you seek, they are not here."

Hunt pushed, "Why should we believe you?"

"I swear upon Cthona's dark crown that no living beings other than yourselves are currently on this island."

Well, vows didn't get much more serious than that. Even the Under-King wouldn't fuck with invoking the earth goddess's name in a vow.

But that left them back at square one. If Emile and Sofie weren't here, and couldn't even enter . . . Danika had to have known that. She'd have been smart enough to look into the rules before sending them here for hiding.

This was a dead end. But it still left Apollion looking for the kid—and them needing to find him before anyone else.

So Hunt said, "You've been enlightening. Thanks for your time."

But Bryce didn't move. Her face had gone stony. "Where's the green and sunlight you showed me? Was that another comforting lie?"

"You saw what you wished to see."

Bryce's lips went white with rage. "Where's the Pack of Devils?"

"You are not entitled to speak to them."

"Is Lehabah here?"

"I do not know of one with such a name."

"A fire sprite. Died three months ago. Is she here?"

"Fire sprites do not come to the Bone Quarter. The Lowers are of no use."

Hunt arched a brow. "No use for what?"

The Under-King smiled again—perhaps a shade ruefully. "Comforting lies, remember?"

Bryce pressed, "Did Danika Fendyr say anything to you before she . . . vanished this spring?"

"You mean before she traded her soul to save yours, as you did with your own."

Nausea surged through Hunt. He hadn't let himself think much on it—that Bryce would not be allowed here. That he wouldn't rest with her one day.

One day that might come very soon, if they were caught associating with rebels.

"Yes," Bryce said tightly. "Before Danika helped to save this city. Where's the Pack of Devils?" she asked again, voice hitching.

Something large growled and shifted in the shadows behind the Under-King, but remained hidden by the mists. Hunt's lightning zapped at his fingers in warning.

"Life is a beautiful ring of growth and decay," the Under-King said, the words echoing through the Sleeping City around them. "No part left to waste. What we receive upon birth, we give back in death. What is granted to you mortals in the Eternal Lands is merely another step in the cycle. A waypoint along your journey toward the Void."

Hunt growled. "Let me guess: You hail from Hel, too?"

"I hail from a place between stars, a place that has no name and never shall. But I know of the Void that the Princes of Hel worship. It birthed me, too."

The star in the center of Bryce's chest flared.

The Under-King smiled, and his horrific face turned ravenous. "I beheld your light across the river, that day. Had I only known when you first came to me—things might have been quite different."

Hunt's lightning surged, but he reined it in. "What do you want with her?"

"What I want from all souls who pass here. What I give back to the Dead Gate, to all of Midgard: energy, life, power. You did not give your power to the Eleusian system; you made the Drop outside of it. Thus, you still possess some firstlight. Raw, nutritious firstlight."

"Nutritious?" Bryce said.

The Under-King waved a bony hand. "Can you blame me for sampling the goods as they pass through the Dead Gate?"

Hunt's mouth dried up. "You . . . you feed on the souls of the dead?"

"Only those who are worthy. Who have enough energy. There is no judgment but that: whether a soul possesses enough residual power to make a hearty meal, both for myself and for the Dead Gate. As their souls pass through the Dead Gate, I take a . . . bite or two."

Hunt cringed inwardly. Maybe he had been too hasty in deeming the being before him not evil.

The Under-King went on, "The rituals were all invented by you. Your ancestors. To endure the horror of the offering."

"But Danika was here. She *answered* me." Bryce's voice broke.

"She was here. She and all of the newly dead from the past several centuries. Just long enough that their living descendants and loved ones either forget or don't come asking. They dwell here until then in relative comfort—unless they make themselves a nuisance and I decide to send them into the Gate sooner. But when the dead are forgotten, their names no longer whispered on the wind . . . then they are herded through the Gate to become firstlight. Or secondlight, as it is called when the power comes from the dead. Ashes to ashes and all that."

"The Sleeping City is a lie?" Hunt asked. His mother's face flashed before him.

"A comforting one, as I have said." The Under-King's voice again became sorrowful. "One for your benefit."

"And the Asteri know about this?" Hunt demanded.

"I would never presume to claim what the holy ones know or don't know."

"Why are you telling us any of this?" Bryce blanched with horror.

"Because he's not letting us leave here alive," Hunt breathed. And their souls wouldn't live on, either.

The light vanished entirely, and the voice of the Under-King echoed around them. "That is the first intelligent thing you've said."

A rumbling growl shook the ground. Reverberated up Hunt's legs. He clutched Bryce to him, snapping out his wings for a blind flight upward.

The Under-King crooned, "I should like to taste your light, Bryce Quinlan."

30

Ruhn had grown up in Crescent City. He knew it had places to avoid, yet it had always felt like home. Like his.

Until today.

"Ephraim must have arrived," Ithan murmured as they waited in the dimness of a dusty alley for Cormac to finish making the information drop. "And brought the Hind with him."

"And she brought her entire pack of dreadwolves? To what end?" Ruhn toyed with the ring through his bottom lip. They'd seen two of the elite imperial interrogators on the way to the meet-up near the Old Square.

Ruhn had veiled himself and Holstrom in shadows while Cormac spoke at the other end of the alley with the cloaked, hooded figure disguised as a begging vagrant. Ruhn could make out the outline of a gun strapped to the figure's thigh beneath the threadbare cloak.

Ithan eyed him. "You think the Hind's onto us?"

Us. Fuck, just that word freaked him out when it came to consorting with rebels. Ruhn monitored the bright street beyond the alley, willing his shadows to keep them hidden from what prowled the sidewalks.

Tourists and city dwellers alike kept a healthy distance from the dreadwolves. The wolf shifters were exactly as Ruhn had expected:

cold-eyed and harsh-faced above their pristine gray uniforms. A black-and-white patch of a wolf's skull and crossbones adorned that uniform's left arm. The seven golden stars of the Asteri shone on a red patch above their hearts. And on their starched, high collars—silver darts.

The number varied on each member. One dart for every rebel spy hunted down and broken. The two that Ruhn had passed had borne eight and fifteen darts, respectively.

"It's like the city's gone quiet," Ithan observed, head cocked. "Isn't this the *least* safe place for this meet-up?"

"Don't be paranoid," Ruhn said, though he'd thought the same.

Down the alley, Cormac finished and strode back to them. Within a blink, the hunched figure was gone, swallowed into the crowds teeming on the main avenue, all too focused on the dreadwolves slinking among them to remark on a hobbling vagrant.

Cormac had veiled his face in shadows, and they pulled away now as he met Ruhn's stare. "The agent told me they think the Asteri suspect that Emile came here after he fled Ophion. It's possible the Hind brought the dreadwolves to hunt for him."

"The sight of those wolves in this city is a disgrace," Ithan snarled. "No one's going to stomach this shit."

"You'd be surprised what people will stomach when they find their families threatened," Cormac said. "I've seen cities and towns fall silent in the wake of a dreadwolf pack's arrival. Places as vibrant as this, now warrens of fear and mistrust. They, too, thought no one would tolerate it. That someone would do something. Only when it was too late did they realize that *they* should have done something."

A chill ran up Ruhn's arms. "I have to make some calls. The Aux and the 33rd run this city. Not the Hind." Shit, he'd have to see his father. He might be a bastard, but the Autumn King wouldn't appreciate having the Hind infringe on his turf.

Ithan's jaw twitched. "I wonder what Sabine and the Prime will do about them."

"No loyalty among wolves?" Cormac asked.

"*We* are wolves," Ithan challenged. "The dreadwolves . . . they're demons in wolves' fur. Wolves in name only."

"And if the dreadwolves request to stay at the Den?" Cormac asked. "Will the Prime or Sabine find their morals holding firm?"

Ithan didn't answer.

Cormac went on, "This is what the Asteri do. This is Midgard's true reality. We believe we are free, we are powerful, we are near-immortals. But when it comes down to it, we're all the Asteri's slaves. And the illusion can be shattered this quickly."

"Then why the fuck are you trying to bring this shit here?" Ithan demanded.

"Because it has to end at some point," Ruhn murmured. He shuddered inwardly.

Cormac opened his mouth, surprise lighting his face—but whirled as a male—towering and muscle-bound and clad in the impeccable uniform of the dreadwolves—appeared at the other end of the alley. So many silver darts covered his collar that from a distance, it looked like a mouth full of razor-sharp teeth around his neck.

"Mordoc," Ithan breathed. Genuine fear laced his scent. Cormac motioned for the wolf to be silent.

Mordoc . . . Ruhn scanned his memory. The second in command to the Hind. Her chief butcher and enforcer. The dreadwolf monitored the alley with golden, glowing eyes. Dark claws glinted at his fingertips. As if he lived in some state between human and wolf.

Cormac's nose crinkled. The prince trembled, anger and violence leaking from him. Ruhn gripped his cousin's shoulder, fingers digging into the hard muscle.

Slowly, Mordoc prowled down the alley. Noting the brick walls, the dusty ground—

Fuck. They'd left tracks all over this alley. None of them dared to breathe too loudly as they pressed into the wall.

Mordoc angled his head, scalp gleaming through his buzzed hair, then crouched, muscles flexing beneath his gray uniform, and ran a thick finger through a footprint. He lifted the dirt to his nose and sniffed. His teeth—slightly too long—gleamed in the dimness of the alley.

Mind-to-mind, Ruhn asked Cormac, *Does Mordoc know your scent?*

I don't think so. Does he know yours?

No. I've never met him.

Ruhn said to Ithan, who jolted slightly at the sound of Ruhn's voice in his mind, *Do you know Mordoc? Have you met him before?*

Ithan's gaze remained on the powerful male now rising to sniff the air. *Yes. A long time ago. He came to visit the Den.*

Why?

Ithan at last responded, eyes wide and pained. *Because he's Danika's father.*

Bryce had enough presence of mind to draw the Starsword. To rally her power even though the thing before them . . . Oh gods.

"Allow me to introduce my shepherd," the Under-King said from the mist ahead, standing beside a ten-foot-tall black dog. Each of its fangs was as long as one of her fingers. All hooked—like a shark's. Designed to latch into flesh and hold tight while it ripped and shredded. Its eyes were milky white—sightless. Identical to the Under-King's.

Her light would have no effect on something that was already blind.

The dog's fur—sleek and iridescent enough that it almost resembled scales—flowed over bulky, bunched muscle. Claws like razor blades sliced into the dry ground.

Hunt's lightning crackled, skittering at Bryce's feet. "That's a demon," he ground out. He'd fought enough of them to know.

"An experiment of the Prince of the Ravine's, from the First Wars," the Under-King rasped. "Forgotten and abandoned here in Midgard during the aftermath. Now my faithful companion and helper. You'd be surprised how many souls do not wish to make their final offering to the Gate. The Shepherd . . . Well, it herds them for me. As it shall herd you."

"Fry this fucker," Bryce muttered to Hunt as the dog snarled.

"I'm assessing."

"Assess faster. *Roast it like a—*"

"Do *not* make a joke about—"

"Hot dog."

Bryce had no sooner finished saying the words than the hound lunged. Hunt struck, swift and sure, a lightning bolt spearing toward its neck.

It screamed, dodging to the left, an obelisk crumbling beneath it. Bryce pivoted to where the Under-King had been, but only mist remained.

Coward.

Hunt struck again, forked lightning splitting the sky before it slammed into the creature's back, but it rolled once more, shaking off the lightning.

"The *fuck*," Hunt panted, drawing his sword and gun as he moved in front of Bryce. The Shepherd halted, eyeing them. Then the hound peeled apart.

First its head split, two other heads joining the first. And then the three-headed dog continued to separate until three hounds snarled at them. Three beasts that shared one mind, one goal: *Kill.*

"Run," Hunt ordered, not taking his focus from the three dogs. "Get back to the river and fucking *swim*."

"Not without you."

"I'll be right behind."

"Just fly us—"

The dog to the left snarled, bristling. Bryce faced it, and in that blink, the one on the right leapt. Hunt's lightning snapped free, and Bryce didn't hesitate before she turned and ran.

Mist swallowed her, swallowed Hunt until he was nothing but light rippling behind her. She sped past obelisks and stone mausoleums. Resting places for the dead, or mere cages to keep them until they could become food, valuable for their firstlight? *Secondlight.*

Thunderous steps crunched behind her. She dared a glance over her shoulder.

One of the hounds rampaged at her heels, closing the distance. Hunt's lightning flashed behind it, along with his bellow of rage. That was her *mate* she was leaving behind—

Bryce cut inland. The beast, apparently convinced she was making a run for the river, pivoted too slowly. It crashed into a mausoleum, sending both structure and hound sprawling. Bryce kept running. Sprinted as fast as she could back toward Hunt.

But the mist was a labyrinth, and Hunt's lightning seemed to launch from everywhere. Obelisks loomed like giants.

Bryce slammed into something hard and smooth, her teeth punching through her lower lip and the Starsword clattering out of her hand. The coppery tang of blood filled her mouth as she hit the ground. Flipping over, she peered up to find herself sprawled before a crystal archway.

The Dead Gate.

A snarl rumbled the earth. Bryce twisted, crawling backward to the Gate. The Shepherd emerged from the mist.

And in the grayish dirt between them lay the Starsword, glowing faintly.

Ruhn's blood iced over at Ithan's declaration. Did Bryce know Mordoc was Danika's father? She'd have mentioned it if she did, right?

It wasn't spoken of, Ithan explained. *Sabine and the others tried to forget. Danika refused to acknowledge Mordoc. Never said his name, or that she even had a father. But a few of us were at the Den the only time he came to see his daughter. She was seventeen and refused to even see him. Afterward, she wouldn't talk about it except to say that she was nothing like him. She never mentioned Mordoc again.*

The male approached, and Ruhn scanned for any hint of Danika Fendyr in him. He found none. *They don't resemble each other at all.*

Ithan said warily, sadly, *The similarities run beneath the surface.* Ruhn waited for the blow. Knew it was coming even before Ithan explained, *He's a bloodhound.*

Ruhn said to Cormac, *Teleport us the fuck out of here.* He should have done it the moment they saw Mordoc coming.

I can only take one at a time.

Mordoc drew closer. *Take Ithan and* go.

I won't be able to pinpoint you in the shadows when I return, Cormac answered. *Be ready to run to the avenue on my signal.* Then he grabbed Ithan and vanished.

Ruhn kept perfectly still as the wolf prowled near. Sniffing, head swaying from side to side.

"I can smell you, Faeling," Mordoc growled, voice like stones cracking against each other. "I can smell the coffee on your breath."

Ruhn kept his shadows tight around him, blending into the dimness along the alley's far wall. He made each step silent, though the dusty ground threatened to betray him.

"What were you doing here, I wonder," Mordoc said, halting to turn in place. Tracking Ruhn. "I saw your agent go in—the vagabond. He slipped my net, but why did you stay?"

Where the Hel was Cormac? Considering that Bryce and Hunt were currently in the Bone Quarter, Ruhn had expected *them* to be the ones in major peril today.

He kept moving, slowly and silently. The bright, open street lay beyond. The crowd might hide him, but not his scent. And his shadows would be of no use out in the sunny open.

"Hunting you all down like vermin shall be diverting," Mordoc said, pivoting in place as if he could see Ruhn through the shadows. "This city has been coddled for far too long."

Ruhn's temper unsheathed its talons, but he willed it down.

"Ah, that annoys you. I can smell it." A savage smile. "I shall remember that smell."

At the other end of the alley, Ruhn's magic picked up the flicker of Cormac arriving—only long enough to scuff his shoes in the dirt—and then vanish.

Mordoc whirled toward it, and Ruhn ran, dropping the shadows around himself.

Cormac appeared in a writhing nest of darkness, grabbed his arm, and teleported them out. Ruhn could only pray to Luna that by the time Mordoc had faced the street again, nothing remained of his scent for the bloodhound to detect.

31

Ruhn nursed his glass of whiskey, trying to calm his frayed nerves. Ithan, seated across from him at a quiet bar in FiRo, was watching the sports highlights on the TV above the liquor display. Cormac had dropped them both here before teleporting away, presumably to warn his rebel counterparts about what had happened with Mordoc.

Danika's father. Bryce would have a fit.

Had her sire's involvement with the dreadwolves been part of what spurred Danika to work with the rebels? She was rebellious and defiant enough to do such a thing.

And Mordoc knew Ruhn's scent now. Knew Ithan's scent had been there. Which was why Cormac had brought them here—so there would be video proof of them far from the Old Square at the time Mordoc would claim Ithan had been in the alley.

Ithan said nothing as the minutes wore on, his whiskey vanishing with them. No matter that it was barely eleven in the morning and only one other person sat at the bar—a hunched female who looked like she'd seen better years. Decades.

Neither of them dared utter a word about what had happened. So Ruhn said to Ithan, "I asked you to join me here so we could chat about something."

Ithan blinked. "Yeah?"

Ruhn said to him, mind-to-mind, *Play along. I have no idea if the cameras have audio, but in case they do, I want our meeting here to seem planned.*

Ithan's face remained casual, intrigued. *Got it.*

Ruhn made sure his voice was loud enough to be picked up as he said, "How do you feel about moving in with me and the guys?"

Ithan angled his head. "What? Like—live with you?" His surprise seemed genuine.

Ruhn shrugged. "Why not?"

"You're Fae."

"Yeah, but we hate the angels more than we hate wolves, so . . . you're only our second-worst enemy."

Ithan chuckled, some color returning to his face. "A winning argument."

"I mean it," Ruhn said. "You honestly want to stay at Bryce's apartment and endure her and Hunt hooking up nonstop?"

Ithan snorted. "Hel no. But . . . why?" *Beyond an excuse for the cameras,* Ithan said silently.

Ruhn leaned back in his chair. "You seem like a decent male. You're helping Dec with the footage stuff. And you need a place to stay. Why not?"

Ithan seemed to weigh his response. "I'll think about it."

"Take all the time you need. The offer stands."

Ithan straightened, his attention darting behind Ruhn. He went wholly still. Ruhn didn't dare look. Not as light footsteps sounded, followed by a second thudding pair. Before he could ask Ithan mind-to-mind what he saw, Ruhn found himself faced with the most beautiful female he'd ever seen.

"Mind if I join?" Her voice was lovely, fair and cool—yet no light shone in her amber eyes.

A step behind her, a dark-haired, pale-faced female malakh grinned with wicked amusement. She was narrow-featured, black-winged, with a wildness like the western wind. "Hello, princeling. Pup."

Ruhn's blood chilled as the Harpy slid into the seat to his left.

An assortment of knives glinted on the belt at her slim waist. But Ruhn peered up again at the beautiful female, whose face he knew well thanks to the news and TV, though he'd never seen it in person. Her golden hair glinted in the dim lights as she sat on his right and signaled the bartender with an elegant hand.

"I thought we'd play a round of cards," the Hind said.

Two against one. Those odds were usually laughable for Hunt.

But not when his opponents were demons from Hel. One of the princes' cast-off experiments, now acting as the Under-King's enforcers, feeding long-dead souls into the Gate for secondlight energy. Like all they were, would ever be, was food to fuel the empire.

The demon to his left lunged, teeth snapping.

Hunt blasted his lightning, forks of it wrapping around the beast's thick neck. It bucked, bellowing, and the one to his right charged. Hunt lashed at it, another collar of lightning going around its neck, a leash of white light clenched in his fist.

Had Bryce made it to the river? The third demon had raced after her before he could stop it, but she was fast, and she was smart—

The demons before him halted. They shuddered and melted back into each other, becoming one beast again.

His lightning remained around its neck. But he could do nothing as it flexed—and shattered the lightning sizzling into its flesh. Something of that size and speed would use the two seconds of slowness it took him to get airborne and swallow him whole.

This wasn't how he'd expected the morning to go.

He rallied his power, focusing. He'd killed Sandriel with this lightning. A demon should be nothing. But before he could act, a scream rent the mists to the southeast. The beast twisted toward the sound, sniffing.

And before Hunt could stop it, faster than his lightning's whip, it raced off into the mist. After Bryce.

* * *

Bryce crouched beside the Dead Gate, sizing up the threats sur-rounding her. Not just the hound, but the two dozen Reapers who'd floated from the mists, encircling her.

The half-lifes' rotting flesh reeked; their acid-green eyes glowed through the mists. Their rasping whispers slithered like snakes over her skin. The Shepherd advanced, cutting her off further.

The crystal of the Dead Gate began to glow white. Not from her touch, but as if—

The Reapers were chanting. Awakening the Dead Gate, somehow.

During the attack on the city, it had channeled her magic against the demons, but today . . . today it would siphon off her power. Her soul. The Gates sucked magic from whoever touched them, and stored it. She'd inherited her power from that very force.

But this one fed that power right back into the power grid. Like some fucked-up rechargeable battery. Somehow, she'd become food. Was that what she'd traded away? A few centuries here, thinking she'd found eternal rest—and then meeting this end? Instead, she'd face a trip straight into the meat grinder of souls immediately when she died.

Which seemed likely to be soon.

There was a good chance that she could draw from the Gate as well, she supposed. But what if the Dead Gate was somehow differ-ent? What if she went to summon power, only to lose all of hers? She couldn't risk it.

Bryce got to her feet, hands shaking. The Starsword lay between her and the Shepherd.

Hunt's lightning had stopped. Where was he? Would a mate know, would a mate feel—

Another dog stepped from the mist. Then peeled apart into two—the ones Hunt had been fighting. No blood stained their muz-zles, but Hunt wasn't with them. Not a sliver of his lightning graced the mists.

The three dogs advanced, sniffing for her location. The Reapers kept chanting as the Dead Gate glowed brighter. That teleporting of Cormac's would have been helpful—she could have grabbed Hunt five minutes ago and vanished.

She glanced at the sword. It was now or never. Live or die. Like, *really* die.

Bryce sucked in a breath, and didn't give herself a chance to second-guess her stupidity. She bolted for the hounds. They charged, leaping for her with three sets of snapping jaws—

Bryce dropped, the rocky ground shredding her face as she slid beneath them, until the Starsword was cradled to her body. Something burning shot down her back.

The world boomed with the impact of the three hounds landing and pivoting. Bryce tried to get up, to hold the sword out, but blood warmed her back. A claw must have raked up her spine while one of the hounds had leapt over her, and the splintering, blistering pain—

Hunt was out there somewhere. Possibly dying.

Bryce dug the tip of the Starsword into the earth, using it to shove herself up to her knees. Her back screamed in agony. She might have screamed with it. The three hounds, the Reapers beyond them, seemed to smile.

"Yeah," Bryce panted, heaving to her feet. "Fuck you, too."

Her legs wobbled, yet she managed to lift the black sword in front of her. The three beasts roared, threatening to split her ears. Bryce opened her mouth to roar back.

But someone else did it for her.

For Hunt, there was only Bryce, bleeding and hurt.

Bryce, who'd made that brash run for the sword, probably thinking it was her only shot. Bryce, who'd gotten to her feet anyway, and planned to go down swinging.

Bryce, his mate.

The three hounds merged back into one. Readying for the killing blow.

Hunt landed in the dirt beside her and let out a bellow that shook the Gate itself.

* * *

Wreathed in lightning from wing tip to toe, Hunt landed beside Bryce so hard the earth shuddered. The power rolling off him sent Bryce's hair floating upward. Primal rage poured from Hunt as he faced down the Shepherd. The Reapers.

She'd never seen anything of the sort—Hunt was the heart of a storm personified. The lightning around him turned blue, like the hottest part of a flame.

An image blasted through her mind. She *had* seen this before, carved in stone in the lobby of the CCB. A Fae male posed like an avenging god, hammer raised to the sky, a channel for his power—

Hunt unleashed his lightning at the Shepherd, the Reapers observing with wide eyes.

Bryce was too fast, even for him, as she leapt in front of the blow, Starsword extended. A wild theory, only half-formed, but—

Hunt's lightning hit the Starsword, and the world erupted.

32

Hunt screamed as Bryce leapt in front of his power. As his lightning hit the black blade, exploding from the metal, flowing up into her arm, her body, her heart. Light flashed, blinding—

No, that was Bryce.

Power crackled from every inch of her, and from the Starsword she clenched in one hand as she barreled toward the Shepherd. It split into three hounds again, and as the first beast landed, Bryce struck. The glowing Starsword pierced the thick hide. Lightning exploded across the beast's body. The other two screamed, and Reapers began scattering into the mist beyond the obelisks.

Bryce whirled as Hunt reached her and said, eyes white with light, "Watch out!"

Too late. The beast who'd fallen snapped its tail at Hunt, catching him in the gut and hurling him into the Dead Gate. He hit the stone and crumpled, his power fizzing out.

Bryce shouted his name as she held her ground against the remaining two beasts. The one she'd injured died, twitching on the ground. Hunt gasped for breath, trying to rise.

She lifted the sword, crackling with remnants of power. Not much. Like the first blow had exhausted most of it. Hunt braced a hand on the Dead Gate's brass plaque as he tried to raise himself once more.

Power sucked from his fingers, pulled into the stone. He snatched his hand back. One of the beasts lunged for Bryce, but bounced away at a swipe of her sword. She needed more power—

Hunt peered at the Dead Gate's archway above him. Firstlight flowed both ways. Into the Dead Gate and out of it.

And here, where the last power of the dead was fed into it . . . here was a well, like the one Bryce had used during the attack last spring.

Sofie and Emile Renast could channel energy, too—and lightning. Hunt was no thunderbird, but could he do the same?

Lightning flowed in his veins. His body was equipped to handle raw, sizzling energy. Was this what Apollion had hinted at—why the prince wanted not only him and Bryce, but Emile and Sofie? Had the Prince of the Pit engineered this situation, manipulating them into coming to the Bone Quarter so that Hunt would be forced to realize what he could do with his own power? Perhaps Emile hadn't even come here at all. Perhaps the Reapers had lied about that at Apollion's behest, just to get them here, to this place, this moment—

Bryce angled her sword higher, ready to fight until the end. Hunt gazed at her for a moment, an avenging angel in her own right—and then slammed his hand onto the brass plaque of the Dead Gate.

Bryce dared only a glance behind her as Hunt bellowed again. He was standing, but his hand . . .

White, blinding firstlight—or was it secondlight?—flowed from the Dead Gate up his arm. Up his shoulder. And on the other side of the archway, the stone began to go dark. As if he were draining it.

The two hounds of the Shepherd merged back together, anticipating the next strike. Hunt's voice was a thunderclap as he said behind her, "Light it up, Bryce."

The words bloomed in Bryce's heart at the same moment Hunt shot a bolt of his power—the Dead Gate's power—into her. It burned and roared and blinded, a writhing ball of energy that Bryce broke to her will and funneled into the Starsword.

Forks of lightning cracked from Hunt, from her, from the sword.

The Shepherd turned tail and fled.

Bryce ran after it.

Wings flapped behind her, and then she was in Hunt's arms. He carried her high above the beast's back, then plunged down, lightning streaming around them, a meteorite crashing—

They slammed into the creature, and Bryce drove the sword into the Shepherd's nape. Into the skull beneath. Lightning and first-light blasted through it, and the hound exploded into smoking smithereens.

Bryce and Hunt hit the ground panting and steaming, soaked with the Shepherd's blood. But Hunt was up again in a moment, running, a hand on Bryce's back as he hauled her with him. "The river," he panted, lightning skittering across his teeth, his cheeks. His wings drooped like he was wholly exhausted. Like flying was beyond him.

Bryce didn't waste breath to answer as they raced through the mist toward the Istros.

"Two more Vanir bodies this morning, Your Excellency," Tharion said by way of greeting, bowing at the waist as he stood in his queen's private study.

It was more biodome than study, really, full of plants and a deep, winding stream, studded with large pools. The River Queen swam among the lily pads, her black hair trailing like ink in the water behind her. Her day of meetings might require her to be inside the building, but she took all of them here, sitting in her element.

She turned toward Tharion, hair plastered down her ample, heavy breasts, her brown skin gleaming with water. "Tell me where." Her voice was lovely, but subdued. Cold.

"One left hanging upside down in an olive grove north of the city—drained and shot the same way as the selkie—the other crucified on the tree next to him. Also shot, with a slit throat. They'd clearly been tortured. Two human scents were present. Seems like this happened yesterday."

He'd gotten the report this morning over breakfast. Hadn't bothered to go to the sites or ask Holstrom to come with him, not when the Aux had been the ones to get the call, and would be the ones to handle the bodies.

"And you still believe the rebel Pippa Spetsos is behind these killings."

"The style is in line with what her Lightfall squad does to its victims. I think she's on Emile Renast's trail, and is torturing anyone who helped him on his way."

"Is the boy here, then?"

"Considering the proximity of the latest site, I have good reason to believe he has arrived." An otter looped and twirled past the windows, a message clenched in his fangs, neon-yellow vest glaringly bright in the cobalt blue.

"And Sofie Renast?" The River Queen toyed with a pink-and-gold lily that brushed against her soft stomach, running her elegant fingers over its petals. "Any sightings of her?"

"Not a ripple." No need to mention Bryce and Athalar going to the Bone Quarter for answers. There was nothing to tell yet. He could only hope the two of them would emerge alive.

"The Hind is here, in Lunathion. Do you believe she's also tracking Emile?"

"She's only arrived today." He'd gotten reports already that her wolves prowled the city, along with the Harpy. At least the Hawk, his spies said, had remained behind in Pangera, left to guard Ephraim's roost, apparently. "Her whereabouts have been public for the last few days—she doesn't have a human scent, and also wasn't in the city to commit these murders. All signs point to Pippa Spetsos."

The river-spirit plucked the lily and tucked it behind her ear. It glowed as if lit by a kernel of firstlight. "Find that boy, Tharion."

He bowed his head. "What about Ophion Command? If they find out we have Emile . . ."

"Make sure they don't find out." Her eyes darkened, and storms threatened. Lightning lashed the surface high above. "We are loyal to the House of Many Waters first and foremost."

"Why the boy?" he finally dared ask. "Why do you want him so badly?"

"You question me?" Only the Ocean Queen, Lady of Waters, Daughter of Ogenas, had that right. Or the Asteri. Tharion bowed.

Lightning illuminated the surface again, and Tharion's brows lowered. That wasn't his queen's power. And since the forecast hadn't called for storms . . .

Tharion bowed again. "I apologize for the impertinence. Your will is mine," he said, the familiar words falling from his lips. "I'll update you when I've apprehended the boy."

He made to leave, risking doing so without dismissal, and had nearly made it to the archway before the River Queen said, "Did you enjoy your punishment last night?"

He closed his eyes for a moment before he turned to face her.

She'd lowered herself into the stream again, no more than a dark, beautiful head among the lily pads. Like one of her sobeks, waiting to make a meal of the unworthy dead.

Tharion said, "It was a wise and fitting punishment for my ignorance and transgression."

Her lips curled upward, revealing slightly pointed white teeth. "It is diverting to see you tug at the leash, Tharion."

He swallowed his retort, his rage, his grief, and inclined his head.

More lightning. He had to go. Knew better than to reveal his impatience, though. "I have only your daughter's best interests in my heart."

Again, that ancient, cruel smile that informed him she'd seen too many males—some far smarter than he—come and go. "I suppose we shall see." With that, she dipped beneath the water, vanishing under the lily pads and among the reeds.

Hunt could barely stand.

The firstlight had flayed him, leaving a smoking ruin inside his body, his mind. But it had worked. He'd taken the power and converted it into his own. Whatever the fuck that meant. Apollion had known—or guessed enough to be right. And Bryce . . . the sword . . .

She'd been a conduit to his power. Fucking Hel.

They staggered through the mists, the obelisks. Screeching and hissing rose around them. Reapers. Would anyplace in Midgard be safe now, even after death? He sure as fuck didn't want his soul in the Bone Quarter.

The bone gates appeared overhead, carved from the ribs of some ancient leviathan, and beyond them, the steps to the river. Hunt's knees nearly buckled as he spied a familiar wave skimmer and the mer male atop it, beckoning frantically as he pivoted the wave skimmer toward Lunathion proper.

"I thought that was you, with all the lightning," Tharion panted as they rushed toward him and leapt down the steps. He slipped off the wave skimmer to make room for them, shifting as he went. The mer looked like Hel: haunted and tired and bleak.

Bryce climbed on first, and Hunt joined her, clasping her from behind. She gunned the engine and sped off into the mist, Tharion shooting under the surface beside them. Hunt nearly collapsed against her back, but Bryce veered to the left, so sharply he had to clutch her hips to keep from falling into the water. "Fuck!" she shouted as scaly, muscled backs broke the surface.

Sobeks.

Only the nutritious souls went to the Under-King. The ones given over to the beasts were snacks. Junk food. A broad snout full of thick, daggerlike fangs shot from the water.

Blood sprayed before the creature could rip into Hunt's leg. Bryce zigged to the right, and Hunt twisted to see Tharion on their tail, a deadly plume of water aimed above him. Pressurized, like a water cannon. So intense and brutal that it had carved a hole right through a sobek's head.

Another beast lunged for them, and again, Tharion struck, water breaking flesh as surely as it could eat away at stone.

A third, and Tharion attacked with brutal efficiency. The other beasts halted, tails lashing the water.

"Hang on!" Bryce shouted toward Tharion, who gripped the side of the wave skimmer as she hurtled them toward the Black Dock. The mist fell away behind them, and a wall of sunshine blinded Hunt.

They didn't stop, though. Not when they hit the dock. Not when Tharion leapt from the water and shifted, grabbing a spare Blue Court aquatic uniform from the seat-hatch in the wave skimmer. The three of them hurried down the streets to Bryce's apartment.

In the safety of her home, Bryce knelt on the floor, wet and bloody and panting. The slice along her spine was long but mercifully shallow, already clotting. It had missed the Horn tattoo by millimeters. Hunt had enough sanity remaining to avoid the white couch as Tharion said, "What happened? Any sign of Emile or Sofie?"

"No—we were stupid to even look for them in the Bone Quarter," Hunt said, sitting at the dining table, trying to reel his mind back in. Bryce filled the mer in on the rest.

When she finished, Tharion dropped onto one of the counter stools, face white. "I know I should be disappointed that Emile and Sofie weren't hiding in the Bone Quarter, but . . . that's what awaits us in the end?"

Hunt opened his mouth, but Bryce asked, "Where's Ruhn? He and Ithan should be back."

Hunt narrowed his eyes. "Call them."

Bryce did, but neither answered. Hunt fished out his phone, grateful he'd gotten the water-repellent spell Quinlan had needled him into purchasing. News alerts and messages filled the screen.

Hunt said a shade hoarsely, "Ephraim just got here. With the Hind."

Tharion nodded grimly. "She brought her pack of dreadwolves with her."

Bryce checked the clock on her phone again. "I need to find Ruhn."

33

Ruhn said nothing as the Hind produced a deck of cards from the pocket of her imperial uniform.

Ithan played the role of confused jock, alternating ignorance with bored distraction as he watched the game above the bar. The Hind shuffled the deck, cards cracking like breaking bones.

On the table's fourth side, the Harpy lounged in her seat and marked his every move. Her wings—a matte black, like they'd been built for stealth—spilled onto the floor. She wore the familiar battle-suit of the 45th—Sandriel's former prized legion. The Harpy, along with the Hammer, had been one of its notoriously cruel leaders.

"I don't believe we've met," the Hind said, flexing and breaking the cards again. Her hands were deft, unfaltering. Unscarred. She wore a gold ring crowned with a square, clean-cut ruby. A subtle hint of wealth.

Ruhn forced himself to smirk. "I'm flattered I was so high on your priority list today."

"You're my half sister's fiancé, are you not?" A lifeless smile. The opposite of Hypaxia's warmth and wisdom. The Hind was only about twenty years older than her sister—forty-seven years old—far closer in age than most Vanir siblings. But they shared nothing in common, it seemed. "It would be rude not to introduce myself upon arrival. I already visited your father's villa. He informed me that you were here."

Cormac must have arrived right before the Hind, to feed the lie to the Autumn King. Thank the gods.

Ruhn snorted. "Nice to meet you. I'm busy."

The Harpy's skin was as pale as the belly of a fish, set off by her jet-black hair and eyes. She said, "You're as impertinent as you appear, princeling."

Ruhn flicked his lip ring with his tongue. "I'd hate to disappoint."

The Harpy's features contorted in anger. But the Hind said mildly, "We'll play poker, I think. Isn't that what you play on Tuesday nights?"

Ruhn repressed his shiver of fear. The standing game wasn't a secret, but . . . how much did she know about him?

Ithan remained the portrait of boredom, gods bless him.

So Ruhn said to the Hind, "All right, you're keeping tabs on me for your sister's sake." Was it mere coincidence she'd sought him out now? What had Mordoc told her about Ithan's whereabouts this morning? Ruhn asked the Harpy, "But why the Hel are *you* here?"

The Harpy's thin lips stretched into a grotesque smile. She reached a pale hand toward Ithan's muscled shoulder as she said, "I wanted to survey the goods."

Without looking at her, the wolf snatched her fingers, squeezing hard enough to show that he could break bone if he wished. Slowly, he turned, eyes brimming with hate. "You can look, but don't touch."

"You break it, you buy it," the Harpy crooned, wriggling her fingers. She liked this—the edge of pain.

Ithan bared his teeth in a feral grin and released her hand. The pup had balls, Ruhn would give him that. Ithan looked at the TV again as he said, "Pass."

The Harpy bristled, and Ruhn said, "He's a little young for you."

"And what about you?" A killer's sharp smile.

Ruhn leaned back in his chair, swigging from his whiskey. "I'm engaged. I don't fuck around."

The Hind dealt the cards with a swift, sure grace. "Except with fauns, of course."

Ruhn kept his face unmoved. How did she know about the female at the party? He met her golden eyes. A perfect match for the Hammer in beauty and temperament. She hadn't been at the Summit this spring, thank the gods. The Harpy had been there, though, and Ruhn had done his damn best to stay away from her.

The Hind scooped up her cards without breaking his stare. "I wonder if my sister shall learn of that."

"Is this some sort of shakedown?" Ruhn fanned out his cards. A decent hand—not great, but he'd won with worse.

The Hind's attention bobbed to her cards, then back to his face. This female had most likely killed Sofie Renast. A silver torque glinted at the base of her throat. Like she'd killed and broken so many rebels that the collar of her uniform couldn't fit all the darts. Did the necklace grow with each new death she wrought? Would his own be marked on that collar?

The Hind said, "Your father suggested I meet you. I agreed." Ruhn suspected that his father hadn't just told her his location to provide an alibi, but also to warn him to keep the fuck out of trouble.

Ithan picked up his cards, scanned them, and swore. The Harpy said nothing as she examined her own hand.

The Hind held Ruhn's gaze as the game began. She was the spitting image of Luna, with her upswept chignon, the regal angle of her neck and jaw. As coldly serene as the moon. All she needed was a pack of hunting hounds at her side—

And she had them, in her dreadwolves.

How had someone so young risen in the ranks so swiftly, gained such notoriety and power? No wonder she left a trail of blood behind her.

"Careful now," the Harpy said with that oily smile. "The Hammer doesn't share."

The Hind's lips curved upward. "No, he doesn't."

"As Ithan said," Ruhn drawled, "pass."

The Harpy glowered, but the Hind's smile remained in place. "Where is your famed sword, Prince?"

With Bryce. In the Bone Quarter. "Left it at home this morning," Ruhn answered.

"I heard you spent the night at your sister's apartment."

Ruhn shrugged. Was this interrogation merely to fuck with him? Or did the Hind know something? "I didn't realize you had the authority to grill Aux leaders in this city."

"The authority of the Asteri extends over all. Including Starborn Princes."

Ruhn caught the bartender's eye, signaling for another whiskey. "So this is just to prove you've got bigger balls?" He draped an arm over the back of his chair, cards in one hand. "You want to head up the Aux while you're in town, fine. I could use a vacation."

The Harpy's teeth flashed. "Someone should rip that tongue from your mouth. The Asteri would flay you for such disrespect."

Ithan drew another card and said mildly, "You've got some nerve, coming to our city and trying to start shit."

The Hind replied with equal calm, "So do you, lusting after the female your brother loved."

Ruhn blinked.

Ithan's eyes turned dangerously dark. "You're full of shit."

"Am I?" the Hind said, drawing a card herself. "Of course, as my visit here will likely entail meeting the princess, I looked into her history. Found quite a chain of messages between you two."

Ruhn thanked the bartender as the male brought over a whiskey and then quickly retreated. Ruhn said into Ithan's mind, *She's trying to rile you. Ignore her.*

Ithan didn't answer. He only said to the Hind, voice sharpening, "Bryce is my friend."

The Hind drew another card. "Years of pining in secret, years of guilt and shame for feeling what he does, for hating his brother whenever he talks about Miss Quinlan, for wishing that *he* had been the one who'd met her first—"

"Shut up," Ithan growled, rattling the glasses on the table, pure feral wolf.

The Hind went on, unfazed, "Loving her, lusting for her from the sidelines. Waiting for the day when she would realize that *he* was the one she was meant to be with. Playing his little heart out on the sunball field, hoping she'd notice him at last. But then big brother dies."

Ithan paled.

The Hind's expression filled with cool contempt. "And he hates himself even more. Not only for losing his brother, for not being there, but because of the one, traitorous thought he had after learning the news. That the path to Bryce Quinlan was now cleared. Did I get that part right?"

"*Shut your fucking mouth,*" Ithan growled, and the Harpy laughed.

Calm down, Ruhn warned the male.

But the Hind said, "Call."

Mind reeling, Ruhn laid out the decent hand he'd gotten. The Harpy put hers down. Good. He'd beaten her. The Hind gracefully spread hers across the table.

A winning hand. Beating Ruhn by a fraction.

Ithan didn't bother to show his cards. He'd already shown them, Ruhn realized.

The Hind smiled again at Ithan. "You Valbarans are too easy to break."

"Fuck you."

The Hind rose, gathering her cards. "Well, this has been delightfully dull."

The Harpy stood with her. Black talons glinted at the angel's fingertips. "Let's hope they fuck better than they play poker."

Ruhn crooned, "I'm sure there are Reapers who'll stoop to fuck you."

The Hind snickered, earning a glare from the Harpy that the deer shifter ignored. The Harpy hissed at Ruhn, "I do not take being insulted lightly, princeling."

"Get the Hel out of my bar," Ruhn snarled softly.

She opened her mouth, but the Hind said, "We'll see you soon, I'm sure." The Harpy understood that as a command to leave and stormed out the door onto the sunny street. Where life, somehow, continued onward.

The Hind paused on the threshold before she left, though. Peered over her shoulder at Ruhn, her silver necklace glinting in the sunlight trickling in. Her eyes lit with unholy fire.

"Tell Prince Cormac I send my love," the Hind said.

Bryce was one breath away from calling the Autumn King when the door to the apartment opened. And apparently, she looked a Hel of a lot worse than her brother or Ithan, because they immediately demanded to know what had happened to her.

Hunt, nursing a beer at the kitchen counter, said, "Emile and Sofie aren't in the Bone Quarter. But we found out some major shit. You'd better sit down."

Yet Bryce went up to her brother, scanning him from the piercings along his ear to his tattooed arms and ass-kicking boots. Not one sleek black hair out of place, though his skin was ashen. Ithan, standing at his side, didn't give her the chance to turn to him before approaching the fridge and grabbing a beer of his own.

"You're all right?" Bryce asked Ruhn, who was frowning at the dirt and blood on her—the wound on her back had thankfully closed, but was still tender.

Tharion said from where he sat on the couch, feet propped on the coffee table, "Everyone is fine, Legs. Now let's sit down like a good little rebel family and tell each other what the Hel happened."

Bryce swallowed. "All right. Yeah—sure." She scanned Ruhn again, and his eyes softened. "You scared the shit out of me."

"We couldn't answer our phones."

She didn't let herself reconsider before throwing her arms around her brother and squeezing tight. A heartbeat later, he gently hugged her back, and she could have sworn he shuddered in relief.

Hunt's phone buzzed, and Bryce pulled away from Ruhn. "Celestina wants me at the Comitium for Ephraim's arrival," Hunt said. "She wants her triarii assembled."

"Oh, Ephraim's already here." Ithan dropped onto the couch. "We learned the hard way."

"You saw him?" Bryce asked.

"His cronies," Ithan said, not looking at her. "Played poker with them and everything."

Bryce whirled on Ruhn. Her brother nodded gravely. "The Hind and the Harpy showed up to the bar where we were lying low. I can't tell if it was because Mordoc sniffed around the alley where Cormac made the intel drop or what. But it was . . . not great."

"Do they know?" Hunt asked quietly, storms in his eyes. "About you? About us?"

"No idea," Ruhn said, toying with his lip ring. "I think we'd be dead if they did, though."

Hunt blew out a sigh. "Yeah, you would be. They would have taken you in for questioning already."

"The Hind is a fucking monster," Ithan said, turning on the TV. "Her and the Harpy, both."

"I could have told you that," Hunt said, finishing his beer and striding to where Bryce stood before the glass dining table. She didn't stop him as he slid a hand over her jaw, cupping her cheek, and kissed her. Just a swift brush of their mouths, but it was a claiming and a promise.

"Rain check?" he murmured onto her lips. Right. The dinner and the hotel—

She frowned pitifully. "Rain check."

He chuckled, but grew deadly serious. "Be careful. I'll be back as soon as I can. Don't go looking for that kid without me." He kissed her forehead before leaving the apartment.

Bryce offered up silent prayers to Cthona and Urd to protect him.

"Glad you two finally sorted it out," Tharion said from the couch.

Bryce flipped him off. But Ruhn sniffed her carefully. "You . . . smell different."

"She smells like the Istros," Ithan said from the couch.

"No, it's . . ." Ruhn's brows twitched toward each other, and he scratched at the buzzed side of his head. "I can't explain it."

"Stop sniffing me, Ruhn." Bryce hopped onto the couch on Tharion's other side. "It's gross. Story time?"

34

"How do I look?" Celestina whispered to Hunt as they stood in front of the desk in her private study. Isaiah flanked her other side, Naomi to his left, Baxian to Hunt's right. Baxian had barely done more than nod to Hunt when he'd entered.

Hunt had taken the flight over here to soothe his nerves, his residual rage and awe at what he and Bryce had done. What they'd learned. By the time he'd alighted on the landing veranda, his face had become impassive once more. The mask of the Umbra Mortis.

It cracked a little, however, upon seeing Pollux a step away from Naomi. Grinning with feral, anticipatory delight.

This was a reunion from Hel. The Hind and the Hammer, back together once more. Never mind the Harpy and the Helhound— things had always revolved around Pollux and Lidia, their twin shriveled souls, and no one else. Thank the gods the Hawk had stayed behind in Pangera.

Hunt murmured to Celestina, "You look like a female about to enter an arranged mating." He was amazed his words had come out so casually, considering how his morning had gone.

The Archangel, clad in dawn-soft pink, gold at her wrists and ears, threw him a sad, *What can you do?* kind of smile.

Hunt, despite himself, added, "But you do look beautiful."

Her smile gentled, light brown eyes with them. "Thank you. And thank you for coming in on your day off." She squeezed his hand, her fingers surprisingly clammy. She was truly nervous.

Down the hall, the elevator doors pinged. Celestina's fingers tightened on Hunt's before letting go. He could have sworn hers were shaking.

So Hunt said, "It's no problem at all. I'll be right here all night. You need to bail, just give me a signal—tug on your earring, maybe—and I'll make up some excuse."

Celestina smiled up at him, squaring her shoulders. "You're a good male, Hunt."

He wasn't so sure of that. Wasn't so sure he hadn't offered only to make her like him so that when shit hit the fan, if Baxian or the Hind or anyone suggested he and Quinlan were up to anything shady, she'd give him the benefit of the doubt. But he thanked her all the same.

The meeting between Ephraim and Celestina was as stiff and awkward as Hunt had expected.

Ephraim was handsome, as so many of the Archangels were: black hair cut close to his head in a warrior-like fashion, light brown skin that radiated health and vitality, and dark eyes that noted every person in the room, like a soldier assessing a battlefield.

But his smile was genuine as he looked upon Celestina, who strode toward him with outstretched hands.

"My friend," she said, peering up into his face. As if seeing it for the first time.

Ephraim smiled, white teeth straight and perfect. "My mate."

She ducked her head right at the moment he went in to kiss her cheek, and Hunt reined in his cringe as Ephraim's lips met the side of her head. Celestina jolted back, realizing the miscommunication, that people were witnessing this, and—

Isaiah, gods bless him, stepped forward, a fist on his heart. "Your Grace. I welcome you and your triarii." Ephraim had only brought Sandriel's triarii with him, Hunt realized. Had left his original members back in Pangera with the Hawk.

Ephraim recovered from the awkward kiss and tucked his blindingly white wings close to his toned, powerful body. "I thank you for your welcome, Commander Tiberian. And hope that your triarii will welcome mine as you so warmly did."

Hunt at last glanced at the Hind, standing a few feet behind Ephraim, and then at Pollux, staring at her with wolfish intensity from across the room. The Hind's golden eyes simmered, focused wholly on her lover. As if she were waiting for the go-ahead to jump his bones.

"Yuck," Naomi muttered, and Hunt suppressed his smile.

Celestina seemed to be searching for something to say, so Hunt spared her and said, "We shall treat your triarii as our brothers and sisters." The Harpy sneered at the last word. Hunt's lightning sparked in answer. "For however long they remain here." *For however long I let you live, you fucking psychopath.*

Celestina recovered enough to say, "Their alliance shall be only one of the many successes for our mating."

Ephraim voiced his agreement, even as he raked his stare over his mate once more. Approval shone there, but Celestina . . . Her throat bobbed.

She'd . . . been with a male, hadn't she? Come to think of it, Hunt didn't even know if she preferred males. Had the Asteri considered that? Would they care what her preferences were, what her experience was, before throwing her into bed with Ephraim?

Baxian's eyes remained on the Harpy and the Hind, cold and watchful. He didn't seem particularly pleased to see them.

"I have some refreshments prepared," Celestina said, gesturing to the tables against the wall of windows. "Come, let us drink to this happy occasion."

Bryce had just finished telling Ruhn and Ithan what had gone down in the Bone Quarter—both of them looking as sick as Tharion had to hear about the real fate of the dead—when someone knocked on the door.

"So Connor," Ithan was saying, rubbing his face. "He's . . . They fed his soul into the Gate to become firstlight? Secondlight? Whatever."

Bryce wrung her hands. "It seems like they'd wait until we're all dust, and even our descendants have forgotten him, but considering how much we pissed off the Under-King, I feel like there's a chance he might . . . move Connor up the list."

"I need to know," Ithan said. "I need to fucking *know*."

Bryce's throat ached. "I do, too. We'll try to find out."

Tharion asked, "But what can be done to help him—any of them?"

Silence fell. The knock on the door came again, and Bryce sighed. "We'll figure that out, too."

Ruhn toyed with one of the hoops through his left ear. "Is there someone we should . . . tell?"

Bryce unlocked the door. "The Asteri undoubtedly know about it and don't care. They'll say it's our civic duty to give back whatever power we can."

Ithan shook his head, looking toward the window.

Ruhn said, "We have to think carefully about this. Was the Prince of the Pit pushing you and Athalar to go there by sending those Reapers? Or by having his Reapers hint that Emile and Sofie might be hiding there? Why? To—activate your combined powers with that Gate trick? He couldn't have known that would happen. We have to think about how the Asteri would retaliate if this *is* something they want kept under wraps. And what they'd do if we do indeed find and harbor Emile and Sofie."

"We'll game it out," Bryce said, and finally opened the door.

A hand locked around her throat, crushing the air from her. "You little cunt," Sabine Fendyr hissed.

Ruhn should have considered who might need to knock on the front door. Instead, he'd been so focused on the truth Bryce had revealed about their lives—and afterlives—that he'd let her open it without checking.

Sabine hurled Bryce across the room, hard enough that she

slammed into the side of the sectional, scooting the behemoth couch back by an inch.

Ruhn was up instantly, gun aimed at the Alpha. Behind him, Tharion helped Bryce to her feet. Sabine's attention remained fixed on Bryce as she said, "What game are you playing, *Princess*?" That title was clearly what had kept Sabine from ripping out Bryce's throat.

Bryce's brows lowered, but Ithan stepped to Ruhn's side, violence gleaming in his eyes. "What the Hel are you talking about?"

Sabine bristled, but she didn't remove her focus from Bryce as she continued, "You just can't stay out of wolf business, can you?"

Bryce said coolly, "Wolf business?"

Sabine pointed a clawed finger toward Ithan. "He was exiled. And yet *you* decided to harbor him. No doubt part of some plan of yours to rob me of my birthright."

"So the big bad wolf came all the way here to yell at me about it?"

"The big bad wolf," Sabine seethed, "came all the way here to remind you that no matter what my father might have said, *you* are no wolf." She sneered at Ithan. "And neither is he. So stay the fuck out of wolf affairs."

Ithan let out a low growl, but pain seemed to ripple beneath it.

Ruhn snarled, "You want to talk, Sabine, then sit the fuck down like an adult." At his side, he was vaguely aware of Bryce thumbing in a message on her phone.

Ithan squared his shoulders. "Bryce isn't harboring me. Perry dropped me here."

"Perry's a moon-eyed fool," Sabine spat.

Bryce angled her head, though. "What about this arrangement, exactly, bothers you, Sabine?" The way her voice had iced over . . . Fuck, she sounded exactly like their father.

Ithan said, "Bryce has nothing to do with you and me, Sabine. Leave her out of it."

Sabine pivoted toward him, bristling. "You're a disgrace and a traitor, Holstrom. A spineless waste, if this is the company you choose to keep. Your brother would be ashamed."

Ithan snapped, "My brother would tell me good fucking rid-dance to you."

Sabine snarled, the sound pure command. "You might be exiled, but you still obey *me*."

Ithan shuddered, but refused to back down.

Tharion stepped forward. "You want to throw down with Holstrom, Sabine, go ahead. I'll stand as witness."

Ithan would lose. And Sabine would gut him so thoroughly there would be no hope of recovery. He'd wind up with his brother, his soul served up to the Under-King and the Dead Gate on a silver platter.

Ruhn braced himself—and realized he had no idea what to do.

Celestina should have laid out some hard alcohol rather than rosé. Hunt wasn't nearly drunk enough to deal with having to keep smiling in a room full of his enemies. To deal with watching two people who had no choice but to make an arranged mating work somehow. They wouldn't officially be mated until the party next month, but their life together was already beginning.

Beside him, at the doors to the private veranda off Celestina's study, Isaiah knocked back his pale pink wine and muttered, "What a clusterfuck."

"I feel bad for her," Naomi said on Isaiah's other side.

Hunt grunted his agreement, watching Celestina and Ephraim attempt to make small talk across the room. Beyond them, the Harpy seemed content to sneer at Hunt the whole night. Baxian lurked by the door to the hall. Pollux and Lidia talked near the Harpy with bent heads.

Naomi followed the direction of his gaze. "There's a terrifying match."

Hunt chuckled. "Yeah." His phone buzzed, and he fished it out of his pocket to see that a text had arrived from *Bryce Sucks My Dick Like a Champ*.

Hunt choked, scrambling to switch screens as Isaiah peered over his shoulder and laughed. "I assume you didn't put that name in there."

"No," Hunt hissed. He'd punish her thoroughly for that one.

After he finally got to fuck her. He hadn't forgotten that he was supposed to be doing exactly that right now. That he'd made dinner and hotel reservations that had been canceled for this awkward-ass shit. Hunt explained to Isaiah, "It's this stupid running joke we have."

"A joke, hmmm?" Isaiah's eyes danced with delight, and he clapped Hunt on the shoulder. "I'm happy for you."

Hunt smiled to himself, opening up her message, trying not to look at the name she'd put in and think about how accurate it was. "Thanks." But his smile faded as he read the message.

Sabine here.

Hunt's heartbeat kicked up a notch. Isaiah read the message and murmured, "Go."

"What about this?" Hunt jerked his chin at Celestina and Ephraim across the room.

"Go," Isaiah urged. "You need backup?"

He shouldn't, but Bryce's message had been so vague, and—shit. "You can't come with me. It'll be too obvious." He turned to Naomi, but she'd drifted off toward the bar cart again. If he grabbed her, it'd draw everyone's attention. He scanned the space.

Baxian looked right at him, reading the tension on his face, his body. Fucker. Now someone *would* know he'd left—

Isaiah sensed it, noted it. "I'll deal with that," his friend murmured, and sauntered off toward the black-winged angel. He said something to Baxian that had them both pivoting away from Hunt.

Seizing his chance, Hunt backed up a step, then another, fading into the shadows of the veranda beyond the study. He kept moving, stealthy, until his heels were at the edge of the landing. But as he stepped off, free-falling into the night, he caught Celestina looking at him.

Disappointment and displeasure darkened her eyes.

35

Bryce cursed herself for opening the door. For letting the wolf in. For letting it get to this so quickly: Ithan and Sabine, about to splatter this apartment with blood. Ithan's blood.

Bryce's mouth dried out. Think. *Think.*

Ruhn swiftly glanced at her, but didn't suggest any bright ideas mind-to-mind.

Sabine snarled at Ithan, "Your brother knew his place. Was content to be Danika's Second. You're not nearly as smart as he was."

Ithan didn't back down as Sabine advanced. "I might not be as smart as Connor," he said, "but at least I wasn't dumb enough to sleep with Mordoc."

Sabine halted. "Shut your mouth, boy."

Ithan laughed, cold and lifeless. Bryce had never heard him make such a sound. "We never learned during that last visit: Was it an arranged pairing between you two, or some drunk decision?"

Mordoc—the Hind's captain?

"I will rip out your throat," Sabine growled, stepping closer. But Bryce saw it—the glimmer of surprise. Doubt. He'd thrown Sabine off her game a little with that volley.

Again, Ithan didn't lower his eyes. "He's here in this city. Are you going to see him? Take him to the Black Dock to bid farewell to his daughter?"

Bryce's stomach dropped, but she kept her face neutral. Danika had never said. Had always claimed it was a . . .

A male not worth knowing or remembering.

Bryce had assumed it was some lesser wolf, some male too submissive to keep Sabine's interest, and Sabine had refused to let Danika see him because of it. Even when Danika had known the truth of Bryce's parentage, she'd never told Bryce about her own lineage. The thought burned like acid.

Sabine spat, "I know what you're trying to do, Holstrom, and it won't work."

Ithan flexed his broad chest. Bryce had seen that same intense expression while facing off against opponents on the sunball field. Ithan had usually been the one to walk away from the encounter. And he'd *always* walked away if a teammate joined in the fight.

So Bryce stepped up. Said to Sabine, "Was Danika a rebel?"

Sabine whipped her head to her. "*What?*"

Bryce kept her shoulders back, head high. She outranked Sabine in position and power now, she reminded herself. "Did Danika have contact with the Ophion rebels?"

Sabine backed away. Just one step. "Why would you ever ask that?"

Ithan ignored the question and countered, "Was it because of Mordoc? She was so disgusted by him that she helped the rebels to spite him?"

Bryce shoved from the other side, "Maybe she did it out of disgust for you, too."

Sabine backed away one more step. Predator turning into prey. She snarled, "You're both delusional."

"Is that so?" Bryce asked, and then took a stab in the dark. "I'm not the one who ran all the way here to make sure Ithan and I weren't plotting some kind of wolf-coup against you."

Sabine bristled. Bryce pushed, getting no small delight out of it, "That's the fear, right? That I'm going to use my fancy princess title to get Holstrom to replace you somehow? I mean, you've got no heir beyond Amelie right now. And Ithan's as dominant as she is. But I don't think the Den likes Amelie—or you, for that matter—nearly as much as they love him."

Ithan blinked at her in surprise. But Bryce smiled at Sabine, who'd gone stone-faced as she snarled, "*Stay out of wolf business.*"

Bryce taunted, "I wonder how hard it would be to convince the Prime and the Den that Ithan is the bright future of the Valbaran wolves—"

"Bryce," Ithan warned. Had he truly never considered such a thing?

Sabine's hand drifted to something at her back, and Ruhn aimed his gun. "Nah," Bryce's brother said, smiling wickedly. "I don't think so."

A familiar ripple of charged air filled the room a moment before Hunt said, "Neither do I," and appeared in the doorway so silently Bryce knew he'd crept up. Relief nearly buckled her knees as Hunt stepped into the apartment, gun pointed at the back of Sabine's head. "You're going to leave, and never fucking bother us again."

Sabine seethed, "Allow me to give you a bit of advice. You tangle with Mordoc, and you'll get what's coming to you. Ask him about Danika and see what he does to get answers out of you."

Ithan's teeth flashed. "Get out, Sabine."

"You don't give me orders."

The wolves faced off: one young and brokenhearted, the other in her prime—and heartless. Could someone like Ithan, if he wanted it, ever win in a battle for dominance?

But then another figure stepped into the apartment behind Hunt.

Baxian. The angel shifter had a gun drawn, aimed at Sabine's legs to disable her if she tried to run.

Only a glimmer of surprise on Hunt's face told Bryce this wasn't a planned appearance.

Sabine turned slowly. Recognition flared in her eyes. And something like fear.

Baxian's teeth gleamed in a feral grin. "Hello, Sabine."

Sabine simmered with rage, but hissed, "You're all carrion," and stormed from the apartment.

"You all right?" Hunt asked Bryce as he looked her over. The redness around her throat was fading before his eyes.

Bryce scowled. "I could have done without being hurled into the side of the couch."

Baxian, still by the door, huffed a laugh.

Hunt turned toward him, lightning at the ready. "You got nothing better to do with your time than follow me around?"

"It seemed like you had an emergency," Baxian retorted. "I figured you might need backup. Especially considering where you were this morning." A slash of a smile. "I worried something had followed you back across the Istros."

Hunt clenched his jaw hard enough to hurt. "What about Isaiah?"

"You mean his pathetic distraction attempt?" Baxian snorted.

Before Hunt could reply, Ithan asked the Helhound, "You know Sabine?"

Baxian's face darkened. "In passing." From the way Sabine had acted, there was definitely more to it than that.

But Bryce suddenly asked Ithan, "Mordoc is . . . was . . . He's Danika's *father*?"

Ithan gazed at his feet. "Yeah."

"As in, the male who sired her. Like, gave her his genetic material."

Ithan's eyes blazed. "Yeah."

"And no one thought to fucking tell me?"

"I only knew because he visited the Den once, a year before we met you. She got her bloodhound gift from him. It was her secret to keep, but now that she's gone—"

"Why wouldn't she tell me?" Bryce rubbed at her chest. Hunt took her hand. Brushed his thumb over her knuckles.

"Would you want that asshole for a father?" Hunt asked.

"I have an asshole father already," Bryce said, and Ruhn grunted his agreement. "I'd have understood." Hunt squeezed her hand in gentle reassurance.

"I don't know why she didn't say anything to you." Ithan dropped onto the couch and ran his hands through his hair. "Danika would have become my Alpha one day, and Sabine ruler of us all, so if they wanted it kept quiet, I had no choice." Until Sabine had exiled him, freeing Ithan from those restrictions.

"Would you have taken Sabine down just now?" Tharion asked.

"I might have tried," Ithan admitted.

Hunt whistled. But it was Baxian who said, "You wouldn't have won tonight."

Ithan growled, "Did I ask for your opinion, dog?"

Hunt glanced between them. Interesting, that Ithan saw him as a dog, not an angel. His animal form took precedence for another shifter, apparently.

Baxian growled right back. "I said you wouldn't have won *tonight*. But another day, give yourself a few more years, pup, and maybe."

"And you're an expert in such things?"

Ithan was still itching for a fight. Perhaps Baxian was about to give him one, sensing his need for it. Baxian's wings tucked in. Definitely primed for a fight.

Bryce massaged her temples. "Go to the gym or the roof if you're going to brawl. Please. I can't afford to lose any more furniture." She scowled at Ithan at that.

Hunt snickered. "We'll get through the mourning process together, Quinlan. Have a proper send-off for the coffee table. Holstrom should give the eulogy, since he broke it."

His phone buzzed, and he checked it to find Isaiah's message. *All ok?*

He wrote back, *Yeah. You?*

She's upset you left. Didn't say anything, but I can tell. Baxian bailed, too.

Fuck. He replied, *Tell her it was an emergency and that Baxian needed to help me.*

He trailed you?

Just busting my balls, Hunt lied.

All right. Be careful.

Ithan said to Ruhn, "I'm accepting your offer."

Hunt's brows twitched toward each other. Bryce asked, "What offer?"

Ruhn sized her up before saying, "To come live with me and the guys. Because of your thin-ass walls."

Tharion said with mock outrage, "I had dibs on the pup as *my* friend."

"Sorry for sexiling you, Ithan," Bryce muttered. Hunt laughed, but Ithan didn't. He didn't look at Bryce at all. Weird.

Ruhn said to Ithan, "All right. You fighting that asshole first, or can we go?" He nodded to Baxian.

Hunt kept perfectly still. Ready to either intervene or referee.

Ithan surveyed the angel with that athletic precision and focus. Baxian only smiled at him in invitation. How many times had Hunt seen that expression on the Helhound's face before he ripped into someone?

But Ithan wisely shook his head. "Another time."

Three minutes later, Ithan was stepping into the hallway with Ruhn and Tharion, who had to go report to his queen once more.

"Ithan," Bryce said before he could leave. From the kitchen, Hunt watched her take a step into the hall, then halt, as if catching herself. "We made a good team."

From his angle, Hunt couldn't see Ithan's face, but he heard the quiet "Yeah," right before the elevator doors dinged. Then, "We did." For all the world, Hunt could have sworn the wolf sounded sad.

A moment later, Bryce walked back into the apartment and aimed right for Hunt, looking like she'd drop into his arms with exhaustion. She drew up short upon seeing Baxian. "Enjoying the view?"

Baxian stopped his surveying. "Nice place. Why'd Sabine come here?"

Bryce examined her nails. "She was pissed that I've been harboring Ithan after she kicked his ass to the curb."

"You know about her and Mordoc, though." It wasn't exactly a question.

"*You* know?" Hunt asked.

Baxian shrugged one shoulder. "I've spent years with the Hind and those who serve her. I picked up a few interesting details."

"What happened when Mordoc visited Danika?" Bryce asked.

"It didn't go well. He came back to Sandriel's castle . . ." Baxian said to Hunt, "Remember the time he ate that human couple?"

Bryce choked. "He *what?*"

Hunt said roughly, "Yeah."

"That was when he'd returned from the visit to the Den," Baxian explained. "He was in such a rage that he went out and killed a human couple he found on the street. Started eating the female while the male was still alive and begging for mercy."

"Burning fucking Solas," Bryce breathed, her hand finding Hunt's.

"Sabine was right to warn you away from him," Baxian said, aiming for the door.

Hunt grunted. "I never thought he'd be in this city."

"Let's hope he's gone soon, then," Baxian said, not looking back.

Bryce said, hand sliding from Hunt's, "Why did *you* come here, Baxian?"

The angel-shifter halted. "Athalar seemed like he needed help. We're partners, after all." His grin was savage, mocking. "And watching Celestina and Ephraim pretend to be into each other was too torturous, even for me."

Bryce was having none of it, though. "You were also at the Black Dock this morning."

"Are you asking if I'm spying on you?"

"Either that or you desperately want in on the cool kids' club."

"A good spy would tell you no, and say you were being paranoid."

"But you're . . . not a good spy?"

"I'm not a spy at all, and you're being paranoid."

Bryce rolled her eyes, and Hunt smiled to himself as she walked to the door, making to shut it behind Baxian. As she closed the door, he heard her say to the Helhound, "You're going to fit right in around here."

"Why'd you say that to him?" Hunt asked as he slumped onto the bed beside her later that night.

Bryce rested her head on Hunt's shoulder. "Say what?"

"That thing to Baxian about fitting in."

"Jealous?"

"I just . . ." His chest heaved as he sighed. "He's a bad male."

"I know. Don't think too much about my nonsense, Hunt."

"No, it's not that. It's . . . He's a bad male. I know he is. But I was no better than him."

She touched his cheek. "You're a good person, Hunt." She'd assured him of that so many times now.

"I told Celestina I'd have her back with Ephraim and then bailed. Good people don't do that."

"You bailed to come rescue your mate from the big bad wolf."

He flicked her nose, shifting onto his side, wings a wall of gray behind him. "I can't believe Mordoc is Danika's father."

"I can't believe our souls get turned into firstlight food," she countered. "Or that the Hind brought her dreadwolves here. Or that the Under-King is a fucking psychopath."

Hunt's laugh rumbled through her. "Rough day."

"What do you think happened in the Bone Quarter—with your lightning and the firstlight and everything?"

"What were you even thinking, jumping in front of my lightning?"

"It worked, didn't it?"

He glared. "You know that scar on Baxian's neck? I did that to him. With my lightning. With a blow a fraction of what I unleashed on the Starsword."

"Yeah, yeah, you're the tough, smart male who knows best and I'm an impulsive female whose feelings get her in trouble—"

"For fuck's sake, Quinlan."

She propped her head on a hand. "So you had no idea you could do that? Take the energy from the Dead Gate and transform it into lightning and all that?"

"No. It never occurred to me to channel anything into my lightning until the Prince of the Pit suggested it the other night. But . . . it made sense: you took the power out of the Heart Gate this spring, and Sofie Renast, as a thunderbird, could do something similar, so . . . even if the push came from the Prince of the Pit, trying it out seemed like a good alternative to being eaten."

"You went . . ." She wiggled her fingers in the air. "All lightning-berserker."

He kissed her brow, running a hand down her hip. "I get a little hysterical when your safety is involved."

She kissed the tip of his nose. "Such an alphahole." But she flopped back on the bed, tucking her arms under her head. "You think there actually *is* a resting place for our souls?" She sighed at the ceiling. "Like, if we died and didn't go to those places . . . what would happen?"

"Ghosts?"

She scowled. "You're not helping."

He chuckled, tucking his hands behind his own head. She crossed her ankle over his shin, and they lay there in silence, staring at the ceiling.

He said after a while, "You traded your resting place in the Bone Quarter for Danika's."

"Given what happens to everyone over there, I feel kind of relieved about that now."

"Yeah." He took one of her hands in his and laid their interlaced fingers atop his heart. "But wherever you're headed when this life is over, Quinlan, that's where I want to be, too."

36

The bridge was blissfully quiet compared to the absolute insanity of Ruhn's day.

He'd brought Holstrom back to his place, where Flynn and Dec had been gobbling down five pizzas between the two of them. The former had arched a brow at Ruhn's announcement that the fourth bedroom—a disgusting heap of crap thanks to years of throwing their messes in there before parties—was now Ithan's. He'd have the couch tonight, and tomorrow they'd clean out all the shit. Declan had only shrugged and tossed Ithan a beer, then pulled his laptop over, presumably to continue combing through the gallery footage.

Flynn had eyed the wolf, but shrugged as well. The message was clear enough: Yeah, Holstrom was a wolf, but so long as he didn't mouth off about Fae, they'd get along just fine. And a wolf was always better than an angel.

Guys were simple like that. Easy.

Not like the female burning across from him on the bridge.

"Hey, Day." He wished he had someplace to sit. For one fucking moment. He was technically sleeping, he supposed, but . . .

Well, damn. A deep-cushioned armchair appeared a foot away. He slumped into it and sighed. Perfect.

Her snort rippled toward him, and another chair appeared. A red velvet fainting couch.

"Fancy," he said as Day draped herself over it. She looked so much like Lehabah that his chest ached.

"Seeing me like this causes you distress."

"No," he said, puzzled as to how she'd read his emotions when night and stars covered his features. "No, it's . . . I, ah, lost a friend a few months ago. She loved to sit on a couch like that one. She was a fire sprite, so your whole fire thing . . . struck a little close to home."

She angled her head, flame shifting with her. "How did she die?"

He checked himself before he could reveal too much. "It's a long story. But she died saving my—someone I love."

"Then her death was noble."

"I should have been there." Ruhn leaned back against the cushions and gazed toward the endless black above them. "She didn't need to make that sacrifice."

"You would have traded your life for a fire sprite's?" There was no condescension in the question—merely bald curiosity.

"Yeah. I would have." He lowered his stare back to her. "Anyway, we made the intel drop-off. Nearly got caught, but we did it."

She straightened slightly. "By whom?"

"Mordoc. The Hind. The Harpy."

She stilled. Her fire guttered to that violet blue. "They are *lethal*. If you're caught, you will be lucky to just be killed."

Ruhn crossed an ankle over a knee. "Believe me, I know that."

"Mordoc is a monster."

"So's the Hind. And the Harpy."

"They're all . . . Where you are now?"

He hesitated, then said, "In Lunathion. Might as well tell you—you could have turned on the news and figured out where they are."

She shook her head, flame flowing. "You say too much."

"And you too little. Any other intel about the shipment on the Spine?"

"No. I thought you called me here to tell me something."

"No. I . . . I guess my mind reached for yours."

She watched him. And even though he couldn't see her face, and she couldn't see his, he'd never felt so naked. She said quietly, "Something's riled you."

How could she tell? "My day was . . . difficult."

She sighed. Tendrils of fire rippled around her. "Mine too."

"Yeah?"

"Yeah."

The word was teasing, a reminder of their earlier conversation. She did have a sense of humor, then.

Day said, "I work with people who are . . . Well, they make Mordoc seem like one of those sweet little otters in your city. There are days when it wears on me more than others. Today was one of them."

"Do you at least have friends to lean on?" he asked.

"No. I've never had a true friend in my life."

He winced. "That's . . . really sad."

She snorted. "It is, isn't it?"

"I don't think I'd have made it this far without my friends. Or my sister."

"For those of us with neither friends nor family, we find ways to make do."

"No family, eh? A true lone wolf." He added, "My father's a piece of shit, so . . . a lot of the time I wish I were like you."

"I have a family. A very influential one." She propped her head on a burning fist. "They're pieces of shit, too."

"Yeah? Your dad ever burn you for speaking out of turn?"

"No. But he did flog me for sneezing during prayers."

She wasn't an Asteri, then. Asteri had no family. No children. No parents. They just *were*.

He blinked. "All right. We're even."

She laughed quietly, a low, soft sound that ran delicate fingers over his skin. "A truly tragic thing to have in common."

"It really is." He smiled, even if she couldn't see it.

She said, "Since you are in a position of power, I'm assuming your father must be as well."

"Why can't I be self-made?"

"Call it intuition."

He shrugged. "All right. What about it?"

"Does he know of your rebel sympathies?"

"I think my work has gone beyond sympathies now, but . . . no. He'd kill me if he knew."

"Yet you risk your life."

"What's the question, Day?"

Her mouth quirked to the side. Or what he could see of it did. "You could use your power and rank to undermine people like your father, you know. Be a secret agent for the rebellion in that sense, rather than doing this message-carrying."

She didn't know who he was, right? Ruhn shifted in his chair. "Honestly? I'm shit at those deception games. My father is the master of them. This is far more my speed."

"And yet your father is allowed to stay in power?"

"Yeah. Aren't all of these assholes allowed to stay in power? Who's going to stop them?"

"Us. People like us. One day."

Ruhn snorted. "That's some idealistic shit right there. You know that if this rebellion is triumphant, we'll likely have a war for dominance between all the Houses, don't you?"

"Not if we play the game well." Her tone was completely serious.

"Why tell me any of this? I thought you were all . . . no-personal-stuff."

"Let's chalk it up to a difficult day."

"All right," he repeated. He leaned back in his chair once more, letting himself fall quiet. To his surprise, Day did the same. They sat in silence for long minutes before she said, "You're the first person I've spoken to normally in . . . a very long time."

"How long?"

"So long that I think I've forgotten what it feels like to be myself. I think I've lost my true self entirely. To destroy monsters, we become monsters. Isn't that what they say?"

"Next time, I'll bring us some psychic beers and a TV. We'll get you normal again."

She laughed, the sound like clear bells. Something male and primal in him sat up at the sound. "I've only ever had wine."

He started. "That's not possible."

"Beer wasn't deemed appropriate for a female of my position. I did have a sip once I was old enough to . . . not answer to my family, but I found it wasn't to my liking anyway."

He shook his head in mock horror. "Come visit me in Lunathion sometime, Day. I'll show you a good time."

"Given who is present in your city, I think I'll decline."

He frowned. Right.

She seemed to remember, too. And why they were here. "Is it confirmed where the rebels are making the strike on the Spine shipment?"

"Not sure. I'm the go-between, remember?"

"You told them what I said about the Asteri's new mech-suit prototype?"

"Yeah."

"Don't forget that it's the most valuable thing on that train. Leave the rest."

"Why not blow up the entire Spine and break their supply lines?"

Her fire sizzled. "We've tried multiple times. With each attempt, we've been thwarted. Either by betrayal or things simply going wrong. An attack like that requires a lot of people, and a lot of secrecy and precision. Do *you* know how to make explosives?"

"No. But there's always magic to do that."

"Remember that the rebellion is mostly humans, and their Vanir allies like to remain hidden. We are dependent on human resourcefulness and abilities. Simply compiling enough explosives to enact a serious hit on the Spine takes a great deal of effort. Especially considering the great losses Ophion has taken to its numbers lately. They're on the ropes." She added, oozing disgust, "This isn't a video game."

Ruhn growled. "I'm aware of that."

Her flame banked a fraction. "You're right. I spoke out of turn."

"You can just say 'I'm sorry.' No need for the fancy talk."

Another soft laugh. "Bad habit."

He saluted her. "Well, until next time, Day."

He half hoped she'd counter with something to keep them talking, keep him here.

But Day and her couch faded into embers drifting on a phantom wind. "Goodbye, Night."

Ithan Holstrom had never been inside a full-fledged Fae's house. There'd only been two Fae males on his CCU sunball team, and both were from cities across the territory, so he'd never had the chance to go to their homes and meet their families.

But Prince Ruhn's house was cool. It reminded him of the apartment Connor and Bronson and Thorne once had—a few blocks from here, actually: crappy old furniture, stained walls with posters of sports teams taped on them, an overly large TV, and a fully stocked bar.

He hadn't minded crashing on the couch last night. Would have slept on the porch, if it meant being far away from where Bryce and Hunt slept together.

The clock beneath the TV read seven in the morning when Ithan rose and showered. He helped himself to Tristan Flynn's array of fancy shampoos and body products, all marked *FLYNN'S. DO NOT TOUCH, RUHN. I MEAN IT THIS TIME.*

Ruhn had written beneath the scribbling on one of the bottles: *NO ONE LIKES YOUR WEIRD SHAMPOO ANYWAY.*

Flynn had scrawled, right along the bottom edge of the bottle, *THEN WHY IS IT NEARLY EMPTY? AND WHY IS YOUR HAIR SO SHINY? ASSHOLE!!!*

Ithan had snickered, even as his heart squeezed. He'd had that kind of dynamic once with his brother.

His brother, who was either already turned into secondlight—or on his way there.

The thought had any rising interest in breakfast melting into nausea. By the time Ithan had dressed and gone downstairs—the three Fae males who lived in the house were still asleep—he'd raised his phone to his ear.

Hey, this is Tharion, if you can't get me, send an otter.

All right, then.

An hour later, after a quick check of the program scanning the gallery footage for Danika, Ithan had headed for the Istros, grabbing an iced coffee on his way. He suppressed a smile as he handed over a silver mark to a whiskery otter whose name tag on his yellow vest said *Fitzroy*. Ithan parked his ass on a bench beside the Istros and stared across the river.

He'd wanted to fight Sabine last night. Had actually contemplated how her blood would taste when he ripped out her throat with his teeth, but . . . the Helhound's words lingered.

Connor had been an Alpha who'd accepted the role of Second because he'd believed in Danika's potential. Ithan had fallen in with Amelie's pack because he'd had nowhere else to go.

But last night, just for a moment, when Bryce had stepped up and the two of them had Sabine backing away . . . he'd remembered what it'd been like. To not only be a wolf in a pack, but a player on a team, working in unison, as if they were one mind, one soul.

Never mind that he'd once thought of himself and Bryce that way.

The fucking Hind could go to Hel. He had no idea how she'd pieced that together, but he'd kill her if she ever mentioned it to anyone again. Especially Bryce.

It was no one's business but his, and it was ancient history now anyway. He'd had two years without Bryce to sort his shit out, and being near her again had been . . . hard, but he'd never told anyone about his feelings before Connor died, and he sure as Hel wasn't going to start now.

The Hind had been right, though: he'd walked into Connor's dorm that day early in his brother's freshman year at CCU, intending to meet the awesome, gorgeous, hilarious hallmate Con talked about endlessly. And on his way down the dingy, carpeted hall, he'd run into . . . well, an awesome, gorgeous, hilarious hallmate.

He'd been struck stupid. She was the hottest person he'd ever seen, no joke. Her smile had warmed some gods-forsaken place in Ithan's chest that had been icy and dark since his parents had died, and those whiskey eyes had seemed to . . . *see* him.

Him, not the sunball player, not the star athlete or anything like that. Just him. Ithan.

They spoke for ten minutes in the hall without exchanging names. He'd just been Connor's little brother, and she hadn't given her name and he'd forgotten to ask for it, but by the time Connor poked his head into the hall, Ithan had decided he was going to marry her. He'd attend CCU, play sunball for them and not Korinth U, who'd already been wooing him, and he'd find this girl and marry her. He suspected they might even be mates, if he was right about that gut tug toward her. And that would be that.

Then Connor had said, "Looks like you met Ithan already, Bryce," and Ithan had wanted to dissolve into that disgusting dorm carpet.

He knew it was fucking stupid. He'd spoken to Bryce for ten minutes before finding out she was the girl his brother was obsessed with, but . . . it had messed with him. So he'd thrown himself into the role of irreverent friend, pretended to be into Nathalie so he had something to complain to Bryce about. He'd suffered on the sidelines watching Connor tiptoe around Bryce for years.

He'd never told Bryce that the reason why Connor had finally asked her out that night was because Ithan had told him to shit or get off the pot.

Not in those terms, and he'd said it without raising his brother's suspicions, as he'd always done when talking about Bryce, but he'd had it. Had just *had it* with his brother hesitating while Bryce dated a string of losers.

If Connor didn't step up to the line, then Ithan had decided he'd finally come forward. Take a gamble and see if that spark between them might lead somewhere.

But Bryce had said yes to Connor. And then Connor had died.

And while Connor was being murdered, she'd been fucking someone else in the White Raven bathroom.

Ithan had no idea how there wasn't some black hole where he'd been standing the moment he'd found out about that night. That was how hard he'd imploded, like the star he'd been gave the fuck up and bailed.

Ithan leaned back against the bench, sighing. These last few days, he'd felt like he was poking his head out of that black hole. Now this bullshit about Connor and the Pack's souls being fed into the Dead Gate threatened to pull him back in.

He knew Bryce was pissed about it. Upset. But she had Athalar now.

And no part of Ithan resented them for it. No, that history was behind him, but . . . he didn't know what to do with himself when he spoke to her. The girl he'd been so convinced would be his wife and mate and mother to his kids.

How many times had he allowed himself to picture that future: him and Bryce opening presents with their children on Winter Solstice eve, traveling the world together while he played sunball, laughing and growing old in this city, their friends around them.

He was glad to not be living in her apartment anymore. He'd had nowhere else to go after Sabine and Amelie had kicked him out, and he sure as fuck wasn't planning to stage any kind of coup with her, as Sabine seemed to fear, but . . . he was grateful Ruhn had offered him a place to stay instead.

"A little early, isn't it?" Tharion called from the river, and Ithan stood from the bench to find the mer treading water, powerful fin swirling beneath him.

Ithan didn't bother with pleasantries. "Can you get me to the Bone Quarter?"

Tharion blinked. "No. Unless you want to be eaten."

"Just get me to the shore."

"I can't. Not if I don't want to be eaten, either. The river beasts will attack."

Ithan crossed his arms. "I have to find my brother. See if he's okay."

He hated the pity that softened Tharion's face. "I don't see what you can do either way. If he's fine or if he's . . . not."

Ithan's throat dried out. "I need to know. Swim me past the Sleeping City and I'll see if I can glimpse him."

"Again, river beasts, so no." Tharion slicked back his hair. "But . . . I need to find that kid, if he's not in the Sleeping City. Maybe we can kill two birds with one stone."

Ithan angled his head. "Any idea where to look instead?"

"No. So I desperately need a hint in the right direction."

Ithan frowned. "What do you have in mind?"

"You're not going to like it. Neither is Bryce."

"Why does she need to be involved?" Ithan couldn't stop his voice from sharpening.

"Because I know Legs, and I know she'll want to come."

"Not if we don't tell her."

"Oh, I'm going to tell her. I like my balls where they are." Tharion grinned and jerked his chin to the city behind Ithan. "Go get some money. Gold marks, not credit."

"Tell me where we're going." Somewhere shady, no doubt.

Tharion's eyes darkened. "To the mystics."

37

Keep holding, hold, hold!" Madame Kyrah chanted, and Bryce's left leg shook with the effort of keeping her right leg aloft and in place.

Beside her, Juniper sweated along, face set with focused determination. June held perfect form—no hunched shoulders, no curved spine. Every line of her friend's body radiated strength and grace.

"And down into first position," the instructor ordered over the thumping music. Totally not the style that ballet was usually danced to, but that was why Bryce loved this class: it combined the formal, precise movements of ballet with dance club hits. And somehow, in doing so, it helped her understand both the movements and the sound better. Merge them better. Let her *enjoy* it, rather than dance along to music she'd once loved and daydreamed about getting to perform onstage.

Wrong body type had no place here, in this bright studio on an artsy block of the Old Square.

"Take a five-minute breather," said Madame Kyrah, a dark-haired swan shifter, striding to the chair by the wall of mirrors to swig from her water bottle.

Bryce wobbled over to her pile of crap by the opposite wall, ducking under the barre to pick up her phone. No messages. A blissfully quiet morning. Exactly what she'd needed.

Which was why she'd come here. Beyond *wanting* to come here twice a week, she needed to be here today—to work out every swirling thought. She hadn't told Juniper what she'd learned.

What could she say? *Hey, just FYI, the Bone Quarter is a lie, and I'm pretty sure there's no such thing as a true afterlife, because we all get turned into energy and herded through the Dead Gate, though some small bit of us gets shoved down the gullet of the Under-King, so . . . good fucking luck!*

But Juniper was frowning at her own phone as she drank a few sips from her water bottle.

"What's up?" Bryce asked between pants. Her legs shook simply standing still.

Juniper tossed her phone onto her duffel bag. "Korinne Lescau got tapped to be principal."

Bryce's mouth dropped open.

"*I know*," Juniper said, reading the unspoken outrage on Bryce's face. Korinne had entered the company two years ago. Had only been a soloist for this season. And the CCB had claimed it wasn't promoting anyone this year.

"This is definitely a *fuck you*," Bryce seethed.

June's throat bobbed, and Bryce's fingers curled, as if she could rip the face off of every director and board member of the CCB for putting that pain there. "They're too afraid to fire me, because the shows where I'm a soloist always bring in a crowd, but they'll do what they can to punish me," June said.

"All because you told a bunch of rich jerks that they were being elitist monsters."

"I might bring in money for the shows, but those rich jerks donate millions." The faun drained her water. "I'm going to stick it out until they *have* to promote me."

Bryce tapped her foot on the pale wood floor. "I'm sorry, June."

Her friend squared her shoulders with a quiet dignity that cracked Bryce's heart. "I do this because I love it," she said as Kyrah summoned the class back into their lines. "They're not worth my anger. I have to keep remembering that." She tucked a stray curl back into her bun. "Any word about that kid?"

Bryce shook her head. "Nope." She'd leave it at that.

Kyrah started the music, and they got back into position.

Bryce sweated and grunted through the rest of the class, but Juniper had become razor-focused. Every movement precise and flawless, her gaze fixed on the mirror, as if she battled herself. That expression didn't alter, even when Kyrah asked June to demonstrate a perfect series of thirty-two fouettés—spins on one foot—for the class. Juniper whipped around like the wind itself propelled her, her grounding hoof not straying one inch from its starting point.

Perfect form. A perfect dancer. Yet it wasn't enough.

Juniper left class almost as soon as it had finished, not lingering to chat like she usually did. Bryce let her go, and waited until most of the class had filtered out before approaching Kyrah by the mirror, where the instructor was panting softly. "Did you see the news about Korinne?"

Kyrah tugged on a loose pink sweatshirt against the chill of the dance studio. Even though she hadn't danced on CCB's stage in years, the instructor remained in peak form. "You seem surprised. I'm not."

"You can't say anything? You were one of CCB's prized dancers." And now one of their best instructors when she wasn't teaching her outside classes.

Kyrah frowned. "I'm as much at the mercy of the company's leadership as Juniper. She might be the most talented dancer I've ever seen, and the hardest-working, but she's going up against a well-entrenched power structure. The people in charge don't appreciate being called out for what they truly are."

"But—"

"I get why you want to help her." Kyrah shouldered her duffel and aimed for the double doors of the studio. "I want to help her, too. But Juniper made her choice this spring. She has to face the consequences."

Bryce stared after her for a minute, the doors to the studio banging shut. As she stood alone in the sunny space, the silence pressed on her. She looked to the spot where Juniper had been demonstrating those fouettés.

Bryce pulled out her phone and did a quick search. A moment later, she was dialing. "I'd like to speak to Director Gorgyn, please."

Bryce tapped her feet again as the CCB receptionist spoke. She clenched her fingers into fists before she answered, "Tell him that Her Royal Highness Princess Bryce Danaan is calling."

Push-ups bored Hunt to tears. If it hadn't been for the earbuds playing the last few chapters of the book he was listening to, he might have fallen asleep during his workout on the training roof of the Comitium.

The morning sun baked his back, his arms, his brow, sweat dripping onto the concrete floors. He had a vague awareness of people watching, but kept going. Three hundred sixty-one, three hundred sixty-two . . .

A shadow fell across him, blocking out the sun. He found the Harpy smirking down at him, her dark hair fluttering in the wind. And those black wings . . . Well, that's why there was no more sun.

"What," he asked on an exhale, keeping up his momentum.

"The pretty one wants to see you." Her sharp voice was edged with cruel amusement.

"Her name is Celestina," Hunt grunted, getting to three hundred seventy before hopping to his feet. The Harpy's gaze slid down his bare torso, and he crossed his arms. "You're her messenger now?"

"I'm Ephraim's messenger, and since he just finished fucking her, I was the closest one to retrieve you."

Hunt held in his cringe. "Fine." He caught Isaiah's attention from across the ring and motioned that he was leaving. His friend, in the middle of his own exercises, waved a farewell.

He didn't bother waving to Baxian, despite his help last night. And Pollux hadn't come up to the ring for their private hour of training—he was presumably still in bed with the Hind. Naomi had waited for him for thirty minutes before bailing and going to inspect her own troops.

Hunt stepped toward the glass doors into the building, wiping the sweat from his brow, but the Harpy followed him. He sneered over a shoulder. "Bye."

She gave him a slashing grin. "I'm to escort you back."

Hunt stiffened. This couldn't be good. His body going distant, he kept walking, aiming for the elevators. If he sent a warning message to Bryce right now, would she have enough time to flee the city? Unless they'd already come for her—

The Harpy trailed him like a wraith. "Your little disappearing act last night is going to bite you in the ass," she crooned, stepping into the elevator with him.

Right. That.

He tried not to look too relieved as the acid in his veins eased. That had to be why Celestina was summoning him. A chewing-out for bad behavior, he could deal with.

If only the Harpy knew what he'd really been up to lately.

So Hunt leaned against the far wall of the elevator, contemplating how he'd best like to kill her. A lightning strike to the head would be swift, but not as satisfying as plunging his sword into her gut and twisting as he drove upward.

The Harpy tucked in her black wings. She'd been built wiry and long, her face narrow and eyes a bit too large for her features. She went on, "You always did think more with your cock than your head."

"One of my most winning attributes." He wouldn't let her bait him. She'd done it before, when they'd both served Sandriel, and he'd always paid for it. Sandriel had never once punished the female for the brawls that had left his skin shredded. He'd always been the one to take the flaying afterward for "disturbing the peace."

The Harpy stepped onto the Governor's floor like a dark wind. "You'll get what's coming to you, Athalar."

"Likewise." He trailed her to the double doors of Celestina's public office. She halted outside, knocking once. Celestina murmured her welcome, and Hunt stepped into the room, shutting the door on the Harpy's pinched face.

The Archangel, robed in sky blue today, was immaculate— glowing. If she'd been kept up all night with Ephraim, she didn't reveal it. Or any emotion, really, as Hunt stopped before her desk and said, "You asked for me?" He took a casual stance, legs apart, hands behind his back, wings high but loose.

Celestina straightened a golden pen on her desk. "Was there an emergency last night?"

Yes. No. "A private matter."

"And you saw fit to prioritize that over assisting me?"

Fuck. "You seemed to have the situation under control."

Her lips thinned. "I had hoped that when you promised to have my back, it would be for the entire night. Not for an hour."

"I'm sorry," he said, and meant it. "If it had been for anything else—"

"I'm assuming it had to do with Miss Quinlan."

"Yeah."

"And are you aware that you, as one of my triarii, chose to assist a Princess of the Fae instead of your Governor?"

"It wasn't for anything political."

"That was not how my . . . mate perceived it. He asked why two of my triarii had ditched our private celebration. If they thought so little of me, of him, that they could leave without permission to help a Fae royal."

Hunt ran his hands through his hair. "I'm sorry, Celestina. I really am."

"I'm sure you are." Her voice was distant. "This shall not happen again."

Or what? he almost asked. But he said, "It won't."

"I want you staying in the barracks for the next two weeks."

"*What?*" Hunt supposed he could always quit, but what the fuck would he do with himself then?

Celestina's gaze was steely. "After that time, you may return to Miss Quinlan. But I think you need a reminder of your . . .

priorities. And I'd like you to fully commit to helping Baxian adjust." She shuffled some papers on her desk. "You're dismissed."

Two weeks here. Without Quinlan. Without getting to touch her, fuck her, lie next to her—

"Celestina—"

"Goodbye."

Despite his outrage, his frustration, he looked at her. Really looked.

She was alone. Alone, and like a ray of sunshine in a sea of darkness. He should have had her back last night. But if it was between her and Bryce, he'd always, *always* pick his mate. No matter what it cost him.

Which was apparently two weeks without Bryce.

But he asked, "How'd it go with Ephraim?" *You don't look too happy for a female who recently bedded her mate.*

Her head snapped up. Again, that distance in her eyes that told him he'd been shut out before she even said, "That's a private matter, to use your words."

Fine. "I'll be around today if you need me." He aimed for the door, but added, "Why send the Harpy to get me?"

Her caramel eyes shuttered. "Ephraim thought she might be the most effective."

"Ephraim, huh?"

"He is my mate."

"But not your master."

Power glowed along her wings, her tightly curling hair. "Careful, Hunt."

"Noted." Hunt strode into the hall, wondering if he'd done something to piss off Urd.

Two weeks here. With all the shit happening with Bryce and the rebels and Cormac . . . Fuck.

As if the mere thought of the word *rebels* had summoned her, he found the Hind leaning against the far wall. There was no sign of the Harpy. The Hind's beautiful face was serene, though her golden eyes seemed lit with Helfire. "Hello, Hunt."

"Here to interrogate me?" Hunt aimed for the elevator that

would take him back to the training ring. He kept his pace casual, arrogant. Utterly unfazed.

Even if Danaan had been freaked out by her, Hunt had seen and dealt with Lidia Cervos enough to know which buttons to push. Which to avoid. And that if he got her away from Mordoc, from Pollux, from her entire dreadwolf retinue, he'd leave her in smoking ruin. Fancy that—she was alone right now.

The Hind knew it, too. That was what made her dangerous. She might appear unarmed, vulnerable, but she carried herself like someone who might whisper a word and have death fly to defend her. Who might snap her fingers and unleash Hel upon him.

He'd been in Sandriel's possession when the Hind had signed on—recruited by the Archangel herself to serve as her spymaster. Lidia had been so young: barely into her twenties. She'd just made the Drop, and had no apparent deep well of magic, other than her swiftness as a deer shifter and her love of cruelty. Her appointment to such a high position had been a blaring alarm to stay the fuck away from her—she was a Vanir who'd cross any line, if she pleased Sandriel so greatly. Pollux had courted her almost immediately.

"What the fuck do you want?" Hunt asked, stabbing the elevator button. He blocked any thought of Ophion, of Emile, of their activities from his mind. He was nothing but the Umbra Mortis, loyal to the empire.

"You're friends with Ruhn Danaan, are you not?"

Burning fucking Solas. Hunt kept his face neutral. "I wouldn't say he's a friend, but yeah. We hang out."

"And Ithan Holstrom?"

Hunt shrugged. Calm—stay calm. "He's a decent guy."

"And what of Tharion Ketos?"

Hunt made himself blow out a loud sigh. It served to loosen the growing tightness in his chest. "Isn't it a little early for interrogating?"

Fuck, had she gone after Bryce already? Was one of her goons—Mordoc, even—at the apartment while she cornered Hunt here, at the elevator?

The Hind smiled without showing her teeth. "I woke up refreshed this morning."

"I didn't realize fucking Pollux is so boring that you could sleep through it."

She snickered, to his surprise. "Sandriel might have done so much more with you, if she'd only had the vision for it."

"Too bad she liked gambling more than torturing me." He could only thank the gods that Sandriel had gotten so buried in her debts that she'd had to sell him to Micah to pay them off.

"Too bad she's dead." Those golden eyes gleamed. Yeah, the Hind knew who was responsible for that death.

The elevator opened, and Hunt stepped in, the Hind following him. "So why the questions about my friends?" How much time would he have to warn them? Or would all of them fleeing the city confirm that they were guilty?

"I thought they were merely people you hung out with."

"Semantics."

Her small, bland smile raked down Hunt's temper. "An unusual group, even in a city as progressive as Lunathion. An angel, a wolf, a Fae Prince, a mer, and a half-human whore." Hunt growled at the last word, rage shaking him from his dread. "It sounds like the start to a bad joke."

"You want to ask me something, Lidia, then fucking say it. Don't waste my time." The elevator opened into the hall of the training floor, bringing the scent of sweat.

"I'm merely observing an anomaly. Wondering what might be so . . . compelling that so many people of power, from different species and Houses, are *hanging out* at Bryce Quinlan's apartment."

"She's got one Hel of a video-gaming system."

The Hind chuckled, the sound laced with menace. "I'll find out, you know. I always do."

"I look forward to it," Hunt said, stalking toward the doors. A dark figure loomed ahead of them—Baxian. His eyes were on the Hind. Stony, and yet seeking.

She stopped short. The *Hind* stopped short.

Baxian said, "Lidia."

The Hind replied flatly, "Baxian."

"I was looking for you." He inclined his head to Hunt in dismissal. He'd take over from here.

"Is it to explain why you vanished into the night with Hunt Athalar?" she asked, folding her hands behind her back in a perfect imperial stance. A good little soldier.

Hunt passed Baxian. "Not a word," Hunt said so softly it was barely more than a breath. Baxian nodded subtly.

Hunt had barely pushed open the doors to the training area when he heard Baxian say carefully to the Hind, as if remembering who she was, "I don't answer to you."

Her voice was smooth as silk. "Not to me, or Ephraim, but you still answer to the Asteri." Her true masters. "Whose will is mine."

Hunt's stomach churned. She was right.

And he'd do well to remember it before it was too late.

38

This is a dumb fucking idea."

"You really love to say that, Legs."

Bryce peered at the two-story iron doors in the back alley of the Old Square, the surface embossed with stars and planets and all matter of heavenly objects. "There's a reason no one comes to the mystics anymore." Hel, she'd suggested it while working on Danika's case this spring, but Hunt had convinced her not to come.

The mystics are some dark, fucked-up shit, he'd said.

Bryce glowered at Tharion and Ithan, standing behind her in the alley. "I mean it. What's behind those doors is not for the faint of heart. Jesiba knows this guy, but even she doesn't mess with him."

Ithan countered, "I can't think of another alternative. The Oracle only sees the future, not present. I need to know what's going on with Connor."

Tharion drawled, "If you can't stomach it, Legs, then sit out here on the curb."

She sighed through her nose, trying again. "Only lowlifes use the mystics these days."

They'd had this conversation twice already on the walk over. She was likely going to lose this round as well, but it was worth a shot. If Hunt had been with her, he'd have gotten his point across in that alphahole way of his. But he hadn't answered his phone.

He'd probably give her Hel for coming here without him.

Bryce sighed to the baking-hot sky. "All right. Let's get this over with."

"That's the spirit, Legs." Tharion clapped her on the back. Ithan frowned at the doors.

Bryce reached for the door chime, a crescent moon dangling from a delicate iron chain. She yanked it once, twice. An off-kilter ringing echoed.

"This is a really bad idea," she muttered again.

"Yeah, yeah," Ithan said, tipping his head back to study the building. The tattoo of Amelie's pack was glaringly dark in the sun. She wondered if he wanted to tear the flesh off and start anew.

Bryce set the question aside as one of the planets carved in the door—the five-ringed behemoth that was Thurr—swung away, revealing a pale gray eye. "Appointment?"

Tharion held up his BCIU badge. "The Blue Court requires your assistance."

"Does it, now?" A croaking laugh as that eye—eerily sharp despite the wrinkles around it—fixed on the mer. It narrowed in amusement or pleasure. "One of the river folk. What a treat, what a treat."

The planet slammed shut, and Tharion stepped onto the slate front step as the doors cracked open a sliver. Cold air rippled out, along with the tang of salt and the smothering dampness of mold.

Ithan trailed Bryce, swearing under his breath at the scent. She twisted, throwing him a reproachful glare. He winced, falling into step beside her with that sunball player's grace as they entered the cavernous space beyond.

A gray-robed old male stood before them. Not human, but his scent declared nothing other than some sort of Vanir humanoid. His heavy white beard fell to the thin band of rope that served as a belt, his wispy hair long and unbound. Four rings of silver and gold glinted on one of his withered, spotted hands, with small stars blazing in the center of each, trapped in the nearly invisible glass domes.

No—not stars.

Bryce's stomach turned over at the minuscule hand that pressed against the other side of the glass. There was no mistaking the desperation in that touch.

Fire sprites. Enslaved, all of them. Bought and sold.

Bryce struggled to keep from ripping that hand clean off the arm that bore it. She could feel Ithan watching her, feel him trying to puzzle out why she'd gone so still and stiff, but she couldn't tear her gaze from the sprites—

"It is not every day that one of the mer crosses my doorstep," the old male said, his smile revealing too-white teeth, still intact despite his age. Unless they'd come from someone else. "Let alone in the company of a wolf and a Fae."

Bryce gripped her purse, mastering her temper, and lifted her chin. "We need to consult your . . ." She peered past his bony shoulder to the dim space beyond. "Services." *And then I'll take all four of those rings and smash them open.*

"I shall be honored." The male bowed at the waist to Tharion, but didn't bother to extend the courtesy to Bryce and Ithan. "This way."

Bryce kept a hand within casual distance of the knife in her purse as they entered the dimness. She wished she had the reassuring weight and strength of Danika's sword, but the blade would have stood out too much.

The space consisted of two levels, bookshelves crammed with tomes and scrolls rising to the dark-veiled ceiling, an iron ramp winding up the walls in a lazy spiral. A great golden orb dangled in the center of the room, lit from within.

And beneath them, in tubs built into the slate floor . . .

To her left, Ithan sucked in a breath.

Three mystics slept, submerged in greenish, cloudy water, breathing masks strapped to their faces. Their white shifts floated around them, doing little to hide the skeletal bodies beneath. One male, one female, one both. That was how it always was, how it had always been. Perfect balance.

Bryce's stomach turned over again. She knew the sensation wouldn't stop until she left.

"May I interest you in a hot tea before we begin the formalities?" the old male asked Tharion, gesturing to a thick oak table to the right of the ramp's base.

"We're pressed for time," Ithan lied, stepping up to Tharion's side. Fine. Let them deal with the old creep.

Ithan set a pile of gold marks on the table with a clink. "If that doesn't cover the cost, give me the bill for the remainder." That drew Bryce's attention. Ithan spoke with such . . . authority. She'd heard him talk to his teammates as their captain, had seen him in command plenty, but the Ithan she'd known these past few days had been subdued.

"Of course, of course." The male's filmy eyes swept around the room. "I can have my beauties up and running within a few minutes." He hobbled toward the walkway and braced a hand on the iron rail as he began the ascent.

Bryce glanced back to the three mystics in their tubs, their thin bodies, their pale, soggy skin. Built into the floor beside them was a panel covered in a language she had never seen.

"Pay them no heed, miss," the old male called, still winding his way toward a platform about halfway up the room, filled with dials and wheels. "When they're not in use, they drift. Where they go and what they see is a mystery, even to me."

It wasn't that the mystics could see all worlds—no, the gift wasn't the unnerving thing. It was what they gave up for it.

Life. True life.

Bryce heard Tharion's swallow. She refrained from snapping that she'd warned him. Ten fucking times.

"The families are compensated handsomely," the old male said, as if reciting from a script designed to calm skittish patrons. He reached the controls and began flipping switches. Gears groaned and a few more lights flickered on in the tanks, further illuminating the mystics' bodies. "If that is of any concern to you."

Another switch flipped, and Bryce staggered back a step as a full holographic replica of their solar system exploded into view, orbiting the dangling sun in the center of the space. Tharion blew out what she could only assume was an impressed breath. Ithan scanned above them, like he could find his brother in that map.

Bryce didn't wait for them before trailing the old male up the walkway as the seven planets aligned themselves perfectly, stars glittering in the far reaches of the room. She couldn't keep the sharpness from her voice as she asked, "Do their families ever see them?"

She really had no right to demand these answers. She'd been complicit in coming here, in using their services.

"It would be upsetting for both parties," the male said distantly, still working his switches.

"What's your name?" Bryce advanced up the ramp.

Tharion murmured, "Legs." She ignored the warning. Ithan kept quiet.

Yet the old male replied, utterly unfazed, "Some people call me the Astronomer."

She couldn't keep the bite from her voice. "What do other people call you?" The Astronomer didn't answer. Up and up, Bryce ascended into the heavens, Tharion and Ithan trailing her. Like the assholes were second-guessing this.

One of the mystics twitched, water splashing.

"A normal reaction," the Astronomer said, not even looking up from his dials as they approached. "Everyone is always so concerned for their well-being. They made the choice, you know. I didn't force them into this." He sighed. "To give up life in the waking world to glimpse wonders of the universe that no Vanir or mortal shall ever see . . ." Stroking his beard, he added, "This trio is a good one. I've had them for a while now with no issues. The last group . . . One drifted too far. Too far, and for too long. They dragged the others with them. Such a waste."

Bryce tried to block out the excuses. Everyone knew the truth: the mystics came from all races, and were usually poor. So poor that when they were born with the gift, their families sold them to people like the Astronomer, who exploited their talent until they died, alone in those tubs. Or wandered so deep into the cosmos they couldn't find their way back to their minds.

Bryce clenched her hands into fists. Micah had allowed it to happen. Her piece-of-shit father turned a blind eye, too. As Autumn King, he had the ability to put an end to this practice or, at the least, advocate to stop it, but he didn't.

Bryce set aside her outrage and waved a hand to the drifting planets. "This space map—"

"It is called an orrery."

"This *orrery*." Bryce approached the male's side. "It's tech—not magic?"

"Can it not be both?"

Bryce's fingers curled into fists. But she said, a murky memory rippling from her childhood, "The Autumn King has one in his private study."

The Astronomer clicked his tongue. "Yes, and a fine one at that. Made by craftsmen in Avallen long ago. I haven't had the privilege to see it, but I hear it is as precise as mine, if not more so."

"What's the point of it?" she asked.

"Only one who does not feel the need to peer into the cosmos would ask such a thing. The orrery helps us answer the most fundamental questions: Who are we? Where do we come from?"

When Bryce didn't say anything more, Tharion cleared his throat. "We'll be quick with our own questions, then."

"Each one will be billed, of course."

"Of course," Ithan said through his teeth, stopping at Bryce's side. He peered through the planets to the mystics floating beneath. "Does my brother, Connor Holstrom, remain in the Bone Quarter, or has his soul passed through the Dead Gate?"

The Astronomer whispered, "Luna above." He fiddled with one of the faintly glowing rings atop his hand. "This question requires a . . . riskier method of contact than usual. One that borders on the illegal. It will cost you."

Bryce said, "How much?" Scam-artist bullshit.

"Another hundred gold marks."

Bryce started, but Ithan said, "Done."

She turned to warn him not to spend one more coin of the considerable inheritance his parents had left him, but the Astronomer hobbled toward a metal cabinet beneath the dials and opened its small doors. He pulled out a bundle wrapped in canvas.

Bryce stiffened at the moldy, rotten earth scent that crept from the bundle as he unfolded the fabric to reveal a handful of rust-colored salt.

"What the fuck is that?" Ithan asked.

"Bloodsalt," Bryce breathed. Tharion looked to her in question, but she didn't bother to explain more.

Blood for life, blood for death—it was summoning salt infused with the blood from a laboring mother's sex and blood from a dying male's throat. The two great transitions of a soul in and out of this world. But to use it here . . . "You can't mean to add that to their water," Bryce said to the Astronomer.

The old male hobbled back down the ramp. "Their tanks already contain white salts. The bloodsalt will merely pinpoint their search."

Tharion muttered to Bryce, "You might be right about this place."

"*Now* you agree with me?" she whisper-yelled as the Astronomer sprinkled the red salt into the three tanks.

The water clouded, and then turned rust colored. Like the mystics were now submerged in blood.

Ithan murmured, "This isn't right."

"Then let's take our money and go," she urged.

But the Astronomer returned and Tharion asked, "Is it safe for the mystics to contact the resting dead?"

The Astronomer typed on the pad mounted on a gold-plated lectern fashioned after an exploding star, then hit a black button on a panel nearby. "Oh yes. They do love to talk. Have nothing else to do with their time." He shot Bryce a sharp glare, gray eyes gleaming like cold knives. "As for your money . . . there is a no-refunds policy. Says so right there on the wall. You might as well stay to hear your answer."

Before Bryce could respond, the floor below slid away, leaving the mystics in their tubs. And creating a considerable gap between the base of the ramp and the entryway.

The tubs rested atop narrow columns, rising from a sublevel lined with more books and another walkway descending down, down—to a black pit in the center of the floor. And filling the sublevel, layer after layer of darkness revealed itself, each one blacker than the last.

Seven of them. One for each level of Hel.

"From the highest stars to the Pit itself." The Astronomer sighed, and typed again into the pad. "Their search may take a while, even with the bloodsalt."

Bryce sized up the gap between the base of the ramp and the entryway. Could she jump it? Ithan definitely could—Tharion, too.

She found Tharion watching her with crossed arms. "Just enjoy the show, Legs."

She scowled. "I think you've lost the right to call me that after this."

Ithan said quietly, face pained, "Bryce. I know this sucks. This is . . . This is not okay." His voice turned hoarse. "But if it's the only way to learn what's going on with Connor . . ."

She opened her mouth to snap that Connor would have condemned this place and told Ithan to find some other way, but . . . she could see him. Connor. Shining right there in Ithan's face, in his eyes—the same hue—and in those broad shoulders.

Her throat ached.

What line wouldn't she cross to help Connor and the Pack of Devils? They would have done the same for her. Connor might have condemned this place, but if their positions were reversed . . .

Tharion jerked his chin to the exit far below. "Go ahead, Princess. We'll see you later."

"Fuck you," Bryce snapped. She braced her feet apart. "Let's get this over with." From the corner of her eye, she saw Ithan's shoulders sag. In relief or shame, she didn't know.

The old male cut in, as if he hadn't heard a word of their hissed argument. "Most astronomers and mystics have been put out of business these days, you know. Thanks to fancy tech. And self-righteous busybodies like you," he spat toward Bryce. She snarled at him, the sound more primal Fae than she liked, but he waved that hateful, ring-encrusted hand toward the mystics in their pools. "*They* were the original interweb. Any answer you wish to know, they can find it, without having to wade through the slog of nonsense out there."

The female mystic twitched, dark hair floating around her in the suspension pool, black tendrils among the red salt. Dried salt water crusted the slate rim of the tub, as if she'd thrashed earlier and soaked the stones. Salt for buoyancy—and to protect them from the demons and beings they spied on or conversed with. But would those protections fade with the bloodsalt in the water?

The mystic who was both male and female jolted, their long limbs flailing.

"Oh," the Astronomer observed, scanning the pad. "They're going far this time. Very far." He nodded to Bryce. "That was high-quality bloodsalt, you know."

"For a hundred marks, it had better be," Ithan said, but his attention remained on the mystics below, his breathing shallow.

Another push of a button, and the holographic planets began to shift, becoming smaller as they drifted away. The sun rose into the ceiling, vanishing, and distant stars came into view. Different planets.

"The mystics made the first star-maps," the Astronomer said. "They charted more extensively than anyone had before. In the Eternal City, I heard they have a thousand mystics in the palace catacombs, mapping farther and farther into the cosmos. Speaking with creatures we shall never know."

Hunt had been in those catacombs—their dungeons, specifically. Had he ever heard a whisper of this?

Something beeped on the screen and Bryce motioned toward it. "What's that?"

"The male is reaching Hel's orbit." The Astronomer clicked his tongue. "He's much faster today. Impressive."

"Connor's soul wound up in *Hel*?" Horror laced Ithan's every word.

Bryce's throat closed up. It—it wasn't possible. How would that have even happened? Had she done something with the Gate this spring that had transported his soul over there?

Silence fell, the temperature dropping with it. She demanded, "Why is it getting colder?"

"Sometimes their powers manifest the environment they're encountering." Before anyone replied, the Astronomer twisted a brass dial. "What do you see, what do you hear?"

The male twitched again, red water splashing over the edge of the tub and dribbling into the pit beneath. Tharion peered over the iron rail. "His lips are turning blue."

"The water is warm." The Astronomer tutted. "Look." He pointed to the screen. A graph of rising and falling lines, like sound waves, appeared. "I'll admit the new tech has some advantages. The old way of transcribing was much harder. I had to reference every single brain wave to find the correlation to the right letter or word. Now the machine just does it for me."

I don't care about brain waves, Bryce thought. *Tell me what's happening with Connor.*

But the Astronomer rambled on, almost absentmindedly, "When you speak, your brain sends a message to your tongue to form the words. This machine reads that message, that signal, and interprets it. Without you needing to say a word."

"So it's a mind reader," Tharion said, face pale in the lights. Bryce drifted closer to Ithan—the wolf radiated dread.

"Of a sort," the Astronomer said. "Right now, it is more of an eavesdropper, listening to the conversation the mystic is having with whoever is on the other end of the line."

Tharion asked, hands behind his back as he peered at the machines, "How does it know what the other person is saying?"

"The mystic is trained to repeat back the words so that we may transcribe them." The screen began to flash a series of letters—words.

"*Too dark*," the Astronomer read. "*It is too dark to see. Only hear.*"

"Can you pinpoint where in Hel your mystic is?" Ithan indicated the holographic levels far below.

"Not precisely, but judging by the cold, I'd say deep. Perhaps the Chasm itself."

Bryce and Ithan swapped glances. His eyes were as wide as her own.

The Astronomer kept reading. "*Hello?*" Silence. Nothing but endless silence. "This is very common," the Astronomer assured them, gesturing them to move closer. Despite herself, despite her objections, Bryce leaned in to read the feed.

The mystic said, *I am searching for the soul of a wolf called Connor Holstrom.*

Someone, something answered.

No wolves have roamed these lands for eons. No wolf by that name dwells here, living or dead. But what are you?

Ithan shuddered, swaying a step. With relief, Bryce realized—because that was the dizzying, rushing sensation in her body, too.

"Strange," the Astronomer said. "Why were we drawn to Hel if your friend isn't there?"

Bryce didn't want to know. Tried and failed to open her mouth to say they should go.

I am a mystic, the male said.

From where?

A faraway place.

Why are you here?

To ask questions. Will you oblige me?

If I can, mystic, then I shall.

What is your name?

A pause. Then, *Thanatos.*

Bryce sucked in a sharp breath.

"The Prince of the Ravine." Tharion fell back a step.

Do you know if Connor Holstrom remains in the Bone Quarter of Midgard?

A long, long pause, the sound waves flatlining. Then—

Who sent you here?

A wolf, a mer, and a half-Fae, half-human female.

How the mystics had known of their presence, Bryce had no idea.

Didn't want to know what sort of perception they possessed while in those isolation tanks.

Thanatos asked, *What are their names?*

I do not know. Will you answer my questions?

Another long pause. "We need to stop this." Ithan nodded toward the male's tub. Ice was beginning to inch over the water.

They are listening, are they?

Yes.

Again, silence.

And then the demon prince said, *Let me see them. Let them see me.*

The mystic's eyes flew open in the tank below.

39

A shuddering inhale was the only sign of discomfort Bryce would allow herself as she stared at the hologram displayed in the center of the orrery. The male now contained inside its dark border.

Thanatos's tightly curled black hair was cropped close to his head, displaying the handsome, unsmiling face above the powerful body bedecked in dark, ornate armor. He gazed right at Bryce. As if he could indeed see through the mystic's eyes.

The Astronomer fell back a step, murmuring a prayer to Luna.

The feed kept going, in time to Thanatos's moving mouth. Hunger filled the demon's expression.

I can smell the starlight on you.

The Prince of the Ravine knew her. Somehow.

The Astronomer took another step back, then another, until he was pressed against the wall behind him, shaking in terror.

Thanatos's dark eyes pierced to her soul. *You're the one my brothers speak about.*

Ithan and Tharion glanced between her and the demon, hands within easy reach of their weapons—little as they could do.

"I came to ask about a friend's soul. I don't know why I'm talking to you," Bryce said, and added a bit quietly, "Your Highness."

I am a Prince of Death. Souls bow to me.

This male had none of Aidas's slickness or what Hunt had told her of Apollion's smug arrogance. Nothing that indicated mercy or humor.

Ithan blurted, teeth clattering with the cold, "Can you tell if Connor Holstrom's soul somehow got lost in Hel?"

Thanatos frowned at his knee-high boots, like he could see all the way down to the Pit levels below.

The wolf is your brother, I take it, he said to Ithan.

"Yes." Ithan's throat bobbed.

His soul is not in Hel. He is . . . His attention snapped again to Bryce. Ripped away skin and bone to the being beneath. *You slew one of my creations. My beloved pet, kept for so long on your side of the Crossing.*

Bryce managed to ask, breath clouding in front of her, "You mean the Reapers? Or the Shepherd?" A shepherd of souls—for a prince who peddled them. "The Under-King said you abandoned it after the First Wars."

Abandoned, or intentionally planted?

Great. Fantastic.

"I had no interest in being its lunch," Bryce said.

Thanatos's eyes flared. *You cost me a key link to Midgard. The Shepherd reported faithfully to me on all it heard in the Bone Quarter. The souls of the dead talk freely of their world.*

"Boo-hoo."

You mock a Prince of Hel?

"I just want answers." And to get the fuck out of here.

Thanatos studied her again—as if he had all the time in the universe. Then he said, *I will give them to you only out of respect for a warrior capable of slaying one of my creations. Shall I meet you on the battlefield, however, I will take vengeance for the Shepherd's death.*

Bryce's mouth dried out. "It's a date."

Connor Holstrom remains in the Bone Quarter. My Shepherd observed him on its rounds the night before you slew it. Unless . . . Ah, I see now. His eyes went distant. *An order was dispatched from the dark. He shall be left alone with the others until the usual amount of time has passed.*

"Who gave the order?" Ithan demanded.

It is not clear.

Bryce demanded, "Is there a way to help souls like Connor?" Whether he was ushered through the Dead Gate tomorrow or in five hundred years, it was a horrible fate.

Only the Asteri would know.

Tharion—the asshole—cut in, "Can you determine the location of a human boy named Emile Renast in Lunathion?"

Bryce stiffened. If Apollion was actually seeking Emile . . . had they just dragged another Prince of Hel into the hunt?

"That is not how this works," the Astronomer hissed from where he still cowered by the wall.

I do not know this name or person.

Thank the gods. And thank the gods the prince's words held no hint of awareness about what Emile was, or what Apollion might want from him.

Tharion drawled, "Know anyone who might?"

No. Those are matters of your world.

Bryce tried and failed to calm her racing heartbeat. At least Connor remained in the Bone Quarter, and they'd gotten a cease-fire.

"Kid's a thunderbird," Tharion said. "Ring any bells?"

"Tharion," Ithan warned, apparently on the same page as Bryce.

I thought the Asteri destroyed that threat long ago.

Bryce cleared her throat. "Maybe," she hedged. "Why were they a threat?"

I grow tired of these questions. I shall feast.

The room plunged into blackness.

The Astronomer whispered, "Luna guard me, your bow bright against the darkness, your arrows like silver fire shooting into Hel—"

Bryce lifted a hand wreathed in starlight, casting the room in silver. In the space where Thanatos's hologram had been, only a black pit remained.

The male mystic jerked violently, submerging and arching

upward. Red liquid splashed. The other two lay still as death. The machine began blaring and beeping, and the Astronomer halted his praying to rush to the controls. "He has snared him," the male gasped, hands shaking.

Bryce flared her light brighter as the feed began running again.

It has been a long while since a mortal fly buzzed all the way down to Hel. I will taste this one's soul, as I once sipped from them like fine wine.

Frost spread over the floor. The male mystic arched again, thin arms flailing, chest rising and falling at a rapid pace.

"Cut him loose!" Bryce barked.

Please, the mystic begged.

How sad and lonely and desperate you are. You taste of rainwater.

Please, please.

A little more. Just a taste.

The Astronomer began typing. Alarms wailed.

"What's happening?" Tharion shouted. Down below, the ice crept over the other two mystics in their tubs.

The prince continued, *You have gone too deep. I think I shall keep you.*

The male thrashed, sending waves of red water cascading into the void below.

"Turn off the machines," Ithan ordered.

"I cannot—not without the proper extraction. His mind might shatter."

Bryce protested, "He's fucked if you don't."

The Prince of the Ravine said, *I do not care for my brothers' agenda. I do not heed their rules and restraints and illusions of civilization. I shall taste all of you like this—you and your masters—once the door between our worlds is again open. Starting with you, Starborn.*

Ice exploded across the walls, crusting over the submerged mystics. The machines groaned, planets flickering, and then—

Every firstlight and piece of tech went out. Even Bryce's starlight vanished. Bryce swore. "What—"

The Astronomer panted in the darkness. Buttons clacked hollowly. "Their respirators—"

Bryce yanked out her phone and fumbled for its light. It was dead. Another curse from Tharion, and she knew his was, too. Every muscle and tendon in her body went taut.

Shimmering, golden light glowed from the Astronomer's upraised hand. The fire sprites trapped in his rings simmered steadily.

Apparently, it was all Ithan needed to see by as he launched himself over the rail and aimed for the male's iced-over tub. He landed gracefully, balancing his feet on either side. A pound of his fist had the ice cracking.

The male was convulsing, no doubt drowning without a functioning respirator. Ithan hauled him up, ripping the mask from his face. A long feeding tube followed. The male gagged and spasmed, but Ithan propped him over the rim, lest he slide back under.

Leaping with that athletic grace, Ithan reached the tub in the middle, freeing the mystic within. Then on to the female in the third.

The Astronomer was shrieking, but it seemed Ithan barely heard the words. The three mystics shook, soft cries trembling from their blue mouths. Bryce shook with them, and Tharion put a hand on her back.

Something groaned below, and the lights sputtered back on. Metal whined. The floor began to rise, pulling toward the tubs again. The sun fixture descended from the ceiling as the Astronomer hobbled down the walkway, cursing.

"You had no right to pull them out, *no right*—"

"They would have drowned!" Bryce launched into motion, storming after the male. Tharion stalked a step behind her.

The female stirred as the slate floor locked into place around the tubs. On reed-thin arms, she raised up her chest, blinking blearily at Ithan, then the room.

"Back," the mystic wheezed, her voice broken and raspy. Unused for years. Her dark eyes filled with pleading. "*Send me back.*"

"The Prince of the Ravine was about to rip apart your friend's soul," Ithan said, kneeling before her.

"*Send me back!*" she screamed, the words barely more than a hoarse screech. "*Back!*"

Not to Hel, Bryce knew—not to the Prince of the Ravine. But into the watery, weightless existence. Ithan got to his feet, inching away.

"Get out," the Astronomer seethed, hurrying toward his mystics. "All of you."

Bryce reached the bottom of the ramp, the Astronomer's still-glowing rings blazing bright. Fury boiled in her chest. "You would have sacrificed them—"

"*BACK!*" the female screamed again. The other two mystics stirred to consciousness, moaning. Bryce reached Ithan's side and looped her arm through his, pulling him toward the doors. The wolf gaped at the mystics, the mess they'd made.

The Astronomer knelt by the female, reaching for the tubes that Ithan had ripped free. "They cannot exist in this world anymore. *Do not want* to exist in this world." He glared at her, cold fire in his pale gray eyes.

Bryce opened her mouth, but Tharion shook his head, already heading to the exit. "Sorry for the trouble," he said over a broad shoulder.

"*Send me back,*" the female whimpered to the Astronomer.

Bryce tried to hustle Ithan along, but the wolf gazed at the female, at the old male. His muscles tensed, like he might very well throw the Astronomer off the girl and haul her away.

"Soon," the old male promised, stroking the young woman's wet hair. "You'll be drifting again soon, my lamb." Each of his rings glimmered, projecting rays around the mystic's head like a corona.

Bryce stopped tugging on Ithan's arm. Stopped moving as she saw the pleading little hands pushing against the glass orbs on the Astronomer's fingers.

Do something. Be something.

But what could she do? What authority did she have to free

the sprites? What power could she wield beyond blinding him and snatching the rings off his fingers? She'd make it a block before the Aux or 33rd were called in, and then she'd have a fucking mess on her hands. And if Hunt was the one called to apprehend her . . . She knew he'd back her in an instant, but he also answered to the law. She couldn't make him choose. Not to mention that they couldn't afford the scrutiny right now. In so many ways.

So Bryce turned, hating herself, towing Ithan along. He didn't fight her this time. The Astronomer was still murmuring to his charges when Ithan shut the heavy doors behind them.

The street seemed unchanged in the light summer rain that had started. Tharion's face was haunted. "You were right," he admitted. "It was a bad idea."

Bryce opened and closed her fingers into fists. "You're a fucking asshole, you know that?"

Tharion threw her a mocking grin. "You're in the gray with us, Legs. Don't get boring now that you've got a fancy crown."

A low growl slipped from her throat. "I always wondered why the River Queen made you her Captain of Intelligence. Now I know."

"What does that mean?" Tharion advanced a step, towering over her.

Like Hel would she back down. "It means that you pretend to be Mr. Charming, but you're just a ruthless backstabber who will do anything to achieve his ends."

His face hardened. Became someone she didn't know. Became the sort of mer that people wisely stayed away from. "Try having your family at the mercy of the River Queen and then come cry to me about morals." His voice had dropped dangerously low.

"My family is at the mercy of *all* Vanir," she snapped. Starlight flared around her, and people down the alley paused. Turned their way. She didn't care. But she kept her voice whisper-soft as she hissed, "We're done working with you. Go find someone else to drag into your shit."

She turned to Ithan for backup, but the wolf had gone pale as he gazed toward a brick wall across the alley. Bryce followed his stare and went still. She'd seen the male before them on the news and in photos, but never in the flesh. She immediately wished she still had the distance of a digital screen between them. Her starlight guttered and went out.

Mordoc smiled, a slash of white in the shadows. "Causing trouble so early in the day?"

40

Nothing of Danika showed in Mordoc's craggy face. Not one shade or curve or angle.

Only—there. The way the wolf captain pushed off the wall and approached. She'd seen Danika make that movement with the same power and grace.

Ithan and Tharion fell into place beside her. Allies again, if only for this.

"What do you want, Mordy?" Tharion drawled, again that irreverent, charming mer.

But the wolf only sneered at Bryce. "Curious, for a little princess to visit a place like this."

Bryce admired her nails, grateful her hands weren't shaking. "I needed some questions answered. I'm getting married, after all. I want to know if there are any blemishes on my future husband's pristine reputation."

A harsh laugh with too many teeth. "I was warned you had a mouth on you."

Bryce blew him a kiss. "Happy not to disappoint my fans."

Ithan cut in, snarling softly, "We're going."

"The disgraced pup," Mordoc said, his chuckle like gravel. "Sabine said she'd thrown you out. Looks like you landed right with the trash, eh? Or is that from lurking in so many alleys lately? Care to explain that?"

Bryce sighed as Ithan bristled and said, "I don't know what you're talking about."

Before Mordoc could reply, Tharion said with that winning smile, "Unless you have some sort of imperial directive to interrogate us, we're done here."

The wolf grinned back at him. "I ran a mer male like you to shore once. Drove him into a cove with a net and learned what happens to mer when they're kept a few feet above the water for a day. What they'll do to reach one drop so they don't lose their fins forever. What they'll give up."

A muscle ticked in Tharion's jaw.

Bryce said, "Awesome story, dude."

She looped arms with Tharion, then Ithan, and hauled them down the alley with her. She might be pissed as fuck at the former, but she'd take the mer any day over Mordoc. They'd always be allies against people like him.

Danika's father . . . She started shaking when they turned the block's corner, leaving Mordoc in the shadows of the alley. She could only pray the Astronomer was as discreet as rumor claimed. Even in the face of one of the empire's worst interrogators.

They walked in silence back into the bustling heart of the Old Square, most of the tourists too busy snapping photos of the various decorations in honor of Celestina and Ephraim to notice them. A block away from the Heart Gate, Bryce halted, turning to Tharion. He looked at her with a frank, cool assessment. Here was the male who'd ruthlessly ripped apart his sister's murderer. The male who . . .

Who had jumped right into Fury's helicopter to come help during the attack last spring.

"Aw, Legs," Tharion said, reading her softening features. He reached out a hand to toy with the ends of her hair. "You're too nice to me."

She quirked her mouth to the side. Ithan remained a few steps away, and made himself busy scrolling through his phone. She said to Tharion, "I'm still mad at you."

Tharion grinned crookedly. "But you also still love me?"

She huffed a laugh. "We didn't get answers about Emile." Only more questions. "Are you going back there?"

"No." Tharion shuddered. She believed him.

"Let me know if you come up with any ideas about where the kid might be hiding."

He tugged on her hair. "I thought we weren't working together anymore."

"You're on probation. You can thank your abs for that."

He took her face in his hands, squeezing her cheeks as he pressed a chaste kiss to her brow. "I'll send you some photos later. Don't show Athalar."

Bryce shoved him. "Send me an otter and we'll be even." She might not approve or agree with Tharion's methods, might not entirely trust him, but they had far more dangerous enemies at their backs. Sticking together was the only choice.

"Done." Tharion flicked her nose with a long finger. He nodded at Ithan. "Holstrom." Then he sauntered down the street, presumably back to the Istros to check in with his queen.

Alone with Ithan on the sun-baked sidewalk, Bryce asked the wolf, "Where are you going now? Back to Ruhn's?"

Ithan's face was shadowed. Bleak. "I guess. You going to search for Emile?"

She pulled a postcard from her purse. Ithan's eyes brightened with recognition at her old tradition. "I'm actually sending this off to my mom." She studied her once-friend as he again turned solemn. "You all right?"

He shrugged. "I got my answers, didn't I?"

"Yeah, but . . ." She rubbed at her forehead, skin sticky with the remnants of sweat from her dance class hours ago. Years ago, it seemed.

"I mean, it all sounds fine, doesn't it? Connor's in the Bone Quarter, and with a don't-touch order, so . . ."

But she could tell, from the way he paced a step, that this

didn't sit well. She squeezed his shoulder. "We'll find something. Some way to help him." And everyone else trapped in the eternal slaughterhouse.

It might have been the worst lie she'd ever told, because as Ithan left, he looked like he actually believed her.

"Two weeks isn't that long," Isaiah consoled Hunt from across the glass table in the 33rd's private cafeteria in the Comitium. They sat at the table reserved exclusively for the triarii, next to the wall-to-ceiling windows overlooking the city.

Normally, Hunt didn't bother with the cafeteria, but Isaiah had invited him for an early lunch, and he'd needed to talk. He'd barely sat down when he burst out with his recap of his conversation with Celestina.

Hunt bit into his turkey-and-Brie sandwich. "I know it's not long," he said around the food, "but . . ." He swallowed, turning pleading eyes to his friend. "Bryce and I decided not to wait until Winter Solstice."

Isaiah burst out laughing, the sound rich and velvety. A few soldiers turned their way, then quickly resumed eating their meals. It might have bothered Hunt any other day, but today . . . "I'm glad you find my blue balls amusing," he hissed at his friend.

Isaiah laughed again, handsome as Hel in his suit. Given how many meetings he attended with Celestina—and now Ephraim—it was a miracle from Urd that his friend had found the time today to grab lunch with him. "I never thought I'd see the day when the Umbra Mortis came crying to me about a relatively light punishment because it interferes with his sex life."

Hunt drained his water. Isaiah had a point there. Of all the punishments he'd ever been given, this was the mildest.

Isaiah sobered, voice quieting. "So what happened last night? Everything okay?"

"It's fine now. Sabine came to the apartment looking for Ithan Holstrom. Bryce got spooked. I arrived in time to convince Sabine not to start shit."

"Ah," Isaiah said. Then asked, "And Baxian?"

"He took it upon himself as my so-called partner to provide backup. However unwanted."

Isaiah snorted. "Points for trying?"

Hunt chuckled. "Sure."

Isaiah dug into his own food, and for a moment, Hunt's chest strained with the effort of keeping every truth inside. Isaiah had been with him throughout the Fallen's rebellion. He'd have valuable insight into this shit with Ophion. Even if his advice was to stay the fuck out of it.

"What's wrong?" Isaiah asked.

Hunt shook his head. His friend was too good at reading him. "Nothing." He scrambled for another truth. "It's weird to think that two weeks without Bryce is a punishment. If I so much as blinked at Sandriel the wrong way, she pulled out my feathers one by one."

Isaiah shivered. "I remember." His friend had been the one to bandage his ravaged wings again and again, after all.

"You like working for her? Celestina, I mean?"

Isaiah didn't hesitate. "Yes. A great deal."

Hunt blew out a long breath. He couldn't tell Isaiah. Or Naomi. Because if they knew, even if they agreed to keep the shit with the rebels secret and stay out of it . . . they'd be killed, too. As it was, they might be tortured a little, but it'd become clear they knew nothing. And they might stand a chance.

"You know you can talk to me about anything, right?" Isaiah asked. Kindness shone in his dark eyes. "Even stuff with Celestina. I know it's weird with the rankings between us, but . . . I'm the middle man between the 33rd and her. Whatever you need, I'm here."

He'd never really deserved a friend like Isaiah. "It's not weird with the rankings between us," he said. "You're the leader of the 33rd. I'm happy to work for you."

Isaiah studied him. "I'm not the one who wields lightning. Or the one with a fancy nickname."

Hunt waved off the weight of what his friend said. "Trust me, I'd rather you be in charge."

Isaiah nodded, but before he could reply, silence rippled through the cafeteria. Hunt looked up on instinct, past all the wings and armor. "Great," he muttered. Baxian, tray in hand, walked toward them. Ignored the soldiers who gave him a wide berth or fell silent entirely as he passed by.

"Play nice," Isaiah murmured back, and made a show of beckoning the male over. Not for Baxian's sake, but for that of all the people witnessing this. The soldiers who needed to be presented with a unified leadership.

Hunt finished off his sandwich just as the shape-shifting angel slid into a chair beside Isaiah. Hunt met his stare. "How'd it go with the Hind?" He knew the male could read between his words. *Did you talk, you fucker?*

"Fine. I know how to handle Lidia." *No, I didn't, you asshole.*

Hunt found Isaiah watching them with raised brows. "What happened with Lidia?"

The Helhound answered smoothly, "She wanted to grill me about why I left last night. I didn't feel like explaining to her that I'm Athalar's understudy, and where he goes, I go."

Isaiah's eyes darkened. "You weren't so antagonistic toward her under Sandriel's rule."

Baxian dug into his platter of lamb kofta and herbed rice. "You've been in Lunathion for a while, Tiberian. Things changed after you left."

Isaiah asked, "Like what?"

Baxian gazed toward the glistening city roasting in the midday heat. "Things."

"I think that means we should mind our own fucking business," Hunt said.

Isaiah snickered. "He's taking a page out of your book, Hunt."

Hunt grinned. "You're confusing me with Naomi. I at least will tell you straight up to mind your own business. She'll only imply it."

"With a death glare."

"And maybe a gun set on the table for emphasis."

They laughed, but Hunt sobered as he noted Baxian observing their volley, something like envy on his face. Isaiah noted it, too, because he said to the Helhound, "You can laugh, you know. We do that kind of stuff here."

Baxian's mouth pressed into a thin line. "You've had more than ten years here. Forgive me if it takes a while to forget the rules of Sandriel's territory."

"As long as you don't forget that you're in Lunathion now." The threat of violence rumbled in Isaiah's every word, belying the impeccable suit he wore. "That scar Athalar put on your neck will be nothing compared to what I do to you if you hurt anyone in this city."

Baxian's eyes glittered. "Just because you weren't interesting enough to merit being part of Sandriel's triarii, don't take it out on me with bullshit threats."

Isaiah's teeth gleamed. "I had no interest in getting that close to a monster."

Hunt tried not to gape. He'd seen Isaiah lay down the law countless times. His friend wouldn't have gotten to where he was without the ability to draw a line and hold it. But it was rare these days to see that vicious warrior shine through. Soldiers were turning their way.

So Hunt cut in, "Sandriel would be thrilled to know that she's still pitting us against each other all these years later."

Isaiah blinked, as if surprised he'd tried to intervene. Baxian watched him cautiously.

Hunt took another deep breath. "Fuck, that sounded preachy." Baxian let out a snort, and the tension dissolved.

Isaiah threw Hunt a grateful smile, then rose. "I need to head out. I have a meeting with the Aux Heads."

Hunt winked. "Give Ruhn my love."

Isaiah laughed. "Will do."

With that, his friend strode off toward the trash receptacles. Angels lifted their heads as he passed; a few waved at him. The white-winged angel waved back, pausing at various tables to swap pleasantries. Isaiah's smile was wide—genuine.

Baxian said quietly, "Your friend was born for this."

Hunt grunted his agreement.

"No interest in leading again?" Baxian asked.

"Too much paperwork."

Baxian smirked. "Sure."

"What's that supposed to mean?"

"You led once, and it went poorly. I don't blame you for not step-ping up again."

Hunt clenched his jaw but said nothing else as he finished off his meal. Baxian was right on his heels as they strode to empty their plates and dump their trays. Hunt didn't dare turn to tell the Hel-hound to back the fuck off. Not with so many eyes on them. He could hear soldiers whispering as they passed.

Hunt didn't bother to engage as Isaiah had. He couldn't bear to look at the other soldiers. The people who'd be summoned to fight against Ophion.

People he'd kill if they threatened Bryce. Fuck, if he replicated what he'd done at the Bone Quarter, he could fry them all in a sec-ond. No wonder the Asteri had considered the thunderbirds a threat—that kind of power was nothing short of lethal.

If Ophion got their hands on Emile . . . Yeah, that was a weapon to kill for.

Hunt reached the elevator bay beyond the doors. The five angels clustered there quickly aimed for the stairs.

"Tough crowd, huh?" Baxian said behind him as Hunt stepped into the elevator. To his displeasure, the Helhound got in with him. The space was wide enough to accommodate many beings with wings, but Hunt kept his tucked in tight.

"You get used to it," Hunt said, pushing the button for the triarii's barracks. He might as well assess his room to see what weapons he had left. What clothes he needed to send for. Knowing Bryce, she'd send him a pair of her underwear along with them.

"I thought you were Mr. Popular," Baxian said, watching the rising numbers above them.

"What the fuck would make you think that?" Hunt didn't wait for a reply as the elevator doors opened and he stepped into the quiet hall.

"You seem friendly with everyone outside this place."

Hunt arched a brow, pausing outside his old room. "What does that mean?"

Baxian leaned against his own door, across from Hunt's. "I mean, I hear you party with Prince Ruhn and his friends, you have a girlfriend, you seem to be on good terms with the wolves . . . But not the angels?"

"Isaiah and I are on good terms." And Naomi.

"I mean the others. The grunts. No friends there?"

"Why the Hel do you care?"

Baxian casually pulled in his wings. "I want to know what's in it for me. What kind of life I can look forward to."

"It's what you make of it," Hunt said, opening his door. Stale, dusty air greeted him. A far cry from the scent of coffee that filled Bryce's apartment.

He peered over a shoulder to find Baxian surveying his room. The emptiness of it. A peek into Baxian's room across the hall revealed an identically empty space.

Hunt said, "That's what my life was like, you know."

"Like what?"

"Vacant."

"Then what happened?"

"Bryce happened."

Baxian smiled slightly. Sadly. Was it—was it possible the Helhound was *lonely*?

"I'm sorry you have to stay apart from her for so long." Baxian sounded like he meant it.

Hunt's eyes narrowed. "Did Celestina punish you?"

"No. She said it was your bad influence, so it was your punishment to take."

Hunt chuckled. "Fair enough." He stepped into his room and made quick work of assessing his weapons and clothes.

When he reemerged into the hallway, Baxian was sitting at the pine desk in his room, going over what appeared to be reports. Every instinct screamed at Hunt to walk out and not say anything, to Hel with this male who'd been more of an enemy than a friend over the years, but . . .

Hunt braced a hand on the doorjamb. "What do they have you working on?"

"Progress reports for the new recruits. Seeing if there are any promising angels to pull up through the ranks."

"Are there?"

"No."

"Angels like us don't come around that often, I guess."

"Apparently not." Baxian went back to his paperwork.

The quiet of the hall, the room, settled on Hunt. Pushed on him. He could hear Bryce saying, *Come on. Try. It won't kill you.* She bossed him around even in his imagination. So Hunt said, "We've still got twenty minutes left of lunch. Want to play some *SUL Sunball?*"

Baxian turned. "What's that?"

"You really don't know anything about modern life, huh?" Baxian gave him a flat look. "SUL," Hunt explained. "Sunball United League. It's their video game. You can play from the point of view of any player, on any team. It's fun."

"I've never played a video game."

"Oh, I know." Hunt grinned.

Baxian surveyed him, and Hunt waited for the rejection, but Baxian said, "Sure. Why not?"

Hunt headed for the common room. "You might regret that in a few."

Indeed, ten minutes later, Baxian was cursing, fingers stumbling over the controller clenched in his hands. Hunt nimbly dodged Baxian's avatar.

"Pathetic," Hunt said. "Even worse than I thought."

Baxian growled, "This is so stupid."

"And yet you keep playing," Hunt countered.

Baxian laughed. "Yeah. I guess I do."

Hunt scored. "It's not even satisfying playing against a novice."

"Give me a day and I'll wipe the floor with you, Athalar." Baxian's thumbs flicked the controls. His avatar ran right into a goalpost and rebounded, sprawling onto the grass.

Hunt snickered. "Maybe two days."

Baxian glanced at him sidelong. "Maybe." They kept playing,

and when the clock above the door read twelve, Baxian asked, "Time to work?"

Hunt listened to the quiet dorm around them. "I won't tell if you don't."

"Didn't I prove this morning that I'm the soul of discretion?"

"I'm still waiting for your motive, you know."

"I'm not here to make an enemy of you."

"I don't get why."

Baxian ran into the goalpost again, his avatar ricocheting onto the field. "Life's too short to hold grudges."

"That's not a good enough reason."

"It's the only one you'll get." Baxian managed to gain control of the ball for all of ten seconds before Hunt took it from him. He cursed. "Solas. You can't go easy on me?"

Hunt let the subject drop. The gods knew he'd had plenty he hadn't wanted to talk about when he first arrived here. And the gods knew he'd done plenty of terrible shit on Sandriel's orders, too. Maybe he should take his own advice from earlier. Maybe it was time to stop letting Sandriel's specter haunt them.

So Hunt smiled roughly. "Where would the fun be in that?"

"This sucks," Bryce muttered into the phone that night, splayed out on her bed. "You really aren't allowed to leave?"

"Only for official 33rd work," Hunt said. "I forgot how crappy the barracks are."

"Your sad little room with its lack of posters."

His laugh rumbled in her ear. "I'm going to be extra good so she'll let me go early."

"I won't have anyone to watch *Beach House Hookup* with. You sure I can't come over there?"

"Not with Pollux and the Hind here. No fucking way."

Bryce toyed with the hem of her T-shirt. "Even if we stayed in your room?"

"Oh?" His voice dropped low, getting the gist of what she was suggesting. "To do what?"

She smiled to herself. She needed this, after the insanity of today. She hadn't even dared tell Hunt what had happened with the mystics, not over the phone, where anyone could listen in. But the next time she saw him face-to-face, she'd tell him about everything.

Including the otter Tharion had sent to her two hours ago, as promised, with a note that said, *Forgive me yet, Legs? Shall we kiss and make up?* She'd laughed—but sent a note back with the screamingly cute otter: *Start with kissing my ass and we'll see how it goes.* Another otter had arrived before ten with a note that said, *With pleasure.*

Now Bryce said to Hunt, mood significantly lifted despite the news, "Things."

His wings rustled in the background. "What kind of things?"

Her toes curled. "Kissing. And . . . more."

"Hmm. Explain what *more* means."

She bit her lip. "Licking."

His laugh was like dark velvet. "Where would you like me to lick you, Quinlan?"

They were doing this, then. Her blood heated. Syrinx must have scented what was up, and took it upon himself to leap off the bed and head into the living room.

Bryce swallowed. "My breasts."

"Mmm. They are delicious."

She slickened between her thighs, and rubbed her legs together, nestling further into the pillows. "You like to taste them?"

"I like to taste all of you." She could barely get a breath down. "I like to taste you, and touch you, and when I can leave these barracks again, I'm going to fly in a straight line to wherever you are so I can thoroughly fuck you."

She whispered, "Are you touching yourself?"

A hiss. "Yes."

She whimpered, rubbing her thighs together again.

"Are you?"

Her hand drifted beneath the waistband of her shorts. "Now I am."

He groaned. "Are you wet?"

"Soaking."

"Gods," he begged. "Tell me what you're doing."

She flushed. She'd never done anything like this, but if she and Hunt couldn't be together . . . she'd take what she could get.

She slid her finger into her sex, moaning softly. "I'm . . . I have a finger inside myself."

"Fuck."

"I wish it was yours."

"Fuck."

Was he close, then? "I'm adding another," she said as she did, and her hips bucked off the bed. "It still doesn't feel as good as you."

His breathing turned sharp. "Open up that nightstand, sweetheart."

Frantic, she grabbed a toy from the drawer. She shimmied off her shorts and her drenched underwear and positioned the vibrator at her entrance. "You're bigger," she said, the phone discarded beside her.

Another primal sound of pure need. "Yeah?"

She pushed the vibrator in, her back arching. "Oh gods," she panted.

"When we fuck for the first time, Quinlan, do you want it hard or do you want a long, smooth ride?"

"Hard," she managed to say.

"You want to be on top?"

Release gathered through her body like a wave about to break. "I want my turn on top, and then I want you behind me, fucking me like an animal."

"Fuck!" he shouted, and she heard flesh slapping against flesh in the background.

"I want you to ride me so hard I'm screaming," she went on, driving the vibrator in and out. Gods, she was going to explode—

"Anything you want. Anything you want, Bryce, I'll give it to you—"

That did it. Not the words, but her name on his tongue.

Bryce moaned, deep in her throat, her pants coming quick and wild, her core clenching around the vibrator as she pumped it in and out, working through her climax.

Hunt groaned again, cursing, and then he fell silent. Only their breathing filled the phone. Bryce lay limp against the bed.

"I want you so badly," he ground out.

She smiled. "Good."

"Good?"

"Yeah. Because I'm going to fuck your brains out when you come home to me."

He laughed softly, full of sensual promise. "Likewise, Quinlan."

Tharion sat atop the smooth rock half-submerged by a bend in the middle of the Istros and waited for his queen to respond to his report. But the River Queen, lounging on a bed of river weeds like a pool float, kept her eyes closed against the morning sun, as if she hadn't heard a single word of what he'd been explaining about the Bone Quarter and the Under-King.

A minute passed, then another. Tharion asked at last, "Is it true?"

Her dark hair floated beyond her raft of weeds, writhing over the surface like sea snakes. "Does it disturb you, to have your soul sent back into the light from whence it came?"

He didn't need to be Captain of Intelligence to know she was avoiding his question. Tharion said, "It disturbs me that we're told we rest in peace and contentment, yet we're basically cattle, waiting for the slaughter."

"And yet you have no problem with your body being sent back to feed the earth and its creatures. Why is the soul any different?"

Tharion crossed his arms. "Did you know?"

She cracked open a warning eye. But she propped her head on a fist. "Perhaps there is something beyond the secondlight. Some-place our souls go even after that."

For a glimmer, he could see the world she seemed to want: a world without the Asteri, where the River Queen ruled the waters, and the current system of soul-recycling remained, because hey, it kept the lights on. Literally.

Only those in power would change. Perhaps that was all she wanted Emile for: a weapon to ensure her survival and triumph in any upcoming conflict between Ophion and the Asteri.

But Tharion said, "The search for Emile Renast continues. I thought I had an easier way to find him, but it was a dead end." Tracking Pippa's string of bodies would have to remain his only path toward the kid.

"Report when you have anything." She didn't look back at him as the river weeds fell apart beneath her and she gently sank into the blue water.

Then she was gone, dissolving into the Istros itself and floating away as glowing blue plankton—like a trail of stars soared through the river.

Was a rebellion worth fighting, if it only put other power-hungry leaders in charge? For the innocents, yes, but . . . Tharion couldn't help but wonder if there was a better way to fight this war. Better people to lead it.

41

A week later, Ruhn stood beside Cormac and smiled as Bryce sweated in the Aux facility's private training ring.

"You're not concentrating," Cormac scolded.

"My head literally *aches*."

"Focus on that piece of paper and simply step there."

"You say that like it's easy."

"It is."

Ruhn wished this were the first time he'd heard this conversation. Witnessed this song-and-dance number between Bryce and Cormac as the prince tried to teach her to teleport. But in the week since all that major shit had gone down, this had been the main highlight. Their enemies had been unnervingly quiet.

When Cormac wasn't attending various Fae functions, Ruhn knew his cousin had been hunting for Emile. Ruhn had even gone with him twice, Bryce in tow, to wander the various parks of Moonwood, hoping the boy was camping out. All to no avail. Not a whisper of the kid anywhere.

Tharion had reported yesterday that he couldn't find the boy, either. From Tharion's unusually haggard face, Ruhn had wondered if the mer's queen was breathing down his neck about it. But no more bodies had been found. Either the kid was here, in hiding, or someone else had gotten him.

Bryce inhaled deeply, then shut her eyes on the exhale. "All right. Let's try this again."

Her brow bunched, and she grunted. Nothing.

Cormac snorted. "Stop straining. Let's return to summoning shadows."

Bryce held up a hand. "Can I have a hall pass, please?"

Ruhn laughed. She'd had little luck with the shadows, either. Starlight, yes. Lots and lots of starlight. But summoning darkness . . . she couldn't manage so much as a bit of shade.

If Apollion wanted an epic opponent, Ruhn was inclined to tell the Prince of the Pit that it might take a while.

"I think my magic's broken," Bryce said, bending over her knees and sighing.

Cormac frowned. "Try again." They'd had no word from anyone, even Agent Daybright, about what had happened with the shipment of ammo and the new mech-suit prototype. The news hadn't covered it, and none of Cormac's agents had heard anything.

That quiet had Cormac worried. Had Ruhn on edge, too.

Ithan had settled easily into Ruhn's house, weirdly enough. He stayed up late playing video games with Dec and Flynn, as if they'd been friends their entire lives. What the wolf did with his time while they were all at the Aux, Ruhn had no idea.

Ruhn hadn't asked him about what the Hind had said at the bar regarding Bryce, and Ithan sure as Hel hadn't mentioned it. If the wolf had a thing for his sister, it wasn't Ruhn's business. Ithan was a good housemate: cleaned up after himself, cleaned up after Flynn, and was excellent at beer pong.

Bryce sucked in a sharp breath. "I can *feel* it—like, this giant cloud of power right *there*." She ran a finger over the eight-pointed star scarred between her breasts. Starlight pulsed at her fingertip. Like an answering heartbeat. "But I can't access it."

Cormac gave her a smile Ruhn assumed he meant to be encouraging. "Try one more time, then we'll take a break."

Bryce began to grumble, but was interrupted by Ruhn's phone ringing.

"Hey, Dec."

"Hey. Bryce with you?"

"Yeah. Right here." Bryce jumped to her feet at the mention of her name. "What's up?"

Bryce leaned in to hear as Declan said, "My program finally finished analyzing all the footage of Danika at the gallery. Jesiba was right. It found something."

Bryce didn't know whether it was a good thing or not that Declan had finally concluded his search. Sitting around her new coffee table—a sad imitation of the original, but one Ithan had paid for—an hour later, she watched Declan pull up the feed.

She hadn't dared call Hunt. Not when one wrong move with Celestina could keep him away even longer.

Declan said to her, Ruhn, and Cormac, "It took so long because once it compiled all the footage I had to go through all the shots with Danika." He smirked at Bryce. "Did you *ever* work?"

Bryce scowled. "Only on Tuesdays."

Declan snorted, and Bryce braced herself for the sight of Danika, of Lehabah, of the old gallery library as he clicked play. Her heart twanged at the familiar corn-silk blond hair with its vibrant dyed streaks, braided down Danika's back. At the black leather jacket with the words *Through love, all is possible* stamped on it. Had the flash drive already been sewn into it?

"This is from two months before she died," Declan said quietly.

There was Bryce, in a tight green dress and four-inch heels, talking with Lehabah about *Fangs and Bangs.*

Danika was lounging at the desk, boots propped up, hands tucked behind her head, smirking at Bryce's regular argument that porn with a plot did not equal award-winning television. Lehabah was countering that sex didn't cheapen a show, and her voice—

Ruhn's hand slid across Bryce's back, squeezing her shoulder.

On the screen, Bryce motioned to Lehabah to follow her upstairs, and the two of them left. She had no memory of this day, this moment. She'd probably gone to grab something and hadn't wanted to leave Lehabah alone with Danika, who was prone to riling the sprite into the hottest of blue flames.

A second passed, then two, then three—

Danika moved. Swift and focused, like she'd been using the time lounging at the table to pinpoint where she needed to go. She headed straight to a lower shelf and pulled off a book. Glancing at the stairs, she flipped it open and began snapping photos with her phone of the inside. Page after page after page.

Then it was back on the shelf. Danika returned to her chair and lounged, pretending to be half-asleep when Bryce and Lehabah returned, still arguing about the stupid show.

Bryce leaned in toward the screen. "What book was that?"

"I clarified the image." Declan pulled up a frame of the book right before Danika's black-sparkle-painted nails grabbed it: *Wolves Through Time: Lineage of the Shifters.*

"You can see her finger going to some text here," Declan went on, clicking to another frame. Danika had opened the book, skimming over the text with a finger. Tapping something right near the top of the page.

As if it were exactly what she'd been looking for.

Bryce, Declan, and Ruhn studied the still frame of the book in Danika's hands. Cormac had departed upon getting a call that he would not—or could not—explain. The book was leather-bound and old, but the title indicated that it had been written after the arrival of the Vanir.

"It's not a published book," Declan said. "Or at least it predates our current publishing system. But as far as I can tell, no other libraries on Midgard have it. I think it must be a manuscript of some sort, perhaps a vanity project that got bound."

"Any chance there's a copy at the Fae Archives?" Ruhn asked her.

"Maybe," Bryce said, "but Jesiba might still have this one at the storage unit." She pulled out her phone and dialed quickly.

Jesiba answered on the second ring. "Yes, Quinlan?"

"You had a book at the old gallery. *Wolves Through Time*. What is it?"

A pause. Ruhn and Dec picked up every word with their Fae hearing.

"So you did look into the footage. Curious, wasn't it?"

"Just . . . please tell me. What is it?"

"A history of wolf genealogy."

"Why did you have it?"

"I like knowing the history of my enemies."

"Danika wasn't your enemy."

"Who said I was talking about Danika?"

"Sabine, then."

A soft laugh. "You are so very young."

"I need that book."

"I don't take demands, even from Starborn Princesses. I've given you enough." Jesiba hung up.

"That was helpful," Declan groused.

But twenty minutes later, Marrin buzzed to say that a messenger had dropped off a package from Miss Roga.

"I'm disturbed and impressed," Ruhn murmured as Bryce opened the nondescript package and pulled the leather tome free. "We owe Jesiba a drink."

"Danika snapped photos of the beginning pages," Declan said, now reviewing the footage on his phone. "Maybe only the first three, actually. But I think the page she tapped was the third."

Bryce opened the book, the hair on her arms rising. "It's a family tree. Going back . . . Does this go all the way back to when the Northern Rift opened?" Fifteen thousand years ago.

Ruhn peered over her shoulder as Bryce skimmed. "Gunthar Fendyr is the latest—and last—name here."

Bryce swallowed. "He was the Prime's father." She flipped to the third page, the one Danika had been most interested in.

"Niklaus Fendyr and Faris Hvellen. The first of the Fendyr line." She chewed on her lip. "I've never heard of them."

Declan tapped away on the computer. "Nothing comes up."

"Try their kids," Bryce suggested, giving him the names.

"Nothing."

They went through generation after generation until Dec said, "There. Katra Fendyr. From here . . . Yeah, there's an actual historical record and mentions of Katra from there on out. Starting five thousand years ago." He ran a finger up the tree, along the generations, counting silently. "But nothing on any of these Fendyrs before her."

Ruhn asked, "Why would Danika feel the need to be secretive about this, though?"

Bryce examined the first two names on the list, the ones Danika had tapped like she'd discovered something, and countered, "Why were their names lost to history?"

"Would Ithan know?" Declan asked.

"No idea." Bryce chewed on a hangnail. "I need to talk to the Prime."

Ruhn protested. "Need I remind you that Sabine tried to kill you last week?"

Bryce grimaced. "Then I'll need you two to make sure she's not at home."

Bryce didn't dare inform Hunt over the phone what she was doing, why she was doing it. She'd risked enough by calling Jesiba. But not having Hunt at her side as she slipped past the guards at the Den's gate felt like a phantom limb. Like she might find him in the shadows beside her at any moment, assessing a threat.

Declan was currently arguing with the Den guards about some imagined slight. And at the Aux headquarters . . . Well, if they were lucky, Sabine had already arrived to meet with Ruhn about an "urgent matter."

Bryce found the Prime without much trouble, sitting in the shade of a towering oak in the park that occupied the central space of the Den. A gaggle of pups played at his feet. No other wolves in the area.

She darted from the shadows of the building's columns to the wooden chair, a few curious pups perking up at the sight of her. Her chest squeezed at their fuzzy little ears and waggly tails, but she kept her gaze on the ancient male.

"Prime," she said, kneeling on his far side, hidden from the view of the guards still arguing with Dec at the gates. "A moment of your time, please."

He cracked open age-clouded eyes. "Bryce Quinlan." He tapped his bony chest. "A wolf."

Ruhn had told her what the Prime had said during the attack. She'd tried not to think of how much it meant to her. "Your bloodline—the Fendyr lineage. Can you think of why Danika might have been interested in it?"

He hesitated, then motioned to the pups and they scattered. She figured she had about five minutes until one of them blabbed to an adult that a red-haired Fae female was here.

The Prime's chair groaned as he faced her. "Danika enjoyed history."

"Is it forbidden to know the names of your first ancestors?"

"No. But they are largely forgotten."

"Do Faris Hvellen and Niklaus Fendyr ring any bells? Did Danika ever ask about them?"

He fell silent, seeming to scan his memory. "Once. She claimed she had a paper for school. I never learned what became of it."

Bryce blew out a breath. There hadn't been any papers about wolf genealogy in the secret coffee table stash. "All right. Thank you." This had been a waste of her time. She got to her feet, scanning the park, the gates beyond. She could make a run for it now.

The Prime halted her with a dry, leathery hand on her own. Squeezed. "You did not ask why we have forgotten their names."

Bryce started. "You know?"

A shallow nod. "It is one scrap of lore most of my people were careful to ensure never made it into the history books. But word of mouth kept it alive."

Brush crackled. Shit. She had to go.

The Prime said, "We did unspeakable things during the First

Wars. We yielded our true nature. Lost sight of it, then lost it forever. Became what we are now. We say we are free wolves, yet we have the collar of the Asteri around our necks. Their leashes are long, and we let them tame us. Now we do not know how to get back to what we were, what we might have been. That was what my grandfather told me. What I told Sabine, though she did not care to listen. What I told Danika, who . . ." His hand shook. "I think she might have led us back, you know. To what we were before we arrived here and became the Asteri's creatures inside and out."

Bryce's stomach churned. "Is that what Danika wanted?" It wouldn't have surprised her.

"I don't know. Danika trusted no one." He squeezed her hand again. "Except you."

A snarl rattled the earth, and Bryce found a massive female wolf approaching, fangs exposed. But Bryce said to the Prime, "You should talk to Sabine about Ithan."

He blinked. "What about Ithan?"

Did he not know? Bryce backed away a step, not letting the advancing female out of her sight. "She kicked him out, and nearly killed him. He's living with my brother now."

Those fogged eyes cleared for a moment. Sharp—and angry.

The female lunged, and Bryce ran, sprinting through the park to the gates. Past the guards still arguing with Declan, who winked at them and then burst into a run beside her, into the bustle of Moonwood. More questions dragged along behind her with each block they sprinted.

She had every intention of collapsing on her couch and processing things for a long while, but when they got back, Cormac was waiting outside her apartment.

Bloody and dirty, and—"What happened to you?" Declan said, as Bryce let them into the apartment, flinging the door open wide.

Cormac helped himself to a bag of ice from the freezer, pressing it to his cheek as he sat at the kitchen table. "Mordoc nearly snared me at an intel pickup. Six other dreadwolves were with him."

"Did Mordoc scent you?" Bryce asked, scanning the battered prince. If he had, if Cormac was tracked back here . . .

"No—I kept downwind, even for his nose. And if any of his soldiers did, they're not a problem anymore." Was the blood on his hands not his own, then? Bryce tried not to sniff it.

"What'd the intel say?" Declan asked, going to the window to scan the street beyond, presumably for anyone who might have followed Cormac.

"The hit on the Spine was successful," Cormac said, face hard beneath the blood and bruises. "The Asteri's new mech-suit prototype was attained, along with an invaluable amount of ammunition."

"Good," Declan said.

Cormac sighed. "They're shipping the prototype here."

Bryce started. "To Lunathion?"

"To the Coronal Islands." Close enough—two hours away by boat. "To a base on Ydra."

"Shit," Dec said. "They're going to start something here, aren't they?"

"Yes, likely with Pippa and her Lightfall squadron at the head."

"Don't they know she's nuts?" Bryce asked.

"She's successful with her ops. That's all that matters."

"What about Emile?" Bryce pushed. "Was she successful with him?"

"No. He's still out there. The agent said the hunt for him continues."

"So what do we do?" Dec asked Cormac. "Go to Ydra and convince them *not* to let Pippa have access to all those weapons?"

"Yes." Cormac nodded to Bryce. "Send an otter to Captain Ketos. And I believe we're also going to need Hunt Athalar's expertise."

42

Bryce was just walking down the shining hallway to Celestina's office when her phone rang.

Juniper. Bryce sent her to audiomail. A message came through instead. *Call back now.*

Dread burning like acid through her, Bryce dialed, praying nothing had happened with Fury—

Juniper answered on the first ring. "How *dare* you?"

Bryce halted. "What?"

"How *dare* you call Gorgyn?"

"I . . ." Bryce swallowed. "What happened?"

"I'm principal, that's what happened!"

"And that's a bad thing?" She was due to meet with Celestina in one minute. She couldn't be late.

"It's a bad thing because *everyone* knows that *Princess Bryce Danaan* put in a call and threatened to pull the Autumn King's donations if CCB didn't *recognize my talent*!"

"So what?" Bryce hissed. "Isn't this the only bit of good that being a princess entails?"

"No! It's the *opposite*!" Juniper was absolutely screaming with rage. Bryce started shaking. "I have worked my entire life for this, Bryce! My *entire life*! And you step in and take that accomplishment away from me! Make yourself—not me, not my talent—into the reason I got this promotion, the reason I made history! *You*, not me. Not me sticking it out, fighting through it, but my Fae Princess friend, who couldn't leave well enough alone!"

The clock chimed in the hallway. Bryce had to go. Had to talk to the Archangel.

"Look, I'm about to go into a meeting," she said as evenly as she could, though she thought she might puke. "But I'll call you back right after, I promise. I'm so sorry if—"

"Don't bother," June snapped.

"Juniper—"

The faun hung up.

Bryce focused on her breathing. She needed one of Kyrah's dance classes. Immediately. Needed to sweat and breathe and majorly unload and analyze the tornado wreaking havoc inside her. But this meeting . . . She squared her shoulders, putting away the fight, the fact that she'd fucked everything up, had been so arrogant and stupid and—

She knocked on the door to Celestina's office. "Enter," came the sweet female voice.

Bryce smiled at the Governor as if she hadn't destroyed a friendship moments ago. "Your Grace," Bryce said, inclining her head.

"Your Highness," Celestina answered, and Bryce reined in a wince. It was how she'd gotten this meeting, too. She'd asked the Archangel to meet not as Bryce Quinlan, but as a Princess of the Fae. It was an invitation even an Archangel had to agree to.

She wondered how it'd come back to haunt her.

"Just for this meeting," Bryce said, sitting down. "I've come to make a formal request."

"For the return of Hunt Athalar, I take it." A tired, sad sort of light gleamed in the Governor's eyes.

"A temporary return," Bryce said, and leaned back in her chair. "I know he bailed on you at your party. If I'd been aware he was doing that, I would never have asked him to assist me that night. So—totally feel free to punish him. You have my blessing."

It was a lie, but Celestina's lips twitched upward. "How long do you want him for?"

"A night." To go to the Coronal Islands and back before Pippa Spetsos and her cabal could get there. To convince whoever Command sent *not* to give Spetsos free rein to unleash those weapons on Valbara. "We figured we'd take the arrow train instead of driving the eight hours each way. I promised my mother I'd bring him home with me. If he doesn't come, there will be Hel to pay." Another lie.

But the Governor smiled fully at that. "Your mother is . . . a fearsome creature?"

"Oh yeah. And if Hunt's not there, every bad thing she thinks about him will be confirmed."

"She doesn't like him?"

"She doesn't like *any* male. No one is good enough for me, according to her. You have no idea how hard dating was when I was younger."

"Try being an Archangel in a small community," Celestina said, and smiled genuinely.

Bryce grinned. "Everyone was intimidated?"

"Some ran screaming."

Bryce laughed, and marveled that she did so. Hated that she had to lie to this warm, kind female.

Celestina hooked a curl behind her ear. "So a great deal is riding on Athalar's visit."

"Yeah. It's not like I need her permission to be with him, but it . . . It'd be nice to have her approval."

"I'm sure it would." Celestina's smile turned sad.

Bryce knew it wasn't her place, but she asked, "How are you and Ephraim getting along?"

A shadow flickered across Celestina's face, confirmation that she wasn't contented. "He's a thorough lover."

"But?"

She said deliberately, warning sharpening her voice, "But he has been my friend for many years. I find that I am now getting to know him in a whole new way."

Celestina deserved so much more than that. Bryce sighed. "I know you're, like . . . an Archangel, but if you ever need some girl talk . . . I'm here."

The last Governor she'd spoken to had tried to kill her. And she'd put a bullet in his head. This was a nice change.

Celestina smiled again, that warmth—and relief—returning to her features. "I'd like that very much, Your Highness."

"Bryce in this instance."

"Bryce." Her eyes twinkled. "Take Athalar home. And keep him there."

Bryce's brows rose. "Permanently?"

"Not at your parents' house. I mean take him with you to your family, and then he may live with you once more. He's been moping around so much that he's bringing down morale. I'll send him your way tomorrow morning. Let him stew one more night before I tell him at dawn."

Bryce beamed. "Thank you. I mean it, thank you *so* much."

But the Governor waved a hand. "You're doing me a favor, trust me."

Bryce made a call on her way to her next stop.

Fury answered right before it went to audiomail. "You fucked up, Bryce."

Bryce cringed. "I know. I'm really sorry."

"I get why you did it. I really do. But she is *devastated.*"

Bryce stepped off the elevator and swallowed the lump in her throat. "Please tell her I'm so sorry. I'm so freaking sorry. I was trying to help, and I didn't think."

"I know," Fury said. "But I'm not getting in the middle of this."

"You're her girlfriend."

"Exactly. And you're her friend. And mine. I'm not playing the messenger. Give her some time, then try to talk it out."

Bryce sagged against a worn wall. "Okay. How long?"

"A few weeks."

"That's ages!"

"Devastated. Remember?"

Bryce rubbed at her chest, the unlit scar there. "Fuck."

"Start thinking of big ways to apologize," Fury said. Then added, "You ever figure that thing out with Danika or the kid?"

"Not yet. Want to help?" It was as much as she'd risk saying on the phone.

"No. I'm not getting in the middle of that shit, either."

"Why?"

"I have a lot of good things going on right now," Fury said. "June is one of them. I'm not jeopardizing any of it. Or her safety."

"But—"

"Big apology. Don't forget." Fury hung up.

Bryce swallowed her nausea, her self-disgust and hatred. She walked down the quiet hall to a familiar door, then knocked. She was rewarded by the sight of Hunt opening the door, shirtless and wearing his backward sunball hat. Gleaming with sweat. He must have just returned from the gym.

He jolted. "What are you—"

She cut him off with a kiss, throwing her arms around his neck.

He laughed, but his hands encircled her waist, lifting her high enough that she wrapped her legs around his middle. He slowed the kiss, his tongue driving deep, exploring her mouth. "Hi," he said against her lips, and kissed her again.

"I wanted to tell you the news," she said, kissing his jaw, his neck. He'd already hardened against her. She went molten.

"Yeah?" His hands roamed over her ass, kneading and stroking.

"Tomorrow morning," she said, kissing his mouth again and again. "You're outta here."

He dropped her. Not entirely, but swiftly enough that her feet hit the ground with a thud. "What?"

She ran her hands down his sweat-slick, muscled chest, then toyed with the band of his pants. Ran a finger up the length of him jutting out with impressive demand. "We're going on a little vacation. So do a good job of seeming like you're still brooding tonight."

"What?" he repeated.

She kissed his pec, running her mouth over the taut brown nipple. He groaned softly, his hand sliding into her hair. "Pack a swimsuit," she murmured.

A male voice chuckled behind them, and Bryce went rigid, whirling to find Pollux, arm slung around a beautiful female's shoulders, walking by. "Is he paying you by the hour?" the Hammer asked.

The female—the *Hind*—snickered, but said nothing as they approached. Solas, she was . . . beautiful and terrible. She'd tortured countless people. Killed them—probably including Sofie Renast. If Cormac saw her, if he got this close, would he take the risk and try to end her?

The Hind's amber eyes gleamed as they met Bryce's, as if she knew every thought in her head. The deer shifter smiled in invitation.

But the Hind and the Hammer continued on, for all the world looking like a normal couple from behind. Bryce couldn't help herself as she said to Pollux's back, "You really need to come up with some new material, Pollux."

He glared over a shoulder, white wings tucking in tight. But Bryce smiled sweetly and he, mercifully, kept walking, his wretched lover with him.

Bryce found Hunt smiling beside her, and it lightened any guilt about Juniper, any frustration with Fury, any fear and dread at being so close to the Hind, even as she yearned to tell him everything. Hunt tugged her hand, making to pull her into his room, but she planted her feet. "Tomorrow morning," she said hoarsely, her very bones aching with need. "Meet me at home."

She'd tell him everything then. All the insane shit that had gone on since they'd last seen each other.

Hunt nodded, hearing what she didn't say. He tugged her again, and she went to him, tilting back her head to receive his kiss. His hand slipped down the front of her leggings. He growled against her mouth as his fingers found the slickness waiting for him.

She whimpered as he rubbed over her clit in a luxurious, taunting circle. "I'll see you at dawn, Quinlan."

With a nip at her bottom lip, Hunt stepped back into his room. And as he shut the door, he licked his fingers clean.

* * *

Ithan blinked at the phone ringing in his hand.

Prime.

Every Valbaran wolf had the Prime's number in their phones. But Ithan had never once called it, and the Prime of Wolves had never once called him. It couldn't be good.

He halted midway down the alley, neon signs casting pools of color on the cobblestones beneath his boots. Sucking in a breath, he answered, "Hello?"

"Ithan Holstrom."

He bowed his head, even though the Prime couldn't see him. "Yes, Prime."

The withered old voice was heavy with age. "I was informed today that you are no longer residing at the Den."

"On Sabine's order, yes."

"Why?"

Ithan swallowed. He didn't dare say why. Sabine would deny it anyway. Sabine was the male's daughter.

"Tell me why." A hint of the Alpha the Prime had been during his younger years came through in his voice. This male had made the Fendyr family a force to be reckoned with in Valbara.

"Perhaps ask your daughter."

"I want to hear it from you, pup."

Ithan's throat worked. "It was punishment for disobeying her orders during the attack this spring and helping the humans in Asphodel Meadows. And punishment for praising Bryce Quinlan's actions during the attack in a magazine article."

"I see." Apparently, that was all the Prime needed. "What do you plan to do now?"

Ithan straightened. "I'm, ah, living with Prince Ruhn Danaan and his friends. Helping them out in the Fae division of the Aux." Helping with a rebellion.

"Is that where you wish to be?"

"Is there an alternative?"

A drawn-out, too-tense pause. "I would make you Alpha of your own pack. You have it in you—I've sensed it. For too long, you have suppressed it so others might lead."

The ground beneath Ithan seemed to rock. "I . . . What about Sabine?" Ithan's head swirled.

"I shall deal with my daughter, if this is what you choose."

Ithan had no fucking idea who'd even be in his pack. He'd locked himself out so thoroughly from old friends and family after Connor's death that he'd only bothered to associate with Amelie's pack. Perry was the closest thing he had to a friend at the Den, and she'd never leave her sister's side. Ithan swallowed hard. "I'm honored, but . . . I need to think about this."

"You have been through a great deal, boy. Take the time you need to decide, but know the offer stands. I would not lose another wolf of worth—especially to the Fae." Before Ithan could say goodbye, the old wolf hung up. Stunned and reeling, Ithan leaned against one of the brick buildings in the alley. Alpha.

But . . . an Alpha in Sabine's shadow, once the Prime was gone. Sabine would be *his* Prime. Amelie would reign as her Prime Apparent. And then Prime, when Sabine herself was gone.

He had little interest in serving either of them. But . . . was it a betrayal of the wolves, of his brother's legacy, to leave the Valbaran packs to Sabine's cruelty?

He brushed his hair back from his face. It was longer than it'd ever been while playing sunball. He couldn't tell if he liked it or not.

Fuck, he couldn't tell if he liked *himself* or not.

Straightening, Ithan pushed off the wall and finished his walk, arriving at his destination. The towering doors to the Astronomer's building of horrors were shut. Ithan pulled the crescent moon door chime once.

No answer.

He pulled it a second time, then pressed an ear to one of the metal doors, listening for any hint of life. Not even a footstep, though he could make out the hum of the machines beyond. He knocked twice, and then pressed his shoulder into the door. It opened with a groan, nothing but darkness beyond. Ithan slipped in, silently shutting the heavy door behind him. "Hello?"

Nothing. He aimed for the faint, pale glow of the three tanks in the center of the cavernous space. He'd never seen anything so strange and unsettling—the three beings who'd been sold into this life. Existence. This sure as fuck wasn't a life.

Not that he'd know. He hadn't had one in two years.

Their visit last week had lingered like an unhealed wound.

He might have walked out of here condemning everything he'd seen, but he'd still given the Astronomer his money. Kept this place running.

He knew it bugged Bryce, but she'd been swept back into the shit with Danika, and as a princess, her hands were tied as far as a public scene. Especially when she walked such a dangerous line these days—any additional bit of scrutiny might be her downfall.

But no one gave a fuck about him. No matter what the Prime had said.

"Hello?" he called again, the word echoing into the dimness.

"He's not here," rasped a hoarse female voice.

Ithan whirled, reaching for his gun as he scanned the darkness. His wolf-sight pierced through it, allowing him to make out the speaker's location. His hand dropped from his hip at the sight of her.

Long chestnut-brown hair draped over her too-thin, pale limbs, her body clad in that white shift that all three mystics wore. Her dark eyes were still—like she was only half-there. A face that might have been pretty, if it weren't so gaunt. So haunted.

Ithan swallowed, slowly approaching where she huddled against the wall, bony knees clutched to her chest. "I wanted to see your . . . boss."

He couldn't say *owner*, even though that's what the old creep was. In the gloom, he could make out a worktable beyond the mystic sitting on the floor, with a small box atop it. Light filtered out from the box, and he had a good idea of what was kept inside it. Who were kept inside, trapped in those four rings, which were apparently valuable enough that the old male had left them behind, rather than risk them in the city at large.

The mystic's rasping voice sounded as if she hadn't spoken in ages. "He put the other two back in, but didn't have the part he needed to fix my machine. He's at the Meat Market, meeting with the Viper Queen."

Ithan sniffed, trying to get a read on her. All he could get from this distance was salt. Like it had brined the scent right out of her. "You know when he'll be back?"

She only stared at him, like she was still hooked up to the machine beyond them. "You were the one who freed me." Solas, she sat with such . . . Vanir stillness. He'd never realized how much *he* moved until he stood before her. And he'd considered himself capable of a wolf's utter stillness.

"Yeah, sorry." But the word stuck—*freed*. She'd been pleading to go back. He'd assumed she'd meant into the between-place where the mystics roamed, but . . . What if she'd meant this world—back to her life before? The family who had sold her into this?

Not his problem, not his issue to solve. But he still asked, "Are you okay?" She didn't look okay. She sat the way he had in his dorm bathroom the night he'd learned that Connor was dead.

The mystic only said, "He will be back soon."

"Then I'll wait for him."

"He will not be pleased."

Ithan offered her a reassuring smile. "I can pay, don't worry."

"You've caused him a great deal of inconvenience. He'll kick you out."

Ithan took a step closer. "Can you help me, then?"

"I can't do anything unless I'm in the tank. And I don't know how to use the machines to ask the others."

"All right."

She angled her head. "What do you want to know?"

He swallowed hard. "Was it true, what the demon prince said, about my brother being safe for now?"

She frowned, her full mouth unnaturally pale. "I could only sense the other's terror," she said, nodding toward the tanks. "Not what was said."

Ithan rubbed the back of his neck. "All right. Thanks. That's all I needed." He had to know for sure that Connor was safe. There had to be some way to help him.

She said, "You could find a necromancer. They would know the truth."

"Necromancers are few and far between, and highly regulated," Ithan said. "But thanks again. And, uh . . . good luck."

He turned back toward the doors. The mystic shifted slightly, and the movement sent a whisper of her scent toward him. Snow and embers and—

Ithan went rigid. Whirled to her. "You're a wolf. What are you doing here?"

She didn't answer.

"Your pack allowed this to happen?" Rage boiled his blood. Claws appeared at his fingertips.

"My parents had no pack," she said hoarsely. "They roamed the tundra of Nena with me and my ten siblings. My gifts became apparent when I was three. By four, I was in there." She pointed to the tank, and Ithan recoiled in horror.

A wolf family had *sold* their pup, and she'd gone into that tank—

"How long?" he asked, unable to stop his trembling anger. "How long have you been in here?"

She shook her head. "I . . . I don't know."

"When were you born? What year?"

"I don't know. I don't even remember how long it's been since I made the Drop. He had some official come here to mark it, but . . . I don't remember."

Ithan rubbed at his chest. "Solas." She appeared as young as him, but among the Vanir, that meant nothing. She could be hundreds of years old. Gods, how had she even made the Drop here? "What's your name? Your family name?"

"My parents never named me, and I never learned their names beyond Mother and Father." Her voice sharpened—a hint of temper shining through. "You should leave."

"You can't be in here."

"There's a contract that suggests otherwise."

"You are a *wolf*," he snarled. "You're kept in a fucking *cage* here." He'd go right to the Prime. Make him order the Astronomer to free this unnamed female.

"My siblings and parents are able to eat and live comfortably because I am here. That will cease when I am gone. They will again starve."

"Too fucking bad," Ithan said, but he could see it—the determination in her expression that told him he wasn't going to pry her out of here. And he could understand it, that need to give over all of herself so that her family could survive. So he amended, "My name is Ithan Holstrom. You ever want to get out of here, send word." He had no idea how, but . . . maybe he'd check in on her every few months. Come up with excuses to ask her questions.

Caution flooded her eyes, but she nodded.

It occurred to him then that she was likely sitting on the cold floor because her thin legs had atrophied from being in the tank for so long. That old piece of shit had left her here like this.

Ithan scanned the space for anything resembling a blanket and found nothing. He only had his T-shirt, and as he reached for the hem, she said, "Don't. He'll know you were here."

"Good."

She shook her head. "He's possessive. If he even thinks I've had contact with someone other than him, he'll send me down to Hel with an unimportant question." She trembled slightly. He'd done it before.

"Why?"

"Demons like to play," she whispered.

Ithan's throat closed up. "You sure you don't want to leave? I can carry you right now, and we'll figure out the other shit. The Prime will protect you."

"You know the Prime?" Her voice filled with whispered awe. "I only heard my parents speak of him, when I was young."

So they hadn't been entirely shut off from the world, then. "He'll help you. I'll help you."

Her face again became aloof. "You must go."

"Fine."

"Fine," she echoed back, with a hint of that temper again. A bit of dominance that had the wolf in him perking up.

He met her stare. Not just a bit of dominance . . . that was a glimmer of an *Alpha*'s dominance. His knees buckled slightly, his wolf instinct weighing whether to challenge or bow.

An Alpha. Here, in a tank. She would likely have been her family's heir, then. Had they known what she was, even at age four? He suppressed a growl. Had her parents sent her here *because* she'd be a threat to their rule over the family?

But Ithan shoved the questions aside. Backed toward the doors again. "You should have a name."

"Well, I don't," she shot back.

Definitely Alpha, with that tone, that glimmer of unbending backbone.

Someone the wolf in him would have liked to tangle with.

And to leave her here . . . It didn't sit right. With him, with the wolf in his heart, broken and lonely as it might have been. He had to do something. Anything. But since she clearly wasn't going to leave this place . . . Maybe there was someone else he could help.

Ithan eyed the small box on the worktable, and didn't question himself as he snatched it up. She tried and failed to rise, her weakened legs betraying her. "He will *kill* you for taking them—"

Ithan strode to the doors, the box of fire sprites trapped inside their rings in hand. "If he's got a problem with it, he can take it up with the Prime." And explain why he was holding a wolf captive in here.

Her throat bobbed, but she said nothing more.

So Ithan stalked outside, onto the jarringly normal street beyond, and shut the heavy door behind him. But despite the distance he quickly put between himself and the mystics, his thoughts circled back to her, again and again.

The wolf with no name, trapped in the dark.

"I'm requesting an aquatic team of twenty-five for tomorrow," Tharion said to his queen, hands clenched behind his back, tail fanning idly in the river current. The River Queen sat in her humanoid form among a bed of rocky coral beside her throne, weaving sea nettle, her dark blue gown drifting around her.

"No," she said simply.

Tharion blinked. "We have solid intel that this shipment is coming from Pangera, *and* that Pippa Spetsos is likely already there. You want me to capture her, to interrogate her about Emile's whereabouts, I'm going to need backup."

"And have so many witnesses mark the Blue Court's involvement?"

What is *our involvement?* Tharion didn't dare ask. *What's your stake in this beyond wanting the kid's power?*

His queen went on, "You will go, and go alone. I take it your current cadre of . . . people will be with you."

"Yes."

"That should be enough to question her, given your companions' powers."

"Even five mer agents—"

"Just you, Tharion."

He couldn't stop himself as he said, "Some people might think you were trying to kill me off, you know."

Slowly, so slowly, the River Queen turned from her weaving. He could have sworn a tremor went through the riverbed. But her voice was dangerously smooth as she said, "Then defend my honor against such slander and return alive."

He clenched his jaw, but bowed his head. "Shall I say goodbye to your daughter, then? In case it is my last chance to do so?"

Her lips curled upward. "I think you've caused her enough distress already."

The words struck true. She might be a monster in so many ways, but she was right about him in that regard. So Tharion swam into the clear blue, letting the current pound the anger from his head.

If there was a chance of attaining Emile's power, the River Queen would snatch it up.

Tharion hoped he had it in himself to stop her.

The chairs had turned into velvet couches on the dream bridge.

Ruhn slid into his, surveying the endless dark surrounding him.

He peered past the fainting couch to Day's "side." If he were to follow her that way, would he wind up in her mind? See the things she saw? Look through her eyes and know who she was, where she was? Would he be able to read every thought in her head?

He could speak into someone's mind, but to actually *enter* it, to read thoughts as his cousins in Avallen could . . . Was this how they did it? It seemed like such a gross violation. But if she invited him, if she wanted him in there, could he manage it?

Flame rippled before him, and there she was, sprawled on the couch.

"Hey," he said, sitting back in his couch.

"Any information to report?" she said by way of greeting.

"So we're doing the formal thing tonight."

She sat up straighter. "This bridge is a path for information. It's our first and greatest duty. If you're coming here for someone to flirt with, I suggest you look elsewhere."

He snorted. "You think I'm flirting with you?"

"Would you say *hey* in that manner to a male agent?"

"Probably, yeah." But he conceded, "Not with the same tone, though."

"Exactly."

"Well, you caught me. I'm ready for my punishment."

She laughed, a full, throaty sound that he'd never heard before. "I don't think you could handle the sort of punishment I dole out."

His balls tightened; he couldn't help it. "We talking . . . restraints? Flogging?"

He could have sworn he got a flash of teeth biting into a lower lip. "Neither. I don't care for any of that in bed. But what do *you* prefer?"

"It's always the lady's choice with me. I'm game for anything."

She angled her head, a waterfall of flame spilling down the side of the couch, as if she draped long, lovely hair over it. "So you're not a . . . dominant male."

"Oh, I'm dominant," he said, grinning. "I'm just not into pressuring my partners into doing anything they don't like."

She studied him at that. "You say *dominant* with such pride. Are you a wolf, then? Some sort of shifter?"

"Look who's trying to figure me out now."

"Are you?"

"No. Are *you* a wolf?"

"Do I seem like one to you?"

"No. You seem like . . ." Someone crafted of air and dreams and cold vengeance. "I'm guessing you're in Sky and Breath."

She went still. Had he struck true? "Why do you say that?"

"You remind me of the wind." He tried to explain. "Powerful and able to cool or freeze with half a thought, shaping the world itself though no one can see you. Only your impact on things." He added, "It seems lonely, now that I'm saying it."

"It is," she said, and he was stunned that she'd admitted it. "But thank you for the kind words."

"Were they kind?"

"They were accurate. You see me. It's more than I can say about anyone else."

For a moment, they stared at each other. He was rewarded by a shifting of her flame, revealing large eyes that swept upward at the edges—crafted of fire, but he could still make out their shape. The clarity in them before her flame veiled her once more. He cleared his throat. "I guess I should tell you that the rebels were successful with their hit on the Spine. They're bringing over the Asteri's mech prototype to the Coronal Islands tomorrow night."

She straightened. "Why?"

"I don't know. I was told by—my informant. A rebel contingent will be there to receive the shipment. Where it goes from there, I don't know." Cormac wanted Athalar to examine the Asteri's prototype—see how it differed from the humans' that the angel had faced so often in battle.

Because Athalar was the only one among them who'd faced off against a mech-suit. Who'd apparently spent time in Pangera taking them apart and putting them back together again. Cormac, as he'd been fighting alongside the human rebels, had never battled one—and he wanted an outside opinion on whether replicating the Asteri's model would be beneficial.

And because Athalar was going, Bryce was going. And because Bryce was going, Ruhn was going. And Tharion would join them, as the River Queen had ordered him to.

Flynn, Dec, and Ithan would remain—too many people going would raise suspicions. But they'd been pissed to learn of it. *You're benching poor Holstrom*, Flynn had complained. Dec had added, *Do you know what that does to a male's ego?* Ithan had only grunted his agreement, but hadn't argued, a distant expression on his face. Like the wolf's mind was elsewhere.

"Who's going to be there?"

He angled his head. "We got word that Pippa Spetsos and her Lightfall squadron will also be present. We have some questions for her about . . . a missing person."

She straightened. "Is Spetsos being given command of the Valbaran front?"

"I don't know. But we're hoping we can convince whoever is there from Command otherwise. We suspect that she and Lightfall have left a trail of bodies all around the countryside."

Day was quiet for a moment, then asked, "Do you know the name of the ship that's carrying the prototype?"

"No."

"What island?"

"Why are you grilling me on this?"

"I want to make sure it's not a trap."

He grinned. "Because you'd miss me if I died?"

"Because of the information they'd squeeze from you before you did."

"Cold, Day. Real cold."

She laughed softly. "It's the only way to survive."

It was. "We're going to Ydra. That's all I know."

She nodded, like the name meant something to her. "If they catch you, running is your best option. Don't fight."

"I'm not programmed that way."

"Then reprogram yourself."

He crossed his arms. "I don't think I—"

Day hissed, bending over. She twitched, almost convulsing.

"Day?"

She sucked in a breath, then was gone.

"Day!" His voice echoed across the void.

He didn't think. Launching over the fainting couch, he sprinted down her end of the bridge, into the dark and night, flinging himself after her—

Ruhn slammed into a wall of black adamant. Time slowed, bringing with it flashes of sensation. No images, all . . . *touch.*

Bones grinding in her left wrist from where it was being squeezed tight enough to hurt; it was the pain that had awoken her, pulled her away from the bridge—

Willing herself to yield, give over, become his, to find some way to savor this. Teeth scraping at her nipple, clamping down—

Ruhn collided with the ground, the sensations vanishing. He surged to his feet, pressing a palm against the black wall.

Nothing. No echo to tell him what was happening.

Well, he *knew* what was happening. He'd gotten the sense of very rough sex, and though he had the distinct feeling that it was consensual, it wasn't . . . meaningful. Whoever slept at her side had woken her with it.

The impenetrable black loomed before him. The wall of her mind.

He had no idea why he waited. Why he stayed. Had no idea how much time passed until a flame once more emerged from that wall.

Her fire had banked enough that he could make out long legs walking toward him. Halting upon finding him kneeling. Then she dropped to her knees as well, flame again swallowing her whole.

"Are you all right?" he asked.

"Yes." The word was a hiss of embers being extinguished.

"What was that?"

"You've never had sex before?"

He straightened at the slicing question. "Are you all right?" he asked again.

"I said I was."

"You weren't—"

"No. He asked, albeit a bit suddenly, and I said yes."

Ruhn's insides twisted at the utter iciness. "You don't seem to have enjoyed it."

"Is it your business whether I find release or not?"

"Did you?"

"Excuse me?"

"Did you orgasm?"

"That's absolutely none of your business."

"You're right."

Again, silence fell, but they remained kneeling there, face-to-face. She said after a tense moment, "I hate him. No one knows it, but I do. He disgusts me."

"Then why sleep with him?"

"Because I . . ." A long sigh. "It's complicated."

"Indulge me."

"Do you only sleep with people you like?"

"Yes."

"You've never fucked someone you hate?"

He considered, even as the sound of her saying the word *fucked* did something to his cock. "All right. Maybe once. But it was an ex." A Fae female he'd dated decades ago, who he hadn't cared to remember until now.

"Then you can think of this like that."

"So he's—"

"I don't want to talk about him."

Ruhn blew out a breath. "I wanted to make sure you're okay. You scared the shit out of me."

"Why?"

"One moment you were here, the next you were gone. It seemed like you were in pain."

"Don't be a fool and get attached enough to worry."

"I'd be a monster not to care whether another person is hurt."

"There's no place for that in this war. The sooner you realize it, the less pain you'll feel."

"So we're back to the ice-queen routine."

She drew up. "Routine?"

"Where's the wild and crazy female I was talking about bondage with earlier?"

She laughed. He liked the sound—it was low and throaty and predatory. Fuck, he liked that sound a lot. "You are such a typical Valbaran male."

"I told you: Come visit me in Lunathion. I'll show you a good time, Day."

"So eager to meet me."

"I like the sound of your voice. I want to know the face behind it."

"That's not going to happen. But thank you." She added after a moment, "I like the sound of your voice, too."

"Yeah?"

"Yeah." She chuckled. "You're trouble."

"Is it cliché if I say that *Trouble* is my middle name?"

"Oh yes. Very."

"What would *your* middle name be?" he teased.

Her flames pulled back, revealing those eyes of pure fire. "Retribution."

He grinned wickedly. "Badass."

She laughed again, and his cock hardened at the sound. "Goodbye, Night."

"Where are you going?"

"To sleep. Properly."

"Isn't your body resting?"

"Yes, but my mind is not."

He didn't know why, but he gestured to her fainting couch. "Then sit back. Relax."

"You want me to stay?"

"Honestly? Yeah. I do."

"Why?"

"Because I feel calm around you. There's so much shit going down, and I . . . I like being here. With you."

"I don't think most females would be flattered to be called 'calming' by a handsome male."

"Who says I'm handsome?"

"You talk like someone who's well aware of his good looks."

"Like an arrogant asshole, then."

"Your words, not mine."

Day rose to her feet, striding to the fainting couch. Her flames rippled as she lay upon it, and Ruhn jumped onto his own couch.

"All I need is a TV and a beer and I'm set," he said.

She snickered, curling on her side. "As I said: typical Valbaran male."

Ruhn closed his eyes, bathing in the timbre of her voice. "You gotta work on those compliments, Day."

Another chuckle, sleepier this time. "I'll add it to my to-do list, Night."

43

Hunt breathed in the cool air off the turquoise sea, admiring the pristine water, so clear that he could see the corals and rocks and the fish darting among them.

Down in the quay, hidden in a massive cavern, the cargo ship was still being unloaded. The sea cave, tucked into an isolated, arid part of Ydra, one of the more remote Coronal Islands, ran at least a mile inland. It had been selected because the water flowing within it ran so deep—deep enough for massive cargo ships to slide into its stone-hewn dock and unload their contraband.

Hunt stood in the shadows just within the mouth of the cave, focusing on the bright, open water ahead and not the reek of the oil on the ancient mech-suits currently helping to unload the ship into the fleet of awaiting vehicles: laundry trucks, food trucks, moving trucks . . . anything that might reasonably inch along one of the island's steeply curving roads or board one of the auto-ferries shuttling vehicles between the hundred or so islands of this archipelago without raising too much suspicion.

Cormac had teleported everyone to Ydra an hour ago. Hunt had nearly puked during the five-minute-long trip with several stops—when they'd finally arrived, he'd sat his ass on the damp concrete, head between his knees. Cormac had gone back, again and again, until all of them were here.

And then the poor fuck had to go head-to-head with whoever was in charge from Command, to convince them Pippa Spetsos shouldn't be anywhere near this shit.

Cormac had been unsteady on his feet, pale from the teleporting, but had left them with the promise to return soon. Bryce, Tharion, and Ruhn all sat on the ground—apparently not trusting their legs yet, either. Hunt hadn't failed to notice that Ruhn kept reaching over his shoulder—as if to seek the reassuring presence of the Starsword. But the prince had left the blade back in Lunathion, not wanting to risk losing it here if all Hel broke loose. It seemed the male was missing his security blanket as their stomachs and minds settled.

"I shouldn't have eaten breakfast," Tharion was saying, a hand on his abs. He wore only tight black aquatic leggings, equipped along the thighs with holsters for knives. No shoes or shirt. If he needed to shift into his mer form, he'd said upon arriving at Bryce's place this morning, he didn't want to lose much.

Tharion's timing had been unfortunate—he'd arrived at the apartment right after Hunt. Bryce was already propped up on the counter, gripping Hunt's shoulders while he lazily licked up her neck. Tharion's knock on the door was . . . unwelcome.

That would all have to wait. But his mate had gotten him out of the barracks—he'd repay her generously tonight.

Bryce now patted Tharion's bare shoulder. "I'm weirdly satisfied that a mer can get airsick, considering how many of us suffer from seasickness."

"*He's* still green, too," Tharion said, pointing to Hunt, who grinned weakly.

But Tharion went back to idly observing the cave around them. Perhaps *too* idly. Hunt knew Tharion's main objective: get Pippa to talk about Emile. Whether that interrogation would be friendly was up to the mer captain.

Ruhn murmured, "Incoming."

They all turned toward the cargo ship to see Cormac striding over to them. Still pale and drained—Hunt had no idea how he'd get them all out of here when this was over.

But Hunt tensed at the fury simmering off Cormac. "What's up?" Hunt said, eyeing the cave interior beyond Cormac. Tharion's attention drifted that way as well, his long body easing into a crouch, ready to spring into action.

Cormac shook his head and said, "Pippa's already got her claws in them. They're all eating out of her hand. The weapons are hers, and she's now in charge of the Valbaran front."

Tharion frowned, but scanned the space behind the Avallen Prince. "Anything about Emile or Sofie?"

"No. She didn't say a word about them, and I couldn't risk asking. I don't want her to know we're on the hunt as well." Cormac paced. "A confrontation about Emile in front of the others would likely lead to bloodshed. We can only play along."

"Any chance of isolating her?" Tharion pressed.

Cormac shook his head. "No. Believe me, she'll be on her guard as much as we are. You want to drag her off for questioning, you're going to have a battle on your hands."

Tharion swore, and Bryce patted his knee in what Hunt could only guess was an attempt at consolation.

Cormac faced Hunt. "Athalar, you're up." He jerked his head to the massive ship. "They're unloading the new prototype right now."

In silence, they followed the prince, Hunt keeping close to Bryce. The rebels—all in black, many with hats or masks on—stared at them as they passed. None of them smiled. One man grumbled, "Vanir pricks."

Tharion blew him a kiss.

Ruhn growled.

"Play nice," Bryce hissed at her brother, pinching his side through his black T-shirt. Ruhn batted her away with a tattooed hand.

"Real mature," Hunt muttered as they halted at the foot of the loading platform. Ruhn subtly flipped him off. Bryce pinched Hunt's side, too.

But Tharion let out a low whistle as four rusty mech-suits emerged from the ship's hold, each carrying the corner of a massive box.

It looked like a metal sarcophagus, carved with the insignia of the Asteri: seven stars around *SPQM*. The humans piloting the old-model mech-suits didn't so much as glance to the side as they carried the box down the ramp, the ground thudding beneath the machines' massive feet.

"Those suits are for battle, not manual labor," Tharion murmured.

"Twelve-gunners. They're the strongest of the human models." Hunt inclined his head to the twin double guns at the shoulder, the guns on each of the forearms. "Six visible guns, six hidden ones—and one of those is a cannon."

Bryce grimaced. "How many of these suits do the humans have?"

"A few hundred," Cormac answered. "The Asteri have bombed enough of our factories that these suits are all old, though. The imperial prototype that they're carrying could give us new technology, if we can study it."

Bryce murmured, "And no one is worried about giving this stuff over to trigger-happy Pippa?"

"No," Cormac replied gravely. "Not one of them."

"But they're cool with us examining the suit?" Bryce asked.

"I told them Athalar would have some insight into how they're constructed."

Hunt clicked his tongue. "No pressure, huh?" He suppressed the memory of Sandriel's face, her cruel amusement as she watched what he'd done to the suits on her orders.

The suits and their pilots reached the concrete quay, and someone barked an order that dispersed the various rebels working the docks until only a unit of twelve rebels—all humans—lingered behind Hunt and the others.

Hunt liked that about as much as the fact that they were here at all, on a fucking rebel base. Officially aiding Ophion. He kept his breathing slow and steady.

The unit of rebels marched past them, climbing into the vessel, and the mech-pilots stomped off, leaving the sarcophagus behind. A heartbeat later, a human female, brown-haired and freckled, emerged from the shadows beside the boat.

From the way Cormac tensed, Hunt knew who it was. He noted that she wore the uniform of the Lightfall squadron. All the rebels who'd gone by had borne armbands with the sinking sun emblem.

Hunt put his hand in easy reach of the gun at his thigh, lightning writhing in his veins. Bryce angled her body, already eyeing up the best shot. Tharion drifted a few feet to the left, positioning Pippa between himself and the water. As if he'd tackle her into it.

But Pippa moved casually to the other side of the sarcophagus as she said to Cormac, "The code to that box is seven-three-four-two-five."

Her voice was smooth and fancy—like she was some rich Pangeran kid playing at being a rebel. She said to Hunt, "We're waiting with bated breath for your analysis, Umbra Mortis." It was practically an order.

Hunt stared at her from under lowered brows. He knew he was recognizable. But the way she said his name definitely carried a threat. Pippa shifted her attention to Cormac. "I wondered when you'd try to turn them against me."

Hunt and Bryce drew close, guns at their fingertips now. Ruhn kept a step back, guarding their rear. And Tharion . . .

The mer had silently shifted positions again, putting himself within a few easy bounds of tackling Pippa.

"I haven't said anything to them about you yet," Cormac said with impressive iciness.

"Oh? Then why were you in such a rush to get here? I can only assume it was for one of two reasons: to convince them to put *you* in charge of the Valbaran front, presumably by slandering me, or to try to capture me so I can tell you everything I know about Emile Renast."

"Who says both can't be true?" Cormac countered.

Pippa grunted. "You needn't have bothered with capturing me. I would have worked with you to find him. But you wanted the glory for yourself."

"We're talking about a child's life," Cormac snarled. "You only want him as a weapon."

"And you don't?" Pippa sneered at them all. "It must make it easier for you if you pretend you're better than I am."

Tharion said, deadly soft, "We're not the ones torturing people to death for intel on the kid."

She frowned. "Is that what you think I've been up to? Those gruesome murders?"

"We found human scents *and* a piece of one of your soldiers on the kid's trail," Tharion growled, a hand drifting to his knives.

Her lips curved into a cold smile. "You arrogant, narrow-minded Vanir. Always thinking the worst of us humans." She shook her head in mock sympathy. "You're too coiled up in your own snake's nest to see the truth. Or to see who among you has a forked tongue."

True to form, Bryce stuck out her tongue at the soldier. Pippa only sneered.

"Enough, Pippa." Cormac punched the code into the small box at the foot of the sarcophagus. Bryce's eyes had narrowed, though. She held Pippa's gaze—and a chill went down Hunt's spine at the pure dominance in Bryce's face.

Pippa drawled, "It is of no concern now. anyway. The boy has been deemed a waste of resources. Especially now that we have . . . better weapons to wield."

As if in answer, the lid popped open with a hiss, and Hunt threw an arm in front of Bryce as it slid aside. Smoke from dry ice billowed out, and Cormac cleared it away with a brush of his hand.

Pippa said, "Well, Umbra Mortis? I await your insights."

"I'd mind how you speak to him, Pippa," Cormac warned her, voice sharp with authority.

Pippa faced Bryce, though. "And you're Cormac's bride, yes?" No kindness, no warmth filled her tone.

Bryce flashed the female a smile. "You can have the job if you want it so badly."

Pippa bristled, but Cormac gestured Hunt forward as the last of the smoke cleared.

Hunt surveyed the suit in the box and swore. "The Asteri designed this?" he asked. Pippa nodded, lips pursed tight. "For Vanir to pilot?" he pushed.

Another nod. Pippa said, "I don't see how it can possess more power than ours, though. It's smaller than our models." The quicksilver-bright suit would stand about seven feet high.

"You know what you're looking at?" Ruhn asked Hunt, scratching his head.

"It's like a robot," Bryce said, peering into the box.

"It's not," Hunt said. He rocked back on his heels, mind racing. "I heard rumors about this kind of thing being made, but I always thought it was a long shot."

"What is it?" Pippa demanded.

"Impatient, are we?" Hunt mocked. But he tapped a finger on the suit. "This metal has the same makeup as gorsian stones." He nodded to Bryce. "Like what they did with the synth—they were seeking ways to weaponize the gorsian stones."

"We already have them in our bullets," Pippa said smugly.

He ground out, "I know you do." He had a scar on his stomach from one.

Perhaps that threat alone was what had kept Tharion from making his move. The mer had a clear shot toward Pippa. But could he run faster than she could draw her gun? Hunt and Bryce could help him, but . . . Hunt really didn't want to outright attack an Ophion leader. Let Tharion and the River Queen deal with that shit.

Pippa shifted a few inches out of Tharion's range once more.

Hunt went on, "This metal . . . The Asteri have been researching a way to make the gorsian ore absorb magic, not suppress it."

Ruhn said, "Seems like ordinary titanium to me."

"Look closer," Hunt said. "There are slight purple veins in it. That's the gorsian stone. I'd know it anywhere."

"So what can it do?" Bryce asked.

"If I'm right," Hunt said hoarsely, "it can draw the firstlight from the ground. From all the pipes of it crisscrossing the land. These suits would draw up the firstlight and turn it into weapons. Brimstone missiles, made right there on the spot. The suit would never run out of ammo, never run out of battery life. Simply find the underground power lines, and it'd be charged up and ready to kill. That's why they're smaller—because they don't need all the extra tech and room for the arsenal that the human suits require. A Vanir warrior could climb inside and essentially wear it like an exoskeleton—like armor."

Silence.

Pippa said, voice full of awe, "Do you know what this would mean for the cause?"

Bryce said dryly, "It means a Hel of a lot more people would die."

"Not if it's in our hands," Pippa said. That light in her eyes— Hunt had seen it before, in the face of Philip Briggs.

Pippa went on, more to herself than to any of them, "We'd at last have a source of magic to unleash on them. Make them understand how we suffer." She let out a delighted laugh.

Cormac stiffened. So did Tharion.

But Hunt said, "This is a prototype. There might be some kinks to work out."

"We have excellent engineers," Pippa said firmly.

Hunt pushed, "This is a death machine."

"And what is a gun?" Pippa snapped. "Or a sword?" She sneered at the lightning zapping at his fingertips. "What is your magic, angel, but an instrument of death?" Her eyes blazed again. "This suit is simply a variation on a theme."

Ruhn said to Hunt, "So what's your take on it? Can Ophion use it?"

"No one should fucking use it," Hunt growled. "On either side." He said to Cormac, "And if you're smart, you'll tell Command to track down the scientists behind this and destroy them and their plans. The bloodshed on both sides will become monstrous if you're all using these things."

"It's already monstrous," Cormac said quietly. "I just want it ended."

But Pippa said, "The Vanir deserve everything that's coming to them."

Bryce grinned. "So do you, terrorizing that poor boy and then deciding he's not worth it."

"Emile?" Pippa laughed. "He's not the helpless baby you think he is. He found allies to protect him. By all means, go retrieve him.

I doubt he'll help the Vanir win this war—not now that we have this technology in our hands. Thunderbirds are nothing compared to this." She ran a hand over the rim of the box.

Tharion cut in, "Where's the kid?"

Pippa smirked. "Somewhere even you, mer, would fear to tread. I'm content to leave him there, and so is Command. The boy is no longer our priority."

Bryce seethed, "You're deluded if you think this suit is anything but a disaster for everyone."

Pippa crossed her arms. "I don't see how you have any right to judge. While you're busy getting your nails painted, Princess, good people are fighting and dying in this war."

Bryce wiggled her nails at the rebel. "If I'm going to associate with losers like you, I might as well look good doing it."

Hunt shook his head, cutting off Pippa before she could retort. "We're talking machines that can make *brimstone missiles* within seconds and unleash them at short range." His lightning now sizzled at his hands.

"Yes," Pippa said, eyes still lit with predatory bloodlust. "No Vanir will stand a chance." She lifted her attention to the ship above them, and Hunt followed her focus in time to see the crew appearing at the rails. Backs to them.

Five mer, two shifter-types. None in an Ophion uniform. Rebel sympathizers, then, who'd likely volunteered their boat and services to the cause. They raised their hands.

"What the fuck are you doing?" Hunt growled, just as Pippa lifted her arm in a signal to the human Lightfall squadron standing atop the ship. Herding the Vanir crew to the rails.

Guns cracked.

Blood sprayed, and Hunt flung out a wing, shading Bryce from the mist of red.

The Vanir crumpled, and Ruhn and Cormac began shouting, but Hunt watched, frozen, as the Lightfall squadron on deck approached the fallen crew, pumping their heads full of bullets.

"First round is always a gorsian bullet," Pippa said mildly in the terrible silence that followed as the Lightfall soldiers drew long knives and began severing heads from necks. "To get the Vanir down. The rest are lead. The beheading makes it permanent."

"Are you fucking *insane?*" Hunt burst out, just as Tharion spat, "You're a murdering psycho."

But Cormac snarled at Pippa, getting in her face, blocking Tharion's direct path. "I was told the crew would be unharmed. They helped us out of their belief in the cause."

She said flatly, "They're Vanir."

"And that's an excuse for this?" Ruhn shouted. Blood gleamed on his neck, his cheek, from where it had sprayed down. "They're Vanir who are *helping you.*"

Pippa only shrugged again. "This is war. We can't risk them telling the Asteri where we are. The order to put the crew down came from Command. I am their instrument."

"You and Command are going to lead these people to ruin." Shadows gathered at Ruhn's shoulders. "And like Hel am I going to help you do it."

Pippa only snickered. "Such lofty morals." A phone buzzed in her pocket, and she checked the screen before saying, "I'm due to report to Command. Care to join me, Cormac?" She smiled slightly. "I'm sure they'd *love* to hear your concerns."

Cormac only glared, and Pippa let out a sharp whistle—an order. With that, she sauntered down the quay toward the side cavern, where the rest of the rebels had gone. A moment later, the human Lightfall squadron walked off the ship, guns at their sides. Ruhn snarled softly, but they followed Pippa without so much as glancing toward them.

The humans were bold as Hel to stride past them, putting their backs to Vanir after what they'd done.

When Pippa and Lightfall had vanished, Tharion said, "She knows where Emile is."

"If you can trust her," Bryce countered.

"She knows," Cormac said. He gestured to Tharion. "You want to interrogate her, go ahead. But with her and Lightfall now in charge of the Valbaran front, your queen will have a mess on her hands if you move against them. I'd think twice if I were you, mer."

Bryce hummed her agreement, mouth twisting to the side. "I'd stay the Hel away from her."

Hunt tucked in his wings. Assessed his mate.

She slid her gaze to him. Innocently. Too innocently.

She knew something.

She dropped the *Who, me?* expression and glared at him. As if to say, *Don't you fucking rat me out, Athalar.*

He was stunned enough that he inclined his head. He'd get the truth out of her later.

Tharion was asking, "All this ammo they unloaded . . . Ophion is bringing it into this region. To do what—stage some big battle?"

"No one would tell me," Cormac said. "If they let Pippa have free rein, she'll commit atrocities that will make that leopard massacre seem merciful."

"You think she'd start shit in Lunathion?" Ruhn asked.

"I don't see why you'd bring in guns and missiles for a tea party," Tharion said, rubbing his jaw. Then he added, "They already had this base set up. How long has it been here on Ydra?"

"Not sure," Cormac said.

"Well, with Pippa at the helm, it seems like they're ready to strike," Ruhn said.

Hunt said, "I can't let them do that. Even if I wasn't in the 33rd, I can't let them attack innocent people. They want to go head-to-head on some muddy battlefield, fine, but I'm not going to let them hurt anyone in my city."

"Me neither," Ruhn said. "I'll lead the Aux against you—against Ophion. Tell Command that if they make one move, they can say goodbye to their contact with Daybright."

Tharion didn't say anything. Hunt didn't blame him. The mer would have to follow the River Queen's orders. But his face was grim.

Cormac said, "You warn anyone in Lunathion, they'll ask how you know."

Hunt observed the bodies slumped against the boat railing. "That's a risk I'm willing to take. And one of us is a master of spinning bullshit." He pointed to Bryce.

Bryce scowled. Yeah, she knew he didn't just mean spinning lies for the authorities about their involvement with the rebels. *As soon as we're out of here*, he silently conveyed, *I want to know everything* you *know*.

She glowered, even if she couldn't read his thoughts. But that glower turned into icy determination as the others noticed the look. She lifted her chin. "We can't let the Asteri get this suit. Or Ophion—especially the Lightfall squadron."

Hunt nodded. At least on this, they were on the same page. "They're going to be so fucking pissed."

"I guess that means it's business as usual," Bryce said, winking despite her pale face. She said to him, "Light it up, Hunt."

Cormac whirled. "What are you—"

Hunt didn't give the prince time to finish before he laid a hand on the suit and blasted it apart with his lightning.

Hunt didn't stop at destroying the suit. His lightning slammed the parked trucks, too. Every single one of them. Bryce couldn't help but marvel at the sight of him—like a god of lightning. Like Thurr himself.

He looked *exactly* like that statuette that had sat on her desk a couple weeks ago—

Ruhn bellowed at her to get down, and Bryce hit the ground, covering her head with her arms as truck after truck exploded across the cavern. The walls shook, stones falling, and then there were wings blocking her, protecting her.

"There are brimstone missiles on those trucks!" Cormac roared.

Bryce raised her head as Hunt pointed to the untouched truck marked *Pie Life*. "Only on that one." He must have somehow figured it out during the few minutes they'd been here. Hunt grinned wickedly at Tharion. "Let's see what you got, Ketos."

Tharion grinned back, pure predator. The male behind the charming mask.

A wall of water slammed into the pie truck, sending it toppling over the quay. Tharion's power sucked it swiftly and deeply below, and then created a small eddy, forming an open tunnel to the truck—

Hunt's lightning speared through it. The water slammed shut in its wake, covering the lightning's path as the truck exploded beneath the surface.

Water sprayed through the cave, and Bryce ducked again.

People were shouting now, rushing from far inside the cave, guns pointed toward where the trucks burned, a wall of flame licking toward the cave's distant ceiling.

"Time to go," Hunt said to Cormac, who was gaping at them. He hadn't gone for his sword, which was a good sign, but—

The prince whirled to the rebels, shouting across the chaos, "It was an accident!"

There was no use in covering their asses, Bryce thought as Hunt grabbed her to him, wings spreading in anticipation of a mad dash through the cave and out into the open air. Like he wouldn't wait for Cormac to teleport them.

"We're leaving," Hunt ordered Ruhn, who fell into a defensive position behind him. Hunt said to Tharion, "You want Pippa, it's now or never."

Tharion scanned the chaos beyond the trucks, the rebels advancing with their guns. No sign of Pippa. "I'm not running a foot closer to that shit," Tharion murmured.

Cormac had raised his hands as he approached his Ophion allies. The prince shouted to them, "The suit came to life, and launched its power—"

A gunshot cracked. Cormac went down.

Ruhn swore, and Hunt held Bryce tight to his side as Cormac struggled on the ground, a hand to his shoulder. No exit wound.

"Fuck," Cormac cursed as Pippa Spetsos emerged from the shadows. She likely wanted the Avallen Prince alive for questioning.

And if Hunt flew into the air . . . he'd be an easy target. Especially while still inside the confines of the cave, no matter how massive. Tharion went for a knife at his side. Water wreathed his long fingers.

"Don't be dumb," Hunt warned Tharion. He whirled on Cormac. "Teleport us out."

"Can't," Cormac panted. "Gorsian bullet."

"Fuck," Bryce breathed, and Hunt prepared to take their chances in the sky, bullets be damned. He was a fast flier. He'd get her out. Then return to help the others. He just had to get her to safety—

Pippa snarled from across the cavern, "You are all *dead*, Vanir filth." Hunt's back muscles tensed, wings readying for a mighty leap upward, then a sharp bank to the left.

But at that moment, Bryce began glowing. A light that radiated from her star, then outward through her body. "Run on my mark," she said quietly, sliding her hand into Hunt's.

"Bryce," Ruhn started.

Stars glinted in Bryce's hair. "Close your eyes, boys."

Hunt did, not waiting to see if the others followed. Even with his eyes shut, he could see light sparking, blinding. Humans screamed. Bryce shouted, "Go!"

Hunt opened his eyes to the fading brightness, clenched her still-glowing hand, and ran toward the wide cave entrance and open sea.

"Grab that boat!" Tharion said, pointing toward a skiff moored a few yards inside the cave—presumably how so many rebels had arrived secretly.

Hunt swept Bryce into his arms and jumped into the air, flapping for it, reaching the boat and untying it before the others could arrive, then gunning the engine. It was ready to go by the time they leapt in, and he made sure Bryce was securely seated before speeding off.

"This boat won't make it back to the coast," Tharion said, taking over the steering. "We'll need to stop at a fuel dock."

Cormac gazed toward the billowing smoke rippling from the broad cave mouth. Like some giant was exhaling a mouthful of mirthroot. "They'll hunt us down and kill us."

"I'd like to see them try," Bryce spat, wind whipping her hair.

"Psychotic *assholes*." She seethed at the prince, "You want to fight alongside those people? They're no better than Philip fucking Briggs!"

Cormac shot back, "Why do you think I was doing all I could to find Emile? I don't want him in their hands! But this is a war. If you can't handle the game, then stay the fuck out of it."

"Their methods mean that even if they do win," Bryce shouted, "there will be nothing left of them that's human at all!"

"This was a bad day," Cormac said. "This whole encounter—"

"*A bad day?*" Bryce yelled, pointing to the smoldering cave. "All those people just got murdered! Is that how you treat your allies? Is that what you'll do to us when we have no more value to you? We'll be pawns for you to murder and then you'll manipulate some other decent people into helping you? You're Vanir, for fuck's sake—don't you realize they'll do this to *you* as well?"

Cormac only stared at her.

Bryce hissed at Cormac, "You can fuck off. You and Pippa and the rebels. Let the Hind tear you to shreds. I want nothing to do with this. We're done." She said to Tharion, "And I'm done with helping you and your queen, too. I'm done with all of this."

Hunt tried not to sag with relief. Maybe they could now wipe their hands clean of any damning association.

Tharion said nothing to her, to any of them, his face grave.

Bryce turned on Ruhn. "I'm not going to tell you what to do with your life, but I'd think twice about associating with Agent Daybright. She'll stab you right in the back, if the way these people treat their allies is any indication."

"Yeah," Ruhn said, but he didn't sound convinced.

For a moment, it seemed like she might fight him on it, but she kept quiet. Thinking it through, no doubt. Along with whatever other secrets she'd been keeping.

Hunt turned to monitor the island's shoreline. No boats came after them, and nothing lay ahead except open water. But—

He went still at the sight of the sleek black dog running along one of the dry, white cliffs of the island. Its coat was a strange, matte black.

He knew that dog. That particular shade of black. Like the wings it bore in its other form. The hound ran along the cliffs, barking.

"Fuck," Hunt said softly.

He lifted an arm to signal to the dog that he'd seen it. Seen him. The dog pointed with a massive paw westward, the direction they were headed. He barked once. As if in warning.

"Is that—" Ruhn asked, seeing the dog as well.

"Baxian." Hunt scanned the western horizon. "Head northward, Tharion."

"If Baxian's on those cliffs . . ." Bryce looped an arm through Hunt's and pressed tight.

Hunt could think of only one enemy Baxian might be summoned to work alongside. "The Hind can't be far away."

44

You have to teleport us out," Bryce ordered Cormac, who pressed a hand to his bloody shoulder. "Let me get that gorsian bullet out of you and—"

"You can't. They're designed to split apart into shrapnel on impact to make sure that the magic is suppressed for as long as possible. I'll need surgery to get every last shard out of me."

"How did the Hind find us?" Bryce demanded, breathing hard.

Cormac pointed to the smoke. "Someone must have tipped her off that there was something going down here today. And Athalar just let her know our precise location."

Hunt bristled, lightning flaring around his head like a bright twin of the halo. Bryce grabbed his shoulder in warning, but said to Cormac, "I'll try, then. Teleporting."

"You'll wind up in the sea," Cormac hissed.

"I'll try," she repeated, and clenched Hunt's hand harder. Only a little guilt stabbed her that it was his and not Ruhn's that she grabbed, but if it came down to it . . . she'd get Hunt out first.

Tharion cut in, "I could protect us in the water, but we'd need to jump in first."

Bryce shut out his voice as the others began arguing, and then—

"*Fuck*," Hunt snarled, and she knew even before she opened her eyes that the Hind had appeared on the horizon. Guns cracked from a distance at a steady beat, but Bryce kept her eyes closed, willing herself to concentrate. Hunt said, "They want to keep me from flying."

Ruhn asked, "Do they know who we are?"

"No," Cormac said, "but the Hind always has snipers do this. You get airborne," he said to Hunt as Bryce gritted her teeth, *ordering* her power to move them away, "and you'll be vulnerable."

"Can we make it to the next island before they reach us?" Ruhn asked Tharion.

Tharion rifled through the compartment beside the steering wheel. "No. They're on a faster boat. They'll be on us when we hit open water." He pulled out a pair of binoculars. "A good two miles from shore."

"Shit," Ruhn said. "Keep going. We'll run until there's no other option."

Bryce tried to calm her frantic breathing. Hunt squeezed her hand in encouragement, lightning zapping into her fingers, but Cormac said to her quietly, "You can't do it."

"I can." But she opened her eyes, blinking at the brightness. This was such a beautiful place to die, with the turquoise sea and white islands behind them.

"Pollux and the Harpy are with the Hind," Tharion announced, lowering the binoculars.

"Get down," Hunt warned, ducking low. They all went with him, the water from the floor of the boat soaking into the knees of Bryce's leggings. "If we can see them, they can see us."

"You say that as if there's a chance of us somehow getting away unseen," Bryce muttered. She said to Tharion, "You can swim. Get the Hel out of here."

"No way." The wind tossed the mer's red hair as they bounded over the swells, the boat steered on a current of his power. "We're in this until the bitter end, Legs." But then the mer stiffened and roared, "*Into the water!*"

Bryce didn't second-guess him. She flung herself over the boat's side, Hunt splashing in with her, wings spraying water wide. The others followed. Tharion used his water magic to propel them a safe distance away, a wave of power that had Bryce sputtering as she emerged, salt stinging her eyes.

Right as something massive and glowing shot beneath her legs.

The torpedo struck the boat.

The tremor in the water rippled through her, and Tharion propelled them farther out as the boat exploded into smithereens, a plume of spray shooting sky-high.

Then it subsided, a field of debris and lashing waves left in its wake.

Exposed and adrift in the water, Bryce scanned for anywhere to go. Hunt was doing the same.

But Ruhn said, "Oh gods."

She looked to where her brother was treading water. Beheld the three massive black shapes aiming for them.

Omega-boats.

Ruhn had never once in his life felt as useless as he did treading water, flotsam drifting past, Ydra distant behind them and the next island not even a smudge on the horizon.

Even if Athalar could manage to get airborne with waterlogged wings, snipers were waiting to down him—and Bryce. Cormac couldn't teleport, and Tharion might be able to move them a little with his water, but against three Omega-boats . . .

He met Hunt's stare over the bobbing swells, the angel's soaking face grim with determination. Hunt asked, "Shadows?"

"Sun's too bright." And the waves shifted them too much.

Two of the Omega-boats peeled off for Ydra, presumably to prevent any Ophion boats from escaping. But that still left one massive submersible against them. And the Hind, the Harpy, and the Hammer on that approaching speedboat.

Once their faces became clear, it'd be over. Sandriel's old triarii would know who they were, and they'd be dead fucking meat. The Helhound, apparently, had tried to help them, but the rest of those assholes . . .

"Get out of here," Bryce scolded Tharion again.

Tharion shook his head, water spraying. "If Athalar can down their boats—"

"I can't," Hunt cut in, and Ruhn raised his brows. Hunt explained, "Even if it wouldn't give away my identity, you're in the water with me. If I unleash my lightning . . ."

Ruhn finished, "We're deep-fried."

Hunt said to Bryce, "You can't blind them, either. They'll know it's you."

"That's a risk I'm willing to take," she countered, treading water. "Lightning, they'd know it's you. But a bright burst of light . . . there are more ways to excuse it. I can blind them, and when they're down, we seize their boat."

Hunt nodded grimly, but Ruhn countered, "That doesn't handle the Omega-boat. It doesn't have windows."

"We'll take our chances," Hunt said.

"Right." Bryce focused on the approaching death squad. "How close do we let them get?"

Hunt eyed their enemies. "Close enough that we can leap on board when they're blinded."

Ruhn muttered, "So really damn close."

Bryce blew out a breath. "All right. All right." Light began flickering from her chest, building, casting the water around her into palest blue. "Just tell me when," she said to Hunt.

"Someone's coming," Tharion said, pointing with a clawed hand to the fleet. A wave skimmer broke away from the speedboat. A familiar golden head appeared atop it, bouncing across the waves.

"The Hind," Cormac said, blanching.

"At least she's alone."

"There goes our plan," Bryce hissed.

"No," Hunt said, though lightning began to glow in his gaze. Burning Solas. "We hold to it. She's coming to talk."

"How do you know that?"

Hunt growled, "The others are holding back."

Ruhn asked, hating that he didn't know, "Why would the Hind do that?"

"To torment us," Cormac guessed. "She toys with enemies before slaughtering them."

Athalar said to Bryce, the general incarnate, "Blind her when I give the signal." He ordered Tharion, "Use one of those knives as soon as she's down." The mer drew a blade. Bryce's light fluttered in the water, reaching down in the depths.

The Omega slowed behind the Hind, but continued to creep closer.

"Say nothing," Cormac warned them as the wave skimmer slowed, engine quieting.

And then the Hind was there, in her impeccable imperial uniform, black boots shining with water. Not one hair on her golden head lay out of place, and her face was the portrait of cruel calm as she said, "What a surprise."

None of them said a word.

The Hind slung one of her lean legs over the wave skimmer so she sat sidesaddle, and braced her elbows on her knees. Put her delicate chin in her hands. "This is the fun part of my job, you know. Finding the rats who nibble away at the safety of our empire."

Such a dead, hateful face. Like she was a statue, flawless and carved, brought to life.

The Hind nodded to Bryce, though. Her red lips curved upward. "Is that little light for me?"

"Come closer and find out," Bryce said, earning a warning look from Hunt. What was he waiting for?

But the Hind surveyed Tharion. "Your presence is . . . troublesome."

The water around him thrashed, roiled by his magic, but the mer kept silent. For some reason, he hadn't yet shifted. Was it some attempt to remain unrecognized for what he was? Or maybe a predator's instinct to hide one of his biggest assets until he could strike?

But the Hind sized up Tharion again. "I'm glad to see the River Queen's Captain of Intelligence is indeed smart enough to know that if he used his power to do something stupid like overturn this wave skimmer, my companions would unleash Hel upon all of you."

Tharion's teeth flashed. But he didn't attack.

Then the Hind met Ruhn's stare, and all that he was diluted to pure, lethal rage.

He'd kill her, and do it gladly. If he could get on that wave skimmer before Tharion, he'd rip out her throat with his teeth.

"Two Fae Princes," the Hind purred. "Crown Princes, no less. The future of the royal bloodlines." She clicked her tongue. "Not to mention that one of them is a Starborn heir. What a scandal this shall be for the Fae. What shame this will bring."

"What do you want?" Hunt challenged, lightning skittering over his shoulders. Bryce twisted toward him with alarm, and Ruhn tensed.

Athalar's power glowed along the tops of his wings, twining in his hair. Each breath seemed to summon more of it, keeping it well above the waves' reach. Readying for the strike.

"I already have what I want," the Hind said coolly. "Proof of your treachery."

Bryce's light shimmered and built, rippling into the depths below. And Hunt . . . If he unleashed his power, he'd electrocute all of them.

Ruhn said to his sister, mind-to-mind, *Get on that wave skimmer and run.*

Fuck that. Bryce slammed her mind shut to him.

The Hind reached into her pocket, and the lightning above Athalar flared, a whip readying to strike whatever gun the deer shifter possessed. Still he didn't give the signal.

But the Hind pulled out a small white stone. Held it up.

She smiled slightly at Cormac. "I showed one of these to Sofie Renast before she died, you know. Made this same demonstration."

Died. The word seemed to clang across the water. The Hind had truly killed her, then.

Cormac spat, "I'm going to rip you to pieces."

The Hind laughed softly. "From where I'm sitting, I don't see much chance of that." She extended her arm over the water. Her

slim, manicured fingers splayed, and the stone plunged. It left barely
a ripple on the waves as it fluttered down, down, down, shimmering white in Bryce's light, and then vanishing into the deep.

"Long way to the bottom," the Hind observed dryly. "I wonder
if you'll drown before you reach it." The Omega-boat surged closer.

"Choose wisely," the Hind crooned. "Come with me," she said
to Hunt, to Bryce, "or see what the seafloor has to offer you."

"Get fucked," Hunt seethed.

"Oh, I plan to, once this is done," she said, smiling wickedly.

Hunt's lightning flickered again. Glowed in his eyes. Shit—
Athalar was walking a fine line of control.

Bryce murmured Hunt's name in warning. Hunt ignored her,
but Tharion cursed softly.

What is it? Ruhn asked the male, who didn't look his way as Tharion replied, *Something big. Gunning for us.*

Not the Omega-boat?

No. It's . . . What the fuck is it?

"Hurry now," the Hind drawled. "Not much time."

Lightning wrapped around Hunt's head. Ruhn's heart stalled a
beat as it lingered—like a crown, making of Hunt an anointed,
primal god. Willing to slaughter any in his path to save the female
he loved. He'd fry every single one of them if it meant getting Bryce
out alive.

Some intrinsic part of Ruhn trembled at it. Whispered that
he should get far, far away and pray for mercy.

But Bryce didn't balk from the knee-wobbling power surging
around Athalar. Like she saw all of him and welcomed it into her
heart.

Hunt, eyes nothing but pure lightning, nodded at Bryce. As if
to say, *Blind the bitch.*

Bryce sucked in a breath, and began to glow.

Something solid and metal hit Bryce's legs, her feet, and before she
could fully release her light, she was hurled up with it. When the
water washed away, she lay on the hull of an Omega-boat.

No—it wasn't imperial. The insignia on it was of two entwined fishes.

Hunt lay beside her, wings dripping wet—lightning still crackling around him. His eyes . . .

Holy fuck, his eyes. Pure lightning filled them. No whites, no irises. Nothing but lightning.

It snapped around him, vines wreathing his arms, his brow. Bryce had the vague sense of the others behind them, but she kept her focus on Hunt.

"Hunt," she gasped out. "Calm down."

Hunt snarled toward the Hind. Lightning flowed like tongues of flame from his mouth. But the Hind had fallen back, revving her wave skimmer and retreating toward her line of boats. Like she knew what kind of death Hunt was about to unleash on her.

"*Hunt*," Bryce said, but something metal clanked against the broad snout of the ship, and then a female voice was bellowing, "*Down the hatch! Now!*"

Bryce didn't question their good luck. Didn't care that the Hind had seen them, knew them, and they'd let the spy-breaker live. She hurtled to her feet, slipping on the metal, but Hunt was there, a hand under her elbow. His lightning danced up her arm, tickling, but not hurting. His eyes still blazed with power as they assessed the unknown female ahead, who—to her credit—didn't run screaming.

Bryce glanced behind to find Ruhn helping Cormac along, Tharion at their backs, a wave of water now towering between him and the Hind. Hiding them from the view of the approaching speed-boat, with Pollux and the Harpy on it.

It didn't matter now. The Hind knew.

A dark-haired female waved to them from a hatch midway along the massive length of the ship—as large as an Omega-boat. Her brown skin gleamed with ocean spray, her narrow face set with grim calm as she gestured for them to hurry.

Yet Hunt's lightning still didn't ease. Bryce knew it wouldn't, until they were sure what the fuck was happening.

"Hurry," the female said as Bryce reached the hatch. "We

have less than a minute to get out of here." Bryce gripped the rungs of a ladder and propelled herself downward, Hunt right behind her. The female swore, presumably at the sight of Hunt's current state.

Bryce kept going down. Lightning slithered along the ladder, but didn't bite. Like Hunt was holding himself in check.

One after another, they entered, and the female had barely shut the hatch when the ship shuddered and swayed. Bryce clenched the ladder as the craft submerged.

"We're diving!" the female shouted. "Hold on!"

Bryce's stomach lurched with the ship, but she kept descending. People milled about below, shouting. They halted as Hunt's lightning surged over the floor. A vanguard of what was to come.

"If they're Ophion, we're fucked," Ruhn muttered from above Hunt.

"Only if they know about what we did," Tharion breathed from the end of their party.

Bryce rallied her light with each step downward. Between facing the two enemies now at their throats, she'd take Ophion, but . . . Could she and Hunt take down this ship, if they needed to? Could they do it without drowning themselves and their friends?

She dropped into a clean, bright white chamber—an air lock. Rows of underwater gear lined it, along with several people in blue uniforms by the door. Mer. The female who had escorted them joined the others waiting for them.

A brown-haired, ample-hipped female stepped forward, scanning Bryce.

Her eyes widened as Hunt dropped to the wet floor, lightning flowing around him. She had the good sense to hold up her hands. The people behind her did, too. "We mean you no harm," she said with firm calm.

Hunt didn't back down from whatever primal wrath he rode. Bryce's breathing hitched.

Ruhn and Cormac dropped on Bryce's other side, and the female scanned them, too, face strained as she noted the injured Avallen Prince, who sagged against Ruhn. But she smiled as Tharion entered on Hunt's right. Like she'd found someone of reason in this giant clusterfuck that had just tumbled down the hatch.

"You called for us?" she asked Tharion, glancing nervously toward Hunt.

Bryce murmured to Hunt, "Chill the fuck out."

Hunt stared at each of the strangers, as if sizing up a kill. Lightning sizzled through his hair.

"Hunt," Bryce muttered, but didn't dare reach for his hand.

"I . . ." Tharion drew his wide eyes from Hunt and blinked at the female. "What?"

"Our Oracle sensed we'd be needed somewhere in this vicinity, so we came. Then we got your message," she said tightly, an eye still fixed on Hunt. "The light."

Ruhn and Tharion turned to Bryce, Cormac nearly a dead weight of exhaustion in her brother's arms. Tharion smiled roughly. "You're a good luck charm, Legs."

It was the stupidest stroke of luck she'd ever had. Bryce said, "I, uh . . . I sent the light."

Hunt's lightning crackled, a second skin over his body, his soaked clothes. He didn't show any signs of calming down. She had no idea *how* to calm him down.

This was how he was that day with Sandriel, Ruhn said into her mind. *When he ripped off her head.* He added tightly, *You were in danger then, too.*

And what's that supposed to mean?

Why don't you tell me?

You seem like you know what the fuck is happening with him.

Ruhn glared at her as Hunt continued to glow and menace. *It means that he's going ballistic in the way that only mates can when the other is threatened. It's what happened then, and what's happening now. You're true mates—the way Fae are mates, in your bodies and souls. That's what was different about your scent the other day. Your scents have merged. As they do between Fae mates.*

She glared right back at her brother. *So what?*

So find some way to calm him down. Athalar's your fucking problem now.

Bryce sent a mental image of her middle finger back in answer.

The mer female squared her shoulders, unaware of Ruhn and Bryce's conversation, and said to Tharion, "We're not out of this yet. There's an Omega on our tail." She spoke like Hunt wasn't a living thunderstorm standing two feet away.

Bryce's heart strained. True mates. Not only in name, but . . . in the way that Fae could be mates with each other.

Ruhn said, *Athalar was dangerous before. But as a mated male, he's utterly lethal.*

Bryce countered, *He was always lethal.*

Not like this. There's no mercy in him. He's gone lethal in a Fae way. In that predatory, kill-all-enemies way. *He's an angel.*

Doesn't seem to matter.

One look at Hunt's hard face, and she knew Ruhn was right. Some small part of her thrilled at it—that he'd descended this far into some primal instinct to try to save her.

Alphaholes can have their uses, she said to her brother with a bravado she didn't feel, and returned to the conversation at hand.

Tharion was saying to the female, "Captain Tharion Ketos of the Blue Court, at your service."

The female saluted as the people with her opened an airtight door to reveal a shining glass hallway. Blue stretched around it, a passageway through the ocean. A few fish shot past—or the ship shot past the fish. Faster than Bryce had realized. "Commander Sendes," the female said.

"What mer court do you come from?" Bryce asked. Hunt walked at her side, silent and blazing with power.

Commander Sendes glanced over a shoulder, face still a little pale at the sight of Hunt. "This one." Sendes gestured to the glass walkway around them, the behemoth of a ship that Bryce could now make out through it.

They hadn't entered along the flat back of the ship as Bryce had thought, but rather at the tip of it. As if the ship had pierced the surface like a lance. And now, with a view of the rest of the ship expanding beyond—below—the glass passage, what she could see of it appeared to be shaped like some sort of squid as it shot into the gloom below. A squid as large as the Comitium, and made of glass and matte metal for stealth.

Sendes lifted her chin. "Welcome to the *Depth Charger*. One of the six city-ships of the Ocean Queen's court Beneath."

45

"All right, so you'll be charged with breaking and entering, and probably theft. Tell me again how you think you've still got grounds to go after this old creep?" Declan's boyfriend, Marc, leaned against the couch cushions, muscled arms crossed as he grilled Ithan.

Ithan blew out a breath. "When you put it like that, I can see what you mean about it being a tough case to win."

Flynn and Declan, beside them, attempted to murder each other in a video game, both cursing under their breath. "It's admirable," Marc admitted. The leopard shifter frowned toward the small black box Ithan had taken from the Astronomer's lair. "But you just waded knee-deep into shit."

"It's not right that she's trapped in there. What choice did she even have as a kid?"

"No arguments from me against that," Marc said. "But there's a legal contract involved, so she's technically owned by the Astronomer. She's not a slave, but she might as well be, legally. And theft of slaves is a big fucking crime."

"I know," Ithan said. "But it feels wrong to leave her there."

"So you took the fire sprites instead?" Marc arched a brow. "You wanna take a guess at how much they cost?" He nodded at the box in the center of the table. "What were you even thinking?"

"I wasn't thinking," Ithan muttered, swigging from his beer. "I was pissed."

Declan cut in, not tearing his attention from the screen and his shooting, "There were no cameras, though, right?"

"None that I saw."

"So it all comes down to whether the girl in the tank tells on you," Declan said, thumbs flying against the controller. Flynn swore at whatever Dec did to his avatar.

"You could return them," Marc suggested. "Say you were drunk, apologize, and send them back."

Ithan opened his mouth, but the box on the table rattled.

Rattled. Like the beings inside had heard. Even Declan and Flynn paused their game.

"Um," Declan said, wincing.

"Hello?" Flynn said, eyeing the box.

It rattled again. They all flinched.

"Well, someone has an opinion," Marc said, chuckling softly, and leaned forward.

"Careful," Dec warned. Marc threw him a wry look and opened the black box.

Light, golden and red, erupted, washing over the walls and ceiling. Ithan shielded his eyes, but the light was immediately sucked back in, revealing four rings nestled in black velvet, the tiny glass bubbles atop them glowing.

The glow inside faded and faded, until . . .

Declan and Marc glanced at each other in horror.

"Solas," Flynn swore, tossing aside his controller. "That old fuck should be crucified for this."

"All right," Marc murmured to Ithan. "I get why you took them."

Ithan grunted in answer, and peered at the four female figures inside the rings. He'd never met Lehabah face-to-face, as Bryce had never let him into the library beneath the gallery, but he'd seen Bryce's photos.

Three of the sprites were just like her—flames shaped into female bodies. Two were slim, one as sinfully curvy as Lehabah had been. The fourth globe was pure fire.

That fourth ring rattled. Ithan recoiled. That was clearly the one who'd shaken the box.

"So do we let them out?" Flynn asked, studying the box and the sprites trapped inside.

"Fuck yeah, we do," Declan said, shooting to his feet.

Ithan stared at the sprites, especially the fourth, radiant one who seemed so . . . angry. He didn't blame her. He murmured to his roommates, "You sure you're cool with freeing a bunch of pissed-off fire sprites in your house?"

But Flynn waved him off. "We've got sprinklers and smoke alarms."

"I'm not reassured," Marc said.

"Got it," Declan called, trotting from the kitchen with a hammer.

Marc rubbed his temples and leaned back against the cushions. "This cannot end well."

"Ye of little faith," Flynn said, catching the hammer as Declan tossed it to him.

Ithan winced. "Just . . . be careful."

"I don't think that word's in either of their vocabularies," Marc quipped, earning an elbow in the ribs from Declan as the male settled onto the couch beside him.

Flynn tugged the box toward him and said to the sprites, "Cover your heads." The three visible ones crouched down. The fourth one remained a ball of flame, but shrank slightly.

"Careful," Ithan warned again. Flynn, with a snap of the wrist, cracked the top of the first ring. It splintered, and he tapped it again. It broke into three pieces on the third rap of the hammer, but the sprite remained crouched.

Flynn moved onto the next, then the next.

By the time he'd cracked open the third ring, the sprites were poking their fiery heads out like chicks emerging from eggs. Flynn moved the hammer above the fourth one. And as it came down, Ithan could have sworn one of the sprites shouted, in a voice almost too hoarse to hear, "*Don't!*"

Too late.

SARAH J. MAAS

All it took was one crack, and the flame within shoved outward, rupturing the glass.

They all leapt over the couch with a shout, and *fuck*, it was hot and bright and wind was roaring and something was screeching—

Then something heavy thudded on the coffee table. Ithan and the others peeked over the couch.

"What the fuck?" Flynn breathed, smoke curling from where the shoulders of his shirt had been singed.

The three sprites cowered in their shattered orbs. All shrinking from the naked, human-sized female smoldering on the coffee table beside them.

The female pushed up onto her arms, hair like darkest iron falling in curling waves around her delicately featured face. Her tan body simmered, the wood table beneath her charring everywhere her nude, luscious form touched. She lifted her head, and her eyes— fucking Hel.

They blazed crimson. More boiling blood than flame.

Her back heaved with each long, sawing breath, ripples of what seemed like red-and-gold scales flowing beneath her skin.

"He is going to kill you," she said in a voice rasping with disuse. But her eyes weren't on Ithan. They were on Flynn, his hammer raised again, as if it would do anything against the sort of fire she bore. "He is going to find you and kill you."

But Flynn, stupid, arrogant asshole that he was, got to his feet and grinned cheerfully down at the curvy female on the coffee table. "Good thing a dragon now owes me a debt."

Athalar was a time bomb—one that Ruhn had no idea how to defuse. He supposed that honor went to his sister, who kept a step away from the angel, one eye on him and the other on the unfolding race for the seafloor.

His sister was *mated*. It was rare enough among the Fae, but finding a mate who was an angel . . . His mind reeled.

Ruhn shook off the thought, approaching Commander Sendes and saying, "I don't hear any engine noise."

"You won't," Sendes said, opening an air lock door at the end of the long glass tunnel. "These are stealth ships, fueled by the Ocean Queen's power."

Tharion whistled, then asked, "So you think we can outrun an Omega in something this big?"

"No. But we're not outrunning it." She pointed through a wall of thick glass to the dimness below. "We're going into the Ravel Canyon."

"If you can fit," Ruhn challenged, hoisting Cormac up a little higher as the male groaned, "then so can the Omega-boats."

Sendes gave him a secret, knowing smile. "Watch."

Ruhn nodded to the prince hanging off his shoulder. "My cousin needs a medwitch."

"One is already coming to meet us," Sendes said, opening another air lock. The tunnel beyond was massive, with halls branching out in three directions like the arteries of a mighty beast. The hall directly ahead . . . "Well, that's a sight," Ruhn murmured.

A cavernous biodome bloomed at the end of the hall, brimming with lush tropical trees, streams winding through the fern-covered floor, and orchids blooming in curling mists. Butterflies flitted around, and hummingbirds sipped from the orchids and neon-colored flowers. He could have sworn he spied a small, furred beast running beneath a drooping fern.

"We have desalinators on this ship," Sendes explained, pointing to the biodome, "but should they ever fail, this is a wholly separate ecosystem that generates its own fresh water."

"How?" Tharion asked, but Sendes had halted at the intersection of the three halls. "The River Queen has a similar one, but nothing that can do this."

"I doubt your bleeding friend would appreciate the lengthy explanation right now," Sendes said, turning down the hallway to their right. People—mer, from their scents—walked past them, a few gaping, a few throwing confused looks their way, some waving to Sendes, who waved back.

Their surroundings had the air of a corporate building—or a city block. People going about their days, dressed in business or casual clothes, some exercising, some sipping from coffee cups or smoothies.

Bryce's head swiveled this way and that, taking it all in. Athalar just kept crackling with lightning.

"No one's concerned about who's on our tail?" Ruhn asked Sendes.

She halted before another massive window, again pointing. "Why should they be?"

Ruhn braced his feet as the ship plowed right for a dark, craggy wall rising from the seafloor. But as easy as a bird shifting directions, it pulled up alongside the wall and drifted down—then halted, hovering.

Ruhn shook his head. "They'll find us like this."

"Look down the body of the ship."

Pressing against the glass, Cormac a ballast on his other side, Ruhn obeyed. Where a mammoth ship had been, now . . . there was only black rock. Nothing else.

"This ship can become invisible?"

"Not invisible. Camouflaged." Sendes smiled with pride. "The Ocean Queen imbued her vessels with many gifts from the seas. This one has a squid's ability to blend into its surroundings."

"But the lights inside—" Tharion started.

"The glass is one-way. It blocks the light and any glimpse within once the camouflaging is activated."

"What about radar?" Ruhn asked. "You might be invisible to the naked eye, but surely the imperial ships would pick you up."

Another one of those proud smiles. "Again, the Ocean Queen's power fuels our ship, not the firstlight that the Omega radar is programmed to pick up. We register no signs of life, either—not even as a whale or a shark might on a radar. We are completely undetectable. To a passing Omega-boat, we are only a cluster of rock."

"What if they run into you?" Tharion asked.

"We can simply drift up or down, to avoid it." She pointed again. "Here they come."

Ruhn's heart leapt into his throat. Athalar's lightning snaked along his body once more. Bryce muttered something to him that apparently did nothing to calm the angel down.

But Ruhn was too busy monitoring the enemy's approach. Like a wolf stepping from the shadows of a kelp forest, the Omega-boat stalked for the canyon. Its firstlights blared into the dark, broadcasting its location.

People continued walking past, a few glancing to the enemy closing in, but not paying it much mind.

What the actual fuck.

The imperial ship plunged right after them. A wolf on the hunt, indeed.

"Watch," Sendes said.

Ruhn held his breath, as if it'd somehow keep them from detection, as the Omega-boat crept closer. A slow, strategic sweep.

He could make out the paint along its sides—the imperial insignia flaking off—the slices and dents from previous battles. Along its hull was written, *SPQM Faustus.*

"The *Faustus*," Tharion breathed, dread in his voice.

"You know the ship?" Sendes asked him.

"Heard of it," Tharion said, monitoring the warship inching past. Utterly unaware of them. "That vessel alone has downed sixteen rebel ships."

"At least they sent someone impressive after us this time," Sendes said.

Tharion ran a hand through his damp hair, claws retracting. "They're drifting right by us. This is incredible."

Cormac grunted, stirring in Ruhn's arms, "Does Ophion know about this?"

Sendes stiffened. "We are not aligned with Ophion." Thank fuck. Bryce sagged, and Hunt's lightning dimmed slightly.

"What about the Asteri? Are they aware of this technology?" Ruhn asked, gesturing to the boat around them, now vanishing into the deep, the Omega-boat blindly passing overhead.

Sendes continued walking, and they followed her. "No. And given the circumstances under which we found you, I trust you will not pass on the information. Just as we shall keep your presence confidential."

You fuck us, we'll fuck you. "Got it," Ruhn said, offering a smile that Sendes didn't return. The ship began drifting farther into the canyon's depths.

"Here she is," Sendes announced as a medwitch came running, a team of three with a stretcher close behind her.

"Cthona spare me," Cormac muttered, managing to lift his head. "I don't need all that."

"Yes, you do," Tharion and Ruhn said together.

If the medwitch and her team recognized any of them, they didn't let on. The next few minutes were a flurry of getting Cormac onto the stretcher and bustled to the medical center, with a promise that he'd be out of surgery within an hour and they could see him soon after that.

Through it all, Bryce kept back with Athalar. Lightning still skimmed over his wings, sparked at his fingertips.

Calm down, Ruhn said into Athalar's mind.

Thunderstorms boomed in answer.

All right, then.

The city-ship began sailing along the floor of the canyon, the seabed unusually flat and broad between the towering cliffs. They passed a half-crumbling pillar, and—

"Are those carvings?" Ruhn asked as Sendes led them back down the hall.

"Yes," she said a shade softly. "From long, long ago."

Tharion said, "What was down here?" He scanned the passing walls of the canyon floor—all of them carved with strange symbols.

"This was a highway. Not as you will find above the surface, but a grand avenue the mer once used to swim between great cities."

"I never heard of anything out here."

"It's from long ago," she said again, a bit tightly. Like it was a secret.

Bryce said from the back, "I used to work in an antiquities gallery, and my boss once brought in a statue from a sunken city. I always thought she was fudging the dates, but she said it was almost

fifteen thousand years old. That it came from the original Beneath."
As old as the Asteri—or at least their arrival in Midgard.

Sendes's expression remained neutral. "Only the Ocean Queen
can verify that."

Ruhn peered through the glass again. "So the mer once had a
city down here?"

"We once had many things," Sendes said.

Tharion shook his head at Ruhn, a silent warning to lay off the
subject. Ruhn nodded back. "Where are we going, exactly?" Ruhn
asked instead.

"I assume you want to rest for a moment. I'm bringing you to
private quarters in our barracks."

"And from there?" Ruhn dared ask.

"We need to wait until the Omegas have cleared the area, but
once that has happened, we'll return you wherever you wish."

"The mouth of the Istros," Tharion said. "My people can meet
us there."

"Very well. We shall likely arrive at dawn, given our need for
secrecy."

"Get me a radio and I'll put out a coded signal."

She nodded, and Ruhn admired the mers' innate trust in one
another. Would she have so easily let *him* use a radio to contact anyone beyond this ship? He doubted it.

But Bryce halted at the hallway intersection. Glanced at Hunt
before saying to Sendes, "You mind if me and my glowing friend
here go into the biodome for a while?"

Sendes warily considered Hunt. "I'll close it to the public tem-
porarily. As long as he does no harm in there."

Hunt bared his teeth, but Bryce smiled tightly. "I'll make sure
he doesn't."

Sendes's gaze drifted down to the scar on her chest. "When you
are done, ask for Barracks Six, and someone will point you that
way."

"Thanks," Bryce said, then pivoted to Ruhn and Tharion. "Stay
out of trouble."

"You too," Ruhn said, arching a brow.

Then Bryce was walking toward the lush biodome, Hunt trailing, lightning in his wake.

Sendes pulled a radio from her pocket. "Clear the biodome and seal off its doors."

Ruhn started. "What?"

Sendes continued onward, boots clicking on the tiled floors. "I think she and the angel should have a little privacy, don't you?"

46

There was only his power, and Bryce. The rest of the world had become an array of threats to her.

Hunt had the vague notion of being brought onto an enormous mer ship. Of talking with its commander, and noticing the people and the Omega-boat and Cormac being wheeled off.

His mind had drifted, riding some storm without end, his magic screaming to be unleashed. He'd ascended into this plane of existence, of primal savagery, the moment the Hind had appeared. He knew he had to take her out, if it meant getting Bryce to safety. Had decided that it didn't matter if Danaan or Cormac or Tharion got cooked in the process.

He couldn't turn away from that precipice.

Even as Bryce walked down a quiet, warm hallway toward a lush forest—pines and ferns and flowers; birds and butterflies of every color; little streams and waterfalls—he couldn't settle.

He needed his magic out, needed to scream his wrath and then hold her and know she was fine, they were fine—

He followed Bryce into the greenery, across a trickling stream. It was dim in here, mist curling along the floor. Like they'd walked into some ancient garden at the dawn of the world.

She halted in a small clearing, the floor covered with moss and small, white flowers shaped like stars. She turned to him, her eyes glowing. His cock stirred at the glittering intent in them.

Her lips curved upward, knowing and taunting. Without saying a word, she lifted her soaked T-shirt over her head. Another second and her purple lace bra was gone too.

The world, the garden, vanished at the sight of her full breasts, dusk-rose nipples already peaked. His mouth watered.

She unfastened her pants. Her shoes. And then she was shimmying out of her purple underwear.

She stood totally naked before him. Hunt's heart pounded so wildly he thought it'd burst from his chest.

She was so beautiful. Every lush line, every gleaming inch of skin, her beckoning sex—

"Your turn," she said huskily.

His magic howling, begging, Hunt had the vague sense of his fingers removing his clothes and shoes. He didn't care that he was already fully at attention. Only cared that her eyes dipped to his cock and a pleased sort of smile graced her mouth.

Naked, they faced each other in that garden beneath the sea.

He wanted to please his mate. His beautiful, strong mate. Hunt must have said it aloud, because Bryce said gently, "Yes, Hunt. I'm your mate." The star on her chest fluttered like an ember sputtering to life. "And you are mine."

The words rang through him. His magic burned his veins like acid, and he grunted against it.

Her eyes softened, like she could sense his pain. She said hoarsely, "I want you to fuck me. Will you do that?"

Lightning sparked over his wings. "Yes."

Bryce ran a hand up her torso, circling the glowing star between her full breasts. His cock throbbed. She took one step toward him, bare feet cushioned by the moss.

Hunt backed away a step.

She lifted a brow. "No?"

"Yes," he managed to say again. His head cleared a fraction. "This garden . . ."

"Closed to the public," she purred, the star's light shining through her fingers. She took another step, and Hunt didn't retreat this time.

He couldn't get a breath down. "I . . ." He swallowed. "My power—"

She paused a foot from him. The scent of her arousal wrapped invisible fingers around his cock and stroked hard. He shuddered. "Whatever you need to throw at me, Hunt, I can take it."

He let out a low groan. "I don't want to hurt you."

"You won't." She smiled softly—lovingly. "I trust you."

Her fingers brushed over his bare chest, and he shivered again. She closed the distance between them, mouth grazing over his pec—his heart. Hunt's lightning flared, casting the garden in silver. Bryce lifted her head.

"Kiss me," she breathed.

Hunt's eyes were pure lightning. His *body* was pure lightning as Bryce opened her mouth to him and his tongue swept in, tasting of rain and ether.

His power flowed over her, around her, a million sensual caresses, and she arched into it, gave herself over to it. He palmed her breast, power zapping at her nipple, and she gasped. He drove his tongue deeper, like he'd lap up the sound.

She knew Hunt needed a way to work off his magic, a way to reassure him that she was safe and his. *My beautiful, strong mate*, he'd growled as he looked at her naked body.

His other hand kneaded her ass, pulling her against him, pinning his cock between their bodies. He groaned at the touch of her stomach against him, and she writhed—just enough to drive him wild.

Lightning danced down her skin, along her hair, and she basked in it. Took it into herself, let herself become it, become *him*, and let him become her, until they were two souls twining together at the bottom of the sea.

Bryce had the vague sense of falling through air, through time and space, and then she found herself laid gently, reverently, on the mossy ground. Like even in his need, his fury, he wanted her safe and well. Feeling only pleasure.

She wrapped her arms around his neck, arching into him as she nipped at his lip, sucked on his tongue. More. She needed more. He clamped his teeth on the side of her throat, sucking hard, and she arched again, right as he settled between her legs.

The brush of his velvety cock against her bare sex had her shaking. Not with fear, but at his closeness, that nothing now lay between them and would never lie between them again.

He slickened himself with her wetness, his wings twitching. Lightning spiderwebbed on the moss around them, then up the trees overhead.

"Hunt," Bryce gasped. They could explore and play later. Right now, when death had been hovering so close, right now she needed him with her, in her. Needed his strength and power and gentleness, needed that smile and humor and love—

Bryce wrapped a hand around the base of his cock, pumping him once, angling him toward where she was absolutely drenched for him.

Hunt stilled, though. Gritted his teeth as she pumped the magnificent length of him again. His eyes met hers.

Only lightning filled them. An avenging god.

The star on her chest flared, merging with his lightning. He laid a hand atop it. Claiming the star, the light. Claiming her.

Bryce positioned him at her entrance, panting at the brush of the blunt head of his cock. But she released him. Let him decide whether this was what he wanted. This final bridge between their souls.

The lightning cleared from his eyes—as if he willed it. As if he wanted her to see the male beneath.

Pure Hunt. No one and nothing else.

It was a question, somehow. As if he were showing her every scar and wound, every dark corner. Asking if this—if he—was what she really wanted. Bryce only smiled softly. "I love you," she whispered. Shuddering, Hunt kissed her and slid home.

Nothing had ever felt so right.

Hunt worked himself into her, filling her deliciously, perfectly. With each gentle thrust, each inch gained into her, her light flared brighter. His lightning cracked, over and around them.

His back flexed beneath her fingers, his wings tucking in tight. His chest heaved in great bellows, pushing against her breasts, the star between them.

Another inch, another shudder of pleasure. And then he slid out. And out. And out.

His tongue flicked against hers as he slammed back, right to the hilt. Light spilled from her like an overflowing cup, rippling across the forest floor.

Bryce clawed at his back, his neck, and Hunt's teeth found her breast, clamping down. She went wild, hips driving up to meet him, power clashing with power.

Hunt set a steady, punishing pace, and she laid her hands on his ass just to feel the muscles clenching with each thrust, to *feel* him pushing into her—

He claimed her mouth again, and Bryce wrapped her legs around his waist. She moaned as he sank in, and his thrusts turned harder, faster. Lightning and starlight ricocheted between them.

She needed him wilder. Needed him to release that edge of fear and rage and become her Hunt again. She tightened her legs around him, and flipped them. The world spun, and then she was staring down at him, his cock buried so deep—

Lightning flowed over his teeth as he panted, all those abs flexing. Gods, he was beautiful. And hers. Utterly hers.

Bryce lifted her hips, rising off his cock—and then plunged back down. She arched as he kissed the star on her chest. She rose again, a steady, taunting slide, and then impaled herself.

He snarled against her skin. "Merciless, Quinlan."

Close. So close. She rose once more, luxuriating in each inch of his cock, nearly pulling herself from his tip. And as she drove down, she clenched her delicate inner muscles around him.

Hunt roared, and she was again on her back as he slammed into her. His power flowed over her, filled her, and she was him, and he was her, and then his cock hit that perfect spot deep in her, and the world was only light—

Release blasted through her, and Bryce might have been laughing, or sobbing, or shouting his name. Hunt rode her through it all, nursing every last drop of pleasure, and then he was moving again, punishing thrusts that sent them sliding across the mossy floor. His wings were a wall of gray above them, his wings were—glowing.

They filled with iridescent light. *He* filled with light.

Bryce reached a hand toward his blazing wings. Her own fingers, her hand, her arm—they radiated the same light. As if they had become filled with power, as if her light had leaked into him, and his into her—

"Look at you," he breathed. "Bryce."

"Look at *us*," she whispered, and lifted up to kiss him. He met her halfway, tongues tangling. His thrusts turned wilder. He was close.

"I want to go with you," he said against her mouth. Sounding . . . almost normal again.

"Then make it happen," she said, hand sliding for his balls. His fingers caressed her clit. Began stroking.

Bryce kneaded his balls, and a shudder went through him. Another. On the third stroke, she squeezed hard, right as lightning streamed from his fingers and—

She was falling. Had the distant sense of screaming her pleasure to the surface miles above, of an orgasm rocking through her, reducing her mind to rubble. She was vaguely conscious of Hunt pumping into her, spilling into her, over and over—

Falling through time and space and light and shadow—

Up was down and down was up, and they were the only beings in existence, here in this garden, locked away from time—

Something cold and hard pushed into her back, but she didn't care, not as she clenched Hunt to her, gasping down air, sanity. He was shaking, wings twitching, whispering, "Bryce, Bryce, Bryce," in her ear.

Sweat coated their bodies, and she dragged her fingers down his spine. He was hers, and she was his, and—

"*Bryce*," Hunt said, and Bryce opened her eyes.

Harsh, blinding light greeted them. White walls, diving equipment, and—a ladder. No hint of a garden.

Hunt was instantly up, whirling to assess their surroundings, cock still jutting out and gleaming. Bryce needed a moment to get her knees operational, bracing against the cold floor.

She knew this room.

Hunt's eyes remained wild, but—no lightning danced around them. No trace of that primal fury. Just a glowing, iridescent handprint on his chest, a remnant of starlight. It faded with each breath.

He asked between pants, "How the *fuck* did we wind up in the air lock?"

"Okay," Flynn said, clapping his hands together. "So to make sure I have this right . . ." He pointed to the slender fire sprite floating in the air to his left. "You're Ridi."

"Rithi!" she squeaked.

"Rithi," Flynn amended with a smile. He pointed to the full-bodied sprite before him. "You're Malana." She beamed. He pointed to the sprite to the right of her. "And you're Sasa. And you're triplets."

"Yes," Malana said, long hair floating in the air around her. "Descendants of Persina Falath, Lady of Cinders."

"Right," Ithan said, as if that meant anything to him. He knew nothing about sprites and their hierarchies. Only that they'd been banished from Sky and Breath ages ago for a failed rebellion. They'd been deemed Lowers ever since.

"And *you*," Flynn drawled, pivoting to the naked female on the other end of the sectional, a blanket draped around her shoulders, "are . . ."

"I haven't given you my name," came the answer, her red eyes now faded to a charred black. She'd stopped burning—at least enough to avoid singeing the couch.

"Exactly," Flynn said, as if the Fae lord weren't taunting a dragon. A fucking *dragon*. A Lower, yes, but . . . fuck. They weren't true shifters, switching between humanoid and animal bodies at will. They were more like the mer, if anything. There was a biological or magical difference to explain it—Ithan vaguely remembered learning about it in school, though he'd promptly forgotten the details.

It didn't matter now, he supposed. The dragon could navigate two forms. He'd be a fool to underestimate her in this one.

The dragon stared Flynn down. He gave her a charming smile back. Her chin lifted. "Ariadne."

Flynn arched a brow. "A dragon named Ariadne?"

"I suppose you have a better name for me?" she shot back.

"Skull-Crusher, Winged Doom, Light-Eater." Flynn ticked them off on his fingers.

She snorted, and the hint of amusement had Ithan realizing that the dragon was . . . beautiful. Utterly lethal and defiant, but—well, damn. From the gleam in Flynn's eyes, Ithan could tell the Fae lord was thinking the same.

Ariadne said, "Such names are for the old ones who dwell in their mountain caves and sleep the long slumber of true immortals."

"But you're not one of them?" Ithan asked.

"My kin are more . . . modern." Her gaze sharpened on Flynn. "Hence Ariadne."

Flynn winked. She scowled.

"How did all of you"—Declan cut in, motioning to Ariadne, her body similar to that of a Fae female's—"fit into that tiny ring?"

"We were bespelled by the Astronomer," Sasa whispered. "He's an ancient sorcerer—don't let him deceive you with that feeble act. He bought us all, and shoved us into those rings to light the way when he descends into Hel. Though Ariadne got put into the ring by . . ." She trailed off when the dragon cut her a scathing, warning look.

A chill went down Ithan's spine. He asked them, "Is there anything to be done to free the others he still controls? The mystics?"

"No," Ariadne answered. She peered down at her tan wrist. The brand there. *SPQM*. A slave's mark. The sprites also bore it. "He owns them, as he owns us. The mystic you spoke to, the wolf . . ." Her black eyes shifted toward red again. "He favors her. He will never let her go. Not until she grows old in that tank and dies."

Centuries from now, possibly. Ithan's gut twisted.

"Please don't make us go back," Rithi whispered, clinging to Malana.

"Hush," Malana warned.

Marc studied them. "Look, ladies. You're in a tough spot. You're not only slaves, but stolen slaves." A warning look at Ithan, who shrugged. He had no regrets. "Yet there are laws about your treatment. It's archaic and nonsensical that anyone can be owned, but if you can prove severe maltreatment, it might allow for you to be . . . purchased by someone else."

"Not freed?" Sasa whispered.

"Only your new owner could do that," Marc said sadly.

"So buy them and be done with it." Ariadne crossed her arms.

"What about you, sweetheart?" Flynn purred at the dragon, like the Fae male literally couldn't help himself.

Her eyes burned crimson. "I'm beyond your pay grade, lordling."

"Try me."

But the dragon turned back to staring at the TV, still paused on the video game. Ithan swallowed and asked her, "It's bad, then— what he does to the mystics?"

"He tortures them," Ariadne said flatly, and Rithi whimpered her agreement. "The wolf female is . . . defiant. She did not lie about his punishments. I've sat on his hand for years and witnessed him send her into the darkest corners of Hel. He lets the demons and their princes taunt her. Terrify her. He thinks he'll break her one day. I'm not so sure."

Ithan's stomach turned.

Ariadne went on, "She spoke true today about the necromancer, too." Flynn, Marc, and Declan turned toward Ithan, brows high. "You want answers about your dead brother, then you should find one."

Ithan nodded. The dragon belonged to the House of Flame and Shadow, even if the slave tattoo removed her from its protections. She'd have knowledge of a necromancer's ability.

Declan announced, "Well, since we're now harboring stolen slaves, we might as well make you ladies comfortable. Feel free to claim Ruhn's room—second bedroom at the top of the stairs."

The three sprites zoomed for the staircase, as if they were no more than three excited children. Ithan couldn't help his smile. He'd done some good today, at least. Even if it would land him in a heap of trouble.

Ariadne slowly got to her feet. They rose with her.

Flynn, standing closest, said to the dragon, "You could run, you know. Shift into your other form and take off. We won't tell anyone where you went."

Her red eyes again dimmed to black. "Don't you know what this does?" She lifted her arm to reveal the tattoo there. She laughed bitterly. "I can't shift unless he allows it. And even if I manage it, anywhere I go, anywhere on Midgard, he can track me in that form."

"You teleported," Cormac said to Bryce an hour later as she and Hunt stood beside his cot in the city-ship's hospital. The prince was pale, but alive. Every shard of the gorsian bullet had been removed. Another hour and he'd be back to normal.

Hunt didn't particularly care. They'd only come to Cormac for answers.

Hunt was still recovering from the sex that had blasted him apart mind and body and soul, the sex that Bryce had known would bring him back from the brink, that had made his magic sing.

Had made their magics merge.

He didn't know how to describe it—the feeling of her magic wending through him. Like he existed all at once and not at all, like he could craft whatever he wished from thin air and nothing would be denied to him. Did she live with this, day after day? That pure sense of . . . possibility? It had faded since they'd teleported, but he could still feel it there, in his chest, where her handprint had glowed. A slumbering little kernel of creation.

"*How?*" Bryce asked. She'd had no shame, not even a blush, striding in here—the two of them wearing navy-blue aquatic body armor they'd taken from the air lock to cover themselves. Ruhn had looked thoroughly uncomfortable, but Tharion had laughed at Hunt's disheveled hair and whatever stupid happiness was on his face, and said, "Good work bringing our boy back, Legs."

Bryce had gone right to Cormac and explained what had happened in the most Quinlan-like way Hunt could imagine: "Right at the end of banging Hunt's brains out, *right* when we came together, we wound up in the air lock."

Cormac studied her, then Hunt. "Your powers merged, I take it."

"Yeah," Bryce said. "We both went all glowy. Not in the way that he was glowing during his . . ." She frowned. "Rage-daze." She waved a hand. "This was like . . . we glowed with my starlight. Then we teleported."

"Hmm," Cormac said. "I wonder if you need Athalar's power for teleporting."

"I can't tell if that's an insult or not," Bryce said.

Hunt lifted his brows. "In what way?"

"If my powers only work if my big, tough male helps me out—"

"It can't be romantic?" Hunt demanded.

Bryce huffed. "I'm an independent female."

"All right," Hunt said, laughing softly. "Let's just say that I'm like some magic token in a video game and when you . . . use me, you level up."

"That is the dorkiest thing you've ever said," Bryce accused, and Hunt sketched a bow.

"So Hunt's magic is the key to Bryce's?" Ruhn asked Cormac.

"I don't know if it's Hunt specifically, or simply energy," Cormac said. "Your power came from the Gates—it's something we don't understand. It's playing by unknown rules."

"Great," Bryce muttered, sinking into the chair beside Ruhn's near the window. Black, eternal water spread beyond.

Hunt rubbed his jaw, frowning. "The Prince of the Pit told me about this."

Bryce's brow scrunched. "Sex teleporting?"

Hunt snorted. "No. He told me that you and I hadn't . . . explored what our powers could do. Together."

Ruhn said, "You think this is what he had in mind?"

"I don't know," Hunt admitted, marking the gleam of worry on Bryce's face. They still had a lot to talk about.

"Is it wise," Tharion drawled, "to do as he says?"

"I think we should wait to see if our theory is correct," Bryce said. "See if it really was our powers . . . merging." She asked Hunt, "How do you feel?"

"Fine," he said. "I think I kept a kernel of your power in me for a while, but it's gone quiet."

She smiled slightly. "We definitely need to do more research."

"You just want to bang Athalar again," Tharion countered.

Bryce inclined her head. "I thought that was a given."

Hunt stalked toward her, fully intending to drag her to some quiet room to test out the theory. But the door to the room slid open, and Commander Sendes appeared. Her face was grim.

Hunt braced himself. The Asteri had found them. The Omegas were about to attack—

But her gaze fell on Cormac. She said quietly, "The medwitch told me that in your delirium, you were talking about someone named Sofie Renast. That name is known to us here—we've heard of her work for years now. But I thought you should know that we were summoned to rescue an agent from the North Sea weeks ago. It wasn't until we reached her that we realized it was Sofie."

The room went utterly silent. Cormac's swallow was audible as Sendes went on, "We were too late. Sofie had drowned by the time our divers picked her up."

47

The morgue was cold and quiet and empty, save for the female corpse lying on the chrome table, covered by a black cloth.

Bryce stood by the doorway as Cormac knelt beside the body, preserved by a medwitch until the ship could hand Sofie over to the Ophion rebels for claiming. The prince was silent.

He'd been this way since Sendes had come to his room.

And though Bryce's body still buzzed with all she and Hunt had done, seeing that slender female body on the table, the prince kneeling, head bowed . . . Her eyes stung. Hunt's fingers found hers and squeezed.

"I knew," Cormac said roughly. His first words in minutes. "I think I always knew, but . . ."

Ruhn stepped to his cousin's side. Put a hand on his shoulder. "I'm sorry."

Cormac leaned his brow against the rim of the examination table. His voice shook. "She was good, and brave, and kind. I never deserved her, not for one minute."

Bryce's throat ached. She let go of Hunt's hand to approach Cormac, touching his other shoulder. Where would Sofie's soul go? Did it linger near her body until they could give her a proper Sailing? If she went to one of the resting places, they'd be dooming her to a terrible fate.

But Bryce didn't say any of that. Not as Cormac slid his fingers beneath the black cloth and pulled out a blue-tinged, stiff hand. He clasped it in his own, kissing the dead fingers. His shoulders began to shake as his tears flowed.

"We met during a recon report to Command," Cormac said, voice breaking. "And I knew it was foolish, and reckless, but I had to speak to her after the meeting was over. To learn everything I could about her." He kissed Sofie's hand again, closing his eyes. "I should have gone back for her that night."

Tharion, who'd been poring over the coroner's files on Sofie at the desk by the far wall, said gently, "I'm sorry if I gave you false hope."

"It kept her alive in my heart a little longer," Cormac said, swallowing back his tears. He pressed her stiff hand against his brow. "My Sofie."

Ruhn squeezed his shoulder.

Tharion asked carefully, "Do you know what this means, Cormac?" He rattled off a series of numbers and letters.

Cormac lifted his head. "No."

Tharion held up a photo. "They were carved on her upper biceps. The coroner thinks she did it while she drowned, with some sort of pin or knife she might have had hidden on her."

Cormac shot to his feet, and Bryce stepped into Hunt's awaiting arms as the Fae Prince folded back the sheet. Nothing on the right arm he'd held, but the left—

The assortment of numbers and letters had been carved roughly an inch below her shoulder, left unhealed. Cut deep.

"Did she know someone was racing to save her?" Hunt asked.

Cormac shook his head. "I have no idea."

"How did the mer know to pick her up?"

"She could have signaled them with her light," Cormac mused. "Or maybe they saw Emile's, like they did with Bryce's. It lit up the whole sea taking down those Omegas. It must have signaled them somehow."

Bryce made a note to ask Commander Sendes. She said to Hunt, "Do those numbers and letters mean anything to you?"

"No." He stroked his thumb over Bryce's hand, as if reassuring himself that she stood there, and wasn't the one on that table.

Cormac covered Sofie with the sheet again. "Everything Sofie did, it was for a reason. You remind me of her in some ways."

Ruhn said, "I'll put Declan on the hunt as soon as we're home."

"What about the Ophion rebels and Pippa?" Bryce asked. "And the Hind?"

Hunt said, "We're everyone's enemy now."

Cormac nodded. "We can only meet the challenge. But knowing for sure that Sofie is gone . . . I must redouble my efforts to find Emile."

"Pippa seemed to know where he was lying low," Tharion said. "No idea if that's the safe place that Danika mentioned, though."

Cormac's eyes flashed. "I'm not letting him fall into your queen's hands. Or Ophion's control."

"You ready to be a single dad?" Bryce drawled. "You're just going to take the kid in and what . . . bring him to Avallen? That'll be a *really* great place for him."

Cormac stiffened. "I hadn't planned that far. Are you suggesting I leave that child alone in the world?"

Bryce shrugged, studying her nails. Felt Hunt looking at her closely. "So do we warn our families?" Gods, if the Hind had already headed to her mom's house—

"The Hind won't go after them," Cormac consoled her. Then amended, "Not yet. She'll want you in her clutches first, so she can breathe in your suffering while you know she's hunting them down."

"So we go home and pretend nothing happened?" Ruhn asked. "What's to stop the Hind from arresting us when we get back?"

"Do you think we could get away with convincing the Asteri that we were at the rebel base to *stop* Pippa and Ophion?" Bryce asked.

Hunt shrugged. "I blasted the shit out of that base, so the evidence is in our favor. Especially if Pippa is now hunting us."

"The Hind won't buy that," Cormac challenged.

But Bryce said, smiling faintly, "Master of spinning bullshit, remember?"

He didn't smile back. Just looked at Sofie, dead and gone before him.

So Bryce touched the prince's hand. "We'll make them all pay." The star on her chest glowed in promise.

The *Depth Charger* glided between the darkest canyons of the sea-floor. In the glass-domed command center, Tharion hung back by the arching doorway into the bustling hall beyond and marveled at the array of tech and magic, the uniformed mer operating all of it.

Sendes lingered at his side, approval on her face as she monitored the team keeping the ship operational.

"How long have you guys had these ships?" Tharion asked, his first words in the minutes since Sendes had invited him down here, where only high-ranking mer officials were allowed. He supposed that being the River Queen's Captain of Intelligence granted him access, but . . . he'd had no idea any of this existed. His title was a joke.

"Around two decades," Sendes said, straightening the lapel of her uniform. "They took twice that to conceptualize and build, though."

"They must have cost a fortune."

"The ocean deeps are full of priceless resources. Our queen exploited them cleverly to fund this project."

"Why?"

She faced him fully. She had a wonderfully curvy body, he'd noticed. With the sort of ass he'd like to sink his teeth into. But . . . the River Queen's cold face rippled through his mind, and Tharion turned to the windows behind the commander.

Beyond the wall of glass, a bioluminescent cloud—some sort of jellyfish—bobbed by. Suitably unsexy.

Sendes asked, "Why does your queen involve herself with the rebels?"

"She's not involving herself with them. I think she merely

wants something that *they* want." Or used to want, if Pippa was to be believed—though after they'd blown the suit to pieces, maybe Ophion would be back on the hunt for the kid. "I don't think her motivations for wanting it are necessarily to help people, though." He winced as he said it. Too bold, too reckless—

Sendes huffed a laugh. "Your opinion is safe here, don't worry. The Ocean Queen is aware that her sister in the Blue River is . . . moody."

Tharion blew out a breath. "Yeah." He took in the control room again. "So all this . . . the ships, the rescuing of rebels . . . Is it because the Ocean Queen wants to overthrow the Asteri?"

"I'm not close enough to her to know whether that's her true motive, but these ships have indeed aided the rebels. So I'd say yes."

"And she intends to make herself ruler?" Tharion asked carefully.

Sendes blinked. "Why would she ever do that?"

"Why not? That's what the River Queen would do."

Sendes stilled, completely earnest as she said, "The Ocean Queen would not set herself up as a replacement for the Asteri. She remembers a time before the Asteri. When leaders were fairly elected. That is what she wishes to achieve once more."

The dark ocean passed beyond the glass. Tharion couldn't suppress his bitter laugh. "And you believe her?"

Sendes gave him a pitying look. "I'm sorry that the River Queen has abused your trust so much that you don't."

"I'm sorry that you're naïve enough to believe everything your queen says," he countered.

Sendes gave him that pitying look again, and Tharion tensed. He changed the subject, though. "What are the odds that either you guys or Cormac will release Sofie's body to me?"

Her brows lifted. "Why do you want it?"

"My queen wants it. I don't get to ask questions."

Sendes frowned. "What use could she have with a thunderbird's corpse?"

He doubted Cormac would appreciate Sofie being referred to as a *corpse*, but he said, "Again, no idea."

Sendes fell silent. "Does . . . does your queen have any necromancers in her employ?"

Tharion started. "What? No." The only one he knew was hundreds of miles away, and she sure as shit wasn't going to help out the River Queen. "Why?"

"It's the only reason I can think of to go to such lengths to retrieve a thunderbird's body. To reanimate it."

Cold horror sluiced through him. "A weapon without a conscience or soul."

Sendes nodded gravely. "But what does she need it for?"

He opened his mouth, but shut it. Speculating on his queen's motives in front of a stranger, even a friendly one, would be foolish. So he shrugged. "Guess we'll find out."

Sendes saw right through him, though. "We have no claim on the body, but Prince Cormac, as her lover and a member of Ophion, does. You'll have to take it up with him."

Tharion knew precisely how that would end. With a giant, burning *NO*. So, short of becoming a body snatcher—not high on his list of life goals—he wasn't delivering the goods. "Time to begin the spin cycle," Tharion murmured, more to himself than to Sendes. He'd have to either lie about ever finding Sofie's body or lie about why he couldn't steal it. Fuck.

"You could be more, you know," Sendes said, seeming to read the dread on his face. "At a place like this. We don't need to lie and scheme here."

"I'm content where I am," Tharion said quickly. His queen would never let him leave anyway.

But Sendes inclined her head knowingly—sadly. "You ever need anything, Captain Ketos, we're here for you."

The kindness stunned him enough that he had no reply.

Sendes was called over by one of the deck officers, and Tharion observed the mer at the controls. Serious, but . . . smiling. No tension, no walking on eggshells.

He glanced at the clock. He should go back to the sleeping quarters Sendes had arranged for them. Check in with the others.

Yet once he did, he'd sleep. And when he woke, he'd return to Lunathion.

To the Blue Court.

It was getting harder to ignore the part of him that didn't want to go home at all.

Ruhn slept miles beneath the surface, a fitful sort of slumber from which he rose frequently to ensure his companions were all piled into the small room with him on the cots and bunk beds. Cormac had opted to remain in the morgue with Sofie, wanting to mourn in private, to say all the prayers to Cthona and Luna that his lover was owed.

Tharion dozed on the bottom bunk across from Ruhn's, sprawled across the top of the sheets. He'd wandered off after dinner to explore the ship, and returned hours later, quiet. He hadn't said anything about what he'd seen other than *It's mer-only*.

So Ruhn had sat with the lovebirds, Bryce nestled between Hunt's legs as they ate dinner on the floor of the room, the sea drifting by their window. They'd reach the mouth of the Istros at dawn, and Tharion's people would be waiting there to transport them upriver to Lunathion.

What would happen then . . . Ruhn could only pray it'd work out in their favor. That Bryce could play their cards well enough to avoid their doom.

Night?

Day's voice floated into his mind, faint and—worried.

He let his mind relax, let himself find that bridge, the two couches. She already sat on hers, burning away. "Hey."

"Are you all right?"

"Worried about me, huh?"

She didn't laugh. "I heard about an attack on the rebel base on Ydra. That people were killed, and the shipment of ammo and the suit destroyed. I . . . thought you might have been among the ones lost."

He surveyed her.

"Where are you now?" she asked.

He let her change the subject. "Somewhere safe." He couldn't say more. "I watched Pippa Spetsos and the Ophion rebels kill innocent Vanir in cold blood today. You want to tell me what the fuck that's about?"

She stiffened. "Why did she kill them?"

"Does it matter?"

She considered. "No. Not if the victims were innocent. Pippa did it herself?"

"A group of soldiers under her command did."

Her flame guttered to hottest blue. "She's a fanatic. Dedicated to the rebel cause, yes—but to her own cause most of all."

"She was a friend of Agent Cypress, apparently."

"She was no friend to Sofie. Or anyone." Her voice had gone cold. Like she was angry enough that she forgot to use Sofie's code name.

"Sofie's dead, by the way."

Day started. "You're sure of this?"

"Yes. She drowned."

"She . . ." Day's legs curled beneath her. "She was a brave agent. Far better and braver than Ophion deserved." Genuine sorrow laced Day's words.

"You liked her."

"She went into the Kavalla death camp to save her brother. Did everything the Ophion commanders asked her just so she could get scraps of information about him. If Pippa serves only herself, then Sofie was her opposite: all the work she did was for others. But yes. I did like her. I admired her courage. Her loyalty. She was a kindred spirit in many ways."

Ruhn slumped against the back of his couch. "So, what—you hate Pippa and Ophion, too? If everyone hates her and the group, why the fuck do you bother working with them?"

"Do you see anyone else leading the cause? Has anyone else stepped up to the line?"

No. No one else would dare.

Day said, "They're the only ones in recent memory to have ever mustered such a force. Only Shahar and General Hunt Athalar ever did anything close, and they were decimated in one battle."

And Athalar had suffered for centuries afterward.

Day went on, "To be free of the Asteri, there are things that we all must do that will leave a mark on our souls. It's the cost, so that our children and their children won't ever need to pay it. So they'll know a world of freedom and plenty."

The words of a dreamer. A glimpse beneath that hard-ass facade.

So Ruhn said, the first time he'd said it aloud, "I'm not going to have children."

"Why?"

"I can't."

She angled her head. "You're infertile?"

He shrugged. "Maybe. I don't know. The Oracle told me when I was a kid that I was to be the last of my bloodline. So either I die before I can sire a child, or . . . I'm shooting blanks."

"Does it bother you?"

"I'd prefer not to be dead before my time, so if her words just mean that I'm not going to be a father . . . I don't know. It doesn't change a lick of who I am, but I still try not to think about it. No one in my life knows, either. And considering the father I have . . . maybe it's good that I won't be one. I wouldn't know the first thing about how to be a decent dad."

"That doesn't seem true."

He snorted. "Well, anyway, that was my stupid way of saying that while I might not be having kids, I . . . I get what you're saying. I have people in my life who will, and for their kids, their families . . . I'll do whatever I have to."

But she was having none of his deflecting. "You are kind, and caring. And seem to love those around you. I can't think of anything else needed to be a father."

"How about growing the Hel up and not partying so much?"

She laughed. "All right. Maybe that."

He smiled slightly. Faint, distant stars glowed in the darkness around them.

She said, "You seem unsettled."

"I saw a bunch of fucked-up shit today. I was having a hard time sleeping before you knocked."

"Knocked?"

"Whatever you want to call it. Summoned me."

"Shall I tell you a story to help you sleep?" Her voice was wry.

"Yeah." He'd call her bluff.

But she only said, "All right."

He blinked. "Really?"

"Why not?" She motioned for him to lie down. So Ruhn did, closing his eyes.

Then, to his shock, she came and sat beside him. Brushed a burning hand through his hair. Warm and gentle—tentative.

She began, "Once upon a time, before Luna hunted the heavens and Solas warmed Cthona's body, before Ogenas blanketed Midgard with water and Urd twined our fates together, there lived a young witch in a cottage deep in the woods. She was beautiful, and kind, and beloved by her mother. Her mother had done her best to raise her, with her only companions being the denizens of the forest itself: birds and beasts and the babbling brooks . . ."

Her voice, lovely and fair and steady, flowed through him like music. Her hand brushed through his hair again and he reined in his purr.

"She grew older, strong and proud. But a wandering prince passed by her clearing one day when her mother was gone, beheld her beauty, and wanted her desperately to be his bride."

"I thought this was supposed to be a comforting story," Ruhn muttered.

She laughed softly, tugging on a strand of his hair. "Listen."

Ruhn figured to Hel with it and shifted, laying his head on her lap. The fire did not burn him, and the thigh beneath was firm with muscle, yet supple. And that scent . . .

Day went on, "She had no interest in princes, or in ruling a kingdom, or in any of the jewels he offered. What she wanted was a true heart to love her, to run wild with her through the forest. But the prince would not be denied. He chased her through the wood, his hounds following."

Ruhn's body relaxed, limb by limb. He breathed in her scent, her voice, her warmth.

"As she ran, she pleaded with the forest she loved so dearly to help her. So it did. First, it transformed her into a deer, so she might be as swift as the wind. But his hounds outraced her, closing in swiftly. Then the forest turned her into a fish, and she fled down one of the mountain streams. But he built a weir at its base to trap her. So she became a bird, a hawk, and soared for the skies. But the prince was a skilled archer, and he fired one of his iron-tipped arrows."

Ruhn drifted, quiet and calm. When was the last time anyone had told him a story to lull him to sleep?

"It struck her breast, and where her blood fell, olive trees sprouted. As her body hit the earth, the forest transformed her one last time . . ."

Ruhn woke, still on the mind-bridge. Day lay on the couch across from him, asleep as well, her body still veiled with flame.

He stood, crossing the distance to her.

A princess of fire, sleeping, waiting for a knight to awaken her. He knew that story. It tugged at the back of his mind. A sleeping warrior-princess surrounded by a ring of fire, damned to lie there until a warrior brave enough to face the flames could cross them.

Day turned over, and through the flame, he glimpsed a hint of long hair draped over the arm of the couch—

He backed away a step. But somehow she heard, and shot upright. Flame erupted around her as Ruhn retreated to his own couch. "What were you doing?"

Ruhn shook his head. "I . . . I wanted to know how the story ended. I fell asleep as the witch was pierced with an arrow."

Day jumped up from her couch, walking around it—putting it between them. Like he'd crossed some major line.

But she said, "The forest turned the witch into a monster before she hit the earth. A beast of claws and fangs and bloodlust. She ripped the prince and hounds who pursued her into shreds."

"And that's it?" Ruhn demanded.

"That's it," Day said, and walked into the darkness, leaving only embers drifting behind.

PART III
THE PIT

48

Ruhn paced in front of Bryce's TV, his phone at his ear. The tattoos on his forearms shifted as he clenched the phone tight. But his voice was calm, heavy, as he said, "All right, thanks for looking, Dec."

Bryce watched Ruhn's face as her brother hung up, and knew exactly what he was going to say. "No luck?"

Ruhn slumped back against her couch cushions. "No. What we saw on Sofie's arm doesn't come up anywhere."

Bryce nestled into Hunt on the other end of the couch while the angel talked to Isaiah on the phone. Upon arriving back in Lunathion courtesy of a few Blue Court wave skimmers, Tharion had gone Beneath to see his queen. It was unlikely that the River Queen would know what the numbers and letters carved onto Sofie's biceps meant, but it was worth a shot.

Cormac had found thirty messages from his father waiting for him, asking after his whereabouts, so he'd gone off to the Autumn King's villa to convince the male—and therefore his father—that he'd been accompanying Bryce to Nidaros.

Bryce supposed she should clue her parents in about the official cover story, but she couldn't quite bring herself to do it. She needed to settle—calm her racing mind—a bit first.

Frankly, it was a miracle the Hind and her dreadwolves hadn't been waiting at the apartment. That the news wasn't broadcasting all of their faces with a *REBEL TRAITORS* banner slapped beneath it. But a skim of the news while Ruhn had talked to Dec showed nothing.

So she'd spent the last few minutes trying hard to teleport from the couch to the kitchen.

Nothing. How had she done it during sex? She wasn't due for her lesson with Ruhn and Cormac until tomorrow, but she wanted to show up with *some* idea.

Bryce concentrated on the kitchen stools. *I am here. I want to go there.* Her magic didn't so much as budge. *Two points in space. I'm folding a piece of paper, joining them. My power is the pencil that punctures through the paper, linking them—*

Hunt said, "Yeah. Ember grilled me, but we're good. We had a nice time." He winked at Bryce, even though the casual gesture didn't quite light his eyes. "All right. I'll see you at the meeting later." Hunt hung up the phone and sighed. "Unless they've got a dagger digging into his back, it seems like Isaiah has no clue about what went down at Ydra. Or that the Hind saw any of us."

"What game is she playing?" Ruhn said, toying with his lip ring. "You really think Isaiah wasn't playing it cool to lure you to the Comitium later?"

"If they wanted to arrest us, they'd have been waiting for us," Hunt said. "The Hind is keeping this to herself."

"But why?" Bryce asked, frowning deeply. "To mess with our minds?"

"Honestly?" Hunt said. "That's a distinct possibility. But if you ask me, I think she knows we're . . . up to something. I think she wants to see what we do next."

Bryce considered. "We've been so focused on Emile and Ophion and the demons that we've forgotten one key thing: Sofie died knowing vital intel. The Hind knew that—was afraid enough of it that she killed her to make sure the intel died with Sofie. And if it didn't take much for Tharion to piece together that Sofie and Danika knew each other and come to us, I bet the Hind has figured that out, too. She has hackers who could have found the same emails between them."

Hunt's wing brushed her shoulder, curving around her. "But how does it even tie to Danika? Sofie didn't get the intel until two years after Danika died."

"No idea," Bryce said, leaning her head against Hunt's shoulder. A casual, steadying sort of intimacy.

The sex on the ship had been life-altering. Soul-altering. Just . . . altering. She couldn't wait to have him again.

But she cleared the thought from her head as Ruhn asked, "Any chance this somehow ties into Danika researching that Fendyr lineage?" Her brother rubbed his temples. "Though I don't see how anything about that would be war-changing intel worth killing to hide."

"Me neither," Bryce said, sighing. She'd slept last night curled beside Hunt in their bunk, limbs and wings and breath mingling, but she was still exhausted. From the shadows under Hunt's eyes, she knew the same weariness weighed on him.

A knock sounded on her door, and Ruhn rose to get it. Hunt's hand tangled in her hair, and he tugged on the strands, getting Bryce to look up at him. He kissed her nose, her chin, her mouth.

"I might be tired," he said, as if he'd sensed her thoughts, "but I'm ready for round two when you are."

Her blood heated. "Good," she murmured back. "I'd hate for you to be unable to keep up in your old age."

They were interrupted by Ruhn standing over them. "Sorry to break up the lovefest, but the Helhound's outside."

Baxian gave them no time to prepare as he burst in after Ruhn, black wings splaying slightly. "How the fuck did you call that ship?"

"What are you doing here?" Hunt asked quietly.

Baxian blinked. "Making sure you're all still in one piece."

"Why?" Ruhn asked.

"Because I want in." Baxian helped himself to a stool at the counter.

Bryce coughed, but said innocently, "On what?"

The Helhound threw her a dry look. "On whatever it was that had you all going to meet with Ophion, then blasting their shit to Hel."

Bryce said smoothly, "We thought to cut off Ophion before they could ruin Valbara's peace."

Baxian snorted. "Yeah, sure. Without backup, without alerting anyone."

"There are rebel sympathizers in the 33rd," Hunt said firmly. "We couldn't risk tipping them off."

"I know," Baxian replied with equal cool. "I'm one of them."

Bryce stared at the shifter and said as calmly as she could, "You realize we could go right to Celestina with this. You'd be crucified before nightfall."

"I want you to tell me what's going on," Baxian countered.

"I already told you. And you just royally fucked yourself over," Bryce said.

"If they start asking questions about how you know I'm a sympathizer, you think anyone's going to buy your bullshit about going there to save Valbara from the big bad human rebels? Especially when you lied to Celestina about going to your parents' house?" Baxian laughed. Hunt had gone so still that Bryce knew he was a breath away from killing the male, even though no lightning zapped around him. "The Asteri will let the Hind start on you right away, and we'll see how long those lies hold up under her ministrations."

"Why isn't the Hind here yet?" Bryce asked. She'd confirm nothing.

"Not her style," Baxian said. "She wants to give you enough rope to hang yourself."

"And Ydra wasn't enough?" Ruhn blurted.

Bryce glared at him. Her brother ignored it, his lethal attention on Baxian.

"If I were to guess, I'd say that she thinks you'll lead her toward whatever it is she wants."

Ruhn growled, "What do *you* want?"

Baxian leaned back against the counter. "I told you: I want in."

"No," Hunt said.

"Did I not warn your asses yesterday?" Baxian said. "Did I not back you up when Sabine came raging in here? Have I said anything to anyone about it since then?"

"The Hind plays games that span years," Hunt countered with soft menace. "Who knows what you're planning with her? But we're not rebels anyway, so there's nothing for you to join."

Baxian laughed—without joy, without any sort of amusement—and hopped off the stool. Aimed right for the front door. "When you fools want actual answers, come find me." The door slammed behind him.

In the silence that fell in his wake, Bryce closed her eyes.

"So . . . we play casual," Ruhn said. "Figure out how to outsmart the Hind."

Hunt grunted, not sounding convinced. That made two of them.

A buzz sounded, and Bryce opened her eyes to see Ruhn scanning his phone. "Flynn needs me back at the house. Call me if you hear anything."

"Be careful," Hunt warned him, but her brother just patted the hilt of the Starsword before striding out. As if the blade would do anything against the Hind.

Alone in their apartment, truly alone at last, Bryce waggled her brows at Hunt. "Want to take our minds off everything with a little tumble in the sheets?"

Hunt chuckled, leaning to brush a kiss on her mouth. He paused millimeters from her lips, close enough that she could feel his smile as he said, "How about you tell me what the fuck you know about Emile?"

Bryce pulled back. "Nothing."

His eyes blazed. "Oh? Spetsos practically blabbed it, didn't she? With her talk about snakes." Lightning shimmered along his wings. "Are you fucking insane? Sending that kid to the Viper Queen?"

49

"How'd it go?"

Ruhn stood before Flynn and Dec, his friends sitting on the sectional with too-innocent smiles. Ithan sat on Dec's other side—and his wary face tipped Ruhn off.

"I'm wondering if I should ask you three the same thing," Ruhn said, arching a brow.

"Well, you're alive, and not captured," Dec said, tucking his hands behind his head and leaning back against the couch. "I'm assuming it went . . . well?"

"Let's leave it at that," Ruhn said. He'd fill them in later. When he was a little less exhausted and a little less worried about those innocent expressions.

"Good, great, fantastic," Flynn said, leaping to his feet. "So, you know how you're always saying that it's pretty sexist that we don't have any female roommates . . ."

"I've never said tha—"

Flynn gestured to the foyer behind him. "Well, here you go."

Ruhn blinked as three fire sprites zoomed in, landing on Flynn's broad shoulders. A full-bodied one cuddled up against his neck, smiling.

"Meet the triplets," Flynn said. "Rithi, Sasa, and Malana."

The taller of the slender ones—Sasa—batted her eyelashes at Ruhn. "Prince."

"Our insurance rates will go sky-high," Ruhn said to Declan, appealing to the slightly-less-insane of his roommates.

"When the fuck did you become a grown-up?" Flynn barked.

Ithan jerked his chin toward the doorway again. "Wait to have your meltdown until after you meet the fourth new roommate."

A short, curvy female walked in, her wavy black hair nearly down to her waist. Most of her tan skin was hidden by the plaid blanket wrapped around her naked body. But her eyes—burning Solas. They were bloodred. Glowing like embers.

"Ariadne, meet Ruhn," Flynn crooned. "Ruhn, meet Ariadne."

She held Ruhn's stare, and he stilled as he caught a glimmer of something molten course beneath the skin of her forearm, making her flesh look like . . . scales.

Ruhn whirled on Dec and Flynn. "I was gone for a day! Sunrise to sunrise! And I come back to *a dragon*? Where did she come from?"

Dec and Flynn, the three sprites with them, pointed to Ithan.

The wolf winced.

Ruhn glanced back at the dragon, at the hand clutching the blanket around her. The slight hint of the brand on her wrist. He studied the sprites.

"Please tell me they're at least here legally," Ruhn said quietly.

"Nope," Flynn said cheerfully.

Hunt had two options: start shouting or start laughing. He hadn't decided which one he wanted to do as they walked down a narrow hallway of the most lethal warehouse in the Meat Market, aiming for the door at the far end. The blank-faced Fae guards at the door didn't so much as blink. If they knew who Bryce was to them, they gave no sign.

"How'd you figure it out?" Bryce's brows bunched. She hadn't denied it on the flight over here. That she'd somehow gotten Emile to the Viper Queen. And Hunt had been too fucking pissed to ask any questions.

So fucking pissed that it had driven away any lingering lust from last night.

Hunt said under his breath, "I told you. You're not as slick as you think. The way you got so tense with Pippa talking about snakes was a dead giveaway." He shook his head. "It wasn't Pippa killing those people to track Emile, was it?"

Bryce winced. "No. It was the Viper Queen's henchmen. Well, henchwoman. She sent one of her human lackeys—some merc—to hunt him down. Hence the female human scent."

"And you were fine with this? Not simply killing those people, but framing Pippa?" Granted, Pippa was awful, but . . . Something crumpled in his chest.

Was this any different from his time with Shahar? Falling for a beautiful, powerful female—only to have her hide her innermost thoughts—

"No," Bryce said, paling. She halted ten feet from the guards. Touched Hunt's arm. "I wasn't fine with that part at all." Her throat bobbed. "I told her to find him by any means necessary. I didn't realize it'd entail . . . that."

"That was a stupid fucking thing to do," Hunt snarled, and immediately hated himself for the bruised look that came into her eyes. But he continued toward the door, pulling out of her grip.

The guards wordlessly let them enter the lushly appointed apartment. Definitely a far cry from her ramshackle office levels below. A foyer of carved wood flowed ahead, the crimson rug leading toward a large sitting room with a massive, floor-to-ceiling interior window overlooking the Viper Queen's notorious fighting pit.

Bryce murmured coldly as they aimed for the sitting room, "I'm not letting this poor kid fall into anyone's hands. Even Cormac's."

"So that night we came here with Juniper and Fury—was Emile here already?"

"The Viper Queen was supposed to have apprehended him by that point. But then Tharion told us about the dead selkie, and it was clear she hadn't yet found him. So I came here to see what the Hel had happened, and to inform her that leaving a trail of bodies . . . that was *not* what I had intended. When I walked past the guards after we separated to search, I might have muttered a few questions for them to convey to their queen. And they might have had one of their undercover guards come up to me at the butcher where I bought the meat for Syrinx and tell me that the kid was still at large, and they'd last seen him near the Black Dock. Which made me doubt everything I'd assumed about him coming here, and I knew that I just . . . I needed to go to the Bone Quarter to make sure he *wasn't* there. While the Viper Queen kept searching. But apparently either she or her henchwoman ignored my demand to stop the killing, and added a few more to the list before they grabbed Emile."

"So coming here that night was a big waste of time?"

She shook her head. "No. I also needed everyone to think I was looking for Emile, and that we'd cleared this space, so if the Viper Queen did manage to get him, no one would come here again. And I needed you and Fury with me so that the Viper Queen would remember who would come fuck her up if she hurt the kid in the process."

That queen now stood before them, a slim female in a neon-green silk jumpsuit beside a large, plush couch. Her glossy black bob reflected the golden flames from the fireplace to her right. And seated on the couch before her, small and thin and wide-eyed, was a boy.

"Come to collect your package or make more threats about Athalar cooking me alive?" the Viper Queen asked, puffing on a cigarette between her purple-painted lips.

"Nice sneakers" was all Bryce said, gesturing to the snake shifter's white-and-gold high-tops. But Bryce offered Emile a gentle smile. "Hey, Emile. I'm Bryce."

The boy said nothing. Rather, he looked up at the Viper Queen, who drawled, "Red's the one who got you here. Ignore the angel. He's all bark, no bite."

"Oh, he likes to bite," Bryce murmured, but Hunt was in no mood to laugh. Or even smile. He said to the Viper Queen, power sparking in his veins, "Don't think for one moment that I'll ever forget how you screwed me over that night with Micah. Vik's suffering and Justinian's death are on you."

The queen had the audacity to look down at herself, as if searching for guilt.

But before Hunt could contemplate roasting her, Emile squeaked, "Hi."

He was just a kid, alone and afraid. The thought doused any lightning in Hunt's veins.

Bryce nodded at the Viper Queen. "I'd like a moment with Emile, please." It was a command. From a princess to another ruler.

The Viper Queen's slitted pupils widened—with amusement or predatory intent, Hunt didn't know. But she said, "Emile, holler if you need anything." She sauntered down an ornate, wood-paneled hallway and vanished through a door.

Bryce plopped onto the couch beside Emile and said, "So what's up?" The boy—and Hunt—blinked at her.

Emile said quietly, "My sister's dead, isn't she?"

Bryce's face softened, and Hunt said, "Yeah. She is. We're so sorry."

Emile gazed at his pale, bony hands. "The Vipe said you were looking, but . . . I knew." Hunt scanned the boy for any hint of that thunderbird gift. Any hint of a magic able to harvest and transform power to his will.

Bryce put a hand on Emile's shoulder. "Your sister was a badass. A brave, brilliant badass."

Emile offered a wobbly smile. Gods, the boy was scrawny. Way too thin for his lanky frame. If this was how thin he remained after a few weeks outside the death camp's barbed-wire fences . . . This boy had seen and endured things that no child—no person—should face.

Shame flooded Hunt, and he sat down beside Bryce.

No wonder she'd worked alone to arrange this—none of the rest of them had really stopped to think about the kid himself. Just his power, and what it might mean if the wrong person got hold of it.

Hunt tried to catch her eye, to show her that he understood, and he didn't hold any of this against her, but she kept her focus on the boy.

Bryce said quietly, "I lost a sister, too. Two years ago. It was hard, and you never stop feeling the loss, but . . . you learn to live with it. I'm not going to tell you time heals all wounds, because for some people it doesn't." Hunt's heart strained at the pain in her voice, even now. "But I get it. What you're feeling."

Emile said nothing. Hunt suppressed the urge to gather both of them in his arms and hug them tightly.

"And look," Bryce went on, "no matter what the Viper Queen says to you, don't take her threats too seriously. She's a psycho, but she's not a kid killer."

"Real reassuring," Hunt muttered.

Bryce scowled at him. "It's true."

But Hunt knew why the Viper Queen wouldn't have harmed the kid. He turned to the fighting pit beyond the window. It was dim and quiet now, too early in the day for the fights that drew hundreds—and made millions—for the snake shifter.

Alarm flared. Hunt blurted, "You didn't sign any contracts with her, right?"

"Why would she want me to sign anything?" Emile said, toeing the carpet.

Hunt said quietly, "Thunderbirds are insanely rare. A lot of people would want that power." He extended a hand toward Emile, and lightning wreathed his fingers, wending between them. "I'm not a thunderbird," Hunt said, "but I've got a similar gift. Made me, ah . . . valuable." He tapped the branded-out slave's mark on his wrist. "Not in any way that counts, deep down, but it made certain people willing to do a lot of bad things to attain me." The Viper Queen would kill—had killed—to own that power.

Emile's eyes widened at the lightning. Like he was seeing Hunt for the first time. "Sofie said something like that about her power once. That it didn't change who she was inside."

Hunt melted a bit at the trust in the kid's face. "It didn't. And your power doesn't, either."

Emile glanced between them. Then down the hall. "What power?"

Hunt slowly, slowly turned to Bryce. Her face revealed nothing. "Your . . . thunderbird power? The power that downed those Omega-boats?"

The kid's face shuttered. "That was Sofie."

Bryce lifted her chin in challenge. "Emile doesn't have any powers, Hunt."

Hunt looked like she'd dumped a bucket of ice water on him.

"What do you mean?" he asked, voice low. He didn't wait for her to reply before he pushed, "How do *you* know, Bryce?"

"I didn't know for sure," Bryce said. The small, scared boy now cringed away from the angel. She continued, "But I figured it was a good possibility. The only thing Vanir care about is power. The only way to get them to care about a human boy was to spin a story about him having powers like Sofie's. The only way to make sure he got to safety was to craft a lie about him being valuable. I had a feeling Sofie knew that all too well." She added with a soft smile to the boy, "Emile was—*is* valuable. To Sofie. To his family. As all loved ones are."

Hunt blinked. Blinked again. Anger—and fear—warred in his eyes. He whispered, "Does the Viper Queen know this?"

Bryce didn't hide her disdain. "She never asked." Bryce had been sure to word the bargain between them very carefully, so Emile could walk out of here whenever he wished.

Hunt's lightning writhed across his brow. "Any protection she's offering this kid will vanish the moment she knows." His gaze shifted to Emile, who watched the lightning not in fear, but with sorrow. The lightning immediately vanished. Hunt rubbed his face. Then said to Bryce, "You did all of this on a guess?"

"Sofie was part-human. Like me." Cormac himself had said they were alike. She explained as gently as she could, "You've never spent a moment of your life as a human, Hunt. You always had value to Vanir. You just said so yourself."

His wings rustled. "And what was the Vipe's asking price?"

"She'd retrieve Emile, hold him here—in comfort and safety—until I came to pick him up. And in return, I'd owe her a favor."

"That was reckless," he said through his teeth.

"It's not like I have piles of gold lying around." This wasn't the time or place for this fight. "You can have your alphahole fit later," she seethed.

"Fine," Hunt shot back. He leaned forward to address the boy, that thunderous expression easing. "Sorry, Emile. I'm glad you're safe, however insanely Bryce acted to make that happen. You game to answer a few questions?"

Emile nodded shallowly. Bryce braced herself.

Hunt gave Bryce another dirty look before he said, "How did you keep the Viper Queen from knowing you don't have any power?"

Emile shrugged. "When she talked about fights and stuff, I didn't answer. I think she thought I was scared."

"Good call," Bryce said. But Hunt cut in, "Were you originally heading to this city to find some sort of meeting place that you and your sister had agreed on beforehand?"

Emile nodded again. "We were supposed to meet here, actually."

Hunt murmured, "A place *where the weary souls find relief . . .*"

Bryce explained, "The Meat Market is drug central. I figured if Danika had suggested it as a hiding spot, then she might have thought the Viper Queen would be . . . amenable to helping them out. Turns out Danika was right."

Emile added, "The Vipe's agent picked me up before I could make it to the city proper. She said it wasn't safe anywhere but with them."

"It wasn't," Bryce said, smiling gently, "but now you're safe with us."

Well, at least they could agree on that. Hunt asked, "Did your sister ever mention anything secret about the Asteri? Anything super valuable to the rebels?"

Emile considered, brow scrunching. "No."

Bryce blew out a heavy breath. It had been a long shot anyway.

Emile wrung his fingers. "But . . . I do recognize that name. Danika. She was the wolf, right?"

Bryce went still. "You knew Danika?"

Emile shook his head. "No, but Sofie told me about her the night we separated. The blond wolf, who died a couple years ago. With the purple and pink streaks in her hair."

50

Bryce struggled to breathe. "How did Danika and Sofie know each other?"

"Danika found Sofie using her Vanir powers," Emile said. "She could smell Sofie's gift, or something. She needed Sofie to do something for her—Danika couldn't do it because she was too recognizable. But Sofie . . ." Emile toed the carpet. "She wasn't . . ."

Bryce cut in, "Sofie was a human. Or passed as one. She'd be ignored by most. What did Danika need her to do?"

Emile shook his head. "I don't know. I wasn't able to talk to Sofie for very long when we were in Kavalla."

Hunt's wide eyes shone with surprise, his anger at her seemingly forgotten for the moment. She pulled a slip of paper from her pocket. "These letters and numbers were found on your sister's body. Any idea what they mean?"

Emile bounced his knee. "No."

Damn it. Bryce twisted her mouth to the side.

Head bowed, Emile whispered, "I'm sorry I don't know anything else."

Hunt cleared his throat. Reached in front of Bryce to clasp the boy's shoulder. "You did good, kid. Really good. We owe you."

Emile offered Hunt a wobbly smile.

Yet Bryce's mind spun. Danika had needed Sofie to find something *big*. And though it had taken her years after Danika had died, Sofie had finally found it. And it had indeed been big enough that the Hind had killed her, rather than risking Sofie spreading it . . .

Hunt said, drawing her from her thoughts, "Bryce."

Her mate nodded pointedly to the window a few feet away.

"Give us a minute," she said to Emile with a smile, and walked over to the window, Hunt trailing her.

Hunt whisper-hissed, "What do we do with him now? We can't leave him here. It's only a matter of time until the Viper Queen figures out that he doesn't have powers. And we can't bring him with us. Pippa might very well come sniffing now that we destroyed that suit and they really do need a thunderbird's power—"

"Pippa Spetsos is a bad woman," Emile said from the couch, paling. Hunt had the good sense to look embarrassed that his little fit had been overheard. "Sofie warned me about her. After I got on the boat, she wanted to question me . . . I ran the moment no one was looking. But she and her Lightfall unit tracked me—all the way to the marshes. I hid in the reeds and was able to shake them there."

"Smart." Bryce pulled out her phone. "And we know all about Pippa, don't worry. She won't get anywhere near you." She glared at Hunt. "You really think I didn't plan this out?"

Hunt crossed his arms, brows high, but Bryce was already dialing. "Hey, Fury. Yeah, we're here. Bring the car around."

"You brought Axtar into this?"

"She's one of the few people I trust to escort him to his new home."

Fear flooded Emile's eyes. Bryce walked back to the couch and ruffled his hair. "You'll be safe there. I promise." She gave Hunt a warning look over her shoulder. She wasn't going to reveal more until they'd left. But she said to Emile, "Go use the bathroom. You're in for a long ride."

Hunt was still sorting through his racing feelings when they walked out of the Meat Market, Emile hidden beneath the shadows of a hooded sweatshirt. As promised, the Viper Queen had let them leave, no questions asked.

She'd only smiled at Bryce. Hunt suspected, with a sinking feeling, that she already knew Emile had no powers. That she'd taken in the kid because, despite his potential, there was one thing that might be more valuable to her one day: Bryce owing her a favor.

Hel yeah, he was going to have his little alphahole fit.

But he tucked away the thoughts when he found Fury Axtar leaning against a sleek black sedan, her arms crossed. Emile stumbled a step. Hunt didn't blame the kid.

Bryce threw her arms around her friend, saying, "Thank you *so* much."

Fury pulled back and turned to survey Emile as if she were looking at a particularly nasty bug. "Not much meat on him."

Bryce nudged her with an elbow. "So get him some snacks on the road."

"Snacks?" Fury said, but opened one of the rear doors.

"You know," Bryce drawled, "garbage food that provides zero nutrition for our bodies, but *lots* of nutrition for our souls."

How could she be so . . . glib about what she'd done? Any number of people would likely kill her for it. If not Cormac, then the River Queen or Ophion or the Hind—

Fury shook her head, chuckling, but beckoned to the boy. "In you go."

Emile balked.

Fury flashed a feral smile, "You're too short for the front. Airbag safety regulations."

"You just don't want him messing with the radio," Bryce muttered. Fury didn't deny it, and Emile didn't say anything as he climbed into the back seat. He had no bag, no belongings.

Hunt remembered that feeling. After his mother had died, he'd had no traces or reminders or comforts of the child he'd been, the mother who had sung him to sleep.

Nausea churned in his gut. Hunt said to the kid, "Don't let Fury boss you around."

Emile lifted wide, pleading eyes to Hunt. Gods, how had everyone forgotten that he was only a kid? Everyone except Bryce.

Shahar would never have done something like this, risked so much for someone who could do her absolutely no good. But Bryce . . . Hunt couldn't stop himself from stepping closer to her. From brushing his wing against her in a silent apology.

Bryce stepped beyond his reach. Fair enough. He'd been an asshole. She asked Fury, "You've got the address?"

"Yes. We'll be there in eight hours. Seven, if we don't bother with snacks."

"He's a kid. He needs snacks," Hunt cut in.

But Fury ignored him and stalked around the car, sliding into the driver's seat. Two handguns were buckled to her thighs. He had a feeling more were in the glove compartment and trunk. And then there was whatever Vanir power she possessed that made Fury Axtar, well . . . Fury Axtar. "You're lucky I love you, Quinlan. And that Juniper didn't want this kid here for another minute."

Hunt caught the way Bryce's throat bobbed, but she lifted a hand in farewell. Then she approached the still-open back door, where she said to Emile, "Your name isn't Emile Renast anymore, okay?"

Panic sparked in the kid's face. Bryce touched his cheek, as if she couldn't help it. The last of Hunt's anger dissolved entirely.

Bryce was saying, "All the documents will be waiting for you. Birth certificate, adoption papers . . ."

"Adoption?" Emile croaked.

Bryce grinned winningly at the kid. "You're part of the Quinlan-Silago clan now. We're a crazy bunch, but we love each other. Tell Randall to make you chocolate croissants on Sundays."

Hunt had no words. She hadn't only found a place for this lost kid. She'd found him a new family. *Her* family. His throat tightened to the point of pain, his eyes stinging. But Bryce kissed Emile's cheek, shut the door, and thumped the car roof. Fury sped off down the cobblestone street, hooked a sharp left, and was gone.

Slowly, Bryce turned back to him.

"You're sending him to your parents," he said quietly.

Her eyes iced over. "Did I miss the memo where I needed your approval to do so?"

"For Urd's sake, that's not why I was mad."

"I don't care if you're mad," she said, flickering with light. "Just because we're fucking doesn't mean I answer to you."

"Pretty sure it's a little bit more than fucking."

She bristled, and his anger bristled with it. But he remembered where they were—right in front of the Viper Queen's headquarters. Where anyone might see. Or try to start shit.

"I have to go to work," Bryce said, practically biting out each word.

"Fine. So do I."

"Fine." She didn't wait for him before striding off.

Hunt rubbed his eyes and shot skyward. He knew Bryce was well aware that he trailed her from above as she wove through the tangle of streets that made up the Meat Market, banking northward toward the CBD only when she'd crossed Crone Street into the safety of the Old Square.

But she didn't look up. Not once.

"I only have ten minutes before I need to go to the archives," Bryce said to her brother as he ushered her into his house an hour later. "I'm already behind as Hel at work."

Steaming at Hunt, she'd used the long walk to process all that had happened with Emile and the Viper Queen. To pray that Fury didn't scare the living daylights out of the kid before he reached her parents' house in Nidaros. And contemplate whether she'd maybe overreacted a smidgen to Hunt's anger at her not telling him.

Bryce had been just turning down the block to the archives when Ruhn called with his vague request to come over immediately. She'd thumbed in a quick message to her boss about a doctor's appointment running late, and raced right over here.

She dumped her purse beside the front door. "Please start explaining why this was so urgent that you needed me to— Oh."

She'd assumed it had something to do with Ithan, or that maybe Declan had found something. Which was why she'd sprinted from FiRo, in her stupid heels, in the stupid heat, and was now a sweaty mess.

She hadn't expected a beautiful female clad in nothing but a blanket, standing against the foyer wall like some trapped animal. Her crimson eyes narrowed with warning.

Bryce offered a smile to the female against the wall. "Uh, hey. Everything . . . all right?" She hissed to Ruhn over her shoulder, *"Where are her clothes?"*

"She wouldn't wear them," Ruhn hissed back. "Believe me, Dec tried." He pointed to an untouched pile of male clothes by the stairs.

But the female was scanning Bryce from her heels to her head. "You came to see the mystics. You blazed with starlight."

Bryce peered back. It wasn't the female mystic, but . . . she turned to see Ithan, looking guilty, on the couch. With three fire sprites floating around his head.

Her blood turned to acid. A plump sprite sprawled on his knee, beaming at Bryce. The memory of Lehabah burned bright and searing.

"So, Ithan *might* have gotten pissed when he went back to the Astronomer and found out that the female mystic is a wolf," Ruhn was saying, "and he *might* have done something rash and taken something he shouldn't have, and then these morons freed them from the rings . . ."

Bryce whirled to the female against the wall. "You were in one of the rings?"

The red eyes flared again. "Yes."

Bryce asked Ithan, "Why did you go back there?"

"I wanted to be sure about Connor," he said. She didn't miss the tone of accusation—that she hadn't been as concerned as he was. Neither did Ruhn, who tensed at her side.

Bryce swallowed hard. "Is he . . . okay?"

Ithan dragged a hand through his hair. "I don't know. I need to find out."

Bryce nodded gravely, then managed to face the three sprites in the living room. Managed to lift her chin and ask, voice shaking only slightly, "Do you know a sprite named Lehabah?"

"No," said Malana, the full-bodied sprite so similar to Lele that Bryce could barely stand to face her. "What clan is she?"

Bryce inhaled a shuddering breath. The males had hushed. "Lehabah claimed she was a descendant of Queen Ranthia Drahl, Queen of Embers."

One of the slender sprites—Rithi, maybe?—puffed with red flame. "An heir of Ranthia?"

A chill went down Bryce's arms. "She said so."

"Fire sprites do not lie about their lineage," said the third sprite, Sasa. "How do you know her?"

"I knew her," Bryce said. "She died three months ago. She gave her life to save mine."

The three sprites floated toward Bryce. "The Drahl line has long been scattered to the winds," Sasa said sadly. "We don't know how many remain. To lose even one . . ." She bowed her head, flame dimming to a soft yellow.

The dragon in the hall said to Bryce, "You were a friend to this sprite."

Bryce twisted to the female. "Yes." Damn her tight throat. To the three sprites, she said, "I freed Lehabah before she died. It was her . . ." She could barely get the words out. "It was her first and final act of freedom to choose to save me. She was the bravest person I've ever met."

Malana drifted to Bryce, pressing a warm, burning hand to her cheek. "In her honor, we shall call you an ally of our people."

Bryce didn't miss the slave tattoo on Malana's wrist. The other two sprites bore the same marking. She slowly turned to Ithan. "I'm glad you stole them from that creep."

"It didn't feel right to leave them."

Something in her chest melted, and she suppressed the urge to hug her old friend, to cry at the glimmer of the male she'd once known. Bryce asked Ruhn instead, "Can't we find some way out of this, Mr. Fancy Prince?"

"Marc's on it," Declan said, holding up his phone. "He thinks you two might be able to use your royal sway to either commandeer them on behalf of the royal household or get the Astronomer to accept payment for them rather than press charges."

"Payment?" Bryce blurted.

"Relax," Flynn said, smirking. "We got the money, Princess."

"Yeah, I've seen your daddy's fancy house," Bryce quipped, earning a scowl from Flynn and an *oooooh* from the sprites.

Bryce suppressed her smile and lifted a brow at Ruhn. She'd fucked up one friendship thanks to pulling princess rank, but this . . . For Lehabah, she'd do it. "You in, Chosen One?"

Ruhn's mouth quirked to the side. "Hel yeah, Starborn."

Bryce waved him off and turned fully to the dragon in the hallway. "I'm guessing you cost . . . a lot."

"More than even a prince and princess can afford," the dragon said with a note of bitterness. "I was a gift to the Astronomer from an Archangel."

"Must have been some reading the Astronomer did for them," Flynn muttered.

The dragon hedged, "It was."

Her eyes cooled to jet-black cinders. To leave her at the Astronomer's mercy, to go back into that tiny little ring to sit on his filthy old fingers . . .

"Look," Bryce said, "if Marc's right about the commandeering slaves thing for royal services, then Ruhn and I can make up some shit to explain why we need you."

"Why help me?" the dragon asked.

Bryce tapped her wrist. "My mate was a slave. I can't turn a blind eye to it anymore. No one should." And since she'd already helped out one lost soul today, why not add a few more?

"Who is your mate?" the dragon said.

"Wait," Flynn objected. "You guys are mates? Like, mates-mates?"

"Mates-mates," Ruhn said.

"Does the Autumn King know?" Declan asked.

Bryce could have sworn Ruhn glanced at Ithan, who was busy with something on his phone, before she said, "Let's say it was officially confirmed last night."

Flynn whistled.

Bryce rolled her eyes, but faced the dragon again. "His name is Hunt Athalar."

Recognition kindled in the dragon's eyes. "Orion Athalar?"

"One and the same," Bryce said. "You know him?"

Her mouth pressed into a thin line. "Only by reputation."

"Ah." Bryce asked, a shade awkwardly, "What's your name?"

"Ariadne."

"Ari for short," Flynn chimed in.

"Never Ari," the dragon snapped.

Bryce's mouth twitched. "Well, Ariadne, expect these idiots to piss you off on an hourly basis. But try not to burn the place down." She winked at the dragon. "Feel free to toast Flynn when he's a smart-ass, though."

Flynn flipped her off, but Bryce turned toward the door—only to find three sprites in her face. "You should speak to our queen about Lehabah's bravery," Sasa said. "Irithys is not a descendant of Ranthia, but she would like to hear your tale."

"I'm pretty busy," Bryce said quickly. "Gotta go to work."

But Malana said to her sister, "She'd need to *find* Irithys first." She explained to Bryce, "Last we heard, before we went into the rings all those years ago, she had been sold to one of the Asteri. But perhaps they'd let you speak to her."

"Why would I need to speak to her?" Bryce asked as she kept heading for the door, aware of Ariadne's keen gaze.

"Because princesses need allies," Rithi said, and Bryce halted.

Bryce sighed. "I'm going to need a really big drink after work," she said, and walked out the door, her phone already at her ear.

"What?" Jesiba said by way of answering.

"The Astronomer. You know him?" Bryce had zero idea what

the old male was, but . . . he seemed like he'd be in the House of Flame and Shadow.

There was silence from the sorceress before she said, "Why?"

"Looking for some strings to pull."

Jesiba laughed quietly. "You're the one who stole his rings?"

Maybe they had some sorcerer message-board support group. "Let's say a friend did."

"And now you want—what? My money to pay for them?"

"I want you to convince him to accept the money my friends will pay for them."

"One of those rings is priceless."

"Yeah, the dragon. Ariadne."

"Is that what she calls herself?" A low laugh. "Fascinating."

"You know her?"

"Of her."

Bryce crossed a busy intersection, keeping her head down as a passing tourist gawked too long in her direction. At least no dread-wolves prowled the streets. "So? Can you help or not?"

Jesiba grunted. "I'll make a call. No promises."

"What are you going to say?"

"That he owes me a favor." Dark promise glittered in the words. "And now you do, too."

"Get in line," Bryce said, and hung up.

By the time Bryce reached her little office in the archives, relieved she hadn't needed to pull her princess rank again, she was ready to bask in the AC and kick back in her chair. Ready to maybe send a message to Hunt to feel out whether he was still pissed. But all plans vanished at the sight of the envelope on her desk.

It contained an analysis of dragon fire, dating back five thousand years. It was in a language Bryce didn't know, but a translation had been included. Jesiba had scribbled *Good luck* at the top.

Well, now she knew why the Astronomer kept Ariadne in a ring. Not for light—but for protection.

Among its many uses, the ancient scholar had written, *dragon fire is one of the few substances proven to harm the Princes of Hel. It can burn even the Prince of the Pit's dark hide.*

Yeah, Ariadne was valuable. And if Apollion was readying his armies . . . Bryce had no intention of letting the dragon return to the Astronomer's clutches.

51

Hunt knew he'd been a fool to think this would end once they found Emile. Once the kid was safe. Bryce clearly had no intention of dropping this. Not with Danika somehow involved.

But he tucked all that aside. He had other shit to take care of right now.

He had to meet with Celestina first. Make an appearance, maintain the facade that all was well. Ensure that the Hind hadn't told the Archangel anything. His meeting with Isaiah wasn't for an hour—plenty of time.

Plenty of time to also stew over Bryce, and how well she'd played all of them. How she'd helped Emile, but she'd hidden her plans from him. Plans that had cost lives. And yeah, Bryce could take care of herself, but . . . He'd thought they were a team.

Again: he knew he'd been a fool.

Hunt soothed his wild blood, and only when he was certain his lightning wasn't about to erupt did he knock on the Governor's door.

Celestina smiled in greeting—a good sign. No hint of Ephraim or the others. Good as well. Her smile widened as Hunt stepped closer. "Congratulations," she said warmly.

Hunt angled his head. "On what?"

She gestured to him. "I take it from your scent that you and Bryce are mated."

He hadn't realized the sex would be broadcast like that. Apparently, the bond between them *had* gone to that biological level. "I, ah. Yeah. Since the overnight at her parents' house."

Even if they'd just been at each other's throats. And not in the good way.

"So visiting her parents went well, then."

"I thought her mom would cut off my balls at one point, but get Ember talking about sunball, and she'll become your best friend." It was true, though he'd learned it months ago. Even if some part of him recoiled at having to answer Celestina's question with a blatant lie.

Celestina laughed merrily. There was no wariness or displeasure in it—no indication that she might know the truth. "Good. I'm happy for you. For both of you."

"Thank you," Hunt said. He added, to cover his bases, "Ruhn and Prince Cormac joined us, though. It made things . . . slightly awkward."

"Because Cormac is technically Bryce's fiancé?" Celestina asked wryly.

Hunt snorted. "That, too, but mostly because Ember isn't . . . a fan of the Fae. She asked Ruhn to come, since she hadn't seen him in years, but it was still tense at times."

"I've heard of her history with the Autumn King. I'm sorry that it still haunts her."

"So am I," Hunt said. "Anything happen here while I was gone?"

"Only if you count overseeing party preparations for the equinox."

Hunt chuckled. "That fun, huh?"

"Riveting," Celestina said, then seemed to remember herself because she added, "Of course, it's for a joyous occasion, so it's not entirely a chore."

"Of course."

The sun through the windows behind her turned her white

wings radiant. "Baxian might have something more interesting to report. He was barely here yesterday."

It took all of Hunt's training to keep his own face neutral as he said, "I've got a meeting with Isaiah, but my next stop after that is to check in with him."

Everything between them was a lie. And one word from the Hind . . . Hunt suppressed the surge of his power as it crackled through him.

Baxian might have claimed he was a rebel sympathizer, might have helped them enough to garner some trust, but . . . he'd be a fool to trust him entirely.

"What's wrong?" Celestina asked, brow furrowing with worry.

Hunt shook his head. "Nothing." He clasped his hands behind his back and asked casually, "Anything for me to do today?"

Hunt emerged from the Archangel's office five minutes later with a stack of preliminary reports on demon activity at the Northern Rift. She wanted his expertise in examining the types of demons caught, as well as an analysis on whether the breeds and frequency meant Hel was planning something.

The answer was a definite yes, but he'd find some way to draw out the task to buy himself more time. To decide how much to tell her about Hel.

Apollion had spoken true, about him and Bryce and their powers. And if the Prince of the Pit had been honest about that, what else had he been honest about? Some shit with Hel was stirring. Hunt's gut twisted.

But he still had one more thing to do before descending into all of that. He hunted down the Hind in ten minutes, finding her in the barracks bathroom, applying red lipliner, of all things. He'd never thought she might actually have to put on her makeup. Somehow, he pictured her permanently coiffed and painted.

"Hunter," she crooned without breaking her stare from the mirror. They were alone.

"Don't call me that."

"You never did like Sandriel's nickname for you."

"I had no interest in being part of her club."

The Hind kept drawing her lipliner with a steady hand. "To what do I owe this pleasure?"

Hunt leaned against the bathroom door, blocking any exit. She slid a kohl-lined eye in his direction.

"What are you going to do about what happened yesterday?" he asked.

She opened a tube of lipstick and began filling in the precise outline she'd drawn. "If you're referring to when I fucked Pollux in the showers, I'm afraid I'm not going to apologize to Naomi Boreas for leaving the stall door open. I did invite her to join, you know."

"That's not what I'm talking about."

She started on her top lip. "Then enlighten me."

Hunt stared at her. She'd seen him. Spoken to him, to all of them, while they'd been in the water. He'd gone ballistic, ready to slaughter her. Had needed his mate's touch and body to calm down afterward.

Hunt growled, "Is this some sort of cat-and-mouse game?"

She set the golden lipstick tube on the counter and pivoted. Beautiful and cold as a statue of Luna. "You're the hunter. You tell me."

This female had killed Sofie Renast. Drowned her. And had tortured so many others that the silver torque around her neck practically screamed the names of the dead.

When Hunt said nothing, the Hind inspected herself in the mirror, tucking a stray tendril of hair into her elegant chignon. She then stalked toward him—to the door. He stepped away silently. The Hind said as she exited, "Perhaps you'll stop prattling on about nonsense once you see what the Harpy did by the Angels' Gate. It's rather extraordinary."

Ten minutes later, Hunt learned what she meant.

The crystal Gate in the heart of the CBD was muted in the midmorning light, but no one was looking at it anyway. The gathered crowd was snapping pictures and murmuring about the two figures lying facedown on the ground beneath it.

It had been a long while since Hunt had seen anyone blood-eagled.

The corpses wore black stealth clothes—or shreds of them. Rebels. That was the Ophion crest on their red armbands, and the sinking sun of the Lightfall squadron above it.

Across the Gate's square, someone vomited, then sprinted away, crying softly.

The Harpy had started down their backs. Taken her knives and sawed through the ribs, cleaving each bone from the spine. And then she'd reached through the incisions and yanked their lungs through them.

Leaving a pair of bloody wings draped over their backs.

Hunt knew the victims would have still been alive. Screaming.

Ephraim had brought this into his city. *This* was what the Hind, the Asteri would unleash upon him and Bryce. It wouldn't be crucifixion. It'd be something far more creative.

Had the Harpy left the blood eagles as a message for Ophion, or for all of Valbara?

Celestina had allowed this to happen here. Allowed the Harpy to do this and then display the bodies. Hadn't even mentioned it in their meeting. Because she agreed with these methods, or because she had no choice?

Hunt swallowed against the dryness in his mouth. But others had noticed him now. *The Umbra Mortis,* they murmured. Like he'd helped the Harpy create this atrocity.

Hunt swallowed his answer. *We might be triarii, but I will* never *be like that monster.*

They wouldn't have believed him.

It had been a weird fucking day, but Ruhn heaved a sigh of relief when Athalar called. *All clear,* the angel had said, and it had eased Ruhn's exhaustion and dread, if only by a fraction. He hadn't told Athalar about the sprites and the dragon. He'd let Bryce tell her mate those details. He wondered if she'd even told him yet about the mystics.

Ruhn toyed with his lip ring as he returned to the living room, where Flynn was flirting with the sprites while Dec asked them questions about their lives in the rings. The dragon sat on the stairs, and Ruhn ignored her, even if it went against every primal instinct to do so. Ithan lifted his brows as Ruhn entered.

"We're good," Ruhn told the males, who all muttered prayers of thanks to the gods. He faced the dragon, bracing himself, but was interrupted by the sound of the doorbell.

Brows lowering, hand drifting to the gun tucked into his back waistband, Ruhn strode to the front door. A lovely, familiar female scent hit him a moment before he registered who stood there, broom in hand.

Queen Hypaxia Enador smiled faintly. "Hello, Prince. I'd hoped to find you here."

52

Tharion finished his report to the River Queen, his fin holding him steady in the current of the river depths. She lounged among a bed of river oysters, long fingers trailing over the ridges and bumps.

"So my sister has a fleet of ships that elude the Asteri's Omega-boats." The waters around them swirled, and Tharion fought to keep in place, tail swishing hard.

"Only six."

"Six, each one the size of the Comitium." Her eyes flashed in the dim depths.

"Does it make a difference?" He'd had no choice but to tell her everything—it was the only way to explain why he'd returned without Pippa Spetsos in tow. Or at least answers regarding Emile Renast's whereabouts.

"Do sisters not share everything?" She dragged a finger along the jagged edge of an oyster and it opened, revealing the pearl within. "They mock me, with these ships. They suggest I am not trustworthy."

"No one said anything like that." He clenched his jaw. "I don't think they've told anyone else."

"Yet this Commander Sendes saw fit to inform *you*."

"Only of the vague details, and only because we stumbled onto her ship."

"They rescued you. They could have let you drown and kept their secrets, yet they saved you." His blood chilled. She would have let them drown. "I want you to find out everything you can about these ships."

"I don't think that will be easy," Tharion cautioned.

"Who is to say my sister won't use them against me?"

She rules the oceans. I doubt she wants one stupid river. But Tharion said, "That didn't seem to be on anyone's mind."

"Perhaps not now, but I wouldn't put it past her."

He refrained from telling her she was being paranoid. Instead, he tried his best weapon: diverting her attention. "Shall I continue hunting for Emile Renast?"

The River Queen eyed him. "Why wouldn't you?"

He tried to hide his relief that she'd pivoted with him, even though he knew she'd return to the subject of the Ocean Queen's ships soon enough. "Even with the ammo and mech-suit prototype destroyed, Pippa Spetsos just became a lot more powerful—her position in Ophion has changed. Capturing her, interrogating her . . . We do that, and we risk having Ophion deem us enemies."

"I do not care what Ophion deems us. But very well." She motioned to the surface. "Go Above. Find another way to collect the boy."

"As you will it," he said, bowing in the current.

She flicked a hand in dismissal. "I shall make your excuses to my daughter."

"Give her my love."

She didn't answer, and Tharion made a beeline to the surface and open world above.

He'd finished tugging on the clothes he'd left in a nook of the quay near Moonwood's River Gate when wings rustled on the walkway above him. He peered over the stone rim to find Athalar standing with crossed arms.

"We need to talk," said the Umbra Mortis.

Ruhn stared at the witch-queen. At his bride.

Hypaxia Enador was as beautiful as he remembered: luxurious, dark hair falling in soft curls down to her slim waist; brown skin that glowed as if moonlight ran beneath it; large, dark eyes that noticed too much. Her mouth, full and inviting, parted in a lovely smile as she stepped into the foyer.

The witch touched a knot in the wood on her broom. It was a stunning piece of art: every inch of its handle carved with intricate designs of clouds and flowers and stars, each twig in the base carved as well and bound together with golden thread.

But with the touch on that knot, the broom vanished.

No, it shrank. Into a golden brooch of Cthona, the earth goddess ripe with child. Hypaxia pinned the brooch onto the shoulder of her gauzy blue robes and said, "A convenient bit of witch-magic. I found that carrying a broom around the city is . . . cumbersome. And attracts the notice of many. Especially a broom such as mine."

"That is . . . really fucking cool," Ruhn admitted.

She began to answer, but her eyes slid to the dragon sitting at the foot of the stairs, and she stopped. She blinked once before turning to Ruhn. "A friend?"

"Yeah," Ruhn lied, and then Flynn and Declan and Ithan were there, sprites in tow, gawking at the queen.

Ithan cleared his throat, likely at the stunning beauty of the witch.

Ruhn hadn't been much better when he'd first seen her. Yet she'd hardly given him the time of day at the Summit. Even if she'd helped out majorly during the shit that had gone down in this city. Had been willing to fly here to help save its citizens—and Bryce.

Ruhn straightened, remembering himself. That he was a prince, and owed her the respect due to her rank. He bowed deeply. "Welcome, Your Majesty."

Flynn smirked, and Ruhn threw him a warning glare as he rose. "Allow me to introduce my . . . companions. Tristan Flynn, Lord Hawthorne." Flynn sketched an irreverent bow—a mockery of the one Ruhn had made. "Declan Emmet, super-genius." Dec grinned, bowing with more gravitas. They'd both been at the Summit when Ruhn had formally met Hypaxia—as a queen, and not the medwitch he'd believed her to be—but had never officially been presented to her. "Ithan Holstrom . . . wolf," Ruhn continued. Ithan gave him a look as if to say, *Really, asshole?* But Ruhn moved on to the sprites, the dragon. "And, uh, our guests."

Hypaxia gave the dragon another wary glance. Flynn stepped forward, slinging an arm around Hypaxia's shoulders. "Welcome. Let's talk about all those times Ruhn tried to talk to you at the Summit and you ignored him."

Declan chuckled, taking up a position at Hypaxia's other side. She furrowed her brow, as if the two males spoke another language entirely.

The queen seemed to note the details of his house as she was escorted to the sectional. His disgusting, beer-soaked house. Solas, a half-smoked mirthroot blunt sat in the ashtray on the coffee table a mere foot from Hypaxia.

Ruhn said to Ithan, *Get that fucking mirthroot out of here.*

Ithan lunged for it.

Not right now! When she's not looking.

Ithan caught himself with that sunball player's grace and relaxed against the cushions as Hypaxia sat, nestled between Flynn and Declan. If Ithan had to pick one word to describe the queen's expression, it would have been baffled. Utterly baffled.

Ruhn rubbed his neck, approaching the couch. "So, ah. Good to see you."

Hypaxia smiled in that wise, knowing way. Fucking Hel, she was lovely. But her voice darkened as she said, "I'd like to have a word with you. Alone."

Ithan rose, subtly swiping the mirthroot from the table. "Room's yours. We'll be upstairs."

Flynn opened his mouth, presumably to say something mortifying, but Ithan grabbed him by the shoulder and hauled him up, shoving the mirthroot into the lord's hands. The sprites fell into line behind them as Declan joined the fray, and then they were all gone, Ariadne stalking up the stairs after them. Ruhn had no doubt they'd try to eavesdrop.

He took a seat on the stained, reeking couch, reining in his cringe as Hypaxia adjusted the folds of her blue robes. "So . . . how are you?"

Hypaxia angled her head. She didn't wear her crown of cloudberries, but every line of her radiated grace and calm and care. She was about fifty years younger than he was, yet he felt like a whelp in front of her. Had she known her fiancé lived in a place like this, had a lifestyle like this?

"I wanted to ask you for a favor." Ruhn stilled. She went on, "I've come to Lunathion for the mating celebration in a few weeks. I'll be staying at the witches' embassy, but . . ." She twisted her hands, the first sign of doubt he'd ever seen from her. "I was wondering if you might spare me an escort."

"Why? I mean, sure, yes, but . . . everything okay?"

She didn't answer.

Ruhn asked, "What about your coven?" They should protect their queen at any cost.

Her long lashes bobbed. "They were my mother's coven. It was one of her last wishes that I inherit them, rather than select my own."

"So you don't like them?"

"I don't trust them."

Ruhn considered. "You want me to give you an escort to protect you from your own coven?"

Her mouth tightened. "You think I'm mad."

"I thought witches lived and died for their loyalty."

"The loyalty of these witches began and ended with my mother. She raised me in isolation—from the world, but also from them. My tutors were . . . unconventional."

It was the most they'd ever spoken to each other. Ruhn asked, "In what way?"

"They were dead."

A chill went down his spine. "Right. Necromancer stuff, huh?"

"Enadors can raise the dead, yes. My mother summoned three ancient, wise spirits to teach me. One for battle and physical training, one for mathematics and sciences, and the other for history, reading, and languages. She oversaw my magical training herself—especially the healing."

"And this freaked her coven out?"

"It estranged us. My only companions while growing up were the dead. When my mother passed, I found myself surrounded by strangers. And they found themselves with a queen whose unorthodox education unnerved them. Whose gifts of necromancy unnerved them further."

"But you're the last Enador. Who would they replace you with?"

"My sister."

Ruhn blinked. "The *Hind*?"

"Lidia has no witch gifts, so she would be a figurehead. She'd wear the crown, but my mother's general, Morganthia, would rule."

"That's insane."

"Lidia was born first. She is the spitting image of my mother." Hypaxia's father must have passed along the genes for her darker coloring, then. "Even while I was growing up, I sometimes heard whispers from my mother's coven wondering if . . . perhaps Lidia should not have been given away."

"Why?"

"Because they're more comfortable with a half-shifter than a half-necromancer. They fear the influence of the House of Flame and Shadow, though I have sworn no vows to any but Earth and Blood. But Lidia is Earth and Blood, through and through. Exactly as they are. They loved my mother, I have no doubt, but they have different plans for the future than she did. That became apparent by the end."

"What sort of plans?"

"A closer bond with the Asteri. Even at the cost of our relative autonomy."

"Ah." That was a potential minefield. Especially considering the shit that he was doing for Ophion. Or had been doing for them—he had no idea where they stood now, after Ydra.

Hypaxia went on, "Your kindness is why I've come here. I know you to be a male of bravery and dedication. While I'm in this city for the Governors' celebration, especially with Lidia in town, I fear my mother's coven might make a move. They presented a unified front with me at the Summit, but the last few months have been strained."

"And since we're technically engaged, it won't be seen as a declaration of your distrust if I send one of my people to look after you. It'll be deemed some protective male bullshit."

Her lips twitched. "Yes. Something like that."

"All right. No problem."

She swallowed, bowing her head. "Thank you."

He dared to touch her hand, her skin velvety smooth. "We'll take care of this. Don't worry."

She patted his hand in a *Thanks, friend* sort of way.

Ruhn cleared his throat, glancing at the ceiling—the distinctive, worrisome *thumping* coming from it. "Since you were raised by ghosts, I'm hoping you won't mind having a bit of an unorthodox guard."

Her brows rose.

Ruhn smiled. "How do you feel about sunball players?"

No one bothered them, but plenty of people stared as Tharion and Hunt meandered through the ornate water garden along the river in Moonwood, a hundred rainbows glimmering in the mists around them. Tharion loved this part of the city—though the Old Square's grit still called to him.

"So what's up?" Tharion said as Athalar paused beneath a towering elm, its leaves shimmering in the spray from a massive fountain of Ogenas lounging in an oyster shell.

The angel pulled his phone from a hidden pocket in his battlesuit. "I had a meeting with the Governor." His fingers flew over the phone, presumably summoning whatever the information was. He handed it to Tharion. "She had me go over some of the latest demon reports from Nena. I wanted to pass them along to the Blue Court."

Tharion took the phone and scrolled through the photos. "Anything interesting?"

"That one. The tail—just out of the shot here." Hunt pointed to the picture, face stony. "It's a deathstalker."

Even the burbling fountain beyond them seemed to quiet at the name.

"What's that?"

"Lethal assassins bred by the Prince of the Pit. He keeps them as pets." Athalar's wings rustled. Had a shadow passed over the sun? "I've only dealt with them once. I've got a scar down my back from it."

If the encounter had left Athalar scarred . . . Cthona spare them all. "One was in Nena?"

"Three days ago."

"Shit. Where did it go?"

"No idea. Report says there's been no breach of Nena's borders. Tell your people to be alert. Warn your queen, too."

"I will." Tharion glanced sidelong at the angel. Noticed that they weren't near cameras or other people. "Any further updates?" Tharion asked carefully.

"Maybe," Hunt said.

"I thought so," Tharion said. The warning about the demons seemed true—but also a convenient cover.

"I know where Emile is," Athalar said quietly.

Tharion nearly stumbled a step. "Where?"

"Can't say. But he's safe." Athalar remained grave despite the beauty of Moonwood around them. "Call off your search. Spin some bullshit to your queen. But you're done hunting for that kid."

Tharion surveyed the angel, the mist beading on the gray wings. "And you think it's wise to tell me that *you* know where he is?"

Hunt bared his teeth in a feral smile. "You going to torture it out of me, Ketos?"

"The thought had crossed my mind."

Lightning licked across Hunt's forehead as he motioned to the fountains, the water all around. "Not the best place for a lightning fight."

Tharion began to pace. "The River Queen won't give up. She wants that kid."

"It's a dead end. And a gigantic waste of your time." Tharion arched a brow. Hunt said, voice low, "Emile Renast has no powers. His sister staged things to make it seem that way, hoping that arrogant Vanir like us would find the kid important enough to look after."

Something glimmered in Athalar's face that Tharion couldn't place. Pain. Sorrow. Shame?

"And I'm supposed to take your word for it," Tharion said.

"Yeah, you are."

Tharion knew that tone. The merciless voice of the Umbra Mortis.

"I can think of only one person who'd make you this intense," Tharion drawled, unable to resist. "Legs knows where the kid is, too, huh?" He laughed to himself. "Did she arrange this? I should have seen that coming." He chuckled again, shaking his head. "What's to stop me from going to ask *her* some questions?"

"Hard to ask Bryce any questions when you don't have a head attached to your body," Hunt said, violence glittering in his eyes.

Tharion held up his hands. "Threat received." But his mind spun with all he'd learned. "Let's say I do trust you. Emile really has no powers?"

"Not even a drop. He might be descended from a thunderbird, but Sofie was the only one with the gifts."

"Fuck." The River Queen would be livid, even if she'd been the one who'd ordered him to spend weeks on a wild goose chase. Hel, she'd be pissed that he hadn't figured out the truth sooner. "And the intel?"

"Kid knows nothing." Hunt seemed to consider, then added, "He confirmed that Danika and Sofie had contact. But nothing else."

Tharion dragged his hands through his still-wet hair. "Fuck," he said again, pacing a step.

Athalar tucked in his wings. "How badly is she going to punish you for this?"

Tharion swallowed. "I'm going to have to spin it carefully."

"Even though none of it is your fault?"

"She'll deem it a failure. Rational thinking is second to her need to feel like she's won."

"I really am sorry." The angel tilted his head to the side. "Any chance she'll fire you and let that be that?"

Tharion let out a humorless laugh. "I wish. But . . ." He paused, an idea sparking. He glanced up and down the sun-baked concrete quay. "Who says she has to know today?"

A corner of Athalar's mouth kicked up. "As far as I know, you and I met up to swap status reports."

Tharion began walking toward the city proper, the hustle and bustle that set his blood thrumming. Athalar fell into step beside him. "It could take days to learn that Emile isn't worth our time. Weeks."

The angel winked. "Months, if you do it right."

Tharion grinned, a thrill shooting through his bones as they entered Moonwood's tree-lined streets. It was a dangerous game, but . . . he'd play it. Milk every second of freedom he could from this. Stay Above as often as he liked, so long as he checked in Below every now and then. "Got any ideas where I can crash?"

53

Ithan didn't think of himself as an eavesdropper. But sometimes he couldn't help it if his keen wolf's hearing picked up stuff being said, even a floor below.

This time, it had been some big, *big* stuff.

Ithan used all his training, all those years of practice and games, to keep from pacing as Ruhn went on and on about the witch-queen needing an escort in the city. Yes, fine, he'd do it, he'd guard her back, but—

"You may speak, Ithan Holstrom," the stunningly beautiful witch said, cutting off Ruhn, who blinked at them. Ithan hadn't realized he'd broadcast his impatience so clearly.

Flynn and Declan had remained upstairs with the sprites and Ariadne, booing when Ruhn had asked only Ithan to come downstairs.

Ithan cleared his throat. "You can talk to the dead, right? You're . . . a necromancer? I'm sorry—I couldn't help but overhear." He offered Ruhn an apologetic look, too. But at Hypaxia's cautious nod, he pressed on, "If I agree to guard you, would you . . ." Ithan shook his head. "Would you try to make contact with my brother, Connor?"

For a long moment, Hypaxia only stared at him. Her dark eyes beheld everything. Too much. "I can feel the disturbance in your heart, Ithan. You don't wish to speak to him merely from longing and loss."

"No. I mean, yeah, I miss him like crazy, but . . ." He paused. Could they tell her everything Bryce had learned?

Ruhn spared him the effort of deciding and said, "Do you know what happens to the dead after they've been in the Bone Quarter for a while?"

Her face paled. "You learned of the secondlight."

"Yeah," Ruhn said, lip ring glinting. "Ithan is pretty worried about what happened to his brother and the Pack of Devils, especially after they helped my sister. If you've got any ability to learn what's happened to Connor Holstrom, or to warn him, even if it's to no avail . . . we'd appreciate it. But Ithan will gladly escort you either way you choose."

Ithan tried not to appear too grateful. He'd spent years thinking Ruhn was a dick, mostly thanks to Bryce and Danika constantly dissing him, but . . . this guy had let him into his house, trusted him with his secrets, and now seemed intent on helping him. He wondered if the Fae knew how lucky they were.

Hypaxia nodded sagely. "There is a ritual I could perform . . . It'd need to be on the Autumnal Equinox, though."

"When the veil between realms is thinnest," Ruhn said.

"Yes." Hypaxia smiled sadly at Ithan. "I'm sorry for your loss. And that you've learned the truth."

"How do *you* know the truth?" Ithan asked.

"The dead have little reason to lie."

Ice skittered down Ithan's spine. "I see." The chandelier rattled above.

Ruhn rubbed at his face, the tattoos on his arm shifting with the movement. He lowered his hand and looked at the witch-queen. His fiancée. Lucky male.

"You cool with a dragon joining you?" the prince asked Hypaxia.

"*That* dragon?" Hypaxia peered at the ceiling.

"A lawyer friend of mine says I need a royal, official reason to commandeer someone else's slave. A very important, powerful slave. Protecting my fiancée is about as important as it gets."

Hypaxia's lips curled, though doubt kindled in her dark eyes. That made two of them. She asked Ithan, "How do you feel about it?"

Ithan gave her a half smile, flattered that she'd even asked. "If you can contact my brother on the equinox, then it doesn't really matter what I feel."

"Of course it does," she said, and sounded like she meant it.

A few weeks until the equinox. And then he could see Connor again. Even if it was just one last time.

Even if it was only to deliver a warning that might do him no good.

Bryce might have avoided going home for as long as possible. Might have stayed at the archives right until closing and been one of the last people exiting the building as night fell. She'd made it down the sweeping marble steps, breathing in the dry, warm night air, when she saw him.

Hunt leaned against a car across the narrow street, wings folded elegantly. People hurrying home from work gave him a wide berth. Some outright crossed the street to avoid him.

He'd worn his hat. That fucking sunball hat she couldn't resist.

"Quinlan." He pushed off the car and approached her where she'd halted at the foot of the stairs.

She lifted her chin. "Athalar."

He huffed a soft laugh. "So that's how it's gonna go, huh?"

"What do you want?" They'd had little fights over the months, but nothing this important.

He waved a hand to the building looming behind her. "I need to use the archives to look something up. I didn't want to disturb you during working hours."

She jabbed a thumb at the building, now beautifully illuminated against the starry night. "You waited too long. The building is closed."

"I didn't realize you'd hide inside until closing. Avoiding something, Quinlan?" He smiled savagely as she bristled. "But you're good at sweet-talking people into doing your bidding. Getting us in will be a walk in the park, won't it?"

She didn't bother to look pleasant, though she pivoted and began marching back up the steps, heels clacking on the stone. "What do you need?"

He gestured to the cameras mounted on the massive pillars of the entrance. "I'll explain inside."

"So you think Hel's planning something?" Bryce asked two hours later when she found Hunt where she'd left him, the massive expanse of the archives quiet around them. There had been no need to sweet-talk her way in after all. She'd discovered another perk to working here: getting to use this place after hours. Alone. Not even a librarian to monitor them. They'd gotten past the security guards with barely a word. And her boss wouldn't show up until night was fully overhead—not for at least another hour.

Hunt had said he needed to peruse some newly translated Fae texts on ancient demons, so she'd gotten him set up at a table in the atrium and then gone back to her office on the other side of the floor.

"The demons in the reports Celestina gave me are bad news," Hunt said. He was working at the desk, sunball hat bright in the moonlight streaming through the glass ceiling. "Some of the worst of the Pit. All rare. All lethal. The last time I saw so many clustered together was during the attack this spring."

"Hmm." Bryce slid into the chair across from him.

Was he going to ignore what happened earlier? That wouldn't do. Not at all.

She casually extended her foot beneath the table. Drifted it up Hunt's muscled leg. "And now they need the big, tough angel to dispatch them back to Hel."

He slammed his legs together, trapping her foot. His eyes lifted to hers. Lightning sparked there. "If Aidas or the Prince of the Pit is planning something, this is probably the first hint."

"Aside from them literally saying that Hel's armies are waiting for me?"

Hunt squeezed her foot harder, those powerful thigh muscles shifting. "Aside from that. But I can't tell Celestina about that shit without raising questions about Hel's interest in *you*, so I need to find a way to warn her with the intel she gave me."

Bryce studied her mate and considered the way he'd spoken of the Archangel. "You like Celestina, huh?"

"Tentatively." His shoulders were tight, though. He explained, "I might like her, but . . . the Harpy blood-eagled two Ophion rebels today. Celestina allowed that shit to go down here."

Bryce had seen the news coverage of it already. It had been enough to turn her stomach. She said, "So you'll play faithful triarii, get her info on the demons, and then . . ."

"I don't know." He released her foot. She traced her toes over his knee. "Stop it. I can't think if you're doing that."

"Good."

"Quinlan." His voice dropped low. She bit her lip.

But Hunt said softly, "Any word from Fury?"

"Yeah. Package was delivered, safe and sound." She could only pray her mom wasn't showing Emile her weird babies-in-plants sculptures.

"Tharion's off the hunt," Hunt said.

She stiffened. "You told him?"

"Not the details. Only that the search isn't worth his time, and he won't find what he's seeking."

"And you trust him?"

His voice went quieter. "I do." He returned to the documents he'd been poring over.

Bryce grazed her toes over his other knee, but he clapped a hand on top of her foot, halting its progress. "If Hel's amassing armies, then these demons must be the vanguard, coming to test the defenses around Nena."

"But they'd need to find a way to open the Northern Rift entirely."

"Yeah." He eyed Bryce. "Maybe Aidas has been buttering you up for that."

Bryce's blood chilled. "Cthona spare me."

He frowned. "Don't think for one moment that Aidas and the Prince of the Pit have forgotten the Horn in your back. That Thanatos didn't have it in mind when you spoke to him."

She rubbed at her temple. "Maybe I should cut it out of my skin and burn it."

He grimaced. "That's a real turn-on, Quinlan."

"Were you getting turned on?" She wiggled her toes beneath his hand. "I couldn't tell."

He gave her a half smile—finally, a crack in that pissed-off exterior. "I was waiting to see how high your foot was going to get."

Her core heated. "Then why'd you stop me?"

"I thought you'd like a little challenge."

She bit her lip again. "There was an interesting book in those stacks over there." She inclined her head to the darkness behind them. "Maybe we should check it out."

His eyes simmered. "Might be useful."

"Definitely useful." She rose from the desk and strode into the dimness, deep enough into the stacks that none of the cameras in the atrium where they'd been sitting could pick them up.

Hands wrapped around her waist from behind, and Hunt pressed against her. "You drive me fucking crazy, you know that?"

"And you're a domineering alphahole, you know that?"

"I'm not domineering." He nibbled at her ear.

"But you'll admit you're an alphahole?"

His fingers dug into her hips, tugging her back against him. The hardness there. "You want to fuck it out, then?"

"Are you still mad at me?"

He sighed, his breath hot against her neck. "Bryce, I needed to process everything."

She didn't turn around. "And?"

He kissed under her ear. "And I'm sorry. For how I acted earlier."

She didn't know why her eyes stung. "I wanted to tell you, I really did."

His hands began to rove up her torso, loving and gentle. She arched against him, exposing her neck. "I understand why you didn't." He dragged his tongue up her throat. "I was . . . I was upset that you didn't trust me. I thought we were a team. It rattled me."

She made to turn around at that, but his hands tightened, holding her in place. So she said, "We are a team. But I wasn't sure if you'd agree with me. That an ordinary human boy was worth the risk."

He let her twist in his arms this time. And—shit. His eyes were wounded.

His voice hoarsened. "Of course I would have thought a human was worth the risk. I was too wrapped up in other shit to see the whole picture."

"I'm sorry I didn't give you enough credit." She cupped his face. "Hunt, I'm really sorry."

Maybe she'd fucked up by not telling him, not trusting him. She regretted that the Viper Queen had killed those people, but she'd be damned if she felt bad about how things had ended up . . .

Hunt turned his head, kissing her palm. "I still don't understand how you pieced it all together. Not just Sofie lying about Emile's powers, but how you knew the Viper Queen would be able to find him."

"She's got an arsenal of spies and trackers—I figured she was one of the few people in this city who could do it. Especially if she was motivated enough by the idea that Emile had powers that could be useful to her. And *especially* when his trail was picked up in the marshes."

He shook his head. "Why?"

"She's a queen of snakes—and reptiles. I know she can communicate with them on some freaky psychic level. And guess what the marshes are full of?"

Hunt swallowed hard. "Sobeks?"

Bryce nodded.

He hooked a strand of her hair behind her ear. Kissed its pointy tip. Forgiveness that she hadn't realized she needed filled the gesture.

Hunt asked softly, "What about the others? Are you going to tell them?"

She slowly shook her head. "No. You and Fury and Juniper are the only ones who will ever know." Not even Ruhn.

"And your parents."

"I meant the other people in this city, currently doing shady shit."

He kissed her temple. "I can't believe your mom didn't freak out and drag you home."

"Oh, she wanted to. I think Randall had to stage an intervention."

"Don't take this the wrong way, but . . . why Nidaros?"

"It's the safest and best place I can think of. He'll be protected there. Hidden. The local sun-priest owes Randall a favor and is having all the relevant documents forged. My parents . . . They weren't able to have a kid of their own. I mean, other than me. So even though my mom was freaked as fuck about the whole rebel thing, she's already gone crazy decorating a room for Emile."

"Emile-who-is-not-Emile-anymore." His smile lit something iridescent in her chest.

"Yeah," she said, unable to stop her answering smile. "Cooper Silago. My half brother."

He studied her, though. "How'd you manage to communicate about it?" There was no way she or her parents would have ever risked discussing this over email or phone.

She smiled slightly. "Postcards."

Hunt choked on a laugh. "That was all a lie?"

"No. I mean, my mom sent me the postcard after our fight, but when I wrote back, I used a code that Randall taught me in case of . . . emergencies."

"The joys of a warrior for a parent."

She chuckled. "Yeah. So we've been swapping postcards about this for the past two weeks. To anyone else, it would have seemed like we were talking about sports and the weather and my mom's weird baby sculptures. But that's why Emile stayed at the Viper Queen's for so long. Sending postcards back and forth isn't the fastest method of communication."

"But it's one of the more brilliant ones." Hunt kissed her brow, wings curling around them. "I love you. You're crazy and shady as all Hel, but I love you. I love that you did this for that kid."

Her smile widened. "Glad to impress, Athalar."

His hands began drifting down her sides, thumbs stroking over her ribs. "I've been aching for you all day. Aching to show you how sorry I am—and how much I fucking love you."

"All is forgiven." She grabbed one of his hands, dragging it down her front, along her thigh—and up under her dress. "I've been wet for hours," she whispered as his fingers brushed her soaked underwear.

He growled, teeth grazing her shoulder. "All this, just for me?"

"Always for you." Bryce turned again and rubbed her ass against him, feeling the hard, proud length of his cock jutting against her.

Hunt hissed, and his fingers slipped beneath her underwear, circling her clit. "You want me to fuck you right here, Quinlan?"

Her toes curled in her heels. She curved back against him, and his other hand went up to her breast, sliding beneath her neckline to cup the aching flesh beneath. "Yes. Right now."

He nipped at her ear, drawing a gasp as his fingers slid down to her entrance, dipping in. "Say please," he breathed.

She arched, moaning softly, and he hushed her. "Please," she gasped.

She trembled with anticipation at the click of his belt buckle, the zip of his pants. Shivered as he set her hands upon the nearest shelf and gently bent her over. Then slid her dress up her thighs. Exposed her ass to the cool air.

"Gods-damn," Hunt breathed, running his hands over her rear. Bryce writhed.

He hooked his fingers in her underwear, sliding the lace down her thighs, letting them fall between her ankles. She stepped out of them, spreading her legs wide in invitation. But Hunt dropped to his knees behind her, and before Bryce could inhale, his tongue was at her sex, lapping and dipping inside.

She moaned again, and he gripped her thighs, holding her in place as he feasted on her. His wings brushed her ass, her hips as he leaned forward, tasting and suckling, and—

"I'm going to come if you keep doing that," she rasped.

"Good," he growled against her, and as he slid two fingers into her, she did exactly that.

She bit her lip to keep from crying out, and he licked her, drawing out each ripple of her climax. She panted, dizzy with pleasure, clinging to the shelf as he rose behind her once more.

"Now be *very* quiet," he whispered in her ear, and pushed inside her.

From behind, at this angle, the fit was luxuriously tight and deep. As he had last night, Hunt eased his way into her with care, and she gritted her teeth to keep from groaning at each inch he claimed for himself. He stilled when he was fully seated, her ass pressed entirely against his front, and ran a possessive hand down her spine.

The fullness of him, the size, simply smelling him and knowing it was Hunt inside her—release threatened again. Bigger and mightier than before. Her star began to glow, silvering the shelves, the books, the darkness of the stacks.

"You like that?" He withdrew nearly to the tip before pushing back in. She buried her face against the hard shelf to stay quiet. "You like how my cock feels in you?"

She could only get out a garbled *yesIdopleasemore*. Hunt laughed, dark and rich, and thrust in—a little harder this time. "I love you undone like this," he said, moving again. Setting the pace. "Utterly at my mercy."

Yesyesyes, she hissed, and he laughed again. His balls slapped against her ass.

"You know how much I thought about doing this all those months ago?" he said, bending to press a kiss to her neck.

"Likewise," she managed to say. "I wanted you to fuck me on my desk at the gallery."

His thrusts turned a little uneven. "Oh yeah?"

She moved her hips back against him, angling him in deeper. He groaned now. She whispered, "I knew you'd feel like this. So fucking perfect."

His fingers dug into her hips. "All yours, sweetheart. Every piece of me." He thrust harder. Faster.

"Gods, I love you," she breathed, and that was his undoing.

Hunt yanked her from the shelf, pulling her to the ground with him, positioning her on all fours. His knees spread her own even wider, and Bryce bit her hand to hold in her scream of pleasure as he rammed into her, over and over and over. "I fucking love you," he said, and Bryce cracked.

Light exploded from her as she came, driving back onto his cock, so deep he touched her innermost wall. Hunt shouted, and his cock pulsed in her, following her into that blinding pleasure like he couldn't stop, like he'd keep spilling into her forever.

But then he stilled, and they remained there, panting, Hunt buried in her.

"No teleporting this time, huh?" he said, bending to kiss her neck.

She leaned her forehead against her hands. "Must need your power to join mine or something," she mumbled. "Good thing you didn't do that, though—probably would have burned the building down. But I don't care right now." She wiggled her ass against him, and he hissed. "Let's go home and have more makeup sex."

Night.

Ruhn opened his eyes, finding himself on the couch on the bridge, with Daybright seated across from him.

"Hey," he said. He'd passed out on the sectional while Declan and Ithan argued about sunball crap. Flynn had been busy fucking a nymph upstairs.

Ariadne and the sprites had claimed Declan's bedroom, as the male had planned to spend the night at Marc's, and gone to sleep soon after a painfully awkward evening meal. The dragon had picked at her dinner like she'd never seen food before. The sprites had drunk an entire bottle of wine between them and spent the meal burping up embers.

How any of them were sleeping with Flynn's escapades down the hall was beyond Ruhn.

Day drummed a flaming hand on the rolled arm of the fainting couch. "I have information for you to pass along."

Ruhn straightened. "Good or bad?"

"That's for you to decide."

She watched him intently. He wasn't sure if he'd see her after that colossal bit of weirdness last night. But she said nothing of it as she declared, "I have it on good authority that Pippa Spetsos is planning something big in retaliation for losing so much ammunition and the imperial mech-suit prototype. Ophion is fully behind her. They believe the unit that sabotaged the shipment has gone rogue, and appointed Spetsos to send a clear message to both those rebels and the empire."

Ruhn kept his face carefully blank. "What's she up to? Where?"

"I'm not sure. But given that her last known location was Ydra, I thought you should pass it along to your cohorts in Crescent City, lest she attack there."

"Do the Asteri know about her plans?"

"No. Only I do."

"How'd you learn about them?"

"That's none of your concern."

Ruhn studied her. "So we're back to the distance. No more bed-time stories?"

Again, she drummed her fingers. "Let's chalk that up to a moment of insanity."

"I didn't see anything."

"But you wanted to."

"I don't need to. I don't give a shit what you look like. I like talking to you."

"Why?"

"Because I feel like I can be real with you, here."

"Real."

"Yeah. Honest. I've told you shit no one else knows."

"I don't see why."

He rose from his couch and crossed to hers. He leaned against the arm of the sofa, peering down at her blazing face. "See, I think you like me, too."

She shot to her feet, and he backed away a step. She came closer, though. Near enough for her chest to brush his. Flame and darkness twined, stars turning into embers between them. "This is not some game, where you can flirt and seduce your way through it," she hissed. "This is war, and one that will claim many more lives before it is through."

A growl worked its way up his throat. "Don't patronize me. I know the cost."

"You know *nothing* of cost, or of sacrifice."

"Don't I? I might not have been playing rebel all my life, but believe me, shit has never been easy." Her words had found their mark, though.

"So your father doesn't like you. You're not the only one. So your father beat you, and burned you. So did mine."

Ruhn snarled, getting in her face. "What the fuck is your point?"

She snarled right back. "My point is that if you are not careful, if you are not smart, you will find yourself giving up pieces of your soul before it's too late. You will wind up *dead*."

"And?"

She stilled. "How can you ask that so cavalierly?"

He shrugged. "I'm nobody," he said. It was the truth. Everything he was, the worth by which the world defined him . . . it had all been *given* to him. By pure luck of being born into the "right" family. If he'd done anything of value, it had been through the Aux. But as a prince . . . he'd been running his entire life from that title. Knew it to be utterly hollow.

And Bryce had kept her power a secret so he might hold on to that scrap of specialness.

Ruhn turned away from Day, disgusted with himself.

Bryce loved him far more than she hated their father. Had given up privilege and power for him. What had he ever done for anyone on that scale? He'd die for his friends, this city—yeah. But . . . who the fuck was he, deep down?

Not a king. His father wasn't a fucking king, either. Not in the way that mattered.

"Message received," he said to Day.

"Night—"

Ruhn opened his eyes.

The living room was dark, the TV off, Ithan presumably long gone to sleep.

Ruhn turned over on the couch, tucking his arms behind his head and staring at the ceiling, watching beams of headlights drift across it from passing cars.

Who the fuck was he?

Prince of Nothing.

54

Sitting in her office at the archives, phone at her ear, Bryce drained the last sips of her third coffee of the day, and debated whether a fourth cup would have her crawling on the ceiling by lunchtime.

"So, um—Cooper's good?" she asked her mother, setting her coffee cup atop the paper that held the sequence of numbers and letters from Sofie's arm. Randall had now deemed it safe enough to discuss the boy on the phone. Bryce supposed it'd be weird not to, since her parents had just publicly adopted the kid.

"He's an exceptionally bright boy," Ember said, and Bryce could hear the smile in her voice. "*He* appreciates my art."

Bryce sighed at the ceiling. "The surest test of intelligence out there."

"Do you know he hasn't been to school in more than three years?" Ember's voice sharpened. "*Three years.*"

"That's awful. Has he . . . ah . . . talked about his . . . previous home?"

Her mom caught her meaning. "No. He won't talk about it, and I'm not going to push. Milly Garkunos said to let him bring it up on his own time."

"Milly Garkunos suddenly became a child psychiatrist?"

"Milly Garkunos is a good neighbor, Bryce Adelaide Quinlan."

"Yeah, and a busybody. Don't tell her anything." Especially about this.

"I wouldn't," Ember hissed.

Bryce nodded, even though her mom couldn't see through the phone. "Let the kid quietly adjust."

"Am I his caretaker, or are you, Bryce?"

"Put Randall on the phone. He's the voice of reason."

"Randall is beside himself with happiness at having another child in the house, and is currently on a walk through the woods with Cooper, showing him the lay of the land."

Bryce smiled at that. "I loved doing that with him."

Ember's voice softened. "He loved doing that with you, too."

Bryce sighed again. "Thanks again, Mom. I know this was a shock—"

"I'm glad you included us, Bryce. And gave us this gift." Bryce's throat ached. "Please be careful," Ember whispered. "I know you think I'm overbearing and annoying, but it's only because I want the best for you. I want you to be safe, and happy."

"I know, Mom."

"Let's plan on a girls' weekend this winter. Someplace nice and cold. Skiing?"

"Neither of us skis."

"We can learn. Or sit by the fire and drink spiked hot chocolate."

Here was the mom she adored, the one she'd worshipped as a kid. "It's a plan."

A ripple of fire, of pure power, shuddered through the building. Silence flowed in its wake, the usual background noise halting. "I gotta get back to work," Bryce said quickly.

"Okay, love you."

"Love you," Bryce said, and had barely hung up when the Autumn King walked in.

"Trash gets dumped in the back," she said without looking up.

"I see your irreverence has not been altered by your new immortality."

Bryce lifted her head. This wasn't how she wanted to start her day. She'd already spent her walk to work with Ruhn, needing him to explain to her twice about the plan to have Queen Hypaxia escorted by Ithan and the dragon in exchange for the witch-queen contacting Connor's spirit on the equinox. She'd been slightly nauseated at that, but had grunted her approval before she left him on the street, telling him to give Hypaxia her number in case she needed anything. A few minutes later, Ruhn had forwarded the queen's contact information.

Her father sniffed her. "Would you like to explain to me *why* you have mated with Athalar, when you are betrothed to a Fae Prince?"

"Because he's my mate?"

"I didn't know half-breeds could have such things."

She bared her teeth. "Real classy."

Fire filled his eyes. "Did you not consider that I arranged for your union with Cormac out of your best interests? The interests of your offspring?"

"You mean *your* best interests. As if I'd ever let you within a hundred miles of any child of mine."

"Cormac is powerful, his household strong. I want you in Avallen because it is a *safehold*. Even the Asteri cannot pierce its mists without permission, so old is the magic that guards it."

Bryce stilled. "You're full of shit."

"Am I? Did you not kill an Archangel this spring? Are you not now at the mercy of the Asteri? Are demons not once more creeping through the Northern Rift—in greater numbers than ever before?"

"Like you give a single fuck about my safety."

Flame rippled around him, then vanished. "I am your father, whether you like it or not."

"You didn't seem to care about that until I surpassed you in power."

"Things change. I found watching Micah harm you to be . . . unsavory."

"Must have really bothered you, since you've seemed to have no issue with harming others yourself."

"Explain."

"Oh, come on. Don't give me that blank fucking look. The last Starborn Prince. You killed him because he was special and not you, and everyone knows it."

Her father threw back his head and laughed. "Is that what you think? That I killed my rival for spite?"

She said nothing.

"Is that what prompted you to hide your gift all these years? Concern that I'd do the same to you?"

"No." It was partly true. Her mother had been the one who'd thought that.

The Autumn King shook his head slowly and sat in the chair opposite her desk. "Ember fed you too many lies born of her irrational fears."

"And what about the scar on her face? Was that a lie, too? Or an irrational fear?"

"I have already told you that I regret that more than you know. And that I loved Ember deeply."

"I don't think you know what that word means."

Smoke curled from his shoulders. "At least I understand what it means to use my household name."

"What?"

"Princess Bryce Danaan. That was the name you gave the Governor, as well as the director of the Crescent City Ballet, isn't it? And what your lawyer—Marc, is it?—called you in his letter to the Astronomer, justifying the fact that you and your brother had commandeered four of his slaves."

"So?"

Her father smiled faintly. "You purchased influence with my name. The royal name. You bought it, and there are no returns, I'm afraid."

Her blood went cold.

"The legal paperwork for your official name change is already filed."

"You fucking change my name and I will *kill* you." Starlight flared at her chest.

"Threatening your king is punishable by death."

"You will never be my king."

"Oh, I am. You declared fealty by using my name, your title. It is done." Rage surged through her, rendering her mute. He went on, enjoying every second of it, "I wonder how your mother shall react."

Bryce shot out of her chair, slamming her hands on the desk. Light shimmered at her fingertips.

Her father didn't so much as flinch. He looked at her hands, then her face, and said blandly, "You are now officially a Princess of the Fae. I expect you to act as such."

Her fingers curled on the desk, her long nails gouging the wood. "You have *no right*."

"I have every right. And you had the right not to use your royal privileges, but you chose otherwise."

"I didn't *know*." He couldn't get away with this. She'd call Marc immediately. See if he and his team could find some way out of it.

"Ignorance is no excuse," her father said, cold amusement frosting his face. "You are now Bryce Adelaide Danaan."

Bile burned her throat. She'd never heard anything more hateful. She was Bryce Adelaide Quinlan. She'd never stop being a Quinlan. Her mother's daughter.

Her father continued, "You will maintain appearances with Cormac for as long as I command you to." He rose, glancing again at her hands—the lines she'd gouged in the desk thanks to that new Vanir strength. His eyes narrowed. "What is that number there?"

She flipped over the piece of paper on which she'd written the sequence of numbers and letters on Sofie's body. But despite her rage and disgust, she managed to ask, "You know it?"

He scanned her face. "I will admit to turning a blind eye to the recklessness of your brother, but I would think you, Princess, would be more careful. The Asteri won't come to kill me first. Or even Athalar. They'll go right to Nidaros."

Her stomach twisted. "I don't know what you're talking about." What did the sequence from Sofie's arm have to do with this? Had he known Sofie? She didn't dare ask. Her father stalked for her office door, graceful as a leopard.

But he paused on the threshold, attention going to the star on her chest. "I know what it is you're searching for. I've been seeking it for a long, long time."

"Oh?" she sneered. "And what is that?"

The Autumn King stepped into the dimness of the stacks. "The truth."

Juniper didn't attend dance class that evening, and Madame Kyrah didn't so much as look at Bryce.

Though everyone else did. There were glares and whispers.

So inappropriate.

What an entitled brat.

Can you imagine *ever doing that to a friend?*

Bryce left class during the five-minute break and didn't return.

She found a bench in a quiet part of the Oracle's Park and slumped onto the wooden slats, tugging her hat low over her face.

She was a fucking princess. Yes, she'd been one before today, but . . .

A folder full of documents had been delivered right before she'd gone to class. In it had been a new scooter registration, proof of name change, and a credit card. A sleek, black credit card with *HRH Bryce Danaan* stamped on the front. A long, golden leash stretched from it to her father. And his bank account. She'd shoved everything into a drawer in her desk and locked it.

How could she tell her mother? How could she tell Randall?

She'd been so fucking *stupid*. She wished Danika were with her. Wished June didn't hate her guts, that Fury wasn't hundreds of miles to the north. With her parents, who already had enough to deal with, without her telling them about this spectacular fuckup.

And yeah, she knew if she called Hunt, he'd find her in two seconds, but . . . She wanted to talk to another female. Someone who might understand.

She dialed before she could second-guess herself.

Thirty minutes later, Bryce waited at a pizza counter, nursing a beer, watching people begin to queue at the alley food stalls as night fell, the baking temperature with it.

The witch-queen entered so casually that Bryce might not have noticed if it hadn't been for Ithan's presence. He sat at one of the small tables in the alley, clad in an old sunball T-shirt and track pants, looking for all the world like a guy out to meet a friend. Except for the outline of the handgun tucked into the back of his waistband. The knife she knew was in his boot.

No sign of the dragon, though. Unless Ariadne was somewhere out of sight.

Bryce said to Hypaxia, "Nice jeans."

The witch peered down at herself, the light green blouse, charcoal biker jacket, and tight black jeans, the sensible flats and pretty gold bracelet. A matching gold brooch of Cthona adorned the lapel of her jacket. "Thank you. Ithan suggested I blend in."

"He's not wrong," Bryce said, glancing at the wolf sizing up every person on the street. She said to Hypaxia, "Order what you want and we'll pay the tab when we leave."

The witch strode the ten feet to the display in the tiny shop, then quietly ordered. If the male behind the counter recognized her, he didn't let on.

Hypaxia took a position at the counter overlooking the alley. Ithan lifted his brows high. She nodded. All was fine.

Bryce said to her, "He's pretty intense about the guard duty."

"Very professional," Hypaxia said approvingly.

Bryce offered a friendly smile. "Thanks for coming. I know my call was super random. I just . . . I had a crazy day. And thought you might have some advice."

Hypaxia smiled at last. "I'm pleased you did. I've wished to see you since our encounter this spring." When the queen had been playing medwitch. And . . .

It all came rushing back.

Hypaxia had freed Hunt from the halo. Had removed it. Had given him the ability to slay Sandriel and come aid Bryce—

"Thank you for what you did," Bryce said, throat tight. "For helping Hunt."

Hypaxia's smile only widened. "From your scent, it seems as if you and he have made things . . . permanent. Congratulations."

Bryce casually rocked back on her heels. "Thank you."

"And how's your thigh?"

"No more pain. Also thanks to you."

"I'm glad to hear it."

Bryce sipped from her beer as the server brought over the queen's pizza. She murmured to him, and the male brought the second slice out to Ithan, who grinned over at Hypaxia and held up the slice in a long-distance cheers. Still no sign of the dragon. Maybe that was a good thing.

When Hypaxia had taken a bite, Bryce said, "So, I, uh . . ."

"Ah. The reason you asked me here?"

Bryce sighed. "Yeah. My father—the Autumn King—visited today. Said that because I used his name for a few things, it meant I had accepted my royal title. I tried to refuse, but he'd already done the paperwork. I'm now officially a princess." She almost choked on the last word.

"Judging from your expression, this is not good news."

"No. I know you're pretty much a stranger, and that you were born into your title and never had the choice to be normal, but . . . I feel like I'm drowning here."

A gentle, warm hand landed atop hers. "I am sorry he did that to you."

Bryce studied a stain on the counter, unsure if she could look at the witch without crying.

Hypaxia said, "Why do you think I came here this spring? I wanted to be normal. If only for a few months. I know what you're feeling."

Bryce shook her head. "Most people wouldn't get it. They'd think, *Oh, poor you, you have to be a princess.* But I've spent my entire life avoiding this male and his court. I *hate* him. And I just walked right into his clutches like a fucking idiot." She heaved a shuddering breath. "I think Hunt's answer to all of this would be to go flambé my father until he reversed this bullshit, but . . . I wanted to see if you had any alternate ideas."

The queen took another bite of her pizza, contemplating. "While I might enjoy the sight of Hunt Athalar flambéing the Autumn King . . ." Bryce's mouth quirked up at that. "I think you're right that a more diplomatic method is required."

"So you think there's a way out of this?" Marc had agreed to help, but hadn't sounded hopeful.

"I think there are ways to manage this. Manage your father."

Bryce nodded. "Ruhn mentioned you had some . . . drama with your coven."

A soft laugh. "I suppose that's a good way to put it."

"He also mentioned that you had some unusual tutors growing up." Ghosts, he'd told her on the phone this morning.

"Yes. My dearest friends."

"No wonder you wanted to bust out and escape, if you had only the dead for company."

Hypaxia chuckled. "They were wonderful companions, but yes. They encouraged me to come here, actually."

"Are they with you on this trip?"

"No. They cannot leave the confines of the keep where I was raised. My mother's summoning spell bound them there. It is . . . Perhaps it's the reason I returned to my homelands again."

"Not to be queen?"

"That too," Hypaxia said quickly. "But . . . they are my family."

"Along with the Hind," Bryce said carefully.

"I do not count her as kin."

Bryce was grateful for the shift in their conversation, even if for a few minutes. She needed time to sort through her raging feelings. "You look nothing alike."

"That is not why I don't consider her a sister."

"No, I know that."

"Our mother was as golden-haired and tan-skinned as she. My father, however—I take after his coloring."

"And who was the Hind's father?"

"A rich and powerful stag shifter in Pangera. My mother never told me the details of how they came to breed. Why she agreed to it. But the Hind inherited her father's powers, not the witch gifts, and thus she was sent at age three to live with him."

"That's horrible." When Bryce had been three . . . her mother had fought nearly to the death to keep her from the Autumn King's clutches. Her mother had done all that, only for Bryce to wind up right here. Shame and dread filled her. She knew it was only a matter of time until her mom found out, but she couldn't tell her— not yet.

"It was part of their deal," Hypaxia explained. "Whatever gift Lidia inherited, that was where she would live. She spent the first three years with my mother, but when the shifter gifts manifested, his kin came to claim her. My mother never saw her again."

"Was your mom bothered by what she became?"

"I was not privy to those thoughts," Hypaxia said tightly enough that Bryce knew to drop it. "But it has never sat well with me."

"Are you going to see her while she's here?"

"Yes. I've never met her before. I was born several years after she was sent away."

Bryce drank again. "I'd suggest not getting your hopes up."

"I'm not. But we digress from your troubles." The queen sighed. "I don't know Fae royal laws, so I'm afraid I can't tell you definitively, but . . . at this point, I think the only ones who might be able to stop your father are the Asteri."

"I was afraid of that." Bryce rubbed her temples. "Just wait until Hunt hears."

"He won't be pleased?"

"Why the Hel would he be pleased?"

"Because you are mated. And now your father has made you a princess. Which makes him . . ."

"Oh gods," Bryce said, choking. "Hunt is a fucking *prince*." She laughed bitterly. "He's going to go ballistic. He'll hate it even more than I do." She laughed again, a bit hysterically. "Sorry. I'm, like, literally imagining his face when I tell him tonight. I need to record it or something."

"I can't tell if this is a good or bad thing."

"Both. The Autumn King expects me to keep up my engagement with Prince Cormac."

"Even though your scent makes it clear you're with another?"

"Apparently." She didn't want to think about that. She finished the beer, then gathered up her plate and Hypaxia's to toss in the trash. She quickly paid their tab, and as she pocketed the receipt, she asked the queen, "Wanna walk a little? It's not as hot as it was."

"I'd like that very much."

They kept silent, unnoticed by those around them as they entered the alley. Ithan fell into step a polite distance behind. The dragon, if she was there, was nowhere to be seen.

"So your brother told you of the situation with my mother's coven, then."

"Yeah. That sucks. I'm sorry."

They reached the river a block away and turned down the quay. Dry, warm wind rustled the palms lining it. Hypaxia studied the stars. "I had such visions for what the future would be like. Of witches returning to power. Of being with the person who I . . ." She cleared her throat.

"You're seeing someone?" Bryce asked, brows lifting.

The queen's face shuttered. "No." Hypaxia blew out a long breath. "The relationship wasn't possible anymore. I might have continued it, but it was not . . . They didn't want to."

Bryce blinked. If Hypaxia was in love with someone else . . . Fuck. "Poor Ruhn," she said.

Hypaxia smiled sadly. "I think your brother wants to marry me as little as I want to marry him."

"Ruhn's hot, though. So are you. Maybe the attraction will kick in." Bryce owed her brother at least an attempt to try to play up his good attributes.

A laugh. "It takes far more than that."

"Yeah, but he's a good guy. Like, a *really* good guy. And I can't believe I'm even saying this, but . . . while I'm sure the person you love is great, you really couldn't do better than Ruhn."

"I'll remember those words." Hypaxia toyed with one of her long curls. "The engagement to your brother was an attempt to prevent my mother's coven from gaining too much power."

Bryce said, "But you said you *want* the witches to return to power. Or is it that you want your people to regain their power—but you want your mother's coven to . . . be excluded from that?" Hypaxia nodded gravely. Bryce's brows knit. "Aren't the witches already powerful?"

"Not as we once were. For generations now, mighty bloodlines have run dry, magic withering. Like they are . . . siphoned into nothing. My mother's coven has no interest in discovering why. They only want us to become even more subservient to the Asteri."

This female had freed Hunt in pure defiance of the Asteri. Was Hypaxia a rebel? Did she dare ask her? How much had Ithan and Ruhn told her yesterday?

Dark mists curled on the other side of the river. She asked quietly, "Did your mom summon your tutors from the Bone Quarter? Or another eternal resting place?"

"Such things did not exist when my tutors walked the earth."

Bryce gaped. "Your tutors predate the Asteri's arrival?"

Hypaxia narrowed her eyes in warning for Bryce to keep her voice down. "Yes. They were already long dead when the Northern Rift opened."

"They remember a time before the Asteri—when Parthos still stood?" Bryce ventured.

"Yes. One of my tutors, Palania, taught mathematics and science at its academy. She was born in the city surrounding it, and died there, too. So did generations of her family."

"The Asteri don't like people talking about these things. That humans accomplished so much before their arrival."

"They are classic conquerors." Hypaxia gazed toward the Bone Quarter. "They have conquered even death in this world. Spirits that once rested peacefully are now herded into these . . . zones."

Bryce started. "You know about that?"

"The dead speak to me of their horrors. When my mother died, I had to do some things that . . . Let's say my mother's coven was not happy that I found a way for my mother to avoid going to an eternal resting place. Even if doing so sacrificed my ability to speak with her forever." Shadows darkened her eyes. "But I could not send her to a zone like the Bone Quarter. Not when I knew what would become of her."

"Why not tell everyone? Why not tell the whole world?"

"Who would believe me? Do you know what the Asteri would do to me? To my people? They would slaughter every single witch to punish me. My mother knew it as well—and also chose not to say anything. If you are wise, you will not, either. I shall help Ithan Holstrom and his kin as best I can on the equinox, but there are limits."

Bryce halted by the rail overlooking the night-dark river. "Where did the dead go before the Asteri arrived? Did your tutors ever tell you that?"

Her mouth softened into a smile. "No. But they told me it was . . . good. Peaceful."

"Do you think the souls that are harvested here ever wind up there?"

"I don't know."

Bryce blew out a breath. "Well, this is the most depressing girl talk I've ever had."

"It's the first girl talk I've ever had."

"Normal girls dish about normal shit."

"You and I are not normal girls."

No, they weren't. They were . . . a queen and a princess. Meeting as equals. Talking about things that could get them killed.

"It can be very lonely, to wear a crown," Hypaxia said quietly, as if reading her thoughts. "But I'm glad to have you to speak with, Bryce."

"Me too." And she might not be anywhere near done fighting her father's bullshit, but . . . it was a comfort to know that she had the witch-queen on her side, at least. And other allies.

Ithan stood guard twenty feet behind. His stare met hers, bright in the dimness. She opened her mouth to call him over, to ask how much he'd heard.

But at that moment, a massive, scaled gray beast leapt over the quay railing.

And before Bryce could shout, it barreled into Ithan and closed its jaws around his throat.

55

Bryce didn't have time to scream. Didn't have time to do anything but fall back on her ass, scrambling away from Ithan, his blood spraying, gurgling as his throat—

The beast—the *demon*—ripped out Ithan's throat.

Tipped back its broad, flat head and swallowed the chunk of flesh between black, curved fangs.

"Get up," Hypaxia ordered from where she stood above Bryce, a knife in her hand. Where it'd come from, Bryce had no idea.

Ithan—

She couldn't do this again. Couldn't endure it.

The demon stepped away from Ithan's twitching, dying body. Would he survive that kind of a blow? If the demon had poison on its fangs like the kristallos—

This thing might have been some relative. Its matte gray scales flowed over a muscular, low-slung body; a tail as long as Bryce whipped back and forth, its spiked end carving grooves in the stone. People along the quay, the streets beyond, started fleeing.

Her body couldn't move. Shock—she knew this was shock, and yet—

Help would come soon. Someone, either in the Aux or the 33rd, would arrive. Hunt—

"*Get up*," Hypaxia said, gripping Bryce under a shoulder to haul her to her feet. Slowly, the witch-queen dragged Bryce back—

A snarl reverberated through the stones behind them.

Bryce twisted to find a second demon, twin to the one that had ripped out Ithan's throat, approaching at their rear. The two of them were closing in on the prey now trapped between them.

Fear, cold and sharp, sliced through her. Shattered the shock rooting her into uselessness. Clarified her fogged, bloody vision.

"Back-to-back," Hypaxia ordered, voice low and calm. One knife—that's all they had. Why the fuck didn't she carry a gun?

But Ithan had a gun. On his lifeless body, Bryce could make out the gun he hadn't had a chance to draw. How many rounds did it hold? If the demon was fast enough to sneak up on him, though, she didn't stand a chance. Not unless . . .

"What kind of magic do you have?" Bryce murmured, pressing her back to Hypaxia as she eyed the second demon. She'd kill these fuckers. Rip them apart piece by piece for this.

"Does it matter?" Hypaxia asked, angling her knife at the first demon.

"Is it energy? Like lightning?"

"Healing and wind—and the necromancy, which I can't even begin to explain."

"Can you pinpoint it? Shoot it into me?"

"What?"

"I need a charge. Like a battery," Bryce said, the scar on her chest glowing faintly.

The demon before her bayed to the night sky. Her ears rang.

"To do what?"

"Just—do it now, or we are going to be royally fucked."

The first demon howled. Like so many beings from the Pit, their eyes were milky—blind. As if they'd been in the dark so long they'd ceased to need them. So blinding wasn't an option. But a bullet . . . "You think a knife is going to work on them?" Bryce demanded.

"I . . ." Hypaxia guided them toward the quay railing. Three feet remained until there was nowhere to go but the water. Bryce shuddered, remembering the sobeks that had attacked them that day fleeing the Bone Quarter.

"Use your healing power and hit my fucking chest," Bryce snarled. "Trust me." They had no other choice. If Hunt's power had charged her up, maybe . . .

The creature nearest the witch-queen lunged, snapping. The two females slammed into the railing.

"Now!" Bryce shouted, and Hypaxia whirled, shoving a shining palm to Bryce's chest. Warmth flowed into her, soft and gentle, and—

Stars erupted in Bryce's mind. Supernovas.

Ithan.

It was as easy as taking a step.

One breath, Bryce stood against the quay. The next, she was beside Ithan's body, behind the creatures, who pivoted toward her, sensing that her scent had shifted away.

Hypaxia tapped the golden brooch on the lapel of her jacket. With a *woomph* of air, her broom appeared before her, and the queen leapt onto it, shooting skyward—

Bryce grabbed the gun from Ithan's waistband, clicked off the safety, and fired at the closest demon. Brain matter splattered as the bullet plowed between its sightless eyes.

The second demon charged at her, Hypaxia forgotten as she hovered on her broom in the air above. Bryce fired, and the beast dodged the blow—as if it could feel the air itself parting for the bullet. It was onto her, aware of what weapon she bore—

The demon leapt for her, and Bryce rallied her power.

Stepped from her place beside Ithan's body to the open walkway behind the charging creature.

It hit the ground and spun, claws gouging deep. Bryce fired again, and the demon used those preternatural senses to veer left at the last millisecond, taking the bullet in the shoulder. The shot did nothing to slow it.

The demon jumped for her again, and Bryce moved. Slower this time—Hypaxia's power was already funneling out of her.

"Thirty feet behind you!" Hypaxia ordered from above,

pointing, and Bryce gritted her teeth, mapping out how to get there. The dance she had to lead the creature into.

It leapt, claws out, and Bryce teleported back ten feet. It leapt again and she moved, body shaking against the strain. Another ten feet back. She could make the last jump. Had to make the last jump as the demon sprang—

Roaring, Bryce flung all of herself, all that remained of the spark of Hypaxia's power, into her desire to step, to move—

She appeared ten feet back, and the creature, sensing her pattern, jumped.

It didn't look up. Didn't see the witch-queen plunging to the earth, dagger aloft.

Bryce hit the ground as Hypaxia jumped from her broom and landed atop the beast, slamming her blade into its skull. Witch and demon went down, the former astride it like a horse from Hel. But the demon didn't so much as twitch.

Scraped palms and knees already healing, Bryce panted, shaking. She'd done it. She'd—

Ithan. Oh gods, Ithan.

On wobbling legs, she scrambled to her feet and rushed for him. His throat was healing—slowly. He stared unseeingly at the night sky.

"Move back," Hypaxia said, breathing heavily, broom discarded beside her. "Let me see him."

"He needs a medwitch!"

"I am a medwitch," Hypaxia said, and knelt.

Wings filled the skies, sirens blaring from the streets. Then Isaiah was there, hands on Bryce's shoulders. "Are you all right? Is that Holstrom? Where's Athalar?" The rapid-fire questions pelted her.

"I'm here," Hunt said from the darkness, landing with enough force that the ground shook. Lightning skittered over the concrete. He assessed Bryce, then Ithan, the wolf's body glowing under Hypaxia's hands. Then he registered the two demons and went pale. "Those . . ." He scanned Bryce again.

"You know what they are?" Isaiah asked.

Hunt rushed to Bryce and tucked her into him. She leaned into his warmth, his strength. He said quietly, "Deathstalkers. Personal pets of the Prince of the Pit. They were seen in Nena four days ago. They somehow crossed the border."

Bryce's stomach hollowed out.

Isaiah held up a hand to keep the other advancing angels and Aux at bay. "You think these two came here all the way from Nena? And why attack Bryce?"

Bryce wrapped her arms around Hunt's waist, not caring that she was clinging. If she let go, her knees might very well give out. Hunt lied smoothly, "Isn't it obvious? Hel's got a score to settle with her after this spring. They sent their best assassins to kill her."

Isaiah seemed to buy that theory, because he said to Bryce, "How did you even bring them down?"

"Ithan had a gun. I got a lucky shot on the first. Queen Hypaxia took care of the second."

It was mostly true.

"There," Hypaxia announced, stepping back from Ithan's healed, limp body. "He'll wake when he's ready." She gathered her broom and, with a touch—or some of her witch-power—it shrank back into the golden brooch of Cthona. She pinned it onto her gray jacket as she pivoted to Isaiah. "Can your soldiers transport him to the witches' embassy? I'd like to tend to him personally until he's conscious."

Bryce couldn't argue with that. But . . . there was no one to call for Ithan. No family, no friends, no pack. No one except—

She dialed Ruhn.

Deathstalkers. He should have sent out a warning the moment he'd IDed the tail of one in that photo from Nena. Should have had every soldier in this city on alert.

But Bryce . . . by some miracle, she didn't have a scratch on her.

It wasn't possible. Hunt knew how fast the deathstalkers were. Even Fae couldn't outrun them. They'd been bred that way by Apollion himself.

Hunt waited to speak until he and Bryce stood in the golden hall of the witches' embassy. Ithan had already been handed over from the two angels who'd flown him here to Ruhn and Declan, who'd gently carried the wolf into a small room to recover. "So, let's hear the real story."

Bryce turned to him, eyes bright with fear—and excitement. "I did it. Teleported." She explained what Hypaxia had done—what she had done.

"That was one Hel of a risk." He wasn't sure whether to kiss her or shake her for it.

"My options were limited," Bryce said, crossing her arms. Through the open doorway, Ruhn and Dec set Ithan on the cot, Hypaxia instructing them to position his body in a certain way. "Where the Hel was the dragon?"

"Fucking coward told Holstrom she'd climb up to the rooftops to provide a second set of eyes, and then bailed," Flynn said, face dark as he stepped into the hall.

"Do you blame her?" Bryce said.

"Yeah." Flynn glowered. "We did her a favor, and she fucked us over. She could have torched those demons." Before Bryce could counter, the lord stalked away with a disgusted shake of his head.

Bryce waited until the hall was empty again before asking Hunt, "You think these were the appetizers the Prince of the Pit threatened to send to test us?"

"Yes. They answer only to him."

"But they were about to kill me. He didn't seem to want us dead. And it seems reckless to do it just to test me." She gestured between them. "His epic opponents, remember?"

Ruhn stepped into the hall and murmured, "Unless you weren't the one they were supposed to kill." He jerked his chin toward Hypaxia, lowering his voice. He assessed the quiet halls of the embassy—no witches in sight—before saying, "Maybe her coven summoned them, somehow."

Bryce frowned. "Why?"

Ruhn paced a step. "You'd be the perfect cover story. She was walking beside someone Hel has a score to settle with—someone who'd pissed Hel off this spring. Deathstalkers imply the Prince of the Pit's involvement. If she'd died, all eyes would be on Hel. Everyone would think they'd targeted you, and she'd be the unfortunate additional loss."

"What about Ithan, though?"

Hunt picked up Ruhn's thread. "Also collateral. After this spring, I doubt Sabine would be stupid enough to summon a demon. That leaves our enemies or Hypaxia's. But given what Apollion threatened . . . I'd say odds are it was him. Maybe he was willing to take the risk that you'd die during his little test—maybe he supposed that if you died, you wouldn't be worthy of battling him anyway."

Bryce rubbed her face. "So where does that leave us?"

Hunt interlaced their fingers. "It leaves us with the realization that this city needs to be on high alert and you need to be armed at all times."

She glared. "That's not helpful."

Ruhn, wisely, kept his mouth shut.

"You didn't have any weapons tonight," Hunt snarled. "You two had *one knife* between you. You were lucky Ithan carried that gun. And you were even luckier in your guess that Hypaxia could charge up your ability to teleport."

Ruhn grunted his agreement.

"So that's how you did it," Declan said, walking back into the hall. The warrior shut the door behind him, giving Hypaxia and Ithan privacy.

Bryce sketched a bow. "It'll be my special solo act during the school talent show."

Declan snorted, but Ruhn was assessing her. "You really teleported?"

Bryce explained everything again, and Hunt couldn't keep himself from tugging her closer. When she finished, Ruhn echoed Hunt's words. "We got lucky tonight. *You* got lucky tonight."

Bryce winked at Hunt. "And I plan to get lucky again."

"Gross," Ruhn said as Declan snickered.

Hunt flicked Bryce's nose and said to Ruhn, "Let's set up watches around the apartment and this embassy—assign your most trusted soldiers. I'll get Isaiah and Naomi on it, too."

"The 33rd and the Aux teaming up to guard little old me?" Bryce crooned. "I'm flattered."

"This is not the time to debate alphahole politics," Hunt ground out. "Those were fucking deathstalkers."

"And I dealt with them."

"I wouldn't be so dismissive," he growled. "The Prince of the Pit will send hordes of them through the Northern Rift if he ever gets it fully open, rather than shoving one or two through at a time for fun. They hunt down whoever they're ordered to stalk. They're assassins. You get marked by them for execution, and you are *dead*."

She blew on her fingers, as if chasing off dust. "All in a day's work for me, then."

"*Quinlan—*"

Ruhn started laughing.

"What?" Hunt demanded.

Ruhn said, "You know who I was talking to before I got your call? My father." Bryce went still, and Hunt knew it was bad. Ruhn grinned at him. "*Your* father in-law."

"Excuse me?"

Ruhn didn't stop grinning. "He told me the wonderful news." He winked at Bryce. "You must be so happy."

Bryce groaned and turned to Hunt. "It's not official—"

"Oh, it's official," Ruhn said, leaning against the wall beside the door.

"What the fuck are you two talking about?" Hunt growled.

Ruhn smirked at Hunt. "She's been bandying about the royal name, apparently. Which means she's accepted her position as princess. And as you're her mate, that makes you son-in-law to the Autumn King. And my brother."

Hunt gaped at him. Ruhn was completely serious.

Bryce blurted, "Did you ask him about Cormac? The Autumn King insists the engagement is still on."

Ruhn's amusement faded. "I don't see how it could be."

"I'm sorry," Hunt cut in, "but what the fuck?" His wings splayed. "You're now officially a *princess*?"

Bryce winced. "Surprise?"

56

Ithan groaned, his body giving a collective throb of pain.

His throat—jaws and fangs and claws, the queen and *Bryce*—

He lunged up, hand at his neck—

"You're safe. It's over." The calm female voice came from his right, and Ithan twisted, finding himself on a narrow bed in a gilded room he'd never seen.

Queen Hypaxia sat in a chair beside him, a book in her lap, wearing her blue robes once again. No sign of the casual, modern female he'd been trailing earlier. His voice was like gravel as he asked, "You all right?"

"Very well. As is Miss Quinlan. You're at my embassy, in case you were wondering."

Ithan sagged back against the bed. He'd been ambushed, like a fucking novice. He'd always prided himself on his reflexes and instincts, but he'd had his ass handed to him. The queen opened her mouth, but he demanded, "What about the dragon?"

Hypaxia's mouth tightened. "Ariadne was nowhere to be found. It appears she has taken her chances with the law and fled."

Ithan growled. "She bailed?" The dragon had claimed she couldn't. That there was nowhere in Midgard she could go without the Astronomer finding her.

Gods. One guarding assignment and he'd fumbled it. Badly.

He deserved to have his throat ripped out. Deserved to be lying here, like a weak fucking child, for his ineptitude.

Hypaxia nodded gravely. "The city cameras picked it up: Ariadne left the moment I entered the pizza shop. But nothing more—even the cameras can't find her."

"She's likely halfway across the planet by now," Ithan grumbled. The Fae males were going to be so pissed.

"You liberated her from the ring. From serving a terrible master. Are you surprised that she is not willing to wait for someone to purchase her again?"

"I thought she'd be grateful, at least."

Hypaxia frowned with disapproval. But she said, "She is a dragon. A creature of earth and sky, fire and wind. She should never have been contained or enslaved. I hope she stays free for the rest of her immortal life."

The tone brooked no room for argument, and—well, Ithan agreed with the queen anyway. He sighed, gently rubbing at his tender throat. "So what the fuck attacked us? A demon?"

"Yes, an extremely deadly one." She explained what had happened.

Ithan eased into a sitting position once more. "I'm sorry I fucked this one up so badly. I . . . I don't like making mistakes like this." Losing grated on his very soul. The queen and Bryce were safe, but he was a fucking *loser*.

"You have nothing to apologize for," the queen said firmly. "Considering the gravity of the situation, I'm assuming your friends know more about the motives behind this attack than they have told me."

Well, she was definitely right on that one. Ithan blew out a breath that set his throat aching. It'd be another few hours until it was totally healed.

He had no idea how long it'd take until he forgave himself for fucking up tonight.

"So you can really contact Connor on the Autumnal Equinox?" he asked quietly, hating that he needed to change the subject. Not that this new one was much better.

"Yes." She angled her head, curls spilling over her shoulder. "You worry for him."

"Wouldn't you? I don't care if we've been told that he's, like, off-limits. I want to make sure he's okay. I heard what you said to Bryce—about ensuring your mom didn't go to one of the sleeping realms. I want you to do that for him." He swallowed, then amended, "If you're cool with that, Your Majesty."

Her eyes twinkled with amusement. "I shall do my best."

Ithan sighed again, staring at the tall windows on the other side of the room, the drapes shut for the night. "I know you're already doing a lot for me, but . . . the Astronomer has a wolf enslaved to him as one of his mystics. Is there anything you could do for her?"

"What do you mean?" He took it as a good sign that she didn't say no.

He said, "I can't just leave her there."

"Why is it your burden to free her?"

"Wolves don't belong in cages. That's what the mystics' tanks are. Watery cages."

"And what if she wants to be in there?"

"How could she?" Before the queen could answer, he plowed on, "I know it's random. There are so many other people suffering out there. But it doesn't sit right with me."

He'd screwed up enough in the past two years—he wouldn't drop the ball on this. An Alpha wolf in captivity—the idea was abhorrent. He'd do whatever he could to help her.

She seemed to read whatever lay on his face. "You're a good male, Ithan Holstrom."

"You met me yesterday." And after tonight, he sure as fuck didn't deserve that claim.

"But I can tell." She touched his hand gently. "I do not think there is much I can do to help the mystic, unfortunately, beyond what your other royal friends might be able to accomplish."

Ithan knew she was right. He'd find another way, then. Somehow. "Well, this is fucked."

"It sure is," said a male voice from the doorway, and Ithan

blinked, surprised to find Flynn and Declan standing there, Tharion a step behind them.

"Hey," Ithan said, bracing for the ridicule, the ribbing, the questioning about how the Hel he'd mangled protection duty.

But Declan bowed his head to the queen before sauntering over to Ithan. "How you feeling, pup?"

"Fine," Ithan said, then admitted, "A little sore."

"Getting your throat ripped out does that to a male," Flynn said. He winked at Hypaxia. "But she fixed you up pretty good, didn't she?"

Hypaxia smiled up at him. Tharion, lingering by the door, chuckled.

Ithan said quietly, "Yeah, she did."

Declan clapped his hands together. "Okay, well, we just wanted to make sure you were all right."

Hypaxia added, "They've been in and out all night."

"You'll give them away as big old softies, Pax," Tharion said to the queen, who shook her head at the name. As if Tharion often used it to annoy her.

Declan asked the queen, "When can he come home?"

Home. The word rang through Ithan. He'd been their roommate for only a week and a half. When had he last had a true home? The Den hadn't been one since his parents had died.

But . . . that was genuine concern on Declan's face. On Flynn's. Ithan swallowed hard.

"Tomorrow morning," Hypaxia said, and rose from her chair. "I'll do my final check then, and if you're cleared, you'll be on your way, Ithan."

"I'm supposed to guard you," Ithan countered, his voice thick.

But she patted his shoulder before walking to the door. Tharion fell into step beside her, like he planned to converse in private. The witch-queen said to Ithan as she and the mer left, "Take tomorrow off."

Ithan opened his mouth to object, but she'd already left, the mer with her.

Flynn slung himself into the seat the queen had vacated. "Don't tell Ruhn, but I'd love to have that female do a check on *me*."

Ithan scowled, but refrained from explaining what he'd over-heard. The queen loved another and seemed pretty cut up about it. But what good was love, in the face of duty?

He'd keep Hypaxia's romance quiet. She'd agreed to her union with Ruhn, and he could do nothing but admire that she'd chosen to do so even when her heart lay with someone else.

Fuck, he knew how that felt. He blocked out Bryce's face from his mind.

Declan was saying to Flynn, "Do yourself a favor and don't hit on her. Or tease her."

"She's Ruhn's fiancée," Flynn said, propping his boots on the edge of Ithan's bed and tucking his hands behind his head. "That entitles me to some ribbing."

Ithan laughed, eyes stinging. No one ever joked in Amelie's pack. He might coax a smile from Perry every once in a while, but mostly they were all serious. Humorless. They never laughed at themselves.

But these guys had come to check on him. Not to rip into him for failing. They didn't even seem to view it as a failure.

Flynn asked a shade seriously, "You're really feeling all right, though?"

Ithan mastered himself. "Yeah."

"Good," Declan said.

Ithan's throat tightened. He hadn't realized how much he missed it—people having his back. Caring if he lived or died. The Pack of Devils had been that for him, yes, but his sunball team, too. He hadn't spoken to any of them since Connor's death.

Flynn's eyes softened slightly, as if seeing something on Ithan's face, and Ithan straightened, clearing his throat. But Flynn said, "We got you, wolf."

"Why?" The question slipped out before Ithan could wonder whether he should ask. But there were probably dozens of Fae who'd spent years trying to squeeze into the trio that was Ruhn, Flynn, and Declan. Why they'd brought Ithan into their little circle was beyond him.

Flynn and Dec swapped glances. The latter shrugged. "Why not?"

"I'm a wolf. You're Fae."

"So old-fashioned." Flynn winked. "I had you pegged as more progressive than that."

"I don't want your pity," Ithan said.

Declan drew back. "Who the fuck said anything about pity?"

Flynn put up his hands. "We're only friends with you because we want good sunball tickets."

Ithan looked between the males. Then burst out laughing.

"All right." He rubbed at his sore throat again. "That's a good enough reason for me."

Ruhn monitored his sister as they waited for Athalar to finish briefing some senior members of the 33rd on what had gone down with the deathstalker.

It felt like last spring all over again. Granted, Micah had been the one summoning those kristallos demons, but . . . this couldn't be good. The Horn was tattooed on Bryce's back now—what wouldn't Hel do to attain it?

"The answer," Bryce said to Ruhn, "is that I'm not going to allow any sort of security detail."

Ruhn blinked. And said silently, *I wasn't thinking that.*

She glared at him sidelong. *I could feel you brooding about the attack. It's the logical conclusion from an overly aggressive Fae male.*

Overly aggressive?

Protective?

Bryce. This is some serious-ass shit.

I know.

And you're a princess now. An official one.

She crossed her arms, watching Hunt talk with his friends. *I know.*

How do you feel about it?

How do you *feel about it?*

Why the fuck would it make any difference what I feel? He scowled at her.

Because now you have to share the crown.

I'm glad I can share it with you. Selfishly, pathetically glad, Bryce. But . . . isn't this what you wanted to avoid?

It is. Her mental voice hardened into sharp steel.

Are you going to do something about it?

Maybe.

Tread carefully. There are so many laws and rules and shit that you don't know about. I can fill you in, but . . . this is a whole new level of the game. You have to be on alert.

She faced him, offering a broad grin that didn't meet her eyes before taking a few steps toward Athalar. "If dear old dad wants a princess," she said, looking more like their father than he'd ever witnessed, "then he'll get one."

"Dreadwolves prowling the Old Square," Hypaxia hissed under her breath to Tharion as she peered out the window of her private suite on the second floor of the elegant embassy.

Despite the plush furniture, the room definitely belonged to a witch: a small crystal altar to Cthona adorned the eastern wall, covered in various tools of worship; a large obsidian scrying mirror hung above it; and the fireplace built into the southern wall had various iron arms, presumably to hold cauldrons during spells. A royal suite, yes, but a workroom as well.

"I hate the sight of them," the queen went on, the streetlights casting her beautiful face in golden hues. "Those uniforms. The silver darts on their collars." He wondered how many people ever saw her so unguarded. "Rebel-hunters. That's what they are."

Indeed, where they walked, revelers fell silent. Tourists stopped snapping photos.

"Tell me how you really feel, Pax," Tharion said, crossing his arms.

The queen whirled toward him. "I wish you'd stop using that nickname. Ever since the Summit—"

"Ever since then, you've missed me using it?" He gave her his most charming smile.

She rolled her eyes, but he caught the slight curl of her lips.

He asked, "Have you kept up the tally? How many times has Prince Ruhn gawked at you since you arrived?"

She flushed. "He doesn't gawk."

"I think our final tally at the Summit was . . . thirty? Forty?"

She whacked him on the chest.

"I missed you," he said, grinning.

She grinned back. "What does your fiancée have to say about that?" She was one of the few people who knew. During their initial meeting at the Summit—an accidental encounter late one night when she'd sought some solitude at one of the mer's subterranean pools and found him seeking the same—they'd spoken of their various . . . obligations. A friendship had immediately sprung up.

Tharion countered, "What does *your* fiancé have to say about it?"

The witch laughed softly, the sound like silver bells. "You're the one who's been associating with him. You tell me."

He chuckled, but his amusement fell away, his voice becoming serious. "He's concerned enough about you that he told some of us about your coven. Why didn't you tell me?" He'd grab any one of them who harmed her and drown them. Slowly.

She searched his face. He let her. "What could you have done?"

Well, that stung. Especially because she was right. He let out a long sigh. He wished he could tell her—about the fact that he'd bought himself a small stretch of freedom. That he would only go back to the Blue Court to keep up appearances, that he'd pretend Emile Renast was still on the loose for as long as he could, but . . . Would he go back after that? *Could* he go back?

Maybe he'd get in touch with the Ocean Queen's people and beg for asylum. Maybe they'd shelter his family, too.

He'd opened his mouth to speak when a ripple went through the street below. People stopped. Some pressed against buildings.

"What the fuck are they doing here?" Tharion growled.

Mordoc and the Hammer stalked down the street, wolf and angel sneering at all in their path. They seemed to savor the quiet and dread that trailed in their wake.

Hypaxia's brows raised. "Not friends of yours?"

He put a hand on his heart. "You wound me, Pax."

The queen's mouth thinned as Pollux and Mordoc crossed the intersection. "It's an ill omen, to see them here."

"Maybe they want to make sure all is well, considering what attacked tonight."

Mighty Ogenas, creatures straight from the Pit. He'd been enjoying a drink with a pride of lioness shifters at a wine bar when he'd gotten the call. He'd come here, claiming an investigative visit from the Blue Court, but . . . "You sure you're all right?" he asked, glad to pivot from the two monsters on the street.

"I'm fine," Hypaxia said, turning weary, sad eyes toward him. "Miss Quinlan proved herself a valuable ally in a fight." He liked the idea of the two of them becoming friendly. They'd be a formidable pair against any opponent.

"What'd your coven say about the attack?" Tharion asked, glancing to the shut double doors across the room. Pollux and Mordoc vanished down the street. As if they'd all been frozen, people suddenly began moving again. None went in the direction the Hammer and the dreadwolf had gone.

"My coven feigned outrage, of course. It's not worth recounting."

Fair enough. "You should get some sleep. You must be exhausted from healing Holstrom."

"Not at all." Her gaze again lifted to his face. "But you . . . you should go. Another few minutes and suspicions will be raised."

"Oh?" He couldn't resist teasing. "Like what?"

She flushed again. "Like we're doing things we shouldn't."

"Sounds naughty."

She playfully shoved him toward the door. He let her, walking backward as he said, "I'll see you soon, okay? You have my number."

Her eyes shone like stars. "Thank you for checking on me."

"Anything for you, Pax." Tharion shut the door behind him and found himself face-to-face with three witches. All members of her coven, if his memory of the Summit served him. All cold-faced and unamused. "Ladies," he said, inclining his head.

None of them answered, and as they converged on the queen's suite with a knock on her door, he suppressed the instinct to return to her side.

But it wasn't his place, and he still had one more task tonight. First, though, he needed a dip in the Istros to make sure his fins stayed intact.

Thirty minutes later, still wet, Tharion walked up to the peeling front door of the near-collapsing house off Archer Street, music blasting from the windows despite the late hour. Tharion knocked, loudly enough to be heard over the bass.

A moment later, the door opened. Tharion smiled crookedly at Ruhn, and waved to Tristan Flynn and Declan Emmet standing in the foyer behind him. "Got space for one more roommate?"

57

Hunt waited until he and Bryce had entered the apartment, the door firmly shut behind them, before he said, "I'm a *prince* now?"

Bryce slumped onto the couch. "Welcome to the club."

"Your father really did this?"

She nodded glumly. "My mom is going to freak."

Hunt stalked to the couch. "What about you, Bryce? Your mom can deal with it. I can deal with this, believe it or not. But . . . are you okay?"

She only stroked Syrinx's coat.

He scented salt and water, then, and sat on the new coffee table, lifting her chin between his thumb and forefinger to find tears running down her cheeks. Ones he had no doubt she'd been holding back for hours.

He'd turn the Autumn King into smoldering carrion for putting those tears, the fear and panic and sorrow, in her eyes.

"I spent my whole life avoiding this. And I just feel . . ." She wiped angrily at her face. "I feel so fucking *stupid* for having walked into his net."

"You shouldn't. He bent the rules to his will. He's a snake."

"He's a snake and now technically, legally, my king." She choked on a sob. "I will never have a normal life again. I'll never be free of him, and—"

Hunt gathered her into his arms, moving to the couch and pulling her into his lap. "We'll fight him on this. You want a normal life, a life with me—we'll make it happen. You're not alone. We'll fight him together."

She buried her face against his chest, tears splashing onto the black armor of his battle-suit. He stroked her silken hair, letting the smooth strands slide through his fingers.

"I could handle the Starborn shit. I could handle the magic," she said, voice muffled against his chest. "But this . . . I can't fucking handle this." She lifted her head, dread and panic flooding her expression. "He *owns* me. I'm chattel to him. If he wanted me to marry Cormac tonight, he could sign the marriage documents without even my presence. If I wanted a divorce, he'd be the one to grant it, not that he would. I'm a commodity—either I belong to him, or I belong to Cormac. He can do whatever he wants, and no amount of bravado from me can stop it."

Lightening skittered down his wings. "I'll fucking kill him."

"And what will that do, beyond get you executed?"

He leaned his brow against hers. "We'll think of a way out of this."

"Hypaxia said only the Asteri could override him. Considering our status with them, I doubt they'll help."

Hunt blew out a long breath. Tightened his arms around his mate. He'd slaughter anyone who tried to take her from him. King, prince, Fae, or Asteri. He'd fucking *kill*—

"Hunt."

He blinked.

"Your eyes went all . . . rage-dazey." She sniffled.

"Sorry." The last thing she needed right now was to have to handle his fury, too. He kissed her cheek, her temple, her neck.

She rested her brow on his shoulder, shuddering. Syrinx whimpered from where he had cuddled up on her other side.

For long minutes, Hunt and Bryce sat there. Hunt savored every place his body touched hers, the warmth and scent of her. Racked his mind for anything he might do, any path out of this.

Her fingers curled against the nape of his neck. He loosened his grip, pulling back to scan her face.

Starlight and fire sparked there. "Tell me that look means you came up with some brilliant yet painless way out of this," he said.

She kissed him softly. "You're not going to like it."

Ruhn wasn't at all shocked when he found himself standing before that mental couch.

After the night he'd had, nothing could shock him.

On the bridge, Day surveyed Ruhn without saying a word. Somehow, he could have sworn she sensed his turmoil.

But Ruhn said, "Anything for me?" He hadn't forgotten their last conversation. She'd told him he was a worthless, do-nothing loser who'd never known sacrifice or pain.

"You're angry with me."

"I don't care about you enough to be angry with you," he said coldly.

"Liar."

The word was an arrow shot between them. The night around him rippled. His temper hadn't improved when he discovered that Ariadne had straight up bailed. Fled the moment no one was looking and gone the gods knew where. He didn't blame the dragon. He was just . . . pissed he hadn't anticipated it.

He asked Day, "What the fuck do you want me to say?"

"I owe you an apology for last time. I'd had a rough day. My temper got the better of me."

"You spoke the truth. Why bother apologizing for it?"

"It's not the truth. I . . ." She seemed to struggle for words. "Do you know when I last spoke honestly with someone? When I last spoke to someone as I do to you, as close to my real self as I've ever come?"

"I'm guessing it's been a while."

She crossed her arms, wrapping them around herself. "Yes."

"Can I ask you a question?"

She angled her head. "What?"

He rubbed his neck, his shoulder. "What do you think makes a good leader?" The question was ridiculous—an essay for a second-grader. But after all that had gone down . . .

She didn't balk. "Someone who listens. Who thinks before acting. Who tries to understand different viewpoints. Who does what is right, even if the path is long and hard. Who will give a voice to the voiceless."

His father was none of those things. Except for thinking before acting. That male had schemes that had been in play for decades. Centuries.

"Why do you ask?"

Ruhn shrugged. "All this rebel stuff has me thinking about it. Who we'd replace the Asteri with. Who we'd *want* to replace them with."

She studied him, her gaze a brand on his skin. "What do *you* think makes a good leader?"

He didn't know. Only that he wasn't entirely sure he fit the bill of what she'd described, either. Where would that leave his people? "I'm trying to figure that out." If he became king one day, what sort of ruler would he be? He'd try to do right, but . . .

Silence fell, companionable and comfortable.

But then Day blew out a breath, blue flame rippling from her mouth. "I'm not used to this sort of thing."

He lowered himself onto his couch. "What sort of thing?"

"Friendship."

"You consider me a friend?"

"In a world full of enemies, you're my only friend."

"Well, maybe I should give you friendship lessons, because you fucking blow at it."

She laughed, and the sound wasn't entirely joyous. "All right. I deserved that."

He gave her a half smile, even if she couldn't see it. "Lesson one: don't shit on your friends when you have a bad day."

"Right."

"Lesson two: Your true friends won't mind when you do, so long as you own up to it and apologize. Usually in the form of buying them a beer."

Another laugh, softer this time. "I'll buy you a beer, then."

"Yeah? When you come to visit me?"

"Yeah," she said, the word echoing. "When I come visit you."

He rose and crossed to her couch, peering down at her. "Which will be when, Day?"

She tipped her head back, as if staring up at him. "On the Autumnal Equinox."

Ruhn stilled. "You . . . What?"

She brought her burning hand to her head—her ear. Like she was tucking a strand of hair behind it. She stood, walking around the couch. Putting it between them as she said, "I must attend the ball for the Archangels. I could . . . meet you somewhere."

"I'm going to that ball," he said, unsure why his voice went hoarse. For her to be invited there, she had to be important, precisely as they'd suspected. "The equinox fete is always a masked ball. We can meet there."

She backed up a step as he rounded the couch. "In front of so many?"

"Why not? We'll both be in masks. And we're both invited to the party, so why would it be suspicious for two people to talk there?"

He could have sworn he heard her heart pounding. She asked, "How will I know you?"

"The party's in the conservatory on the rooftop garden of the Comitium. There's a fountain on the western side of it—right off the stairs from the conservatory. Meet me there at midnight."

"But how can I be sure not to mistake someone else for you?"

"If I think it's you, I'll say 'Day?' And if you answer 'Night,' we'll know."

"We shouldn't."

Ruhn took a step toward her, his breathing uneven. "Is it so bad if I know who you are?"

"It jeopardizes everything. For all I know, you could be baiting me for the Asteri—"

"Look at me and tell me you think that's true."

She did. Ruhn came close enough that the heat of her flame warmed his body.

And, deciding to Hel with it, he reached for her hand. The flame warmed his night-skin, but did not burn. The hand beneath the fire was slender. Delicate.

Her fingers contracted against his own, but he held firm. "I'll be waiting for you."

"And if I'm not what you expect?"

"What do you think I'm expecting?"

Again, her fingers twitched, like she'd yank away. "I don't know."

He tugged on her arm, pulling her a little closer. When was the last time he'd had to work for a female's attention like this? Fuck, he *was* working for it, wasn't he? He wanted to see her face. Know who was bold and brave enough to risk her life again and again to defy the Asteri.

Ruhn stared down at the veil of flame between him and Day. "I want to smell your scent. See you. Even for a moment."

"That ball will be swarming with our enemies."

"Then we won't stay long. But . . . just meet me, all right?"

She was silent, as if she were trying to pierce the blanket of stars he wore. "Why?"

His voice dropped. "You know why."

She hesitated. Then she said softly, "Yes."

Her flames seemed to reach for his stars and shadows. "Midnight."

She faded into embers on the wind. "Midnight," she promised.

58

Two weeks later, Hunt scowled at his reflection in the mirror. He tugged at the white bow tie of his tux, already feeling strangled by the stupid thing.

He'd wanted to wear his battle-suit to the party, but Bryce had staged an intervention last week and demanded he wear something "halfway normal." *Then you can go back to being the predator-in-the-night we all love so much*, she'd said.

Hunt growled, giving himself a final once-over before calling across the apartment, "I'm as good as I'm going to get, so let's leave. The van's downstairs."

He sure as fuck couldn't cram his wings into the usual black sedan the Autumn King would have sent for Bryce. But at least the asshole had sent a van instead. Cormac was her official escort to the party, and was no doubt waiting in the vehicle. It had likely been Cormac who'd convinced the Autumn King to switch to a van so Bryce's "plus-one" could join them.

Bryce had bristled at every new order that had come from the Autumn King: the jewelry she was expected to wear, the clothes, the height of her heels, the length of her nails, the type of car they'd take, who would exit the car first, how *she* would exit the car— apparently, her ankles and knees were to be forever glued together in public—and lastly, most outrageously, what and how she was allowed to eat.

Nothing. That was the short answer. A Fae Princess did not eat in public, was the long answer. Maybe a sip of soup or one solitary, small bite to be polite. And one glass of wine. No hard liquor.

Bryce had read the list of commandments one night after they'd fucked in the shower, and had been so wound up that Hunt had gone down on her to take the edge off. He'd taken his time tasting her, savoring each lick of her delicious, enticing sex.

Even fucking her at night and before work, he couldn't get enough. Would find himself in the middle of the day aching for her. They'd already fucked twice in her office, right on her desk, her dress bunched at her waist, his pants barely unbuckled as he pounded into her.

They hadn't been caught, thank the gods. Not just by her coworkers, but by anyone who'd report it to Cormac, to the Autumn King. She'd already had one battle with her father over Hunt still living here with her. But after tonight . . .

He scooped up the golden mask from where he'd left it on the dresser—so fucking ridiculous and dramatic—and stepped into the great room, toes wriggling in his patent leather shoes. When was the last time he'd worn anything but his boots or sneakers? Never. He'd literally never worn shoes like this. When he was young, it had been lace-up sandals or boots—and then it had been boots for centuries.

What would his mother make of this male in the mirror? He strained to recall her smile, to imagine how her eyes might have sparkled. He wished she were here. Not only to see him, but to know that all she'd struggled to provide had paid off. To know that he could take care of her now.

Bryce let out a whistle from the other side of the great room, and Hunt looked up, tucking away the old ache in his chest.

All the breath left his chest. "Holy shit."

She was . . .

"Holy shit," he said again, and she laughed. He swallowed. "You're so fucking beautiful."

She blushed, and his head began roaring, cock aching. He wanted to lick that blush, wanted to kiss every inch of her smile.

"I couldn't bring myself to wear the tiara," Bryce said, lifting a wrist and twirling the crown around it with typical irreverence.

"You don't need it."

She really didn't. The sparkling black dress hugged every luscious curve before loosening around the knee, spilling into a train of solid night. The plunging neckline stopped below her breasts, framing the star between them, drawing the eye to the remarkable scar.

Black gloves flowed up to her elbows, and her satin-clad fingers toyed with one of the diamond chandelier earrings sparkling against the column of her neck. She'd left her hair down, a diamond comb pinning back one side, the silken mass of hair draping over her opposite shoulder. In her other hand she clutched the stem of a silver mask.

Full, bloodred lips smiled at him beneath eyes framed with a swoop of kohl. Simple makeup—and utterly devastating.

"Solas, Quinlan."

"You clean up pretty good yourself."

Hunt straightened the lapels of his tux. "Yeah?"

"Want to stay home and fuck instead?"

Hunt laughed. "Very regal of you. Any other night, my answer would be yes." He offered his arm. "Your Highness."

Bryce smirked and took it, pressing close to him. Hunt breathed in her scent, the jasmine of her perfume. She set her tiara on her head at a jaunty angle, the little peak of solid diamond glittering as if lit by starlight. Hunt straightened it for her, and led her out the door.

Toward the world waiting for them.

Ruhn bowed before the seated Archangels. Hypaxia, at his side, bowed as well.

He was a lying piece of shit, he'd thought ruefully as he'd donned a black-on-black tux an hour ago. He'd agreed to be Hypaxia's date to this thing—as her fiancé, and as Crown Prince he didn't really have a choice but to be here—but he hadn't been able to stop thinking about Day. About whether she'd show up in a mere few hours.

He'd already scoped out the fountain through the western doors. It lay in shadow beyond the massive glass conservatory, about fifteen feet from the stairs leading out of the building and into the starry night.

He hadn't spoken to Day since they'd made their arrangement. He'd tried to talk to her, but she hadn't answered. Would she be here tonight, as promised? Was she already in the packed conservatory?

He'd removed his carved black mask to make his formal greeting to the Archangels, and as he turned from Celestina and Ephraim, Ruhn scanned the crowd once more.

Beautiful gowns, beautiful ladies—they were masked, but he knew most of them. Of course, Day could be someone he knew. He had no idea what to look for. *Where* to even look for her in the vast, candlelit space, bedecked in garlands and wreaths of autumnal leaves brought from the colder climes up north. Winged skulls and scythes were interspersed with a rainbow of fall gourds on every table. Day could be anywhere.

Security had been insane getting in here. It was the 33rd's show, and they ran it like the paranoid psychos they were. Soldiers stood stationed outside the doors and hovered in the skies. Baxian and Naomi had checked IDs and invites at the doors. They'd remain there all night, even while other members of the triarii reveled. None of Ephraim's people had been tapped to stand guard. Either from a lack of trust or as a privilege, Ruhn didn't know.

There had been no sign of Pippa Spetsos or her Lightfall squadron, or any other Ophion unit recently, but dreadwolves still prowled the streets. And this ballroom.

Ruhn slipped on his mask and said to Hypaxia, "Can I get you anything?"

She was resplendent in a royal-blue ball gown, her cloudberry crown gleaming amid her dark, upswept hair. Heads turned to remark on her beauty, visible even with the white-winged mask she'd donned. "I'm fine, thank you." She smiled pleasantly.

Ithan, in a traditional tux behind her, stepped up, his silver wolf mask glittering in the little firstlights strung throughout the lush conservatory. "The River Queen's daughter wishes to meet you," he murmured, gesturing to where Tharion stood stone-faced beside a stunning, curly-haired young female. The former looked a bit stiff for once, but the female, clad in gauzy turquoise, brimmed with energy. Excitement.

That had been a minor bomb the other night. Tharion had settled quite comfortably into life with Ruhn and his friends . . . until he'd gotten the otter's note from the River Queen instructing him to come to this ball with her daughter.

Apparently, the leash only stretches so far, Tharion had said when Ruhn had asked, and that had been that.

Hypaxia smiled at Ithan. "Of course. I'd love to meet her." Ithan offered his arm, and Hypaxia said to Ruhn, "I suppose we'll dance later?"

"Yeah," Ruhn said, then bowed quickly. "I mean, yes. I'd be honored." Hypaxia gave him a strange, assessing glance, but left with Ithan.

He needed a drink. A big fucking drink.

He was halfway to one of the six open bars throughout the space, each one of them packed, when his sister and Cormac walked in.

Bryce looked like a princess, and it had nothing to do with the crown, an heirloom of the Danaan house that their father had ordered her to wear tonight. People stared at her—many unkindly.

Or maybe their attention was on Athalar. The angel entered a few steps behind the royal couple. Apparently, he'd been given the night off by Celestina. But how the male could stand walking behind them, seeing Bryce's hand on another male's arm . . .

Athalar's face revealed nothing, though. He was the Umbra Mortis once more.

A flash of red across the space drew Ruhn's gaze. His father made his way toward Bryce and Cormac. The Avallen Prince seemed inclined to meet him halfway, but Bryce tugged on his arm and steered them right to the Archangels instead.

A few Fae gasped at the snub—Flynn's parents among them. Flynn, the traitor, had claimed he had a headache to avoid coming tonight. From his parents' pinched faces upon seeing Ruhn arrive without Flynn in tow, he knew his friend hadn't told them. Too bad for all the eligible young ladies they'd no doubt lined up to woo their son tonight.

Ignoring the dismayed Fae, Bryce strode right up to the dais where the Archangels sat, bypassing the line of well-wishers. No one dared call her out for it. Athalar followed her and Cormac, and Ruhn noted his father's stormy face and moved closer, too.

Bryce and Cormac bowed before the Archangels, Celestina's brows high as she turned between Hunt and Cormac. Bryce said, "My congratulations to you both."

"Thank you," Ephraim answered, bored and eyeing the bar.

Cormac added, "Avallen extends its wishes and hopes for your happiness."

It had been a relief to discover that Mordoc wouldn't be attending the party tonight—wouldn't be able to put faces to the scents he'd probably detected in the alley all those days ago. But the Hind was here. Ruhn had already warned his cousin to stay away from the female, no matter how his blood might howl for vengeance.

"And we extend our wishes to you, too," Celestina said.

"Thank you," Bryce said, smiling widely. "Prince Hunt and I plan to be quite happy."

A gasp rippled through the room.

Bryce half turned toward Hunt and extended a hand. The angel walked to her, eyes dancing with wicked amusement. Cormac seemed caught between surprise and fury.

The room seemed to be spinning. Bryce wouldn't dare. She wouldn't fucking dare pull a stunt like this. Ruhn swallowed a laugh of pure shock.

"Prince?" Celestina asked.

Bryce looped her arm through Hunt's, pressing close. "Hunt and I are mates." A charming, brilliant smile. "That makes him my prince. Prince Cormac was good enough to escort me tonight, as we've become close friends this month." She turned to the crowd. Immediately pinpointed the Autumn King, glaring white-faced at her. "I thought you told her, Father."

Holy shit.

She'd played along with the rules so far to reach this point. A public declaration that she was with Hunt. That Hunt was a prince—a Prince of the Fae.

And their father, who hated public scenes . . . he could either risk calling his own daughter a liar—thus embarrassing himself—or play along.

The Autumn King said into the stunned crowd, "My apologies, Your Graces. My daughter's union must have slipped my mind." His eyes threatened Helfire as he glowered at Bryce. "I hope her excitement in announcing her union with Hunt Athalar is not interpreted as an attempt to upstage your joy tonight."

"Oh, no," Celestina said, covering her mouth with a hand to hide a smile. "I congratulate and bless you and Hunt Athalar, Bryce Quinlan." It didn't get more official than that.

Ephraim grunted and motioned to the nearest server for a drink. Taking that as her cue, Bryce bowed to them again, and pivoted Hunt toward the crowd. Cormac had the wits to follow, but left them near a pillar after a word to Bryce. He stalked for the Autumn King.

So Ruhn went up to them, and Bryce snorted. "Nice crown."

He jerked his chin at her. "That's all you have to say?"

She shrugged. "What?"

But she frowned over his shoulder. Right. There were a lot of people with Vanir hearing listening. He'd yell at her later.

Though . . . he didn't really need to yell at all. She'd found her way out of this clusterfuck. Her own brilliant, daring way. "I'm really glad you're my sister," Ruhn said.

Bryce smiled so broadly it showed all her teeth.

Ruhn shook off his shock and said to Athalar, "Sweet tux." He added, just to be a dick, "Your Highness."

Athalar pulled at his collar. "No wonder you got all those piercings, if this is how you're expected to dress at these things."

"First rule of being a prince," Ruhn said, grinning. "Rebel where you can." Considering what they were all doing these days, it was the understatement of the year.

Hunt growled, but Ephraim and Celestina stood from their thrones at the rear of the conservatory, a massive screen dropping from a panel in the glass ceiling. A projector began to hum.

"Friends." Celestina's clear voice rang out over the crowd. Anyone still speaking shut the fuck up. "We thank you for coming to celebrate our union this lovely evening."

Ephraim's deep voice boomed, "It is with much joy that Celestina and I announce our mating." He smiled faintly at his gorgeous mate. "And with much joy that we remotely welcome our guests of honor."

The lights dimmed, leaving only soft candlelight that made the decorative skulls all the more menacing. Then the screen flickered on, revealing seven thrones. A sight more harrowing than any skull or scythe.

Six of the thrones were full. The seventh had been left vacant, as always—thanks to the Prince of the Pit.

A chill skittered up Ruhn's arms as the Asteri coldly surveyed the party.

59

Bryce couldn't get a breath down.

The Asteri stared at them all like they could see through the screen. See them gathered here.

They must be able to, Bryce realized. Her hand slipped into Hunt's, and he squeezed tight, a gray wing tucking around her. Gods, he was gorgeous tonight.

She'd figured this party was the only setting where her father wouldn't dare challenge her. Where any union with Hunt could be verified and recognized by Archangels. She'd worn and done everything he'd ordered . . . all so she could get here tonight. Had raced up to the dais upon arriving so that she could announce Hunt as her mate before her father could introduce her as Cormac's bride.

Relief and excitement—and a bit of smugness—had coursed through her. Her father would bring down the hammer later. But tonight . . . she'd celebrate her victory. She knew Hunt had as little interest in being a prince as she did in being a princess. But he'd done it. For her. For them.

She'd been about to drag Hunt into a closet or a cloakroom to fuck his brains out when the screen descended. And now, staring at the six immortal figures, at Rigelus's boyish face . . .

Thankfully, other people in the room were shaking, too. Her heart pounded like a drum.

Celestina and Ephraim bowed, and everyone followed suit. Bryce's legs wobbled on her heels as she did so. Hunt squeezed her hand again, but she kept her focus on the ground, hating the primal fear, the terror of knowing that these beings judged them, and with one word they might slay everyone, might slay her family—

"Our congratulations to you, Celestina and Ephraim," Rigelus crooned in that voice that didn't belong to the teenage body his twisted soul inhabited. "We extend our wishes for a happy mating, and a fertile one."

Celestina and Ephraim lowered their heads in thanks. "We are grateful for your wisdom and kindness in pairing us," Celestina said. Bryce tried and failed to detect the undercurrent of her tone. Was it sincere? Was the slight tightness from a lie, or from being before the Asteri?

Octartis, the Southern Star—the Asteri to Rigelus's right—spoke, her voice like ancient, cracking ice. "I understand other congratulations are in order, too."

A chill shot along Bryce's spine as Rigelus said, "Princess Bryce Danaan and Prince Hunt Athalar." It was an order. A command.

The crowd fell back. Giving the Asteri a clear shot at them.

Oh gods. Bryce's blood rushed from her face. How did they already know? Had the cameras on their end been running the whole time, letting the Asteri watch and listen unseen?

But then the Autumn King was there, bowing at her side. "I present my daughter to you, Holy Ones," he intoned.

She wondered if he hated bowing to them. It satisfied the fuck out of her to see him do it, but there was no time to dwell on that now. Bryce bowed, too, as she murmured, "Hail the Asteri."

Cormac appeared on her father's other side, bowing low. As Crown Prince of Avallen, he had no other choice.

He'd been furious at her stunt. Not that she'd ended their engagement, but that she hadn't warned him ahead of time. *Any other surprises tonight, Princess?* he'd snapped at her before striding off to speak to her father. *You broke our deal. I won't forget that.*

She hadn't responded, but . . . Did the Asteri know one of their fiercest rebels stood before them, playing prince? Did they know how she'd helped him, worked with him? She supposed if they did, they'd all be dead.

"And I present her mate and consort, Prince Hunt Athalar," the Autumn King was saying sharply, his disapproval palpable. He might very well kill her for this. If Cormac didn't do it first.

But, according to Fae law, she was now Hunt's property. Recognized in the past few minutes by both Archangels and the Asteri. If it made Hunt uncomfortable, if he resented his new title or the beings before him, he showed no sign as he bowed, his wing brushing over her back. "Hail the Asteri."

"Rise," the Asteri said, and so Bryce, Hunt, and her father did. There were so many eyes upon them. In this room, in that chamber in the Eternal City. Rigelus's, especially, bore into her. He smiled slightly. Like he knew everything she'd done these weeks. Every rebel activity, every mutinous thought.

Bryce hated herself for lowering her gaze. Even as she knew Hunt stared Rigelus down.

But the Bright Hand of the Asteri said, "So many happy unions tonight. It is our wish that you all partake in the revelry. Go, and celebrate Death's Day in peace."

Everyone bowed again, and the screen went dark. More than a few people whimpered, as if they'd been holding in the sound.

No one spoke for several seconds as the lights brightened. Then the band began once more slightly off-tempo, like the musicians needed a minute to get their shit together. Even the Archangels were a little pale as they took their seats.

Bryce faced her father. The Autumn King said in a voice so low no one else could hear, "You little bitch."

Bryce smiled broadly. "It's 'You little bitch, *Your Highness.*'" She stalked into the crowd. She didn't miss Hunt smirking at the king, throwing him a wink that clearly said: *Make a move and I'll fry you, asswipe.*

But she had to suck down a few long breaths as she halted at the edge of the dance floor, trying to regain her composure.

"You all right?" Hunt asked, gripping her shoulder.

"Yes, Your Highness," she muttered.

He chuckled, and leaned to whisper in her ear, "I thought you only called me that in bed, Quinlan." She did. *You are my fucking prince*, she'd panted last night as he drove his cock up into her.

Bryce leaned against him, shaking off the last of the Asteri's ice. "I can't believe we did it."

Hunt let out a low laugh. "There's going to be Hel to pay." From her father. But tonight, he could do nothing. Here, in front of all these people, he could do nothing at all.

So Bryce said, "Dance with me?"

He raised a brow. "Really?"

"You do know how to dance, right?"

"Of course I do. But . . . It's been a long while since I've danced with anyone."

Since Shahar, probably. She interlaced their fingers. "Dance with me."

The initial steps were stilted, hesitant. His arm slid around her waist, his other hand clutching hers as he led her into the sweet ballad coming from the band. With so many watching, it took a verse or two to get their rhythm.

Hunt murmured, "Just look at me, and fuck all the rest of them."

His eyes shone with desire and joy, and that spark that was pure Hunt. The star on her chest gleamed, on full display. Someone gasped, but Bryce kept her attention on Hunt. He smiled again.

It was all that mattered, that smile. They fell into easy movement, and when Hunt spun her, she smiled back.

She whipped into his arms, and Hunt didn't falter a step, sweeping her around the floor. She had the vague sense of Ruhn and Hypaxia dancing, Celestina and Ephraim, too, of Baxian and Naomi—Isaiah now with them—on guard by the doors, but she couldn't look away from Hunt.

He pressed a kiss to her mouth. The entire universe melted away with it. It was only them, would only be them, dancing together, souls twining. "Everything that ever happened to me, it was all so I could meet you, Quinlan. Be here with you. I'm yours. Forever."

Her throat tightened, and the star on her chest flared, lighting up the entire conservatory like a small moon. Bryce kissed him back, not caring who saw, only that he was here.

"Everything I am is yours," she said against his lips.

Hypaxia seemed distracted as Ruhn danced with her, trying his best to avoid watching Hunt and Bryce make moon-eyes at each other. To avoid hearing the comments that trailed in their wake.

The Umbra Mortis—now a Fae Prince. What a disgrace. The slurs and nastiness flowed past Ruhn from Fae mouths, bold enough to run free behind the safety of their masks. Not that the masks would hide their scents. Ruhn marked each one of them.

Athalar was his brother now, by law. And Ruhn didn't put up with people talking shit about his family. The family he liked, anyway.

Cormac had already left, slipping into a shadow and teleporting out. A small mercy—Cormac had been so distracted by Bryce's little surprise that he hadn't bothered to confront the Hind. But Ruhn didn't blame his cousin for bailing. After the stunt Bryce had pulled, Cormac would have been swarmed by Fae families eager to present their daughters. Flynn's parents—a sharp-eyed Sathia in tow—were clearly scouring the ballroom for any hint of the Avallen Prince.

Ruhn suppressed his smile at the thought of their fruitless hunt and focused on his partner. Hypaxia seemed to be scanning the crowd.

His heart skipped a beat. He asked quietly, "You looking for someone?"

She cleared her throat. "My sister. The Hind."

His chest loosened. "Over by the foot of the dais. Next to Pollux."

Hypaxia glanced over on their next turn. The Hind and the Hammer stood together, both in matte black masks, the angel in a white imperial uniform edged in gold. The Hind's golden, sparkling dress clung to her hips before falling to the floor. Her blond hair had been swept up, and for once, no silver torque adorned her neck. Only slender gold earrings brushed her shoulders.

"They make a beautiful pair," Hypaxia murmured. "As monstrous inside as they are lovely outside, though."

Ruhn grunted. "Yeah."

Hypaxia chewed on her lip. "I was waiting until tonight to approach her."

He studied her face. "You want me to go with you?" He could offer nothing less.

"Do you think she'll . . . react badly?"

"She's too smart to cause a scene. And I don't think the Hind is the sort to do that anyway. She's cut from the same cloth as my father. The worst thing that happens is that she ignores you."

Hypaxia stiffened in his arms. "I suppose you're right. I'd rather get this meeting over with. It will spoil the rest of my night to stew over it."

"Why meet with her at all?"

"Because she is my sister. And I've never spoken to her. Or seen her in the flesh."

"I felt that way when I learned about Bryce's existence."

She nodded distractedly, her eyes darting around the room again. "You're sure you don't mind coming with me?"

Ruhn checked the massive clock at the rear of the conservatory. Eleven fifty. He had time. A few minutes. He needed something to distract himself with anyway. "I wouldn't have offered if I didn't mean it."

They slipped from the dance floor, the crowd parting for the beautiful queen as she aimed for her sister. The Hind marked her approach without smiling. Pollux, however, grinned at Hypaxia, then at Ruhn.

Hypaxia, to her credit, squared her shoulders as she halted. "Lidia."

The Hind's mouth curled upward. "Hypaxia." Her voice was low, smooth. It was a blatant show of disrespect, not to use the queen's title. Not to even bow.

Hypaxia said, "I wished to formally greet you." She added, "Sister."

"Now, *that* is a name no one has ever called me," Lidia said.

Pollux sneered. Ruhn bared his teeth in warning and received a mocking smile in return.

Hypaxia tried once more. "It is a name that I hope we can both hear more often."

Not one ounce of kindness or warmth graced the Hind's beautiful face, even with the mask. "Perhaps," Lidia said, and went back to staring at the crowd. Bored and disinterested. A dismissal and an insult.

Ruhn glanced at the clock. He should go. Make his way slowly to the garden doors, then slip outside. But he couldn't leave Hypaxia to face her sister alone.

"Are you enjoying Lunathion?" Hypaxia tried.

"No," the Hind drawled. "I find this city tediously plebian."

The Hammer snickered, and Hypaxia said to him with wondrous authority, "Go lurk somewhere else."

Pollux's eyes flashed. "You can't give me orders."

But the Hind turned her cool, amused gaze on the Hammer. "A minute, Pollux."

The Hammer glared at Hypaxia, but the witch-queen remained unbowed before a male who'd slaughtered his way through the world for centuries.

Ruhn saw his opening and said to Hypaxia, "I'll give you two a moment as well."

Before the queen could object, he backed into the crowd. He was a piece of shit for abandoning her, but . . .

He walked, unnoticed and unbothered, to the western doors. Slipped out of them and down the five steps to the gravel ground. He strode to the fountain bubbling away in the shadows beyond the reach of the conservatory's lights and leaned against it, his heart pounding.

Two minutes now. Would Day be here?

He monitored the doors, forcing himself to breathe in and out slowly.

Maybe this was a bad idea. He'd been talking to the Hind and the Hammer, for fuck's sake. This place *was* swarming with enemies, all of whom would slaughter him and Day if they were found out. Why had he risked her like this?

"Looking for someone?" a female voice crooned.

Ruhn whirled, his stomach bottoming out as he beheld the masked figure before him.

The Harpy stood in the shadows beyond the fountain. As if she'd been waiting.

60

Ruhn scanned the face in the darkness. It couldn't be her.

The fucking *Harpy*? He took in her dark hair, the lean body, the taunting mouth—

"What are you doing out here?" the Harpy asked, stalking closer, her dark wings blacker than the night.

Ruhn forced himself to take a breath. "Day?" he asked quietly.

The Harpy blinked. "What's that supposed to mean?"

The breath nearly whooshed from him. Thank the fucking gods it wasn't her, but if the Harpy was here, and Agent Daybright was about to appear . . . The Harpy and the Hind had shown up at the bar that day, but he'd seen nothing of the former since. And yeah, meeting by the fountain with another person wouldn't scream *rebel liaison*, but if the Harpy had any suspicions about him, or whoever Daybright was, if she saw them meeting together . . .

He had to get out of here. Walk back into the conservatory and not endanger Day.

What an idiot he was.

"Enjoy the party," Ruhn said to the Harpy.

"No stolen kisses for me in the garden?" she mocked as he stormed up the steps.

He'd explain to Day later. The clock read two minutes past

twelve—she hadn't come. Or maybe she'd seen who was in the garden and decided to hang back.

Seen who also observed from the shadows at the top of the stairs.

The Hind's golden eyes gleamed in the dimness through her mask. She'd followed him. *Fuck.* Had she suspected that he was slipping away to meet with someone? She hadn't said a word, as far as he knew, about the shit that had gone down at Ydra—was it so she could ultimately follow them to a bigger prize?

To the greatest prize a spy-catcher could find. Agent Daybright.

Ruhn stared down the Hind as he passed her. She watched him with serene indifference.

He tugged at his collar as he entered the noise and heat of the party. He'd come that close to being caught by the Hind and the Harpy—to getting Day caught by them.

Ruhn didn't say goodbye to anyone before bailing.

Hunt licked his way up Bryce's neck, a hand sliding over her mouth to muffle her moan as he tugged her down the dim hallway. "You want someone to find us?" His voice was guttural.

"We're official now. I don't care." But she fumbled with the handle of the cloakroom door. Standing behind her, mouth at her throat, Hunt suppressed a groan of his own as her ass pushed into his aching cock. Another few seconds, and they'd be in the cloakroom. And within a few seconds of that, he planned to be balls-deep in her.

He knew Baxian and Naomi had been well aware they weren't going down this hall to use the bathroom, but the angels guarding the door had only smirked at them.

"It's locked," she mumbled, and Hunt huffed a laugh against her warm skin.

"Good thing you've got a big, tough alphahole with you, Quinlan," he said, pulling away from her. Gods, if anyone walked down this hallway, they'd get a glimpse at his pants and know what was about to go down. He'd lasted all of three dances before needing to slip away with her. They'd return to the party soon. Once they got in a good, solid fuck.

He'd be damned if he'd ever call himself Prince Hunt, but . . . it had been worth it. The wild plan she'd spun for him more than two weeks ago, when she'd honored him by asking if he'd do this.

Hunt dragged his teeth down the column of her neck, then tugged her a step back. Bryce, panting softly, face flushed with desire that set his cock pounding, grinned fiendishly at him.

"Watch and learn, sweetheart," Hunt said, and rammed his shoulder into the door.

The lock splintered, and Hunt didn't hesitate before tugging her in with him. Her arms slid around his neck, all of her lining up with him, and he hefted her leg to wrap around his waist, bracing to hoist her up—

A squeak of surprise halted him.

Hunt whirled, mind trying to match up with what his senses were blaring.

But there it was. There they were.

Celestina's dress had been tugged down, baring one full, round breast. Gleaming as if someone had been licking it.

But it wasn't Ephraim who stood before the Archangel, positioned between the female and Hunt. It wasn't Ephraim whose own clothes were askew, hair mussed, lips swollen.

It was Hypaxia.

Hunt had no idea what to say.

Bryce cleared her throat and stepped in front of Hunt, blocking his raging erection from view. "I guess the locked door means *already occupied*, huh?"

Hypaxia and Celestina just stared at them, their hair half falling out of their elegant arrangements.

Hunt slowly, quietly shut the door behind them. Lifted his hands. Because that was a faint glow of power beginning to shimmer around Celestina. An Archangel's wrath, priming to strike down any enemy.

Hunt couldn't stop his own lightning from answering, its zap searing through him. If Celestina was going to throw down, he'd match her.

Bryce said breathlessly to Hypaxia, as she sensed the brewing storm in the cloakroom, "I've, uh, never been in this kind of situation before."

Hypaxia glanced to the Governor, whose eyes had turned white, flaring with power, and said to Bryce, an attempt at casualness, "Me neither."

The only way in and out was the door at Hunt's back. Unless Celestina blasted apart the entire top of the building. Hunt put a hand on Bryce's shoulder.

But his mate said brightly, "In case we need to clarify, we aren't going to say anything."

Hypaxia nodded sagely. "We thank you." She peered up at the Archangel—at her lover. "Celestina."

The Governor didn't take her gaze from Hunt. If he so much as breathed wrong, she'd kill him. In two fucking seconds. Hunt grinned, though. She could *try* to kill him. "My lips are sealed."

Her wings glowed, so bright the entire cloakroom was illuminated. "You endanger the person I love," Celestina said, her voice echoing with power. "For infringing on what he considers his, Ephraim will end her. Or the Asteri will kill her to make a statement."

Bryce kept her hands up. "The Asteri are probably going to kill me, too, at some point." Hunt whipped his head to her. She wouldn't— "I like you," she said instead, and Hunt tried not to sag with relief that she hadn't explained their rebel activities. "I think you're good for this city. Ephraim and his loser cabal, not so much, but once he's gone home, I think you're going to make Lunathion even more . . . awesome." Hunt threw her an incredulous look. She shrugged. Bryce's eyes met Celestina's. Her star flared.

Power to power. Female to female. Governor to . . . *Princess* wasn't the right word for the expression that came across Bryce's face, the shift of her posture.

Another word formed on his tongue, but Hunt didn't let it

take root, didn't let himself think of all the deadly implications that the other word would entail.

Bryce said, with that more-than-princess bearing, "I have no plans to fuck you over. Either of you." She faced Hypaxia, who was giving Bryce that more-than-princess look, too. "We're allies. Not only politically, but . . . as females who have had to make some shitty, hard choices. As females who live in a world where most powerful males see us only as breeding tools." Hypaxia nodded again, but Celestina continued to stare at Bryce. A predator surveying the best place to strike.

Hunt rallied his power again. Bryce continued, "I'm no one's prize mare. I took a gamble with this idiot"—she jerked a thumb toward Hunt, who gaped at her—"and luckily, it paid off. And I just want to say that"—she swallowed—"if you two want to make a gamble with each other, say fuck it to the arrangements with Ephraim and Ruhn, then I'm with you. We'd have to go against the Asteri, but . . . look what I did tonight. Whatever I can do, whatever clout I have, it's yours. But let's start by walking out of this closet in one piece."

Silence fell.

And slowly, like a setting sun, the Archangel's power dimmed until only her silhouette glowed with it. Hypaxia laid a hand on her lover's shoulder, proof that they were safe.

Celestina said, setting her fine clothing to rights, "We weren't without choices in this. When the Autumn King came asking for Hypaxia's hand for his son, I was the one who encouraged her to accept. But who I love, who I am mated to . . . those are decisions that I am not entitled to make, as an Archangel."

Hunt grunted. "I know how that feels." At Celestina's arched brow, he pointed to his branded-out wrist. "Slave, remember?"

"Perhaps there's a thin line between Governor and slave," Hypaxia mused.

Celestina admitted, "I thought that Hypaxia might wed the prince, perhaps in a political sense, and when enough time had passed, we could . . . resume our relationship. But then the Asteri gave the order about Ephraim, and I found myself with little choice but to say yes."

Bryce asked quietly, "Did Ephraim . . ."

"I agreed to it," the Governor said firmly. "Though I can't say I found it enjoyable." Hypaxia kissed her cheek.

That was why Celestina had seemed so unsettled before her first night with Ephraim, so haunted afterward—because her heart lay elsewhere.

Bryce said to the females, "For however long you want and need to keep this secret, we won't breathe a hint to anyone. You have my word."

And it occurred to Hunt, as both females nodded, that Bryce had somehow earned their trust—had become someone who people trusted unfailingly.

A more-than-princess, indeed.

Hunt smiled at his mate and said, "Well, we should probably leave. Before someone comes in and finds us all in here and thinks I'm having the night of my life." Hypaxia and Bryce laughed, but Celestina's answering smile was subdued.

Bryce seemed to note that, and looped her arm through the witch-queen's, steering her toward the door and murmuring, "Let's discuss how much this evening will piss off the Autumn King and how wonderful that will be," as they left, leaving Hunt and Celestina alone.

His Archangel observed him. Hunt didn't dare move.

"So you're truly a prince now," Celestina said.

Hunt blinked. "Uh, yeah. I guess."

The Governor walked past him, toward where her lover had gone into the hall. "There's a fine line between prince and slave, too, you know."

Hunt's chest tightened. "I know."

"Then why accept the burden?" she asked, pausing.

Bryce seemed thick as thieves with the witch-queen as they walked arm-in-arm. "She's worth it."

But Celestina said, face solemn, "Love is a trap, Hunt." She shook her head, more at herself than at him. "One I can't figure out how to free myself from."

"You *want* to be free of it?"

The Archangel stepped into the hall, wings still glowing with a remnant of power. "Every single day."

Tharion tried not to glance at his watch—technically his grandfather's waterproof watch, given to him upon high school graduation—as the night wore on. Bryce's betrothal coup had provided five minutes of glorious amusement before he'd been sucked into boredom and impatience.

He knew it was an honor to be here, to escort the River Queen's daughter, who was sparkling with delight and joy. But it was hard to feel that privilege when he'd been ordered to attend the ball at her side.

Tharion had waited at the docks by the River Gate at sundown, dressed to the nines. The River Queen's daughter had emerged from the mists in a pale oak boat pulled by a bevy of snow-white swans. Tharion hadn't failed to notice the sobeks lurking fifty feet beyond them. Sentinels for this journey of their queen's most precious daughter.

"Is it not magical?" his companion was saying for the fifth time that night, sighing at the lights and dancing couples.

Tharion drained the rest of his champagne. *She is allowed to have one glass of wine,* her mother had said in her letter via otter. *And she is to be home by one.*

Tharion finally glanced at his watch. Twelve twenty. Another fifteen minutes and he could start ushering her toward the door. He handed his flute to a passing server, but found his companion's expression had turned dangerously pouty.

He offered her a charming, bland smile, but she said, "You do not seem to be enjoying yourself."

"I am," he assured her, taking her hand and pressing a kiss to her knuckles.

"Your friends do not come to speak with us."

Well, considering that he'd seen Bryce and Hunt slip off somewhere, that was no surprise. Ithan was chatting with Naomi Boreas and the Helhound at the doors, and the others . . . Ruhn and Cormac had bailed. No sign of Hypaxia.

Though the witch-queen had already come to speak with them. He'd had a hard time meeting her gaze throughout the awkward conversation, while she could see how stupid he'd been in tying himself to this female. But Hypaxia had been kind to the River Queen's daughter, who herself had been all smiles. Tharion hadn't dared call her Pax.

"My friends have a lot of glad-handing to do," he hedged.

"Oh." She fell silent, lurking on the edge of the dance floor as couples swept past. Maybe it was all the champagne, but he really looked at her: the dark eyes full of longing and quiet happiness, the eager energy buzzing from her, the sense that she was some creature crafted into mortal form only for this night, and would dissolve into river silt as soon as the clock struck one.

Was he any better than her mother? He'd been stringing this girl along for ten years now. Had held her back tonight because *he* didn't feel like enjoying himself.

She must have felt the weight of his stare, because she twisted to him. Tharion offered her another bland smile, then turned to one of the bodyguards lurking in the shadows behind them. "Hey, Tritus, can you take over for this dance?"

The guard glanced between them, but Tharion smiled down at the River Queen's daughter, whose brows were raised. "Go dance," he told her. "I'll be right back." He didn't let her object before handing her off to the guard, who was actually blushing as he extended his arm.

And Tharion didn't look back as he strode off into the crowd, wondering how much shit he'd be in for this. But . . . even if he was flayed for it, he wasn't going to string her along any further.

He paused on the outskirts of the crowd, finally turning to see the guard and the River Queen's daughter dancing, both of them smiling. Happy.

Good. She deserved that. Mother or not, temper or not, she deserved someone to make her happy.

Tharion made his way over to the nearest open bar, and was about to order a whiskey when he noticed a curvy female—a leopard shifter from the scent of her—lounging against the counter beside him.

He'd always noticed a good ass, and this female . . . Hel yes.

"Come here often?" he asked her with a wink. The leopard turned her head toward him, light brown skin radiant in the soft lights. Her eyes were thick-lashed, utterly gorgeous above high cheekbones and full lips, all of it framed by golden-brown hair that fell around her heart-shaped face in soft waves. She had the ease and grace of a movie star. Probably was one, if she was important enough to be here. That full mouth curled in a smile. "Is that your attempt at a pickup line?"

He knew that sultry tone. So Tharion ordered his whiskey and said to the stranger, "You want it to be?"

61

Are you all right?" Ithan asked Hypaxia as the clock neared three thirty in the morning. She'd complained of some stomach cramps and had left the party for about twenty minutes, returning pale-faced.

The witch-queen now tucked a dark curl behind her ear, then adjusted the fall of her jet-black robes, having pulled them over her gown moments before. Even standing in the small clearing of an olive grove nestled in the hills beyond the city, the sounds of revelry reached them: booming bass, cheering, strobing lights. A far cry from the whispering leaves and dry ground around him, the stars glinting beyond the silvery canopy.

Another world away from that glittering party where so many powers had come together tonight. Where Bryce had somehow outmaneuvered the Autumn King and had declared Hunt her prince. He hadn't known what to think in that moment.

He'd done his best to stay the fuck away from Sabine and Amelie tonight. Thankfully, they had been present only long enough to see the Asteri speak, then left. He hated himself for being so relieved about it. The Prime hadn't attended—he usually avoided such functions.

"So this is it?" Ithan asked Hypaxia, gesturing with a hand to the seven candles she'd arranged on the ground. "Light the candles and wait?"

Hypaxia drew out a long dagger. "Not quite," she said, and Ithan kept a step back as she used the knife to draw lines between the candles.

Ithan angled his head. "A six-pointed star," he said. Like the one Bryce had made between the Gates this spring, with the seventh candle at its center.

"It's a symbol of balance," she explained, moving away a foot, but keeping the dagger at her side. Her crown of cloudberries seemed to glow with an inner light. "Two intersecting triangles. Male and female, dark and light, above and below . . . and the power that lies in the place where they meet." Her face became grave. "It is in that place of balance where I'll focus my power." She motioned to the circle. "No matter what you see or hear, stay on this side of the candles."

A chill went up Ithan's spine, even as his heart lightened. If he could just talk to Connor . . . He'd thought over and over about what he'd say, but he couldn't remember any of it.

Hypaxia read whatever lay in his gaze, her face again solemn.

But a bargain was a bargain. Hypaxia lifted both arms, holding the dagger aloft, and began chanting.

Day appeared far down the bridge and stayed there, like she didn't want to come near him.

Ruhn sat on his couch, forearms on his knees. He'd been reeling from what had gone down in the garden for hours now. Was surprised he'd even fallen asleep in his physical body.

He rushed to her. "I'm sorry I endangered you."

Day said nothing. Just stood there, burning.

He tried again. "I . . . It was a really dumb idea. I'm sorry if you showed and I wasn't there. I got to the garden and the Harpy and the Hind had trailed me, and I think they might have suspected me, or I don't know, but I'm . . . I'm so sorry, Day."

"I was there," she said quietly.

"What?"

"I saw you," she said, and stalked forward. "Saw the threat, too. And stayed away."

"Where? In the garden?"

She came closer. "I saw you," she said again. Like she was still processing it.

"You came." He shook his head. "I thought you might not have, and we didn't talk since we made that plan, and I was worried—"

"Ruhn." His name on her lips rocked through him.

He shuddered. "You know who I am."

"Yes."

"Say my name again."

She came closer. "Ruhn." Her flames parted enough for him to get a glimpse of a smile.

"Are you still in the city? Can I meet you somewhere?" It was the middle of the night—but it was the equinox. People would be partying until dawn. But they'd be masked—he and Day could fit right in.

"No." Her voice flattened. "I'm gone."

"Liar. Tell me where you are."

"Did you learn nothing tonight? Did you not see how close we came to disaster? The Asteri's servants are everywhere. One mistake, even for a moment, and we are *dead*."

His throat worked. "When the Harpy came out of the shadows, I thought she was you. I . . . I panicked for a moment."

A quiet laugh. "That would have been awful for you? To have me be someone you hate so much?"

"It would take some adjustment."

"So you do have a notion of what you expect me to be like."

"I don't. I just . . . don't want you to be *her*."

Another laugh. "And you're a Fae Prince."

"Does it gross you out?"

"Should it?"

"It grosses me out."

"Why?"

"Because I've done nothing to deserve that title."

She studied him. "The Autumn King is your father. The one who hurt you."

"The one and only."

"He's a disgrace of a king."

"You should talk to my sister. I think she'd like you."

"Bryce Quinlan."

He tensed at her knowing Bryce's name so readily, but if she'd been at the party tonight, she'd know without a doubt. "Yeah. She hates my father even more than I do."

But Day's flame dimmed. "You're engaged to Queen Hypaxia."

He almost laughed it off, but her voice was so grave. "It's complicated."

"You danced with her like it wasn't."

"You saw me?"

"Everyone saw you."

That sharpness in her voice . . . was it jealousy? He said carefully, "I'm not the two-timing sort. Hypaxia and I are betrothed in name only. I don't even know if we'll marry. She has as little attachment to me as I do to her. We like and admire each other, but . . . that's about it."

"Why should I care?"

He studied her, then took a step closer, until only a handsbreadth separated them. "I wanted to see you tonight. I spent the entire time watching the clock."

Her breathing hitched. "Why?"

"So I could do this." Ruhn lifted her chin and kissed her. The mouth beneath the fire was soft, and warm, and opened for him.

Flaming fingers twined through his hair, tugging him close, and Ruhn slid his arms around a slim, curving body, hands feeling her ample backside. Fuck yes.

His tongue brushed over hers, and she shuddered in his arms. But she met him stroke for stroke, as if she couldn't hold back, as if she wanted to know every inch of him, his every taste and nuance.

Her hand slid along his jaw, fingers exploring the shape of his face. He willed his night to pull back to show his eyes, his nose, his mouth. Thankfully, it obeyed him. Beyond the veil of flame covering her features, he could feel her watching him. Seeing his bared face.

Her fingers traced the bridge of his nose. The bow of his lips. Then she kissed him again, with sheer abandon, and Ruhn gave himself entirely to it.

"You remind me that I'm alive," she said, voice thick. "You remind me that goodness can exist in the world."

His throat ached. "Day—"

But she hissed, stiffening against his grip. She glanced back toward her end of the bridge.

No. That male who'd once dragged her from sleep to have sex with her—

Day whipped her head back to Ruhn and the flame rippled, revealing pleading eyes of solid fire. "I'm sorry," she whispered, and vanished.

Hunt was still drunk when he and Bryce returned to the apartment at three in the morning. She carried her heels in one hand, the train of her dress in the other. They'd left the party soon after Ruhn had bailed, and headed to a dive bar in the heart of the Old Square, where they'd proceeded to play pool and drink whiskey in their ridiculous finery.

They didn't talk about what they'd discovered in the cloakroom. What more was there to say?

"I'm plastered," Bryce announced to the dim apartment, slumping onto the couch.

Hunt chuckled. "Very princess-ish."

She removed her earrings, chucking the diamonds onto the coffee table as if they were cheap costume jewelry. The comb in her hair followed, gems glinting in the soft firstlights.

She stretched out her legs, bare feet wiggling on the coffee table. "Let's never do that again."

"The whiskey or outsmarting your father or the party?" Hunt

tugged his white bow tie free of its knot as he approached the couch and peered down at her.

She huffed a laugh. "The party. Outsmarting my father and the whiskey will *always* be a repeat activity."

Hunt sat on the coffee table, adjusting his wings around it. "It could have been a lot worse."

"Yeah. Though I can't think of anything much worse than gaining multiple enemies for the price of one." That the Asteri's appearance had only been a footnote said plenty about their night. "Though Celestina isn't our enemy, I guess."

Hunt picked up one of her feet and began rubbing the insole. She sighed, sinking back into the cushions. Hunt's cock stirred at the pure pleasure she radiated.

"Can I tell you something?" Hunt said, massaging the arch of her foot. "Something that might be deemed alphahole-ish?"

"As long as you keep rubbing my foot like that, you can say whatever the Hel you want."

Hunt laughed. "Deal." He picked up her other foot, starting on that one. "I liked being at the party tonight. Despite all the fancy clothes and the Asteri and the stuff with Hypaxia and Celestina. Despite all the prince bullshit. I liked being seen. With you."

Her mouth quirked to the side. "You liked staking your territory?"

"Yeah." He let her see the predator in him. "I've never had that with anyone."

She frowned. "Shahar never showed you off?"

"No. I was her general. At public functions, we didn't appear together. She never wanted that. It would have positioned me as an equal, or at least someone she deemed . . . important."

"I thought your movement was all about equality," Bryce said, frown deepening.

"It was. But we still had to play by the old rules." Rules that continued to govern and dictate people's lives. Celestina's and Hypaxia's lives.

"So she never came out and said, *Hey, world! He's my boyfriend!*"

Hunt laughed, and marveled that he did so. He'd never thought he'd be able to laugh about anything related to Shahar. "No. It's why I was so . . . honored when you asked me to do this."

Bryce studied him. "Do you want to go outside so we can get caught fooling around in public by the press? That'll make us *really* official."

"Maybe another time." Hunt lifted her foot to his mouth, pressing a kiss to the instep. "So, we're, like . . . married."

"Are we?" She held out a hand before her, studying her splayed fingers. "I don't see a ring, Athalar."

He nipped at her toes, earning a squeal from her. "You want a ring, I'll get you one." Another kiss. "You want iron, steel, or titanium?" Wedding bands in Lunathion were simple, their value derived from the strength of the metal used to forge them.

"Titanium all the way, baby," she crowed, and Hunt bit her toes again.

She squirmed, but he held her firm. "These little toes make me think some dirty things, Quinlan," he said against her foot.

"Please tell me you don't have a foot fetish."

"No. But everything where you're involved is a fetish for me."

"Oh?" She leaned back farther into the cushions, her dress slipping up her legs. "So I make you want to get a little kinky?"

"Uh-huh." He kissed her ankle. "Just a little."

She arched into the touch. "Want to have drunk, sloppy sex, Prince Hunt?"

He rumbled a laugh against her calf. Only from her lips would he tolerate that title. "Fuck yeah."

She pulled her leg from his touch and stood with that dancer's grace. "Unzip me."

"Romantic."

She gave him her back, and Hunt, still seated, reached up to tug at the zipper hidden down the length of her spine. The tattoo of the Horn appeared, along with inches of golden skin, until the first tendrils of lace from her thong were revealed. The zipper ended before he could get a view of what he wanted.

But Bryce peeled the dress from her front, letting it drop. She hadn't worn a bra, but the black thong . . .

Hunt ran his hands over the firm cheeks of her ass, bending to bite at a delicate strap of her underwear. She let out a soft, breathy sound that had him kissing the base of her spine. Her long hair brushed his brow, silken and as lovely as a caress.

Bryce turned in his grip, and—what luck—he found himself right where he wanted to be. From where it sat high on her hips, her thong plunged into a dramatic vee, a veritable arrow pointing to paradise.

He kissed her navel. Flicked her nipples with his thumbs as he licked up toward them. Her fingers slid into his hair, her head tipping back as he closed his mouth around a taut bud. He rolled her nipple over his tongue, savoring the weight and taste of it, his hands drifting around her waist, tangling in the straps of her thong. Tugging it down her hips. Her thighs. He moved to her other breast, sucking it into his mouth. Bryce groaned, and his cock pushed against the front of his dress pants.

He liked having her at his mercy. Liked this image, of her wholly naked and resplendent before him, his to touch and pleasure and worship. Hunt smiled against her breast. He liked it a lot.

He rose, scooping her into his arms and carrying her to the bedroom, his bow tie dangling around his neck.

He laid her on the mattress, cock pulsing at the sight of her heavy-lidded with desire, sprawled there naked and his for the taking. He pulled the tie free. "Want to get a little kinky with me, Quinlan?"

She glanced to the iron posts of the headboard, and her red lips parted in a feline grin. "Oh yes."

Hunt made quick work of binding her hands to the bedposts. Light enough not to hurt, but tight enough that getting any ideas about touching him while he feasted on her was out of the question.

Bryce lay stretched out before him, and Hunt could hardly get a breath down as he unbuttoned his shirt. Then his pants. He shed his shoes, his socks—all the trappings of civility, until he stood before her naked, and Bryce bit her lip. Then he propped up her knees and spread them wide.

"Fuck," he said, taking in her gleaming sex, already drenched for him. Its heady scent hit him, and he shuddered, cock now a steady ache.

"Since I can't touch myself," she said huskily, "maybe you'll do the honors."

"Fuck," he said again, unable to think of anything else. She was so beautiful—every single part of her.

"Are you articulating what you'd like to do to me, or has your brain short-circuited?"

He snapped his gaze to her own. "I wanted to draw this out. Really torment you."

Her legs spread a little wider, a taunting invitation. "Oh?"

"I'll save that for another day," he growled, and crawled on top of her. The tip of his cock nudged at her wet, hot entrance, and a shiver of anticipatory pleasure went down his spine. But he ran a hand down the length of her torso, fingers tracing the silken swells of her breasts, the plane of her stomach. She writhed, tugging on the restraints.

"So defiant." He dipped to kiss her neck. He pushed in a little, his mind blacking out at the perfect tightness. But he withdrew—and eased back in a little more. Even when every instinct screamed to plunge into her, unless she asked for it, he'd be careful. He wanted her to feel only ecstasy.

"Stop teasing," she said, and Hunt raked his teeth down her left breast, sucking in her nipple as he sank a bit further into her sheer perfection. "*More*," she snarled, hips rising as if she'd impale her-self on him.

Hunt laughed. "Who am I to deny a princess?"

Her eyes flashed with desire hot enough to sear his soul. "I'm issuing a royal decree for you to fuck me, Hunt. Hard."

His balls tightened at the words, and he gave her what she wanted. They both groaned as he sank all the way home in a thrust that had him seeing stars. She felt like bliss, like eternity—

Hunt withdrew and thrust again, and there were indeed stars around them—no, it was her, she was glowing like a star—

Her hips undulated, meeting his, driving him deeper.

Fuck yes. She was his, and he was hers, and now the whole fucking world knew it—

He sent out a fizzle of his lightning, snapping the restraints on her wrists. Her hands instantly came around his back, fingers grappling hard enough to draw sweet slices of pain. Hunt's wings twitched, and she wrapped her legs around his middle. He sank even deeper, and holy *fuck*, the squeeze of her—

She flexed those inner muscles. His eyes nearly rolled back in his head.

"Solas, Quinlan—"

"*Hard*," she breathed in his ear. "Fuck me like the prince you are."

Hunt lost it. He pulled back enough to grip her ass in both hands, tilting her pelvis upward—and plunged in. She moaned, and everything he was transformed into something primal and animalistic. *His*. His mate to touch and fuck and fill—

Hunt let himself go, pounding into her again and again and again.

Bryce's moans were sweet music, a temptation and a challenge. She glowed, and Hunt looked at his cock, sliding in and out of her, shining with her wetness—

He was glowing, too. Not with her starlight, but . . . fuck, his lightning was crackling down his arms, his hands, skittering over her hips, up to her breasts.

"Don't stop," she gasped as his lightning flared. "Don't stop."

Hunt didn't. He yielded to the storm, riding it, riding her, and there was only Bryce, her soul and her body and the flawless fit of them—

"Hunt," she pleaded, and he knew from her breathy tone that she was close.

He didn't let up. Didn't give her one ounce of mercy. The slap and slide of their bodies meeting filled the room, but the sounds were distant, the world was distant as his power and essence flowed into her. Bryce cried out, and Hunt turned frenzied, pounding once, twice—

On the third, mightiest thrust, he ruptured, his power with him.

Lightning filled the room, filled her as surely as his seed, and he kissed her through it, tongues meeting, ether flooding his senses. He could never get enough of this—this connection, this sex, this power flowing between them. He needed it more than he needed food, water—needed this sharing of magic, this twining of souls; he'd never stop craving it—

Then he was falling, amid black wind and lightning and stars. He came through all of it, roaring his pleasure to the skies.

Because those *were* skies above them. And city lights. Booming bass from a nearby party.

Hunt stilled, gaping down at Bryce. At the surface beneath her— the apartment building's roof.

Bryce grinned sheepishly. "Oops."

62

Hypaxia's chants rose in volume and complexity, the full moon with them. It silvered the orchard.

Ithan shivered against the cold. He knew that it wasn't due to the night around them, or the autumn unfolding. No, the air had been pleasantly warm a moment ago. Whatever Hypaxia's magic was doing, it was bringing the frigid temperatures with it.

"I can feel . . . a presence," the witch-queen whispered, arms lifted toward the moon, beautiful face solemn. "Someone is coming."

Ithan's mouth dried out. What would he even say to Connor? *I love you* would likely be the first. *I miss you every minute of every damn day* would be the second. Then the warning. Or should it be the warning first? He shook out his trembling fingers at his sides.

"Get ready to say your piece. Your brother's spirit is . . . strong. I'm not sure how long I can hold the star."

Something weirdly like pride rose in him at that. But Ithan stepped closer, breathing evenly. Exactly as he had before important games, during game-winning shots. Focus. He could do this. He'd deal with the repercussions later.

The star she'd drawn glowed a faint blue, illuminating the trees around them.

"One more moment . . ." Hypaxia hissed, panting, a faint sheen on her temples. Like this was draining the power out of her.

Light ruptured from the star, blinding and white, a great wind shaking the trees around them, sending olives scattering in a pitter-patter. Ithan squeezed his eyes shut against it, letting his claws slide free.

When the wind stopped, he blinked, adjusting his vision. His brother's name died in his throat.

A creature, tall and thin and robed, lurked in the center of the six-pointed star. Hypaxia let out a soft gasp. Ithan's stomach clenched. He'd never seen the male, but he'd seen drawings.

The Under-King.

"You were not summoned," Hypaxia said, mastering her surprise. She lifted her chin, every inch the queen. "Return to the misty isle over which you rule."

The Under-King laughed at the witch. Her body shimmered with pale blue light. Like she was rallying her power. But the Under-King slowly turned his head to Ithan. Let out another dry, husky laugh.

"Young fools. You play with powers beyond your ken." His voice was horrible. Full of dusty bones and the pleading screams of the dead.

Yet Hypaxia didn't back down an inch. "Be gone, and let us see the one whom I have summoned."

Ithan's hand drifted toward his gun. It wouldn't do anything. His wolf form would protect him better with its speed, but even losing that split second to shifting might make him vulnerable, and cost Hypaxia her life.

The Under-King extended a bony hand. Light rippled where it met the edge of the star. "Do not fear, wolf pup. I cannot harm you. Here, at least." He grinned, exposing too-large brown teeth.

Ithan bristled and he found his voice at last as he growled, "I want to speak to my brother."

Beside him, Hypaxia was murmuring under her breath, the light around her building.

"Your brother is well cared for." Dark fire danced in the Under-King's milky eyes. "But whether that remains so now depends entirely on you."

"What the Hel does that mean?" Ithan demanded. But the

witch-queen had tensed. Wind stirred her curly hair, as if she were readying her defenses.

The Under-King lifted a bony hand, and an eerie, greenish light wreathed his fingers. Ithan could have sworn ancient, strange symbols swirled in that light. "Let's play a little game first." He inclined his head to Hypaxia, whose face had gone stony—anticipatory. "The House of Flame and Shadow has long been curious about your . . . abilities, Your Majesty."

Bryce knew she was dreaming. Knew she was physically in her bed. Knew she was currently tucked up against Hunt's side. But she also knew that the being in front of her was real—even if the setting was not.

She stood on a vast, dusty plain before an azure, cloudless sky. Distant dry mountains studded the horizon, but she was surrounded only by rock and sand and emptiness.

"Princess." The voice was like Hel embodied: dark and icy and smooth.

"Prince." Her voice shook.

Apollion, Prince of the Pit, had chosen to appear in a golden-haired, golden-skinned body. Handsome in the way that ancient statues were handsome, in the way that Pollux was handsome.

His black eyes, however, gave him away. No whites anywhere. Only unending darkness.

The Star-Eater himself.

She asked, trying to master her shaking, "Where are we?"

"Parthos. Or what remains of it."

The barren land seemed to stretch on forever. "In the real world, or in, like, dreamworld?"

He angled his head, more animal than humanoid. "Dreamworld. Or what you consider to be dreams."

She wasn't going to touch that one. "All right, then. Um . . . nice to meet you."

Apollion's mouth curved upward. "You do not cower before me."

"Aidas kind of ruined your scary-monster vibe."

A soulless laugh. "My brother has the tendency to be a thorn in my side."

"Maybe he should join this conversation."

"Aidas would be angry with me for speaking with you. That's why I picked this moment, when he is conveniently occupied."

"With what?"

"Raising Hel's armies. Readying them."

Her breath hitched. "To invade Midgard?"

"It's been long in the making."

"I'm going to make a request on behalf of my planet and say please stay in your own world."

Another twitch of his mouth. "You do not trust us. Good. Theia did. It was her downfall."

"The Starborn Queen?"

"Yes. Aidas's great love."

Bryce started. "His *what*?"

Apollion waved a broad hand to the ruined world around them. "Why do you think I slew Pelias? Why do you think I went on to devour Sirius? All for him. My foolish, lovesick brother. In such a rage over Theia's death at Pelias's hands. His folly lost us that phase of the war."

Bryce had to blink. "I'm sorry, but please back up. You summoned me into this dream to tell me about how Aidas, Prince of the Chasm, was the lover of Theia, the first Starborn Queen, even though they were enemies?"

"They were not enemies. We were her allies. She and some of her Fae forces allied with us—against the Asteri."

Her mouth dried out. "Why didn't he tell me this? Why are *you* telling me this?"

"Why are you not yet master of your powers? I was very clear: I told your mate you must both explore your potential."

"Did you send those Reapers to jump me and Ruhn?"

"What Reapers?" She could have sworn his confusion was sincere.

"The ones who told me the same exact thing, to master my powers."

"I did no such thing."

"That's what the Under-King said. I'm guessing one of you is lying."

"This is not a useful debate. And I do not appreciate being called a liar." Pure threat laced the words.

But Bryce steeled herself. "You're right—it's not a useful debate. So answer my question: Why the Hel are you telling me any of this stuff about Aidas and Theia?" If he spoke true, and Hel hadn't been their enemy back then . . . Whatever side Theia had ruled, she'd been . . . against the Asteri. And Pelias had killed her—fighting *for* the Asteri.

Her mind spun. No wonder nobody knew about Theia. The Asteri had likely erased her from history. But a Fae Queen had loved a demon prince. And he had loved her enough to . . .

"I am telling you this because you are racing blind toward your doom. I am telling you this because tonight the veil between our worlds is thinnest and I might finally speak to you."

"You spoke to Hunt before."

"Orion was bred to be receptive to our kind. Why do you think he is so adept at hunting us? But that is of no matter. This night, I might appear to *you*—as more than a vision." He reached out a hand, and Bryce flinched as it touched her. Truly *touched* her, ice so cold it ached. "Hel is nearly ready to finish this war."

She took a step back. "I know what you're going to ask, and my answer is *no*."

"Use the Horn. The power Athalar gives you can activate it." His eyes danced with storms. "Open the doors to Hel."

"Absolutely fucking not."

Apollion chuckled, low and lethal. "What a disappointment." The plain that had been Parthos began to fade into nothing. "Come find me in Hel when you learn the truth."

Ithan pivoted slowly, eyeing the shadows where the Under-King had stood—and vanished.

"Don't move from this spot," Hypaxia warned him, voice low.

"I can feel his power all around us. He's turned this clearing into a labyrinth of wards."

Ithan sniffed, as if it'd give him some sense of what the Hel she was talking about. But nothing appeared to have changed. No creatures jumped out at them. Still, he said, "I'll follow your lead."

Hypaxia scanned the sky. "He warded above us, too. To keep us grounded." She crinkled her nose. "Right. On foot it is."

Ithan swallowed. "I, ah . . . got your back?"

She chuckled. "Just keep up, please."

He gave her a determined smile. "You got it."

Ithan braced himself as Hypaxia took a step forward, hand extended. Her fingers recoiled at whatever ward she encountered, right as a low snarl sounded from the trees beyond.

The hair on his neck rose. His wolf senses told him it wasn't an animal's snarl. But it sounded . . . hungry.

Another one rippled from nearby. Then another. All around them.

"What is that?" Ithan breathed, even his Vanir eyes failing to pierce the darkness.

Hypaxia's hands glowed white-hot with magic. She didn't take her gaze off the trees ahead of them. "The hunting hounds of the House of Flame and Shadow," she said grimly before slamming her hand against the ward in front of them.

63

He was a micromanaging fucking nightmare," Bryce ranted the next day as she stood with Hunt, Ruhn, and Declan in the Aux training center during her lunch break. Tharion lay sprawled on a bench against the wall, napping. Cormac, standing across the space, frowned.

Her brother was pale. "You really think Theia and a bunch of Fae sided with Hel during the war?"

Bryce suppressed a shiver of cold at the memory. "Who knows what's true?"

Across the vast, empty room, Hunt rubbed his jaw. She hadn't even mentioned what Apollion had said—that little tidbit about Hunt being *bred*. She'd tackle that later. Hunt mused, "What's the benefit in convincing us of a lie? Or the truth, either, I suppose. All that matters is that Hel is definitely on the move."

Declan said, "Can we pause for a moment and remark on the fact that both of you have *spoken* to the Prince of the Pit? Is no one else about to puke at the thought?"

Ruhn held up a hand, and Tharion lazily lifted one from the bench, but Bryce high-fived Hunt. "Special kids club," she said to the angel, who winked at her. She leapt back a step, rallying her power. "Again." They'd been in here for twenty minutes already, practicing.

Hunt's lightning flared at his fingertips, and Bryce set her feet apart. "Ready?" he asked.

Tharion roused himself enough to turn over, propping his head on a fist. Bryce scowled at him, but the mer only waggled his brows in encouragement.

She faced Hunt again, right as the angel hurled his lightning at her like a spear. It zinged against her chest, a direct hit, and then she was glowing, power singing, soaring—

Two feet in front of the windows.

She'd no sooner thought the command than she appeared across the space. Exactly two feet from the windows. *Back to a foot before Hunt.*

She appeared before him, so suddenly that he staggered back.

Ruhn. She moved again, slower this time. But her brother yelped.

Declan braced himself, like he thought he'd be next, so Bryce thought, *A foot behind Hunt.*

She pinched her mate's butt so fast he didn't have time to whirl before she'd moved again. This time in front of Declan, who cursed when she poked him in the ribs, then teleported once more.

Cormac called from where he'd been standing in the far corner, "You're slowing." She was. Damn it, she was. Bryce rallied her power, Hunt's energy. She appeared in front of Tharion's bench, but the mer was waiting.

Fast as a striking shark, Tharion grabbed her face and planted a smacking kiss on her lips.

Hunt's laugh boomed across the space, and Bryce joined him, batting the mer away.

"Too slow, Legs," Tharion drawled, leaning back against the bench and crossing an ankle over a knee. He draped an arm along the back of the plastic bench. "And too predictable."

"Again," Cormac ordered. "Focus."

Bryce tried, but her bones weighed her down. Tried again to no avail. "I'm out."

"Concentrate, and you could hold on longer. You use too much at once, and don't reserve the energy for later."

Bryce put her hands on her hips as she panted. "Your teleporting works differently than mine. How can you know that?"

"Mine comes from a source of magic, too. Energy, just a different form. Each jump takes more out of me. It's a muscle that you need to build up."

She scowled, wiping her brow as she walked back over to Hunt.

"It does seem like he's right," Declan said to Bryce. "Your teleporting works when your power gets charged up by energy—considering what I heard about how quickly you ran out of steam with Hypaxia, Hunt's is the best form of it."

"Damn right it is," Hunt growled, earning a smack on the arm from Bryce.

"Do you think the power will . . . stay in me if I don't use it?" she asked Dec.

"I don't think so," Dec said. "Your power came from the Gate—with a shit-ton of firstlight mixed in. So your magic—beyond the light, I mean—needs to be powered up. It relies on firstlight, or any other form of energy it can get. You're literally a Gate: you can take in power and offer it. But it seems the similarity ends there. The Gates can store power indefinitely, while yours clearly peters out after a while." He faced Hunt. "And your power, Athalar, as pure energy, is able to draw from her, like she did from the Gate. Bryce, when you draw from a source, it's the same way the Gates zap power from people using them to communicate."

Bryce blinked. "So I'm like some magical leech?"

Declan laughed. "I think only of certain kinds of magic. Forms of pure energy. Throw in the Horn, which relies on a blast of power to activate it . . ."

"And you're a liability," Ruhn said darkly. Tharion grunted his agreement.

Declan rubbed his chin. "You told Ruhn after the attack that Hypaxia aimed for your scar to supercharge your powers, right? I wonder what would happen if you were struck on the Horn."

"Let's not find out," Bryce said quickly.

"Agreed," Cormac said from across the room. He pointed to the obstacle course he'd laid out in the center of the space. "Back to work. Follow the track."

Bryce pivoted toward the Avallen Prince, and said as casually as she could, "I'm shocked you're even here."

Cormac said icily, "Because you decided to end our engagement without consulting me?"

Hunt muttered to her, "Anything to avoid your exercises, huh?"

She glared at her mate, especially as Ruhn chuckled, but said to Cormac, "I had no other choice."

Shadows rippled around Cormac. "You could have let me know while you were plotting."

"There was no plotting. Athalar and I decided, and then just waited."

The Avallen Prince snarled low. Hunt let out a warning growl of his own. Tharion said nothing, though she knew the mer was monitoring every breath and word. But Cormac didn't take his eyes from her. "Do you have any idea what the phone call with my father was like?"

"I'm assuming it was similar to the Autumn King telling me I'm a little bitch?"

Cormac shook his head. "Let's be clear: I'm only here today because I'm well aware that if I'm not, then your brother will cease contacting Agent Daybright."

"I'm flattered you know me so well," Ruhn drawled, his arms crossed. He'd moved into a position on Cormac's other side—without her even noticing. Placing himself between the Avallen Prince and Bryce. Oh please.

Cormac glowered at him, but then focused upon Bryce again. "I'm willing to move beyond this, on the condition that you don't surprise me again. We have too many enemies as it is."

"One," she said, "don't give me conditions. But two . . ." She made a show of examining her bare arms. "Nothing up my sleeves. No other secrets to hide, I swear."

Except for that itsy-bitsy thing about Emile. Hunt gave her a dry look, as if to say, *Liar*, but she ignored him.

Cormac, however, did not. Catching that look, the Avallen Prince said, "There's something else."

"Nope."

But even Ruhn now lifted his brows at her. Hunt said casually, "Don't be paranoid."

"You have something planned," Cormac pressed. "For fuck's sake, tell me."

"I don't have anything planned," Bryce said, "other than figuring out this teleporting crap."

One moment, Cormac was glancing between her and Hunt. The next, he'd vanished.

Only to reappear at Bryce's back with a knife to her throat.

Bryce stiffened. "Come on, Cormac. There's no need for this." Lightning shone in Hunt's eyes. Ruhn had drawn his gun. Tharion remained sprawled across the bench, but—that was a knife now gleaming in his hand. His focus was fixed on the Avallen Prince.

"*Tell me*," Cormac snarled, and cool metal bit into her throat.

Trying not to breathe too deeply, Bryce laid a finger on the blade. "I made the Drop. I'll survive."

Cormac hissed at her ear. "Tell me what the fuck you have planned, or you'll lose your head. Good luck growing that back."

"You draw blood and you lose your head, too," Hunt growled with lethal menace.

She could blind Cormac, she supposed. But would his shadows muffle the impact? She doubted he'd truly kill her, but if he tried . . . Hunt would definitely attack. Ruhn would, too.

And she'd have an even bigger mess on her hands.

So Bryce said, "Fine. It's about Emile."

Hunt started. So did Tharion as the mer said, "Bryce."

Cormac didn't remove the knife. "*What* about Emile?"

"I found him. At the Viper Queen's warehouse." She sighed loudly. "I learned he was there, that all the reptiles and gross things in the marshes had told her where he was and she'd gone to retrieve him. She was the one who killed the people who helped him, and intended to control him. But when I went to the warehouse two days ago, he was already gone."

Cormac whirled her to face him with rough hands. "Gone where?"

"Somewhere safe. Apparently, the Vipe found it in herself to put him into the care of people who will look after him."

"*Who?*" His face was white with rage. Tharion's eyes had widened.

"I don't know. She wouldn't tell me."

"Then I'll make her tell *me*."

Ruhn laughed. "No one makes the Viper Queen do anything."

Into her mind, her brother said, *Cormac might not know you well enough to tell when you're lying, but I do.*

It's not a lie. Emile is safe.

He's just not where you're claiming.

Oh, he was with the Viper Queen. And now he's somewhere else.

Cormac shook his head. "Why would the Viper Queen have any interest in that boy?"

"Because she likes to collect powerful beings to fight in her pits," Hunt snarled. "Now put the fucking knife away."

To her relief, the prince lowered the knife from her neck with an easy flip of the blade. "But why would she let go of someone so powerful, if she likes to use them in fights?"

Bryce said, "Because Emile has no powers."

Are you shitting me? Ruhn asked.

Nope. Kid's totally human.

Cormac's eyes narrowed. "Sofie said—"

"She lied," Bryce said.

Cormac's shoulders slumped. "I need to find him. I shouldn't have put off questioning Spetsos—"

"Emile is safe, and cared for," Bryce interrupted, "and that's all you need to know."

"I owe it to Sofie—"

"You owe it to Sofie to keep Emile out of this rebellion. Your life is hardly what I'd call a stable environment. Let him stay hidden."

Cormac said to Tharion, "What are *you* going to tell your queen?"

Tharion offered him a razor-sharp smile. "Absolutely nothing." A threat of violence simmered beneath the words. If Cormac breathed anything to the mer, to the River Queen, the Avallen Prince would find himself in a watery grave.

Cormac sighed. And to her shock, he said, "I apologize for the knife." To Hunt, he said, "And I apologize for threatening your mate."

Ruhn asked, "Don't I get an apology?" Cormac bristled, but Ruhn grinned.

Bryce caught Hunt watching her, his expression proud. Like she'd done something worthy. Had it been her smooth weaving of lies and truth?

"Apology accepted," Bryce said, forcing herself to sound chipper. Steering away from the topic of Emile. "Now back to training."

Cormac shrugged, pointing to the spots he'd taped off: X's on the floor, atop chairs, atop piled mats, beneath a table.

Bryce groaned, but marked them, cataloged the path she'd take.

"Well, that was exciting," Tharion announced, groaning as he got to his feet. "Right. I'm out."

Hunt arched a brow. "Where to?"

"I'm still technically employed by the River Queen. Regardless of what happened with Emile, there are other matters to attend to."

Bryce waved at him. But Ruhn said, "Dinner tonight?"

Tharion winked. "You got it." Then he sauntered through the metal doors and was gone.

"All right, Athalar," Bryce muttered when the mer had shut the doors. "Time to level up."

Hunt laughed, but his lightning flared again. "Let's do this, Your Highness."

There was something in the way he said *Your Highness* that made her realize that the expression on his face a moment before hadn't been pride in her manipulation—it had been pride in the way she'd defused things without violence. Like he thought she might actually deserve the title she now bore.

Bryce tucked the thought aside. By the time the bolt of lightning slammed into her chest, she was already running.

Despite the exhaustion weighing on his very bones, despite the urgency that had sent him and Hypaxia racing here, Ithan couldn't help gaping from the doorway as the party girl he'd loved moved through the Aux training space like the wind, vanishing and appearing at will. At his side, Hypaxia monitored the remarkable feats, studying Bryce intently.

Bryce finished the obstacle course and halted at Hunt's side, bending over her knees to catch her breath.

Hypaxia cleared her throat, stepping into the gymnasium. Even the queen looked . . . ruffled after the endless, terrifying night they'd had.

They'd passed Tharion on his way out. The mer had been speaking in low tones to someone on the phone, and had raised his brows with concern at the sight of the dirt and sweat on them. But whoever had been on the phone must have been important enough that he couldn't hang up, and Tharion had only continued on after Hypaxia had given him a gesture that seemed to assure him that she was fine. The mer had stopped and peered back over a shoulder at Ithan, as if needing to confirm the queen's claim, but Ithan had nothing to offer him. What the Hel could he say? They weren't fine. Not at all. So they'd left Tharion in the hall, the mer staring after them for a long moment.

"What's up?" Ruhn asked Ithan, waving his greeting to Hypaxia. Then the prince did a double take. "What the Hel happened to you two? I thought you were summoning Connor."

The others in the training space halted.

"We did indeed try to summon Connor Holstrom last night," Hypaxia said gravely.

Bryce paled as she hurried over. "What happened? Is Connor all right? Are you guys all right?"

Ithan's throat worked. "Ah . . ."

Hypaxia replied for him, "We did not encounter Connor. The Under-King answered."

"What happened?" Bryce asked again, voice rising.

Ithan met her stare. Pure predatory wolf gleamed there. "He detained us for his amusement. Sicced Flame and Shadow's nightmare dogs on us and warded us into an olive grove with them. It took Hypaxia until now to figure out an exit through the wards that wouldn't get us ripped to shreds. We're fine, though." Ruhn whirled with alarm to his fiancée, and the witch-queen nodded solemnly, shadows in her eyes. Ithan scrubbed at his face before he added, "He wants to see you at Urd's Temple."

Hunt's lightning sparked at his fingertips. "Fuck no."

Ithan swallowed hard. "You don't have a choice." He turned, pleading and exhausted, to Bryce. "Connor is safe for right now, but if you don't show within an hour, the Under-King will throw him and the rest of the Pack of Devils through the Gate immediately. He'll make secondlight of them all."

64

Tharion strolled through the Meat Market, casually browsing the stalls. Or at least, he tried to appear casual. While surveying an array of luck stones, he kept an ear open. In the midday bustle, the general assortment of lowlifes had come here for lunch, shopping, or fucking, and at this point, they'd likely have downed at least a few drinks. Which meant loose tongues.

I hear the bitch is already pregnant, one satyr grunted to another as they sat around a barrel converted into a table, smoked kebabs half-eaten in front of them. *Ephraim's been fucking her good.*

Tharion pushed aside his disgust at the crude words. He hated that word—*bitch.* How many times had it been thrown at his sister whenever she'd ventured Above? She'd always laughed it off, and Tharion had laughed it off with her, but now . . . He shook off the pang of guilt and moved to the next stall, full of various types of mushrooms from the damp forests to the northeast.

He checked his phone—the quick message exchange between him and Pax.

What happened? Are you all right? he'd written nearly an hour ago, after running into her and Holstrom in the hall of the Aux training center. She'd been dirty and tired-looking, and he hadn't been able to so much as ask if she was okay, because he'd been on the phone with the River Queen. Who had wanted updates on Emile.

Which was why he had come here. To maintain the fiction that he was hunting for the kid. He figured he'd do some listening to the idle chatter while pretending, though. Pick up gossip from the city creeps.

His phone buzzed, and Tharion scanned the message on the screen before loosing a long breath. Hypaxia had written, *I'm fine. Just some Flame and Shadow posturing.*

He didn't like that one bit. But what the Hel could he do about any of it?

"Lion's head is in season," said the gnome perched on a stool behind the baskets of fungi, drawing Tharion from his thoughts. "Morels finished their run, but I've got one last basket left."

"Only browsing," Tharion said, flashing a smile at the rosy-cheeked, red-capped male.

"Let me know if you have any questions," the gnome said, and Tharion again tuned in to the tables behind him.

Fight last night was brutal. There was nothing left of that lion after—

I drank so much I can't remember who the Hel I was fucking—

—that dragon finished with them. Only embers—

I need more coffee. They should give us the day off after *a holiday, you know?*

Tharion stilled. Slowly turned, pinpointing the speaker who'd snagged his attention.

Dragon.

Well, *that* was interesting. And . . . fortunate.

He'd been lounging on that bench while Legs trained, needing the company of others as a distraction from the shuddering earthquake of nerves after last night. He'd fucked the leopard shifter in the garden shadows. Had enjoyed every second of it, and from her two orgasms, she had, too.

He might have walked away from the River Queen's daughter last night, but he hadn't told her that. As far as the River Queen and her daughter knew, and judging by the former's tone on the phone earlier when she'd called to ask about the hunt for Emile, they were still engaged. But if either of them found out . . .

If they found out, wouldn't it be convenient to have a dragon to offer as an apology present? Wouldn't a dragon be perfect in lieu of Emile?

"This place isn't nearly as fun when you're sober," Flynn observed from behind him thirty minutes later as he approached in civilian clothes, precisely as Tharion had requested. The attire did little to hide the gun tucked down the back of his shorts.

Tharion hadn't dared say much on the phone when he'd asked the Fae lord to meet him here. And while Flynn might act like an unworried frat boy, Tharion knew he was too smart to risk asking questions on an open phone line.

Tharion rose from a table in the midst of the food stalls, where he'd been sipping coffee and filing old emails, and began a casual walk through the market. Low enough that no one—not even the fennec-fox shifter working a row over—would be able to hear, he said, "I found something you might be interested in."

Flynn feigned typing into his phone. "Yeah?"

Tharion muttered out of the corner of his mouth, "Remember how your new best friend with the . . . fiery temperament went missing?"

"You found Ari?" Flynn's voice had become dangerously solemn. A voice that few ever heard, Tharion knew. Unless they were about to die.

Tharion pointed toward the wooden walkway built above the market. Leading toward an ordinary door that he knew opened into a long hallway. Two blank-faced Fae guards armed with semi-automatic rifles stood before it. "I've got a wild guess about where she might be."

Now he had to figure out how to get the dragon Beneath.

Tharion eyed the bare-bones wooden hallway as he and Flynn strode down the worn planks, aiming for a round door at its far end. It looked like the entry to a vault, solid iron that didn't reflect the dim firstlights.

They'd been halted at the first door by the Viper Queen's guards. Flynn had snarled at them, but the males had ignored him, their drug-hazed eyes unblinking as they radioed their leader. That Tharion knew of this door at all told her guards he was important enough to warrant a call.

And here they were. About to go into the Viper Queen's nest.

The massive vault door swung open when they were about ten feet away, revealing ornate red carpets—definitely Traskian—over marble floors, three tall windows with heavy black velvet drapes held back with chains of gold, and low-slung couches designed for lounging.

The Viper Queen was sitting on one of them in a white jumpsuit, feet bare, toenails painted a purple so dark it was almost black. The same color as her lipstick. Her gold-tipped nails, however, glinted in the soft lights as she lifted a cigarette to her mouth and puffed away.

But beside her, sprawled on the couch . . .

He'd been right. The Viper Queen did like to collect valuable fighters.

"Ari," Flynn said tightly, halting just beyond the door. Mirthroot hung heavy in the air, along with a secondary, cloying scent that Tharion could only assume was another drug.

The dragon, clad in black leggings and a tight black tank top, didn't take her eyes off the massive TV mounted above the dark fireplace across the room. But she replied, "Tristan."

"Good to see you," Flynn said, voice taking on that dangerously low quality that so few lived to tell about. "Glad you're in one piece."

The Viper Queen chuckled, and Tharion braced himself. "The lion she fought last night can't say the same. Even confined to her humanoid form, she is . . . formidable."

Tharion grinned sharply at the ruler of the Meat Market. "Did you capture her?" He needed to know how she'd done it. If only so he could do it himself.

The Viper Queen's snake eyes flared to a nearly neon green. "I'm not in the business of snatching slaves. Unlike some people I know." She smirked at Ariadne. The dragon continued to stare at the TV with fixed intent. "She sought me out and asked for asylum, since she realized there was nowhere on Midgard she might flee from her captor. We reached a bargain that suited us both."

So the dragon had come of her own free will. Maybe he could convince her to go Beneath. It'd be a Hel of a lot easier.

Even if once he got her down there, she'd never get out again.

"You'd rather be here," Flynn asked the dragon, "fighting in her pit, than with us?"

"You threw me on guard duty," Ari spat, at last snapping her attention from the TV to Flynn. Tharion didn't envy the male as she fixed her burning gaze on him. "Is that any better than fighting in the pit?"

"Uh, yeah. A fuck-ton better."

"You sound like someone who's grown accustomed to his life being dull as dust," Ari said, turning back to the TV.

"You've been trapped inside a *ring* for the gods know how long," Flynn exploded. "What the Hel do you know about anything?"

Molten scales flowed under her skin, then vanished. Her face remained placid. Tharion wished he had some popcorn. But he caught the Viper Queen's narrowed eyes on him.

She said coolly, "I remember you: dead sister. Rogue shifter."

Tharion suppressed the flicker of ire at the casual reference to Lesia and threw the snake shifter his most charming smile. "That's me."

"And the River Queen's Captain of Intelligence."

"The one and only." He winked. "Care to have a word?"

"Who am I to deny the wishes of the River Queen's daughter's beloved?" Tharion tensed, and her purple lips curled, the razor-sharp bob swaying as she rose. "Don't roast the Faeling," she said to Ariadne, then curled a finger at Tharion. "This way."

She led him through a narrow hall lined with doors. He could see ahead that the corridor opened into another chamber. All he could make out of it was more carpets and couches as they approached. "Well, mer?"

Tharion huffed a laugh. "A few questions."

"Sure." She tapped ash from her cigarette into a glass ashtray atop the coffee table.

He opened his mouth, but they'd reached the room at the other end of the hall. It was a near-twin to the other, only its windows overlooked the fighting pit.

But sitting on one of the couches, with a pile of white powder that seemed a Hel of a lot like lightseeker on a small brass scale on the table before her . . .

"Let me guess," Tharion drawled at the Harpy, who lifted her head from where a Fae male weighed out the drugs, "it's not yours; it's for a friend."

The Harpy's dark eyes narrowed with warning as she eased to her feet. "Here to narc on me, fish?"

Tharion smiled slowly. "Just paying a friendly visit."

She turned her menacing stare to the Viper Queen, who slid her hands into her pockets and leaned against the far wall. "Did you sell me out?"

"This pretty hunk of meat waltzed in. Wanted a word. He knows the rules."

Tharion did. This was the Viper Queen's space. Her word was law. He had as little authority over her as he did the Asteri. And if he pulled anything, she had as much authority as the Asteri to end him. Likely by throwing him into that fighting pit and seeing how many of her fighters it took to kill him.

Tharion gestured to the doorway in a mockery of a bow. "I won't trouble you."

The Harpy glanced at the male who now scooped her lightseeker into a black velvet bag lined with plastic.

"VIP service, huh?" Tharion said to the Viper Queen, whose lips curved again.

"Only the best for my most valued clients," she said, still leaning against the wall.

The Harpy snatched the bag from the Fae male, her black wings rustling. "Keep your mouth shut, mer. Or you'll wind up in pieces like your sister."

He let out a low growl. "Keep talking, hag, and I'll show you what I did to the male who killed her."

The Harpy chuckled, tucking her drugs into the pocket of her jacket, and walked out, wings a black cloud behind her.

"Buying or selling?" the Viper Queen asked him quietly as the Fae male packed up his drugs and scale and bustled out.

Tharion turned to her, willing the rage riding his temper to ease off. "You know that psychopath made blood eagles out of two rebels, don't you?"

"Why do you think I invited her to be a client? Someone who does that kind of shit needs to take the edge off. Or keep it on, I suppose."

Tharion shook off his disgust. "She talk to you about what those rebels were doing in this city?"

"Are you asking me to play spy, Captain?"

"I'm asking you whether you've heard anything about Ophion, or a commander named Pippa Spetsos." He needed to know if and when Pippa and her Lightfall unit would make a move, even without that mech-suit prototype. If he could save innocent lives in this city, he would.

"Of course I have. Everyone's heard of Ophion."

Tharion ground his teeth. "You know what they're up to?"

She took a long drag from her cigarette. "Information isn't free."

"How much?"

"The dragon's good for business." Her snake eyes didn't move from his. "Fight last night brought in a lot of money. I worked out a deal with her: she'll get a portion of profits from her wins, and it can go toward buying her freedom."

"You don't own her." No matter that *he* wanted to hand her over to his queen like . . .

Fuck, like a slave.

"No, I don't. That's why I'll need you to spin whatever bullshit your friends and their lawyer gave to the Astronomer. Something about royal commandeering?" The Viper Queen admired her immaculate nails. "Tell everyone her fighting here is a matter of imperial security."

"No one will believe that." And fuck, he needed that dragon. He needed her as an exit strategy out of this Emile situation. And any fallout for leaving the queen's daughter.

"People believe anything when presented correctly."

Tharion sighed at the mirrored ceiling. The dragon had at least agreed to be here, to fight toward her freedom, but . . .

The Viper Queen said, as if somehow reading or guessing his thoughts, "Even in that humanoid form, she can turn you into ashes if you try to bring her to the Blue Court." Tharion glowered, but said nothing. She went on, "You and your little gaggle of friends have been awfully active lately. I might have let Quinlan talk me into a bargain for the kid, but I have no plans to let this dragon slip out of my hands." A sharp smile. "You fools should have kept a tighter leash on her."

Tharion gave her a sharp smile of his own. "It's not my call whether she can stay here or not."

"Get your royal friends and their legal team to spin their bullshit and we'll be good, mer."

Fuck. He was really going to walk out of here empty-handed, wasn't he. His mind raced as he tried to think up some other prize to bring back to his queen, something to save his hide . . .

He'd figure it out later. When he wasn't in front of a notoriously lethal Vanir.

He sighed and said, "If the dragon agrees, then whatever. We'll spin our bullshit."

"She already has." Another sly smile.

"So tell me what Spetsos is up to." If he could appear competent in his job as Captain of Intelligence, maybe the information about a rebel threat would keep his queen's wrath at bay.

The Viper Queen pulled out her phone, checking the digital clock. "Call your friends and find out."

"What?"

But the Viper Queen had already turned back to the hall, to the dragon and Flynn at its other end.

Tharion dialed Hypaxia. Hunt. Then Bryce. Ithan. Ruhn. No one answered.

He didn't dare put it into a message, but . . . He dialed Hunt again. "Pick the fuck up," he murmured. "Pick the fuck up."

For a moment, he flashed back to another day, when he'd tried and tried to call his sister only to get her audiomail, so he'd called his parents, asking if they'd spoken to her, if they knew where she was—

Tharion reached Flynn, who was sitting on the couch, engaging in a silent staring contest with Ariadne. He couldn't keep the edge from his voice as he said, "Call Ruhn. See if he'll pick up for you."

"What's wrong?" Flynn was instantly on his feet.

"Not sure," Tharion said, heading for the door. He swallowed down those awful memories and his rising dread. "Any idea where they were today?"

The Viper Queen said behind them, sinking onto the couch again, "Good luck."

Tharion and Flynn paused at the doorway. The Fae lord pointed to the dragon. "We're not done here."

Ariadne only watched the TV again, ignoring him.

Flynn snarled. "I'm coming back for you."

Tharion tucked away the knowledge of what he'd done, what he'd bargained for this measly tip-off about Ophion and Spetsos. He'd tell Flynn later.

Ariadne's stare turned to Flynn as the vault door swung open again. Black turned to red. "Spare your high-handedness for someone who wants it, lordling."

Tharion stepped into the hall, phone again at his ear. Bryce didn't answer.

But Flynn looked back at the dragon lounging in the Viper Queen's nest. "We'll see about that, sweetheart," the Fae lord growled, and followed Tharion out.

Bryce had been to Urd's Temple in Moonwood all of one time since moving to Crescent City years ago. She and Juniper had drunkenly taken a cab over here one night during college to make an offering to the goddess of fate to make sure their destinies were epic.

Literally, that was what she'd said.

Benevolent and Farseeing Urd, please make our destinies as epic as possible.

Well, she'd gotten it, Bryce thought as she strode up the steps of the gray marble temple. So had June, though . . . Sorrow and guilt and longing swarmed her at the thought of her friend.

The quiet street was empty of cars. Like the Under-King had cleared everything out.

Or maybe that was due to the other menacing presence they'd dodged near the intersection of Central and Laurel on their walk over here from the training center: Pollux and Mordoc. Two monsters abroad in the city, a unit of the Hind's dreadwolves trailing behind them.

Searching for something. Or someone.

Hunt made sure no one was on the street behind the temple as Bryce, Ruhn, and Hypaxia entered. The Under-King had been very specific—only those four people were permitted to come. Ithan and Cormac hadn't been happy to stay behind.

Beyond the temple's courtyard—not a priestess in sight— the open doors to the inner sanctum beckoned, shadows and smoke within.

Bryce checked that the rifle across her back was in place, the handgun ready at her hip. Ruhn, on her left, carried the Starsword. She'd argued that it was impolite to arrive at a meeting bearing a weapon designed to kill Reapers, but the others overruled her. Ruhn would stay within arm's reach at all times, in case she needed to draw the blade. Lightning crackled around Hunt as they stepped into the gloom.

Not trusting how long it could last—or whether she could even contain it within herself—she hadn't asked him to transfer a charge to her. If it was needed, he could power her up in seconds.

A pyre smoked atop a black stone altar in the center of the temple. A stone throne on a dais loomed at the rear of the space. No statues ever adorned Urd's Temple—no depiction of the goddess had ever been made. Fate took too many forms to capture in one figure.

But someone *was* sitting on the throne.

"Punctual," the Under-King intoned, his bony fingers clicking on the stone arm of the throne. "I appreciate that."

"You desecrate that throne," Ruhn warned. "Get your rotting carcass off it."

The Under-King rose, black robes drifting on a phantom wind. "I thought the Fae bowed to Luna, but perhaps you remember the old beliefs? From a time when Urd was not a goddess but a force, winding between worlds? When she was a vat of life, a mother to all, a secret language of the universe? The Fae worshipped her then."

Bryce feigned yawning, earning an alarmed look from Ruhn, who'd blanched at the sight of the Under-King descending from the dais. Hunt, at least, didn't seem surprised. He'd grown accustomed to her antics, she supposed.

Hypaxia monitored every movement from the Under-King, wind stirring her hair. She had a score to settle after last night, it seemed.

"So," Hunt drawled, "here to finish our business?"

The Under-King drifted to the black altar, his horrific face contorting with pleasure as he breathed in the smoldering bones atop it. "I wished to inform you that the Reapers you so hatefully accused me of sending after you were in fact not Apollion's at all. I've discovered that they hailed from the Eternal City."

Bryce stiffened. "Reapers can cross oceans?"

"Reapers once crossed worlds. I don't see how some water might deter them."

"Why come here to attack us?" Hunt demanded.

"I don't know."

"And why tell us this at all?" Bryce went on.

"Because I do not appreciate my territory being infringed upon."

"Bullshit," Ruhn said. Hypaxia trailed a few steps behind him. "You told them the horrible truth about what happens after death, and yet you're willing to let them live now because you're pissed that someone stepped on your toes?"

His eyes—his dead, milky eyes—fixed on Bryce. "You are officially a princess now, I hear. I suspect you will learn a great deal of equally unpleasant truths."

"You're hedging," Ruhn growled.

But Bryce asked, "Did Jesiba speak to you?"

"Who?"

"Jesiba Roga. Antiquities dealer. She has—had—a few Death Marks. She must know you. She knows everyone."

The Under-King's eyes glowed. "I do not know her by that name, but yes. I know of her." His gaze drifted behind her, to Hypaxia at last. "You did well last night. Few could have worked their way through that labyrinth of spells. The House of Flame and Shadow will welcome you."

The breeze around Hypaxia rose to a chill wind, but she didn't deign to speak. Bryce made a note to herself to never get on the queen's bad side.

Hunt cut in, "You summoned us here to give us this convenient update about those Reapers, and now you want to play nice? I don't buy it."

The Under-King only smiled, revealing those too-large brown teeth.

Bryce said, "What does this sequence mean?" She rattled off what had been on Sofie's arm.

The Under-King blinked. "I don't know." He smiled again, wider. "But perhaps you should ask them." He pointed behind her to the doorway. The world beyond.

Where Pippa Spetsos was marching into the courtyard of the temple, flanked by Lightfall soldiers.

Hunt's lightning flared. "You tipped off Ophion," he snarled, even as he began calculating the fastest route out of the temple.

Ruhn, already at the inner sanctum doors, slammed them shut and barred them. Locking them in with the Under-King.

Pippa's voice came through the doors. *"Come play, Vanir scum. We'll show you what happens when you turn on us."*

Hypaxia's face paled. "You were . . . working with the rebels?"

"Emphasis on *were*," Bryce muttered. Not that it made a difference right now.

The Under-King's figure began to fade away. An illusion. A projection. Hunt didn't bother to wonder how he had done it, had made the details seem so real. "War means death. Death means souls—and more secondlight. Who am I to turn away from a feeding trough? Commander Spetsos's first act upon arriving in Crescent City was to kneel before me. When she mentioned the enemies in their ranks, I took it upon myself to inform her of our . . . altercation. We made a deal that is in both of our best interests."

The rebels would claim the kill, sparing the Under-King any political fallout, but the creep would be satisfied that he'd played a role in slaughtering them, and receive whatever souls would wind up in his realm. A whole lot of them, if Pippa was on the move.

Bryce bristled, starlight shimmering from her. "And were you lying when you claimed you didn't send the Reapers after me and Ruhn those weeks ago?"

"I spoke true then and I speak true now. I had no involvement in that. Why should I lie to you, when I have already revealed so much?"

"Keep playing these games, and you'll make enemies of all of us," Ruhn warned the king.

The Under-King faded into shadows. "Death is the only victor in war." Then he was gone.

A bullet boomed against the metal door. Then another. Pippa was still shouting her vitriol.

"Any ideas?" Hunt asked. If the rebels had gorsian bullets, this would get messy very quickly. And bring a huge crowd to witness the disaster.

Bryce grabbed Hunt's hand. Pushed it on her chest. "Level me up, Athalar."

Ruhn jerked his chin toward Hypaxia. "Take her with you."

The witch-queen glared at the Fae Prince in reproach, but Bryce shook her head, keeping her hand over Hunt's. Her fingers tightened, the only sign of her nerves as she said, "I've never brought anyone along. I need all my focus right now."

Good. At least she was being smart about this. Hunt held his mate's gaze, letting her see his approval, his encouragement. He wouldn't waste time asking what she planned. Bryce was brilliant enough to have something figured out. So Hunt let his lightning flow, setting it zinging through his hand and into her chest.

Her star began glowing beneath his fingers, as if in greedy anticipation. Another barrage of bullets clanged against the door.

His lightning flowed into her like a river, and he could have sworn he heard a beautiful sort of music between their souls as Bryce said, "We need reinforcements."

Ruhn contained his panic as his sister, charged up with a spike of Athalar's lightning, vanished into nothing.

An impact rocked the metal doors into the inner sanctum. Why hadn't the Aux been summoned yet? He reached for his phone. If he called in help, there would be questions about why they'd even been here in the first place. He'd already tried Cormac, but the male had sent him to audiomail, and then messaged that he was talking to the King of Avallen. There was no way the prince would interrupt that call.

They were trapped.

He pivoted to Hypaxia, who was scanning the sanctum, searching for any hidden doors. "There has to be another exit," she said, running her hands over the walls. "No temple ever has just one way in and out."

"This one might," Hunt grumbled.

Bryce reappeared, and Ruhn marked every detail of his panting sister. "Easy peasy," Bryce declared, but her face was sweaty, her eyes dim with exhaustion. What the Hel had she gone off to do?

Another bang on the doors, and the metal dented.

"What the fuck was that?" Ruhn drew the Starsword.

"We need to get out of here now," Bryce said, going to Hunt's side. "We have time, but not much."

"Then teleport us out."

She shook her head. "I don't know if I can do it—"

"You can," Athalar said, absolutely certain. "You just teleported in and out. You've got this. Steady your breathing, block out the noise, and focus."

Her throat bobbed. But she reached for Athalar's hand.

Hunt took a step away. "Hypaxia first. Then Ruhn."

"I might not have enough strength—"

"You do. Go."

Wariness and apprehension flooded his sister's face. But Bryce kissed Athalar's cheek, then grabbed the witch by the arm. "Hold on. I've never taken anyone with me like this and it might be . . ." Her words cut off as they disappeared.

Thank the gods. Thank the gods Bryce had made it out again, with Hypaxia in tow.

Hunt held his breath.

Ruhn said, "You should go next. You're her mate."

"You're her brother. And heir to the Fae throne."

"So is she."

Hunt blinked at the prince, but then Bryce was back, panting. "Oh gods, that fucking sucked." She retched, and reached a hand for Ruhn. "Come on."

"Rest," her brother ordered, but the doors dented further inward. Another few blows and they'd be open. And if Bryce's plan didn't get them a little more time . . .

Bryce grabbed Ruhn's arm and before her brother could object, they vanished. Alone, Hunt monitored the door, rallied his lightning. He could charge her up again, but she was clearly exhausted. Would it do any good?

The doors shuddered, and light cracked in as they peeled apart a few inches.

Hunt ducked behind the altar, away from the spray of bullets that followed, blindly aiming for whoever was within. "*There!*" Pippa shouted, and guns trained on him.

Where the fuck was Bryce—

The doors blew open, throwing three Lightfall soldiers to the ground.

Pollux stood between the doors, white wings luminescent with power, laughing to himself as he brought a clenched fist down upon the head of a female rebel sprawled before him. Bone and blood sprayed. Beyond him, in the courtyard, rebels fired at Mordoc and the dreadwolves. And out in the street, standing beneath a palm tree, away from the fray, Hunt could see the Hind, surveying the brawl.

Bryce appeared and slid behind the altar. Her skin had gone ashen, her breaths uneven. Sharp. She lifted a shaking hand toward him. "I . . ." She collapsed to her knees. She didn't need to say the rest. She was tapped out. Yet she'd come back to him. To fight her way out with him.

"Another charge?" he asked, lightning twining down his arms as he lifted her to her feet.

"I don't think my body can take it." She leaned against him. "I feel like overcooked meat."

Hunt peered around the altar. "How'd you manage to buy us time?"

"The Gates," Bryce panted. "I had to teleport to a few of them before I found one that was pretty empty and unwatched. I used the dial pad to broadcast a report that Ophion was sacking Urd's Temple—right in the middle of one of those stupid daily announcements. I figured a unit would be sent here. Probably the biggest and baddest they had, which happened to also be the closest."

He remembered now—they'd avoided Pollux and Mordoc, along with the Hind's dreadwolves, on the walk over here. "Your voice will be recognized—"

"I recorded the message, then played it through the Gate using a voice-warping app," she said with a grim smile. "And I made sure to move fast enough that the cameras couldn't pick it up as more than a blur, don't worry."

He could only gape at her, his clever, brilliant Bryce. Gods, he loved her.

Crouching behind the altar again as the fighting pressed into the temple, Hunt breathed, "We have to find some way to get through those doors unseen."

"If you can give me a minute . . ." She brushed a shaking hand to her chest. The scar there.

But Hunt knew. Only time would allow her to gain back her strength, and it would sure as fuck take longer than they had to spare.

Hunt banked his lightning, fearful Pollux would spy it. The Hammer drew closer, Mordoc a menacing shadow behind him. Where they walked, rebels died. Hunt couldn't get a visual on Pippa.

Bryce panted, and Hunt scented her blood before he looked. Her nose was bleeding. "What the fuck?" he exploded, covering her with his body as a stray spray of bullets shot over the top of the altar.

"My brain might be soup," she hissed, though fear shone in her eyes.

If he could unleash his lightning, he might be able to fry their way out. No matter that everyone would know who'd been there, especially if Mordoc picked up on the scents afterward, but . . . he'd take that chance. For Bryce, he'd risk it.

They could, of course, say that they had been fighting Ophion, but there was a chance that the Hind would decide this was the moment to reveal what she knew.

"Hold on to me," Hunt warned, reaching for Bryce as something crept out of the shadows behind Urd's throne.

A black dog. Massive, with fangs as long as Hunt's hand.

The Helhound motioned to the throne with a clawed paw. Then he vanished behind it.

There was no time to think. Hunt scooped up Bryce and ran, ducking low through the shadows between the altar and the dais, praying no one saw them in the chaos and smoke—

He whipped behind the throne to find the space empty. No sign of Baxian.

A growl came behind him, and Hunt whirled to the back of the throne. It wasn't solid stone at all, but an open doorway, leading into a narrow stairwell.

Hunt didn't question their luck as he sprinted through the stone doorway. Baxian, now in angelic form, shoved it shut behind him. Sealing them entirely in darkness.

Baxian lit the tight steps downward with his phone. Hunt held on to Bryce. From the way she clung to him, he wasn't entirely certain she could walk.

"I heard Pollux give the order to come here over the radio," Baxian said, hurrying ahead, wings rustling. Hunt let the male lead, glancing behind them to ensure the door didn't open. But the seal was perfect. Not so much as a crack of light shone. "Given how pissed Pippa was after Ydra, I figured it was you lot involved. I researched the history of this temple. Found rumors about the door hidden in the throne. It's what took me some time—finding the tunnel entrance in. Some priestess must have used it recently, though. Her scent was all over the alley and fake wall that leads in here."

Hunt and Bryce said nothing. That was twice now that Baxian had interfered to save them from the Hind and Pollux. And now Pippa.

"Is Spetsos dead?" Baxian asked, as they reached the bottom of the stairs and entered a long tunnel.

"Don't know," Hunt grunted. "She probably escaped and left her people to die."

"Lidia will be pissed she didn't catch her, but Pollux seemed to be enjoying himself," Baxian said, shaking his head. They walked until they hit a crossroads flanked by skulls and bones placed in tiny alcoves. Catacombs. "I don't think they had any clue you were there," Baxian went on, "though how they got tipped off—"

Bryce moved, so fast Hunt didn't have time to stop her from dropping out of his arms.

To stop her from unslinging her rifle and pointing it at Baxian. "Stop right there."

Bryce wiped the blood dripping from her nose on her shoulder as she aimed the rifle at the Helhound, paused in the catacombs' crossroads.

Her head pounded relentlessly, her mouth felt as dry as the

Psamathe Desert, and her stomach was a churning eddy of bile. She was never teleporting again. Never, ever, *ever*.

"Why the fuck do you keep popping up?" Bryce seethed, not taking her attention off the Helhound. Hunt didn't so much as move at her side. "Hunt says you're not spying for the Hind or the Asteri, but I don't fucking believe it. Not for one second." She clicked off the safety. "So tell me the gods-damned truth before I put this bullet through your head."

Baxian walked to one of the curved walls full of skulls. Didn't seem to care that he was a foot away from the barrel of her gun. He ran a finger down the brown skull of what seemed to be some fanged Vanir, and said, "Through love, all is possible."

The rifle nearly tumbled from her fingers. "What?"

Baxian peeled back the collar of his battle-suit, revealing brown, muscled flesh. And a tattoo scrawled over the angel's heart in familiar handwriting.

Through love, all is possible.

She knew that handwriting. "Why," she asked carefully, voice shaking, "do you have Danika's handwriting tattooed on you?"

Baxian's dark eyes became pained. Empty. "Because Danika was my mate."

65

Bryce aimed the rifle at Baxian again. "You are a fucking *liar*."

Baxian left his collar open, Danika's handwriting inked there for all to see. "I loved her. More than anything."

Hunt said harshly, words echoing in the dry catacombs around them, "This isn't fucking funny, asshole."

Baxian turned pleading eyes to him. Bryce wanted to claw the male's face off. "She was my mate. Ask Sabine. Ask her why she ran the night she burst into your apartment. She's always hated and feared me—because I saw how she treated her daughter and wouldn't put up with it. Because I've promised to turn her into carrion one day for what Danika endured. That's why Sabine left the party last night so fast. To avoid me."

Bryce didn't lower the gun. "You're full of shit."

Baxian splayed his arms, wings rustling. "Why the fuck would I lie about this?"

"To win our trust," Hunt said.

Bryce couldn't get a breath down. It had nothing to do with the teleporting. "I would have known. If Danika had a mate, I would have *known*—"

"Oh? You think she would have told you that her mate was someone in Sandriel's triarii? The Helhound? You think she'd have run home to dish about it?"

"Fuck you," Bryce spat, focusing the scope right between his eyes. "And fuck your lies."

Baxian walked up to the gun. To the barrel. Pushed it down and against his heart, right up against the tattoo in Danika's handwriting. "I met her two years before she died," he said quietly.

"She and Thorne—"

Baxian let out a laugh so bitter it cracked her soul. "Thorne was delusional to think she'd ever be with him."

"She fucked around," Bryce seethed. "You were no one to her."

"I had two years with her," Baxian said. "She didn't fuck anyone else during that time."

Bryce stilled, doing the mental tally. Right before her death, hadn't she teased Danika about . . .

"Two years," she whispered. "She hadn't gone on a date in two years." Hunt gaped at her now. "But she . . ." She racked her memory. Danika had hooked up constantly throughout college, but a few months into their senior year and the year after . . . She'd partied, but stopped the casual sex. Bryce choked out, "It's not possible."

Baxian's face was bleak, even in the dimness of the catacombs. "Believe me, I didn't want it, either. But we saw each other and knew."

Hunt murmured, "That's why your behavior changed. You met Danika right after I left."

"It changed *everything* for me," Baxian said.

"How did you even meet each other?" Bryce demanded.

"There was a gathering of wolves—Pangeran and Valbaran. The Prime sent Danika as his emissary."

Bryce remembered that. How pissed Sabine had been that Danika had been tapped to go, and not her. Two weeks later, Danika had come back, and she'd seemed subdued for a few days. She'd said it was exhaustion but . . .

"You're not a wolf. Why were you even there?" Danika couldn't have been with Baxian, couldn't have had a *mate* and not told her about it, not smelled like it—

She was a bloodhound. With that preternatural sense of smell, she'd know better than anyone how to hide a scent—how to detect if any trace of it had remained on her.

"I wasn't at the gathering. She sought me out while she was there."

"*Why?*"

"Because she was researching shifter ancestry. Mine is . . . unique."

"You shift into a dog," Bryce raged. "What's unique about that?" Even Hunt gave her a disapproving frown. She didn't care. She was sick of these surprises about Danika, about all the things she'd never known—

"She wanted to know about my shifter ancestry. Really old shifter ancestry that manifested in me after years of lying dormant. She was examining the most ancient bloodlines in our world and saw a name on an early ancestor's family tree that could be traced all the way to the last living descendant: me."

"What the Hel could you even tell her if it was that ancient?" Hunt asked.

"Ultimately, nothing. But once we knew we were mates, once we'd sealed it . . . She started to open up about what she was looking into."

"Was it about the synth?" Bryce asked.

"No." Baxian clenched his jaw. "I think the synth was a cover for something else. Her death was because of the research she was doing."

Through love, all is possible. One last clue from Danika. To look where she'd stamped the phrase—right on this male.

So Bryce said, "Why did she care about any of this?"

"She wanted to know where we came from. The shifters, the Fae. All of us. She wanted to know what we'd once been. If it might inform our future." Baxian's throat worked. "She was also . . . She told me she wanted to find an alternative to Sabine."

"*She* was the alternative to Sabine," Bryce snapped.

"She had a feeling she might not live long enough for that," Baxian said hoarsely. "Danika didn't want to leave the wolves' future in Sabine's hands. She was seeking a way to protect them by uncovering a possible alternative in the bloodline to challenge Sabine."

It was so . . . so *Danika.*

"But after we met," Baxian went on, "she started hunting for a way into a world where we could be together—since there was no way Sabine or Sandriel, or even the Asteri, would have allowed it."

Bryce clicked the safety back on the gun and lowered it to the ground.

Baxian said with quiet ferocity, "I was so fucking glad when you killed Micah. I knew . . . I had this *feeling* that prick was involved in her death."

Glad someone finally put a bullet through Micah's head, Baxian had said when they'd first met. Bryce surveyed the male who'd loved her friend—the male she'd never known about. "Why wouldn't she have told me?"

"She wanted to. We didn't dare talk on the phone or write to each other. We had a standing agreement to meet at a hotel in Forvos— I could never get away from Sandriel for long—on a given day every two months. She worried that the Asteri would use me against her to keep her in line, if they found out about us."

"Did she tell you she loved you?" Bryce pushed.

"Yes," Baxian replied without a moment of hesitation.

Danika had once claimed she'd only said those words to Bryce. To *her*, not to this . . . stranger. This male who'd freely and willingly served Sandriel. Hunt had been given no choice in that matter. "She didn't care that you're a monster?"

Baxian flinched. "After I met Danika, I tried my best to counteract all I did for Sandriel, though sometimes all I could do was . . . lessen Sandriel's evil." Yet his eyes softened. "She loved you, Bryce. You were the most important person in the world to her. You were—"

"Shut up. Just . . . shut the fuck up," Bryce whispered. "I don't want to hear it."

"Don't you?" he challenged. "Don't you want to know all of it? Isn't that why you've been digging around? You want to know—*need* to know what Danika knew. What she was up to, what she kept secret."

Her face hardened into stone. She said flatly, "Fine. Let's start with this one, if you knew her so well. How did Danika meet Sofie

Renast? You ever hear that name in all your secret little conversations? What did Danika want from her?"

Baxian bristled. "Danika learned about Sofie's existence while investigating thunderbird lineage as part of her research into shifters and our origins. She traced the bloodlines—and then confirmed it by tracking her down and scenting her. Being Danika, she didn't let Sofie walk away without answering some questions."

Bryce stilled. "What kind of questions?" Hunt put a hand on her shoulder.

Baxian shook his head. "I don't know. And I don't know how they pivoted to working together on the Ophion stuff. But I think Danika had some theories about thunderbirds beyond the lineage thing. About their power in particular."

Bryce frowned. "Do you know why Sofie Renast might have felt the need to carve a series of numbers and letters on herself while she drowned a few weeks ago?"

"Solas," Baxian murmured. And then he recited the sequence from Sofie's body, down to the last numeral. "Was that it?"

"What the fuck are you playing at, Baxian?" Hunt growled, but Bryce snapped at the same time, "What *is* it?"

Baxian's eyes flashed. "It's a system of numbering rooms used in only one place on Midgard. The Asteri Archives."

Hunt swore. "And how in Urd's name do you know that?"

"Because I gave it to Danika."

Bryce was surprised enough that words failed her.

"Sandriel was the Asteri's pet." Baxian turned to Hunt. "You know that, Athalar. She made me serve as escort on one of her visits to their palace. When they brought her down to the archives for a meeting, I saw them go through that door. When Sandriel emerged, she was pale. It was odd enough that I memorized the series of numbers and letters and passed it to Danika later as something to look into. Danika became . . . obsessed with it. She wouldn't tell me why, or what she thought might be in there, but she had theories. Ones that she said would alter this very world. But she couldn't go in herself. She was too recognizable. She knew the Asteri were already watching her."

"So after she met Sofie, Danika gave her the information, and had Sofie sneak in to investigate," Bryce murmured. "Since Sofie's record wouldn't have shown anything suspicious about her."

Baxian nodded. "From what I gleaned from the Hind's reports, it took Sofie three years of work to get in. Three years of spying and going undercover as one of the archivists. I'm assuming she finally found a way to sneak into that room—and ran to Kavalla soon after. By that time, Danika was . . . gone. She died without ever learning what was in the room."

"But Sofie did," Bryce said quietly.

"Whatever she learned was in that room," Hunt agreed. "That must have been the intel Sofie planned to use as leverage against Ophion—and against the Asteri."

"Something war-changing," Bryce said. "Something big."

"Why wouldn't this room identifier come up on search engines?" Hunt asked Baxian.

The Helhound tucked in his wings. "The Asteri don't have any of their palace blueprints on the interweb. Even their library cataloging system is secret. Anything digitized is highly encrypted."

"And if we had someone who could hack into anything?" Bryce asked.

Baxian again smiled bitterly. "Then I guess you'd have a chance at finding out what was in that room."

"This is a totally nonsensical way of numbering rooms," Declan muttered, typing away on the sectional couch in Ruhn's house. Bryce had run there with Hunt after leaving Baxian in the alley the tunnel had led to, a few blocks from Urd's Temple. She was still reeling.

She'd turned on her phone to find several missed calls from Tharion. The Viper Queen had given him a heads-up about Ophion—only a few minutes too late. Flynn had nearly thrown a fit when Ruhn had explained what had happened.

At least no word had emerged about their connection to the rebel attack on Urd's Temple, as the news was calling it. Pollux, Mordoc, and the Hind were hailed as heroes for stopping Pippa's forces from desecrating the sacred space. The only failure: Pippa had escaped.

Bryce would deal with that later. Would deal with a lot of other shit later.

Declan scratched his head. "You realize that what we're doing right now amounts to treason."

"We owe you big-time," Hunt said, sitting on the arm of the sofa.

"Pay me in booze," Declan said. "It'll be a comfort while I worry about when the dreadwolves will show up at my door."

"Here," Ruhn said, handing the male a glass of whiskey. "This'll start you off." Her brother dropped onto the cushions beside her. Across the couch, Hypaxia sat next to Ithan, quiet and watchful.

Bryce had let Hunt explain what they'd learned from Baxian. And let Ruhn explain the whole truth to the witch-queen and the sprites, who had draped themselves around Flynn's shoulders where he sat on Declan's other side.

But it was to Ithan that Bryce's attention kept returning. And as Declan focused, Bryce said quietly to the wolf, "Did you know about Danika and Baxian?" His face had revealed nothing.

"Of course not," Ithan said. "I thought she and Thorne . . ." He shook his head. "I have no idea what to make of it. I never once scented anything on her."

"Me neither. Maybe she was able to hide it with her bloodhound gift somehow." She cleared her throat. "It wouldn't have mattered to me."

"Really? It would have mattered to me," Ithan countered. "To everyone. Not only is Baxian not a wolf, he's . . ."

"An asshole," Hunt supplied without looking up from his phone.

"Yeah," Ithan said. "I mean, I get that he just saved your hides, but . . . still."

"Does it matter now?" Flynn asked. "I mean, no offense, but Danika's gone."

Bryce gave him a flat look. "Really? I had no idea."

Flynn flipped her off, and the sprites *ooohed* at his shoulder.

Bryce rolled her eyes. Exactly what Flynn needed: his own flock of cheerleaders trailing him at all hours. She said to Flynn, "Hey, remember that time you set a dragon free and were dumb enough to think she'd follow your orders?"

"Hey, remember that time you wanted to marry me and wrote *Lady Bryce Flynn* in all your notebooks?"

Hunt choked.

Bryce countered with, "Hey, remember when you pestered me for years to hook up with you, but I have something called standards—"

"This is highly unusual behavior for royals," Hypaxia observed.

"You have no idea," Ruhn muttered, earning a smile from the queen.

Noting the way her brother's face lit up, then dimmed . . . Did he know? About Hypaxia and Celestina? She had no idea what else might dampen his expression.

"Where's Tharion?" Hunt asked, surveying the house. "Shouldn't he be here?"

"He's upstairs," Ruhn said. They could fill Tharion in later, she supposed. And Cormac, once he'd finished with whatever his father wanted.

Declan suddenly cursed, frowning. Then he said, "There's good news and bad news."

"Bad news first," Bryce said.

"There's no way in Hel I can ever hack into this archival system. It's ironclad. I've never seen anything like it. It's gorgeous, actually."

"All right, tone down the fanboying," Ruhn grumbled. "What's the good news?"

"Their camera system in the Eternal Palace is *not* ironclad."

"So what the fuck does that get us?" Hunt asked.

"At the very least, I can confirm whether Sofie Renast ever gained access to that room."

"And where that room might be," Bryce murmured. Ithan and Hypaxia both nodded. "All right. Do it."

"Settle in," Declan warned. "We're in for a long night."

Ithan was dispatched to get Tharion after an hour, and Bryce was rewarded with the sight of a sleep-tousled mer entering the living room wearing nothing but his jeans.

Tharion plopped onto the couch beside Hypaxia, slinging his arm around the queen's shoulders and saying, "Hi, Pax."

Hypaxia waved off the mer. "Sleeping all afternoon?"

"Life of a playboy," Tharion said. Apparently, they'd become fast friends during the Summit. Bryce might have wondered if there was more between them, had she not found the witch with the Archangel the night before. She wondered if Tharion knew.

Wondered if it rankled her brother that the witch and the mer had stayed in touch since the Summit, and he'd had only silence from her. Ruhn didn't so much as frown.

Around midnight, Declan said, "Well, holy shit. There she is."

Hunt nearly trampled Ruhn as they hurried over. Bryce, of course, made it to Declan's side first, and swore. Hunt shoved Ruhn out of the way with an elbow and claimed the seat next to his mate. Ithan, Tharion, Hypaxia, and Flynn—sprites in tow—pressed in around them.

"She looks so young," Hunt murmured.

"She was," Ruhn said. Dec had pulled up the photo from Sofie's old university ID and had the program search for any faces that resembled hers in the footage.

Bryce had tried to call Cormac, but the prince hadn't answered his phone.

So they kept silent as Declan played the footage of the wood-and-marble subterranean library. From the camera mounted on the ceiling, they could see Sofie Renast, clad in some sort of white uniform that could only belong to one of the archivists, stalk by the ancient shelves.

"Door Seven-Eta-Dot-Three-Alpha-Omega," Declan said, pointing to a wooden door beyond the shelf. "You can make out the writing faintly beside it."

They could. Sofie slipped inside the room, using some sort of ID card to bypass the modern lock, then shut the carved door behind her.

"Fifteen minutes pass," Declan said, zooming ahead. "And then she's out again." Sofie walked from the room the same way she had entered it: calmly.

"She doesn't have anything on her," Hunt observed.

"I can't make out anything under her clothes, either," Ruhn agreed.

"Neither did the computer," Declan said. "She carried nothing in, nothing out. But her face is white as death." Just as Baxian claimed Sandriel's had been.

"When is this dated?" Bryce asked. Hunt squeezed her knee, like he needed to touch her, remind himself she was here and safe with him.

"Two months ago," Declan said. "Right before she went into Kavalla."

"It took *three years* of working undercover to get access to this room?" Ruhn said.

"Do you know how intense the security is?" Hunt asked. "I can't believe she made it in at all."

"I know it's fucking intense, Athalar," Ruhn said tightly.

Bryce said, "Well, we're going to have to beat her time."

They all faced her. Bryce's attention remained fixed on the screen, though. On the young woman walking out of the ancient library.

Hunt's stomach twisted. He had a feeling he knew what she was going to say even before Bryce declared, "We need to get to the Eternal City—and into those archives."

"Bryce," Hunt started, dread rushing through him. He might have made peace with their involvement with Cormac and Ophion, but this . . . this was on a whole new level. Perilously close to what he'd done leading the Fallen.

"I want to know what Sofie knew," Bryce said through her teeth. "What Danika was willing to risk so much to discover."

After the truth Baxian had dropped, she needed the full story more than ever. It didn't only have to do with wanting to use the intel as leverage against the Asteri. Danika had thought this information could change the world. Save it, somehow. How could she walk away from it now?

"You're talking about breaking into the most secure place on Midgard," Tharion interjected carefully. "Breaking into an enemy's stronghold."

"If Sofie Renast did it, I can, too."

Ruhn coughed. "You realize none of us know our way around the palace, Bryce. We'll be operating blind."

Hunt tensed beside her, and Bryce knew that particular sort of tautness on his face. Knew he was shutting out his vivid memories of the throne room, the dungeons. Blood and screaming and pain— that's all he recalled, he'd told her.

She leaned into his side. Offered what love she could through the touch.

"We won't be operating blind," Bryce said to Ruhn, lifting her chin. "I know someone who's intimately familiar with its layout."

Ithan sat on the couch long after Bryce and Athalar had gone home, and Ruhn, Dec, and Flynn had left for their Aux duties. The sprites had opted to follow Flynn, leaving Ithan and Tharion alone in the house.

"You ready for the shitshow we're about to enter?" the mer asked him, forearms on his knees as he leaned forward to play the video game on the big screen.

"I don't really have a choice but to be ready, right?" Ithan, playing on the split screen beside him, jammed his thumbs onto the controller buttons.

"You're probably used to high-stakes situations. You went to finals a couple times."

"Twice. And three times in high school."

"Yeah, I know. I mean, I watched you." Tharion flicked the switch on the controller, seemingly content to focus on the game. Like he wasn't a male who'd walked in and out of the Viper Queen's lair today. "You seem remarkably calm about everything that's been going down."

"Flynn said it doesn't make a difference if Danika was Baxian's mate, since she's, you know, dead." His chest ached. "I guess he's right."

"I meant about the rebels and the Under-King, but that's good to know."

Ithan shrugged. "After this spring, what the fuck is normal anyway?"

"True." They played for a few more minutes.

"What's the deal with you and the River Queen's daughter?" Ithan asked finally.

Tharion didn't take his eyes off the screen. "I've been betrothed to her for years. End of story."

"You love her?"

"Nope."

"Why get engaged to her, then?"

"Because I was horny and stupid and wanted to fuck her so badly that I swore myself to her, thinking I could undo it in the morning. Turns out, I couldn't."

"Rough, dude."

"Yep." Tharion paused the game. "You seeing anyone?"

Ithan had no idea why, but the wolf in the Astronomer's tank emerged before him. But he said carefully, "Ruhn didn't tell you about, uh, my past?"

"You mean about you having a thing for Bryce? No."

"Then how the fuck do you know?"

"She's Bryce. *Everyone* has got a thing for her."

"I used to like her."

"Uh-huh."

Ithan exposed his teeth. "I don't feel that way about her anymore."

"Good, because Athalar would probably kill you, then barbecue your corpse."

"He could try."

"He'd try, and he'd win, and I doubt slow-roasted wolf would taste that good, even doused in sauce."

"Whatever."

Tharion chuckled. "Don't do anything tragically romantic to prove yourself to her, okay? I've seen that shit go down before and it never works. Definitely not if you're dead."

"Not on my agenda, but thanks."

Tharion's expression turned serious. "I mean it. And . . . look, I bet Bryce will kick my balls into my throat for this, but if you have any unresolved business with anyone, I'd get it done before we go to the Eternal City. Just in case."

In case they didn't come back. Which seemed likely.

Ithan sighed. Set down his controller. Got up from the couch. Tharion arched a brow.

Ithan said, "There's something I have to do."

66

Y ou have to be ten kinds of stupid," Fury hissed at Bryce from where they sat at the dive bar's counter, nursing their drinks. Fury had initially refused to meet up when Bryce had called her last night, but Bryce had pestered her enough throughout the following morning that she'd agreed to meet here.

Bryce had barely been able to sleep, though Hunt had done a good job exhausting her. Her mind couldn't stop turning over the things she'd learned. Danika had a *mate*. Sabine had known about it. Danika's mate still loved her.

And Danika had never told Bryce about any of it.

"I know it's insane," Bryce murmured, swirling her whiskey and ginger beer. "But any help you can give me . . ."

"You need a *shit*-ton of help, but not with this. You're out of your mind." Fury leaned closer, getting in Bryce's face. "Do you know what they'll do to you if you're caught? What they might do to your family, to Juniper, to punish you? Did you see what the Harpy did to those rebels? Do you know what Mordoc likes to do to *his* victims? I make sure to stay well out of his path. These people are soulless. The Asteri will gladly let them go to work on you and everyone you love."

"I know," Bryce said carefully. "So help me make sure I don't get caught."

"You're assuming I just have blueprints of the crystal palace lying around."

"I know you've been there. You have a better memory than anyone I know. You mean to tell me you didn't take mental notes while you were there? That you didn't notice the exits, the guards, the security systems?"

"Yeah, but you're talking about the archives. I can only give you a vague layout. I've only ever walked the halls—never gone into the rooms."

"So don't you want to know what's *in* those rooms? What Danika suspected might be inside that one room in particular?"

Fury swigged from her vodka on the rocks. "Don't try to convert me to your bullshit cause. I've done work for both sides and neither is worth the time of day. They're certainly not worth your life."

"We're not working for either side."

"Then what side are you working for?"

"Truth," Bryce said simply. "We want the truth."

Fury studied her, and Bryce withstood the searing assessment. "You've definitely lost your mind, then. I'm going to take June out of this city for a while. Lie low."

"Good." Bryce wished she could warn her parents without raising suspicions. She tapped her foot on the bronze footrest beneath the bar.

"Can you take Syrinx with you?" She wouldn't leave without knowing he'd be cared for.

"Yeah." Fury sighed and signaled the bartender for another vodka. "I'll get you what intel I can."

Tharion found his fiancée sitting on the edge of the quay off the Bone Quarter, her delicate feet dipping into the turquoise water, sending waves splashing in the sunlight. Her black hair was unbound, cascading down her slim back in a luxurious fall.

Once, that beauty had staggered him, snagged him. Now it merely . . . weighed.

"Thank you for meeting me." He'd sent the otter an hour ago. She twisted, looking back at him, a pretty smile lighting her face.

Tharion swallowed hard. She'd been so . . . starry-eyed at the party the other night. So elated to be there, dancing and laughing.

A decade. A decade wasted for him—and for her.

He'd advised Holstrom to settle any unfinished business. He needed to do the same.

"I, ah . . ." Tharion paced a step, keenly aware of the sobeks lurking in the river, appraising them with slitted eyes. The mer guards positioned near the dock, spears within throwing range, ready to impale him. "I wanted to talk to you."

Her look turned wary. He could have sworn the sobeks drifted closer. Tourists spotted them and began snapping photos along the quay. Saw the River Queen's daughter and began snapping photos of the beauty, too.

This was an awfully public place for this kind of meeting, but he knew if he did this at the Blue Court, if her mother got word of it before he could leave, she'd keep him Beneath, as trapped as any of the mortals who'd once been dragged below by the mer.

"You wish to call off our betrothal," she said. Thunderclouds threatened in her eyes.

Instinct had him fumbling for soothing lies to comfort her. But . . . if he was going to die, either at the Asteri's or her mother's hand, he wanted to do it knowing he'd been honest. "Yes."

"You think I did not know? All this time? A male who wanted to marry me would have acted by now." Her nose crinkled in anger. "How many years did I spend trying to coax some affection, some intimacy from you? Something to heal this?"

He refrained from saying that she'd also been vindictive and childish and sullen.

The water at her feet thrashed. "Yet it was always *I'm busy working on a case.* Then it was the next case, and the next. Then your wave skimmer would break, then your mother would need you, then your friends would require you." Power stirred around her. "You believe it is not obvious to all of the Blue Court that you don't *want* to come back home?"

His breathing stalled. He'd vastly underestimated her. He dared ask, "Why didn't you call it off, if you knew all that, then?"

"Because I harbored a shred of hope you might change. Like a fool, I prayed to Ogenas every day that you might come to me of your own free will. But that hope has withered now." She stood, somehow towering over him even though she was more than a foot shorter. Her words were a chill wind skittering over the water. "You want to stay here, amid this filth and noise?"

"I . . ." He scrambled for the words. "I do."

But she slowly shook her head. "My mother warned me of this. Of you. You do not have a true heart. You never did."

Good. At least she finally knew the truth. But he said as gently as he could, "I have to leave the city for a while, but let's talk about this more when I'm back. I feel like there's a lot of air to clear here."

"No more talking." She retreated a step to the edge of the quay, bristling with power. Waves crashed against the stones, spraying her feet. "Come Beneath with me."

"I can't." He wouldn't.

Her teeth flashed, more shark than humanoid. "Then we'll see what my mother has to say about this," she hissed, and leapt into the river.

Tharion debated jumping in after her, but—why? His palms slickened with sweat. He had thirty minutes, he supposed. Thirty minutes until he was hauled Beneath by his fin, and he'd never, ever leave again.

Tharion dragged his hands through his hair, panting. He peered westward toward the low-lying buildings beyond the CBD. Celestina would never interfere, and Bryce and Ruhn didn't have the authority. And there was no chance in Hel that Commander Sendes and the *Depth Charger* would get here in thirty minutes.

Only one person in Crescent City might stand up to the River Queen and survive. One person even the River Queen might balk at crossing. One person who valued powerful fighters and would hide them from their enemies. And one person he could reach in thirty minutes.

Tharion didn't think twice before he began running.

"Thanks again for getting me in here," Ithan said to Hypaxia, who sat in the waiting room of the Prime's study at the Den. It was weird to have needed to ask a veritable stranger to get him safely into his own home, but . . . this was the only way.

The witch-queen offered him a soft smile. "It's what friends do, isn't it?"

He bowed his head. "I'm honored to be called your friend." He'd been proud to walk through the gates moments before at the side of this strong, kind female. No matter that the wolves on duty had sneered as he'd passed.

A reedy voice grunted his name, and Ithan rose from the leather chair, offering Hypaxia a smile. "I'll be quick."

She waved him off, and Ithan braced himself as he entered the old wolf's formal study. Wood-paneled walls crammed with bookshelves gleamed in the midday light. The Prime sat at his desk, hunched over what seemed to be a stack of paperwork. Sabine stood above him. Monitoring every shaking stroke of his hand.

Ithan stiffened. Sabine's teeth gleamed.

Yet the old wolf lifted his head. "It is good to see you, boy."

"Thank you for meeting with me." Sabine knew that Danika had been sworn to a mate. That Baxian was in this city. Ithan shoved the thought away. "I know you're busy, so—"

"Out with it," Sabine snarled.

Ithan let her see the wolf in him, the dominance he didn't shove down like he always had. But the Prime said, "Go ahead, Ithan."

Ithan squared his shoulders, tucking his hands behind his back. The same pose he'd taken when getting instructions from Coach. To Hel with it, then.

"One of the Astronomer's mystics is a wolf. An *Alpha* wolf." The words were met with silence, but Sabine's eyes narrowed. "She's from Nena—sold so young she doesn't know her name, or her age. I'm not even sure if she knows she's an Alpha. But she's a wolf, and she's no better than a slave in that tank. I . . . We can't leave her there."

"What business is it of ours?" Sabine demanded.

"She's a wolf," Ithan repeated. "That should be all we need to help her."

"There are plenty of wolves. And plenty of Alphas. They are not all our responsibility." Sabine exposed her teeth again. "Is this part of some scheme you and that half-breed whore are concocting?"

She sneered as she said it, but . . . Sabine had come to Bryce's apartment that night to warn her to stay out of wolf business. Out of some fear, however unfounded, that Bryce would somehow back Ithan—as if Sabine herself could be at risk of being overthrown.

Ithan tucked that aside. Tossing out wild accusations wouldn't help his cause right now. So he said carefully, "I just want to help the mystic."

"Is this what you've dedicated your time to now, Holstrom? Charity cases?"

Ithan swallowed his retort. "Danika would have done something."

"Danika was an idealistic fool," Sabine spat. "Don't waste our time with this."

Ithan looked to the Prime, but the old wolf said nothing. Did nothing. Ithan turned to the door again and strode out.

Hypaxia rose to her feet as he appeared. "Done so soon?"

"Yeah, I guess." He'd told someone about the mystic. He supposed . . . Well, now he supposed he could go to Pangera with few regrets.

Sabine strutted out of the study. She growled low in her throat at Ithan, but faltered upon seeing Hypaxia. Hypaxia held the wolf's stare with steely calm. Sabine only snorted and stalked away, slamming the hall door behind her.

"Let's go," Ithan said to Hypaxia.

But the door to the study opened again, and the Prime stood there, a hand on the jamb to support himself. "The mystic," the

— 715 —

Prime said, panting slightly, as if the walk from his desk to the door had winded him. "What did she look like?"

"Brown hair. Medium brown, I think. Pale skin." A common enough description.

"And her scent? Was it like snow and embers?"

Ithan stilled. The ground seemed to sway. "How do you know that?"

The old wolf bowed his silvery head. "Because Sabine is not the only Fendyr heir."

Ithan rocked back on his heels at that. Was that why Sabine had come to the apartment that night to warn off Bryce? Not to keep Ithan from becoming the Prime Apparent, but to scare Bryce away before she could discover there was a true alternative to Sabine. A legitimate one.

Because Bryce would stop at nothing to find that other heir.

And Sabine would kill them to prevent it.

67

Tharion burst into the Viper Queen's nest. He had only minutes until all Hel broke loose.

Ariadne was sprawled on her belly on the carpet, a book splayed open before her, bare feet bobbing above her ample backside. The sort of ample backside that on any other day, he'd truly appreciate. The dragon didn't remove her focus from her book as she said, "She's in the back."

Tharion ran for the rear room. The Viper Queen lounged on a couch before the window overlooking the fighting pit where the current match was unfolding, reading something on her electronic tablet. "Mer," she said by way of greeting.

"I want to be one of your prize fighters."

She slowly turned her head toward him. "I don't take freelancers."

"Then buy me."

"You're not a slave, mer."

"I'll sell myself to you."

The words sounded as insane as they felt. But he had no other options. His alternative was another form of slavery. At least here, he'd be away from that stifling court.

The Viper Queen set down her tablet. "A civitas selling himself into slavery. Such a thing is not done."

"You're law unto yourself. You can do it."

"Your queen will flood my district for spite."

"She isn't dumb enough to fuck with you."

"I take it that's why you're rushing into my care."

Tharion checked his phone. Ten minutes left at most. "It's either be trapped in a palace down there or trapped up here. I choose here, where I won't be required to breed some royal offspring."

"You are becoming a *slave*. To be free of the River Queen." Even the Vipe looked like she was wondering if he'd gone mad.

"Is there another way? Because I'm out of ideas."

The Viper Queen angled her head, bob shifting with the movement. "A good businessperson would tell you no, and accept this absurd offer." Her purple lips parted in a smile. "But . . ." Her gaze swept across the room, to the Fae males standing guard by an unmarked door. He had no idea what lay beyond. Possibly her bedchamber. Why it needed to be guarded when she wasn't inside was beyond him. "They defected from the Autumn King. Swore allegiance to me. They've proved loyal."

"So I'll do it. I hereby defect. Give me some way to immerse myself in water once a day and I'm set."

She chuckled. "You think you're the first mer fighter I've had? There is a tub a few levels down, with water piped in right from the Istros. It's yours. But defecting . . . That is not as easy as simply saying the words." She stood, rolling back the sleeve of her black jumpsuit to expose her wrist. A tattoo of a snake twining around a crescent moon lay there. She lifted her wrist to her mouth and bit, and blood—darker than usual—welled where her teeth had been. "Drink."

The floor began rumbling, and Tharion knew it wasn't from the fight. Knew something ancient and primordial was coming for him, to drag him back to the watery depths.

He grabbed her wrist and brought it to his mouth.

If he defected from the River Queen, then he could defect from the Viper Queen one day, couldn't he?

He didn't ask. Didn't doubt it as he laid his lips on her wrist, and her blood filled his mouth.

Burned his mouth. His throat.

Tharion staggered back, choking, grabbing at his neck. Her blood, her venom dissolved his throat, his chest, his heart—

Cold, piercing and eternal, erupted through him. Tharion crashed to his knees.

The rumbling halted. Then retreated. Like whatever it had been hunting for had vanished.

Tharion panted, bracing for the icy death that awaited him.

But nothing happened. Only that vague sense of cold. Of . . . calm. He slowly lifted his eyes to the Viper Queen.

She smiled down at him. "Seems like that did the trick." He struggled to his feet, swaying. He rubbed at the hollow, strange place in his chest. "Your first fight is tonight," she said, still smiling. "I suggest you rest."

"I need to help my friends finish something first."

Her brows rose. "Ah. This business with Ophion."

"Of a sort. I need to be able to help them."

"You should have bargained for that freedom before swearing yourself to me."

"Allow me this and I'll come back and fight for you until I'm chum."

She laughed softly. "Fine, Tharion Ketos. Help your friends. But when you are done . . ." Her eyes glowed green, and his body turned distant. Her will was his, her desires his own. He'd crawl through coals to fulfill her orders. "You return to me."

"I return to you." He spoke in a voice that was and wasn't his own. Some small part of him screamed.

The Viper Queen flicked a hand toward the archway. "Go."

Not entirely of his own volition, he stalked back down the hallway. Each step away from her had that distance lessening, his thoughts again becoming his own, even as . . .

Ariadne peered up from her book as he stalked past. "Are you mad?"

Tharion retorted, "I could ask the same of you." Her face tightened, but she returned to her book.

With each step toward his friends, he could have sworn a long, invisible chain stretched. Like an endless leash, tethering him—no matter where he went, no matter how far—back to this place.

Never to return to the life he'd traded away.

Ithan sat on a park bench in Moonwood, a few blocks from the Den, still reeling from the world-shattering revelation the Prime had dropped on him.

The wolf mystic was a Fendyr. An *Alpha* Fendyr.

Ithan hadn't been able to get any more than that out of the Prime before the male's gaze had gone murky, and he'd needed to sit down again. Hypaxia had worked some healing magic to ease whatever pains ailed him, and he'd been asleep at his desk a moment later.

Ithan breathed in the fall day. "I think I've put her in grave danger."

Hypaxia straightened. "In what way?"

"I think Sabine knows. Or has already guessed." Another Alpha in the heritage bloodline could destroy the wolves. But how the fuck had she wound up in that tank? And in Nena? "Sabine will kill her. Even if Sabine thinks she *might* be a Fendyr Alpha, if there have been rumors about it before now . . . Sabine will destroy any threat to her power."

"So the mystic isn't some sister or long-lost daughter?"

"I don't think so. Sabine had an elder brother, but she defeated him in open combat decades before I was born. Took his title as Prime Apparent and became Alpha. I thought he died, but . . . maybe he was exiled. I have no idea."

Hypaxia's face turned grave. "So what can be done?"

He swallowed. "I don't like going back on my promises."

"But you wish to leave my side to look into this."

"Yes. And"—he shook his head—"I can't go to Pangera with the others. If there's a Fendyr heir who isn't Sabine . . ." It might mean that the future Danika had hoped for could come to pass. If he could find some way to keep the mystic alive. And get her free of the Astronomer's tank.

"I need to stay here," he said finally. "To guard her." He didn't care if he had to camp on the street outside of the Astronomer's place. Wolves didn't abandon each other. Granted, friends didn't abandon each other, either, but he knew Bryce and the others would get it.

"I need to find the truth," Ithan said. Not just for his people. But for his own future.

"I'll tell the others," Hypaxia offered. "Though I'll miss you as my guard."

"I'm sure Flynn and his backup singers will be happy to protect you." Hypaxia laughed softly. But Ithan said, "Don't tell them—don't tell Bryce, I mean. About the other Fendyr heir. She'd be distracted by it, at a time when she needs to focus elsewhere."

And this task . . . this task was *his*.

He hadn't been there to help Danika that night she'd died. But he was here now. Urd had left him alive—perhaps for this. He'd fulfill what Danika had left unfinished. He'd protect this Fendyr heir—no matter what.

"Just tell the others that I need to stay here for wolf stuff."

"Why not tell them yourself?"

He got to his feet. He might already be too late. "There's no time to waste," he said to the queen, and bowed to her. "Thanks for everything."

Hypaxia's mouth curled upward in a sad smile. "Be careful, Ithan."

"You too."

He broke into a jog, pulling out his phone as he did. He sent the message to Bryce before he could second-guess it. *I've got something important to do. Hypaxia will fill you in. But I wanted to say thanks. For not hating my guts. And having my back. You always had my back.*

She replied immediately. *Always will.* She added a few hearts that had his own cracking.

Pocketing his phone, breathing in that old ache, Ithan shifted.

For the first time in weeks, he shifted, and it didn't hurt one bit. Didn't leave him feeling the ache of exile, of being packless. No, his wolf form . . . it had focus. A purpose.

Ithan darted through the streets, running as fast as he could toward the Astronomer's place to begin his long watch.

Ruhn hadn't seen Day since the night of the ball. Since he'd kissed her. Since that other male had dragged her away, and pain had filled her voice.

But now she sat on the couch before him. Quiet and wary.

"Hey," Ruhn said.

"I can't see you anymore," she said in answer.

Ruhn drew up short. "Why?"

"What happened between us on the equinox is never to happen again." She rose. "It was dangerous, and reckless, and utter madness. Pippa Spetsos was in your city. Attacked your temple with her Lightfall unit. Lunathion is soon to become a battlefield."

He crossed his arms. Drew his focus inward, to the instinctual veil of night and stars. He'd never figured out where it had come from, why his mind had automatically hidden him, but—there. A neat little knot in his mind.

A tug on it, and it fell away, dropping all the night and stars. Letting her see all of him. "What happened to you? Are you hurt?"

"I'm fine." Her voice was tight. "I can't jeopardize all I've sacrificed for."

"And kissing me is a threat to that?"

"It distracts me from my purpose! It throws me from my vigilance! *It will catch up to me.*" She paced a few feet. "I wish I were normal. That I had met you under any other circumstances, that I had met you long ago, before I got tangled in this." Her chest heaved, flames flickering. She lifted her head, no doubt meeting his stare through the barrier of flames. "I told you that you remind me that I am alive. I meant that. Every word. But it's because of that feeling that I'll likely wind up dead, and you with me."

"I don't understand the threat," he said. "Surely a kiss that's good enough to distract you isn't a bad thing." He winked, desperate for her to smile.

"The male who . . . interrupts us. He will slaughter you if he finds out. He'll make me watch."

"You fear him." Something primal stirred in Ruhn.

"Yes. His wrath is terrible. I've seen what he does to enemies. I wouldn't wish it upon anyone."

"Can't you leave him?"

She laughed, harsh and hollow. "No. My fate is bound to his."

"Your fate is bound to mine." The words echoed into the darkness.

Ruhn reached for her hand. Took the flames within his own. They parted enough for him to see her slim, fiery fingers as he stroked his thumb over them. "My mind found yours in the darkness. Across an ocean. No fancy crystal required. You think that's nothing?"

He glimpsed enough of her eyes to see that they were closed. Her head bowed. "I can't."

But she didn't stop him when he stepped closer. When his other hand slid around her waist. "I'm going to find you," he said against her burning hair. "I'll find you one day, I promise." She shuddered, but melted into him. Like she'd yielded any attempt at restraint. "You remind me that I'm alive, too," he whispered.

Her arms came around him. She was slender—on the taller side, but with a delicate frame. And insane curves. Lush hips, full breasts that pushed against his chest with tantalizing softness. That sweet, tempting ass.

She murmured against his pec, "I never told you the ending of the story from the other night."

"With the witch-turned-monster?"

"It didn't end badly." He didn't dare breathe. "As the witch fell to the earth, the prince's arrow through her heart, the forest transformed her into a monster of claws and fangs. She ripped the prince and his hounds to shreds." Her fingers began trailing up his spine. "She remained a monster for a hundred years, roaming the forest, killing all who drew near. A hundred years, so long that she forgot she had once been a witch, had once possessed a home and a forest she loved."

Her breath was warm against his chest. "But one day, a warrior arrived in the forest. He'd heard of the monster so vicious none could kill it and live. She set out to slaughter him, but when the warrior beheld her, he was not afraid. He stared at her, and she at him, and he wept because he didn't see a thing of nightmares, but a creature of beauty. He saw her, and he was not afraid of her, and he loved her." She released a shuddering breath. "His love transformed her back into a witch, melting away all that she'd become. They dwelled in peace in the forest for the rest of their immortal lives."

"I like that ending much better," he said, and she huffed a soft laugh.

He dipped his head, kissing her neck, breathing in the subtle scent of her. His cock instantly hardened. Fuck yes. This scent, this female—

A sense of rightness settled into his bones like a stone dropped in a pond. Her hand began stroking up his spine again. His balls tightened with each trailing caress.

Then her mouth was on his pec, flaming lips grazing over the swirling tattoo there. The pierced nipple on his left pec. Her tongue flicked at the hoop, and his brain went haywire as he realized he was naked, or had somehow willed his clothes gone, because that was his bare skin she was touching, kissing.

And she . . . He ran his hands over her waist again. Smooth, velvety soft skin greeted him.

"You want to do this?" he ground out.

She kissed his other nipple. "Yes."

"I'm not even sure we can have sex like this."

"I don't see why not." Her fingers skated down to the top of his ass, taunting.

Ruhn's cock throbbed. "Only one way to find out," he managed to say.

Day huffed another breathy laugh and lifted her head. Ruhn just took her face between his hands and kissed her. She opened for him, and their tongues met, and she was as sweet as summer wine, and he needed to be in her, needed to touch and savor all of her.

Ruhn hoisted her up, and she wrapped her legs around his middle, his cock dangerously close to where it wanted to be. But he carried her to the fainting couch, gently laying her down before climbing atop her. "Let me see your face," he breathed, sliding a hand between her legs.

"Never," she said, and Ruhn didn't care, not as his fingers slicked through her soaked sex. Utterly ready for him.

He spread her knees and knelt between them. Dragged his tongue up her center—

He bucked, like his cock had a mind of its own, like it *needed* to be in her, or it was going to fucking erupt right there—

Ruhn fisted himself, pumping slowly as he licked her again.

Day moaned, her chest heaving, and he was rewarded with the sight of her breasts. Then her arms. Then her stomach and legs, and finally—

She was still crafted of fire, but he could clearly see the body now. Only her head remained in those flames, which shrank until they were no more than a mask over her features.

Long hair cascaded down her torso, and he ran a hand through it. "You're beautiful," he said.

"You haven't seen my face."

"I don't need to," he said. He laid a hand on her heart. "What you do, every minute of every single day . . . I've never met anyone like you."

"I've never met a male like you, either."

"Yeah?"

"*Yeah*," she said, and he punished her for the sass in her voice by licking her again, drawing another gasp. "Ruhn."

Fuck, he loved his name on her lips. He slipped a finger into her, finding her mind-meltingly tight. She was going to drive him wild.

She tugged on his shoulders, hauling him up. "Please," she said, and he hissed as her fingers wrapped around his cock and guided him to her entrance.

He halted there, poised on the brink. "Tell me what you like," he said, kissing her neck. "Tell me how you want it."

"I like it true," she said, hands running down his face. "I want it real."

So Ruhn slid home, crying out at the sheer perfection of her. She groaned, arching, and Ruhn stilled. "Did I hurt you?"

"No," she whispered, hands framing his face as he hovered above her. "No. Not at all."

The pressure of her around his cock was too much, too gloriously intense—"I can go slow." He couldn't. He really fucking couldn't, but for her, he'd try.

She laughed softly. "Please don't."

He withdrew nearly to the tip and pushed back in with a smooth, steady thrust. He nearly leapt out of his skin at the rippling pleasure.

Her hands dug into his shoulders, and Day said, "You feel better than I even dreamed."

Ruhn smiled into her neck. "You dreamed about this?"

He thrust again, sinking to the hilt, and she gasped. "Yes," she said, as if his cock had wrung the word from her. "Every night. Every time I had to . . ." She trailed off. But Ruhn claimed her mouth, kissing her as deeply as he fucked her. He didn't need her to say the rest, the part that would smash something in his chest.

Ruhn angled her hips so he could drive deeper still, and she reached up above her to clutch at the rolled arm of the chaise. "Ruhn," she moaned again, a warning that she was close—and echoed it with a flex of her delicate inner muscles.

The squeeze had him grabbing her hands in his and slamming home. Her hips undulated in perfect rhythm with his, and nothing had ever felt so good, so real as their souls twining here—

"Come for me," he breathed against her mouth, as he reached between them to rub the bud of her clit in a taunting circle.

Day cried out, and those inner muscles fluttered and clenched around his cock, milking him—

Release barreled through him, and Ruhn didn't hold back as he pounded into her, wringing the pleasure from both of them.

They kept moving, one orgasm rolling into the next, and he had no fucking idea how it was even possible, but he was still hard, still going, and he needed more and more and more of her—

He erupted again, hauling her with him.

Their breaths echoed against each other like crashing waves, and she was shaking as she held him. He lowered himself so his head rested upon her chest. Her heartbeat thundered into his ear, and even the melody of that was beautiful.

Her fingers tangled in his hair. "I . . . ."

"I know," Ruhn said. It had never been like that with anyone. Sex had been good, yeah, but this . . . He was fairly certain his soul lay in splinters around them. He kissed the skin above her breast. "I should have asked you if you had anything to report first."

"Why?"

"Because my mind's too fried to remember anything after this point."

Another one of those soft laughs. "All is quiet. No word on Pippa Spetsos after she eluded capture at Urd's Temple."

"Good. Though I guess we could use a distraction to keep attention elsewhere."

"From what?"

Ruhn toyed with the strands of her long hair, trying to make out the texture, the color. All was pure flame. "I'm coming your way."

She stilled. "What do you mean?"

"We need to get into the Asteri Archives."

"Why?"

"The vital intel Sofie Renast possessed is likely in one of the rooms there."

She pushed up onto her elbows. "What?"

He pulled out of her and said, "Any intel on the layout of the crystal palace or the archives, since you're so familiar with them . . . we'd appreciate it."

"You're going to break into the crystal palace. Into the archives."

"Yes."

"Ruhn." She grabbed his face in her hands. "Ruhn, do *not* go there. They will kill you. All of you."

"Hence the need for attention to be elsewhere while we break in."

Her fingers dug into his cheeks, and her heart pounded so wildly he could hear it. "It's got to be a trap."

"No one knows except people I trust. And now you."

She shot to her feet, again wholly veiled in flame. "If you're caught, I cannot help you. I won't be able to risk saving you. Or your sister. You're on your own."

His temper began simmering. "So you won't tell me anything useful about the layout."

"Ruhn, I—"

Again, that awful hiss of surprise and pain. That glance behind her.

To him. The male.

Ruhn grabbed her hand, like she could stay with him. But she began panting, wild and frantic. Terrified. "Ruhn, they know. *I*—" Her voice cut out for a moment. "The dungeons—"

She vanished.

Like she'd been snatched away.

68

We leave for the crystal palace tomorrow," Ruhn snarled at Hunt in the great room of Bryce's apartment. "At dawn."

"Let me get this straight," the angel said with maddening calm. "You've been meeting mind-to-mind with Agent Daybright—and dating her?"

Bryce sat at the dining table as she nursed a cup of coffee—which she needed desperately, since Ruhn had burst in at four in the morning. "Banging her, apparently."

Ruhn growled at his sister. "Does it matter?"

"It does," Hunt said, "because you're suggesting that we break into the crystal palace not only to get into the archives, but to save your lady love. That adds a shit-ton of risk."

"I'll get her myself," Ruhn shot back. "I just need to get in with you two first."

"Absolutely not," Bryce countered. "I get that you want to play rescuing hero, but what you're talking about is suicide."

"Would you hesitate to go in after Athalar?" He pointed to the angel. "Or you to go after Bryce?"

"You've known her for a month," Bryce protested.

"You knew Athalar for barely more than that before you offered to sell yourself into slavery for him." Ruhn snapped before they could speak, "I don't need to justify my feelings or my plans to you. I came here to tell you that I'm going with you. Once we're inside the palace, we'll go our separate ways."

"See, that's the part that bugs me," Bryce said, draining her coffee. "This whole 'separate ways' thing. We all go in, we all go out."

Ruhn blinked, but Bryce said to the angel, "Honestly, you should stay here."

"*Excuse me?*" Hunt demanded.

Ruhn kept silent as Bryce said, "The more of us go in, the better the chance of getting noticed. Ruhn and I can manage."

"One, no. Two, fuck no. Three . . ." Hunt grinned wickedly. "Who's going to level you up, sweetheart?" She scowled, but Hunt plowed on, "I'm going with you."

She crossed her arms. "It'd be safer with two people."

"It'd be safer not to go at all, but here we are, going," Hunt said. Ruhn wasn't entirely sure what to do with himself as the angel crossed the room and knelt before Bryce, grabbing her hands. "I want a future with you. *That's* why I'm going. I'm going to fight for that future." His sister's eyes softened. Hunt kissed her hands. "And to do so, we can't play by other people's rules."

Bryce nodded, and faced Ruhn. "We're done playing by Ophion's rules, or the Asteri's rules, or anyone else's. We'll fight our own way."

Ruhn smirked. "Team Fuck-You." Bryce grinned.

Hunt said, "All right, Team Fuck-You." He stood and patted a hand-drawn map of the crystal palace on the dining table. "Fury dropped this off earlier, and now we're all wide awake, so time to get studying. We need to create a distraction to make the Asteri look elsewhere, and we need to know where we're going once we're in there."

Ruhn tried not to marvel at the commander mode Athalar had slipped into. "It has to be something big," he said, "if it'll buy us enough time to get into the archives and find Day."

"She's probably in the dungeons," Hunt said. He added, as if reading Ruhn's worry, "She's alive, I'm sure of it. The Hind will be dispatched to work on her—they're not going to kill her right away. Not when she's got so much valuable information."

Ruhn's stomach churned. He couldn't get the sound of Day's panicked voice out of his mind. His very blood roared to go to her, find her.

Bryce said a shade gently, "We'll get her out, Ruhn."

"That doesn't give us much time to plan something big, though," Hunt said, sliding into the seat beside Bryce.

Ruhn scratched his jaw. They didn't have time to wait weeks. Even hours might be lethal. Minutes. "Day said that Pippa is lying low—but she has to have something planned. Ophion has taken enough hits to its numbers and bases lately that they'll likely let her do whatever she wants, either as some final-stand effort or to rally old and new recruits. Maybe we can prompt Pippa to do whatever she's planning a little earlier."

Bryce drummed her fingers on the table. "Call Cormac."

Bryce was fully awake when Cormac arrived thirty minutes later, Tharion in tow. She'd called him, too. He'd started them on this bullshit—he could damn well help finish it.

Yet Tharion . . . something was off about his scent. His eyes. He said nothing when Bryce asked, so she dropped it. But he seemed different. She couldn't place it, but he was different.

Cormac said when Ruhn had filled them in, "I have it on good authority as of last night that Pippa is planning a raid in a few weeks on the Pangeran lab where the Asteri's engineers and scientists work—where they made that new mech prototype. She wants their plans for it, and the scientists themselves."

"To build the new mech-suits?" Tharion asked.

Cormac nodded.

"And you were going to tell us this when?" Ruhn challenged.

Cormac's eyes blazed. "I heard at midnight. I figured it could wait until morning. Besides, you lot haven't bothered to loop me in on anything since the ball, have you?" He directed this last bit at Bryce.

She smiled sweetly. "I thought you were licking your wounds."

Cormac seethed, "I've been dealing with my father, finding a way to convince him to let me remain here after the *humiliation* of my engagement being called off."

Tharion let out a whistle at that. Bryce asked, "And did you?"

"I wouldn't be here if I hadn't," Cormac hurled back. "He thinks I'm currently trying to woo you from Athalar."

Hunt snorted at this, earning a glare from Cormac. Bryce cut in before it could escalate to blows, "So how do we convince Pippa to make her move now? We're not exactly on good terms with her."

Tharion said, "What if she's not the one initiating the raid?"

Bryce angled her head. "You mean . . . *us?*"

"I mean me and Cormac and whoever else we can trust. *We* carry out the raid, and Pippa and her cronies come running before we can steal the plans and suits they want."

"And where does that get us?" Hunt asked.

"It gets us in a lab with Pippa and Ophion—and if we time it right, a pack of dreadwolves will arrive right after they do."

"Solas," Bryce said, scrubbing at her face. "How are you going to get out of that?"

Cormac smiled at Tharion, as if sensing the direction of his thoughts. "That's the big distraction. We blow it all to Hel."

Ruhn blew out a breath. "That'll certainly get the Asteri's attention."

"The lab's twenty miles north of the Eternal City," Cormac said. "It might even draw them out to inspect the site. Especially if Pippa Spetsos has been captured."

"You're cool with handing over a fellow rebel?" Hunt asked the prince.

"I don't see any other options."

"Keep the casualties to a minimum," Hunt said to Cormac, to Tharion. "We don't need their blood on our hands."

Bryce massaged her chest. They were really doing this. She got to her feet, and they all looked at her as she said, "I'll be right back," and padded into her bedroom.

She shut the door and strode to a photo on her dresser, staring at it for several long minutes. The door opened behind her, and Hunt was there. "You all right?"

Bryce kept staring at the photo. "We were really happy that night," she said, and Hunt approached to study the photo of her, Danika, Juniper, and Fury, all grinning in the White Raven nightclub, drunk and high and gorgeous. "I thought we were really happy, at least. But when that photo was taken, Fury was still . . . doing what she does, Juniper was quietly in love with her, and Danika . . . Danika had a *mate*, had all these secrets. And I was stupid and drunk and convinced we'd party until we were dust. And now I'm here."

Her throat ached. "I feel like I have no idea who I am. I know that's so fucking cliché, but . . . I *thought* I knew who I was then. And now . . ." She lifted her hands, letting them fill with starlight. "What's the end goal in this? Somehow, someway, overthrowing the *Asteri*? What then? Rebuilding a government, an entire world? What if it triggers another war?"

Hunt tugged her into his arms and rested his chin atop her head. "Don't worry about that shit. We focus on the now, then deal with everything else afterward."

"I thought a general always planned ahead."

"I do. I am. But the first step in making those plans is finding out what the fuck Sofie knew. If it's nothing, then we reassess. But . . . I know how it feels to wake up one day and wonder how you got so far from that carefree person you were. I mean, yeah, my life in the slums with my mom wasn't easy, but after she died . . . It was like I'd had some illusion ripped away from me. It's how I wound up with Shahar. I was reeling and angry, and . . . it took me a long, long while to sort myself out. I'm still sorting it out."

She leaned her brow against his chest. "Can I admit that I'm scared shitless?"

"Can I admit that I am, too?"

She laughed, squeezing him tight around the middle, breathing in his scent. "I'd be slightly less scared if you were staying here, and I could go in knowing you're safe."

"Likewise."

She pinched his ass. "Then I guess we're stuck with each other, venturing into the lion's den."

"More like a sobek nest."

"Great. Really reassuring."

He chuckled, the sound rumbling into her bones, warming them. "Ruhn talked to Declan. He's going to hack into the security cameras at the palace—turn away the cameras while we're in there. We need to give him our route through the building so he can turn them without being noticed by anyone monitoring the system. Flynn will run support for him."

"What if we wind up needing to take a different hall?"

"He'll have backup plans, but . . . we'll really need to try to stick to ours."

Nausea roiled her gut, but she said, "Okay."

Hunt kissed her cheek. "Take your time, Quinlan. I'll be with the others." Then he was gone.

Bryce stared at the photo again. She pulled out her phone from her bathrobe and dialed. Unsurprisingly, Juniper's phone went to audiomail. It was five thirty in the morning, but—she knew Juniper would have picked up before.

"Hey, this is Juniper Andromeda. Leave a message!"

Bryce's throat closed up at her friend's lovely, cheerful voice. She took a breath as the audiomail beeped. "Hey, June. It's me. Look, I know I fucked up, and . . . I'm so sorry. I wanted to help, but I didn't think it through, and everything you said to me was absolutely right. I know you might not even listen to this, but I wanted you to know that I love you. I miss you so much. You've been a rock for me for so long, and I should have been that for you, but I wasn't. I just . . . I love you. I always have, and always will. Bye."

She rubbed at her aching throat as she finished. Then removed the photo from the frame, folded it, and slipped it inside her phone case.

69

Ruhn found Cormac sitting alone in an Old Square dive bar, face stony as he watched the late-night news show, a glossy-haired celebrity laughing her way through some interview—a shameless promo for her recent movie.

"What are you doing here?" the Avallen Prince asked him as Ruhn slid onto the stool beside him.

"Flynn was notified of your location. Thought I'd see why you were up so late. Considering our appointment tomorrow."

Cormac studied him sidelong, then drained his beer. "I wanted some quiet."

"And you came to a dive in the Old Square for that?" Ruhn indicated the blasting music, the wasted patrons around them. The sylph puking green liquid into the trash can by the pool table in the back.

His cousin said nothing.

Ruhn sighed. "What's wrong?"

"Does it matter to you?" Cormac signaled for another beer.

"It matters to me when we're relying on you tomorrow." When Day and Bryce were relying on the prince to be alert and ready.

"This isn't my first big . . . appointment." Ruhn glanced at the male—the immaculate blond hair, the unfailingly arrogant angle of his chin.

Cormac caught him looking and said, "I don't know how your father never managed to do it."

"Do what?" Ruhn leaned his forearms on the oak bar.

"Break you. The kindness in you."

"He tried," Ruhn choked out.

"My father did, too. And won." Cormac snorted, taking his fresh beer from the bartender. "I wouldn't have bothered to check on you."

"Yet you expended a lot of time and risk on finding . . . her."

The prince shrugged. "Perhaps, but deep down, I am what I've always been. The male who would have gladly killed you and your friends."

Ruhn tugged on his lip ring. "You're telling me this right before we head off?"

"I suppose I'm telling you this to . . . to apologize."

Ruhn tried not to gape. "Cormac—"

His cousin blankly watched the TV. "I was jealous of you. Then and now. For your friends. For the fact that you have them. That you don't let your father . . . corrupt what is best in you. But had I been forced to marry your sister . . ." His mouth twisted to the side. "I think, with time, she might have undone the damage my father did to my soul."

"Bryce has that effect on people."

"She will be a good princess. As you are a good prince."

"I'm starting to get disturbed by all this niceness."

Cormac drank again. "I'm always pensive the night before an appointment."

For a glimmer, Ruhn could see the male his cousin might have become—might yet become. Serious, yes, but fair. Someone who understood the cost of a life. A good king.

"When all this shit is done," Ruhn said hoarsely, tucking even thoughts of Day aside as he settled himself more comfortably on the stool, "I want us to start over."

"Us?"

"You and me. Prince to prince. Future king to future king. Screw the past, and screw that shit with the Starsword. Screw our fathers.

We don't let them decide who we get to be." Ruhn extended his hand. "We'll carve our own paths."

Cormac smiled almost sadly. Then took Ruhn's hand, clasping firmly. "It'd be an honor."

The barracks were dim. No one lounged in the common area, from what Hunt could tell down the hall as he entered his room.

Good. No one but the cameras to see him come and go.

He'd left Quinlan sleeping, and hadn't told anyone where he was going.

His room was cold and soulless as he shut the door behind him. Just as he'd been when he'd first met Quinlan. He'd displayed no traces of his life, put no art on the walls, done absolutely nothing to declare that this space was his. Perhaps because he'd known it truly wasn't.

Hunt strode to his desk, setting his empty duffel on it. He made quick work of loading up the extra knives and guns he'd kept in here, not wanting to be noticed checking out a stock of weapons from the armory. Thank the gods Micah had never bothered with enforcing the sign-out rules. Hunt had enough here to . . . well, to sneak into the crystal palace, he supposed.

He zipped the duffel, his gaze catching on the helmet on his desk. The skull painted on its front stared at him, unholy Hel in its black pits for eyes. The face of the Umbra Mortis.

Hunt picked up the helmet and set it on his head, the world shading into hues of red and black through the visor. He didn't let himself second-guess it as he stalked out of his room and into the night.

Celestina was standing at the elevator bay.

Hunt drew up short. Did she know? Had someone tipped her off? The duffel of weapons burned against his hip. He reached to pull off the helmet.

"Leave it," she said, and though her words were firm, her expression was contemplative. "I've always wondered what it looked like."

Hunt lowered his hand. "Everything all right?"

"I'm not the one sneaking in at five in the morning."

Hunt shrugged. "I couldn't sleep." The Archangel remained in front of the elevator bay, blocking his access. Hunt asked, "How are things with Ephraim?"

Her wings snapped shut. A clear warning. Whether it was to keep his mouth shut about Hypaxia or something else, he didn't know. Celestina only said, "He departs tomorrow. I shall visit his keep next month if there is not . . . a change in my situation by then."

If she hadn't gotten pregnant.

"Your silence speaks volumes about your dismay, Athalar." Power crackled in her voice. "I go to the mating bed willingly."

Hunt nodded, even as disgust and rage curled through him. The Asteri had ordered this, done this. They'd make Celestina keep going to Ephraim until she was pregnant with the child they wanted her to bear. Another little Archangel for them to mold into a monster. Would Celestina fight to keep her child free from their influence? Or would Ephraim hand the kid over to the Asteri and the secretive training centers they had for young Archangels? Hunt didn't want to know.

Celestina asked, "Why couldn't you sleep?"

He blew out a breath through his nose. "Is it pathetic to say it's because of the prince stuff?"

She offered him a pitying wince. "I thought that might come up."

Hunt tapped the side of his helmet. "I . . . weirdly missed it. And I wanted to clear out the last of my stuff from the room before it became a public spectacle." It was partially true.

She smiled softly. "I haven't had the chance to ask, but will you be leaving us?"

"I honestly have no idea. Bryce and I are giving the Autumn King a few days to cool down before asking him to define my royal duties. The thought of having to act fancy and take meetings with a bunch of assholes makes me want to puke."

Another quiet laugh. "But?"

"But I love Bryce. If doing that shit is what will allow us to be together, then I'll grin and bear it."

"Does she want to do such things?"

"Hel no. But . . . we don't really get much say. The Autumn King forced her hand. And now we're pretty much stuck with things as they are."

"Are you? The Umbra Mortis and the Starborn Princess don't seem the types to accept things as they are. You proved that with your surprise at the party."

Was there an edge to her voice? A gleam of suspicion?

They'd trusted Hypaxia not to say a word of their activities to her lover, had believed the witch when she said Celestina didn't know, but . . . the gods knew he talked when Bryce fucked the Hel out of him. Mistakes happened. Especially with a gorgeous set of tits involved.

But he made himself shrug again. "We're trying to get a better picture of the battle ahead before deciding where to start fighting the royal nonsense."

Her mouth quirked to one side. "Well, I hope that if you need an ally, you'll come to me."

Was that code for something? He scanned her face but could pick up nothing beyond reserved concern. He had to get out of here. So Hunt bowed his head. "Thank you."

"A prince doesn't need to bow to a Governor, you know." She walked over to the landing veranda doors, opening them for him. All right. He'd fly home.

Hunt stalked into the night, that bag of weapons a millstone hanging off his shoulder. He spread his wings. "Old habits."

"Indeed," she said, and a shiver went down his spine.

He didn't look back as he launched skyward.

Hunt slowly sailed over the city. Dawn remained a whisper on the horizon, and only a few delivery trucks rumbled along to bakeries and coffee shops. He had the skies to himself.

Hunt tugged off his helmet, tucking it into the crook of his elbow, and breathed in the open, clean breeze off the Istros. In a few hours, they'd leave for Pangera—Tharion had already reached out to Commander Sendes and arranged for transport across the ocean.

By tomorrow morning, they'd reach the Eternal City.

Tomorrow morning, he'd again wear this helmet. And pray that he and his mate walked away alive.

70

Tharion had commanded plenty of raids for the River Queen. He'd gone in solo, led teams small and large, and usually emerged unscathed. But riding shotgun beside Prince Cormac in the open-air jeep as they approached the security checkpoint down the cypress-lined road, he had the distinct feeling that he might not get so lucky today.

The imperial uniform they each wore lay heavy and smothering in the sun, but at least the hot day would disguise any glimmer of nervous sweat on them.

No one had seemed to notice the change he felt with every breath: the invisible tether, now stretched tight, linking whatever remained of his heart—that cold, dead thing—to the Viper Queen in Valbara. A constant reminder of his promise. His new life.

He tried not to think of it.

He'd been grateful for the wonders of the *Depth Charger*'s swift submersible-pod as it hurtled their group across the ocean. Sendes had told him when he contacted her that the city-ship was too slow to make it in time, but one of its makos—sleek little transport pods—could do it. So they'd boarded the pod at the coast, then spent their time either planning or sleeping, keeping themselves mostly separate from the mer who steered the ship.

Cormac waved with impressive casualness to the four guards—ordinary wolves, all of them—at the gate. Tharion kept his right hand within swift reach of the gun strapped to the side of his seat.

"Hail the Asteri." Cormac spoke with such offhanded ease that Tharion knew he'd said it a thousand times. Perhaps in similar settings.

"Hail the Asteri," the female guard who stepped forward said. She sniffed, marking what her eyes confirmed: a Fae male and a mer male, both in officer's uniforms. She saluted, and Tharion nodded for her to stand down.

Cormac handed over their forged papers. "We're to meet with Doctor Zelis. Have they radioed that he's ready?"

The guard scanned the clipboard in her hands. The three others with her didn't take their attention off the car, so Tharion gave them a glare he usually reserved for field agents who'd royally fucked up. The wolves, however, didn't back down.

"There's no appointment on here with Zelis," the guard said.

Tharion drawled, "It wouldn't be in writing."

She studied him, and Tharion smirked. "Rigelus's orders," he added.

The female's throat bobbed. To question the actions of an Asteri, or to risk letting two officers in who weren't on the security roster . . .

Cormac pulled out his phone. "Shall I call him?" He showed her a contact page that merely read: *Bright Hand*.

The wolf paled a little. But she saluted again, waving them through.

"Thank you," Cormac said, gunning the engine and driving through the gates before they'd finished lifting.

Tharion didn't dare speak to Cormac. Not with the wolves so nearby. They just stared ahead at the dirt road winding through the forest. At the sprawling concrete compound that appeared around the next bend, where guards were already waving them through the barbed-wire fencing.

He had to keep an eye on the clock today. The spray of the water from the mako's passage had extended the amount of time he could stay Above, but a familiar itching had started an hour ago. Another fucking headache to deal with: five more hours until he had to truly submerge. The coast was a two-hour drive from here. So . . . they'd better get this shit done within three. Two, to be safe.

Tharion nodded to the wolves in front of the lab and took in the enormous, low building. It hadn't been built for beauty, but for function and storage.

Smokestacks billowed behind the lab, which seemed to be at least half a mile long and perhaps twice as wide. "Look at this place," Tharion murmured as Cormac pulled up to the steel front doors. They opened as if by invisible hands—another guard must have pressed the security button to allow them in. Tharion whispered, "You think Pippa's going to come?" How the Hel would she get in?

Cormac cut the engine and threw open his door, stepping crisply into the morning sun. "She's already here."

Tharion blinked, but followed Cormac's military-precise motions as he climbed from the car. Cormac turned toward the open doors to the lab. "They're in the trees."

Declan had spent the previous day covertly planting information on rebel networks: the anti-Ophion rebels who'd destroyed the base on Ydra were making a move on this lab before Pippa and her agents could do so. She must have had Lightfall hauling ass to get here in time.

Tharion suppressed the urge to peer into the trees. "What about the dreadwolves?"

"This place reeks of humans, can't you smell it?"

"No."

Cormac stalked toward the open doors, black boots shining. "They're using human labor. Carted in and out every dawn and dusk. Pippa would have timed their arrival with it, so their scents are hidden from the dreadwolves below."

Solas. "So why wait for us to arrive, then?"

Cormac growled, "Because Pippa has a score to settle."

Bryce had no idea why anyone would want to live in the Eternal City. Not simply because it lay in the shadow of the crystal palace of the Asteri, but because it was . . . old. Dusty. Worn. No skyscrapers, no neon lights, no music blasting from passing cars. It seemed to have been trapped in time, stuck in another century, its masters unwilling to bring it forward.

As she, Hunt, and Ruhn lurked in the shadows of an olive grove a mile to the west of the palace, she steadied her nerves by imagining the Asteri as a bunch of cranky old people, shouting for everyone to keep the noise down, complaining that the lights were too bright and the youngsters too whippersnappery.

It definitely helped. Just a little.

Bryce glanced at Hunt, who kept his attention on the olive grove, the skies. He'd worn his black battle-suit, along with the Umbra Mortis helmet, to her shock. A warrior going back into battle.

Was this the right move? This risk, this danger they were plunging into? Maybe they'd have been better off staying in Lunathion, keeping their heads down.

Maybe she was a coward for thinking that.

She flicked her attention to Ruhn, her brother's face tight as he monitored the olive grove as well. He'd worn his Aux battle-suit, too, his black hair tied back in a braid that flowed down his spine, along the length of the Starsword strapped there. He clutched the comm-crystal in a fist, occasionally opening his fingers to study it. As if it might offer some hint about Day's welfare. He'd said he hadn't used it since that first contact with her, but he'd grabbed it before they left in case it could help locate her, if she had its twin on her.

Ruhn shifted from foot to foot, black boots crunching on the rocky, dry earth. "Cormac should be here by now."

She knew every second since Agent Daybright had gone dark pressed on her brother. Bryce didn't want to think about what was probably happening to the agent Ruhn seemed to care so much for. If they were lucky, she'd be alive. If they were luckier, there would be enough of her to salvage. Any attempts Ruhn had made to contact her—even going so far as to use the crystal—had been futile.

"Give him a minute," Bryce said. "It's a long jump." Too far for her to make—or attempt. Especially with others in tow. She needed all her strength for what was to come.

"You're a teleporting expert now?" Ruhn asked, brows high. The ring in his bottom lip glinted in the hot morning light. "Dec's on standby. I don't want to throw off his calculations. Even by a minute."

Bryce opened her mouth, but Cormac appeared in the small clearing ahead. They'd studied a satellite map of the grove yesterday and Cormac had committed the location to memory, plotting out the jumps he'd need to make to get here from the lab. And the jumps he'd need to make from this grove into the palace itself.

Cormac announced, "We're in. Tharion's in the waiting room. I slipped off to the bathroom. All plans are a go. Ready, Athalar?"

Hunt, then Bryce, then Ruhn. That had been the order they'd settled on, after an hour of arguing.

Hunt drew his gun, keeping it at his thigh. That helmeted head turned to Bryce, and she could feel his gaze even through the visor. "See you on the other side, Quinlan," Hunt said, taking Cormac's gloved hand.

Prince to prince. She marveled at it.

Then they were gone, and Bryce struggled to get down a breath.

"I feel like I can't breathe, either," Ruhn said, noticing. "Knowing that Day's in there." He added, "And knowing that you're about to go in there, too."

Bryce gave him a wobbly smile. And then decided to Hel with it and threw her arms around her brother, squeezing him hard. "Team Fuck-You, remember? We'll kick ass."

He chuckled, holding her tightly. "Team Fuck-You forever."

She pulled away, scanning her brother's violet-blue eyes. "We'll get her out. I promise."

Ruhn's golden skin paled. "Thanks for helping me, Bryce."

She nudged him with an elbow. "We Starborn have each other's backs, you know?"

But her brother's face turned grave. "When we get home, I think we need to talk."

"About what?" She didn't like that serious expression. And didn't like that Cormac was taking so long.

Ruhn's mouth tightened. "All right, since we might very well die in a few minutes—"

"That is *so* morbid!"

"I wanted to wait until shit had calmed down, but . . . You outrank the Autumn King in power."

"And?"

"I think it's time his reign comes to an end, don't you?" He was completely serious.

"You want me to back you in a coup? A Fae coup?"

"I want to back *you* in a Fae coup. I want you as Autumn Queen."

Bryce recoiled. "I don't want to be a queen."

"Let's ditch the whole reluctant royal thing, okay? You saw what the Fae did during the attack this spring. How they shut out innocents and left them to die, with our father's blessing. You mean to tell me that's the best our people can do? You mean to tell me that's what we're supposed to accept as normal Fae behavior? I don't buy that for a second."

"*You* should be king."

"No." Something else shone in his eyes, some secret she didn't know, but she could sense. "You have more power than I do. The Fae will respect that."

"Maybe the Fae should rot."

"Tell that to Dec. And Flynn. And my mother. Look at them and tell me that the Fae aren't worth saving."

"Three. Out of the entire population."

Ruhn's face turned pleading, but then Cormac appeared, panting and covered in sweat. "Athalar's waiting."

"Think about it," Ruhn murmured as she approached Cormac. "All clear?"

"No issues. The intel was right: they don't even have wards around the place," Cormac reported. "Arrogant worms." He extended a hand to Bryce. "Hurry."

Bryce grabbed the prince's hand. And with a last look at her brother, she vanished into wind and darkness, stomach whipping around and around. Cormac said over the roaring of the space between places, "He asked you to be queen, didn't he?"

Bryce blinked up at him—though it was difficult with the force of the storm around them. "How did you know?"

"I might have caught the end of your conversation." Bryce clung harder as the wind pressed. Cormac said, "He's right."

"Spare me."

"And you were right, too. When we first met, and you said the Oracle's prophecy was vague. I understand that now. She didn't mean our union in marriage would bring prosperity to our people. She meant our union as allies. Allies in this rebellion."

The world took form at the edges of the darkness.

"But after today . . ." Cormac's words grew heavy. Weary. "I think the choice about whether to lead our people forward will be up to you."

Hunt couldn't shake the tremor from his hands. Being here, in this palace . . .

It smelled the same. Even in the hallway directly outside the archives, where he hid in an alcove, the stale odor of this place dragged claws down his temper, set his knees wobbling.

Screaming, pain blinding as they sawed off his wings slowly—

Shahar was dead, her broken body still dust-covered from Sandriel dragging it through the streets on her way in here—

Pollux laughing as he pissed on Shahar's corpse in the middle of the throne room—

His wings, his wings, his wings—

Hunt swallowed, shutting out the memories, focusing his mind on the hall. No one was around.

Bryce and Cormac appeared, and she'd hardly thanked him before he vanished, off to grab Ruhn before teleporting back to the lab. Sweat gleamed on the prince's face, his skin sallow. He had to be exhausted.

"All right?" Hunt murmured, brushing back her hair with a gloved hand. She nodded, eyes full of worry—and something else. But Hunt flicked her chin and went back to monitoring.

They stood in tense silence, and then Ruhn was there, Cormac with him. Cormac's skin was ashen now. He disappeared immediately, back to the lab.

"Tell Declan we're a go," Hunt said.

Ruhn's shadows cloaked them from sight as he thumbed in a message on a secure phone that Declan had retrofitted against tracking. In five minutes, Tharion would contact them on it to tell them whether or not to move.

Bryce's fingers slid into Hunt's, clutching tight. He squeezed back.

He had no idea how five minutes passed. He was barely breathing, monitoring the hall ahead. Bryce held his gloved hand through all of it, her jaw tense.

Then Ruhn lifted his head. "Tharion said Cormac just blew up the jeep."

Hunt nudged her with a wing. "Your turn, Quinlan."

Ruhn said, "Remember: Every minute in there risks detection. Make them count."

"Thanks for the pep talk," she said, but smiled grimly up at Hunt. "Light it up, Athalar."

Hunt pressed a hand to her heart, his lightning a subtle flare that was sucked into the scar. As the last of it faded, Bryce teleported into the archives.

To find whatever truth might lie within them.

71

Bryce's breathing turned so jagged that she could barely think as she tumbled alone through the darkness.

They were in the Asteri's palace. In their sacred, forbidden archives.

And she was . . . in a stairwell?

Bryce took steadying inhales as she surveyed the spiral staircase, crafted entirely of white quartz. Firstlight glimmered, golden and soft, lighting the carved steps downward. At her back was a door—the other side of the one they'd watched Sofie walk through on the surveillance footage.

The one labeled with the number Sofie had etched into her biceps.

Bryce began to creep down the stairs, her black utility boots nearly silent against the quartz steps. She saw no one. Heard no one.

Her heart raced, and she could have sworn the veins of firstlight in the quartz throbbed with each beat. As if in answer.

Bryce halted after a turn in the stairs and assessed the long hallway ahead. When it revealed no guards, she stepped into it.

There were no doors. Only this hall, perhaps seventy feet long and fifteen feet wide. Likely fourteen feet, to be a multiple of seven. The holy number.

Bryce scanned the hall. The only thing in it was a set of crystal pipes shooting upward into the ceiling, with plaques beneath them, and small black screens beside the plaques.

Seven pipes.

The crystal floor glowed at her feet as she approached the nearest plaque.

Hesperus. The Evening Star.

Brows rising, Bryce strode to the next pipe and plaque. *Polaris.* The North Star.

Plaque after plaque, pipe after pipe, Bryce read the individual names of each Asteri.

Eosphoros. Octartis. Austrus.

She nearly tripped at the penultimate. *Sirius.* The Asteri the Prince of the Pit had devoured.

She knew what the last plaque would say before she reached it. *Rigelus.* The Bright Hand.

What the Hel was this place?

This was what Danika had felt was important enough for Sofie Renast to risk her life for? What the Asteri had wanted to contain so badly they'd hunted Sofie down to preserve the secret?

The crystal at her feet flared, and Bryce had nowhere to go, nowhere to hide, as firstlight, pure and iridescent, ruptured.

She squeezed her eyes shut, dropping into a crouch.

But nothing happened. At least, not to her.

The firstlight faded enough that Bryce cracked open her eyes to see it shooting up six of the pipes.

The little black screens beside each plaque flared to life, filled with readings. Only Sirius's pipe remained unlit. Out of commission.

She went rigid as she read the Bright Hand's screen: *Rigelus Power Level: 65%.*

She whirled to the next plaque. The screen beside it said, *Austrus Power Level: 76%.*

"Holy gods," Bryce whispered.

The Asteri fed on firstlight. The Asteri . . . *needed* firstlight. She looked at her feet, where light flowed in veins through the crystal before funneling into the pipes. The quartz.

A conduit of power. Exactly like the Gates in Crescent City.

They'd built their entire palace out of it. To fuel and harness the firstlight that poured in.

She'd studied Fury's rough map of the palace layout. This area was seven levels below the throne room, where the Asteri sat on crystal thrones. Did those thrones fill them with power? In plain sight, they fueled up like batteries, sucking in this firstlight.

Nausea constricted her throat. All the Drops people made, the secondlight the dead handed over . . . All the power of the people of Midgard, the power the people *gave* them . . . it was gobbled up by the Asteri and used against its citizens. To control them.

Even the Vanir rebels who were killed fighting had their souls fed to the very beasts they were trying to overthrow.

They were all just food for the Asteri. A never-ending supply of power.

Bryce began shaking. The veins of light wending beneath her feet, glowing and vibrant . . . She traced them down as far as she could see through the clear stone, into a brilliantly shining mass. A core of firstlight. Powering the entire palace and the monsters that ruled it.

This was what Sofie had learned. What Danika had suspected.

Did the Asteri even possess holy stars in their chests, or was it firstlight, stolen from the people? Firstlight that they *mandated* be given over in the Drop to fuel cities and technology . . . and the overlords who ruled this world. Secondlight that was ripped from the dead, squeezing every last drop of power from the people.

Cut off the firstlight, destroy this funnel of power, get people to stop handing over their power through the Drop in those centers that funneled off their energy, stop the dead from becoming secondlight . . .

And they could destroy the Asteri.

72

Athalar paced in a tight circle. "She should be back."

"She's got two minutes," Ruhn growled, clenching the comm-crystal so hard in his fist it was a wonder the edges weren't permanently etched into his fingers.

Hunt said, "Something happened. She should be here by now."

Ruhn eyed the watch on his wrist. They had to make it down to the dungeons. And if they didn't start immediately . . . He peered at the crystal in his hand.

Day, he said, throwing her name out into the void. But no answer came. Like every other attempt to reach her recently.

"I'm going to get a head start," he murmured, pocketing the crystal. "I'll cloak myself in my shadows. If I'm not back in ten minutes, leave without me."

"We all go together," Hunt shot back, but Ruhn shook his head. "We'll come find you."

Ruhn didn't reply before he slipped down the hall, blending into the darkness, and aimed for the passageways that would take him across the palace compound. To the dungeons and the agent trapped within them.

* * *

Bryce raced back to the top of the stairs, bile burning her throat.

She'd been here too long. Could only spare a minute or two more.

She reached the door and the landing, rallying what remained of Hunt's charge to teleport back to him and Ruhn, but the door handle seemed to gleam. What else lay down here? What else might she uncover? If this was her only opportunity . . .

Bryce didn't let herself doubt as she slipped into the main archives hallway. It was dim and dusty. Utterly silent.

Shelves crammed with books loomed around her, and Bryce scanned their titles. Nothing of interest, nothing of use—

She sprinted through the library, reading titles and names of sections as fast as she could, praying that Declan had kept up and was moving the cameras away from her. She scanned the vague section titles above the stacks. *Tax Records, Agriculture, Water Processing* . . .

The doors along this stretch had been named similarly to each other—not in code, but along a theme.

Dawn. Midnight. Midday. She had no idea what any of the names meant, or what lay behind the door. But one in the center snared her eye: *Dusk.*

She slipped inside.

Bryce was late. Hunt stayed put only because his secure phone had flashed with a message from Declan. *She's okay. She went into a room called Dusk. I'll keep you posted.*

Of course Quinlan was doing *extra* research. Of course she couldn't listen to the rules and be back when she was supposed to—

Then again, *Dusk* could have something to do with Dusk's Truth. No wonder Bryce had entered.

Hunt paced again. He should have gone with her. Made her teleport him in, even if it would have drained her at a time when they'd need all her gifts.

Ruhn had already been gone for three minutes. A lot could happen in that time.

"Come on, Bryce," Hunt murmured, and prayed to Cthona to keep his mate safe.

Cloaked in shadows, Ruhn raced down the halls, encountering no one. Not one guard.

It was too quiet.

The hall opened into a wide fork: To the left lay the dungeons. To the right, the stairs up to the palace proper. He went left without hesitation. Down the stairs that turned from cloudy quartz to dark stone, like the life had been sucked from the rock. His skin chilled.

These dungeons . . . Athalar had made it out, but most never did.

Ruhn's stomach churned, and he slowed his pace, readying himself for the gauntlet ahead. Checkpoints of guards—easy enough to avoid with his shadows—locked doors, and then two halls of cells and torture chambers. Day had to be somewhere in there.

Screams began leaking out. Male, thankfully. But they were wrenching. Pleading. Sobbing. He wished he could plug his ears. If Day was making a similar sound, in such agony . . .

Ruhn kept going—until Mordoc stepped into his path with a feral grin. He sniffed once, that bloodhound gift no doubt feeding him a host of information before he said, "You're a long way from cavorting with spies in the alleys of Lunathion, Prince."

Tharion raced behind Cormac, a shield of water around them as the prince hurled ball after ball of fire into the chaotic, smoky lab. Chunks of rupturing machines flew toward them, smoldering—and Tharion intercepted them as best he could.

The doctor had led them right into the lab without a second thought. Cormac had put a bullet through the male's head a moment later, then ended the lives of the screaming scientists and engineers around him.

"Are you fucking insane?" Tharion screamed as they ran. "You said we'd limit the casualties!"

Cormac ignored him. The bastard had gone rogue.

Tharion snarled, half debating whether to overpower the prince. "Is this any better than what Pippa Spetsos does?"

Tharion got his answer a second later. Gunfire crackled behind them, and rebels stormed in. Right on time.

Imperial Vanir reinforcements roared as they rushed in—and were drowned out by the barrage of guns. An ambush.

Would it be enough to draw the Asteri's attention away? Cormac had incinerated the jeep with his fire magic moments before they'd shot the doctor—surely that would warrant a message to the Asteri. And this shitshow unfolding . . .

Cormac skidded to a stop, Tharion with him. Both of them fell silent.

A familiar female, clad in black and armed with a rifle, stepped into their path.

Pippa pointed the gun at Cormac. "I've been looking forward to this." Her rifle cracked, and Cormac teleported, but too slowly. His powers were drained.

Blood sprayed a moment before Cormac vanished—then appeared behind Pippa.

The bullet had passed through his shoulder, and Tharion launched into movement as Pippa twisted toward the prince.

Tharion was stopped by shaking ground, though. A glowing, electrified sword plunged into the floor in front of him.

A mech-suit sword.

Cormac shouted to Tharion, "*Get out of here!*" The prince faced off against Pippa as the woman fired again.

Tharion knew that tone. Knew that look. And it was then that he understood.

Cormac hadn't just gone rogue. He'd never intended to get out of here alive.

The door marked *Dusk* had been left unlocked. Bryce supposed she had Declan to thank for the dead electronic keypad.

Braziers of firstlight glowed in the corners of the room, dimly illuminating the space. A round table occupied the middle. Seven seats around it.

Her blood chilled.

A small metal machine sat in the center of the table. A projection device. But Bryce's attention snagged on the stone walls, covered in paper.

Star-maps—of constellations and solar systems, marked up with scribbled notations and pinned with red dots. Her mouth dried out as she approached the one nearest. A solar system she didn't recognize, with five planets orbiting a massive sun.

One planet in the habitable zone had been pinned and labeled. *Rentharr. Conq. A.E. 14000.*

A.E. She didn't know that dating system. But she could guess what *Conq.* meant.

Conquered . . . by the Asteri? She'd never heard of a planet called Rentharr. Scribbled beside it was a brief note: *A bellicose, aquatic people. Primordial land life. Little supply. Terminated A.E. 14007.*

"Oh gods," Bryce breathed, and went to the next star-map.

Iphraxia. Conq. A.E. 680. Lost A.E. 720.

She read the note beside it and her blood iced over. *Denizens learned of our methods too quickly. We lost many to their unified front. Evacuated.*

Somewhere out in the cosmos, a planet had managed to kick out the Asteri.

Map to map, Bryce read the notes. Names of places that weren't known in Midgard. Worlds that the Asteri had conquered, with notations about their use of firstlight and how they either lost or controlled those worlds. Fed on them until there was nothing left.

Fed on their power . . . like she had with the Gate. Was she no better than them?

The rear wall of the chamber held a map of this world.

Midgard, the map read. *Conq. A.E. 17003.*

Whatever *A.E.* was, if they'd been on *this* planet for fifteen thousand years, then they'd existed in the cosmos for far, far longer than that.

If they could feed off firstlight, generate it somehow on each planet . . . could they live forever? Truly immortal and undying? Six ruled this world, but there'd originally been a seventh. How many existed beyond them?

Pages of notes on Midgard had been pinned to the wall, along with drawings of creatures.

Ideal world located. Indigenous life not sustainable, but conditions prime for colonization. Have contacted others to share bounties.

Bryce's brow furrowed. What the Hel did that mean?

She peered at a drawing of a mer beside a sketch of a wolf shifter. *The aquatic shifters can hold a hybrid form far more easily than those on land.*

She read the next page, with a drawing of a Fae female. *They did not see the old enemy who offered a hand through space and time. Like a fish to bait, they came, and they opened the gates to us willingly. They walked through them—to Midgard—at our invitation, leaving behind the world they knew.*

Bryce backed away from the wall, crashing into the table.

The Asteri had lured them all into this world from other planets. Somehow, using the Northern and Southern Rifts, or whatever way they traveled between worlds, they'd . . . drawn them into this place. To farm them. Feed off them. Forever.

Everything was a lie. She'd known a lot of accepted history was bullshit, but this . . .

She twisted to the projector device in the center of the table and stretched an arm to hit the button. A three-dimensional, round map of the cosmos erupted. Stars and planets and nebulas. Many marked with digital notes, as the papers on the walls had been.

It was a digital orrery. Like the metal one she'd glimpsed as a kid in the Autumn King's study. Like the one in the Astronomer's chamber.

Was this what Danika had learned in her studies on bloodlines? That they'd all come from elsewhere—but had been lured and trapped here? And then fed on by these immortal leeches?

The map of the universe rotated above her. So many worlds. Bryce reached out to touch one. The digital note immediately appeared beside it.

Urganis. Children were ideal nutrition. Adults incompatible.

She swallowed against the dryness in her throat. That was it. All that remained of a distant world. A note about whether its people made for good eating and what the Asteri had done to its young.

Was there a home planet? Some original world the Asteri had come from, bled so dry that they'd needed to go hunting in the wilds of space?

She began flicking through planets, one after another after another, clawing past the stars and cosmic clouds of dust.

Her heart stopped at one.

Hel.

The ground seemed to slide away from beneath her.

Hel. Lost A.E. 17001.

She had to sink into one of the chairs as she read the note. *A dark, cold world with mighty creatures of night. They saw through our lures. Once warring factions, the royal armies of Hel united and marched against us. We were overwhelmed and abandoned their world, but they gave chase. Learned from our captured lieutenants how to slip between the cracks in realms.*

Bryce was dimly aware of her shaking body, her shallow breaths.

They found us on Midgard in 17002. Tried to convince our lured prey of what we were, and some fell to their charms. We lost a third of our meals to them. War lasted until nearly the end of 17003. They were defeated and sent back to Hel. Far too dangerous to allow them access to this world again, though they might try. They developed attachments to the Midgard colonists.

"Theia," Bryce whispered hoarsely. Aidas had loved the Fae queen, and . . .

Hel had come to help, exactly as Apollion had said. Hel had kicked the Asteri from their own world, but . . . Tears stung her eyes. The demon princes had felt a moral obligation to chase after the Asteri so they might never prey upon another world. To spare others.

Bryce began sifting through planets again. So many worlds. So many people, their children with them.

It had to be here—the Asteri's home world. She'd find it and tell the Princes of Hel about it, and once they were done beating these assholes into dust here on Midgard, they'd go to that home world and they'd blow it the fuck up—

She was sobbing through her teeth.

This empire, this world . . . it was just one massive buffet for the six beings ruling it.

Hel had tried to save them. For fifteen thousand years, Hel had never stopped trying to find a way back here. To free them from the Asteri.

"Where the *fuck* did you come from?" she seethed.

Worlds ripped past her fingertips, along with the Asteri's dispassionate notes. Most planets were not as lucky as Hel had been.

They rose up. We left them in cinders.

Firstlight tasted off. Terminated world.

Denizens launched bombs at us that left planet and inhabitants too full of radiation to be viable food. Left to rot in their waste.

Firstlight too weak. Terminated world but kept several citizens who produced good firstlight to sustain us on travels. Children proved hearty, but did not take to our travel method.

These psychotic, soulless *monsters*—

"You will not find our home world there," a cold voice said through the intercom on the table. "Even we have forgotten where its ruins lie."

Bryce panted, only rage coursing through her as she said to Rigelus, "*I am going to fucking kill you.*"

73

Rigelus laughed. "I was under the impression that you were only here to access the information for which Sofie Renast and Danika Fendyr died. You're going to kill me as well?"

Bryce squeezed shaking hands into fists. "Why? Why do any of this?"

"Why do you drink water and eat food? We are higher beings. We are *gods*. You cannot blame us if our source of nutrition is inconvenient for you. We keep you healthy, and happy, and allow you to roam free on this planet. We have even let the humans live all this time, just to give you Vanir someone to rule over. In exchange, all we ask is a little of your power."

"You're parasites."

"What are all creatures, feeding off their resources? You should see what the inhabitants of some worlds did to their planets—the rubbish, the pollution, the poisoned seas. Was it not fitting that we returned the favor?"

"You don't get to pretend that this is some savior story."

Rigelus chuckled, and the sound knocked her from her fury enough to remember Hunt and Ruhn, and, oh gods, if Rigelus knew she was here, he'd find them—

"Isn't that what you're doing?"

"What the fuck is that supposed to mean?"

"You left such a noble audiomail to your friend Juniper. Of course, once I heard it, I knew there was only one place you could be going. Here. To me. Precisely as I had hoped—and planned."

She shut away her questions, instead demanding, "Why do you want me here?"

"To reopen the Rifts."

Her blood froze. "I can't."

"Can't you?" The cold voice slithered through the intercom. "You are Starborn, and have the Horn bound to your body and power. Your ancestors wielded the Horn and another Fae object that allowed them to enter this world. Stolen, of course, from their original masters—our people. Our people, who built fearsome warriors in that world to be their army. All of them prototypes for the angels in this one. And all of them traitors to their creators, joining the Fae to overthrow my brothers and sisters a thousand years before we arrived on Midgard. They slew my siblings."

Her head spun. "I don't understand."

"Midgard is a base. We opened the doors to other worlds to lure their citizens here—so many powerful beings, all so eager to conquer new planets. Not realizing we were *their* conquerors. But we also opened the doors so we might conquer those other worlds as well. The Fae—Queen Theia and her two foolish daughters—realized that, though too late. Her people were already here, but she and the princesses discovered where my siblings had hidden the access points in their world."

Rage rippled through his every word. "Your Starborn ancestors shut the gates to stop us from invading their realm once more and reminding them who their true masters are. And in the process, they shut the gates to all other worlds, including those to Hel, their stalwart allies. And so we have been trapped here. Cut off from the cosmos. All that is left of our people, though our mystics beneath this palace have long sought to find any other survivors, any planets where they might be hiding."

Bryce shook. The Astronomer had been right about the host of mystics here. "Why are you telling me this?"

"Why do you think we allowed you to live this spring? You are the key to opening the doors between worlds again. You will undo the actions of one ignorant princess fifteen thousand years ago."

"Not a chance."

"Are your mate and brother not here with you?"

"No."

Rigelus laughed. "You're so like Danika—a born liar."

"I'll take that as a compliment." She lifted her chin. "You knew she was onto you."

"Of course. Her quest for the truth began with her bloodhound gift. Not a gift of the body's strength, but of *magic*, such as the shifters should not have. She could scent other shifters with strange powers."

Like Sofie. And Baxian. Danika had found him through researching his bloodline, but had she scented it, too?

"It prompted her to investigate her own bloodline's history, all the way back to the shifters' arrival in this world, to learn where her gifts came from. And she eventually began to suspect the truth."

Bryce's throat worked. "Look, I already did the whole villain monologuing thing with Micah this spring, so cut to the chase."

Rigelus chuckled again. "We shall get to that in a moment." He went on, "Danika realized that the shifters are Fae."

Bryce blinked. "What?"

"Not your kind of Fae, of course—your breed dwelled in a lovely, verdant land, rich with magic. If it's of any interest to you, your Starborn bloodline specifically hailed from a small isle a few miles from the mainland. And while the mainland had all manner of climes, the isle existed in beautiful, near-permanent twilight. But only a select few in the entirety of your world could shift from their humanoid forms to animal ones. The Midgard shifters were Fae from a different planet. All the Fae in that world shared their form with an animal. The mer descended from them, too. Perhaps they once shared a world with your breed of Fae, but they had been alone on their planet for long enough to develop their own gifts."

"They don't have pointed ears."

"Oh, we bred that out of them. It was gone within a few generations."

An isle of near-permanent twilight, the home world of *her* breed of Fae . . . A land of Dusk.

"Dusk's Truth," Bryce breathed. It wasn't just the name of this room that Danika had been talking about with Sofie.

Rigelus didn't answer, and she didn't know what to make of it. But Bryce asked, "Why lie to everyone?"

"Two breeds of Fae? Both rich in magic? They were ideal food. We couldn't allow them to unify against us."

"So you turned them against each other. Made them two species at odds."

"Yes. The shifters easily and swiftly forgot what they had once been. They gladly gave themselves to us and did our bidding. Led our armies. And still do."

The Prime had said something similar. The wolves had lost what they had once been. Danika had known that. Danika had *known* the shifters had once been Fae. Were still Fae—but a different kind.

"And Project Thurr? Why was Danika so interested in that?"

"Thurr was the last time someone got as far as Danika did in learning about us. It didn't end well for them. I suppose she wanted to learn from their mistakes before acting."

"She was going to tell everyone what you were."

"Perhaps, but she knew she had to do it slowly. She started with Ophion. But her research into the bloodlines and the origins of the shifters, her belief that they'd once been a different type of Fae, from a different Fae world, was important enough that they put her in touch with one of their most talented agents: Sofie Renast. From what I gather, Danika was *very* intrigued by Sofie and her powers. But Sofie, you see, had a theory, too. About energy. What her thunderbird gifts sensed while using firstlight. And even better for Danika: Sofie was an unknown. Danika would be noticed poking about, but Sofie, as a passing human working in the archives, was easily missed. So Danika sent her to learn more, to go undercover, as you call it."

She'd made an enormous mistake coming here.

"We were eventually notified by one of our mystics here, who learned it from prying into the mind of one of Ophion's Command. So we did a little tugging. Pointed Micah toward synth. Toward Danika."

"No." The word was a whisper.

"You think Micah acted alone? He was a brash, arrogant male. All it took was some nudging, and he killed her for us. Had no idea it was on our behalf, but it played out as we planned: he was eventually caught and killed for disturbing our peace. I thank you for that."

Bryce shot from her chair. They'd killed Danika—to keep all of this secret. She would rip them to shreds.

"You can try to run," Rigelus said. "If that will make you feel better."

Bryce didn't give him a chance to say more before she teleported back to the alcove, Hunt's power fading like a dimming flame inside her.

No sign of Ruhn. But Hunt—

He was on his knees, Umbra Mortis helmet discarded on the stone floor beside him. Hands behind his head, bound with gorsian manacles.

His eyes turned wild, pleading, but there was nothing Bryce could do as freezing stone clamped around her wrists as well, and she found herself face-to-face with a grinning Harpy.

74

Tharion ran—or tried to. The mech-suit blocked his exit with a giant gun.

The pilot inside grinned. "Time to fry, fish."

"Clever," Tharion ground out, and leapt back as the cannon-gun fired. Only a smoking pile of rubble remained of the concrete where he'd stood.

"*Go!*" Cormac yelled again, and Pippa's rifle thundered.

Tharion twisted to see the prince collapse to his knees, a gaping hole in his chest.

He had to get him out. Couldn't leave him like this, where recovery would likely be thwarted by a beheading. But if he stayed, if he wasn't killed outright . . .

He had four hours to reach water. The rebels would use that against him. And he might have sold his life away to the Viper Queen, but to live without his fins . . . He wasn't ready to lose that piece of his soul.

Cormac's eyes rippled with fire as he met Tharion's stare. *Run*, that gaze said.

Tharion ran.

The mech-suit behind him fired again, and he rolled between its massive legs. Shooting to his feet, he sped for the hole the mech-suit had made in the wall. Daylight poured in through the billowing smoke.

That tether in his chest—the Viper Queen's leash—seemed to whisper, *Get to water, you stupid bastard, then return to me.*

Tharion dared a glance back as he leapt through the opening. The mech-suit was advancing on Cormac. Pippa marched beside it now, smiling in triumph.

Beyond them, row after row of half-made mech hybrids slumbered. Waiting for activation and slaughter. It didn't matter which side they fought for.

Cormac managed to lift a bloody hand to point behind Pippa. She drew up short and whirled to face the five glowing beings at the far end of the space.

The Asteri. Oh gods. They'd come.

Cormac gave no warning as he erupted into a ball of fire.

Pippa was consumed by it first. Then the mech-pilot, who burned alive in his suit.

But the ball kept growing, spreading, roaring, and Tharion began running again, not waiting to see if it could somehow, against all odds, take out the Asteri.

He ran into the open air, following the tug of that leash back to the water, to Valbara, dodging the wolf guards now racing to the building. Sirens blared. White light rippled into the sky—the Asteri's rage.

Tharion cleared the trees. Kept running for the coast. Maybe he'd get lucky and find a vehicle before then—even if he had to steal it. Or put a gun to the driver's head.

He was half a mile away when the entire building exploded, taking Cormac, the suits, and the rebels with it.

Slumped on the cell floor, Ruhn's body ached from the beating he'd taken. Mordoc had surrounded him with dreadwolves—no shadows would have been able to hide Ruhn from the bloodhound anyway. He'd have been sniffed out immediately.

Had Day betrayed him? Pretended to be captured so he'd come here? He'd been so blind, so fucking *blind*, and now—

The door to the cell far beneath the Asteri's palace opened. Ruhn, chained to the wall with gorsian shackles, looked up in horror as Bryce and Athalar entered, similarly shackled. His sister's face was wholly white.

Athalar bared his teeth at the Harpy as she shoved him in. Since Mordoc still lurked by the cell archway, grinning at them both, Ruhn had no doubt that the Hind was somewhere close by—that she'd be the one who got to work on them.

Neither Athalar nor Bryce fought their captors as they, too, were chained to the wall. Bryce was shaking. With fear or rage, Ruhn didn't know.

He met Mordoc's stare, letting the dreadwolf see just who the fuck he was tangling with. "How did you know I'd be here?"

The dreadwolf captain pushed off from the archway, violence in every movement. "Because Rigelus planned it that way. I still can't believe you walked right into his hands, you stupid fuck."

"We came here to assist the Asteri," Ruhn tried. "You've got the wrong idea."

From the corner of his eye, he could sense Bryce trying to catch his attention.

But Mordoc's face twisted with cruel delight. "Oh? Was that the excuse you were going to use in that alley? Or with the mystics? You forget who you're speaking to. I never forget a scent." He sneered at Bryce and Hunt. "I tracked you all around Lunathion—Rigelus was all too happy to hear about your activities."

"I thought you reported to the Hind," Athalar said.

The silver darts along Mordoc's collar glinted as he stepped closer. "Rigelus has a special interest in you lot. He asked me to sniff around." He made a show of smelling Hunt. "Maybe it's because your scent is wrong, angel."

Athalar growled, "What the fuck does that mean?"

Mordoc angled his head with mocking assessment. "Not like any other angel I've scented."

The Harpy rolled her eyes and said to the captain, "Enough. Leave us."

Mordoc's lip curled. "We're to wait here."

"*Leave us*," the Harpy snapped. "I want a head start before she ruins my fun. Surely you know a thing or two about that, if you're sneaking around her to report to Rigelus." Mordoc bristled, but stalked off with a low snarl.

Ruhn's mind raced. They should never have come here. Mordoc *had* remembered his scent—and tracked them these past weeks. Had fed every location to Rigelus. Fuck.

The Harpy grinned. "It's been a while since I've played with you, Athalar."

Hunt spat at her feet. "Come and get it."

Ruhn knew he was trying to keep her from going for Bryce. Buying them whatever time he could to find a way out of this shitstorm. Ruhn met Bryce's panicked look.

She couldn't teleport, thanks to the gorsian shackles. Could Cormac get back here? He was their only shot at getting out of these chains—their only shot at survival. Had Dec seen the capture? Even if he had, there were no reinforcements to send.

The Harpy drew a short, lethal knife. The kind so precise that it could carve skin from the most delicate places. She flipped it in her hand, keeping back from Athalar's reach, even with the chains. Her focus slid to Ruhn. Hate lit her eyes.

"Not so cocky now, are you, princeling?" she asked. She pointed her knife toward his crotch. "You know how long it takes for a male to grow back his balls?"

Pure dread shot through him.

Bryce hissed, "Keep your fucking hands off him."

The Harpy laughed. "Does it bother you, Princess, to see your males so roughly handled?" She approached Ruhn, and he could do nothing as she ran the side of the blade down his cheek. "So pretty," she murmured, her eyes like blackest Hel. "It will be a shame to ruin such beauty."

Hunt growled, "Come play with someone interesting."

"Still the noble bastard," the Harpy said, running the knife down the other side of Ruhn's face. If she came close enough, he could try to rip out her throat with his teeth, but she was too wary. Kept far enough back. "Trying to distract me from harming others. Don't you remember how I cut up your soldiers piece by piece despite your pleading?"

Bryce lunged against her chains, and Ruhn's heart cracked as she screamed, "*Get the fuck away from him!*"

"Listening to you squeal while I carve him will be a delight," the Harpy said, and slid the knife to the base of Ruhn's throat.

It was going to hurt. It would hurt, but because of his Vanir blood, he wouldn't die—not yet. He'd keep healing while she sliced him apart.

"*GET OFF HIM!*" Bryce bellowed. A guttural roar thundered in the words. As Fae as he'd ever heard his sister.

The tip of the knife pierced Ruhn's throat, its sting blooming. He dove deep, into the place where he'd always run to avoid his father's ministrations.

They'd walked in here so foolishly, had been so blind—

The Harpy sucked in a breath, muscles tensing to shove in the knife.

Something golden and swift as the wind barreled into her side and sent the Harpy sprawling.

Bryce shouted, but all the noise, all the thoughts in Ruhn's head eddied away as a familiar, lovely scent hit him. As he beheld the female who leapt to her feet, now a wall between him and the Harpy.

The Hind.

75

You fucking *cunt*," the Harpy cursed, rising to draw a long, wicked sword.

Ruhn couldn't move from the floor as the Hind unsheathed her own slim blade. As her beckoning scent floated to him. A scent that was somehow entwined with his own. It was very faint, like a shadow, so vague that he doubted anyone else would realize the underlying scent belonged to him.

And her scent had been familiar from the start because Hypaxia was her half-sister, he realized. Family ties didn't lie. He'd been wrong about her being in House of Sky and Breath—the Hind could claim total allegiance to Earth and Blood.

"I knew it. I always *knew* it," the Harpy seethed, wings rustling. "Traitorous bitch."

It couldn't be.

It . . . it couldn't be.

Bryce and Hunt were frozen with shock.

Ruhn whispered, "Day?"

Lidia Cervos looked over a shoulder. And she said with quiet calm in a voice he knew like his own heartbeat, a voice he had never once heard her use as the Hind, "Night."

"The Asteri will carve you up and feed you to your dreadwolves," the Harpy crooned, sword angling. "And I'm going to help them do it."

The golden-haired female—Lidia, *Day*—only said to the Harpy, "Not if I kill you first."

The Harpy lunged. The Hind was waiting.

Sword met sword, and Ruhn could only watch as the shifter deflected and parried the angel's strike. Her blade shone like quicksilver, and as the Harpy brought down another arm-breaking blow, a dagger appeared in Lidia's other hand.

The Hind crossed dagger and sword and met the blow, using the Harpy's movement to kick at her exposed stomach. The angel went down in a pile of wings and black hair, but she was instantly up, circling. "The Asteri will let Pollux have at you, I think." A bitter, cruel laugh.

Pollux—the male who'd . . . A blaring white noise blasted through Ruhn's head.

"Pollux will get what's coming to him, too," the Hind said, blocking the attack and spinning on her knees so that she was behind the Harpy. The Harpy twirled, meeting the blow, but backed a step closer to Ruhn.

Their blades again met, the Harpy pressing. The Hind's arms strained, the sleek muscles in her thighs visible through her skintight white pants as she pushed up, up, to her feet. She kept her black boots planted—the Harpy's stance was nowhere near as solid.

Lidia's golden eyes slid to Ruhn's. She nodded shallowly. A command.

Ruhn crouched, readying.

"Lying filth," the Harpy raged, losing another inch. Just a little further . . . "When did they turn you?"

Ruhn's heart raced.

The two females clashed and withdrew with horrifying skill, then clashed again. "Liar I might be," Lidia growled, smiling savagely, "but at least I'm no fool."

The Harpy blinked as the Hind shoved her another inch.

Right to the edge of Ruhn's reach.

Ruhn grabbed the Harpy's ankle and *yanked*. The angel shouted, tumbling down again, wings splaying.

The Hind struck.

Swift as a cobra, Lidia plunged her sword into the top of the Harpy's spine, right through her neck. The tip of her blade hit the floor before the Harpy's body collided with it.

The Harpy tried to scream, but the Hind had angled the blow to pierce her vocal cords. The next blow, with her parrying dagger, plunged through the Harpy's ear and into the skull beneath. Another move, and her head rolled away.

And then silence. The Harpy's wings twitched.

Ruhn slowly lifted his gaze to the Hind.

Lidia stood over him, splattered with blood. Every line of the body he'd seen and felt was taut. On alert.

Hunt breathed, "You're a double agent?"

But Lidia launched into motion, grabbing Ruhn's chains, unlocking them with a key from her imperial uniform. "We don't have much time. You have to get out of here."

She'd sworn she wouldn't come for him if he got into trouble. But here she was.

"Was this a trap?" Bryce demanded.

"Not in the way you're thinking," Lidia said. As the Hind, she'd kept her voice low and soft. Day's voice—*this* person's voice—sounded higher. She came close enough while she freed Ruhn's feet that he could scent her again. "I tried to warn you that I believed Rigelus *wanted* you to come here, that he knew you would, but . . . I was interrupted." By Pollux. "When I was finally able to reach out to you again, it was clear that only those of us in Sandriel's triarii knew about Rigelus's plan, and that Mordoc had been feeding him information regarding your whereabouts. To warn you off would have been to give myself away."

Hunt glowered as Ruhn stared at the Hind. "And we couldn't have that," the angel said.

Mordoc—how had the bloodhound not noticed the subtle shift in Lidia's scent? In Ruhn's? Or had he, and been biding his time to spring the trap shut?

Lidia shot Hunt a glare, not backing down as she started on Bryce's chains. "There is a great deal that you do not understand."

She was so beautiful. And utterly soulless.

You remind me that I'm alive, she'd told him.

"You killed Sofie," Bryce hissed.

"No." Lidia shook her head. "I called for the city-ship to save her. They arrived too late."

"What?" Athalar blurted.

Ruhn blinked as the Hind pulled a white stone from her pocket. "These are calling stones—beacons. The Ocean Queen enchanted them. They'll summon whatever city-ship is closest when dropped into the water. Her mystics sense when the ships might be needed in a certain area, and the stones are used as a precise method of location."

She'd done it that day in Ydra, too. She'd summoned the ship that saved them.

"Sofie drowned because of you," Ruhn growled, his voice like gravel. "People died at your hands—"

"There is so much to tell you, Ruhn," she said softly, and his name on her tongue . . .

But Ruhn looked away from her. He could have sworn the Hind flinched.

He didn't care. Not as Hunt asked Bryce, "Did you find out the truth?"

Bryce paled. "I did. I—"

Steps sounded down the hall. Far away, but approaching. The Hind went still. "Pollux."

Her hearing had to be better than his. Or she knew the cadence of the bastard's steps so well she could tell from a distance.

"We have to make it appear real," she said to Bryce, to Ruhn, voice pleading, utterly desperate. "The information lines *can't* be broken." Her voice cracked. "Do you understand?"

Bryce did, apparently. She smirked. "I shouldn't enjoy this so much."

Before Ruhn could react, his sister punched the shifter in the face. Sent her sprawling. He shouted, and those footsteps down the hall turned into a run.

Bryce leapt upon the Hind, fists flying, and the Harpy's blood on the floor smeared all over them both. Hunt struggled against his chains, and Ruhn got to his feet, lunging toward the females—

Pollux appeared in the doorway.

He beheld the dead Harpy, beheld Bryce bloodied with the Hind beneath her, being pummeled, beheld Ruhn advancing, and drew his sword.

Ruhn could have sworn the Hind whispered something in Bryce's ear before Pollux grabbed Bryce by the neck and hauled her off the other female.

"Hello, Princess," the monster crooned.

Hunt had no words in his head as the male he hated above all others grabbed his mate by the neck. Held her off the floor so that the tips of her sneakers dragged on the bloodied stone.

"Look what you did to my friend," Pollux said in that dead, soulless voice. "And to my lover."

"I'll do the same to you," Bryce managed to say, feet kicking blindly.

"*Put her the fuck down,*" Hunt snarled.

Pollux sneered at him, and did no such thing.

The Hind had managed to pull her sword from the Harpy's body and point it at Ruhn. "Back against the wall or she dies." Her voice was flat and low—as Hunt had always heard it. Not at all like the softer, higher register of a moment before.

Agent Daybright hadn't needed saving after all. And the Hind . . . the female that Hunt had seen so mercilessly stride through the world . . .

She was a rebel. Had saved their asses that day in the waters off Ydra by summoning the city-ship with the calling stone. It hadn't been Bryce's light at all. *We got your message,* they'd said.

Ruhn looked like he'd been punched in the gut. In the soul.

But Pollux finally lowered Bryce to the ground, an arm wrapping around her middle as he grinned at Hunt. He sniffed Bryce's hair. Hunt's vision went black with rage as Pollux said, "This is going to be so satisfying."

Bryce was shaking. She knew—whatever the truth was about the Asteri, about all of this, she knew. They had to get her out, so that information wouldn't die here.

So she wouldn't die here.

The next few minutes were a blur. Guards flowed in. Hunt found himself being hauled to his feet, Bryce chained beside him, Ruhn on her other side, the Hind stalking next to Pollux as they walked from the dungeons to an elevator bay.

"Their Graces await you," the Hind said with such unfeeling ice that even Hunt bought it, and wondered if he'd imagined the female helping them. Imagined that she'd risked everything to save Ruhn from the Harpy.

From the way Ruhn was glaring at the Hind, Hunt could only guess what the prince was thinking.

They entered the elevator, the Hind and Pollux facing them. The Hammer smirked at Hunt.

If they could kill Pollux . . . But cameras monitored this elevator. The halls. The Hind would be revealed.

Bryce was still shaking beside him. He hooked his fingers through hers, sticky with blood—as much movement as his chains would allow.

He tried not to glance down when he felt her own chains. The manacles were loose. Unlocked. Only Bryce's fingertips held them in place—the Hind hadn't secured them. Bryce met Hunt's stare. Pained and full of love.

The Hind had known it, too. That Bryce, with the intel she carried, had to get out.

Was the Hind planning something? Had she whispered a plan in Bryce's ear?

Bryce said nothing. Just held his hand—for the last time, he realized as the elevator shot up through the crystal palace.

He was holding his mate's hand for the last time.

Ruhn stared at the female he'd thought he knew. At her impassive, beautiful face. Her empty golden eyes.

It was a mask. He'd seen the real face moments ago. Had joined his body and soul with hers days ago. He knew what fire burned there.

Night.

Her voice was a distant, soft plea in his mind. Like Lidia was trying to find a way to link their thoughts again, like the crystal in his pocket had yet again forged a path. *Night.*

Ruhn ignored the begging voice. The way it broke as she said, *Ruhn.*

He fortified the walls of his mind. Brick by brick.

Ruhn. Lidia banged on the walls of his mind.

So he encased it with iron. With black steel.

Pollux smiled at him. Slid a hand around the Hind's blood-splattered throat and kissed under her ear. "Do you like the way my lover looks, princeling?"

Something lethal snapped free at that hand on her neck. The way it squeezed, and the slight glimmer of pain in Lidia's eyes—

He'd hurt her. Pollux had hurt her, again and again, and she'd voluntarily submitted so she could keep feeding the rebels intel. She'd endured a monster like Pollux for this.

"Maybe we'll put on a show for you before the end," Pollux said, and licked up the column of Lidia's neck, lapping up the blood splattered there.

Ruhn bared his teeth in a silent snarl. He'd kill him. Slowly and thoroughly, punishing him for every touch, every hand he'd put on Lidia in pain and torment.

He had no idea where that landed him. Why he wanted and needed that steel-clad wall between him and Lidia, even as his blood howled to murder Pollux. How he could abhor her and need her, be drawn to her, in the same breath.

Pollux laughed against her skin, then pulled away. Lidia smiled coolly. Like it all meant nothing, like she felt nothing at all.

But that voice against the walls of his mind shouted, *Ruhn!*

She banged against the black steel and stone, over and over. Her voice broke again, *Ruhn!*

Ruhn locked her out.

She'd taken countless lives—but she'd worked to save them, too.

Did it change anything? He'd known Day was someone high up—he'd have been a fool to think anyone with that level of clearance with the Asteri would come without complications. But for it to be her . . . What the Hel did it even say about him, that he was capable of feeling what he did for someone like *her*?

His ally was his enemy. His enemy was his lover. He focused on the gore splattered on her.

Lidia had so much blood on her hands that there would never be any washing it away.

Bryce knew no one was coming to save them. Knew it was likely her fault. She could barely stand to feel Hunt's fingers against hers as they walked down the long crystal hallway. Couldn't stand the stickiness of the Harpy's blood as it dried on her skin.

She'd never seen a hall so long. A wall of windows stretched along one side, overlooking the palace grounds and ancient city beyond. On the other side, busts of the Asteri in their various forms frowned down upon them from atop pedestals.

Their masters. Their overlords. The parasites who had lured them all into this world. Who had fed off them for fifteen thousand years.

Rigelus wouldn't have told her so much if he planned to ever let her go again.

She wished she'd called her mom and Randall. Wished she could hear their voices one more time. Wished she'd made things right with Juniper. Wished she'd lain low and been normal and lived out a long, happy life with Hunt.

It wouldn't have been normal, though. It would have been contented ignorance. And any children they had . . . their power would one day have also been siphoned off to fuel these cities and the monsters who ruled them.

The cycle had to stop somewhere. Other worlds had managed to overthrow them. *Hel* had managed to kick them out.

But Bryce knew she and Hunt and Ruhn wouldn't be the ones to stop the cycle. That task would be left to others.

Cormac would continue to fight. Maybe Tharion and Hypaxia and Ithan would pick up the cause. Perhaps Fury, too.

Gods, did Jesiba know? She'd kept Parthos's remaining books—knowing the Asteri would want to wipe out the narrative that contradicted their own sanctioned history. So Jesiba *had* to know what kind of beings ruled here, didn't she?

The Hind led their group down the hall, Pollux at their backs. At the far, far end of the passage, Bryce could make out a small arch.

A quartz Gate.

Bryce's blood chilled. Did Rigelus plan to have her open it as some sort of test before cracking wide the Rifts?

She'd do it. Rigelus had Hunt and Ruhn in his claws. She knew her mate and brother would tell her that their lives weren't worth it, but . . . weren't they?

The Hind turned a third of the way down the hall, toward a pair of colossal open doors.

Seven thrones towered on a dais at the far end of the cavernous, crystal space. All but one lay empty. And the center throne, the occupied one . . . it glowed, full of firstlight. Funneling it right into the being who sat atop it.

Something feral opened an eye in Bryce's soul. And snarled.

"I suppose you're pleased to have added yet another angel to your kill list with the death of the Harpy," the Bright Hand of the Asteri drawled to Bryce, stare sweeping over the blood caked on her. "I do hope you're ready to pay for it."

76

Hunt stared at his severed wings, mounted on the wall high above the Asteri's thrones.

Shahar's pristine white wings were displayed above his, still glowing after all these centuries, right in the center of the array. Isaiah's were to the left of Hunt's. So many wings. So many Fallen. All preserved here.

He'd known the Asteri had kept them. But seeing them . . .

It was proof of his failure. Proof that he should never have come here, that they should have told Ophion and Tharion and Cormac to fuck off—

"I did you a favor, killing the Harpy," Bryce said to Rigelus, who watched her with lifeless eyes. At least the five others weren't here. "She was a drag."

Hunt blinked at his blood-splattered mate. Her eyes smoldered like coals, defiant and raging. She'd seen his wings, too.

Rigelus propped his slender chin on a fist, leaning a bony elbow against his throne. He appeared as a Fae boy of seventeen or so, dark-haired and gangly. A weak facade to veil the ancient monster beneath. "Shall we banter some more, Miss Quinlan, or can I get to the part where I order you to confess the names of your allies?"

Bryce smirked, and Hunt had never loved her more. On her

other side, Ruhn glanced between the Asteri and his sister, as if trying to formulate a plan.

Hunt caught a familiar scent, and he twisted to see Baxian and Mordoc enter behind them. They walked to where the Hind and the Hammer stood by the pillars. Blocking the way out.

Rigelus had known of their mission here before they'd even reached Pangera's shores—before they'd even set out. Mordoc had tracked their scents with that bloodhound's gift all around the city, marking each location and reporting directly to the Bright Hand.

And Hunt had left his phone in Lunathion, for fear of it being tracked here. Baxian wouldn't have been able to warn him, if he'd even been willing to risk doing so.

Hunt's eyes met Baxian's. The male revealed nothing. Not one bit of recognition.

Had everything he'd told them been a trap? A long con to get them here?

Bryce said to Rigelus, drawing Hunt's attention away, "There is no one else. But let's talk about how you're intergalactic parasites who trick us into making the Drop so you can feed off our firstlight. And then feed off our souls' secondlight when we die."

Hunt went still. He could have sworn someone behind him—Baxian or the Hind, perhaps—started.

Rigelus snorted. "Is this your way of telling your companions what you know?"

Bryce didn't avert her gaze. "Hel yeah, it is. Along with the fact that if we destroy that core of firstlight beneath this palace—"

"Silence," Rigelus hissed, and the room shuddered with power.

But Hunt's mind reeled. The Asteri, the firstlight . . . Bryce caught his stare, her eyes brimming with rage and purpose. There was more, she seemed to say. So much more to be used against the Asteri.

Rigelus pointed at Ruhn. "I'm sure you could enlighten me as to who has been helping you. I know of Prince Cormac—I'd hoped his rebel activities might be of use someday. When we learned of his treachery, the others wanted to kill him and be done with it, but I thought it might be . . . valuable to see where and to whom he led us. A Prince of the Fae would no doubt wind up around other powerful Vanir, perhaps even try to recruit some of them, and thus root out the corruption among our most loyal subjects. So why kill one traitor, when we could eventually kill many? Alas, he's dead now. That's where my other siblings are—drawn out to the lab, as you no doubt expected. But they reported that another male was with the prince, and fled."

Bryce made a low sound in her throat.

Rigelus turned to her. "Oh yes. Cormac incinerated himself and the lab. A great setback, considering how useful he was, but one we shall overcome, of course. Especially with Pippa Spetsos among the dead."

At least Tharion had escaped unidentified.

"Perhaps we shall call in your father to assist with the questioning," Rigelus went on to Ruhn, bored and cool. "He was so skilled at wielding his fire to get things out of you when you were a boy."

Ruhn stiffened.

Hunt took in Bryce's blood-flecked features. He'd only once seen this level of rage on her face. Not toward Rigelus, but the male who'd sired her. It was the same rage he'd beheld that day she'd killed Micah.

"Isn't that what so many of the tattoos are for?" Rigelus continued. "To hide the scars he left on you? I'm afraid we'll have to ruin some of the ink this time around."

Fucking Hel. Bryce's lips had gone white from pressing them together so hard. Her eyes were bright with unshed tears.

Ruhn looked at his sister and said softly, "You brought so much joy into my life, Bryce."

It was perhaps the only goodbye they'd be able to make.

Hunt reached for Bryce's fingers, but she stepped forward. Lifted her chin in that defiant, fuck-you way he loved so much. "You want me to open a portal for you? Fine. But only if you let them go and agree to leave them unharmed. Forever."

Hunt's blood iced over. "That was why you lured us here?" he found himself demanding of the Asteri, even as he roared with outrage at Bryce's offer.

Rigelus said, "I couldn't very well snatch you off the streets. Not such notorious, public figures. Not without the right charges to bring you in." A smirk at Bryce. "Your friend Aidas will be terribly disappointed to learn you couldn't tell the difference between the real Prince of the Chasm and myself. He's terribly vain in that way."

Hunt started, but Bryce seethed, "You pretended to be Aidas that night."

"Who else could break through the wards on your apartment? You didn't even suspect anything when he encouraged you toward rebellious activities. Though I suppose credit for that goes to me—I played his rage about Theia and Pelias quite well, don't you think?"

Fuck. He'd anticipated their every move.

Rigelus went on, "And you didn't even look that hard into the Reapers I sent from this city to nudge you. The Bone Quarter was a testing ground for your true power, you see—since you seemed to have little awareness or interest in it all summer. You were to hone your powers, all so we might put them to good use. You played along beautifully."

Hunt's fingers curled into fists. He should have seen it—should have pushed Bryce away from this mess, should have taken her at the first hint of trouble and gone to a place where no one could ever find them.

But this was Midgard. No matter where they went, no matter how far from Lunathion or the Eternal City, the Asteri would always find them.

Rigelus sighed dramatically at their stunned silence. "This all seems very familiar, doesn't it? A Starborn queen who allied with a Prince of Hel. Who trusted him deeply, and ultimately paid the price."

Hunt mastered himself enough to nod toward the seventh, always empty throne. "Hel got one on you in the end, though, I think."

Rigelus's body glowed with ire, but his voice remained silky smooth. "I look forward to facing Apollion again. Mordoc suspected that the Star-Eater had been trying to get your attention these past weeks—to prod you along in his own way."

So one Prince of Hel had been a fake, the other true. Apollion really had sent the deathstalkers, presumably to test Bryce's powers—just as Rigelus also wanted—and Hunt's own. And wanted it so badly that he was willing to risk her death should she not be up to the task.

But she'd teleported that night. Used that ability to defeat the deathstalkers. Had started to grasp the gift and progressed in leaps and bounds since then. Literally.

Apollion must have known she'd need those skills. Perhaps for this very moment.

The gorsian chains on Bryce's wrists were unlocked. If she could throw them off, she could get out. If the Hind could somehow get his own chains off, he'd block the Asteri and Bryce could keep running.

Hunt said, one last try, "You're full of shit, and Mordoc should get his nose checked. We're not rebels. Celestina can vouch for us."

Rigelus laughed, and Hunt bristled. "Celestina? You mean the Archangel who reported to me that you'd lied about going to visit Miss Quinlan's family a few weeks ago, and then reported to me immediately when she saw you leave the barracks heavily armed?" The words landed like a phantom punch to Hunt's gut.

Love is a trap, Celestina had told him. Was this her way of protecting what she loved? Proving her trustworthiness to the Asteri by selling Hunt and his friends out so that they might react kindly if they learned about Hypaxia? Had she any idea the witch she loved was involved?

Rigelus seemed to read those questions on Hunt's face, because he said, "She might have once been a friend of Shahar, Orion, but with so much personally on the line for her, she is no friend to you. At least, not when it comes to protecting those she cherishes most."

"Why are you doing this?" Ruhn asked hoarsely.

Rigelus frowned with distaste. "It is a matter of survival." A glance at Bryce. "Though her first task for us shall be one of . . . a personal matter, I think."

"You're going to attack Hel," Hunt breathed. Was that what Apollion was anticipating? Why he'd kept telling them, again and again, that Hel's armies were readying?

Not to attack this world, but to defend Hel itself. To ally with any who'd stand against the Asteri.

"No," Rigelus said. "Even Hel is not at the top of our list of those from whom we shall exact vengeance." Again, that smile at Bryce. "The star on your chest—do you know what it is?"

"Let's assume I know nothing," Bryce said grimly.

Rigelus inclined his head. "It's a beacon to the world from which the Fae originally came. It sometimes glows when nearest the Fae who have undiluted bloodlines from that world. Prince Cormac, for example."

"It glowed for Hunt," Bryce shot back.

"It also glows for those who you choose as your loyal companions. Knights."

"So what?" Bryce demanded.

"So that star will lead us back to that world. Through you. They overthrew our brethren who once ruled there—we have not forgotten. Our initial attempt at revenge was foiled by your ancestor who also bore that star on her chest. The Fae have still not atoned for the deaths of our brothers and sisters. Their home world was rich in magic. I crave more of it."

Bryce shook, but Hunt's heart cracked as she squared her shoulders. "My bargain holds. You let Hunt and Ruhn go freely and unharmed—forever—and I'll help you."

"Bryce," Ruhn pleaded, but Hunt knew there was no arguing with her.

"Fine," Rigelus said, and smiled, triumph on every line of his lanky body. "You may say goodbye, as a sign of my gratitude for your assistance."

Bryce turned to Hunt, and the terror and pain and grief on her gore-splattered face threatened to bring him to his knees. He slipped his chained hands around her head, pulling her close. Whispered in her ear. Her fingers bunched in his shirt, as if in silent confirmation.

So Hunt pulled back. Stared into his mate's beautiful face for the last time.

He laughed softly, a sound of wonder at odds with the crystal throne room and the monsters in it. "I love you. I wish I'd said it more. But I love you, Quinlan, and . . ." His throat closed up, his eyes stinging. His lips brushed her brow. "Our love is stronger than time, greater than any distance. Our love spans across stars and worlds. I will find you again. I promise."

He kissed her, and she shuddered, silently crying as her mouth moved against his own. He savored the warmth and taste of her, etching it into his soul.

Then he stepped back, and Bryce faced Ruhn.

She couldn't do this.

Her heart was shattering; her bones were screaming that this was *wrong, wrong, wrong.*

She couldn't leave them. Couldn't go through with what Hunt had whispered to her.

She clung to her brother, unable to stop her sobbing. Even as a small weight dropped into her pocket.

But Ruhn whispered in her ear, "I lied to the Autumn King about what the Oracle told me as a boy." She stilled. Ruhn went on, swift and urgent, "The Oracle told me that the royal line would end with me. That I am the last of the line, Bryce." She tried to pull back to gape at him, but he held her firm. "But maybe she didn't see that *you* would come along. That you would walk this path. You have to live. I can see it on your face—you don't want to do any of this. But you *have* to live, Bryce. You have to be queen."

She'd guessed what the Autumn King had done to Ruhn, how he'd tortured him as a boy, though she'd never confirmed it. And that debt . . . she'd make her sire repay it, someday.

"I don't accept that," Bryce breathed to Ruhn. "I *don't.*"

"I do. I always have. Whether I die right now or whether I'm just infertile, I don't know." He chuckled. "Why do you think I partied so hard?"

She couldn't laugh. Not about this. "I don't buy that bullshit for one second."

"It doesn't matter now."

Then Ruhn said into her mind, *Grab the Starsword when you go.*
Ruhn—

It's yours. Take it. You'll need it. You got the chains unhooked?

Yes. She'd used the key the Hind had slipped her to unlock Hunt's
and Ruhn's manacles while she held them.

Good. I told Athalar the signal. You're ready?

No.

Ruhn pressed his brow against hers. *We need armies, Bryce. We
need you to go to Hel through that Gate, and bring Hel's armies back with
you to fight these bastards. But if Apollion's cost is too high . . . don't come
back to this world.*

Her brother pulled away. And Ruhn said, shining with pride,
"Long live the queen."

Bryce didn't give the others a chance to puzzle it out.

She flicked her wrists, chains falling to the floor as she grabbed
the Starsword from Ruhn and whirled toward Rigelus.

She plunged into her power in a blink. And before the Bright
Hand could shout, she blasted him with starlight.

Hunt threw his chains to the ground the moment Ruhn said the
word *queen.* And as his mate launched her blinding power at Rigelus, Hunt hurled his at the male, too.

Lightning struck the marble pillar just above the crystal throne.

It was a gamble: directing his initial blast of power at Rigelus,
to keep him down, rather than charging up Bryce and risking an
attack from Rigelus before it was done.

Behind them, shouting rose, and Hunt twisted to see Bryce running toward the doors, Starsword in hand.

Pollux lunged for her, but Baxian was there. He tackled the male
to the crystal floor. Behind him, Mordoc was bleeding from a gash
in his throat. The Hind was on the floor, unconscious. Had Baxian's
treachery been a surprise to her? Hunt supposed he didn't care. Not
as Baxian got Pollux down, and Bryce raced through the doors, out
into the endless hallway. She turned left, red hair streaming behind
her, and then she was gone.

Hunt whirled back toward Rigelus, but too late.

Power, hot and aching, blasted him into a nearby pillar. Glowing like a god, Rigelus leapt off the dais, the crystal floor splintering beneath him, and barreled after Bryce, death raging in his eyes.

Bryce's heart cracked piece by piece with each step she ran from that throne room.

As she sped down the long hall, the busts of the Asteri damned her with their hateful faces.

A tidal wave of power rose behind her, and she dared a look over her shoulder to find Rigelus on her tail. He blazed white with magic, fury radiating from him.

Come on, Hunt. Come on, come on . . .

Rigelus sent out a blast of power, and Bryce zoomed left. The Asteri's power smashed through a window, glass spraying. Bryce slipped on the shards, but kept running toward the arch at the end of the hall. The Gate she'd open to take her to Hel.

She'd take her chances with Aidas and Thanatos and Apollion. Get their armies and bring them back to Midgard.

Rigelus shot another spear of power, and Bryce ducked, sliding low just as it shattered a marble bust of Austrus. Fragments sliced her face, her neck, her arms, but then she was up and running again, clenching the Starsword so hard her hand ached.

The slide had cost her.

Rigelus was ten feet behind. Five. His hand stretched for her trailing hair.

Lightning speared down the hall, shattering windows and statues in its wake.

Bryce welcomed it into her heart, her back. Welcomed it into the tattoo there as Hunt's power singed her very blood—and left it sparking.

Lightning ruptured from her scar like a bullet passing through. Right into the archway of the Gate.

She didn't dare see if Hunt still stood after his flawless shot. Not as the air of the Gate's arch turned black. Murky.

Rigelus's fingers snared in her hair.

Bryce gave herself to the wind and darkness, and teleported for the Gate.

Only to land ten feet ahead of Rigelus, as if her powers had hit a wall. Bryce could sense them now—a series of wards, like those Hypaxia had said the Under-King had used to entrap her and Ithan.

But Rigelus shouted in rage and surprise, as if shocked she'd even managed to get that far, and slung his power again.

Ten feet at a time, then. Bryce teleported, and another statue lost its head.

Again, and again, and again, Rigelus shot his power at her and Bryce leapt through space, ward to ward, zigging and zagging, glass and countless statues to the Asteri's egos shattering, the Gate nearing—

Bryce leapt *back*—right behind Rigelus.

He whirled, and she blasted a wall of light into his face. He howled, and she teleported once more—

Bryce landed ten feet from the Gate's gaping maw and kept running.

Rigelus roared as Bryce jumped into the awaiting darkness.

It caught her, sticky like a web. Time slowed to a glacial drip.

Rigelus was still roaring, lunging.

Bryce thrust her power out, willed the Gate to take her and her alone, and she was falling, falling, falling while standing still, suspended in the archway, sucked backward so that her hair trailed outward, toward Rigelus's straining fingers—

"*NO!*" he bellowed.

It was the last sound Bryce heard as the darkness within the Gate swallowed her whole.

She fell, slowly and without end—and sideways. Not a plunge down, but a yank *across*. The pressure in her ears threatened to pulp her brain, and she was screaming into wind and stars and emptiness, screaming to Hunt and Ruhn, left behind in that crystal palace. Screaming—

77

Hunt could barely get a breath down around the stone gag. A gorsian stone, to match the ones clamped around his wrists and neck. The same kind contained Ruhn and Baxian as the two males were led toward the doors of the throne room by Rigelus and his underlings.

Not one flicker of lightning remained in Hunt's body.

The Hind strode beside Rigelus, speaking softly as they walked past where Hunt was on his knees outside the doors. She didn't so much as look at Ruhn. The prince only stared ahead.

Baxian was escorted over, bloodied and bruised from the fight with Pollux. Mordoc was recovering from his slit throat, hate simmering from him as he lay bleeding on the floor. Hunt gave the bloodhound a savage smile as a ribbon of Rigelus's power hauled Hunt to his feet.

"A short stop before the dungeons, I think," Rigelus announced, turning left—toward the shattered ruin along the hall. Toward the now-empty Gate.

Hunt was powerless to do anything but follow, Ruhn and Baxian with him. He'd been at the end of the hall when Bryce had made her spectacular run, teleporting as fast as the wind toward the black hole that had opened within the small Gate. No trace of the blackness or Bryce remained now.

Hunt could only pray that Bryce had reached Hel. That she'd

locate Aidas and he'd protect her as they rallied Hel's armies and brought them back through the Rift into Midgard. To save them.

Hunt doubted he'd be around to see it. Doubted Ruhn or Baxian would, either.

Rigelus halted before the Gate. "Get the angel on his knees."

Bryce's scent still lingered in the air of the empty space framed by the Gate. Hunt focused on that scent and that scent alone as Pollux shoved him to the floor before the Gate.

If this was it, he could die knowing Bryce had gotten away. She'd gone from one Hel to a literal one, but . . . she'd gotten away. Their last chance at salvation.

"Go ahead, Hammer," Rigelus said, smiling at Hunt, cold death in his ageless eyes.

Hunt could feel Ruhn and Baxian watching in muted horror. Hunt bowed over his knees, waiting for the blow to his neck.

Bryce, Bryce, Bryce—

Pollux's hands clamped onto either side of his face. Holding it upright, like he'd snap Hunt's neck with his bare hands.

Pollux laughed softly.

Hunt knew why a moment later as Rigelus approached, a hand lifted and near-blinding with white light. "I don't think I need one of the crones this time," the Bright Hand said.

No. *No.* Anything but this.

Hunt thrashed, but Pollux held him firm, smile unfaltering.

Rigelus laid his glowing hand on Hunt's brow and pain erupted through his skull, his muscles, his blood. As if the very marrow of his bones were being burned into mist.

The Asteri's power slithered and spiderwebbed across Hunt's brow, piercing into him with every spike of the halo's thorns that Rigelus tattooed there.

Hunt screamed then. It echoed off the stones, off the Gate.

Beside him, Baxian started inhaling sharp, jagged breaths. Like the Helhound knew he was next.

The pain across Hunt's brow became blinding, his vision splintering.

The halo kept spreading over his skull, worse than any gorsian shackle. His power writhed in its iron grip, no longer his to fully command. Just as his own life, his freedom, his future with Bryce . . . Gone.

Hunt screamed again, and as darkness swept in to claim him, he wondered if that soul-scream, not the halo, was what Rigelus wanted. If the Asteri believed the sound of his suffering might carry through the Gate and into Hel itself, where Bryce could hear him.

Then Hunt knew nothing at all.

78

Hel had grass. And mist.

Those were Bryce's first two thoughts as she landed—or appeared. One moment she was falling sideways, and then her right shoulder collided with a wall of green that turned out to be the ground.

She panted, mind spinning so violently she could only lie amid the drifting, chill fog. Her fingers dug into the verdant grass. Blood coated her hands. Crusted beneath her nails.

She had to get up. Had to start moving before one of Hel's creatures sniffed her out and ripped her to shreds. If those death-stalkers found her, they'd kill her in an instant.

The Starsword—

There. A foot beyond her head.

Bryce trembled as she eased onto her knees, bending to hold them tight.

Hunt . . . She could have sworn she heard his screams echoing in the mist as she fell.

She had to get up. Find a way to Aidas.

Yet she couldn't move. To get up would be to walk away from her world, from Hunt and Ruhn, and whatever the Asteri were doing to them—

Get up, she told herself, gritting her teeth.

The mists parted ahead, peeling back to reveal a gentle turquoise river perhaps fifty feet from where she knelt, flowing right past the . . . lawn.

She was on someone's clipped, immaculate lawn. And across the river, emerging from the mist . . .

A city. Ancient and beautiful—like something on a Pangeran postcard. Indistinct shapes meandered through the mist on the other side of the river—the demons of Hel.

Get up.

Bryce swallowed hard, as if she could drink down her shaking, and slid out a leg to rise. The Harpy's blood still soaked her leggings, the fabric sticky against her skin.

Something icy and sharp pressed against her throat.

A cool male voice spoke above her, behind her, in a language she did not recognize. But the curt words and tone were clear enough: *Don't fucking move.*

Bryce lifted her hands and reached for her power. Only splintered shards remained.

The male voice demanded something in that strange language, and Bryce stayed on her knees. He hissed, and then a strong hand clamped on her shoulder, hauling her up and twisting her to face him.

She glimpsed black boots. Dark, scalelike armor over a tall, muscled body.

Wings. Great, black wings. A demon's wings.

But the male face that stared through the mists, grave and lethal . . . it was beautiful, despite the fact that his hazel eyes held no mercy. He spoke again, in a soft voice that promised pain.

Bryce couldn't stop her chest from heaving wildly. "Aidas. I need to see Aidas. Can you take me to him?" Her voice broke.

The winged male swept his gaze over her—assessing and wary. Noted that the blood covering her was not her own. His attention drifted to the Starsword lying in the grass between them. His eyes widened slightly.

Bryce lunged a step toward him, making to grab the front of

his intricate armor. He easily sidestepped the move, face impassive as she asked, "Can you take me to Prince Aidas?" She couldn't stop her tears then. The male's brows knitted.

"Please," Bryce begged. "Please."

The male's face didn't soften as he picked up the sheathed Star-sword, then gestured for her to step closer.

Bryce obeyed, shaking, wondering if she should be fighting, screaming.

With scarred hands, the demon pulled a scrap of black cloth from a hidden pocket in his armor. Held it up to his face, feigning putting it on. A blindfold.

Bryce breathed in, trying to calm herself as she nodded. The male's hands were gentle but thorough as he fitted it tightly over her eyes.

Then hands were at her knees and back, and the ground was gone—they were flying.

Only the flap of his leathery wings and the sighing mist filled her ears. So different from the rippling hush of Hunt's feathers in the wind.

Bryce tried to use the time in the air to stop shaking, but she couldn't. Couldn't even form a solid thought.

They glided downward, her stomach tipping with the movement, and then they landed, the thump of the demon's boots hitting the ground echoing through her. He set her down, taking her by the hand. A door creaked open. Warm air greeted her, then the door shut. He said something she didn't understand, and then she was toppling forward—

He caught her, and sighed. She could have sworn he sounded . . . exasperated. He gave no warning as he hauled her over a shoulder and tromped down a set of stairs before entering somewhere . . . nice-smelling. Roses? Bread?

They ate bread in Hel? Had flowers? *A dark, cold world*, the Asteri had said in their notes on the planet.

Floorboards groaned beneath his boots, and then Bryce found herself again on solid ground, carpets cushioning her feet. He led her by the hand and pushed her downward. Bryce tensed, fighting it, but he did it again, and she sat. In a comfy chair.

He spoke in that silken voice, and she shook her head. "I don't understand you," she said rawly. "I don't know Hel's languages. But . . . Aidas? Prince Aidas?"

He didn't reply.

"Please," she repeated. "I need to find Prince Aidas. My world, Midgard—it's in grave danger, and my mate . . ." Her voice broke, and she doubled over in the darkness. *I will find you again*, Hunt had promised.

But he wouldn't. He couldn't. He had no way to get here. And she had no way to get home.

Unless Aidas or Apollion knew how to use the Horn. Had magic that could charge it.

She'd left Hunt and Ruhn. Had run and left them, and . . . Bryce sobbed. "Oh gods," she wept. She tore off the blindfold, baring her teeth. *"Aidas!"* she shouted at the cold-faced male. "Get fucking *AIDAS*."

He didn't so much as blink. Didn't reveal one hint of emotion, that he cared.

But—this room. This . . . house?

Dark oak wood floors and furniture. Rich, velvet fabrics. A crackling fire. Books on the shelves lining one wall. A cart of liquor in crystal decanters beside the black marble fireplace. And through the archway beyond the winged male, a foyer and a dining room.

Its style could have fit in with her father's study. With Jesiba's gallery.

The male watched cautiously. She swallowed down her tears, straightening her shoulders. Cleared her throat. "Where am I? What level of Hel?"

"Hel?" he said at last.

"Hel, yes, Hel!" She gestured to the house. The complete opposite of what she'd expected. "What level? Pit? Chasm?"

He shook his head, brow furrowing. The front door in the foyer opened, and multiple people rushed in, males and females, all speaking that strange language.

Bryce beheld the first one and shot to her feet.

The petite, dark-haired female with angular eyes like Fury's drew up short. Her red-painted mouth dropped open, no doubt at the blood all over Bryce's face and body.

This female was . . . Fae. Clad in beautiful, yet thoroughly old-fashioned clothes. Like the stuff they wore on Avallen.

Another winged male, broader than the other, swaggered in, a pretty female with brown-gold hair at his side. Also Fae. Also wearing clothes that seemed out of some sort of fantasy film.

Bryce blurted, "I've been trying to ask him, but he doesn't understand. Is this Hel? I need to see Prince Aidas."

The dark-haired one turned to the others and said something that had them all angling their heads at Bryce. The swaggering male sniffed, trying to read the scent of the blood on her.

Bryce swallowed hard. She knew only one other language, and that one . . .

Her heart thundered. Bryce said in the ancient language of the Fae, of the Starborn, "Is this world Hel? I need to see Prince Aidas."

The petite, dark-haired female staggered back, a hand to her mouth. The others gaped. As if the small female's shock was a rare occurrence. The female eyed the Starsword then. Looked to the first winged male—Bryce's captor. Nodded to the dark-hilted knife at his side.

The male drew it, and Bryce flinched.

Flinched, but—"What the fuck?" The knife could have been the twin of the Starsword: black hilted and bladed.

It *was* its twin. The Starsword began to hum within its sheath, glittering white light leaking from where leather met the dark hilt. The dagger—

The male dropped the dagger to the plush carpet. All of them retreated as it flared with dark light, as if in answer. Alpha and Omega.

"Gwydion," the dark-haired female whispered, indicating the Starsword.

The broader male sucked in a breath. Then said something in

that language she couldn't comprehend. The brunette at his side snapped something back that sounded like a reprimand.

"Is this Hel?" Bryce asked again in the old tongue of the Fae.

The dark-haired female observed Bryce from head to toe: the clothes so thoroughly at odds with their own attire, the blood and cuts. Then she replied in the old tongue, "No one has spoken that language in this world for fifteen thousand years."

Bryce rubbed at her face. Had she traveled in time, somehow? Or did Hel occupy a different time and—

"Please," she said. "I need to find Prince Aidas."

"I do not know who that is."

"Apollion, then. Surely you know the Prince of the Pit."

"I do not know of such people. This world is not Hel."

Bryce slowly shook her head. "I . . . Then where am I?" She surveyed the silent others, the winged males and the other Fae female, who stared coolly. "*What world is this?*"

The front door opened again. First, a lovely female with the same brown-gold hair as the one already standing before Bryce entered. She wore a loose white shirt over brown pants, both splattered with paint. Her hands were tattooed to the elbows in intricate swirls. But her blue-gray eyes were wary—soft and curious, but wary.

The winged, dark-haired male who stepped in behind her . . .

Bryce gasped. "Ruhn?"

The male blinked. His eyes were the same shade of violet blue as Ruhn's. His short hair the same gleaming black. This male's skin was browner, but the face, the posture . . . It was her brother's. His ears were pointed, too, though he also possessed those leathery wings like the two other males.

The female beside him asked the petite female a question in their language.

But the male continued to stare at Bryce. At the blood on her, at the Starsword and the knife, the blades still gleaming with their opposite lights.

He lifted his gaze to her, stars in his eyes. Actual stars.

Bryce pleaded with the petite female, "My world . . . Midgard . . .

It's in grave danger. My mate, he . . ." She couldn't get the words out. "I didn't mean to come here. I meant to go to Hel. To get aid from the princes. But I don't know what this world is. Or how to find Hel. I need your help."

It was all there was left to do: throw herself at their mercy and pray they were decent people. That even if she'd come from another world, they'd recognize her as Fae and be compassionate.

The petite female seemed to repeat Bryce's words to the others. The female with the tattooed hands asked Bryce a question in their language. The petite one translated: "She wants to know what your name is."

Bryce glanced from the tattooed female to the beautiful male at her side. They both possessed an air of quiet, gentle authority. The others all seemed to wait for their cues. So Bryce addressed the two of them as she lifted her chin. "My name is Bryce Quinlan."

The male stepped forward, tucking in his wings. He smiled slightly and said in the Old Language, in a voice like glorious night, "Hello, Bryce Quinlan. My name is Rhysand."

EPILOGUE

Ithan Holstrom crouched, a hulking wolf among the rain-lashed shadows outside the Astronomer's building, monitoring the few people in the alley braving the storm.

No word had come from Pangera. Just a mention of an explosion at a lab outside the city, and that was it. He didn't expect to hear anything from Bryce and the others at least until the next day.

But he couldn't help the urge to pace, even as he guarded the doors across the alley. He'd seen no glimpse of the Astronomer. No patrons had entered. Had Mordoc dragged the wretch off for an interrogation about why Ithan and his friends had visited him? And left the mystics here—unguarded and alone?

He'd fucked up guard duty with Hypaxia. He wouldn't make that mistake again. Not with the mystic caged beyond those doors.

Another Fendyr heir to the Prime. An Alpha to challenge Sabine.

Something moved in the shadows far down the alley, beyond the neon glow of the signs above the tattoo parlors and bars. Swift and hulking and— He sniffed the air. Even with the rain, he knew that scent. Knew the golden eyes that glowed in the rainy darkness.

Ithan's growl rumbled over the slick cobblestones, his wet fur bristling.

Amelie Ravenscroft, his former Alpha, only snarled back, sending whatever patrons were on the streets scattering into the buildings, and melted into the dimness.

Ithan waited until her scent had faded before letting out a breath. He'd been right to come here, then. If he hadn't been here . . . He glanced to the doors again.

He couldn't stay here indefinitely. He'd need others to keep watch while he rested.

His phone rang from where he'd left it on the stoop of an alley doorway, and Ithan shifted into his humanoid body before answering. "Flynn. I was about to call you." To beg for a massive favor. If Sabine came here, or Amelie returned, packs in tow . . .

The Fae lord didn't reply immediately. Ithan could have sworn he heard the male swallow.

He stilled. "What is it?" Flynn's breathing turned harsh. Jagged. "Flynn."

"Shit went down." The Fae lord seemed to be struggling for words. And to hold back tears.

"Is . . ." He couldn't face this. Not again. Not—

"Ruhn and Athalar have been taken prisoner by the Asteri. Dec saw it on the palace feeds. Tharion called from the *Depth Charger* pod to say Cormac's dead."

Ithan began shaking his head, even as he contemplated the risk of discussing this on the phone. Breathing was somehow impossible as he whispered, "Bryce?"

A long, long pause.

Ithan slid to the soaking ground.

"She disappeared. You . . . you gotta come hear it from Dec."

"Is she alive?" Ithan's snarl tore through the rain, bouncing off the bricks.

"The last we saw her in this world . . . she was."

"What do you mean, *in this world*?" But he had a terrible feeling that he already knew.

"You have to see it for yourself," Flynn croaked.

"I can't," Ithan bit out. "I've got something to do."

"We need you," Flynn said, and his voice was full of an authority that people outside the Aux rarely heard. "We're friends now, wolf. Get your furry ass over here."

Ithan peered toward the towering doors. Felt himself being pulled apart by Urd herself.

"I'll be there in fifteen," Ithan said, and hung up. Slid his phone into his pocket. Stalked across the street.

A blow from his fist dented the metal doors. The second one broke the locks. The third sent them crumpling inward.

No sign of the Astronomer. Too bad. He was in the mood for blood tonight.

But Ithan stormed to the nearest tub. The wolf mystic floated in the murky, salt-laden water, hair spread around her, eyes closed. Breathing mask and tubes back in place.

"Wake up." His words were a low growl. "We're going."

The mystic didn't respond, lost to wherever her mind took her.

"I know you can hear me. I need to go somewhere, and I'm not leaving you behind. People are lurking out there who want you dead. So you can either get the fuck up right now or I can do it for you."

Again, no response. His fingers flexed, claws sliding free, but he kept his hand at his side. It was only a matter of time until someone came to investigate why the doors had been ripped open, but to tear her from that dream state . . . she'd been so tormented the last time.

"Please," he said softly, head bowing. "My friends need me. My . . . my pack needs me."

That's what they'd become.

He'd lost his brother, his brother's pack—the pack that would have one day been his—but this one . . .

He wouldn't lose it. Would fight until the bitter end to protect it.

"Please," Ithan whispered, voice breaking. Her hand twitched, the water rippling. Ithan's breath caught in his throat.

Her brow furrowed. The feeds on her tank began blaring and beeping, flashing red. The hair on Ithan's arms rose.

And then, lids fluttering, like the Alpha fought for every inch toward awakening, the lost Fendyr heir opened her eyes.

ACKNOWLEDGMENTS

To Robin Rue: How can I even convey my gratitude for all that you do as both an agent and a friend? (Dedicating this book to you is a feeble attempt at doing so!) Thank you from the bottom of my heart for your wisdom and encouragement, and for being there at the drop of a hat. And thank you, as always, for being a kindred spirit in all things fine food and wine!

To Noa Wheeler: I thank the universe every single day that our paths crossed. From your brilliant feedback to your unparalleled attention to detail, you are the most incredible editor I've ever worked with. (And the only person out there who truly understands my *NYT* crossword and Spelling Bee obsessions.) Here's to many more books together!

To Erica Barmash: Working with you again is such a pleasure! Thank you for all the years spent championing my books and being such a great friend!

To Beth Miller, an all-around gem of a human being, and a fellow marine biology fangirl: Thank you for all your hard work and for being a constant ray of sunshine! (And for the amazing marine wildlife photos!)

To the global Bloomsbury team: Nigel Newton, Kathleen Farrar, Adrienne Vaughn, Ian Hudson, Rebecca McNally, Valentina

Rice, Nicola Hill, Amanda Shipp, Marie Coolman, Lauren Ollerhead, Angela Craft, Lucy Mackay-Sim, Emilie Chambeyron, Donna Mark, David Mann, Michal Kuzmierkiewicz, Emma Ewbank, John Candell, Donna Gauthier, Laura Phillips, Melissa Kavonic, Oona Patrick, Nick Sweeney, Claire Henry, Nicholas Church, Fabia Ma, Daniel O'Connor, Brigid Nelson, Sarah McLean, Sarah Knight, Liz Bray, Genevieve Nelsson, Adam Kirkman, Jennifer Gonzalez, Laura Pennock, Elizabeth Tzetzo, Valerie Esposito, Meenakshi Singh, and Chris Venkatesh. I can't imagine working with a better group of people. Thank you for all your dedication and tremendous work! And tons of gratitude and love to Grace McNamee for jumping on board so quickly to help with this book! An especially big thank-you to Kaitlin Severini, copyeditor extraordinaire, and to Christine Ma, eagle-eyed proofer!

Cecilia de la Campa: You are one of the hardest-working and loveliest people I know. Thank you for all that you do! To the entire Writers House team: You guys are incredible, and I'm honored to work with you.

Thank you to the fierce and lovely Jill Gillett (and Noah Morse!), for making so many of my dreams come true and being an absolute delight to work with! To Maura Wogan and Victoria Cook: I'm so grateful to have you in my corner.

To Ron Moore and Maril Davis: working with you two rock stars has been the highlight of my *life*. And thank you so much to Ben McGinnis and Nick Hornung—you guys are amazing!

To my sister Jenn Kelly: What would I do without you? You bring such joy and light into my life. I love you.

I could write another thousand pages about the marvelous and talented women who keep me going, and who I am honored to call friends: Steph Brown, Katie Webber, Lynette Noni, and Jillian Stein. I adore you all!

Thank you, as always, to my family and in-laws for the unwavering love.

To Annie, faithful friend and writing companion: I love you forever, babypup.

To Josh and Taran: Thank you for always making me smile and laugh. I love you both more than there are stars in the sky.

And thank *you*, dear reader, for reading and supporting my books. None of this would be possible without you.

DISCOVER MORE OF THE WORLD OF SARAH J. MAAS!

CRESCENT CITY

THRONE OF GLASS

A COURT OF THORNS AND ROSES